ASHES
OF THE
TYRANT

FORGOTTEN REALMS®

ERIN M. EVANS

ASHES
OF THE
TYRANT

ASHES OF THE TYRANT
©2015 Wizards of the Coast LLC.

Published by Wizards of the Coast LLC. Manufactured by: Hasbro SA, Rue Emile-Boéchat 31, 2800 Delémont, CH. Represented by Hasbro Europe, 2 Roundwood Ave, Stockley Park, Uxbridge, Middlesex, UB11 1AZ, UK.

Lineage Diagram by: Mike Schley
Cover art by: Min Yum
Original Hardcover Edition First Printing: December 2015
First Mass Market Paperback Printing: February 2016

9 8 7 6 5 4 3 2 1

ISBN: 978-0-7869-6590-8
ISBN: 978-0-7869-6583-0 (ebook)
620-B65150000-001-EN

The Hardcover edition cataloging-in-Publication data
is on file with the Library of Congress

Contact Us at Wizards.com/CustomerService
Wizards of the Coast LLC, PO Box 707, Renton, WA 98057-0707, USA
USA & Canada: (800) 324-6496 or (425) 204-8069
Europe: +32(0) 70 233 277

Visit our web site at **www.DungeonsandDragons.com**

To Kevin and all we can do as one.
To my boys, and all we can do better.

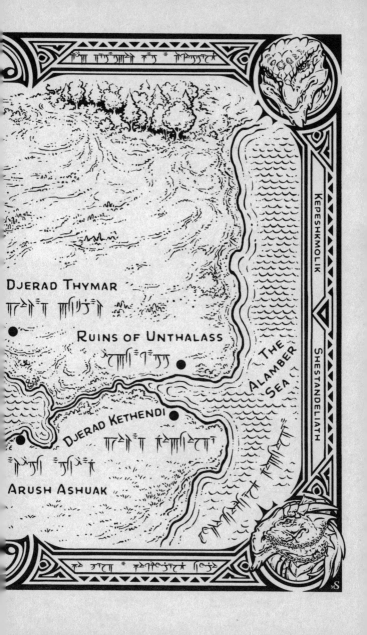

DJERAD THYMAR

RUINS OF UNTHALASS

DJERAD KETHENDI

ARUSH ASHUAK

THE ALAMBER SEA

KEPESHKMOLIK

SHESTANDELIATH

PROLOGUE

15 Nightal, the Year of the Nether Mountain Scrolls (1486 DR)
Djerad Thymar, Tymanther

IN EVERY ANCESTOR STORY LAY THE TRUTH. WHETHER YOU heard them in the stolen language of the *Vayemniri* or from some human rattling on about "dragonborn" tales in the common tongue, it could not be denied that the sacrifice and honor, bravery and cunning of the ancestors of Djerad Thymar bore powerful lessons to all who would listen.

And indeed the means to live those stories out, for those brave enough, Shestandeliath Zaroshni thought, watching her cousin pour lines of mithral dust through her trembling, scaly hands. The handful in the ancient crypt would be bold enough to make ancestor stories of their own.

Parvida's hands shook too hard to finish the circle. Zaroshni stepped forward and took the mithral dust into her own scaled palms and gestured for the younger dragonborn to step back, to rejoin the others along the wall of the ancient Clan Verthisathurgiesh crypt. In the flickering light of the torches, a dozen other faces watched, waited.

"It must be perfect," she heard Baruz whisper as Parvida came to stand beside him. Zaroshni poured the rare powder into the shapes of strange runes. A second dragonborn, Versvesh, made the farther edge of the circle. Baruz was right: the runes had to be perfect, or they wouldn't make the portal. Ravar's notes had been quite clear about that.

It can be nothing less, Zaroshni told herself. So it will be perfect. And then we can return home.

1

• • •

15 Nightal, the Year of the Nether Mountain Scrolls (1486 DR)
The Upperdark, beneath the Earthfast Mountains

SO FAR FROM the sun, the dark was nearly complete. Only the fluorescent dots of strange fungi traced the passages' walls, the shining lines of otherworldly insects hanging from the cavern's ceiling like strands of stars. A person could go mad there, and the Underdark went so much farther down.

Louc never took his hand off his weapon when he stood guard by the Zhentarim outpost, just ahead of the line of torches. If it didn't give him the crucial few seconds that saved his life when gods-only-knew-what burst out of the dark tunnels, all teeth and tentacles and madness, then at least the familiar feeling of the sword's hilt in his hand warded off the creeping sense that the Underdark was devouring his thoughts, morsel by morsel, singing in the strange wind that whistled down the passages and stirred the glowing strands of insects high above.

"Stlarning wind," muttered the guard beside him, a woman called Feiyen. She kept her bow out, an arrow already poisoned and nocked. They'd both been at the outpost a tenday, already too long.

The wind picked up, a keening note in the soft wailing, and Louc shuddered.

• • •

THE RUNES SHONE silvery blue against the smooth granite floor. The crypt was Baruz's family's, the list of names—those lost and left behind when the dragonborn were torn away from Abeir a century before—taking up most of one wall. Clan Verthisathurgiesh's matriarch—Baruz's mother—would not mind its use, he insisted.

And if she did, then she ought to be ashamed for the sake of those names.

Zaroshni hadn't bothered to make such entreaties to her own parents, her own patriarch. She knew they would cite tradition, precedent, and eventually the fact that they were her elders, and she must therefore listen. Parvida had dared and been told under no uncertain terms that her association with a group like the Liberators was bound to cause her and the clan harm. Zaroshni had reassured her—their rebuke meant little in the long run.

Of the dozen of them there that night, three had been cast out from their clans and another six had been threatened with exile. What had happened was a tragedy for those left behind, that much even the hardest of elders would agree to. But there was no going back, not now.

The elders thought because they were all young that they didn't understand, that they didn't appreciate the gift in the sacrifice. That they didn't understand what Abeir had been like.

"Neither do they," Zaroshni had pointed out to her friend, Dumuzi, as they walked through Djerad Thymar's winding passages, down to the base of the pyramid city and the entrance to the crypts. "They're only afraid of angering their elders, of being too soft to stand up and fix things. We don't belong here. You can't say we do."

"Do you believe that?" Dumuzi had asked. And she'd said she did. But curled in the center of Zaroshni's heart was the hope that they would return to Abeir, that their success tonight would serve to convince people like Dumuzi and their elders that there were other ways of doing things, other sources of strength and honor and throtominarr. She hoped, as she finished the circle, that she would see Dumuzi again, and be able to prove she was right. That Abeir held possibilities they would never have in Djerad Thymar.

That faraway plane where the dragonborn had been created, a land where they would not be strangers, where their ancestors had risen up, thrown off the shackles that the dragon lords weighed

3

them down with, and birthed the civilization of Tymanchebar. "A world," she'd said, "where we can rule ourselves and not make unwelcome overtures to elves and genies."

"A world," Dumuzi had said, "where dragons and titans and strange monsters wait to wipe you away."

"What of the Lost?" Zaroshni had said. "If it's so bad, shall we leave them there?"

Dumuzi had shrugged. "If you think you can bring them back, then bring them. But you should stay on Toril. We should all stay on Toril. This is our world now."

He doesn't know, Zaroshni thought, watching Baruz scatter a pungent powder over the space. It caught fire in tiny motes as it floated down. *None of us know.*

Yet, she amended, as magic began to fill the Verthisathurgiesh crypt.

• • •

"PISS AND HRAST!" Feiyen shouted as the wind howled higher. Sparks snapped in the dark. Louc took a step back, not meaning to, as the wind suddenly filled his mouth with the taste of salt and ashes, the stink of brimstone and thick perfume. Louc gripped his sword. The air turned cool and thick, as though a rainstorm were coming, and the wailing rose in pitch. Feiyen's arrows clattered into the darkness—there was nothing for her to hit.

Louc's pulse raced like a rabbit's, suddenly flooding him with fear and rage, flight and fight. This outpost was his to guard, and damned if he was going to let the wind steal it away—He caught himself within the wild scramble of those thoughts.

Something was coming.

• • •

BARUZ SPOKE THE incantations over the hovering sparks, a sound that made Zaroshni's scales shiver. Soon, the portal would open. Soon, Abeir would appear. Soon, she would see the place where her ancestors had shaped all their futures. She checked her

4

haversack, her short sword in its scabbard. Parvida took hold of her arm, all nervous excitement.

Within the circle the light brightened, and the sudden smell of cherries and bracing ashkarhz leaves hit Zaroshni's nostrils. The air shivered, like heat upon the horizon.

The light flashed, popped, and flashed again—golden and green this time. The sudden smell evaporated, replaced by a tang of blood, a stink of sulfur, and a cloud of dense perfume. The air turned cold, and a different sort of shiver ran over Zaroshni's scales. Her mouth tasted of ashes and salt. She pushed her younger cousin back, away from the portal, and reached for her sword.

The portal tore open, but the land Zaroshni glimpsed was not a plain beneath a steel sky. A blue sun, a line of violet flames, a burst of chilly, rain-soaked wind—the portal had failed to lead them to Abeir.

The air cracked as if the stones of Djerad Thymar had broken.

And then, the brief, inane thought that Parvida's parents were right after all—they had somehow brought the worst upon themselves, their clans, their city.

After, it was only teeth and claws and screaming.

• • •

THE DARKNESS WAS complete, and then it wasn't. Miles from the sun, untold distances from the Abyss, two eyes as bright as stars opened in the cavern and looked down at the Zhentarim outpost from a face as black as night, as handsome as the Morninglord—a face, a body that was suddenly there.

Louc's heart was ready to burst out of his chest as the eyes fell upon him, as a voice as musical as a blade upon a whetstone threatened to retune his pulse to suit its meter.

Someone, it said with a patience that Louc knew down to his marrow it didn't have, has a lot of explaining to do. Let's begin with you.

PART I

KEPESHKMOLIK
THE DEATHS OF THE ELDERS
IN RAUROKH

· · ·

Let us sing of one who brought wisdom and honor to the blood of the Kepeshkmolik clan: Shasphur Who-Would-Be-Kepeshkmolik. Let us sing of the deaths of the elders in Raurokh, the Citadel of Endings.

Under the claw of Raurokhymdhar the Golden, where Kepeshkmolik's first bones are buried and first shells are dust, Shasphur Who-Would-Be-Kepeshkmolik hatched and came of age. Strong-limbed and quick of mind, scales as green as emeralds, Shasphur was a prize for Raurokhymdhar the Golden, set as the wyrm was on gaining an army of slaves. Seven elders watched over their bloodlines in that prison—called Nazari, Baishiria, Rahishu, Hurashum, Zerath, Ana-Mashhal, and Qinnaz. Shasphur gave them all the devotion that was possible in that place of evil, and their wily wisdom protected many.

In the dark times of Raurokh, Shasphur saw that the lesser dragons who served the Golden would travel to and from the Citadel of Endings through a hole cut into the roof, carrying messages to other tyrants and bringing water and gems to Raurokhymdhar. One day he came to the seven wise elders with a heavy heart, and Nazari Who-Would-Be-Kepeshkmolik, wisest among them, asked "What troubles you so?"

"Oh my elders," he said. "I have found a hole in the Golden's grip. Three foolish ausiri carry her messages and weapons to the

northern citadels. They do not watch as the slaves load their cargo. They do not mind when the load is uneven, and they do not check to see what they carry. Many could flee on their backs. Many could be saved. But as I thought this, I realized it would be folly indeed. Not all could be saved, and especially not the elders. It would take great strength to cling to the harness, great stillness not to catch the eyes of even a foolish ausir. Forgive me, I forgot myself."

Nazari went away with the other elders, and when they returned, she said to Shasphur, "You are among our wisest and most honorable. Prove it now. Raurokhymdhar the Golden plans to keep you in her claws for all time, to better breed strong-limbed slaves. You must flee. Take as many of the young ones, as many of the eggs as you can, onto the backs of the ausiri. Bring them down as they fly, and flee into the mountains."

"You will be killed," Shasphur said.

"We will die so you may live," Nazari said. "Listen to your elders."

Shasphur obeyed, and on the day he and the beginnings of Kepeshkmolik would flee, the elders came one by one into the presence of Raurokhymdhar the Golden, in place of the young ones. Each tested her patience with tales of other dragons' follies. Each died beneath her claws. By the time the last of the elders had been slain, Raurokhymdhar the Golden hurried to check on her slaves, sure of a trick. But Those-Who-Would-Be Kepeshkmolik had listened to their elders, and with Shasphur they were gone, into the mountains with the blood of three foolish ausiri warming their claws.

They never forgot the Seven Wise Elders, whose names are foremost on the rolls of the lost, and when we became the Vayemniri, the Citadel of Endings was among the first to fall.

. . .

1

16 Nightal, the Year of the Nether Mountain Scrolls (1486 DR)
One day from Djerad Thymar, Tymanther

C LANLESS MEHEN NEVER SPOKE OF DJERAD THYMAR TO
his daughters except by accident, and so the shadows of
a thousand half-spoken memories implied the shape of
the City-Bastion in Farideh's mind. She had been raised with its
language in her ears, its customs in her home, its stories lulling
her to sleep as a child, but the city of the dragonborn itself
remained little more than a legend, until now. The pyramid city
of her father's birth loomed on the horizon, as real and gleaming
red as spilled blood in the sunset. It left Farideh uneasy, and
she wasn't alone.

"Is there anything I can do?" Clanless Mehen asked.

Farideh glanced back at her adoptive father, standing on the ridge
of the riverbank, shifting from one foot to the other. The faint steam
of his breath curled around his scaled nostrils in the evening chill.

"You can stop watching," Farideh said, and smiled wanly at
the dragonborn. "I don't want you to see."

"I've seen it," Mehen reminded her, looking down his snout.
"It doesn't bother me."

It *should*, Farideh thought.

She looked down into the River Alamber brushing the tips of
her boots, its muddy waters painted by sunset. *Kuhri Ternhesh*,
she thought, the name of the river in Tymantheran Draconic.
The River of Stone. Her reflection looked back—one silver eye,
one gold beneath a ridge of horns—broken by the ripples of the
water. Does a thing change when you change what you call it?

9

Or do the names just uncover other layers, other truths, other ways of seeing something?

Farideh, she thought. Or Chosen of Asmodeus.

Both, she thought. There's no running from it, and you know that.

She shut her eyes, turning her attention to the roiling powers of Asmodeus, the god of sin, that tugged on her nerves like a pack of wild hounds, threatening to break what control she had over them. Four days of holding on so tightly and it felt almost impossible to loose that grip.

But if she didn't now, the powers that came from being a Chosen of Asmodeus would pry it loose for her.

The dark horror of Asmodeus burst out of Farideh, a corona of fear, just before the flames raced over her bronze skin, gathering and unfolding from her back in wings of fire. Anger burned through her—she didn't want this, she didn't ask for this, *any* of this. She steeped in it for a moment—the fury was hers, and yet it wasn't. She had to remember that.

A few breaths later, she let the flames die.

"Better?" Mehen said, as if Farideh had only thrown up in the river. She climbed up the bank, taking Mehen's hand to pull herself up over the rise.

"For now."

Mehen hesitated, then embraced her with a suddenness and strength that crushed the air from her lungs. She hugged him back.

"It scares you," Farideh said. "Don't pretend it doesn't. Not to me."

"The whole business scares me," he said. "But *karshoj* to that burning-angel nonsense. Just a conjurer's trick when you get down to it."

The blessings of Asmodeus couldn't be ignored, couldn't be undone, and every time she tapped into them, the wave of fear took hold of everyone around her, friend or foe, family or stranger. Or lover. She shied from that thought and wondered what the dragonborn would make of it.

"Do you need more time?" Mehen said, a little too quickly. "Would a stroll help? Wear you out a bit? It's not a bad walk, along the river."

She looked back over her shoulder at her father. "You're stalling."

His fearsome teeth parted. "If caring about my daughter's well-being is stalling—"

Farideh tucked an arm around him. "You know it is. Come on. It's better to have it all out."

They walked together back to where the caravan had camped for the night, a stone's throw from the path the human caravan master called the Road of Dust and Mehen called *Ossa Choshk*. The wagons, laden with copper bars, in locked and lashed chests, and goods to tempt the dragonborn of faraway Djerad Thymar, had been circled loosely around a handful of campfires, and at their edge, a guard post had been set. A small fire crackled between a tiefling leaning against an enormous, muzzled black dog, a human man stretched out on the ground listening to her, and a young dragonborn man standing with his back to the fire, looking out at the plains of Tymanther. Beyond them, Djerad Thymar waited, impossibly large, and still a day's ride away.

The hellhound, Zoonie, came up on her feet as Mehen and Farideh approached, jostling Farideh's twin, Havilar. She broke off whatever she'd been saying to Brin with a curse. "*Tiamash*! Zoonie, lie down! It's just Mehen and Farideh. How'd it go?" she added to her sister.

"Same as always," Farideh said. As Djerad Thymar should have been familiar, so should the powers of Asmodeus have become less alien over time. It had been the better part of a year since that first time the flames had taken her over, but it still felt like a violation when it did.

"Well?" Havilar said, as Mehen settled down beside the fire. He ignored her, scratching the empty piercings along his jaw frill. Then he heaved a great sigh and poured himself a mug of watered-down wine.

"All right," he said. "Ask your questions."

11

Just beyond the firelight, Dumuzi turned, looking back as if something on the road had drawn his eye and not as if he were listening to the conversation. That would be improper, Farideh was fairly sure, and Kepeshkmolik Dumuzi was never improper.

"Who's Anala?" Havilar asked. "Why did she call you back? Are you rich now? Are we staying?"

"How long are we staying?" Farideh asked.

"Anala is my father's younger sister," Mehen said. "She's the matriarch of Verthisathurgiesh now."

"How is she?" Havilar asked. "Do you like her?"

"Slow down," Mehen said. He drank some of the wine. "In my youth, I would say she was dear to me. She minded me and my siblings often. She was the elder I went to with my troubles, the one who cared for me."

"Like your mother?" Brin asked.

Mehen sighed again. "Yes and no. Things are different in Djerad Thymar. But keep in mind, I haven't seen her in almost thirty years. I don't *know* Anala anymore."

"Is your mother alive?" Farideh asked, surprised she didn't know the answer already.

"She died before I hatched." He drummed his thick fingers against the mug, eyes on the fire. "To your other question, Anala called me back because my father's dead, and so his exile doesn't stand. I doubt very much we're getting any coin out of this."

"We know *that*." Havilar pointed her chin at the dragonborn in the darkness. "Dumuzi said as much in Suzail. But that's a lot of trouble just to say sorry when you've never asked to come back. What's she want, do you think?"

"There is no telling," Mehen said. He fell silent again, as if he were trying to sort out words. "You know the ancestor stories? 'Khorsaya and the Thigh Bone Sword,' 'Clever Nala and the Ten Thousand Shadows,' 'The Battle of the Crippled Mountain'? Verthisathurgiesh prizes wiliness and action, and while Anala may have been like a mother to me, she is matriarch for a reason. She might say calling me back is only to right Pandjed's wrongs."

"But you wouldn't be here if it might not be more," Farideh said.

Mehen nodded. "That *doesn't* mean we're staying, and if I have my way, we'll hardly be here long enough to shake the dust from our boots." He hesitated. "I don't want you three to be unprepared. Djerad Thymar is a dragonborn city. You'll be as strange as you were in Suzail, girls, and Brin . . ." He sighed once more. "Well, I suppose you'll see."

"What do we call her?" Havilar asked. "Anala? Matriarch? Auntie?"

Mehen looked as if he hoped beyond hope they would call Anala nothing at all, and it made Farideh's heart squeeze. "Call her Matriarch Anala, and then see what she says," Mehen said. Then, "I'm not going to lie to you, she likely doesn't know about you girls, and I don't know how she'll feel about my adopting tieflings. Mind, anyone says a word against you and I'll make them regret it, but I can't promise words won't be said."

"Well," Havilar said a little briskly, "we're used to that. Better or worse than Cormyr, do you think?"

Farideh sneaked a look at Brin and marked the abashed look that crossed his face. Just a tenday ago, they had been in Cormyr, the kingdom of his birth and birthright, a place where Farideh and Havilar had stood out worse than ever before—even setting aside the racing gossip that accompanied Brin, a nobleman in line for the throne, having a tiefling for a lover despite his engagement to the princess of Cormyr. The stress of it had proved too much for Havilar, and she'd broken things off. What was happening between them now, Farideh couldn't say. She couldn't say she wanted to know either—it was beyond private—but it would have helped to know what to say and what to bite her tongue about.

"It's complicated," Mehen said again. "I'd guess the same as Cormyr. Worse than Waterdeep, but better than it would've been in . . ." He trailed off suddenly, and Farideh's heart twisted around the omission. *Better than it would have been in Harrowdale.*

A month ago, standing in the Royal Gardens, the air thick with the scent of lemon balm and the sound of bees. Dahl standing beside the hedge, fiddling with the leaves. Nervous, she'd thought, because of the impending siege, but no. "Would you consider coming to Harrowdale?"

"It's been three days," she'd pointed out. "Are you sure?"

"Three days since I told you I loved you," Dahl had said. "We've been all but courting for months—false or not, I don't think there's much I haven't learned about you by now. You can hardly pretend I'm rushing. Besides," he said after a moment, "I have to go." War spilling out over the North and the Heartlands, with no regard for border or boundary—how could he not go, with his mother, his family in danger's path? Farideh had agreed—even if doubt had made its own little nest in her thoughts, she was sure she loved him.

But then he'd gone without her and without a word to say why.

Before they'd left Cormyr, she'd had one last message from Dahl in Harrowdale: *I love you. I will fix this.* Farideh had borrowed enough coin to gather the components for a sending ritual. She'd laid the lines of powdered metals and salts and dried blood, conjuring up the magic Dahl himself had taught her years and years ago that would let her speak with him on the other edge of the continent.

"I got your message," she'd said. "Mehen wants to go to Djerad Thymar. We leave tomorrow, unless you tell me why I should stay?" She hesitated. "I love you."

But only silence had followed. Farideh had sat, perfectly still, until the magic that powered the spell fizzled and crackled out of the air, a snow of dying power. The response hadn't come.

Because Dahl couldn't answer? Because Dahl didn't want to answer? Because she hadn't cast the spell right?

Because someone in the Nine Hells was keeping her from him?

There was only one way of knowing at her disposal. One way of being sure, one way of saving Dahl, of bringing him back to her, and it tore at Farideh.

All I want is your happiness, Farideh. The one who gets hurt doesn't have to be you.

Asmodeus, the god of sin, king of the Nine Hells, could give her Dahl, *would* give her Dahl, if she just stayed quiet, stayed calm, stayed out of his business and stopped wondering what it was that made her dream of both the king of devils and the long-dead god of wizards.

She rubbed her thumb over her bleached ring finger, the remnant of another hasty decision, another attempt to fix things that had wound up hurting more people. What was to say Dahl wanted to come back to her anyway? She thought of Lorcan then, the half-devil who held her pact and who she still thought of with complicated feelings. *Don't you think it's more likely that he left of his own accord? I suppose he's just not our kind.*

Hush, she told herself. He loves you. He can take care of himself. Stop worrying about this right now.

She eyed Havilar, still sprawled across the hellhound. There was plenty to worry about that was far more pressing.

"People will say things," Dumuzi piped up, "but you won't know it."

"Cryptic," Havilar said.

"*Sjashukri,*" Dumuzi said as if he were correcting her. "No one will be directly rude. Not even Anala. That's not our way." Mehen's teeth gapped, his tongue hammering a nervous rhythm against the roof of his mouth.

"Shjash-oo-kree," Brin repeated. "Sounds like nobles in Cormyr." Dumuzi looked back over his shoulder at Mehen.

"No," the older dragonborn said, as if the whole business annoyed him. "*Sjashukri* is subtler. Trickier. *You'll* suspect it's an insult or a criticism, but you cannot call it out. If . . . If I were to praise Havilar's skill with a blade, and then say how nice Farideh's script is—"

"Then you'd be lying," Havilar interrupted, "because her script is *terrible.*"

"You have no room to talk," Mehen said sternly. "But the *sjashukri* is in the way the compliments are arranged. It implies Farideh's skills are not worth mentioning, that the only thing that comes near is her scriptwork. But no one can say that's an insult. It's two compliments." Mehen coughed. "Your blade work's come along nicely," he added to Farideh.

"It's not worth complimenting," Farideh said dryly. "I see what you mean. Should keep us on our toes." She wrapped her hands around each other, nervous and uneasy. "Are you sure she doesn't know about us?"

"I haven't been back in thirty years," Mehen said again. "How in the broken planes would she know?"

Farideh gave her father a significant look. He might not have returned to Djerad Thymar in thirty years . . . but some part of Djerad Thymar had come to find him not sixteen years earlier. Verthisathurgiesh Arjhani, Dumuzi's father, the man Mehen had loved enough to choose exile over, had come to the hidden village of Arush Vayem and joined their patchwork little family for all of a summer, before fleeing back to the City-Bastion.

Mehen frowned and said nothing, and Farideh squeezed her hands together more tightly. The one thing they needed a plan for and there was no plan. She glanced at Havilar scratching Zoonie under the jaw, remembering the summer, the following autumn and winter. Havilar, unsettled, uncertain, fragile as an ice crystal, and more heartbroken even than Mehen. She had loved Arjhani the way she loved all things, wholly and unreservedly, and he'd left without a word. What would happen this time?

We won't stay long, she told herself. We won't run into Arjhani.

"Here's something I've always wondered," Brin said lightly. "You all hate the dragons so much, right? Why do you call yourselves dragonborn?"

Mehen turned a cold eye on Brin. "We don't," he said. "We just gave up trying to convince you all to stop."

"It's *Vayemniri,* in Draconic," Havilar said.

"Vie-yem-near-ee," Brin repeated. "What's it mean?"

" 'The Ash-Marked Ones,' " Farideh said, prodding the campfire and sending up a swirl of embers as the last of the sun dipped below the horizon.

• • •

THE LAST TIME Clanless Mehen had passed through the gates of the city of Djerad Thymar, he had vowed to never return, cursing his father's name and his lover's cowardice, two wounds he never thought would heal. Melodramatic, he thought. He'd been too young to know plenty of people lived with wounds like that.

"Come on," he muttered to Brin. The young man nodded once, climbing down from the wagon seat. "What are you going to do?"

"Ask if he needs anything else and hold out my hand," Brin recited. "No niceties."

Mehen nodded back. When they'd left Cormyr behind, and Brin's royal life with it, Mehen knew that he'd have to make sure the lad could survive this unkind life he'd chosen. He might not have been Mehen's son, but whatever happened between Brin and Havilar, the boy was in his heart.

Besides, he thought, looming over the much shorter human and glaring at the caravan master, humans always paid their own kind better.

"Will there be anything else?" Brin asked. The bearded caravan master looked him up and down, a faint sneer on his face.

"Didn't really have much need of you it seems," he said. "You oversold the dangers of the Road of Dust more than a little."

"A fortunate season," Brin said. "I think we agreed on fifty-eight gold."

The caravan master handed over a purse of coins. "Thirty. You didn't give me fifty-eight's worth. And those devil-children and their great hound spooked my horses."

Brin turned his head, as if to look back at Mehen the way they'd agreed upon, punctuating the discussion with the threat of Brin's monstrous right hand. But then he turned back to face the caravan master.

"You're coming from Tsurlagol, isn't that right?" The caravan master narrowed his eyes. "You're not the first to bring copper to Djerad Thymar," Brin went on. "I'm guessing . . . you want a deal with the glassworks. Do you know that my dragonborn friends here are associated with two of the most powerful clans in the city?" He dropped his voice. "Do you even *know* which of the clans is powerful? Who invited you?"

The caravan master's eyes darted from the young man to Mehen and back. "Clethtinthtiallor," he said, naming one of the score or so clans in Djerad Thymar.

Brin turned back to Mehen then as though this answer wasn't to be believed, and the dragonborn allowed himself a small smile. It was a newer clan, but its reputation didn't suffer. Not that the caravan master knew that.

"Listen," Brin said. "I don't want to ruin your livelihood so long as you don't ruin mine. Pay what we're owed, and I don't tell Kepeshkmolik and Verthisathurgiesh you shorted their kin." He shrugged and the caravan master's scowl deepened. "It's coin now or coin later. Your decision."

"I see Cormyr hasn't left you as completely as you'd like," Mehen said, as they walked back to the twins with their full fee. "What happened to the plan?"

"To be honest? There's so many of you here." Brin gestured at the dragonborn milling around the gates and the outer city. "I figured he's not going to be as frightened of my dragonborn guard, and if he were, he'd see a value in fighting that fear. But coin—he'd be scared of losing more coin. It's a risky venture already, diving into a market no one's successfully tapped."

"Hmph. Well done. Next time, leave the clan names out," Mehen said. "You don't want to stir that pot."

"How'd he do?" Farideh asked as they approached.

"Full fee," Mehen said. "He put the fear of the clans into him."

"Nicely done, Brin," Havilar said.

Brin's smile grew a little. "Thanks."

Dumuzi said nothing, only frowned in disapproval, arms folded across his chest. Kepeshkmolik to the core, thought Mehen.

But Verthisathurgiesh under the scales—Dumuzi could have been your son, he thought. If he'd married Kepeshkmolik Uadjit the way his father had planned, if he hadn't chosen love and exile over duty and honor, then who knew how many Kepeshkmolik eggs he would have reluctantly sired.

Some ancient part of him, awakened as he crossed through Djerad Thymar's gates, noted he ought to feel regretful, ought to wish for a strapping child of his own blood.

But there was nothing of the sort in Clanless Mehen. There was no path he wanted that left those two babies to die in the snow.

He gave Dumuzi and Brin their shares, and the two young men collected their belongings from the caravan wagon. Mehen held out two shares of the coins to Farideh and Havilar. They traded a glance.

"We get our own?" Havilar asked, as if there were some trick here.

"You're grown," Mehen said. "You handle your own coin from here on out. That means you pay for your own supplies too," he pointed out, seeing a dangerous gleam in Havilar's eye. "You waste it on a fancy blade or a gown you don't need, you'll be the one selling at a loss when you can't afford trail rations." He cleared his throat, dropping into Draconic. "And don't forget you need to . . . buy the herbs, regardless of what . . . of who . . . of where your day-count is—"

"*Thrik!*" Havilar cried, keeping the tongue. "Gods, Mehen, we *understand.*"

"You all but bought out the stall in Suzail for us," Farideh said, her cheeks scarlet. "We're set for a good while."

Mehen scowled. "Either of you get a child, I'm not paying for that either." A lie, he thought, even as he said it. Still if he were the praying sort, he'd have told the gods to keep their blessings to themselves. They might be grown, but they were still too young.

"No one is getting pregnant," Havilar hissed. "*Neither* of us has a lover, and maybe if you'd taken up Kallan on his *obvious* interest—"

"That is not your business," Mehen snapped.

"Well mine's not yours!" Havilar said. "Neither is Fari's. So if you want to get obsessed with someone's love life, then *yours* is the only fair option."

Mehen growled, and tapped his tongue against the roof of his mouth to ease his agitation. "You're paying to stable the dog for tonight," he said.

"You can use Verthisathurgiesh's stables," Dumuzi piped up. "Matriarch Anala gave permission."

"For horses," Mehen pointed out. "I doubt she'll be pleased about a fire-breathing hellhound bedding down amongst her prized brood mares."

Zoonie scratched her ear and sneezed. "Yeah, she's a killer," Havilar said dryly. "The stables will be fine for now."

Until Verthisathurgiesh finds out about you, Mehen thought. Until someone says something cruel or callous or thinks to use you against me. He blew out a breath. His daughters didn't have to exchange a word to Anala or any of the Verthisathurgiesh clan. Mehen would make it clear he wanted nothing to do with Verthisathurgiesh or Djerad Thymar, and they could be on their way tomorrow.

"I'll take you," Dumuzi offered to Havilar. "Then we can all go to the enclave—"

"No," Mehen said. Dumuzi clamped his mouth shut, stiff and startled. "I mean," Mehen said, a little more gently, "it's not necessary for all of us to go tramping through the City-Bastion. I don't expect this will take long."

The twins exchanged skeptical glances, which only made Mehen's resolve firmer. It wouldn't take long. It couldn't.

"The stables are on the western edge of the pyramid," he said. "Dumuzi will give you whatever insignia Anala handed off to him." He spared a dark look for Dumuzi that all but forced the brass disk etched with Draconic from his pocket and into Farideh's hand. "After the dog's settled, wait for me in the . . ." The *Munthrarechi* word eluded him. "Tavern," he decided. "There's a tavern near there, Reshvemi's Shield—"

"They can't go there," Dumuzi interrupted. "*Chaorkartels* are for warriors."

Mehen blinked. The memories of uncountable evenings spent in that *chaorkartel,* the farthest place in Djerad Thymar from his father's reach besides the barracks—laughing with his friends, laughing with Arjhani, late into the night—tripped him up. His girls were warriors, he almost said—but no, not by Djerad Thymar's standards. They were not pierced, they had no status swords, they hadn't served in the Lance Defenders or killed a dragon.

"I . . . ," he started. But his memories refused to give him the name of a single other place the twins and Brin could wait, snagged as they were on Reshvemi's Shield and the taste of watered apple brandy.

"You could wait at, umm, the Horn of Shasphur?" Dumuzi asked. "It's on the market floor. My cousin owns it—they have the sort of things you like to drink. It's nice enough," he said to Mehen.

It's inside the city, Mehen thought. He held his tongue. They would just be tieflings, travelers, passersby. Kepeshkmolik wouldn't know who they were either. "Fine," Mehen said. Then, "You're not to have whiskey."

Havilar's eyes danced. "Too late!" she teased. "It's our coin now."

"I think she's joking," Dumuzi offered as Zoonie cut a path for the three of them through the crowd of dragonborn. "She's probably joking. Shall we go?"

Mehen snorted and turned, heading toward the pyramid's entrance. There were more buildings beyond the city's massive main structure than he remembered, more people—dragonborn and otherwise—milling around the gates and through the outer city. At a glance, Mehen was left with the impression that the city had become something entirely new.

But as he walked, his eyes would find a chink in the stone, a stain of lichen, a shape of the ground, and he'd suddenly be a boy all over again. It was as if Djerad Thymar were stirring in his blood.

The first time Mehen had ventured into a human city, he'd been struck by the overwhelming sense of the sky. Although there had been comfort to be found in the closeness of people, the embrace of dwellings and shops squeezed against one another, the way everything just *stopped* around twice or three times his height had been disorienting. Returning didn't throw him in the same way—it felt *right* to have the stone over his head again.

In Djerad Thymar, the base of the pyramid city supported a sprawling network of shops and stalls, taverns and offices and homes for those who had displeased their clan. Rather than spreading out, the city ran up the pyramid's walls, with balcony after balcony jutting out over the city, clan enclaves linked by arching staircases and walkways, all dripping with plants that grew in the magical light that flooded the City-Bastion. More dragonborn than he had seen in twenty years passed by him.

Staring, Mehen realized, at the empty holes along his jaw. One thing that hasn't changed, Mehen thought. *What did he do?* their frank gazes wondered. *What was worthy of exile?* He caught a pair whispering to one another, and glared at them fiercely enough to cut them off.

He looked back over his shoulder, at Dumuzi straggling ten steps behind him as if he hoped not to be noticed by the passersby or by Mehen. Mehen rolled his eyes. "Your task's almost done," he said. "Thought you'd quit being skittish by now."

"You have my apologies," Dumuzi said, picking up his pace. "Here I . . . I'll lead."

Mehen muttered a curse under his breath as the younger dragonborn pushed past him. He'll grow out of it, he told himself. Most of us do. And Dumuzi wasn't his to worry about anyway.

Neither were the girls—Havilar's rebuke still needled at him. They were grown enough to manage their own coin and their own lives. They didn't need him like they once did—even Brin didn't need him anymore, without a network of nobles trying to assassinate him. Once he'd sorted himself out, he'd be fine on his own.

You were someone before you were a father, he thought. If they don't need you, you can always find something else.

A handsome sellsword was a poor substitute. Even if he still found his thoughts wandering to Yrjixtilex Kallan more often than he was willing to admit.

22

Done is done, he thought, weaving through the passersby.

Mehen stretched his jaw twice as Dumuzi approached the staircase that led up the pyramid's northwestern wall, into the enclaves of half a dozen clans—most importantly Verthisathurgiesh. But his thoughts rattled with memories of the Lance Defenders' barracks, of riding bat-back over the plains, of crossing swords with Uadjit. Of kissing Arjhani. It slid into his thoughts like a knife, the heart-shattering memory of a slim, brassy dragonborn boy in his arms.

The Verthisathurgiesh Enclave's doors loomed deep into the passages through the thick walls of Djerad Thymar, their enormous faces hung with a mock red dragon skull carved of lusturl root, mottled brown and gleaming and split down the center. The real skull had been lost, they said, when the Blue Fire came, but Verthisathurgiesh's name was still present many times over in the Hall of Trophies. Mehen wondered if the skull of the green dragon he had killed to finally earn his long sword still hung there, or if Pandjed had destroyed it in his pique. He wouldn't put anything past the old man, and if he said one word about the girls—

He is dead, Mehen reminded himself as they entered his childhood home. Pandjed is dead and his bones are gathered. He can say nothing at all.

And the girls will stay far, far from here.

Dumuzi stopped in the large entryway and turned to Mehen so suddenly the older man almost crashed into him. "I have to tell you something," he blurted. "Your forgiveness, I should have told you before, but . . . I was advised not to, but I suspect Matriarch Anala will have it all out and then you'll know—"

"Spit it out," Mehen said with a sigh. A thousand possibilities—none of them mattered. Kepeshkmolik opposed him returning, surely, he thought. Or perhaps the Lance Defenders would not have him—as if it mattered to Mehen. Or maybe—

"I came for you because my father was . . . he didn't think it was his place," Dumuzi said. "But Matriarch Anala sent him at first, and he passed the task to me. To prove myself. But I think also to excuse himself."

Mehen raised his brows. Bold words from such a correct and proper hatchling. "So you think she's going to chastise your father."

Dumuzi shook his head, his tongue fluttering in an agitated way. "If so, she already has," he said. "I should have told you when I . . . My father is Verthisathurgiesh Arjhani."

Mehen's heart stuttered, and he saw it. The boy had his mother's coloring, the steel-blue scales and amber eyes of Kepeshkmolik Uadjit, daughter of Narghon of the line of Shasphur, scion of Kepeshkmolik. But in the shift of his scale ridges, in the crooked shape of his smile, there was a man whose claws still dug into Clanless Mehen's heart. How had he missed such a thing?

Because for all Arjhani had done, he realized, he could never have expected a slight this deep. He had turned from *everything* because he loved Arjhani . . . and then Arjhani had taken his place beside the bride Mehen wouldn't abandon Arjhani for.

"I see," Mehen said. Then, "Do the girls know?"

Dumuzi nodded, looking abashed. "I told Farideh, before you returned. And Havilar guessed."

"She has an eye for such things," Mehen said, crushing down everything he wanted to say instead. He gestured at the door. "Shall we?"

Dumuzi didn't move. "Are you angry?"

"You cannot help your parents," he said, chillier than he meant to. "Farideh told you to hold your tongue, didn't she?" Dumuzi nodded. "It was wise." Mehen would have words with her later. "Lead on."

Let's get this over with, Mehen thought. An elder who would send Arjhani to find him, to apologize, would have nothing Mehen wanted, so at least he knew that much.

Thirty years had wrought their changes on the clan's quarters—hangings faded, statues replaced or moved, rugs now lying upon the granite floor. It was as if Mehen moved through a dream, his memories jumbled together into nonsense, while he tried vainly to refit them.

The audience chamber on the other hand, looked exactly as Mehen remembered, the skull of a colossal red dragon hanging high on the slanting outer wall, so that it looked as if the beast bowed its head over the elder's throne. The floors were uncovered, built of bloodred stone. On every wall, the weapons of past elders hung, testaments to their strength and protection. It had not changed a bit from Mehen's last day in Djerad Thymar.

His father had sat upon the elder's throne, all the gray-scaled aunties and uncles arrayed around him, cheated of the patriarch's position by their line and their own elders. A potent audience for the scion of Khorsaya's line.

I don't wish to marry Kepeshkmolik Uadjit.

Your wishes don't enter into it, you spoilt hatchling. The agreement is made. You live at my pleasure. You will wed her, or you will be no son of mine.

Verthisathurgiesh Anala did not sit upon the elder's throne, but stood over a stack of scrolls on a table to the side, a filmy wrap draped over her shoulders. Her greatsword lay across the throne in her place. She had the height Mehen and his father had inherited, but not the bulk. Lithe and loose-limbed, her scales the color of damp brick, and her plumes nearly black and hanging neatly to her shoulders, Pandjed's youngest sister seemed not to have aged a day.

Dumuzi started to speak an introduction. No more than a syllable had crossed his teeth but Anala raised her head, eyes bright, and clapped her hands.

"Mehen," she said warmly. "You came."

"I've . . . I found . . . ," Dumuzi stumbled.

"Thank you, Dumuzi. You are a credit to your sire's line. Give your clan our deepest appreciations for your help," Anala said with a polite bow. "And if you see your father, kindly remind him of your success."

The younger dragonborn nodded. "Thank you." Dumuzi's eyes darted to Mehen again, and Mehen's annoyance at the boy softened slightly. But Dumuzi turned and fled the room before Mehen could think of a single thing to say.

Anala crossed to him without warning and embraced Mehen tightly, rubbing the frill of her jaw against his shoulder. "You won't want to hear it, but it must be said: You look exactly like your father." She held him at arm's length, dropping her voice. "Though, I do hope you're happier than he was. Miserable old *henish*."

"That's not hard, but I think I've managed it."

"Please sit. May I offer you some refreshments?" Mehen didn't answer and didn't sit. Anala poured two glasses of something ruby colored and steaming from a clay teapot. "You must be buzzing with questions."

"Not really," Mehen said. "I'll save you the trouble. I'm not coming back."

Anala smiled. "You always were a stubborn one. I agreed with your father about that much. Have a drink and talk a bit if you're so sure you won't change your mind. Give an old woman the comfort of hearing her favorite nephew is well."

Mehen took up the cup from the table. "How did he die?"

Anala's smile fell from her eyes. "Pandjed? An excess of bile, one presumes. It caused a heartstop and he didn't recover."

Mehen recalled his powerful, furious father and imagined the old man clutching his broad chest, imagined the roars, imagined him looking for someone to blame death on.

"Should have seen that coming," Mehen said.

"I wish I could say he mentioned you at the end," Anala said. "But we both know that would be untrue and unkind to you."

"It wouldn't matter," Mehen said. "Pandjed's regrets don't matter to me." He drained the cup—a mild wine, heavy with spices that bloomed up more memories. You couldn't find these in Cormyr. "How'd you end up matriarch? If I recall, Pandjed didn't love you either."

Now her eyes smiled. "Nor did he hate me. I annoyed him—every day of my life—but I never angered him, never enough to warrant exile. When he lay on his deathbed, he had me and a great bunch of *pothachi* and hatchlings to choose from." She set her cup down, leaned against the table. "Between you and me," she said in conspiratorial tones, "he's left us in quite the bind. Verthisathurgiesh is damaged, no doubt, and every other clan marks it."

"So you want me to come back," Mehen finished. He sat in the chair beside the table, to spare his tired knees. "Shore up your numbers. That didn't work out so well for Pandjed."

"I'm only asking for *you*," Anala promised. "You represent, Mehen, the days before Pandjed's anger twisted us. The glorious young scion returned. That's more than enough, and—selfishly—it would do my heart good to know you weren't out in the wilds. Although," she added, sitting against the table," I won't say no to more eggs. Maybe we'll find you a handsome fellow with an over-fertile sister or cousin. Broker something clever."

"What would the other clans say to *that*?"

"Does it matter? I want to remind the others, after all, that Verthisathurgiesh has always adapted when others made themselves stagnant. Besides, I suspect that you aren't the only one who'd prefer a marriage brokered that way."

Mehen studied the matriarch, wondering if she meant to surprise him, or entice him. Wondering, briefly, if Kallan had sisters, before he brushed it aside. Anala wouldn't catch him off guard like that.

"I think you'll find I'm less of a catch for Verthisathurgiesh than ever before."

"Ah, Mehen," Anala said. "I think you'll find Verthisathurgiesh less choosy than ever before. What is it you've done that's so insurmountable?"

The doors to the rest of the enclave squealed open, and a rusty-colored dragonborn man came flailing through them. When he caught sight of Anala, he skidded to a stop, making a hasty bow.

"Matriarch Anala!" he said, breathless. "There's been a . . . a crime, a terrible crime! Baruz is dead! Murdered!" He glanced at Mehen, at the missing piercings, as if realizing how incautious he'd just been, and then continued anyway. "You must come. Right now. It's terrible."

Anala became still, as if her whole spirit had left her, as if she were the one to discover the murdered body of Verthisathurgiesh Baruz, her third-hatched son, and not this stranger. She was not the matriarch in that moment, and Mehen watched her, just as still, just as startled, his heart aching as it wrapped itself in memories, warding off the imaginary pain of losing his own children.

Baruz. Baruz had been just a baby when he left, just starting to walk, overbalancing on his clawed toes. Mehen could remember minding him and his two clutchmates in the summer before he left—knowing Pandjed would have said that wasn't a warrior's task. Pulling faces and making puppets of dollies, the same way he would for the twins, years later. Baruz had laughed loudest, always.

"Matriarch Anala?" the frantic man said. "Please?"

"Of course," Anala said, her voice shifted, as if she were speaking through the mask of Verthisathurgiesh. She turned to Mehen. "I . . . I have to take care of this. Would you . . . Would you mind—"

"I'll come with you," Mehen said, standing.

"That's not necessary," Anala said. "You're a guest."

"That's not what you were saying a moment ago," Mehen said, taking his aunt by the arm. "This is what I do now. A bounty hunter. If someone's . . . If Verthisathurgiesh has been wronged," he amended, sliding into that safer, less personal position, "I can find them. Get you justice."

Anala nodded, her expression closing swiftly as the enclave's heavy doors. "I'll pay," she said, and named a sum that meant nothing to Mehen in that moment, snarled as he was between the past and the present. Imagining Baruz the hatchling and the twins' in the same moment. Imagining the agony of hearing his daughters were gone.

"We'll discuss it," Mehen said. "Maybe you should stay here."

"No," Anala said, retrieving her arm. "I am Verthisathurgiesh. I need to be present. But I'd be glad to have you with me," she added softly. She nodded to the young man, "Lead on."

Mehen followed her from the enclave, all thoughts of fleeing Djerad Thymar pushed aside as death made him a member of Verthisathurgiesh once more.

• • •

Turn. Turn. Down into the shadows. Blood smells so sweet, so thick—no, must follow orders, must find the—oh such fury, such passion. Just a taste, just a morsel, just one more . . .

No, no, no. These must be enough for now. More later. More soon. Too many eyes and too many weapons mean meanness. Mean using what you have.

Must find the weaknesses, must find the holes, must make the path or the Dark Prince will be displeased and then death, death, death. Unless unlucky. Then worse. He made the deal, not me—could tear that surly mortal all to pieces I could, king of figments, king of dust. But the Dark Prince says he is ally, he is more than mortal, so turn, turn, down in the shadows, down where it's darker than the spot a soul leaves behind. Now we have a little fun.

Think like her. *Think like the screaming one. Soak it all in, fill out the skin, wear it like my own. Pull the words together, remind the tongue how to speak, the face how to move. Possess it all—the memory of the sword, the memory of a kiss, fears and loathings and wishes—she's mine. They'll never see a thing. How lucky that king of dust is to have such a one as the maurezhi on his side!*

Until the Dark Prince changes his mind. He won't even see a thing, that king of figments, king of dust.

2

IN THE DOMES OF REASON, WHERE HE'D TAKEN HIS VOWS AS a paladin of the god of knowledge, Dahl Peredur had made a habit of praying several times a day—to clear his mind, to hone his focus, to still his heart. After he'd fallen, cast from Oghma's favor for losing sight of what it truly meant to serve the search for knowledge, Dahl had kept the practice in a haphazard way, trying to right a faltering heart, to steer a fractured soul, even if the god didn't answer aloud anymore. There was a peace that he couldn't find elsewhere, even if he had sometimes gone days without praying.

Now—with Dahl returned to Oghma's grace, and knowledge he desperately needed out of reach—it felt like nothing but cruelty that he couldn't find that same balance.

Lord of All Knowledge, he implored, kneeling in the corner of a rented, overcrowded set of rooms in New Velar. *Binder of What Is Known: Make my eye clear, my mind open, my heart true.*

"I take you to Harrowdale," Lorcan's words snapped across the chant out of Dahl's memories, "and you never, ever speak to Farideh again. You don't whisper in her ear, you don't yell across the room. Not with a spell, not with handsigns. Never."

Give me the wisdom to separate the lie from the truth, Dahl prayed. *My word is my steel, my reason my shield.*

When the cambion had offered Dahl the chance to reach Harrowdale ahead of the Shadovar army Lorcan had almost certainly set on Dahl's family in the first place—the price had nearly stopped him. If he spoke to Farideh again, his soul was Lorcan's, and he could never tell anyone the deal existed.

In that moment, Dahl could only hope he would find a loophole. His family's lives outweighed his own heart.

There would be an answer—there had to be. He just had to find someone who knew how to deal with devils. Call Lorcan back to him. Demand to see the deal written out—was it written out? Were there only the words they'd spoken to bind Dahl? If he did speak to Farideh, would his soul truly be forfeit, or was that a threat Lorcan couldn't follow through on, not without a contract?

And I shall fear no deception, he all but shouted out loud, *for the truth remains.*

Who was there in New Velar—in all of Harrowdale—that Dahl could ferret out the secrets of dealing with devils? Who wouldn't gossip if he asked the wrong person, carrying back the taint of evil magic to his family? He could easily imagine other farmers, other tradesmen, whispering unfair rumors about the farmstead and its inhabitants—how fast would that ruin his mother and his brothers' and their families?

It is my duty to find what is hidden, Dahl prayed, *and my gift to know what is unknown.*

His soul in the balance—was this why Oghma hung distant as the moon? The presence of the god of knowledge had flooded him in Suzail, in the moment where he realized how pride and arrogance had stolen his paladinhood from him, in the moment where he realized the same need to be right had made him unable to see how deeply in love with Farideh he was. Now Oghma seemed to watch, to wait: Could he solve this?

No, he thought. No, no, no. You can't. You can't possibly—

He took a deep breath, stretching his lungs to their very limits. And began again.

But what went through Dahl's mind wasn't the prayer he'd practiced for years on end. A memory, a moment—Farideh and he, tangled together still, flushed and sated, close enough to share their panted breath. Dahl had kissed her, and everything had fallen together, too perfect to question, until that moment, spent and clinging to each other. He felt emptied out, washed of shock and worry but also of the faint presence of Oghma.

Farideh had been the one to break the silence. "I don't want you to leave," she'd breathed against his ear. So many things caught in those words—a plea, a gasp, a laugh. It felt as if they stood on a tipping point, between grief and hope and happiness.

Dahl already knew which way he would fall. But he held the moment, thinking how so much of life was holy, how so many things were worth knowing. He buried his face against her neck. "Where would I go?" he chided.

My champion, my wayward son, Farideh's voice murmured in his memories, the words of prophecy etched upon his soul by Oghma himself. The words that only the blessings of Asmodeus, the soul sight the god of sin had given to Farideh, could unlock. *The path's well trod, the hunting's poor. From heav'ns to Hells, the plane will ring. Reflect, and after, my priest speaks.*

Dahl shivered and his breath stopped. The middle of his mind felt warm and glowing as a lantern in the gloom.

There's an answer, a voice in his thoughts said, whether the god's or his own better sense. *There is always an answer.*

"Wass he doo-nee?" a little voice chirped, severing the moment of reverie.

"Dunno," a boy said. Then, "Maybe he's sleeping?"

Dahl opened his eyes to the too-bright room and blinked, dizzy at the shift. His nephew, Wilmot, stood a little ways away, hand-in-hand with his cousin, Aggie.

The chubby little girl, her cheeks jammy, grinned. "Unca Dahl is you seepy?"

"Sleep*ing*," Wilmot said, at five and a half years, his little cousin's conscientious tutor. "Are you? Because no one's in the beds. You could nap there. You can have my blanket."

"Aggie, Wil, leave your uncle be!" Meribelle, Aggie's mother, swept in behind the children, and scooped Aggie off the ground. "He's . . ." She smiled vaguely at Dahl. "Busy."

"I said he could sleep in the beds upstairs," Wilmot reported.

Meribelle hitched Aggie up a little higher on her hip. "Apologies, Dahl. They're just curious."

"It's fine."

"No, you need your space and we'll give it to you. Children, go play with the others."

"Oh don't buy that cow, Meri," Dahl's brother Bodhar said, as he came down the stairs. "You *know* he's just sleeping." Meribelle swatted at her husband as he leaned in to kiss her cheek.

"Be good. Your brother's a holy man."

"Better to practice napping on his knees."

"Why in the stlarning Hells would I sleep on my knees?" Dahl asked, straightening. "That doesn't make sense."

"Uncle Dahl *swore*," Wilmot said, eyes like saucers.

"Sorry." Dahl had been crammed into the three hastily rented rooms with thirteen other people for a tenday already, and every time he found the space to take a breath by himself, one or another of his family would interrupt—one of his nieces and nephews would ask what he was doing, one of his two brothers would prod at him, his mother would ask if he'd eaten, his granny would tell him to stop being a layabout. At least Bodhar hadn't—

"Or," Bodhar went on, as if hearing Dahl's thoughts, "he's doing that magic talk with his mysterious brightbird. Since apparently, little Dahl's a wizard too."

No—Dahl had no components left for sendings. One back to Lord Vescaras Ammakyl, the Harper agent he'd been teamed with in Cormyr, as soon as he'd gotten to Harrowdale—partly to make contact, partly to pass a message to Farideh. One to Tam Zawad, the High Harper in Waterdeep, to sort out where the agents he handled were.

Lorcan had not left him room for anything else.

I got your message, Farideh had said through her own sending. *Mehen wants to go to Djerad Thymar. We leave tomorrow, unless you tell me why I should stay?*

And he couldn't. He couldn't speak a single sound, without breaking his deal and giving his very soul to the Nine Hells. He'd stood there, waiting for the spell to run out, holding the sound of her voice in his thoughts. That half-hesitant *I love you.*

"Thost thinks she's from Hillsfar," Bodhar said to his wife. "That's why Dahl's being so cryptic."

Meri clucked her tongue. "He wouldn't take up with a Hillsfar woman."

"He might. Not as if he's got throngs of Harran girls fighting for him."

"Why would they fight for him?" Wilmot asked.

"It's means something different with adults," Bodhar said. "Except with Uncle Dahl."

"Gods' books, I'm right here," Dahl snapped.

"He's wight deer!" Aggie shouted. Bodhar and Meribelle laughed, and even Dahl had to smile.

"It's not a Hillfarian name."

Bodhar and Dahl straightened like guilty boys at the sound of Granny Sessaca's voice. The old woman, her snow-white hair in long braids, stood in the doorway, delicate as a rapier and just as sharp.

"Farideh," the old woman said, leaning on her wooden cane. "Wasn't that it?"

"Yes, Granny." He smiled down at Wilmot who was studying the hilt of Dahl's dagger in his belt.

"*Look* at me when you're talking, boy."

Dahl made himself look into his grandmother's steely eyes. "Yes, Granny."

She muttered something under her breath and shook her head, as though there were no bigger disappointment than her youngest grandson. "You going out again today?"

"Yes, later."

"Find me some tea. Chessenta black. None of that rubbish with petals in it, mind." Her eyes flicked over Dahl. "Your brothers can't manage better than dusty Kara-Turan leavings."

"Granny," Bodhar said, "the trade roads are closed and the sea's half-full of pirates. There just aren't the goods coming in that there used to be."

"Oh?" Sessaca said. "What was your excuse before the war?"

"Fair winds now, Mother." Eurdila, Dahl's mother, came in from the back door, a basket of laundry on her hip, her graying hair knotted atop her head. She gave her youngest son a fond smile. "I'm sure Dahl will find your tea."

"I'll try," Dahl said.

"And a book," Sessaca added. "Since mine weren't worth carrying away, apparently."

"There's my good lad," Eurdila said. She patted Dahl's cheek. "Can you manage a few other things as well? I've a pie in the embers, and the lack of a fire-iron is going to doom it. We've also run off without a good whetstone. And the children didn't grab enough underthings," she added, dropping her voice, "so a few yards of linen would not be unappreciated."

"I'll find what I can," Dahl said. His mother smiled.

"It's so good to have you home again." She turned and hooked her mother-in-law's arm in hers. "Would you come sit with me while I undo what all those thorns did?"

Meribelle hugged Aggie a little closer. Only Eurdila could make fleeing through the edges of the Cormanthor forest in darkest night sound like a minor nuisance. Eurdila and Sessaca headed into the back room, where the fire burned, and Meribelle took Aggie and Wilmot out to where the other children played.

"My excuse is that tea tastes like the bottom of a rain barrel," Bodhar muttered to Dahl. "Nobody sells it." He sniffed and considered the door his wife had gone through. "Why don't you let me tag along? Getting a little cottage-crazed, and maybe I can help you with your errands."

Dahl hesitated. "It's . . . I've got to find some components. Spells and things. It's going to take a while, maybe involve shops you don't want to go to."

Bodhar's brows went up. "That sounds interesting."

"It won't be."

"Come on." Bodhar clapped Dahl on the back. "There's a reason I'm the one they send to market, and t'isn't because I don't know which end of the sheep to geld. I know folks. I'll bet I can help. We can stop by a tavern on the way back, if you like. Catch up."

Dahl inhaled slowly, trying to calm his pulse. "All right. Let's go."

In the road, Dahl's nieces and nephews played, soaking up the meager winter sun. The little ones made forts of firewood along the house's side. His eldest brother, Thost, and his sister-in-law, Dellora, shouted corrections and encouragements at lanky Jens and fifteen-year-old Sabrelle, sparring with sticks of wood.

"You're skirting her," Dellora called to her son. "You're going to both tire out that way." She smiled at Dahl and Bodhar, while Wilmot rebraided her long chestnut hair.

Thost nodded at them, towering over the children. Their own father had loomed like that, a mountain of a man, making even Dahl and Bodhar seem small as they jabbed at each other with their own sticks. "Where you headed?" Thost asked.

"Getting Granny some tea and Ma a whole list of things," Bodhar called back. "And Dahl's got secret errands again."

Thost sniffed and tugged his reddish beard. "Your secret errands giving you any notion of when we can go back? I don't like to think of how many sheep we're going to lose to the forest."

Better sheep than children, Dahl thought. His niece yelled as she lunged at her cousin, jabbing his midsection with the stick. "If I find out," Dahl said. "I'll tell you."

"Knock 'em down, Sabrelle!" Bodhar called. "That's my girl."

New Velar had grown since Dahl had last visited. The port city gleamed with fresh plaster and new faces, the prosperity the council of burghers brought to Harrowdale evident at every turn. Still, to Dahl it seemed cramped and false, a village playing at something grander.

Maybe, he thought as they left a blacksmith's with Eurdila's whetstone and fire irons, it's you who's grown. How many years had he lived in Waterdeep, with its ancient streets and massive population? How many cities had he made a temporary home in, carrying out one Harper mission or another? Westgate. Proskur. Baldur's Gate. Suzail.

Farideh moved in the edges of his thoughts again, all the many days they'd roamed Suzail looking for connections and secrets and ways to save the city. His arm around her waist. Her head on his shoulder. All their conversations turning back to the Shadovar, to the reason they were pretending to be lovers.

Wasting time, Dahl thought, pretending you didn't love her in fact.

"You're worrying her, you know?" Bodhar said suddenly.

Dahl stopped, puzzled, at the crossroads. "Who?"

"Ma. Maybe she doesn't know about that message in the night"—he tapped the side of his nose—"but you turn up out of nowhere, shouting about Shadovar raiders, and then you're right?" He shook his head. "Everyone's figured out you're not just a secretary out in Waterdeep at this point. Question is, what are you?"

A simple question with a tangled answer. His allegiance to the Harpers was secret, and so then were the sort of skills that would mark him as an agent and a handler. For years, his family had assumed Dahl worked as a secretary for a priest in Waterdeep, a cover that Dahl bore with gritted teeth. Already he'd slipped, sending a message to another agent after his family escaped the Shadovar attack, making sure Vescaras knew where he was and that he could tell Farideh what Dahl couldn't. He should have waited until Thost and Bodhar were gone, but he couldn't bear to risk it.

"It's complicated," Dahl said, moving again.

"Complicated as your distant dove?" Bodhar squinted at him. "She's *not* Hillfarian, is she?"

"No," Dahl said. And if his family was so concerned that Farideh might hail from a nearby kingdom that had always had a little bit too much interest in New Velar's port for comfort, what would they say about her having horns and a tail and the attention of an undeniably evil god?

If she were here, Dahl told himself, it would be different. They'd see.

Bodhar kept pressing, as Dahl threaded his way down an alley. "So why didn't you bring her? And why's Granny giving you the dagger-eyes about her name?"

"It's Granny," Dahl said. "Has she ever not given me the dagger-eyes?" He exhaled hard again. "Look, I need . . . some things that aren't going to necessarily be easy to come by. I rather expect I'm looking for someone—a caster preferably—who does business with less-savory folks."

Bodhar sniffed. "All right. I maybe know a fellow. Dark Reyan."

Dahl frowned. "You know a wizard called Dark Reyan?"

"He drinks at the Drowning Goat sometimes," Bodhar said. "I've diced with him. I've diced with just about everybody in this city—mind, you don't need to be telling Meri about that in much detail. I always keep it even enough." Bodhar glanced at the crossroads. "Come on."

He led Dahl down an alleyway behind a bakehouse, the ambient heat enough to melt the ice into muddy slush. Another turn and Dahl found himself looking at a dismal little shop set into an even danker little alley. A sign with a raven perched on a mortar and pestle hung over the door.

Bodhar stopped him. "I'll make you a deal?"

The word sent a shudder down Dahl's spine. "What's that?"

"I'll help you out, talk Reyan down for you—talk the rest of these people down too. And you tell me three things about your new dove."

"So you'll have something new to nip my heels over? No thanks."

"No," Bodhar said. "So I know a thing or two about my own brother. Your decision."

Dahl was silent for a long moment, biting his tongue and debating how badly he needed Bodhar's help. How merciless his brothers would be.

"She's adopted. She has a twin sister." He hesitated. "She puts a ridiculous amount of sugar in her tea."

Bodhar's face fell. "Watching Gods. That's the best you can do? What do you love about her?"

Everything, Dahl thought. The image of Farideh, fiery and terrible, missiles streaming from her fingers—almost everything—he shook it away. "You said 'three things.' That was three things. Come on."

The interior of the shop was dim and thick with the acrid smells of guano and brimstone. Dark Reyan stood behind a counting table, eyeing the brothers as though they might be lost or they might be brigands, but there was no chance they might be customers. He was thin as a reed and sallow-skinned, and his shoulder-length hair was an improbably deep black.

"Oh, Bodhar," Reyan said. "Well met."

"Heya, Reyan," Bodhar called, as though they'd just wandered into a taproom. "Well met, yourself. How ye farin'?"

"Well enough."

"You remember my little brother? Dahl?" Bodhar asked, jerking a thumb toward Dahl. "He's visiting. Helped us get out of the army's reach."

"I heard about that. Beshaba pass you over."

"Already did, already did," Bodhar said, his cheer undampened. "Thanks to this one's quick thinking. *He's* been in Waterdeep," Bodhar added proudly.

Reyan nodded. "You've said. The learned secretary. Always figured if one of Barron's boys left that farm, it'd be to sellsword."

Dahl's temper flared. "Yes, well. It's complicated." Complicated in all the ways he couldn't discuss—the fence between his life out in the wider world, and his life in Harrowdale hemmed him in. Easier to be a secretary and let them assume what they want.

"Don't mind him," Bodhar said. "We've been giving him all the trouble he's missed out on in the big city, me and Thost. What's a brother for after all?"

Reyan cracked a smile. "Well, Dahl, you're one up on most if you haven't cracked this plinth-head one yet."

"Ma would thrash us all if he started a fight," Bodhar said with mock seriousness.

"Your mother is a lamb," Reyan said "From what I hear, your granny, on the other hand . . ."

"String us right up," Dahl said.

Reyan chuckled. "If you're lucky. What can I get for you?"

Dahl hesitated, the boundary between his past in Harrowdale and his present and Harper oath feeling as solid as a fence in that moment. "Components," he said. "To begin with."

"And what after that?" Reyan asked.

"Have you got books," Dahl asked carefully, "about planar entities?"

Reyan's eyes cut to Bodhar. "Got some texts on the Feywild."

"He says he wants something dark, but t'isn't for dark reasons," Bodhar supplied. Reyan made a face. He considered Dahl a moment more.

"You shouldn't dirty your hands with that," he said.

"I know," Dahl said. "It's not for me. It's for someone I think is in trouble."

Reyan shook his head and muttered something. "I don't carry that sort of trouble. Anything else?"

Dahl blew out a breath. There will be an answer. It might not be here. "A ritual? I need something to get a message to someone far away—"

"Simple," Reyan said. "A sending will get you—"

"No," Dahl said. "I need to get a message to them, but I can't talk to them." He pursed his mouth. "You have anything that could maybe send a letter or scribe a message if I don't know where the person's at exactly?"

Reyan frowned. "Usually the sending's good for folks."

"I can't use it," Dahl said. "Otherwise I wouldn't be here."

The sorcerer scratched his nose. "I have one that charms an animal to carry a message for you."

Dahl shook his head. Such a spell would take ages—how long would it take a squirrel or a cat or a jay to reach Djerad

Thymar from Harrowdale? Longer than the spell could reliably last, he thought.

"A really large distance," he tried again. "A tenday's journey, maybe two."

Reyan looked to Bodhar, who shrugged. "I think in that case you use the sending."

"The sending doesn't—" Dahl bit off the repeated protest— this was going nowhere and he couldn't say too much, not without risking the edges of the deal. "Never mind. I need some components too."

He ran down the short list of things he needed, Bodhar chiming in to needle at the prices, and by the end, Dahl had half of his list—including the dried formian blood he hadn't been able to find, procured from Reyan's private stores—and a third of his coin purse. Not ideal, he thought. But better than expected.

"Many thanks," he said to Bodhar. "You kept him down."

Bodhar shrugged. "Reyan's easy. Bluffs like Aggie, all giddy he's lying."

"Why do you call him Dark Reyan?"

"Come on—that hair? Looks like he dunks his head in a vat of ink." Bodhar patted his own salt-and-pepper crop. "Can't say I enjoy this, but having seen the alternative, I'll accept it. Yours going yet?"

"Not yet."

"Let it go. It'll make you look less like a pup," Bodhar advised. He grinned at Dahl. "So you can't talk to her. That it?"

Dahl turned on his heel, heading south through the city without a word.

"Oh come on," Bodhar called. "What is it? She got a husband or something?"

Dahl gritted his teeth. Worse, he thought. Lorcan's laugh echoed in his memory. *You're not the hero of her story. You're an impediment. A sidetrack.* He needed a damned drink—his hand reached like a reflex for the flask in his pocket. He balled it into a fist instead.

"Hey!" Bodhar shouted, running to catch up. "Look, everyone's just worried about you."

"They don't need to be."

"Why can't you talk to her?"

Because my soul is forfeit if I do, Dahl thought. "I can't tell you that. It's complicated."

"Everything's 'complicated,'" Bodhar said. "But this girl's the one you let your guard down to get a message to. *Don't* tell me it was about telling your employer where you were," he said, when Dahl started to speak. "One of those things could have waited until morning."

Dahl spun. "I don't know why you care so much about—"

The cloaked figure beyond his brother caught his eye as it suddenly turned, too interested in a stall selling roasted apples. The seller held out one in offer, and the figure waved it away with a slim, dark arm.

"Let's go," Dahl said, pulling Bodhar along.

He turned a corner, not knowing where he was heading anymore, his path determined by the shadowy figure following behind. Sure enough, as the brothers passed a hearth house in the middle of the block, the figure turned the same corner, their face invisible in the shadows of a hood.

Little shorter than him, he thought, lighter frame. Probably a woman, maybe an elf? Who would be following him? Who would know he was in New Velar?

How dangerous was this going to be to Bodhar?

"Come on," Bodhar said. "You can talk to me, little brother. I'm not going to tell you I know everything about women, but I haven't forgotten what I do know." He looked around. "Where are we going?"

"A moment," Dahl said, turning down a narrow road. The path was short—his shadow would need to catch up quick to stay on his tail. Partway up, another alley broke off to the left between a fuller's and a candle maker. "Stick close," he said to Bodhar, and darted through the passersby and detritus of the city toward the alley.

Dahl turned the corner fast, yanking Bodhar back out of the way. He motioned for silence and drew his dagger from his boot, listening for rapid footfalls. When the stranger in the cloak came to the corner, he seized them by one arm, swinging them around and up against the stone wall, bending the arm behind.

"Gods above!" Bodhar cried out.

"Whatever you're thinking of trying," Dahl started, "whoever sent you—"

"Well met to you too," a woman's voice said. A familiar woman's voice. "If you break my arm, I'm going to have to tell my father."

"Gods' books!" Dahl spat. He let go of his captive. Mira Zawad turned, pulling back her hood enough to reveal her brown face and the dark edge of her hair. Her black eyes looked hollow, tired, but they glittered with amusement.

"What are you doing here?" Dahl demanded.

"Looking for you, obviously," Mira said. "And, one hopes, finding you before the Zhentarim do."

"Zhentarim?" Bodhar said, eyes wide. He shot Dahl a look. "Well met indeed."

Dahl cursed. "Not here," he said. "We need a quiet place to talk. What's close?"

Bodhar clicked his tongue a few times. "The Gilded Rune's near to here and open, but nobody goes until late." He turned to Mira. "Not that I do either," he said conversationally. "Bit rich."

"I'm paying," Mira said.

"Lead on," Dahl said, sheathing the dagger. He leaned close to her as he walked. "Did your father send you?"

"Not this time," she said apologetically. "Nor am I here for my own pleasure, before you ask."

Dahl turned his eyes to Bodhar's back. "Yes. Well."

Holding tight to Mira's arm, Dahl followed Bodhar to the taproom and back to the darkest, quietest corner it could offer.

"Not bad?" Bodhar said. "Since you're talking to each other, I'll assume she's not your secret brightbird?"

Mira laughed once. "Beg your pardon?"

"Bodhar," Dahl said, ignoring the question, "why don't you go find Granny's things?" The boundary between Harper and Harran tilted dangerously, threatening to topple. "I'll find you after."

Bodhar looked from Mira to Dahl, skeptical. "Yeah, I'll wait at that table by the door."

"He's your brother?" Mira asked as the shorter man left.

"One of them," Dahl said, as he sat beside his Zhentarim double agent, the only daughter of the High Harper of Waterdeep, ready for the worst. Mira wasn't the sort of agent to come to him with less. Neither spoke as he ordered two ales, plus one for Bodhar.

"Who's your secret brightbird?" Mira asked, in a conversational way.

"There are Zhentarim chasing me and you want to make chatter?" Dahl asked, pulse speeding. "Every breath we sit here is one we lose preparing for whatever nonsense they've brought down on us now. So tell me."

Mira bit her upper lip, thoughtful a moment, before asking. "Have you heard of the Master's Library?"

"The lost temple of Deneir?" Dahl asked. More than a temple—a library, the biggest, they said, in all of Toril. Larger than Candlekeep. Larger than the Library of Curna. Larger than anything Shou Lung could boast of. And since the Spellplague and the death of the god of records, the Scribe of Oghma, no one had seen it. "What do your employers want with that?"

Mira hesitated again. "Portal magic. Or so they tell me. The Weave is being repaired—somehow. They'd like the portal system they had in olden days back up and running, but there's a lack of information in this day and age as to how to manage it. So they hired me to find the library."

"Since you did so well the last time," Dahl said. He'd met Mira while searching for another lost library. And Farideh, he thought, that first time ages ago, when he'd gotten everything wrong.

"The Shadovar have better things to do than chase us this time," Mira said. "Should be fun, if you want to come along."

And there would be portal magic, strong enough to cross the continent. Spells that could send a message long distances, and maybe ways to undo pacts with devils? Dahl shook his head—dealing with the Zhentarim always had a price. "Why are you asking me?"

Mira smiled in that small, secret way she had. "I don't think they're telling me everything. They came to me three days ago. Pulled me off another project they said was paramount—giant artifacts, believe it or not. I haven't slept since, and they're willing to use the very expensive portal magic they do have to jump me around hunting—and still, that's not quick enough. This isn't about books."

"Do you need extraction?"

"And leave all those lovely records to rot?" Mira said, eyes glittering. "I haven't found a way in. But what I found is information about the last person my employers know entered the library—one of theirs obviously, but sixty-three years ago—and it's very interesting, because you share a surname."

Dahl frowned, embarrassed. "I think you're wrong."

Mira leaned over the table before he could explain. "Her name was Sessaca Peredur."

For a moment Dahl couldn't speak at all. "Sessaca?" Dahl repeated. "*Sessaca* Peredur."

"Ring any bells? A black sheep of a grandaunt perhaps? Maybe you have an old chest full of gear she left behind? Or, Watching Gods favor us, a map in her hand?"

Dahl said nothing at all for several breaths. It was a mistake, he thought. It had to be a mistake. Mira raised her eyebrows. "We are talking about my head here, and maybe yours. Tell me you have something."

"I might have . . . her," Dahl finally said.

"Her?" Mira asked. "Sessaca Peredur is still alive?"

Dahl nodded, still gobsmacked. "But . . . there has to be a mistake. My grandmother . . ."

"She come from a big family?" Mira asked. "Peredur's not a common name, so far as I can tell."

It wasn't—and Sessaca had no one outside of the farm in Harrowdale, they knew that well enough. Bodhar was staring at them from his table by the door. Dahl couldn't begin to think of how to explain this to him.

Karshoj—only one of Farideh's Draconic curses sounded ripe enough for the occasion, and if his pronunciation had been anything to speak of, it would have come right out. Dahl raked a hand through his hair. "I'm going to need you to help me track down some Chessentan black. And finish your ale," he suggested, picking his up as well. "You're going to need it."

• • •

EVEN WITH THE promise of good Chessentan black, Granny Sessaca did not take kindly to being roused from her seat by the fire, especially not when Dahl insisted that she go upstairs to the chilly third room where the children all slept, the only room of the little house that was abandoned this time of day. She insisted, wearily, that she had to stir the fire until her husband came home with the good haunch of venison he promised.

Bodhar winced. "She gets like that sometimes lately," he whispered to Dahl. "Forgets things. Maybe we should wait." He tapped his hand against his leg. "You going to tell me what's going on?"

What was going on, Dahl thought, was that Mira was already scaling the drainpipe, letting herself in the window upstairs. And the barrier between Dahl's Harper life and his Harran life was growing dangerously thin.

"Go get Thost," Dahl said. "And don't breathe a word of this to anyone."

As much as Dahl didn't want any more members to this conspiracy, Thost was strong enough and swift enough to scoop Granny from her chair and bring her upstairs. Bodhar carried up the rocker after him and a rug for her lap besides.

"What is this?" Sessaca demanded. "Your father will be very upset with you boys. You'll get the switch, I'll make sure of it."

Dahl pursed his mouth. Barron, Sessaca's only son, had been dead for several years now—bringing him up, forgetting the passage of time. She was upset and there was all the chance Mira was about to upset her more. *Maybe Bodhar's right*, he thought.

But Mira remained, the question remained—the Zhentarim remained. They were coming one way or another, and if he didn't have an answer to hand them before then—

Thost stopped dead in the doorway at the sight of Mira. "Who in the sodden Hells is that?"

"A friend," Dahl said, setting down the teapot. "She's got questions for Granny."

Sessaca looked up at Mira, adding the shriveled tea leaves to the hot water, as Thost set her carefully down in the rocking chair. "And who's this? A little playmate? I don't like the look of her." She peered at Mira. "Who're your parents, girl? I'll not have my grandsons bringing urchins into this house."

"The Black Network sent me, old mother," Mira said flatly. "And I brought you tea."

"What the *sodden Hells?*" Thost hissed. "Godsdamn it, Dahl, what are you doing?"

For a moment, Dahl wondered the same thing. But then Sessaca's expression shifted—if he hadn't trained himself to spot such things, he might never have noticed. She still watched Mira, puzzled, weary, but Dahl couldn't deny that a certain cunning had overtaken her.

"I beg your pardon, girl? The what now?"

"Old mother, don't play that game," Mira said. "Maybe your grandsons will believe your mind's not sharp, but I've read the records. I think I know you better."

Sessaca leaned back in her rocking chair, silent for a moment. Weighing the odds. Dahl nearly cursed aloud. Mira was right.

"Sounds wicked," Sessaca said, not conceding but not speaking in that trembling way she'd used before. "Sounds like a pack of rogues who might try and kill me where I sit." She set the chair rocking, toying with the heavy gold locket she always wore. "But that hardly seems wise, girl, when I have my three strapping grandsons on guard like this. Do you think you can take all three of them on?"

"I don't hunt people," Mira said. "Just secrets."

Sessaca chuckled. "I've forgotten more than you'll ever know. And I don't break the covenant. Your masters have aught to fear from me."

"My masters would agree. Although they'd prefer to come line your family up and make you remember with a good bit more blood on the floor, just to be certain. I need to know where the Master's Library is. You want to keep yours safe. Can you help us both, old mother?"

Sessaca turned to Dahl. "Is this what you've been mixed up in? What are you bringing into this house?"

Dahl nearly laughed. There was never a border, Dahl realized in that moment, never a division between the life of secrets and the life of simplicity. He'd been born into a world where they were already blurred and blended in a thousand ways.

"She wants to know where the Master's Library is," he said, "because a Zhentarim agent named Sessaca Peredur was the last to see it, sixty years ago. And if there were another explanation in the planes above and below, I'd like to hear it. But it was you, wasn't it? You were the agent. You probably never left. That's how we always get the best prices on the rye crop, why the burgher's collectors would miss Grandda in lean years. You're the same Sessaca Peredur, agent of the Black Network."

"Sodden Hells," Thost said.

Sessaca folded her bony hands together, looking irritated. For a long moment, she said nothing, and Dahl found himself hoping beyond hope that he was wrong.

Bodhar's eyes looked as though they might pop out of his head. "Granny?"

"Is it so hard to believe?" she asked. "I was someone before I ever came to this dale, after all, before I ever met your grandfather, gods care for his soul. Why would I throw all that away when he needed it, when *we* needed it? Don't paint me a blackguard though, lambkin. I haven't earned that." She turned to Mira. "You, on the other hand, I still don't like the look of. The Master's Library is nothing but an empty tomb. What do you want there?"

"Does it matter?"

"Of course, it matters. It's something serious if you've managed to track me down all the way out here. If your superiors are willing to kill for the answer."

Mira hesitated and Sessaca nodded sagely. "They're not telling you everything, are they? Typical. But if you won't tell me, then I've no way to decide if you *need* it."

"Old mother, please," Mira said. "I'm no killer, but my employers are dangerous souls. They won't ask you nicely or bargain with tea. They'll—"

A crash from downstairs, a startled cry. The sound of booted feet.

"Piss and hrast," Mira said. "They caught up."

3

Havilar looked up at the core of Djerad Thymar, bathed in a light that seemed to come from nowhere at all. The four walls, slanting into a peak so impossibly far off they seemed to be midcollapse, somehow looked more solid than a mountain too. Balconies dripping with plants protruded from every side, the space between crisscrossed by walkways as the sides neared one another. It was like something out of a chapbook story, she thought, an alien palace from a far-off world, and she grinned.

She'd dreamed of Djerad Thymar for so many years, the nearest city to the village she and Farideh had grown up in, the source of most luxuries, gossip, stories. This was the result of Khorsaya and the thighbone sword, of Nala and the ten thousand shadows, of the battles of Arambar Gulch and the Crippled Mountain.

This, she thought, is where you'll belong.

"Watching Gods," Brin breathed beside her. "It goes up forever."

Her arm wanted to reach for him, her hand to take his, but Havilar kept her eyes on the pyramid's peak. They weren't doing that anymore. Not for a while at least. Not until she'd figured things out. She made a fist of that hand. "It's like a mountain," she said. "Do you think it was a mountain? Maybe they hollowed it out."

Brin reached across her, pointed at the nearest wall. "There's seams," he said. "Tight ones, but it was built of blocks. Somehow." He grinned at her. "It's like something out of a chapbook isn't it?"

50

Havilar smiled at him despite herself. "Exactly."

He cleared his throat awkwardly and looked back up. "What's at the top?" Brin asked. "Do you know?"

Together they squinted up at the dark square that marred the granite near the peak. "Maybe that's how you get up to the top?" Havilar said. "Or . . . it's a window?"

"They don't need a window with this light." He shook his head. "They always say dragonborn don't like magic, but this is all pretty glim." He gave Havilar a worried look. "Can I say 'dragonborn' here, or is that rude?"

She shrugged. "I've never met anyone who was bothered by it. They think it's stupid, but it's not like it's an *insult*."

"You're hardly going to talk to anyone," Farideh said beside them. She gave Havilar a dark look. "And it's not about disliking magic, just preferring using your own two hands. Come on. The teahouse is this way."

Havilar bit her tongue and shot a look at Brin. Ever since they'd left Suzail, Farideh had been distant, prickly. Pining for Dahl probably, Havilar thought. *Henish.* Bastard.

"There's no harm in *looking*. It's not like we're expected."

Farideh looped her arm through Havilar's, pulling her near. "If we could predict harm, we'd be a lot better off."

"Worrywart." As they entered the edge of the market square, spoken Draconic rattled across her ears—too fast for her to catch every word. It made her feel slow. Havilar dropped her voice as they walked. "Are you doing all right? That was enough, the fire thing on the road?"

"I'll be all right for another few days," Farideh said. "The imps?"

"I haven't needed anything to make them come," Havilar said. If there was one thing to be grateful about, it was the fact that the meager powers Asmodeus had bestowed on her didn't need any attending to—aside from making sure Zoonie had a chance to run a bit, which wasn't the same. "I'll just keep not needing anything."

Farideh snorted. "Why didn't we think of that before?" Then she added, "We're not staying long. Here and gone."

Havilar rolled her eyes, but only nodded. None of it was all that important—they were safe, they were together, she knew what mattered, and she was someplace *interesting* and new. She admired a display of bright colored cloths, shot through with silver and gold thread, and a stall of glass bottles in as many colors as the dragonborn milling through the market. The scents of spices she couldn't name mixed together into something new and different. She wondered what they'd have to eat at the Shield of Shasphur and whether Brin would like it.

Beside her, Farideh kept sweeping her gaze over the crowd, as if she were watching for an ambush. "What are you doing?" Havilar whispered. "You look like a lunatic. What are you looking for?"

"Nothing," Farideh murmured. Havilar looked past her, along the row of stalls to where a tiefling man slouched against a column. He was handsome in a weathered kind of way, his eyes the pale blue of a cold, clear sky. He smiled at Havilar, looked her over in an appreciative way, and she smiled back. She could, after all, she thought. Brin'd had romances while she was gone. She could make up for lost time, if she wanted.

"There's a lot more tieflings here than I would have thought," she said in a careless way, gazing up at the pyramid's peak again.

Something unfolded from the high-up passage, gray and enormous. It dropped like a stone, and Havilar picked out the greenish dragonborn riding on its back before wings unfolded and the creature swooped down through the pyramid and out of sight. Havilar jumped, releasing Farideh.

"That was a *bat*!" she said. "That was a giant *karshoji* bat! Gods." She turned to Brin, elated. "What do you think you have to do to ride a bat? Do you think it costs?"

"You already have a hellhound," Farideh said. "Is that not terrifying enough?"

"She doesn't *fly*."

"She does jump from awful high," Brin said, in a worried sort of way. "The rider had a badge of some kind on. You think it's their army?"

"Lance Defenders." Havilar looked back to the dark passage, stories whirling in her thoughts. Farideh grabbed her arm again and hugged her close.

"Here and gone," she reminded Havilar gently. "Come on. I'll bet we can get an ale."

That's what she's looking for, Havilar realized. Arjhani. And the idea that something so far away and faded would chase her from this chance at making a life for herself made Havilar's chest tight, her cheeks hot. "Don't treat me like a little girl," she said to Farideh. "Not you."

"We just have plenty to worry about," Farideh said. "Chosen, clans, the ghost."

"We haven't seen her for ages." The ghost of their ancestor, Bryseis Kakistos, had tracked Havilar down, possessing a pair of sellswords and then Brin, before being turned. All that bloodshed, all that danger, and they had no idea what she was after. *You have something I need, locked deep inside you.*

Havilar stole a glance back at Brin. He never spoke of those moments when the ghost of the Brimstone Angel had ridden him, breaking his fingers to try and motivate Havilar to do her bidding. She wondered if she ought to ask him.

Leave him be, she thought. You're not sweethearts anymore. She hugged Farideh's arm closer.

"I still think we should tell Lorcan," Havilar said. "We already know as much as we're going to know without someone from the Nine Hells helping," Havilar went on. "And it's *not* going to be Sairché." Lorcan's sister was more trouble even than he was.

"It's not going to be Lorcan either," Farideh said. "Not now."

Havilar spat a little curse. "I'd say you shouldn't have slept with him, but *that* was never going to happen. And I'd say you shouldn't have broken off with him, but that was bound to happen too."

Farideh flushed. "Oh, so I had no say in any of it?"

"Be reasonable—I've seen what Lorcan looks like. Dahl," Havilar went on. "You could have not slept with Dahl. I imagine that only riled Lorcan up worse." And then stupid Dahl had vanished and left her sister with just enough to make her hope he was coming back—but not enough to be sure.

"And you could have had done with Brin a lot sooner," Farideh said testily, dropping into Draconic so Brin wouldn't hear. "Decided not to be in love with him, and then we wouldn't have been in Suzail."

Havilar glanced back at Brin again, trailing them and watching as if gauging the sisters' conversation. Since Suzail, since they'd set aside their relationship, he did that a lot. She wanted to protest that it wasn't the same, that Farideh wasn't being fair—to her or to Brin. But she only sighed. "Romance is the worst."

Farideh squeezed her arm. "Devils are the worst."

"Fair," Havilar agreed as they arrived.

The Shield of Shasphur was much like a tavern, but open on one side to the market, and half the tables were just boards of polished wood upon the ground, surrounded by cushions. A mix of people, mostly dragonborn, drank from glass flagons and clay cups, nibbling at platters of grilled breads. A dragonborn woman with the same pearly piercings Dumuzi wore greeted them and showed them to a table. She poured them each a small cup of steaming liquid, fragrant with spices and faintly gold. It tasted of apples and anise and strange perfume.

"*Sukriya*," Farideh and Havilar said over each other. Brin smiled nervously.

"Sookree-ah." The dragonborn woman gave him a patient smile. "Um, thank you."

"You are welcome," she said to him with care. To the twins she said in Draconic, "You speak very well."

"Our father's Thymari," Havilar said. "More or less."

The woman's smile froze, as though she were no longer certain Havilar wasn't mad. "How nice."

"Can we just get three ales?" Farideh asked quickly. She handed over a small pile of coins, and the woman left.

Brin frowned. "Sookree-ah."

"*Sook-ree-yah*," Havilar said. "Three sounds."

"Sook-ree-yuh."

"If you just say 'thank you,' you'll probably be fine," Farideh pointed out. "I think just about everyone speaks Common too."

"I'd like to know anyway," Brin said. "I wouldn't mind learning to speak it. Especially if everyone here speaks it. You all speak it. How do you sasy 'Do you speak the common tongue?' in Draconic?"

"You don't have to ask that," Farideh said. "They all speak it."

"*Wux renthish Munthrarechi*," Havilar said.

"Wooks rent-theesh mun-thrar-etch-ee," Brin repeated carefully. Havilar smiled, his accent was adorable. "Mun-thrar-etch-ee."

"We're not staying that long," Farideh reminded him as the woman returned with their ales. "*Sukriya*."

"*Nar viraka*," the woman said.

"If you say so," Brin said once she'd left, and Havilar felt a little flutter of triumph. "I mean . . ." He gestured out at the marketplace. "Everyone looks like Mehen. Even if he thinks he doesn't want to be here, isn't that a comfort of sorts? I can see him wanting to stay longer. And I wouldn't mind. I'm curious."

"Me too," Havilar said.

Farideh drank a little of her ale. "He doesn't like his clan. There's nothing for him here."

"Who even knows what's here?" Havilar said. "Aside from dragonborn and giant bats."

"You're not going to ride a bat," Farideh said. "Are you even considering—"

Before she could finish her thought, Havilar spotted Mehen beyond Brin's head, striding after a dragonborn woman with reddish scales and black plumes, a gauzy wrap floating around her like a pair of wings. He looked faintly gray, and Havilar stood without thinking. "*Karshoj*. Look."

"Come on," Farideh said, but Havilar was already up and heading for Mehen. Something was wrong, very wrong—and all at once she found herself picturing Mehen coming face-to-face with Arjhani again and then—

No. Calm down, she told herself.

"Mehen?" she called. "Mehen, are you all right?"

He stopped as if startled by her voice. All around him, dragonborn had slowed, staring back at Mehen and now Havilar approaching. "Go back to the Shield," he said. "Something's happened, and . . . I'll be a little longer. Go back."

"What happened?" Havilar demanded as Farideh and Brin caught up to them. She looked toward the dragonborn woman. "Is that *her*? Anala?"

The woman glanced back over her shoulder, slowing as she spotted Mehen still beside the twins and Brin. Beyond her, Havilar saw another man stop and look back, as if waiting for them to follow.

"A moment, Anala," Mehen called. To the twins, he said, "Just go to the Shield. I will be back in an hour, no more."

"Are these your assistants?" Anala asked, coming over. Beneath her gauzy wraps she wore proper armor, Havilar noticed. She wondered briefly if there were a shop you could buy the wraps at.

"I would hire them too," Anala said.

Havilar's attention came back to the moment. "What for?"

Mehen's tongue tapped the roof of his mouth. "Go back to the Shield."

Like Hells, Havilar thought. She wasn't leaving a chance to stay longer on the table, and she wasn't leaving Mehen on his own when he looked so upset. "I thought we had to earn our own coin? I'd like to earn some more coin."

"Havi," Farideh warned. "Maybe we should—"

"Come with us then," Anala said. "But quickly."

"Of course," Havilar said, feeling maybe a little more pleased with herself than necessary. The gauze would look amazing on bat-back, she thought. "What's the job?"

"They're not my assistants." Mehen hesitated. "These are my daughters."

Anala's golden eyes darted from one horned woman to the other, her hands pressed together as if she needed something to occupy them. "Well," she said after a moment. "I see what you mean by insurmountable."

"Leave it there," Mehen said. "I'm not a catch, and I don't care to be."

"Don't underestimate me," Anala said. She squared her shoulders and gave the girls a little bow. "Good afternoon," she said in perfect Common. "I'm Verthisathurgiesh Anala, daughter of Gharizani." The briefest hesitation. "Verthisathurgiesh's matriarch and Mehen's aunt. Your . . . grandaunt, I suppose." Havilar looked to Farideh, but her twin looked just as uncertain.

"This is Farideh and Havilar," Mehen said.

"Very pretty," Anala said. "I've always been fond of the old names. And this?" She gestured at Brin. "A son too?"

"This is Brin. Just a friend."

"A pleasure to make your acquaintance, saer," Brin said with a bow that would have been quite proper in Cormyr. Anala gave him a curious look.

"Matriarch Anala?" the young man who'd been leading them called. "Please, the others will have gotten there already."

"Shall we?" Anala said. "Or do you need to discuss terms?"

"No," Mehen said. "We'll settle it later."

Havilar hurried to keep up with Mehen as they wound back down the pyramid's stairways and passages, following Matriarch Anala, a thousand questions dancing on her tongue, but she knew better than to ask them now. Now there was a job. Now was the time to make sure she looked seasoned.

Behind a forge, a door opened into the pyramid's wall, a dark portal into the depths below. Mehen stopped dead before it and drew a deep, labored breath.

"Mehen?" Farideh said softly. "Did someone die?"

"Several someones," he said a moment later. "Anala's son is one. Baruz. He's . . . He was just a hatchling, a baby, when

I left." He cleared his throat. "He could hardly walk. And now he's dead. In the catacombs. I said we'd find the killer."

Havilar's stomach dropped. They'd tracked killers before. She'd seen the dead, and added to the number. But the story of a baby Mehen knew being dead made her heart hurt—even if he was grown by now. And poor Anala—

Though she didn't seem too overtaken, Havilar had to say. Anala disappeared down into the base of the pyramid, and with another sigh, Mehen followed. Farideh watched with a troubled expression, the faint flags of shadow wafting off her. Havilar brushed her arms as if she could dust them off, as if she could soothe her sister's worries.

"I feel like he's not telling us something," Farideh said.

"Probably," Havilar sighed. Brin caught up to them and gave her a questioning look—she didn't feel like explaining it all just then, so she just said, "Come on." They entered the dark mouth of the catacombs of Djerad Thymar.

• • •

BEFORE SHE COULD register what the smell was, Farideh's stomach twisted, as if it were trying to escape out her back. In the hall of the catacombs, she looked back at Havilar, who threw up a hand to stop Brin.

"Brin, maybe you should stay back here," Havilar said.

"I've seen a dead body before."

"These . . . have been dead for some time," Farideh said. A few days, by the smell.

"You're going to vomit," Havilar said bluntly. Brin's mouth tightened. "You *know* you are."

"I can handle myself."

Havilar looked as if she were going to protest further, but she shook her head. "Fine," she said. "It's your stomach." Brin started to reply, but Havilar was already striding off. He watched her with an expression that suggested he'd let his stomach turn inside out before he threw up.

Farideh struggled to find *something* reassuring to say. She hardly knew what to do with the two of them these days. Brin regarded her as though he knew there was nothing she could say. "What are you worried about?" he asked. "With Havi, I mean. You're getting jumpy. Why do we need to leave so fast?"

Farideh bit her lip. "Has she ever told you about Arjhani?"

"A little. He was Mehen's lover?"

Farideh watched her sister heading down the passageway. Its height and breadth had been carved for dragonborn, and so Havilar seemed dwarfed and delicate. "It would be bad if she were to see Arjhani again."

"Why?" Brin asked. "What happened?"

Farideh shook her head. It was complicated, snarled and tangled around the time and the place. How could she explain without making her or Havilar sound mad, without explaining everything Arjhani had meant and represented? "Not now."

"And not later," Brin finished. "Since you two say we have to leave right away. I get it."

The stink of death became stronger with each doorway, until they ended in a long room dominated by a series of sepulchers and lined with niches. On the far wall, names in Draconic etched the granite surface. *The Roll of the Lost,* the runes over it read. Those ancestors who remained in Abeir, Farideh thought, whose bones were never recovered. A handful of dragonborn already stood around the room, holding torches.

On the floor lay the bodies, or what was left of them.

Someone had drawn sheets over the dead, but even at a glance Farideh could tell they were many and they were none of them intact. Blood stained the stone around the bodies, great pools of it, drying against the polished granite. Farideh pressed her sleeve against her nose and mouth, and counted ten skull-sized lumps.

Brin turned gray and gritted his teeth. He quickly left the room, Havilar watching him with a sympathetic expression she dropped as soon as she saw Farideh watching her.

"Here now," someone said. A dragonborn man with graying, rusty scales and long tasseled plumes. Silver chains draped from the piercings on his face, and the right sleeve of his shirt was tacked up where his arm had been lost. At his feet, a dead woman with the same silver-chain piercing lay on a stretcher, half covered by a cloth. Blood spots oozed through the sheet at her midsection. "This is a matter for clans—"

"Oh, Gesh," Anala said, pressing a handkerchief to her snout. "Don't be ridiculous. Did you think I stroll around trailing miscreants?" She looked back at Farideh and smiled in a way Farideh couldn't decipher. "They've come with me."

"May I present," Anala said to Mehen, "Shestandeliath Geshthax, son of Orothain and patriarch of his clan." She gestured to a second dragonborn standing against the far wall, her patina-green scaled hands clutching a walking stick. Two jade rings pierced the scales on the side of her neck, and a deep scar marked her chest. "And Ophinshtalajiir Kaijia, daughter of Laerysth and matriarch of her clan. You remember my nephew?" she asked. "Mehen?"

The dragonborn elders hid their surprise better than their followers—two women and a man who were seeing to the bodies. "Pandjed's son?" the younger woman said, earning her a sharp look from Geshthax.

"The very same," Anala said, as though no insult worth such a look were offered. Farideh and Havilar glanced at each other—Djerad Thymar wouldn't be so simple as they'd hoped. Anala turned back to the circle of bodies. "Which is Baruz?" she asked softly.

Verthisathurgiesh Baruz lay a short distance away from the others, against one of the smaller tombs, a wand lying at the fingertips of one outstretched hand and his sword half-drawn from its sheath. Anala lifted the covering from his face. The bronze scales of his throat had been torn away in a deep, brutal wound. She let out a soft, shuddering breath, and Mehen reached over to pull the cloth back up.

"No," she said. "I want to know what we're up against."

Havilar slipped up beside Farideh, sleeve over her nose. "I should get credit for not telling Brin I told him so. I can barely manage." She looked down at Baruz. "Oh. Wizard?"

Farideh shook her head, eyes on Anala. "I don't know."

Farideh looked over the other bodies. They had fallen in a rough circle, four fleeing out into the crypt before dying. All of them bloodied. Something or someone fast indeed, she thought. Something that surprised them. She wasn't sure how old the others were, but if Mehen had known Baruz, he was old enough to have trained as a Lance Defender. He was old enough to have some skill with a weapon and maybe with spells.

And someone had still killed him as if he were helpless.

"It smells disgusting in here," Havilar whispered. "Do you smell that?"

Farideh shook her head—besides the strange odor of rot, only the flinty smell of blood overlay the kind of dampness she expected from being underground.

"It smells like the kind of perfume you buy from a tinker." Havilar wrinkled her nose. "And *Lorcan*."

Farideh turned fully to her sister, alarmed, but before she could ask what that meant, another dragonborn trailing followers entered the crypt.

His scales were the color of tarnished brass, green and dark, and the row of piercings along his brow ridges traced the waxing and waning of silvery, miniature moons, just like Dumuzi's. Kepeshkmolik, Farideh thought. Every one of the dragonborn watched him, watched Mehen.

"Narghon," the Ophinshtalajiir matriarch said, nodding to the man. Anala straightened, spun, still smiling but suddenly stiff as a poker. Mehen kept his eyes down, locked on Baruz's corpse.

Kepeshkmolik Narghon's gaze swept over the room, the carnage, the other elders. Mehen. "I see your guest arrived, Anala," he said coldly.

"And in good health," Anala said. "Better than I can say for these young ones."

Narghon's nostrils flared over his curled lip. He scanned the room once more, spotting Havilar and Farideh. Surprise overtook his features, and he stared at Farideh with bald confusion. Farideh stared back, unwilling to blink first, and the powers of Asmodeus nipped at her temper. She made herself look away, slow her breathing.

"Which of them called you down, Kepeshkmolik?" Kaijia asked. She shook her head. "These hatchlings running wild, hither and yon, carrying gossip like it's water from the river." Her own followers traded glances, as if they were used to such dressing-downs.

"Atchni," Narghon spat. "I don't know where she heard it from. I grieve your losses."

Beside Farideh, Havilar exhaled noisily, nervously. Her fingers drummed against her thighs, and the faint sheen of sweat stood out on her upper lip. Farideh nudged her—was she all right? Havilar swallowed hard and gave her head a little shake.

"Cover your nose," Farideh said. "And go stand with Brin."

"It's not that," Havilar whispered. "It's . . . I can handle it. Stop fussing."

"Has anyone sent for the Adjudicators?" Narghon asked. Anala's brow ridges shifted, and she turned to the other two elders. Geshthax tapped his tongue to the roof of his mouth, very deliberately, and Kaijia's hands closed more tightly over the walking stick.

"I don't see how that's necessary at this point," she said. "It's not clear to me that we're dealing with anything so dire. A falling out, perhaps?"

How it could be anything but dire, Farideh couldn't imagine. The smell of rot, the lack of survivors. She turned to Mehen, but her father said nothing, only kept his eyes locked on the sarcophagus against the wall.

"A matter for clans," Geshthax agreed. "Someone should send a message to Yrjixtilex and Daardendrien. Theirs are here as well."

Farideh sidled up beside her father. "Are we . . . Should we be here while they're seeing to their dead? What is it Anala wants us to do?"

Mehen didn't answer. He was staring at the largest of the tombs, draped with a cloth of gold. Carvings lined the sides, a relief of dragonborn warriors dying in battle and bringing terrible beasts with them.

"Is that where he is?" Farideh asked, softly. "Pandjed?"

"*Thrik*," he murmured. "She wants us to see what the others are missing. Or ignoring." He looked past her, at Havilar looking peaked, and cursed. "What's wrong with her?"

"I think the smell's bothering her. I'll look," Farideh said, easing around him, her cuff pressed to her nose and mouth. The dragonborn bundling the bodies of their clan-kin eyed her as she kneeled beside him.

At first, she saw only the horrible injuries, the blood—the way these dragonborn had surely died. She peeked beneath one of the sheets and wished she hadn't. Kaijia was wrong—whatever had killed them wasn't normal. She'd wager the whole of her take on it. The wounds were rough and ragged, torn flesh, not sliced. An animal, she thought. But what beast would be running free in the catacombs? So maybe a pet? She thought of Zoonie—Zoonie could kill someone like this, and would the dragonborn even think to look for something like that? How could they help it? Farideh thought, replacing the cloth. A hellhound wouldn't be ignored for long.

And then she spotted something out of the ordinary.

Poking out from the edge of the blood pool, the jagged edge of strange runes outlined in silvery powder caught the torchlight. Farideh leaned nearer, tracing the path of them as it curved . . . a circle.

The scent of brimstone threaded through the sweet-sour smell of death, and a chill ran down Farideh's spine. The smell of a portal. A smell like Lorcan's, she thought.

But the runes weren't the ones she knew—if it were a portal, where was it set to go?

Or maybe the question is, she thought, what had come out?

"What were they doing down here?" Farideh called. The dragonborn all stared at her, as if she had sat up from among the dead to speak. "Do you know?"

"Your guest's manners leave something to be desired, Verthisathurgiesh," Geshthax said crisply. Farideh felt her cheeks burn. Anala wouldn't look at her.

The Shestandeliath patriarch beckoned his followers. "Come. Parvida deserves a better rest than this." Two of the dragonborn hauled a litter bearing its sad load from the crypt, and the Ophinshtalajiir contingent followed with their fallen. Kepeshkmolik Narghon left with them, deliberately not looking at Mehen or Farideh now.

Anala made a little sound, deep in her throat. "Solving these murders," she said, "would ease many minds when it comes to counting tieflings among Khorsaya's line."

Farideh turned to Mehen in shock. Mehen kept his eyes on the tomb.

"That's what you think to tempt me with?" Mehen said.

"It's an offer," Anala said. "Make no mistake, first and foremost I want justice for Baruz. But I still want you to come back."

"You think it was one of his companions?"

Anala shook her head. "I don't know. But I know none of the elders wishes to make this a matter for Vanquisher Tarhun or his Adjudicators. I know they are all embarrassed that their clan-kin were found dead in Verthisathurgiesh's vault. They know something else is going on."

"Were any of them dabbling in magic?" Farideh asked, thinking of the portal marks. "Other than Baruz?"

Anala smiled at her thinly. "That is what I need you to discover."

The sound of Havilar emptying her stomach interrupted them. She straightened, one hand on the carved stone wall, looking paler than Farideh had left her.

"Oh *karshoj*! Did Brin hear that?" she said, wiping her mouth. Then she clapped a hand over her mouth again and crouched down, head between her knees.

Anala's smile fell slightly. "Well," she said. "Better out than in, they say." More dragonborn arrived, the representatives of still more clans, come to collect their dead before the Adjudicators could arrive. Anala greeted them each as though they were walking into her sitting room, all her grief stuffed down someplace deep.

Mehen came up beside Havilar and rubbed her back as she straightened. "It's all right," he said. "Happens to everyone."

"It didn't happen to you," she said a little thickly. "But at least I found something." She held up a thin silver chain. On one end, a bloodied ring, where it had been torn from someone's skin. At the other, the chain was twisted, mangled, as if it had gone through some sort of grinder. Mehen took it from her, frowning.

"It looks like jewelry," Havilar said.

"It is," Mehen said. "It's a clan piercing. Must have been the Shestandeliath girl's."

"No," Farideh said. "She was still wearing her piercing." The silver chain swung gently from her father's fist. "Do any of the others wear a chain?"

"Not like that. Just Shestandeliath."

"Could it be the killer's?"

"Don't say that too loudly," Mehen murmured. He pooled the chain into his hand and slipped it into a pocket, eyes on the dragonborn elders.

"There's a circle of runes too," Farideh whispered. "Under the blood."

Mehen's expression hardened. "You recognize it?"

She shook her head. "The runes that are left are different. But it doesn't look like they used silver. That would . . ." She faltered. Missing silver was why Lorcan had been able to get out of the circle, the first time she met him. "It would keep the circle from holding something bad in," she finished.

"Anything else?"

"He's casting out of the circle." They turned to Brin, who stood just behind Mehen, still looking a little green. He pointed down at Baruz's body. "I don't see how he could have fallen that way if he was casting at something in the center there." He frowned. "Havi, are you all right?"

"Fine!" Havilar said, with a hard glare at Mehen.

Farideh traced the line of Baruz's wand, out toward the far side of the tomb. Three more sarcophagi rested near that wall, where a hundred niches held a hundred lead ossuaries, the resting bones of Mehen's ancestors. Another door led deeper into the catacombs.

"So if it was a falling out, someone got away."

"Mehen?" Anala called. The nervous young man who'd led them down was joined by another with a stretcher. "We ought to go. Give them space."

Mehen nodded and turned to go, but Farideh caught him. "I want to check something," Farideh whispered. "All right?"

"Be quick," Mehen whispered. "And careful." He and Brin followed Anala out. Farideh slid her arm through Havilar's as she turned to go.

"Come with me a moment," she whispered. "I have an idea."

"Are you going to stir up that portal?" Havilar demanded as they stepped into the dark hallway beyond the sarcophagi.

"No," Farideh watched the dragonborn secure their dead. None of them gave any notice to the two tieflings. "It's not a Hellsportal."

Havilar snorted. "Small favors."

Farideh took a deep breath. "But it's *something*. I think you should call the imps."

"What?"

"The dragonborn aren't going to admit what was going on down here. But whatever they were doing, we have to know, or we're missing the most important detail."

"We can figure that out without the imps. What happened to staying out of trouble?" Havilar shook her head. "*Why* are *you* the one suggesting we get into trouble?"

"I'm not," Farideh said. "But we need help—otherwise we'll end up stuck here for ages. Do you want that?"

Havilar stared at her as if she'd gone right out of her mind. "Wouldn't it work better to call Lorcan? I mean—trust me—he's smarter than these imps."

Farideh bit off her reply. "Call the imps. Please."

Havilar scowled at her, as if she heard everything Farideh didn't say and everything she'd thought as well. "Fine," she spat. Then a little louder, "I need some help."

The air behind them *popped*. Havilar spun around, pulling her glaive in front and moving to block Farideh from . . .

A pair of imps who sat on the ground, their stinger-laden tails curved over their heads as if they were no more than curious cats. One was red as clay and the other was deepnight blue.

"What do you want?" the red one said.

Havilar sighed. "Well met, Mot." She glanced at the blue imp. "Who's that?"

"Olla," Mot said with utter disgust. "He's Dembo's replacement."

"Why are there two of you?" the deepnight blue imp asked in a nasal voice. "There's only supposed to be one. That's what they said."

"We're only supposed to take care of this one," Mot said. "The gold-eyed one. I don't know why." He looked up at Havilar. "So what do you want?"

"That depends. Can either of you read?"

"Blistering archlords, what do you think we are? Dogs?"

"I don't know!" Havilar said. She folded her arms. "There's some kind of a portal in the other room. And a lot of dead bodies. Can you tell where the portal was supposed to go? Without being seen—that's important."

Olla looked anxiously at Mot. "Is that meddling?"

"No," Mot said through his teeth.

"Because we're not supposed to meddle."

"It's not meddling." Mot seemed to roll back into himself, disappearing into the air. Olla made a little irritated noise, but he followed.

Farideh kept her eyes on the tomb, her nerves thrumming. The imps would be fine, she thought. This could stop more murders from happening. This could protect Djerad Thymar. This would mean she didn't have to call Lorcan down and ask him what else smelled the way he did. She blew out a breath.

Havilar was leaning against the wall again, one arm wrapped around her stomach.

"Are you going to throw up again?" Farideh asked. "Is it nerves or just the smell?"

"Oh gods, if you don't just forget that, I swear," Havilar started. The imps interrupted her, returning with another *pop*.

"It stinks in there," Mot said as soon as he landed. "What is that?"

"Dead bodies?" Havilar said.

"No," Olla said. "It smells like—"

"Nobody cares," Mot interrupted. "The runes are Dethek, but that's not Dwarvish. Not anything I've ever seen."

"It looks like Abyssal."

"It's not godsbedamned Abyssal, Olla," Mot said. "Do you think I can't spot Abyssal?"

"Where did it go?" Farideh asked.

"Boil me alive if I know, Lady," Mot said. "Honestly, it looks like it didn't open all the way."

"Then why does it smell like brimstone?" Farideh asked.

Mot shrugged. "It opened enough? If I had to guess, someone shut it down."

"It smells like dretches," Olla piped up. "That's what that smell reminds me of."

Mot looked back over his shoulder, glowering at Olla. "It's not shitting Abyssal!"

"We should report the smell in any case. That's protocol."

"You don't have to report everything you think you smell," Mot said. He shook his head at Havilar. "This is your fault, you know. You still got the hellhound?"

"I'm not done with her."

Mot muttered something that made Farideh's skin crawl. "Fine. Tell us if you need something again." And with that, he and Olla vanished into the ether.

"Well, great spitting lot of help *that* was," Havilar said.

"Maybe whatever killed them came out of the portal partway?" Farideh said. "Maybe they closed it before it could get through?"

"Maybe the portal's not the important part," Havilar said. She sighed and tugged her braid nervously. "Come on, I feel sick again. Whatever a dretch is, I don't want to ever find one."

• • •

FROM THE SHADOWS of the passage beyond the Verthisathurgiesh crypt, Dumuzi watched Ophinshtalajiir and Shestandeliath dragonborn carry bodies past on stretchers, covered with sheets of cloth. Dread uncoiled in his heart. He should have been here to talk them out of it. He should have never left with Baruz putting madness in the others' ears, with Ravar giving them tools they couldn't manage. He should have never left Zaroshni.

"What will the elders say if they find out what you're planning?" Dumuzi had demanded of her, before his father had sent him to hunt for Clanless Mehen. "You are throwing every generation's struggle in their faces. You are tilling up the very concept of *throtominarr*!"

"They have already tilled it up and thrown it in the midden," Zaroshni said haughtily. "They've given up. They've traded true integrity to play at this world's games, giving tyrants and enemies honors they did not earn, bowing to the disrespect of nations who did not fight as we did."

What price is that honor now? Dumuzi thought as Shestandeliath carried a stretcher by. Zaroshni or Parvida or Ravar? They were all masked and hidden by the sheets. How could they have saved the Lost if they weren't prepared for what lay between the worlds?

You don't know what happened, Dumuzi thought.

But he knew this much: they were dead. Zaroshni was gone. Zaroshni and Parvida and Baruz and ancestors only knew who else.

Footsteps whispered through the stone, the faintest disturbance of Djerad Thymar. Dumuzi whirled toward them, drawing the dagger from his sleeve. Zaroshni stood in the shadows of a cross-passage a stone's throw away, and Dumuzi nearly dropped the weapon as he shoved it back into its sheath.

He took a step forward, ready to embrace her, every part of him needing to feel Zaroshni solid in his arms. "You're alive!"

Zaroshni blinked. "Yes. And so are you."

At that, Dumuzi remembered himself. He stopped, folded his hands together. "I . . . I don't know who else. The bodies . . ." He swallowed against the lump in his throat. "*Chaubashk vur kepeshk karshoji, this* is what I warned you about. What were they thinking?"

Zaroshni considered him a moment. "Perhaps they weren't."

Dumuzi's heart clenched at her distance, but he masked it. There was too much now to think of. "Listen, we have to see the others, the other Liberators. Find out who's alive still and who knows what happened. Make sure all the dead are accounted for in case one of them . . ." He trailed off. It was too awful to consider that one of his misguided friends might have become a murderer. It was too awful to consider letting them roam free if that was so. "There were more than twelve of you fools. I know that much."

Zaroshni's brow ridges scrunched up, and she tilted her head, sending her silver piercing chain swinging. He looked away from that silent rebuke. "Wouldn't someone have said if they were missing?"

Dumuzi frowned—perhaps she was in shock? "You said you were being careful. That no one knew what you were planning. I assumed you were among them—why wouldn't I?" He clacked his teeth once, as if he could shake the tension building, building in his stomach. "I'm so glad you're safe," he blurted.

Zaroshni nodded, her mouth twisting as if she were trying to smile and scream in the same moment. She took a step toward him. "Can you help me remember who will not be missed?"

Shocked, Dumuzi thought, surely shocked. He risked impropriety, stroked a hand down her arm. "You will recover, I swear. I'll help you, though—we have to move fast. We have to tell the elders."

Zaroshni moved close, close enough Dumuzi stepped back. "I don't think that's wise," she said.

Footfalls again—but these were so much nearer. Dumuzi leaped back against the wall and saw Clanless Mehen standing there, looking down at the two young people. He looked so like Patriarch Pandjed that Dumuzi's heart leaped up with old fear—

"What are you doing here?" Mehen demanded.

Dumuzi mastered himself. "Apologies," he said. "I overheard . . . Are they . . . Are they all dead?"

At that, Mehen's fierce expression softened. "I'm sorry. You were agemates with them, weren't you?" His teeth gaped a moment, anxious and riled, before he laid a hand on Dumuzi's shoulder, something Pandjed never did. "We'll find out what happened. We'll catch the one who did this."

Dumuzi met Zaroshni's dark eyes—he feared they would and they wouldn't in equal measure. This is where the Liberators' selfish "honor" had brought them. Zaroshni's expression didn't waver.

"This is Shestandeliath Zaroshni," Dumuzi said. "Daughter of Baishir. I think . . . She might be in shock." I might be in shock, Dumuzi thought.

"Come on," Mehen said to the both of them. "Let's get you home."

Zaroshni smiled that strange-sick smile. "Of course. Thank you."

4

PHRENIKE MADE FOR A SORRY LICH, THE GHOST OF BRYSEIS
Kakistos thought. Where once her confederate had
seemed a sleek and lovely Amnian woman, whose features
were perhaps a bit too pointed, whose gaze was perhaps a bit
too penetrating, whose movements were perhaps a bit too
abrupt, now the tiefling warlock was little more than bones
held together by gaudily gilded sinews, draped in a fitted
lavender gown that mocked her fleshless body. Her gaze
still penetrated, two motes of violet light in the depths of
her cavernous eyes.

"I would say it's astonishing to see you in such a state, but let
us be honest," Phrenike drawled, "you were always more a zealot
than a pathfinder. Not eager for risk, but blind to it."

And you were a toady, Bryseis Kakistos snapped, trapped
inside the skull of a cambion woman who stood before the
lich on her throne.

"Do you want me to repeat that?" Sairché said under her
breath. Brazen little pretender, Bryseis Kakistos thought.

Ask her about the spell, she said. *If this is where we* must *begin,
then begin it already.*

Sairché bristled all around the ghost, but she smiled at
Phrenike. "We're in search of a spell. Something that can
divide a soul. The Brimstone Angel says you know it."

"Did something happen with Alyona?" Phrenike
asked, too sweetly.

The name sent a cascade of memories over the ghost. The bone-deep tug of another spirit bound to hers. A filthy city street, buildings whose bones were sap-stained pine logs, and her child-hand in a passing pocket. Herself, younger, wide-eyed, saying, *Bisera, we shouldn't be here—*

Bryseis Kakistos snapped back to the tower in the hinterlands, the lich, and the cambion, the edges of her stitched-together soul feeling frayed and fragile. A moment passed while she focused on sealing herself up.

Stop, she told Sairché. *This will go better if I do the talking.*

The cambion's mind darted along the wall she'd built of her thoughts. Bryseis Kakistos might once have been the most powerful warlock packed to the Nine Hells, might still be imbued with the powers of Asmodeus, but Sairché was proving to be as canny as her sire. She'd made her offer of aid, partitions already in place. Bryseis Kakistos would not be able to read her thoughts, to wrest control away, with such boundaries in place.

At least, that was what Sairché thought.

Phrenike can manage it, Bryseis Kakistos said instead. *Tell her to cast the spell.*

"She wishes to speak to you directly," Sairché said. "She says you have a spell that could manage it."

The lich chuckled, and Bryseis Kakistos seethed at the reversal of their positions. The last time she'd spoken to the tiefling warlock had been more than sixty years ago, in Chondath, shortly before Bryseis Kakistos met her end. They had been friendly—never friends—and Phrenike had promised to see to all of Bryseis's lingering plans with all her usual fulsome praise and promises.

Now, Phrenike waved her wand over Sairché, as though she were nothing but a haunted bit of armor. The spell wrapped around the ghost like a burning fist—not only could she speak, she would *have* to speak. How times changed.

"She looks familiar," Phrenike said, conversationally. "She's one of Caisys's get, isn't she?"

Patently, Bryseis Kakistos said.

Phrenike chuckled again. To Sairché she said, "Your papa was something else."

Simmering annoyance and uncertainty surrounded Bryseis Kakistos—Sairché didn't like the reminder of that fact she could never tease out on her own. "So I hear," she said, as if it didn't matter in the least. "Knowing my mother, he'd have to be."

Quiet. It's not Alyona, Bryseis Kakistos said, bringing them back to the matter at hand. *It's Asmodeus.*

"Well," Phrenike said after a moment. "You *have* gone mad. You can't undo what we did."

That's what you think.

Phrenike laughed. "Delightfully, delightfully mad. I can tell you right now, that spell won't work on a god."

"It's not for the god," Sairché said.

I need the rest of my soul, Bryseis Kakistos said, ignoring Sairché. *Two parts of it are trapped in what should have been my vessel.*

"You mean Caisys's seditious little leaving wasn't your first choice?" Phrenike drawled. What was left of her face grinned at Sairché, the violet lights of her eyes twinkling. "Don't worry—she loves seditious. Don't let her pretend she doesn't."

"Hand over the spell," Sairché said, as if she could channel her fearsome mother.

I told you to stay quiet, Bryseis Kakistos said. To Phrenike she said, *I know you remember it.*

"I don't," the lich said. "Besides, do you forget? That spell didn't work the way you expected it to, after the Spellplague came. Times may have changed, but not that much. The gods still don't want you to have it." The remnants of her flesh twitched. "One in particular, eh, cambion?"

All around the ghost, Sairché's rage flickered, incandescent. The presence of two magic rings flit through her thoughts, too quick for the ghost to assess what they might do. Bryseis Kakistos felt her thoughts coil in. This was not going as she'd planned.

When the cambion had offered her assistance—seeking to gain the favor of her archduchess, she said without saying—she'd been silver-tongued and smooth, persuasive in the way the devils of the Nine Hells always were, with the faint air of desperation that meant she was willing to reach beyond the hierarchy.

Now, it seemed more and more, Sairché reached because she did not understand her place.

"I suggest you find another solution—your last one might suffice." Phrenike tilted her head. "What did you do with her when you decided to roam free?"

"Who?" Sairché asked under her breath.

Don't concern yourself, Bryseis Kakistos said, not knowing what Phrenike meant.

"If you are keeping things from me," Sairché began.

Quiet, Bryseis Kakistos said. She considered Phrenike, considered all the things the lich wouldn't say in front of Sairché, and all the secrets her former follower might know. Phrenike kept smiling at Sairché, as she flicked her wrist and let the spell that gave Bryseis voice fade.

It was time to take a risk.

Bryseis Kakistos struck, swift as an arrow, shifting herself past the magical barriers Sairché had erected in her own mind. The walls were strong, but they were common, the sort of spells Bryseis Kakistos had been familiar with before Sairché was ever born, before Caisys the Vicelord ever lay down with Exalted Invadiah. A few tendays of study and testing were all that Bryseis Kakistos had needed to bring the limitations clear in her broken thoughts, and she'd had practice enough lately to make the possession firm.

Sairché's consciousness flashed in a burst of panic, then went still and numb. Bryseis Kakistos flexed the cambion's red fingers, her batlike wings. For the moment, Sairché was sleeping, but the ghost didn't have long before the cambion regained control.

"Well," Phrenike said, looking faintly surprised after all. "I take it she doesn't know you can do that?"

"Not yet," Bryseis Kakistos said with the cambion's voice. The lights of Phrenike's eyes danced, and Bryseis Kakistos thought perhaps she wasn't the only one who was a little mad, a little zealous. The lich inclined her head.

"O Brimstone Angel," she said, with a familiar hint of mockery Phrenike always had, "what can I do for you?"

"Who else still lives?" Bryseis said. "I need the spell." It wasn't the most important part—she felt sure of that, even if she couldn't quite remember why—but it would become necessary soon enough.

"I told you the truth," Phrenike said. "None of us can help you with this—the Weave is broken."

"They say it's repairing itself."

The lich shrugged. "How long will that take? And will it all be the same? It's a lot of waiting and no less risk. I still don't understand how you wound up like this. Wasn't that the point of the brats? What happened to that new-grown body you always planned?"

"Beshaba," Bryseis Kakistos said, spitting at the name of the goddess of foul luck. "I'm seeing to it. But I need the spell. I'm running out of time."

Phrenike sighed. "I didn't mention this," she said significantly, "but there's only a few . . . entities one can really expect to hold onto that kind of magic come Sundering or Spellplague."

Bryseis Kakistos felt Sairché's face reflect her surprise. "Archlords?"

Phrenike gave her a look that might have been contemptuous with a little more skin. "Please," she said. "They'll turn on you all over again. I'm talking about the demon lords."

"No," Bryseis Kakistos said. "They can't be bargained with."

"But they do tear souls up. If you want a spell like this, you'd better be prepared to ride your cambion down into the Abyss and get down on your knees for Orcus himself again." Phrenike considered the cambion. "How seditious is she really?"

"I'm still finding out," Bryseis Kakistos said.

Phrenike stood, her bony feet clacking on the stone floor as she crossed the room to a chest against the far wall. From within, she collected a small jar, half-filled with glass capsules. She gave it a little shake, and the core of every one lit with a faint green flame.

"Here," she said. "Never say I didn't help you."

"What are they?"

"Let's say they'll make her a little less fussy about being seditious," Phrenike said. "When she's ready to wake up, snap one under her nose and inhale the vapors. Whatever has changed, whatever's unfamiliar or missing, she'll accept it as how things ought to be. So you can go where you need to, get what you need to, talk to who you wish. They're very handy when it comes to minions." Her violet eyes glittered coldly. "Cleans up a lot of messes before they happen."

Bryseis Kakistos took the jar. "Thank you, Phrenike."

"Don't let her find them, though," Phrenike added. "She might accept them, but then she might use them up."

The capsules glowed in the cambion's red hands. Bryseis Kakistos weighed her options, the plethora of pathways that lay open to her suddenly. *Each one leads to Asmodeus's comeuppance,* she thought, smiling to herself. She did need the spells—so she would need her old books, and so she would need to track down which of her descendants had access to them. She needed the staff, no doubt still lost in the Nine Hells, and enough warlocks to fill out a circle.

She needed a new body. That was the most important.

"Fare well, Phrenike," she said. "I hope we never see one another again."

"Likewise," the lich said, as Bryseis Kakistos plucked up the portal ring Sairché wore, and cast the portal that drew her back into the Nine Hells.

Something at the core of her grew frantic and animal as she stepped into the nightmarish layer of Malbolge. It always did, a tenacious and powerful memory of her time trapped in Asmodeus's realm. She pushed it down.

"You and I need to have a chat."

Bryseis Kakistos fought not to grin as she turned to find Lorcan crouched in the corner. A memory jolted through her: the cambion man's sire, the source of those obscenely handsome features, standing over the remains of one of those first sacrifices. *Well,* he'd said, *this is going to take time, isn't it?*

"About what?" she asked as the memory faded.

"About where in the Hells you keep running off to." Lorcan straightened, long and lean and muscular, clad in black leathers. "Our agreement means we each can't hurt the other, or let them come to harm, but if you're trying to run the sands through the glass by preparing something, might I remind you that none of those strictures matter if His Majesty decides we've wasted his time. I need you here."

"What for?"

Lorcan peered at her, his black eyes puzzled. "Have you lost your mind?"

Bryseis Kakistos shrugged. "Of the matters you've been tasked with, His Majesty cares about none of them so much as those two Chosen. You have that in hand . . . or do you?"

Lorcan's wings flicked in an irritable way and flames sparked between his fingers, the beginnings of a fireball. "Oh go ahead, Sairché. Prod it. See where it gets you."

Bryseis Kakistos clucked her tongue. Here was a moment to be glad she held the reins once more. When she'd pressed Sairché to put her manipulative skills to use on her brother's fond feelings, Sairché had been all but incapable of doing anything besides throwing barbs.

"This is a waste of time," Sairché had said when the Brimstone Angel had upbraided her. "Even if he manages to get back into Farideh's good graces—and I think there's even coin on the table in that wager—and then he manages to talk her into an unwise assignation, you will still have to wait the better part of a score of years before you have a body that can manage anything remotely like what you're talking about—during which you are of absolutely no use to anyone. Focus on the spell to split the twins' souls. Get the information you need first, so we can set things in motion."

Sairché didn't understand, Bryseis Kakistos thought . . . even though the ghost wasn't sure she understood either. She didn't have to understand—she *knew* this was the most important step, the one she couldn't fail at.

She needed another heir.

"It's simply a question," she said to Lorcan. "I have to imagine she's not the usual sort you spend your time on. Mortals are always more . . . finicky than one expects. But, too, they're more tractable. You ought to try making amends. Admit you were wrong. That goes a lot further than it ought to."

Lorcan's eyes narrowed, but the fire in his hands went out. "What's your game?"

Bryseis Kakistos made Sairché smile. "I like the idea of you humbling yourself? And more, I like the idea of keeping her in line. You know perfectly well you have to fix this." She leaned in. "I'm sure Mother has some artifacts to make her a little more compliant."

He started to reply—no doubt a declamation that he wasn't a shitting demon, to judge by the furious sneer—but Bryseis cut him off. "No," she said. "You have charm enough if you opt to use it. You can convince her of your more tolerable qualities. Shall *I* go and check on her?"

Something jolted Bryseis Kakistos, like a burst of vertigo. Sairché was waking. She held perfectly still.

Lorcan hesitated. "No. See to the *pradixikai*. The archduchess has guests planned." He looked discomfited, as if he meant to say something else but thought better of it, and left the little room.

Bryseis Kakistos took the jar from Sairché's pocket as another jolt went through her. Tymora favors the reckless, she thought, taking one of the hollow beads out. She considered the room, the marrow-weeping walls. Crossing to a particularly fleshy section beside the portal, she tested the tissues there. A shuddering wail howled through the fingerbone tower, and she felt a pang of disgust at this other, trapped spirit.

Not so strongly that she didn't plunge the jar into the flesh of the wall, marrow and blood oozing over her borrowed hand. As she pulled free, the wall closed over the wound, leaving behind the faintest scar. She wiped Sairché's hand clean on her crimson skirts.

Another jolt—

The world lurched as if all of Sairché's bones shifted, an earthquake of the self—the cambion was waking. Bryseis Kakistos crushed the capsule between her fingers, releasing a glowing green vapor that snaked up the cambion's nostrils as she inhaled. The ghost slipped back behind the walls of Sairché's magic, moments before the cambion's consciousness stirred and settled, dizzied and bemused.

"Well," she said, a few moments later, "that was a spectacular waste of time. I dearly hope the rest of your former confederates are less odious than that one."

• • •

"How many?" Dahl demanded, moving toward the top of the stairs. The door below was ajar, and highsun light shaded and flashed through the gap as bodies moved through the front room. Someone shouted, then several voices barked orders, followed by the clatter of feet. A child—Aggie—wailed. The Zhentarim had arrived—there was no doubt.

"I don't know," Mira said. "Depends who came. Grathson rides with a dozen, all soldiers—they clear out ruins and knock skulls—"

More shouts, more children shrieking, Wilmot's little voice rising above the chaos—"Don't hit my brother!"

Thost nearly bowled Dahl over, rushing for the stairs. "Wait," Dahl hissed, bracing against his brother's arm. "You run down there and scare them—"

"Xulfaril's force will be smaller, few of them are really fighters," Mira said quickly. "But she's got spells." She blew out a breath. "Go out the window. Get your brothers out of the way, come around the front. I'll distract them."

Dahl shook his head. "They've got too many held hostage." He considered the numbers. "Would they flinch if you're a hostage on our end?"

"Not a chance. They don't need me if they have your grandmother."

Sessaca rose to her feet. "Stop yammering and get down there."

There wasn't another option—but this was no option Dahl wanted. Too many chances for someone to get hurt, for someone to get killed. "No sudden moves," he ordered. "No threats. See what they want, and we'll get in the way if we need to. Mira first, then me, Thost and Bodhar at the back. Granny," he said firmly, "*don't* leave that chair."

If Sessaca had anything to say to that, Dahl didn't hear it as they moved swiftly down the stairs.

On the lower floor, black-armored mercenaries had arranged themselves around the clustered family. Dahl's mother, his sisters-in-law, and the eldest of the children made a second circle around the smallest members of the family. Aggie peered out at him from behind Eurdila's skirts. Jens sported a swollen cheekbone and Dellora's lip dripped blood—but one of the mercenaries was clearly favoring her shoulder, another had an angry red line across his jaw where something hard had cracked him, and a third sat to the side, trying to reset a shoulder pulled free of its socket. A halfling man in a high-collared cloak perched on the kitchen table, well out of reach—he whistled as he spotted Dahl and Mira.

All the mercenaries' eyes turned to their leaders, two humans: a middle-aged man in scarred armor and scarred skin, with graying sandy curls; and a woman in robes with a shock of dark hair and a patch over her left eye. Grathson and Xulfaril.

"There you are, Mira dear," Xulfaril said, without a hint of real concern. "We were wondering where you'd gotten to."

"Obviously it wasn't hard to guess," Mira said lightly. "You'll be happy to know I'm close."

"You've been close for long enough." Grathson's gaze swept over Dahl and his brothers. "You," he said, pointing at Dahl. "You're the one feeding her information, aren't you? You have the look of someone who knows too much." He pointed his sword at Dellora's throat. "So share a little. Where's the Master's Library?"

"He doesn't know," Mira said.

"I really don't," Dahl said. He held his empty hands up, as if to placate Grathson, all the while calculating how quickly he could draw his sword, his dagger, what in reach might make a weapon. "We're still looking for an answer."

Xulfaril clucked her tongue. "That's not what I want to hear."

"Let's start with the little ones," Grathson said. "Get everyone on the same page."

A flicker of images—how it would look if he grabbed Aggie, Wilmot. Slow breath—he's baiting you. Dahl gritted his teeth. "We *are* on the same page."

"I don't know that we're even in the same book," Grathson said, swinging his sword between Dellora and Jens, pointed at the little ones like the needle of a compass. "Which one, which one?" Dellora's expression darkened, Meribelle tensed. None of them would let Grathson's blade touch a child without leaping to action, and then everything would fall apart fast.

"A moment," Xulfaril said. Grathson kept sliding his sword over the children, as if he hadn't heard her.

Xulfaril drew her wand, the tip dancing with a spark of gold energy. "Put your sword down, Captain," she said, enunciating. "No need to leap in."

Grathson sneered at her. "Thought we were short of time? Thought this was an emergency?"

"And I thought you could follow simple directions. Put the sword down."

"You want my help, we do things my way."

The wand's spark built. "Your way is going to keep anything from getting done at all."

"*Enough!*"

Sessaca's order cut through the din, as sharp and demanding as a swung battle-axe, and with the same effect on the tension in the room. Xulfaril's wand brightened as Sessaca pushed past her grandsons, near enough a sneering Grathson turned his sword point to her crepey throat.

"Are you volunteering, my beldam?"

Sessaca turned to the one-eyed wizard, ignoring the blade. "Watching Gods, you have no control over him at all, do you?"

The woman tilted her head. "My apologies if he offends your sense of propriety, old mother."

"You should be so lucky," Sessaca said, "as to offend my sense of propriety. This is the work of idiot striplings who've been handed their first swords. Blundering around, bellowing threats. Have you been taught nothing? *This* is not the Black Network I recall."

Xulfaril's smirk faltered. "You recall?"

Grathson's sword touched Sessaca's throat. She only raised her eyebrows. "You have one clue, you little donkey shit," she pointed out. "Are you prepared to lose it just to show off what a sharpjaw you are? You can't very well talk to me if you cut my throat."

Xulfaril lowered her wand, the spark dying out. "You're Sessaca Peredur? The Viper of the Earthfasts?"

"The very same." Sessaca pushed Grathson's blade away as if it were a stick wielded by one of her great-grandchildren. "I made my bones before you were even *born,* so let's have a little courtesy."

"You *were* the Viper of the Earthfasts," Grathson said. "Now you're a sack of skin." He flicked a hand at one of his subordinates, a thick, ugly fellow who pointed a blade at Dellora's heart. "Now tell us where the Master's Library is, or I start motivating you." Thost went tense all over. Dellora's eyes met her husband's, and she drew a deep breath. Thost gave the smallest of nods.

Hrast, Dahl thought.

Sessaca only sighed and shook her head. In the same moment, Thost moved. "Don't you touch her! Please! I'm begging you!"

He clutched his fists together, as if frantic for some aid. "Granny, for gods' sakes!"

Grathson smirked. The brute with the blade laughed, as if this big man's helplessness was the height of humor. He laughed, and he let his grip soften.

Which was when Dellora's arm came up, flinging the sword aside, and her booted foot slammed into the Zhentarim's underarm. Grathson turned, giving Thost a heartbeat to crash his massive fist into the side of the Zhentarim leader's head. A grunt of surprise and pain, a moment of confusion. Dahl pulled his sword and slashed at the woman holding her knife on his mother and Aggie. She parried, pulling her blade away from Eurdila's neck. Dahl's mother twisted away, pushing Aggie out of reach.

Xulfaril pulled a wand, thrust it into the air with a sibilant word, and a torus of energy burst out around her, knocking Dahl, the Zhentarim he fought, and Eurdila to the ground. Mira, Thost, and Bodhar had toppled as well, and Dellora and the big Zhentarim. Only Sessaca, Grathson, and Xulfaril kept their feet.

"Welcome," Sessaca said, "to the Viper's Nest. Or did you think I'd tuck myself away and become soft? Did you think farmers were only for stolen supplies and watering the wheat with their spilt blood? My children may not be the Black Network's, but there is nothing weak in them, and you were *fools* to count on that."

Dahl eased back onto his feet, and stood beside his grandmother, heart pounding, thoughts buzzing. His father had taught him to use a sword, just as he'd taught Thost and Bodhar. Who taught Barron? Sessaca, of course. Why had Dahl ever thought it was his grandfather?

He thought of the dagger his mother always wore, the time he watched his mother humming a little tune to herself as she butchered the body of a boar that had come down, all wild out of the Cormanthor to antagonize the sows. She'd killed it herself, with an axe, as you did. For all his nightmares swirled around marauders attacking the farm, an axe could kill a soldier same as a boar.

He thought of watching his father and brothers teach Meribelle to swing a sword—of course they had. It was safer if everyone could use a blade. He thought of his grandmother's satisfied expression when Thost brought home Dellora, a former soldier who came with her own blades. He thought of the children sparring giddily between chores.

Always figured if one of Barron's boys left that farm, it'd be to sellsword, Reyan had said. And he wasn't the first to say it. *My father wouldn't have really understood giving up farming for books alone,* Dahl had told Farideh. Because the land and the blade were in their blood. The land from his grandfather, Lamhail . . . the blade from Sessaca Peredur.

He thought of Sessaca watching over all of this, surveying her oblivious army. Picking at techniques, because—he'd thought— she always had *something* to criticize. He'd known she'd come from far off Chessenta, and always assumed that was the source of her displeasure, her opinions about how they fought—her people knew better.

It never would have occurred to him that "her people" might have been the Zhentarim. That she was preparing them for this very moment.

"Now," the Viper of the Earthfasts said, "are we going to negotiate like civilized folks, or are you going to persist in acting like children?"

"Here's our negotiations," Grathson said. "You tell us, or we start killing your kin."

Sessaca didn't flinch. Quick as a flash, she yanked the dagger from Dahl's belt and pressed its tip against her belly. "You shed one drop of blood," she said calmly, "and you're not getting so much as the name of a continent."

Grathson's eyes narrowed. "You wouldn't dare."

"I'm eighty-eight years old," Sessaca said. "Gods only know how much time I have left, but I'd give it all up just to spit in your eye, you little donkey shit. You hurt my family, you get nothing."

Grathson started to speak again, but Xulfaril cut him off. "What do you want, old mother?"

Sessaca gave her that cunning smile. "Well now, you've made it clear I can't just tell you where the Master's Library lies. Once you have your answer, you've got no reason to keep this fool in check, and I think you'll be happy to hope that my grandchildren haven't kept their sword practice up." She gave Xulfaril a pitying look. "But it's been a bad year for leucrotta. I wouldn't take that wager if I were you.

"Plus, my memory's not what it used to be. The path is tricky. Who's to say that the markers I give you won't be the wrong ones? That I can't guess what remains behind?"

"What do you want?" Xulfaril repeated.

Sessaca spread her hands, the dagger cutting a shaky arc through the air. "Simple. You bring me along."

"No," Dahl burst out.

"Don't be an idiot, lambkin," Sessaca chided, never taking her eyes from Xulfaril's. "There's not really a better option. We need out of this mess, and that's the path."

"Granny," Bodhar said. "You could die."

"As if you're not all waiting for it," Sessaca said dismissively. "Any day now, any year. I've outlasted two children, three grandchildren, and my man. I'm running short of time to have any kind of adventure left, and gods bless us all, I'm tired of watching people mend. Bless you, Eurdila, but you know it's dull."

"Consider our side," Xulfaril said. "You've just shown you have little concern for your own safety. What's to stop you from throwing yourself into the Dragon Reach as soon as we're away from New Velar? We'll have to leave some of ours behind to make sure you stay motivated."

"I'll go as well." Dahl sheathed his sword. "There. You have a way to motivate her. Let the rest of them go."

"Lambkin," Sessaca warned.

"You said it yourself: we need out of this mess and this is the path."

Xulfaril tilted her head again, considering Dahl, then Bodhar, then Thost with her single eye. "All three of you," she said. "Obviously the lovebirds need separating—I'm not about to leave the two of you here to play that trick again. I assume the big one can help you along, old mother?"

Sessaca considered her grandsons. Thost nodded once. Bodhar's eyes darted to Meri's, and she sighed, and though she looked worried, she nodded too. Shit, Dahl thought. Shit, shit, shit.

"You get me some potions," Sessaca said. "They'll keep me moving, and Thost can take up the slack. I get you into the Master's Library, and you'll let all of us walk away. Deal?"

"You have my word, Goodwoman Peredur," Xulfaril said.

" 'Swordcaptain,' if you please," Sessaca said. "Now you have supplies to gather, a boat to charter, and my grandsons and I need to pack. If you're going to leave some behind, I'd appreciate—"

"Yes, yes," Xulfaril said. "Where shall we tell the captain we're sailing?"

Sessaca smiled. "Make for Raven's Bluff."

• • •

Two hours later, as the sun set, Dahl stood on the deck of a ship, New Velar's lights glowing on the edge of the horizon as they sailed eastward, and the whole of his life a jumble. On the forecastle, the halfling man, Volibar, freed the winged serpent hidden beneath that high collar and tied a note to its back. The creature looped around the ship once, its body flattening as it slithered over the air, its batlike wings catching the currents.

"What if they don't let them go?" Dahl murmured to his grandmother. "Do you have a plan for that?" She folded her shawl more tightly around her thin shoulders. The potion Xulfaril had acquired for her had straightened her back and let her move more easily as the ship rocked beneath them.

"They will. For all they got greedy back there, they aren't idiots. They've left three guards on ten people, five of whom will absolutely put up a fight. They didn't leave their best, and none of them were spellcasters. Even if you set the little ones aside, that's not enough to be sure of so many in such a small space. They have what they want, and so they'll leave. Or they'll get themselves beaten bloody and shitless by farmers for the trouble and have to answer for it." Sessaca gave him a disapproving look. "They're none of them mincing delicates."

"You made very sure of that, didn't you?"

"You're welcome."

It grated at Dahl how smoothly everything fit together—how had he missed this? You miss everything, he thought. You've lost what edge you had.

Be fair—Farideh's voice echoed in his thoughts, and he sighed. No one thinks their grandmother is secretly a retired Zhentarim swordcaptain. He found himself wishing Farideh were here. She would have kept him steady.

Sessaca eyed him a moment. "Is this what you've been mixed up in? Are you an agent of theirs?"

"No stranger than my grandmother being one," Dahl said, dancing around the answer.

"So, no," Sessaca said. "Pity. They ought to have grabbed you before you got all starry-eyed about serving Oghma. Could have put some sense into you *and* them, and made you some extra coin to send your mother." She sighed. "Whatever you are, have you any idea what this is really about?"

Dahl shook his head. "Not a one."

"Don't let on," Sessaca advised. "Never give them the upper hand." She pulled her shawl tighter again, eyes on New Velar. "The dark girl, the one waiting upstairs. Mira. You know her."

"I did," Dahl said. He knew that tone. "Old acquaintance."

"She's pretty enough," Sessaca said. "Calm in a crisis."

"If you say so."

"And steady. You'd do well with steady. Better than the girl you've taken up with," Sessaca added. "And here besides."

"You have no idea what kind of girl I've taken up with." Dahl turned on her. "Perhaps you're out of practice, but you might have deduced I'm not interested in talking about my love life."

"Of course not," Sessaca said. "*Farideh*. It's a dragonborn name. You thought I wouldn't know that?"

Dahl frowned. "I did. Although I don't see how . . . Oh Gods' books," he swore. "You think she's a *dragonborn*?"

"You're going to break your mother's heart."

Dahl gave a short, bitter laugh. "Well now she has worse things to worry about than whether I'm in love with someone who lays eggs. Well done, us." He left her on the deck and headed down into the ship's belly.

Eurdila had not taken their plan well—frail Sessaca and all three of her sons, hostages for these horrible people? Dahl had told her it would be fine, but he couldn't imagine how. She'd wept, and he'd held her tightly and promised he knew what he was doing, even if he couldn't tell her why. It was Sessaca's fault, but it was his too—or would he have ever come to the Harpers if his grandmother had not instilled the things she had in his heart and mind?

While Sessaca had garnered an officer's bunk, the Zhentarim had left Dahl and his brothers a trio of hammocks right in the middle of the lower decks. As Dahl approached the hatch, he heard Thost and Bodhar talking down below.

"Course it does!" Thost rumbled. "He shows up, sudden as you please and trailing trouble. What else do you call it?"

"I'm just saying let him talk," Bodhar said. "You know there's got to be more here."

"Oh aye, that he's no rich man's scribe?" Thost said. "That's plain enough."

Dahl cursed. Suddenly there was nothing more refreshing than the sea breeze and his grandmother's opinions on what women would suit him. Or he could sit here, on the steps between both, him and a half-filled flask of whiskey.

He made a fist of his hand and went down anyway, fighting the sensation of being ten again, amid his grown brothers, everything he said and did ripe for correction or teasing.

Thost and Bodhar sat on a pair of hammocks strung opposite each other. The Zhentarim sailors gave them a wide berth, yet still on guard. Still listening.

"I didn't tell him everything that happened," Bodhar said, as Dahl approached. "But you should."

Dahl sighed, eyeing the sailors. He crouched down between the hammocks and spoke in a low voice. "Mira came looking for me first. I know her."

"Gathered that," Thost said, even terser than usual. "How?"

The sailor mending a rope by the bulkhead a little too deliberately. The fellow counting water barrels slower than a student. There would be nowhere on the ship they could safely speak. "Secretary work," he settled on. Bodhar looked at him as if he'd gone mad. Thost sniffed.

"I'm not slow," he said. "Granny made it very clear who these folks are. But not who *you* are."

"They said you were feeding her information," Bodhar pointed out. "That Mira." When Dahl didn't answer, he went on. "You're not working with the Zhentarim, are you?"

Dahl hesitated—assuming Mira hadn't slipped, the Zhentarim didn't know he was a Harper. Once they did—if they did—everything would become a great deal more urgent. "It's complicated."

Thost stood. "Complicated just got us hauled off to gods-know-where with a bunch of wolves nipping our heels and sitting guard on our families. You're working for the stlarning Black Network? Gods above, Dahl, and you're meant to be the smart one."

He started toward the deck, and Dahl cursed. "Thost!" He sprinted after. "Thost, damn it." He caught his brother's arm—too many eyes, too many ears, and Thost was furious. He wet his mouth. "Do you remember," he said, quietly, "the stories you and Bodhar used to tell me? Like . . . Like 'The

Unfaithful Servant'?" He gave Thost a significant look. "Or 'The Shepherd and the Giants'? About Oehmur Laskaling, and the Bard of Shadowdale and Those Who Harp." He held Thost's gaze, willing him to pick out the references—secret identities and fighting from the inside, loyalty disguised as disloyalty and Harpers besides. "I'm still your little brother," he added. "Still the boy you told stories to.

"I listened," he added, mouthing the words.

Thost frowned, searching Dahl's face. "Don't you claim blood, not now."

"I don't blame you for being angry," Dahl said. "Be angry. But you want to know who I am. I'm your brother. That's what's important."

Thost shook his head. "It's not what's going to keep us safe." He turned and climbed the stairs to the deck. Dahl swallowed a curse and turned back to Bodhar, who was watching him now with interest.

"You always liked those stories," he said conversationally, as Dahl sat on the empty hammock. "Though I thought you went in for the noble hero slays the monster more than the ones full of lessons."

"It's funny what stays with you."

"Thost never told you 'The Unfaithful Servant,'" he said. "That was Da."

"I forgot," Dahl lied.

"Right," Bodhar said, studying Dahl. "I don't think you've earned the right to secrets. Not now. Not when it's plain they're there. Not when it's cost us our family's safety."

"Are you mad at Granny too?"

"For all the good it will do." Bodhar shook his head. "Have to tell you, this isn't the adventure I was hoping for."

"I'll fix it. Somehow I'll get us out of this."

Bodhar sighed. "Well, you're not going to get us off this ship until it's across the Reach." He grinned at Dahl. "Plenty of time for old stories. Or new ones—you still owe me three things."

• • •

ILSTAN NYARIL WATCHED his reflection waver in the sunlit ripples of the River Alamber, dizzying himself as he looked through his own face into the murky depths.

Who you are and who you were and who you will be, the rambling voice of a not-dead god said in his thoughts. *Magic accounts for all of these and none of these . . . We are and we were and we will be and so shall it.*

"Is that better than the water skins?" the slim dragonborn man said as he squatted down beside Ilstan. Ilstan looked up at him, forgetting where he'd come from.

"The water of the rivers is alive with the breath of Mystra," he said, the words tumbling out of his mouth as though they were liquid themselves. "It's more than a body can bear."

The dragonborn smiled kindly at him. "Bend down to the surface and make a cup of your hand. Do you want me to get Wick? We've got another day or two of traveling, and it's been a while since you . . . you know . . . sorted yourself out."

Ilstan stared at the dragonborn, as if he could see through the layers of scale and muscle and bone and into his soul. He trusted the fellow, he found, as much as Ilstan trusted anyone, but he couldn't remember his name. And he couldn't remember Wick.

. . . The wizard is but the channel that magic flows through, but the vessel for the goddess's blessings, but the parchment the spell is written upon . . .

The dragonborn man reached over and flipped Ilstan's cloak back over his sleeve. Crude embroidery picked out a series of runes there: *Give the magic to another caster.*

Ilstan covered the message he'd written to himself with the cloak again, clutching his arm to his chest. Wick was the caster, he remembered, a gnome woman with hair the color of the sunset on the walls of Suzail. He'd hired her and the dragonborn when he'd left Proskur, heading after . . .

Farideh.

The seal is weakened . . . the key is found . . . the Lady of Black Magic is searching, searching . . . how is a devil like a wizard? . . . both bleed until they don't . . .

Ilstan's whole brain turned electric at the memory of the tiefling, the Chosen of Asmodeus, god of sin and murderer of Ilstan's true master. "I have to find the Lady of Black Magic," he said. "It's imperative."

The dragonborn frowned. "I'll get Wick."

Djerad Thymar, he thought. Djerad Thymar is where she's heading. She'll be there, she has to. And then . . .

And then, my man, what will you do? Crush the breath from her lungs? Boil the blood from her veins?

Ilstan startled. The voice of the god . . . it was seldom so specific. So melodic. So merciless.

There are spells, he thought, tracing the pattern of their casting on the cool air. Would it come to that? Would he be ready for such action?

"All right, saer. You ready?" The gnome woman stood on the stony bank beside him, coming just to his shoulder where he sat. Her eyes, blue as broken magic, seemed to take up half her face as Ilstan peered into their depths.

"The Lord of Spells has made me ready," Ilstan said. "To find the key, to break the prison. To end the Knight of the Devil."

Wick sighed and took hold of his hand, setting it on her shoulder. She rummaged through her pockets for a small brown bean. She dropped it, and her own hands flitted before her, separate creatures marking their own separate paths through the air, a dance to lure that power along the Weave. She spoke a word of benediction, a word of strength, a word of pure magic, and Ilstan's mind stilled.

The blessings of Azuth flowed through him in the same heart-beat that Wick's spell completed. What should have been a stiff gust of wind became a squall that whipped the River Alamber's waters back upstream. Ilstan watched the river grow shallower and shallower, as if the wind would blow it all away—

He woke at the top of the riverbank, a score of steps from the road. The god's voice was a gentle murmur. Magic eased through his body, slow and rolling as the River Alamber. He remembered who he was, where he was, where he needed to be.

"Thank you," he said. "Without you two, I don't know what I would do." The dragonborn clasped his forearm and pulled him to his feet. "Thank you," Ilstan said again.

"Thank *you*," Wick said, a little wild. Her big blue eyes seemed to spark and crackle, her grin wide enough to crack her skull. She flexed her hands, in an agitated way. "How's the road between here and the City-Bastion? Monsters? Brigands?"

"More caravans," the dragonborn said with a chuckle. "We're past the worst of it all. Gonna have to wear yourself out with the boring sort of spell. Maybe teach yourself Draconic for a bit before we get there?"

Wick made a face. "You're no fun."

"Yrjixtilex Kallan," Ilstan said. The dragonborn sellsword turned. "That's your name," the wizard explained. "I've just remembered."

Kallan smiled in a friendly way. "That's right. You remember yours?"

"I'm no one," Ilstan lied. It was better that way. He already knew that the servants of the Raging Fiend could hide behind even the kindest smiles.

5

Instead of the inn Havilar had been expecting, Anala set them up in a cluster of rooms, deep in the Verthisathurgiesh enclave. One for her, one for Mehen, one for Farideh, and one for Brin—all centered around a sitting room with a little fire pit that vented out the ceiling. Havilar considered her room, annoyed at its expanse and its emptiness.

"Do you think I could bring my puppy in here?" she asked Anala. "She's in the stables right now."

"I don't see a problem with that," Anala said.

"She's . . . big," Farideh said from behind them. "And she's not a regular dog."

Havilar shot Farideh a look. "She's a hellhound. But she's obedient and she wears a muzzle all the time. The worst you'd have to worry about is her drool burning the rug, and I'll roll it up."

Anala's brow ridges rose. "How big?"

"She rides it," Farideh said.

"She'll fit in the room," Havilar said quickly. "I won't let her in the bed."

Anala considered Havilar for such long moments that she couldn't help but wonder if she'd revealed the wrong thing. She didn't break her gaze—it was stupid to try and hide. Especially something the size of Zoonie.

"The muzzle stays on," Anala said cautiously.

"Always," Havilar said. Which was a lie, but not a big one. She wouldn't take the muzzle off for anything short of an emergency, but there was no planning for an emergency, after all. "Also," Havilar added, "who would I talk to about riding a bat?"

A small smile curved Anala's mouth. "My, you're an adventurous one. The giant bats are for Lance Defenders and—occasionally—their guests. I could arrange something."

"That's not necessary," Farideh said quickly. To Havilar she said, "Do you want to go get Zoonie?"

Havilar scowled at her. "What is your problem?" she demanded once they were out of earshot. "I could ride a bat! Maybe I could spar with some Lance Defenders even. Not that you and Brin aren't good . . . You're just . . ."

"Have you considered *who* is likely to be in the Lance Defender barracks?" Farideh whispered.

Havilar felt herself blush hot. "Is that why you're acting like this? *Karshoj* to Arjhani."

"I just think it's better if we keep our distance. Like a truce."

"I don't care about Arjhani. I don't need a truce because he doesn't matter."

Farideh looked at her as though Havilar had denied anything hurt with a torn-off leg and staved-in ribs. "It was a long time ago," Havilar said hotly. Not that anyone would let her forget it. Not that anyone would think she'd moved past it.

They'd been eleven, nearly twelve, when Arjhani had come to Arush Vayem. The summer right when she'd started to notice the future, possibilities and adventures and adulthood there on the edge of her life. The summer she'd started daydreaming about who she would be and how. Even still, the smell of alfalfa left to blossom sent her back to that time and place as if it cast a spell on her.

And into that summer of possibility, her father's long-lost love had come, full of apologies and promises, stories and more possibilities. He had come carrying his glaive, and Havilar had chosen the first path of her future. She loved Arjhani like a second father, and maybe more. Her future started shaping itself around him as he claimed Arush Vayem for a new home, and their family as his. For a summer, everything had been as happy and nearly perfect as Havilar could remember.

But winter came eventually.

"I'm not going to crack again," she said, cheeks still burning. "I'm grown. I've got my own life. I've got nothing to do with him." Farideh said nothing, and in the silence, Havilar wondered if she was thinking about how much Havilar's life had come apart—her true love broken by fighting and distrust, her adventures determined by others, her life decided by the whims of an evil god.

"If Arjhani shows up," she said a little loudly, "I'll tell Zoonie to sit on him."

A smile slipped through her sister's serious expression. "I like that idea. But I don't think it's a good idea to walk around with Zoonie. People might realize what she is. She could burn your whole room down—"

They came to the market floor, and Havilar wondered if she could find that tiefling fellow again. "My room is all stone, same as yours, same as everything. If the whole place is full of dragonborn, then what happens when a windchill fever sweeps the place? Everybody hacking fire and lightning? They wouldn't last long if the city could burn—Hey, if Zoonie can't burn my room down, then you can't burn down yours! You don't have to go far to do your fire thing!"

Farideh's expression was grim. "We're not staying that long."

"Well we'd be gone a lot quicker if you called Lorcan and asked him about that portal."

Farideh's expression turned grimmer and her tail lashed. "He's not going to help us."

"Please. He's just as stuck as we are. If Brin and I can be friends, you and he can be allies. Anyway, if Dahl's gone—"

"*Thrik!*" Farideh spat. "I'm not calling him down." They walked in silence the rest of the way to the Verthisathurgiesh stables.

Zoonie was overjoyed to see Havilar and would have knocked her on her rump if she weren't chained. As it was, the wooden beam creaked as Zoonie yanked against it. The stablehands all peered around their nervous charges as the hellhound yelped, her tail thumping a wild tattoo against the stable walls.

"Sit!" Havilar cried. "Sit, Zoonie!" Zoonie obeyed, scrabbling back into the stable, bouncing on her still-wagging tail. Havilar unlatched the chain and wrapped the length around her waist. Through the muzzle the hellhound licked her face gleefully, scattering sparks.

"Quit it!" Havilar laughed, patting out an ember that had caught, glowing, on her blouse sleeve. "Did she do any damage?" she asked the nearest stablehand, a broad-shouldered dragonborn woman with reddish scales.

"Just burnt up some hay," she said. "What kind of dog is that?"

"A Nessian warhound," Havilar said, scratching Zoonie's neck. "Good girl, good girl." The stablehand ventured a hand forward to pet her.

Zoonie turned, snarling and baring teeth the size of iron nails. "Hey!" Havilar yanked on her muzzle, pulling the hellhound away. "No! She's friendly. We don't growl at friendly people." Zoonie dropped her head, but eyed the stablehand mistrustfully. Havilar smiled at the woman, holding tight to the muzzle. "Maybe don't pet her just now. She's not *completely* trained yet."

She kept hold of the muzzle as she and Farideh walked back through the streets around the pyramid. The sun was setting, and their breath clouded on the chilly air. Steam wafted from Zoonie's coal-black coat.

"You're still planning to send her back, right?" Farideh said.

"When she's ready."

Farideh sighed. "Havi."

"What? You can't say she's unruly—she obeys me."

"She's a hellhound."

"You kept Lorcan around a lot longer than I've kept Zoonie," Havilar retorted.

Farideh turned scarlet. "What happened to 'You have to call him down'?"

Havilar bit her tongue. It was too easy to snap back, to say something she didn't mean, just to push her sister. Lorcan wasn't worth the argument. "I'm taking Zoonie for a run so she'll sleep better," Havilar said instead.

Farideh frowned. "She walked all morning."

"Tell Mehen and Brin I'll be back later," Havilar said, unstrapping her glaive and attaching it to Zoonie's harness. She clucked her tongue and started down the Road of Dust, Zoonie loping alongside.

The air had warmed with the rising sun, but as it set, it grew chilly and sharp in Havilar's nose. She ran until the effort of moving her legs was all she could think about, and panting, she stopped beside an outcropping of rock that looked down over the river. Zoonie trotted over to her, nudging at her to get up.

"I don't want a ride right now," Havilar said. "Sit with me." The hellhound nudged again, but when Havilar pushed her off, she obeyed, laying her enormous head across Havilar's sweaty lap, her side heaving.

"Are you going to tell me if you want to go back?" Havilar asked, scratching Zoonie's coal-black coat over her ribs. The hellhound licked the air happily. Havilar giggled. "I'm not going to make you," she promised.

She'd thrown Lorcan in Farideh's face before, but in a way, he and Zoonie were the same—Lorcan was useful, until he wasn't. Zoonie was harmless, until she wasn't. But then again, who was to say Lorcan *wasn't* still useful? Assuming you just talked to him and kept your knees together, *Fari,* she thought with a little venom.

She sighed. It was better she hadn't said that to Farideh.

The last of the sunlight glittered on the river, making silhouettes of the boats crossing to the other bank. She thought of the dead dragonborn, of the stink and the dread and the cold nausea that upended her stomach. It wasn't just a matter of a disagreement gone bloody, she felt sure down to her bones—as sure as she was that Farideh would be much, much happier if they could leave Djerad Thymar sooner rather than later.

And you're not going to convince her of the best way to do that, Havilar thought, scratching Zoonie behind the ear.

Havilar sighed again, her mind made up. "I need help."

• • •

THE BONE DEVIL ran through its feints of gossip too quickly for Lorcan's tastes, and it agitated him to acknowledge he'd developed any kind of opinion on such things. They stood on a parapet over the mound known as the birthing pit, watching new-made lemures scrabble down the sides to wander the plain of Malbolge.

"I *hear*," the bone devil said, "that Lady Malcanthet requested to leave the Nine Hells in order to put down a faction of her exiled sister, the Lady Xinivrae, claiming that *she* is the queen of the succubi. But Asmodeus denied it. One can hardly imagine why."

Lorcan considered the circling imps overhead, the peculiar cries of the devils born from the pit, and cursed how he'd gotten there. Entertaining a bone devil of all things, while its mistress, Lady Fierna, ruler of the Fourth, attended the archduchess. When Lorcan's mother had been in power, he would have made a point to be far, far away from Malbolge when another archdevil visited. But circumstances had brought the cambion solidly under the notice of the archdevils and forced him up the hierarchy against his will.

"Because he doesn't trust her?" Lorcan guessed, knowing it wasn't the answer the creature wanted. Knowing exactly why Fierna had suggested this connection. He flicked his wings in irritation.

"Well who would?" The bone devil shifted, its scorpion-like tail clattering as it did. It towered over Lorcan, skinless, sinewless, but unspeakably strong. Any other time, Lorcan might have been afraid to be so near one of the brutal enforcers, but this one's motives were as clear as the bones of its spine: *Something is happening in Nessus. Something is happening to the king of the Hells. Everyone knows Invadiah's spoiled son is caught in it. Find out more.*

"But given the rebellion of the succubi in Stygia," the bone devil went on, "the fact that the Abyss has grown more of the defectors since their defeat, one would assume that His Majesty would be glad to allow Lady Malcanthet to show where the true succubi stand."

Lorcan met the creature's green-ember eyes within its hollow sockets. "Or loath to let her conspire with her sister."

The bone devil's teeth twisted in something like a grin. "You give the succubi too much credit. The ones who remain must know it's in their interests to reaffirm their loyalties."

You don't give them enough credit, Lorcan thought. If the succubi were as foolish as most of the Nine Hells believed, they never would have escaped the Abyss when Asmodeus ascended—and if they were wise enough to see which way the wind blew a hundred years ago, they were wise enough to see it now.

His mother, Invadiah, had been an erinyes all his life, until a succubus under her command had turned traitor and earned Invadiah the displeasure of Glasya and Asmodeus alike. For her crime she'd been demoted into the form of a succubus herself, and there was no denying Invadiah had grown more terrifyingly clever even as she was weakened.

"I will lay a balance of thirty souls," Lorcan said flatly, "that we find the 'succubus queens' have all been playing us—demons, devils, and all else alike—into thinking their loyalties are something that persist beyond their current needs."

"How bold," the bone devil chortled. "Does that notion come from His Majesty?"

If Lorcan ever found the person who had let slip that the king of the Nine Hells, the god of sin, had spoken to him personally, he would throttle them merrily and crush their bones into the ravenous plane of Malbolge. Twice—two shitting times—Asmodeus had made Lorcan his audience, and half the Hells seemed to think Lorcan was the path to the god's ear.

More and more, if the gossip was to be believed, the king of the Hells fell silent and turned away any and all petitioners. Not even his closest advisors seemed to know what was happening.

More and more, Lorcan feared that *he* did.

"You say that as though His Majesty brings me into his confidence," Lorcan said, aiming for louche, aiming for useless. "And I hear that circle is quite diminished as it is. My only fortune lies in being the pact holder for a few Chosen." He made himself smile at the bone devil. "Do you collect?"

There was no denying the bone devil's disdain—of course it didn't collect warlocks. "So I hear. What is His Majesty's interest in that Chosen?"

Lorcan kept his eyes on the bubbling lake, but his thoughts were on Farideh, that first night together—the fury in her eyes and the tremor in her voice, the roughness of her breath and the glint of the amulet she wound around her hand. "You remember how this works?" she'd said. "You hurt me and it hurts you." He'd let his temper get the better of him—there had been no plan in his head, only the fact that he did not want Dahl near her, didn't want her to forget that she wanted him. Lorcan hadn't expected her to turn his bluff on him, to dare him to act on the lust he taunted her with. Which made him all the more eager.

He thought of Asmodeus saying, *Keep her alive. Keep her sated. Keep her quiet.*

For a time, they all aligned so nicely. Not anymore.

"I know better than to ask that," Lorcan said.

"That's not what I hear." The bone devil's tail clattered behind Lorcan. "You're cleverer than you make yourself seem."

"You'd be the first to say that."

What did you do to him? Farideh had cried—Lorcan should have kept his distance, should have waited until she'd become certain that Dahl must have left of his own accord. *What did you do to him?* And the truth was as unmanageable, untwistable as Farideh was becoming. So Lorcan did the previously unthinkable: he looked her in the eyes and lied.

What did you do to him?
Absolutely nothing.

The lie still danced on his tongue, the urge to do it again, not to twist the facts but to invent new ones. He could tell the bone devil Farideh was dead. He could tell it Asmodeus was looking to obliterate the Fourth Layer. He could tell it anything at all, and it made him feel as if he were looking down into the bottomless Abyss.

"Weaker too," the bone devil went on. The scorpion tail twisted behind Lorcan's legs, rattling against the stone, a reminder of the creature's purpose. "I hear your Chosen isn't corrupted. I hear you've lost all your other warlocks."

"How funny," Lorcan said, forcing his voice to remain level and dry. "I hear nothing at all about you."

The bone devil's grin twisted once more. "I don't tend to leave many tongues to wag." Its tail curved more closely around Lorcan. "Does this deliberate obtuseness work with lesser devils?"

It can't kill you, Lorcan told himself. It doesn't dare. "Quite frequently," Lorcan said. "Or else they realize that they're treading terribly close to things they shouldn't know."

The air beside him *popped* and Lorcan and the bone devil turned to see a dark blue imp hanging in the air over the Birthing Pit.

"Greetings," it said in a nasal voice. "You are Lorcan, yes? You are the one who holds the pact with the Chosen of Asmodeus." It wet its lips. "*Chosens* of Asmodeuses."

Lorcan suppressed a curse. "What is it?"

"There's been an incident."

Fear seized Lorcan's heart like the claws of the bone devil itself. "What? What happened?" She was dead, he thought. She was wounded. She was apostate and Asmodeus wanted her head—

"I think there's a dretch in the city where they are," the imp said. "She wants you to come. Right away, if possible." Its eyes darted to the bone devil.

Lorcan went perfectly still—fear and rage and relief and desire clutching at his heart. The bone devil didn't need to know, the imp didn't need to know, but it was very hard in that moment not to laugh. "Does she?" he said carefully.

"Trouble?" asked the bone devil.

"Possibly," Lorcan drawled, seeing an escape. "If you'll excuse me, I'll just find out for myself." He turned to the erinyes guards who followed him everywhere now—dark-skinned Neferis, ugly Axona, Pandosia with her broken nose, and silver-haired Ctesiphon, whom he'd promoted to the elite *pradixikai* to replace their dead sister, Noreia. The closest he could come among his half sisters to a loyal guard.

"Ctesiphon, would you escort our guest back to Osseia? I'll return shortly. Neferis, to me."

The erinyes fell in behind him, and Lorcan found himself all too aware of the proximity of her blade. But—like himself—Neferis had been singled out by Glasya, lord of the Sixth. When Noreia had been sacrificed to the Dragon Queen to destroy the secrets she knew, only Neferis had been spared among the erinyes who dragged Noreia there. Her life, she had to know, was a gift, and it would not do to throw that away with foolish actions.

"What did she say?" Lorcan asked the imp that still flapped alongside him. "What exactly did she tell you?"

"That you should come and see for yourself," it said. "That she wants to be sure, but that the other one—that Farideh shouldn't know you came."

Lorcan stopped walking. "Havilar sent you."

"Yes," the imp said. "Because she thinks you can deal with the dretch."

Of course, he thought. Of course. He kept his expression still, his back stiff. There was no humiliation here, because no one needed to know he'd ever thought anything else.

Havilar, he told himself, was better than nothing.

"Where did the dretch come from?" Lorcan said, walking toward the tower again. "I assume she didn't call it up herself?"

"I don't know," the imp said. "I didn't see it. I only smelled it."

Farideh could handle herself against a dretch. The whining dregs of the Abyss, even the imp could probably hold its own against one. Havilar did not need Lorcan.

But where one dretch appeared, there would be more. There would be a summoner. There would be something to fear. If Farideh wasn't supposed to know Havilar had sent for him, did she even know demons were involved? Or was she angry enough that she was willing to risk it?

Or, he thought, was the imp a little idiot?

"She's in Djerad Thymar with Mot," the imp said as they approached the fingerbone tower where Lorcan's scrying mirror hung.

"I know."

"The dragonborn city."

"I know what Djerad Thymar is. Get out of my way before I break your shitting neck."

A spell of protection cloaked Havilar from the scrying mirror's magic, but the imp directed him to seek out a second imp, the afore-mentioned Mot, who was still with Havilar. Lorcan hid himself in the guise of a human before waking the portal in the wall. A ghostly screech scraped the air as he stepped through it onto a grassy patch beside an outcropping of rock. Havilar waited there with a bright red imp and that blasted hellhound. The beast snarled as he appeared.

"Hush, Zoonie," Havilar said. "Well met."

"Well met. I hear you have a problem with dretches."

"Oh blistering archlords, Olla!" the other imp cried. "You boot-sucker—who said to tell him dretches?"

"I don't know what I have a problem with," Havilar said. "But something strange is happening and you're possibly the only person who can help."

"I doubt that," Lorcan said. "Where's your sister?"

"In her room," Havilar said. "She's not happy with you."

"Well I'm not happy with her either," Lorcan said, ignoring the trickle of panic that ran through his thoughts. "What is it you think I can do?"

Havilar blew out a breath. "I'll tell you inside. You can go," she said to the red imp. "Thank you."

It rubbed its hands nervously. "You sure? We could come along. In case."

"He's fine," Havilar said, looking up at Lorcan. "Mostly."

"You shouldn't impugn a greater devil like that," the blue imp said.

"Who's impugning?" the red one snapped. "And in case you didn't notice, he's a cambion. Wild card, that one." The little imp narrowed its eyes at Lorcan.

Lorcan smiled at Havilar. "My, but you seem to have a penchant for undersized defenders."

"Shut up," Havilar said. "And Mot, go away and take Olla. Thank you for helping, but I can do this on my own." The imps popped out of existence, the little red one's eyes fading out last, still glaring at Lorcan.

"If by chance," Lorcan said, "you've taken to thinking of me as a surprisingly large imp, I'd like to remind you that if you order me around like that, I'll make my Brimstone Angel more valuable in one stroke."

Havilar shook her head. "*Pothachi*—as if you wouldn't lose Farideh the second you killed me."

"You make it sound like your sister always knows what I do."

"She'd find out eventually. She always does." Havilar clicked her tongue at the hellhound. She dropped to her belly beside Havilar, standing the moment Havilar's leg swung over. "Careful, Zoonie!" she cried, catching her balance. "I'll tell her not to run if you stop being a *henish*."

They didn't speak again until they were nearly to the city. "You couldn't have asked me to come somewhere a bit closer?" Lorcan said as the gates of Djerad Thymar came into sight. "Tell me what you want and let's get this over with."

"First," Havilar said, "I think you ought to apologize to Farideh. Whatever it is you've done."

"I did."

"Right. Sure you did."

"Like it or not, your sister isn't innocent in our dealings. I've forgiven her, she ought to forgive me. What I did was trivial, anyway."

"Maybe if you're in the Hells." Havilar shook her head. "Don't talk to her if you're not going to apologize, you'll just make it worse."

"How wonderful that you thought it worth my time and magic to haul myself across the planes to hear this. Especially when I could have gotten it free from my own sister."

"*Second*," Havilar said forcefully, "it'll help you if you help me. Because she wants to leave Djerad Thymar as soon as possible, and we can't leave until Mehen finds out who killed some people. I called you because I think it's something Abyssal."

Lorcan frowned. She climbed off the dog and took the chain around her waist. "Look," he said, "just as you shouldn't consider me an oversized imp, you shouldn't think that those imps know anything at all—"

"It's not the imps," Havilar said. "It's me."

Though the dragonborn guarding the gates of the city eyed Havilar and the hellhound as they passed, the little token she flashed at them seemed to ensure their goodwill. They skirted the edge of a market, more crowd than streets, and nearly every face among them a dragonborn's. Twice Lorcan's eyes lit on tiefling women, islands in that sea of scales, but neither one was Farideh.

Havilar led him to a door set into the stone floor of the city, and they descended into a network of catacombs. Havilar dismounted from the hellhound and led both it and Lorcan through the tunnels some distance, before stopping in a large tomb dominated by a quartet of sepulchers.

The smell of rot lingered, though whatever bodies had been there had long since been carted away. The fine hairs on the back of Lorcan's neck prickled—more than rot. Lorcan drew his sword.

"That's the first thing," Havilar said. "It smells bad. I know someone died in here, but—"

"Zoonie?" The hellhound lifted her head. "*Parosh renoutaa*," he said in Infernal.

Zoonie lowered herself, growling, to the floor, ready to spring. She bared her iron-gray teeth, sparks raining from her jaws.

"Zoonie, stop it!" Havilar snapped. Zoonie straightened and backed toward her, still tense, still watching Lorcan. "Stop giving my dog orders!"

"Hush." Lorcan racked his memory, searching the scattering of lessons his erinyes sisters had given him. "*Chizaći chizaći gerje ghod ze!*" he called, a rough string of Abyssal that echoed through the tomb.

"What's that?" Havilar whispered.

"The all clear," Lorcan said. Or he hoped at least—he had never been the most attentive pupil where the erinyes were concerned, especially not when it came to information only suited for the long-ended Blood War.

The echoes faded. "*Ah! Lhayox'ales!*" he called.

Lhayox'xales? The mewling voice nudged into Lorcan's thoughts, echoing strangely. *Takhi okhznay? Ang ostarkija murta . . .* Something rustled at the other end of the tomb. A chill ran down his spine.

"Zoonie? *Renoutaa*."

The hellhound didn't move. Lorcan looked back over his shoulder—Zoonie stared at Havilar, who was watching Lorcan, looking fairly peaked. He gestured at the tomb, the source of the strange voice.

Havilar nodded. "*R-renoutaa*."

Zoonie raced forward, toward the sarcophagus. She slammed into it with all her weight, knocking the lid ajar. She pounced it once, twice, and the stone slab crashed against the granite. Something within screeched as the hellhound lunged in and pulled out a scrabbling, screaming little beast. Gray and hairless with long, clawed arms and tapered ears, it shivered, clutching a piece of a partly mummified dragonborn corpse that it struck Zoonie with over and over as she returned it to Lorcan.

Ja naghinuxara! Ja naghinuxara! its little voice said, and Lorcan struggled to pick out words that he knew. *Ang ostarkija murta! Khanakho ni, ni Graz'zt znayat san xi! Graz'zt ja naghpadakha! I'm alone. The others are dead.*

A cloud of green gas spread off it, and Zoonie dropped it, coughing sparks. "Dretch," Lorcan spat. Of course that smarmy little imp had to be right. *"T'Ikaw sijusa ka?"* Who summoned you?

The dretch jibbered more Abyssal, protesting that it had not been summoned and that a great demon lord would devour Lorcan and it both if he didn't—

Zoonie lunged again and grabbed the little demon by one arm. Before Lorcan could so much as take a step, she shook it furiously and *snap*—the arm broke, her jaws closed, and the rest of the dretch went flying. The dretch screamed like a creature ten times the size, and vanished in a puff of fire as it hit the wall.

"I wasn't finished," Lorcan said. Zoonie coughed and licked the roof of her mouth before trotting back over to the sarcophagus.

Havilar crouched down on the floor, gray-faced and shaking. Lorcan frowned. "It's just a dretch."

In answer she heaved again and sprinted toward the corner where she vomited noisily. Zoonie whined and looked from Lorcan to Havilar.

"We should go," Lorcan said. "That noise is likely to call people."

"Wait," Havilar said. She straightened, wiping her mouth and breathing hard. "Why does it make me sick?"

"Because it smells like a pile of corpses washed in vomit and dogshit?"

"It happened before," Havilar said. "Not this bad, but I know what it feels like. She said it was the Abyss that made my skin crawl and my bones itch. She called it a gift befitting the Chosen of the king of devils. What kind of gift is throwing up at demons?"

Lorcan's wings twitched. *"Who* said that?"

"The ghost," Havilar said "Bryseis Kakistos. Which you would know if you hadn't mucked everything up with Farideh."

Lorcan's heart nearly stopped. "The ghost of *Bryseis Kakistos* contacted you?"

"She came to Farideh in the internment camp, only Fari didn't know who it was. She went after me while we were traveling, possessed some people. Including Brin."

"Why didn't you tell me this?" Lorcan demanded. "What in the name of the shitting Nine does she want? What did you tell her? Why did you not tell me?"

"Because Farideh said not to!" Havilar shouted back. "Anyway, I'm telling you now. Because she also made me sick and that thing made me sick and I can't really live my life throwing up at odd moments, especially when its people I need to be able to fight that make it happen." She folded her arms over her stomach. "Anyway, she hasn't come back since Constancia turned her after she possessed Brin. Unless she's involved with *this*—I don't understand how any of this works."

This was not a development Lorcan particularly knew how to contend with. The Brimstone Angel had been one of the greatest champions of Asmodeus, but she'd died in conflict with the god, and her soul had vanished from the Nine Hells nearly fifty years before. What she might be up to, what she might want now, whether she still existed as the same soul—no one knew the answers to these questions. No one, outside the very foolish, wanted to know. Bryseis Kakistos was a special sort of anathema. A problem that could not be ignored but that must not be dug into.

"It is very unlikely that the Brimstone Angel is skulking the catacombs murdering dragonborn," Lorcan said. "I wouldn't rule it out completely, but signs suggest someone got a boon from some demon in the form of a cluster of dretches dropped on their enemies. This was the last of them—I gathered that much before your unruly hound stepped in. The others are dead or pulled back to the Abyss by now. Again, we should go."

"So there's nothing to worry about?"

"No one sicced demons on you, I assume? The worst you could do is bother yourself looking for the one who summoned them, or had them sent. You'll likely know them because you'll vomit on their boots, so I would just steer clear of anyone who makes you feel sick."

"Will I get used to it? Do I have to practice?"

"Why in the world would I know?" Lorcan said. "It's not as if this is a common skill. Presumably at some point your stomach will tire of vomiting." That was true of almost everything—given time, anything could be tolerable. "Until then, you can always stay back."

Havilar made a face at him. "I don't stand at the back."

"Stand where you like. I assume your sister's waiting on you. Zoonie! *Eshata*!"

The hellhound didn't move. She glanced back at Havilar, whining and scratching at the sarcophagus. "What is it?" Havilar asked, crossing to the dog. "Is there something—Oh *karshoji* gods! There's a body."

"It's a sarcophagus," Lorcan said. "They tend to have those."

"No, a *fresh* body." She peered over the stone edge again. "I think it's one of the young ones . . . It . . ."

Lorcan came to stand beside her. Lying on the withered bones of the sarcophagus's previous occupant was a young dragonborn man. Small cuts raked his yellowish scales, and a row of red-jasper piercings arched over his wide, staring eyes.

"How did he get inside?" Havilar asked. "That lid's not light."

"Perseverance?" Lorcan said. He marked the exits, the sound of distant feet and cursed. "Come on. You don't want to be caught here with a fresh body, do you?"

"I should tell Mehen." Havilar clicked her tongue at Zoonie, urging the hellhound to follow, and hurried after Lorcan. "Do you want me to pretend we didn't talk?"

"Do as you like," Lorcan said, trying for careless. "If she's still sulking, let her sulk." Near the exit to the catacombs he plucked a ring from the chain he wore around his neck, blowing through the center to cast the whirlwind that sucked him back to the Nine Hells and the fingerbone tower. Letting the disguise fall, Lorcan flicked his wings, agitated and off-balance.

The iron-framed scrying mirror hung on a wall of weeping marrow. With the portal shut and the lock of sinews sealed over the door, Lorcan stood before the scrying mirror, the scourge pendant he wore clutched in one hand.

Farideh's blood soaked the charm, and through it, the magic of the scrying mirror raced across the planes, slipping past the protection spell that still hung heavy around Farideh, preventing anyone from locating her with spells alone.

The magic sought out the wound that Lorcan had stolen the blood from, and as Farideh appeared—alone, sitting on the edge of an enormous bed in a stone-walled room, hair unbound, and garbed only in a plain shift—she gasped and clapped a hand over the brand on her upper arm.

She went completely still, as if bracing for something. He tugged the lines of magic that bound them, gentler this time, a caress of power. She shut her eyes, but still she didn't move.

"What do you want?" she asked the empty room.

Lorcan sat a long moment, staring at the mirror, staring at the tiefling woman sitting on the edge of the bed. There were a hundred answers to that question, and not all of them agreed with one another. What would happen if he went? If he was charming? If he was kind? If he lied again? Would things go back the way they were supposed to, or would he regret rushing in?

He thought of the fight they'd had, the image in the mirror of her and Dahl together. The rage that had overtaken him, like a tide of erinyes blood in his veins. Almost as if another devil altogether had stepped into his skin. He'd moved too quickly, too *devilishly*. What worked in the Nine Hells wasn't what worked on Toril, with Farideh.

He didn't regret it. Not exactly. With Dahl out of the way, the Harper could hardly pretend to be a rival. But he shouldn't have gone back to make sure Farideh knew Dahl was gone, he shouldn't have rubbed it in her face. Now she was angry at him, regardless of everything else.

He should *never* have promised Farideh he wouldn't hurt Dahl. He'd lied once—how different was breaking a promise? Would it unmake him the way it might a full devil?

He waited. He watched. The vein at the curve of her throat pulsed, a flutter of blood and heat and life.

She's safe, he assured himself. You're not out of chances. And you'll have to go to her, sooner or later.

But he sat for a long time, watching the last of his warlocks wait for him to return, fiddling with the scourge pendant and the lines of connection that bound Farideh to him, pointedly not thinking about how much he'd weakened them.

With Neferis at his back, Osseia welcomed Lorcan with the howls of the long-dead Hag Countess whose skull formed the palace. The pit fiends guarding the gate of its mouth eyed Lorcan and his guard, but they knew better than to stop them. Everyone knew better, it seemed, and it made Lorcan a little giddy. You are all but a devil here, he thought. No one knows how far you can step from the Hells' grasp.

But then Ctesiphon stopped him at the entrance to the apartments, her face pale. "There's a . . . problem."

"What?" Lorcan said. "Does it want a tour of the pleasure gardens now?"

The powerful erinyes wet her mouth. "You have a visitor . . . *The* visitor."

Lorcan's blood ran cold. "Is he still here?"

Ctesiphon only nodded. Lorcan looked past her, into the audience chamber where only the bone devil should have waited for him. There was no running, he reminded himself. There was nowhere to flee.

He entered the room as if in a dream, saw the goblet resting on a table beside a cushioned iron chair, saw the lacunae windows that opened out onto the plains of Malbolge. Heard the faint rustle of cloth—

Lorcan's vision went black and his knees buckled, his body suddenly slammed prostrate on the bone-tiled floor.

One would assume, came a voice like a landslide speaking from the center of Lorcan's brain, *that you understand your position, Lorcan. That you understand what is required of you. And yet, you come perilously close to failing me, over and over and over.*

Lorcan could not speak. Asmodeus had no interest in his excuses, his explanations. Invadiah did not matter, Glasya did not matter, the Brimstone Angel did not matter. None of those things were Lorcan, after all.

She cannot die, the god said. *She cannot be allowed to ask too many questions. She . . .*

The god's voice faded, as did the supernatural grip on Lorcan's senses. His left eye saw once more, fuzzy and distorted. Without thinking, he lifted his head, enough to see the edge of Asmodeus, the eye-searing existence of something that belonged to the Nine Hells and yet outstripped it. He closed his eyes again.

You have no idea how much power you hold, said a voice Lorcan had heard only once before; a voice that was the god of sin's and yet not at all Asmodeus. *You have no idea . . . It will be you that determines if she succeeds or she succeeds . . . If she has the tools and the weapons she needs to untangle . . . to right . . . or destroy . . . But then,* the voice went on as if it had completed its thought, *it would be unwise to hang* all *ones hopes on what is, in essence, a house divided . . .*

Lorcan's pulse felt like a constant vibration, hard enough to rattle his every vein. I don't want to know this, he thought over and over. I don't want to know this.

Suddenly the god's will over him surged again, pressing him briefly into oblivion before he found himself once more, blind and prostrate on the bone-tile floor. Asmodeus's presence was a palpable thing, a swarm of wasps, a building thunderhead.

This time, he said, and Lorcan felt a trickle of blood run from his ear down his jaw, *I took care of it for you. See that it doesn't happen again.*

All at once the presence lifted. Lorcan was whole again and Asmodeus was no longer in the Sixth Layer. The cambion straightened, carefully, cautiously. There was no sign of the bone devil.

Save one: As Lorcan stood, he saw the long bone lying in the chair, the half-moon shape of its end hooked over the chair's armrest. He stared at it for long moments, as if it might disappear if he didn't touch it. He wasn't so lucky. He plucked it up—a bone of the forearm, slender and gently twisted. Along the length of the shaft, burned in lacy glyphs, was a message:

You all live at my mercy.

Lorcan dropped the bone, staring at his open hands as though they might burst into flames by the contact alone.

Why? Lorcan's whole being screamed the question. Why did he care about a bone devil? Why care about Farideh in the first place? What was so important it needed this much attention? What was going to happen to Lorcan if he didn't make sure all of those issues were dealt with?

And who in all the Nine Hells was calling him a house divided?

It will be you that determines if she succeeds or she succeeds. Farideh. Glasya. Invadiah. Bryseis Kakistos. There could hardly be a less useful bit of babbling. And yet the strange speaker's words rattled through his thoughts.

Lorcan left the room, aware that he was shaking to the tips of his wings. For once, his sisters didn't mock his weakness, his fragile nature. They only watched, wide-eyed, waiting for orders from the one who had skimmed so close to Asmodeus's displeasure and survived.

You won't survive long if you don't know what you're avoiding, Lorcan thought, a little wildly. You need to know what the other Kakistos heirs are doing. You need to know why these are so special. You need to know what he's hiding, without him finding out.

The ghost, Havilar had said. *Bryseis Kakistos. Which you would know if you hadn't mucked everything up with Farideh.* Asmodeus wasn't the only one with an interest in his warlock that Lorcan couldn't ignore.

Lorcan thought a moment, about warlocks, about arch-devils, about the Blood War and the Ascension. Bryseis Kakistos and the Brimstone Angels. There was only one collector devil in the Sixth Layer who might have the keys to this puzzle. "Send a message to Shetai," he said finally. "I would speak with it."

"Shetai?" Ctesiphon said. "Invadiah never—"

"Invadiah is not here," Lorcan snapped.

Ctesiphon's eyebrow arched, a glimmer of the distaste his sisters normally dealt him. "Invadiah could never match the Vulgar Inquisitor. Be wary."

"Tell Shetai I would speak with it," Lorcan said once more. "About Brimstone Angels." In the meantime, he would have to make certain to gather enough information to sate the Vulgar Inquisitor. Shetai gave nothing without a price being paid.

• • •

FARIDEH DREAMS, A patchwork of panic—voices, monsters, the ghost of the Brimstone Angel dogging her. One moment she's trying to follow Dahl through a cavern full of twisting passages, the next she's standing in Arush Vayem, the village on no one's maps, and the snow is thick around her ankles. She calls for Dahl—he must be here somewhere—but she only hears the merry voices of her childhood neighbors, celebrating. She moves from house to house, fighting through the drifting snow, looking for Dahl.

But every house she reaches is cold and empty. The villagers are somewhere else. Dahl is somewhere else. She can't find them.

And something is following her through the shadows.

She starts to run, floundering in the snow, managing somehow to take the wrong paths through a village of only a dozen houses. She turns a corner, into Old Garago's house and the smell of brimstone hits her like a brick. A tiefling woman with small sharp horns like a mountain goat's, her golden eyes hard, stands in the middle of the wizard's empty study. Bryseis Kakistos, the Brimstone Angel, her robes splattered with blood.

"What is the secret?" she whispers. "One of us knows how to defeat him—is it you?"

"Don't think about that," Lorcan's voice says.

Farideh turns and finds him standing, inches from her.

"I don't want to be here," she says.

He holds out a hand to her, and she wants to take it—can remember the feeling of those hands on her arms, on her hips, on her breasts. For a moment, she might be somewhere else, tangled in another life, wrapped in his arms and sheltered by his wings.

He poisoned you, she remembers.

And it isn't Lorcan. She's sure down to her bones. Someone else is watching her through those black, black eyes.

"There is a weakness in the god of sin," she hears herself say. "We can punish him for his treachery. We can unseat him." She looks down at her hands, realizes they aren't cold. "This is a dream." She looks up at the thing that isn't Lorcan, and knows who it is. "Are you checking up on me?"

Asmodeus blinks with Lorcan's eyes. The village is suddenly on fire, the cheerful voices screaming, and above them all Dahl shouts—

Farideh sat up, Dahl's shout changing into a shrill note. The powers of Asmodeus, primed by the dream, flooded into Farideh and only instinct propelled her from the bed before flames erupted from her skin. As it was, the edge of the rug smoldered, and once she'd calmed herself enough to extinguish the fire, she stamped it out. She tested the edges of the pact, but in the same moment she realized the source of the sound—a flute, played in the little sitting room by idle hands.

Farideh said a little curse and stormed out into the sitting room. "Brin, it's the middle of the *karshoji* night, will you give the flute a rest, please."

He startled at her appearance and sheepishly let the flute he'd inherited from his father drop into his lap. "Sorry," he said. He nodded at the open door, the darkened room beside Farideh's. "Havi's not back yet. I can't sleep. I came out to wait for her."

"She's still taking Zoonie for a run?"

Brin nodded, drumming his fingers against the holes of the flute. "Look, I have to ask you something. And you don't have to answer, but if you can . . . ye gods, please tell me. Because . . . Look. Is she pregnant?"

For a heartbeat, Farideh thought she hadn't woken after all. "What?"

"She threw up—she never throws up," Brin said. "Even I didn't throw up. And . . . she's acting cagey about it. I don't know if it's the only time. She seems like she's sleeping a lot. Have you asked her? Why she was sick?"

Havilar's irritated dodge the other night made Farideh's stomach tighten. "She's embarrassed," she said. "I mean, you're right she doesn't get sick and then she was the only one . . ." It sounded false and flimsy. "She can't be, right? I mean . . . you two . . . It was well before the siege the last time . . ."

Brin looked away.

"Are you *joking*? You were hardly talking to each other!" Farideh said. "You were giving it a break! How could you have slept together?"

"Don't try to tell me that things weren't . . . complicated by the fact that there was an army trying to kill us all on the other side of the gates," Brin said hotly. "We made up. A bit. Twice." He blew out a breath. "I don't know what day she was on and she wasn't taking those herbs yet, so it's possible. I don't know."

Farideh covered her face with both hands. "I don't know either," she said after a moment. "She would have told me."

"I'd hope so," Brin said. "Of course, I would have hoped she'd tell me too."

Farideh didn't know what to say to that.

The jangle of Zoonie's muzzle broke her reverie. The hellhound trotted into the room, followed by Havilar. And Mehen.

"When did you leave?" Brin asked Mehen.

"Before," Mehen answered. "Go to bed."

"I woke him up," Havilar said, sounding rattled and punchy. "Our murder got stranger. I found another body in the tomb. Also a demon. So I got Mehen so he would get Anala, so she would get the guards. Adjudicators." She looked up at Mehen for confirmation, then added, "I don't actually know who she got. I had to go walk Zoonie again. She ate the demon and I had to wait for her to pass it. Worse than shades."

"I . . . You," Brin fumbled, "you were in a tomb with a demon?"

"And Zoonie," Havilar said. Then, "And Lorcan." Her eyes darted up to Farideh's. "I sent the imps for him. I . . . had a hunch. And I figured he might know things about demons."

Farideh found she couldn't breathe for a moment. Lorcan had been here. Lorcan had been in this very city, and he hadn't spoken to her. She folded her arms across her stomach. But he'd been watching her. He'd pulled on the brand. "Oh," she said. "Did he help?"

"He knows a lot of commands for Zoonie that I don't," Havilar said irritably. "But yeah, he found the demon. Not a big one." She glared at Mehen. "But it came from somewhere."

"We can worry about where in the morning."

"Was the body one of the hatchlings'?" Farideh asked.

Mehen's nostrils flared. "Right age for it. A Yrjixtilex boy. But he wasn't killed like the others. Hardly a scratch on him. Looks like he died of shock."

"Inside a stone sarcophagus it took Zoonie three tries to unlid," Havilar said.

"We will worry about it in the morning," Mehen said more firmly. "Everyone go to bed." Without waiting for them, he went to his own room and slammed the door.

"Well," Brin said with a false-sounding briskness. "I'm glad you're all right. Are you feeling any better, from earlier?"

Havilar scowled at her sister. "Gods! Did you tell him I threw up?"

"Give me a little credit," Brin said. "You were gray when I came in." A pause. "I care if you don't feel well is all. If there's something . . .You know, if you need to take it slow—"

"It's fine," Havilar said firmly. "Look, it's late. I'll see you in the morning."

Havilar clicked her tongue, and Zoonie trotted after her, her nails clicking across the stone floor.

"Hrast," Brin said. "That's not good." Farideh said nothing, and he wished her a good night, and went into his room. Farideh didn't move from where she sat. Every edge of Farideh's brand hummed with the memory of Lorcan's summons.

If he left her, she'd be in worse straits than she was now, without a patron or a pact. But every time she thought of him, she remembered the shaking fever, the threats to Dahl before they were anything but friends, and the cruel way he'd rubbed Dahl's absence in her face. *Don't cry for him,* Lorcan had said. *You were never his.*

He'd been so close to kind before that, Farideh thought. She couldn't help feeling as if she'd somehow broken Lorcan.

Farideh covered her face with both hands and cursed into her palms. You didn't make Lorcan what he is, she told herself. Maybe you just made him a little less like himself for a time.

And if she agreed to Asmodeus's offers, then she could make Lorcan into whatever she wanted. Her stomach turned. You don't want that.

Farideh went back to bed and lay staring at the cold, false moonlight for longer than she could gauge. It might have been a few minutes, it might have been all of the night, when she finally stood, realizing she wouldn't sleep. Her chest felt hot and tight as she found her way to Havilar's door and let herself in. "Havi?"

Zoonie sat up, her muzzle jingling. Havilar turned over, groggy and puzzled. "What is it? What's wrong?"

A lump built in Farideh's throat, and when she tried to speak, a shuddering sob went through her and she clapped a hand over her mouth. Havilar sprang out of bed and wrapped her arms around Farideh.

"What happened?" she demanded. "Why are you crying?"

"The usual reasons," Farideh managed. "Can I stay with you?"

"Yes," Havilar said, tucking an arm around her and walking her back. "These beds are too big in every way. It's like floating in a lake. I almost let Zoonie in," she admitted, "just so it didn't feel so lonely." Farideh climbed in beside Havilar, just like old times, and pulled the sheets up over her shoulder. Havilar studied her face. "I'm sorry about Lorcan. Do you want me to sic Zoonie on him? I will." As if on cue, the hellhound laid her enormous head on Havilar's hip and snuffled.

"Not yet," Farideh said.

"I told him he has to talk to you. For what it's worth."

"I don't want to talk to him," Farideh lied. "So you killed a demon?"

"Zoonie killed it. It was just a little grubby thing. Like maybe a demon's version of an imp. It looked kind of like a shaved dog. Lorcan said it was probably part of a group, but the rest of them are gone. That someone probably had another demon drop them on the group to punish an enemy or something."

Farideh frowned. "It doesn't make sense that a handful of little demons could have killed ten or twelve people who all had to have been trained to weapons at least a little. And what about the sarcophagus lid?"

"Maybe there were a hundred of them? Anyway, someone summoned them. I think we'll have to figure that out too."

Farideh cursed to herself. "We're never leaving here, are we?"

"Killers are easier than fellows, at least. At least it's not Dahl *and* Lorcan this time. Romance is the worst," Havilar said again. "Waste of energy. You should be done with both of them."

"As if you're really done with Brin," Farideh pointed out. "Anyway, I can't be done with Lorcan, not while we're both *karshoji* Chosen and every devil in the Hells wants a pact. We're stuck with him."

"And Dahl?"

"He's on the other side of the world," Farideh said, her stomach twisting. "So . . . I can hardly worry about him as much as the problems at my feet."

But she did. Oh, gods, she did. Where was he and who was he caught by? Why didn't he talk to her and was it because of devils or something new and worse? "Don't tell me to forget him. Please."

Havilar snuggled down into the bed. "Fine. And . . . I don't know if I'm done with Brin. I'm gauging my options," she said, a little loftily.

"What is that supposed to mean?"

Havilar was quiet a moment. "It means I'm wasting energy," she said. Before Farideh could press her further, she went on, "Which of them is better in bed?"

Farideh blushed to her temples. "*No*."

"I'm not asking for details! I'm just curious. You've got something to compare—I don't. Not yet anyway," she added quickly. "So . . . is it that different? Or is it all basically—"

"Oh *karshoji* gods!" Farideh pulled the blanket over her head. "It's different, all right?"

"I figured. I figure, too, that Dahl has to be a little interesting because I can't imagine that Lorcan is anything but ridiculously good. I suspect if you asked him, he wouldn't understand why anybody would bother being bad at it. But then you like Dahl better, so—"

"I'm going to go sleep in my room if you don't stop." Farideh pulled the blanket down. "Sleeping with Lorcan is like . . ." She shut her eyes tight. "Watching someone in a fighting exhibition, like at a fair or something. You can't pretend he's not really skilled, but after a while, it feels like it doesn't matter that much who's on the other side of the blade. And Dahl . . . it matters. A lot." She held tight to that knowledge—whatever else, he did love her and she loved him. "I miss him," she said quickly. "It's . . . so strange to miss him this much. I don't know what's going on. I don't know where he is or if it's my fault or if he misses me, and I still miss him so much."

"Because he's better with his 'blade,' " Havilar snickered.

If it were as simple as that, Farideh thought, I would be done with all of this. But instead she kept looking for him before she could remember he was gone, thinking of things she wanted to tell him before she could recall he wouldn't hear them. Looking up at the impossible bulk of Djerad Thymar, she'd thought about how dazzled Dahl would have been by it . . . and then remembered he wasn't coming.

"I didn't tell Brin, you know. Are you feeling better?"

"Why are you two so obsessed with me throwing up!"

"You *never* throw up," Farideh reminded her. "Did you catch something in Djerad Kethendi?"

"It's passed," Havilar said after a moment. "And good thing, because we don't need anything else to worry about. Ghosts and gods and murders and . . ." She trailed off, and the name neither of them wanted to speak hid in the silence. "I suppose we'll leave soon."

"I hope so," said Farideh, even though she couldn't begin to guess what would come next.

• • •

FEIYEN WANTED TO believe the man made of night was just some kind of drow, just another madman, another monster that the Underdark spat out. But in the moments of lucidness that came—between bouts of rage, bouts of passion, bouts of emotion so wild and animal that Feiyen was sure she was watching someone else—she knew it wasn't so. It couldn't be so. Where the drow were alien and terrible, the man made of night was nothing of this world.

I want an answer, he said, his voice angry and beautiful as he dug through the Zhentarim's minds, one by one. *These things don't happen by accident.*

How many of them were dead now? How many of them were compromised? Feiyen eyed Louc beside the man made of night, a puppet of his whims—in that moment, a reflection of his coiled rage, his fierce hungers. What did she look like to Louc?

The man made of night turned and met Feiyen's eyes. Her mind seemed to break apart into scrabbling, animal reactions—fear, fury, lust, an urge to claw her way up by blood or bed or cunning. Each fought against the others, churning her thoughts into a maddening cacophony.

And then the man made of night blinked and everything in her froze.

Is this truly all you've ever striven for? he said in her mind. *All you've craved? To be the guard of a trading outpost so remote even your superiors don't realize it's fallen? You could be more, much more, Feiyen . . .*

If she were only willing to claim her place. To use everything she had, regardless of how well it suited others, how well it suited her image of herself. To the Abyss with the rules and order. Tooth and claw and desire were all that ruled in the end.

Show me what you're made of, the man made of night said. *What's behind that civilized facade?*

Feiyen looked down at her blood-soaked hands, closing them into fists.

6

19 Nightal, the Year of the Nether Mountain Scrolls (1486 DR)
Raven's Bluff

DUMUZI RACES THROUGH THE VERTHISATHURGIESH ENCLAVE, chased by the roars of a ghost. He can't remember the passages, can't remember the exits. The walls are somehow not so towering as they seemed in his youth, but not the height he knows them to be now.

Pandjed shouts again—stupid weakling shitbrain broken-egg—Dumuzi's heart is ready to explode. He ducks into someone else's living area and, finding it empty, races through the door into the tallhouse in Suzail. The wrongness strikes him the moment he crosses the threshold, but Pandjed is still coming and he cannot stop.

He throws open the door to the garden and sprints across Westgate's dark and dangerous streets.

He bursts into a taproom and dodges tables, then he leaps through a window into Djerad Kethendi's harbor. He's drowning, drowning, drowning—

Someone grabs him by the collar and heaves him up out of the water, flinging him high into the sky. Dumuzi clutches at the air, but there is no slowing him, no controlling his rise. Beneath him, autumn kisses Tymanther's waving fields golden. Clouds race alongside him, burning red and roiling with rain and storm. Dumuzi searches, searches—where can he land, where can he come down?

Nowhere, he realizes. Because Djerad Thymar is gone.

There is no escaping its absence. The hole where the pyramid should be draws him in like a vortex, and his heart is screaming.

Pandjed's roars rival the distant thunder. Wasted *qalim.* Wasted *koshqal.* Get back to your mother.

The building rises out of the plain as he slows, a beast built of stacked, polished granite layers. Six fortresses crouched atop each other, shining red in the sunset. The thunder builds and overtakes Pandjed's roars, and Dumuzi's panic ebbs as he considers the building.

It has always been here; it has never left.

A chorus of voices whispers on the wind: Enlil lugal kur-kur-a ab-ba dingir-dingir-re-ne-ke . . . lugal-e Unther-ah ba-gi-shey.

Dumuzi turns—searching for the voices, searching for his home, but nothing is familiar and there is only the strange language singing in his ears. Djerad Thymar is gone. He cannot see the homesteads scattered across the plain of Tymanther. All along the horizon, more of the fortresses rise. Ziggurats—*the word rises in his thoughts as certain and permanent as the structure.* Tombs.

Enlil lugal kur-kur-a ab-ba dingir-dingir-re-ne-ke . . . I-men ur-sag enlil-la-ke? . . . *The singsong voices send a shiver over his scales.*

When he turns back to where Djerad Thymar should be, a man is waiting for him. A human with a thick, curly beard, floating beside him as if there were no simpler thing. The thunder keeps rumbling, the lightning building.

"Who are you?" Dumuzi asks.

The man watches his mouth, curious and puzzled, as if he cannot understand what Dumuzi has said. He reaches out a tentative hand and brushes the tip of his finger along the bridge of Dumuzi's nose.

Ushumgal-lú I-ngeshtugh-ngar-ngar, *the man's voice rumbles like the lightning.* Untherah Tymantherah i-tehi . . .

Dumuzi woke with a blistering headache that made his stomach threaten to upend. He staggered to his dresser and splashed cold water over his scales. The dream clung to his thoughts, filmy and tenacious as cobwebs.

The *ziggurats.* The human man with the curly beard. Watching him.

Dumuzi felt sure he'd seen that man before. Somehow. Somewhere. But the harder he tried to place the man—Westgate? Proskur? Suzail?—the more the image of him slipped away.

Maybe you dreamed that too, *pothachi*, he thought.

What did it mean if you invented people and things in your dreams? Dumuzi dressed himself with shaking hands and thought of Zaroshni. She would tease him and say they were only dreams. Or maybe suggest they were visions of Abeir. He had never been able to get his bearings with Zaroshni, but he enjoyed trying.

Now the dead lay between them. Every time he spoke to Zaroshni she felt numb and cold and distant, as if something fundamental had died within her. He shut his eyes, clenched his jaw tight as if it could seal in the pain of that thought.

They are dreams, he thought. They are only your mind turning circles while you sleep. The frenzy of a heart overwhelmed with grief. Your friends are dead. You cannot figure out how to help Zaroshni. Of course you have nightmares. He pulled his white mourning shirt on, covering the silvery, fernlike scars that wrapped around his ribs from his back before he could linger on them and remember all the other things he'd lost.

He had done what he could to track down the rest of the Liberators, but try as he might, he could not seem to pin Zaroshni down. No matter when he went to the Shestandeliath enclave, she was not there.

When they'd talked last, after that awful day, she'd agreed to speak with a handful of Liberators—each of whom, Dumuzi discovered, had gone missing, down in the catacombs after all. Except Shestandeliath Ravar. Of all the fools who thought they could save all the Lost and Abeir as well, Ravar was—to be fair—the most sensible.

"It's hard to say if he takes it seriously," Zaroshni had told Dumuzi, long before he'd left to find Mehen. They'd sat in a teahouse, discussing the Liberators and whether she would leave them or throw in with their wild plans. It was hard to tell if Zaroshni had taken it seriously too—it was hard to tell if Zaroshni had taken anything seriously, and Dumuzi often wondered if that was what he found so enchanting about her. He sighed. She would talk to Ravar and maybe that would help. Maybe he would know what had happened.

Dumuzi went out into the Kepeshkmolik enclave, his home for most of his life—aside from a month when he was ten and the time he'd spent searching for Clanless Mehen. All those days and he still could not shake the sensation that he had yet to earn his place within Kepeshkmolik. As he walked, the stair-step edges of the ziggurat seemed to ghost over his vision. Dumuzi rubbed his eyes, and walked straight into someone as he did.

Kepeshkmolik Uadjit, in full black scale armor, grabbed hold of his shoulders. "Careful there."

"My apologies. I was preoccupied." Dumuzi made a little bow to his mother. A lopsided white ribbon had been tied around her long sword's hilt. "Good morning, Uadjit. Did you just arrive?"

Uadjit smiled. "Not an hour ago. It's good to see you're back, and all in one piece."

"Thank you," Dumuzi said. "I succeeded."

Uadjit's smile fractured. "Did you? Then . . . you brought him back?"

"He's at the Verthisathurgiesh enclave. With his daughters. And . . . one of their lovers. It's confusing." Dumuzi searched his mother's face for a hint of her reaction. He'd gleaned enough—between Kepeshkmolik whispers and Pandjed's tirades—to know what had happened, why Mehen was not in favor with Kepeshkmolik or Verthisathurgiesh, why his father might be circumspect about seeking Mehen out. But Dumuzi never could tell what Uadjit truly felt about the matter. She was a mirror, a mask. It made her an excellent diplomat, and a sometimes puzzling mother.

For a moment, she looked distant, calculating. He wondered if she was going to ask him what he thought of Mehen, to see if Dumuzi could give the right opinion in the right way, when such a fractious situation presented itself. But when she spoke, Uadjit only asked, "Have you seen your father since you came back?"

"I thought it would be better that I didn't," Dumuzi said. Arjhani stayed high up in the Lance Defender barracks, training his students. No doubt Anala had sent a message telling him not to bother making appearances. Arjhani would only upset her plans.

Or make them, Dumuzi thought a little bitterly. Arjhani had a way of convincing people to love him, even while he was stealing the rugs from beneath their feet.

"He's your father," Uadjit reminded Dumuzi.

"I don't want to take up his time," Dumuzi said. "I'll try today." His tongue fluttered behind his teeth, betraying his frustration. "Did they tell you about the murders?" he blurted. "Down in the catacombs."

Uadjit's pierced brows rose. "Murders?"

"Baruz, Parvida, Mirji, Versvesh, and some others."

"Murders? Are you sure? Does Narghon know?"

Dumuzi nodded. Uadjit regarded her son with such sadness. "I'm so sorry, Dumuzi. Losing friends, comrades is never easy. But with time——"

"Thank you."

Uadjit pulled him into a stiff embrace, rubbing her jaw frill along the crown of Dumuzi's forehead. Dumuzi hugged her back——she smelled of leather and oil, *panjar* gum and stale guano. "Everything will be all right. We'll be sure of it."

"Matriarch Anala hired Mehen to find the murderers," Dumuzi said, releasing his mother. "I don't know if Narghon knows that."

"I see." Uadjit studied him another moment. "So he has daughters?"

"Adopted," Dumuzi said, not sure why that made him nervous. "They're tieflings. Twins. Same-egg twins, or . . . however they call it. Well mostly. One of them is . . . Farideh has an odd-eye. Silver and gold. And they're very different from each other."

He clamped his mouth shut, as the moons along his mother's brow rose and her dark eyes seemed to sharpen—surprise at his babbling or something he'd said. "The lover is a human. Only they're not really lovers."

"It's confusing," Uadjit finished for him, suddenly warm again. She smoothed a hand over the top of his head. "I have things to see to, before I can call myself settled, but tomorrow let's plan for highsunfeast together. You can tell me about your many months in the world beyond, *noachi*."

Uadjit left, and guiltily Dumuzi felt a weight come off his shoulders. Kepeshkmolik Uadjit was like something out of an ancestor story: powerful, distant, and almost unreal. Her regard—her *approval*—felt far more precious and unreachable than her mere affection.

"If you are going to be Kepeshkmolik," she had said to him once, the first, worst time he'd disappointed her, "then you must never refuse your duty like this again. The clan is only as strong as the weaknesses each of us shows."

Dumuzi knew he ought to go and seek out Arjhani, to let him know face-to-face that he'd completed the task Arjhani had laid upon him. But as he left the Kepeshkmolik enclave, he couldn't imagine anywhere he'd rather go less.

The elders had not fit him back into the assignments of chores. His friends were all dead or beginning their Lance Defender service. Looking down at the busy walkways and market of Djerad Thymar, Dumuzi couldn't remember a time he had felt so alone, so ill at ease.

Because you were right at home in Suzail, he could imagine Zaroshni teasing, and he longed for those days.

He had felt alone in his search for Mehen, in the streets of Suzail—but there had been a self-righteousness to his alone-ness, a sort of security in it. It would make him stronger, wiser, better for Kepeshkmolik. And then he had settled in, beside the woman Clanless Mehen called daughter, one of the few people who could truly understand why Dumuzi didn't want to go see his father at the peak of Djerad Thymar.

Was it odd he missed her company and Dahl's? That he even found himself missing Havilar and her mercurial reactions, Brin and his odd manners? Mehen . . .

He remembered Pandjed's roars, echoing through his dreams, through his memories, and shuddered.

Farideh, he told himself, would not be too busy. If Mehen was engaged in the search for the killer, then she would still be here, still be waiting, still be at loose ends as much as he was. Before he could talk himself out of it, Dumuzi began walking toward the Verthisathurgiesh enclave, deliberately not thinking about the other times he had been there.

• • •

WHEN FARIDEH WOKE, every nerve of her body screamed with another nightmare. The pale light of Djerad Thymar's false morning glowed through the curtains, calm and rosy, and grating as a rasp against her rattled brain. Beside her, Havilar snored softly, echoed by Zoonie stretched out on the floor. For the third night in a row, she'd slept over.

For the third night in a row, Lorcan had been needling at her brand, watching Farideh, still keeping his distance.

For the third night in a row, she'd dreamed of Asmodeus.

Or Asmodeus had visited her. She couldn't ever be sure of the difference. Farideh dressed, trying to shake off the lingering buzz of fear that still jangled her nerves. She combed the braid from her hair before the tarnished mirror hanging beside the door. The skin under her eyes was puffy and bruised looking.

For a long moment, she watched her reflection. Then she took hold of the powers Asmodeus had granted her, the magic sliding through her brain like the sharp talons of an unspeakable beast. When she opened her eyes with the soul sight cast across them, her reflection wavered and blurred. But once more there was no sign of Asmodeus's mark upon her, no hint of how corrupted her soul had become, no sense of how deeply in peril she really was.

She let go of the powers. *No one else gets to know,* she reminded herself. *Not really. You have to just try to do your best and hope.*

But what hope would there be for the tiefling Chosen of Asmodeus?

The soft notes of Brin's flute wafted through the door along with the scent of food—onions and bread and spices. In the sitting room, Brin sat perched on a low sofa, playing a meandering tune and looking at a spread of food, as though it were a puzzle. He spotted Farideh and stood too fast—*he thought I was Havilar,* Farideh realized.

"Good morning," she said, as his smile fell a little. "What did she send today?"

"Good morning. Um, let's see." He pointed to the plates in turn. "That's some kind of mutton pasty. These are stuffed bread. I think these are pickles, and I have no idea what's in this"—he picked up a sort of fritter from a stack—"what that wiggly thing is"—he pointed at a wide bowl of yellow custard—"or what in all the planes above and below is in the red bowl. Also, there's that spicy tea. Do you want a cup?"

"Please." Farideh sat down and put a pasty and a fritter on a plate, as well as a small pile of pickles. She scooped up some of the custard. "Steamed eggs," she said. "With . . . um . . ." She plucked one of the morsels of meat from the custard—it had a creamy texture and a faint metallic taste. "It's just lamb brains." Brin turned a little pale. "Have you never eaten lamb's brains?"

"There's a lot of other parts of the lamb I prefer," Brin said. "What's in the red bowl?"

"*Yochit,*" Farideh said. "You put it on the *farothai*—um, the stuffed bread." She considered the lumpy white mixture flecked with spices and green herbs, knowing that telling Brin the ingredients would only give him trouble. "I don't think you'll like it."

Brin shook his head and handed her a cup of tea. She added several lumps of golden sugar to her tea. "Did you sleep all right?" she asked, stirring.

Brin shook his head. "You? I didn't wake you, did I?"

"No. Just bad dreams." She took a bite of the fritter. "Mm. Gourd and egg," she said around a mouthful. Brin made a face, and she shook her head, dipping the fritter into a vinegary sauce. "It's good. I promise."

He took several of the mutton pasties instead. "I want you to tell me about Arjhani."

Farideh stared at her plate. "What's there to tell?"

"Don't," Brin said. "Look, I know she and I are . . . That things are complicated right now, but this seems like it's serious. I should know. I could help. Please."

Farideh broke her fritter into pieces. "Arjhani . . . He's the one who taught her to use the glaive. He came and lived with us for a summer, when we were eleven. Almost twelve. Havilar adored him, of course."

"Did you like him?"

No, she thought. Never. It was a lie—she'd wanted to love him as dearly as Havilar had, to feel like she fit into this new version of their family. But Arjhani knew what to do with her even less than Mehen had at times, and Farideh's doubts about Arjhani made him snappish and distant. "I don't get along with people as easily as she does. Anyhow, he left. And she didn't take it well."

Brin set down his plate, and for a moment, he said nothing. "And you're afraid it will come back to her the same way? It was a long time ago."

As long as it was, Farideh felt tears crowd her throat. The memory of the fight they'd had, of the childish anger that filled her knowing Havilar was willing to fall apart because of that *henish*, because of someone who wasn't even family. Of finding Havilar gone, of the empty bottles and the building storm. Of how pale she was when Mehen brought her back. "All the same," Farideh said. "It was bad enough the first time."

Brin shook his head. "Why doesn't she talk about this?"

"Some things are better to forget." Farideh gave him a stiff smile. "I don't suppose you've heard from Dahl? Or Tam?"

"No. Sorry. Keep in mind," he added, "Tam's put me down as wandering, and Dahl's likely out of scrolls. He'll have to track down components and find a way to pay for them."

Assuming he's safe enough to search, Farideh thought, her throat closing tight. Assuming he's alive.

Brin moved to sit beside her and clasped an arm around her. "He'll be all right, you know? People can survive without you being there to rescue them."

Farideh laughed and it chased off the tears. "Fair point."

He hugged her tighter. "I do know what it feels like. Just . . . have to keep going and believe it will be all right."

Farideh blushed. For nearly eight years, she and Havilar had been imprisoned in the Nine Hells, leaving Brin and Mehen behind. He *did* know what he was talking about. "Thank you."

"You want advice for how to do that, I don't have a lot to offer. I was terrible to be around."

"I'll bet your advice is better than Havi's." Farideh reached for another fritter. "She thinks I ought to cut my losses with Dahl."

Brin gave her a wan smile. "I think maybe Havilar's not being entirely unbiased there. Sorry."

Romance is the worst. Farideh speared a pickle with her fork, a chunk of purple root slick with oil and brine and speckled with spice. But Havilar didn't get sick. You can't fix this, she told herself.

"Did she tell you anything?" Brin asked. "About . . . you know . . ."

"Not yet. But we'll find out one way or another, right?" she said, trying for careless as she took a bite of the fritter.

Brin sighed. "I just want everything to sort out. I just want her to be happy, and—"

Farideh gagged and clapped a cloth to her mouth as the spices in the pickle gripped her tongue. She spat out the bitter, musky-tasting root, and washed her mouth with tea, as Mehen came into the room. He raised a scaly brow ridge.

"What's in the pickles?" Farideh asked.

Mehen peered at the plates and sniffed. "*Türkhaari*. You won't like those. Peppers, gourd, *charchuka* root, lemon, and some herbs. *Talsch*—it's . . . a resin," he said, switching to Common at the word. "Comes from an herb, *nychaki*. That's in there too. Kind of . . . *kiskartchi*," he decided, switching back to Draconic for the right adjective. "It's a taste you have to grow up with."

"If you say so," Farideh said.

"Stick to the hand pies," Mehen advised Brin.

"Are we going to go anywhere today?"

Mehen only grunted and sat beside Brin. The last two days, Anala had insisted they couldn't properly search, because the enclave was in mourning and would be for the rest of the tenday. Every Verthisathurgiesh dragonborn wore a white ribbon tied around their weapons, leaving behind all jewels but for the clan piercings. Anala's plumes fell loose and unarranged around her shoulders, and she'd left her gauzy wraps behind for plain armor over a white sheath.

"When the mourning period's ended, then I'll make arrangements," Anala had said. "You ought to tie your weapon."

"I know this is hard and I know this is tradition. But you're giving them time to hide what they might know," Mehen had said. "We're losing proof as we speak." Anala had not wavered, and a white ribbon appeared on the hilt of Mehen's falchion.

The mourning didn't apply to the twins and Brin, but still it found a way to trip them up. Farideh and Brin had gone down to explore the market one morning while Havilar took Zoonie running. She'd found a shop that sold components, but without Verthisathurgiesh's blessing, the prices were steep.

"We go out today," Mehen said. "You and Havi find Dumuzi. The dead were mostly his agemates. He followed us down into the catacombs. Maybe he knows what they were up to."

"Wouldn't he have told Anala?" Farideh asked. "Or Narghon?"

Mehen lifted his head and looked down his snout at her. "Do you tell me everything you get up to?"

"Mostly," Farideh said. Eventually, she added to herself. "If we're really not finished, shouldn't we be looking for a wizard? Someone who could have opened a portal?"

"There aren't a lot of wizards in Djerad Thymar," Mehen said. "So don't get ideas."

"What is that supposed to mean?"

"It means that I'm well aware you want to leave and why you want to leave," Mehen said. "And where you want to go and what a wizard might be able to help you with. We will get to it. Start with the hatchlings in the catacombs. Figure out why they were there and you can verify this notion about monsters crawling out of portals and dead demons, if it's right."

Farideh frowned. "What else could it be?"

"Look," Mehen said, "*Vayemniri* don't truck with things from other worlds."

"Well *that's* not true," Farideh said. "Just because you don't like what Havilar found the other night doesn't mean there aren't—"

Havilar stuck her head out of the door, bleary-eyed, with her purplish-black hair a nest. Zoonie nearly knocked her over as she tried to peer past. "What are you two yelling about?" she asked. "Some of us are trying to sleep."

Mehen scowled. "You two, staying up, gabbing all *karshoji* night—how are we supposed to do anything when you're a slugabed?"

Farideh's stomach tightened, and from the corner of her eye she glanced at Brin. They hadn't been up late—was it a bad sign that Havilar overslept? Maybe there was a ritual of some sort, a spell to check. Maybe Havilar would tell her soon. She ran through a count of her own days, and found she wasn't sure anymore if they were anywhere close to Havilar's.

A tenday, she reminded herself, maybe two, and they'd know for sure. But when the last two days had felt like an eternity, languishing in Djerad Thymar, Farideh wasn't sure how they'd manage.

"Do you know," Brin said, in a conversational way, "that the three of you have been speaking Draconic since Mehen woke up? All I've managed to catch is 'Dumuzi,' 'night,' 'wizard,' and something nasty that—to speak the truth—I still don't know what it means, for all the three of you say it."

Farideh blushed, and Mehen looked abashed. "Sorry," Mehen said. "Force of habit." He repeated his plans for the three of them.

"What are *you* going to do?" Havilar asked.

"Invite myself over to the Shestandeliath enclave," Mehen said. "And make a little trouble."

"Fun," Havilar said dryly. She spotted the red bowl. "Ooh! *Yochit!*" She piled several spoonfuls on one of the flatbreads. "Did you try them?" she asked Brin around a mouthful. "You'd never think ant eggs would taste so good."

Brin set the mutton pasty down without another word.

They had hardly finished preparing to go out into the city when Dumuzi arrived, unannounced. "I thought perhaps you might be looking for something to do," he said. "I haven't anything particular to do today myself."

Farideh thought of her own hollowed face when she looked at Dumuzi. His sharp scale armor seemed as if it held him up.

"We're supposed to come find you, actually," Havilar said, as she pulled on a boot. "Did you know the ones that died?"

Dumuzi looked away. "I did."

Havilar started to ask another question, but Farideh gestured sharply at her. "Would you like to have some tea or something?"

"You can ask me about them," he said. "I'll tell you what I know."

Brin poured a cup of tea for Dumuzi, but the dragonborn only took it and set it back on the table. "They were trying to go to Abeir."

Havilar's eyes widened. "*Karshoj.* Really?"

"The other world or the other continent?" Brin asked.

"The other world. They called themselves . . ." He hesitated as if searching for the right words in the common tongue. "The Liberators of the Steel Sky. They thought . . . They had this mad notion that that was the place where we belonged. Where we ought to return. They thought they could go there and it would be like the ancestor stories."

"I've heard those stories—that sounds like a good reason to stay far away," Brin said. "Isn't it better here?"

Dumuzi shook his head, as if Brin were being deliberately obtuse. "It is and it isn't. Like anywhere."

"Well, no dragon tyrants attacking you," Havilar said. "Better than that."

"Was Baruz the one who made the circle?" Farideh asked.

Dumuzi gave her an odd look. "No. I don't think he could do that sort of magic. It's difficult, isn't it?"

"Quite," Brin said.

"Who made the circle then?" Farideh asked. *Do they have a ritual book? Can they make another circle? Can they make a sending?*

Gods' books, someone's distracted, she thought, and it was Dahl's dry voice. *You need a killer, not a way to run.* She sat opposite Dumuzi, and folded her hands in her lap, as if crushing the thought between them.

"Shestandeliath Ravar is the only one who could have," Dumuzi said. "He was sympathetic to their goals, or maybe he just found them amusing. I don't know. I don't think he was there that night, though."

"Could he have just told them how?" Havilar asked her sister.

Farideh nodded. "He could have made a scroll. If he had those skills. Would Ravar have turned on them?"

"On the Liberators?" Dumuzi asked. "I don't think so. I mean . . ." He scowled again at the table's edge, lost in thought. "Do you know the word *throtominarr?* It's . . . it's the honor you pay your ancestors by building and . . . *improving* what they did. You owe them, and your descendants owe you. Leaving Djerad Thymar, leaving behind their clans and their futures for this silly dream? That would be a disgrace. It would be ignoring that responsibility. It's the sort of thing elders might exile you for."

"Is that what Mehen did?" Havilar whispered.

That startled Dumuzi. "You don't . . . Don't you *know*?"

From the corner of her eye, Farideh saw Havilar turn to her, but her own gaze was locked on Dumuzi. "Not really," Havilar said lightly. "I know it was to do with Arjhani. Probably."

"He was supposed to marry," Dumuzi said. "He was supposed to marry my mother, Kepeshkmolik Uadjit, but he refused in favor of Arjhani. But you didn't tell Pandjed no, even if you were his scion, and refusing a match like that . . . For a reason like that . . ." He shook his head. "Mehen was exiled. And Arjhani did not go with him. He stayed and wed Uadjit." He shook his head. "I thought you knew."

They did, Farideh thought. They knew all the pieces, scattered to the winds. A comment there, a sore spot there. Narghon's glare in the Verthisathurgiesh tomb. *What sthyarli did they find to satisfy choosy Uadjit?* Mehen had demanded when Dumuzi had named his mother. If not Mehen, then who?

The one man Verthisathurgiesh Pandjed could punish his wayward son with.

For a long, awkward moment, no one spoke.

"It sounds like Ravar is the man to talk to," Brin said briskly. "Can you make an introduction?"

Dumuzi cleared his throat. "I can try."

The Shestandeliath enclave was on the other side of the pyramid, down two staircases and across a wide walkway. The city bustled beneath the warm midmorning light streaming down from nowhere, the smell of plants and strange herbs warming in the magical light threaded through the air.

"This is what Suzail was like, isn't it?" Brin asked as they descended from the City-Bastion toward the market floor. "For you two, I mean."

"How do you mean?" Havilar asked.

"I haven't seen a single human since we got here," Brin said. "Everyone stares. No one speaks the same language as me, unless I start talking first. Everything," he added, coming down off the stairs with a heavy thump, "is meant for someone a good deal taller than I am. I don't fit. That's what it was like, wasn't it?"

Havilar shrugged in a diffident way. "That's how it is most places."

Shestandeliath enclave's doors were hung with falchions, carved with twisting dragons and a strange-looking bow on its side, wide as the whole portal. Slices of colorful stone decorated the spaces between. The doorguards told them that Ravar had left not long before.

"Meeting someone down in the clan tomb," one said. "I don't know when he'll be back."

"That will be Zaroshni, I hope," Dumuzi said, sounding perturbed. "She's one of them too . . . a friend of mine. Her cousin was among the dead. She's helping me find the remaining Liberators," he went on. "I haven't seen her since that day." He turned to Farideh. "Do you mind going down there again?"

"I think we'd best," Farideh said.

* * *

THEY NEVER, NEVER notice—oh they always think they will! But whatever difference they believe they'll surely mark, I've marked it too. This one remembers two tongues, the way the chain across her face swings, the way her feet walk the paths through this city of stone, the names of the ones who might go missing—but oh, oh, nothing to eat, not truly. It's a buzzing city, a rumbling city, a too-crowded place. Down, down in the catacombs is the only peace and quiet, the only place to eat, so that's where she—sweet as a dewdrop hanging on a thorn—asks to meet the chain-marked wizard and he doesn't notice. They never notice. Tasty, tasty magics on this one. Seasons the flesh so well.

Turn, turn, down into the shadows, to wait and wait and wait, until the smell of blood that puts the dewdrops to shame becomes too much to bear . . .

7

R AVEN'S BLUFF EMBRACED THE ZHENTARIM SHIP, WRAPPING
it in the waiting arms of its harbor. On the rising cliffs
over the Dragon Reach, the city glinted with innumerable
torches as the sun set. None of the Zhentarim spoke, the tension
on the ship's deck as thick as a fog across the water until the ship
moored between a trireme and a big caravel with its sails all furled.

"What now?" Dahl asked Grathson. He'd been on the
deck of the ship since Thost had stormed off, hovering between
his brothers and his grandmother and Mira, not coming too
close to any of them.

"We switch to a river boat," Grathson said. "Make sure yours
are ready to move as soon as we've secured it."

"Any chance of visiting the market while we're here?" Dahl
asked.

"Why? You need new dancing slippers?"

"I need components," Dahl said, gesturing at his haversack.
"I can't cast rituals without them."

Grathson chuckled. "Boy, keep your sorry spells to yourself.
We don't need a ritual caster for this mission. Just a little motiva-
tion for your granny." He strolled away.

Dahl considered the torches of the city beyond, the distant
glow of the nightmarket. Chances were good he wouldn't find
the ritual he needed anyway—not at a price he could pay. The
knowledge sent his pulse racing. Every day that passed without
Farideh felt like another cut, another slice through the ties

between them, and how long would she wait before she gave up? How long before Lorcan lured her back?

Stop, he told himself, rubbing a hand over his face. She's not a stlarning dog.

His brothers and Sessaca had retreated to his grandmother's cabin, shutting themselves away from the Zhentarim—they'd done so nearly every night. Dahl had left them to it, with everything lying sharp and uneven between himself and them. For a moment, he considered letting it lie, staying the villain and keeping his secrets so they could all remain safe and sound—

It's too late for that, Dahl thought as he crossed the ship. So you have to fix this first. Then figure out how to get off this ship before they find a boat. Stock up on components. Steal some grog.

Not that one—Even if his head ached and his temper simmered, not that one. Keep your wits about you.

Dahl pushed into the cabin without knocking. Bodhar sat on the floor, Thost at the foot of the narrow bed. Sessaca occupied a narrow wooden chair. Every one of them looked up at Dahl as he entered, as stonily as if Dahl had been one of the Zhentarim sailors. Dahl found the latch and shut it.

"Did you check for spells?" he asked Sessaca. "Listening, scrying, that sort of thing?"

She gave him a withering look. "Please."

Dahl nodded once, his pulse rattling. He rolled his sleeve up. "Look, I'm sick of secrets and lying—"

"Oh, cry for the Fallen!" Sessaca said. "No one lied to you, lambkin."

"Really? What do you call it? I'm sick of the lying," Dahl went on firmly, "and so it's not fair to do it to you." He laid two fingers on his forearm. "*Vivex prujedj.*" A dark blue sigil of a harp and moon rose out of his skin.

"I'm not a Zhentarim agent, I'm a Harper," he said, dropping his voice. "That's what I do in Waterdeep, that's what I was doing in Suzail, that's . . ." He faltered. That wasn't how he knew they were in danger. That had been all Lorcan's doing. "That's who I was contacting in the wood. That's how I know Mira," he said. "She's a flipcloak agent, I'm her handler. She tells me what the Black Network get up to and helps me keep them in sights. But the Zhentarim think I'm just a contact of hers, an Oghmanyte come to hard times, so none of this can ever, ever leave this cabin." He hid the tattoo and rolled his sleeve back down, eyes on the floor. "Now," he said. "Thost, do you want to talk to Dellora?"

"I *knew* it!" Bodhar cried. "I *knew* there was something squirrelly. You're a *Harper*? How long have you been a Harper?"

"Give me a breath, Bodhar. Do you want to talk to Dellora?" Dahl asked. He glanced at his brother. Thost's expression was ice.

"You can," Dahl said. "The sending ritual I used before. I can make it so you can talk to her. You can tell her you're all right and make sure she is too. I can't undo what happened, but this I can do."

Dahl took his ritual book out, the packets of components. He kneeled on the floor. "You get twenty-five words, that's it. Once the spell takes effect, the next twenty-five words out of your mouth are what she'll hear, all right?" He laid the lines of powdered metals and dried blood out in careful succession. "You might want to write them down first," he added. "It's easy to lose count."

Still, Thost didn't speak. Dahl bit back a curse and settled into the rhythm of the ritual, shifting threads of the Weave with careful application of the components and murmured words. Everything else faded away.

When he'd finished, the magic hung in the air, a bird, a sprite ready to carry Thost's voice all the way back to New Velar, to a three-room house just a little less crowded than it had been two days ago.

Dahl lifted his head, regarding the circle of faces around him. He held out a hand to Thost, who still watched him, grim and unflinching. His eldest brother wet his lips, glanced at the lines on the floor, at Dahl.

He leaned forward. "Dellora?" He paused as if waiting for an answer. Dahl gestured at him to keep speaking. "I'm . . . we're all right, all of us. In Raven's Bluff. On a boat." He trailed off, wide-eyed.

Eleven more, Dahl mouthed. *Tell her: twenty-five words. Are they all right?*

"Tell me you're all right? In twenty-five words." He exhaled. "I love you."

The air fizzled, popped. A moment so long panic began to edge up Dahl's nerves—what if something had happened? What if Dellora was dead?

Oh gods, his sister-in-law's voice came, scratchy and thin. *Oh . . . We're fine. We're all fine. They left.* She exhaled, as at a loss for words as her husband. *Watching Gods, Thost, you don't come back in one piece, I'll hunt your ghost down.*

Thost chuckled. "Don't doubt it one bit. Kiss the children for me?" Silence answered.

"She can't hear you," Dahl said, apologetically. "It's . . . it's just those twenty-five words."

"Ah," Thost said, nodding. "Better'n nothing." He sniffed, nodded twice. "Many thanks."

"Least I could do."

"Cost a shiny copper too," Bodhar pointed out, sounding surprised. "Figured that mess you bought was for a lot more than a quick back and forth. How much coin you take as a Harper?"

"You don't do it for the coin. Nor secretary work. But it was important," Dahl said, sweeping away the lines.

"A handy little spell," Sessaca agreed. "Suppose it wasn't an entire waste, sending you off to the Oghmanytes." Then, "You talk to your brightbird that way?"

"Nah," Bodhar said. "He can't talk to her."

Sessaca frowned. "What do you mean he can't talk to her?"

"He can't do that"—Thost gestured at the scattered powders on the wooden floor—"thing again?"

"He can't talk at all," Bodhar said. "Needs a way to send a letter or something, he says. Like maybe a talking animal—oh wait, no, that didn't work either."

"Could you stop talking over my head like I'm Wilmot?" Dahl cried.

"Put it on a ship," Thost suggested. "Like Ma sent yours."

"Where is she anyway?" Bodhar asked.

Dahl hesitated. "Djerad Thymar. Way down south. Not a common passage, New Velar to Tymanther."

"How did you get yourself into such a stupid spot," Sessaca demanded. "Falling for a girl on the arse-end of the continent, with some crazy barrier on her?"

"Stlarn it!" Dahl shouted. "Enough! It's not your business, and—" He bit off the words he was going to say. "Anyway, Bodhar's right. I can't talk to her, so it's out of my hands and like as not you'll wind up getting your way. Happy?"

No one spoke, and in the silence, Dahl felt once more the border between his Harran life and his life in the world beyond rise up as palpable as a wooden palisade. On one side him, on the other side Farideh. A dark surge of melancholy rose up in his soul. You can't win.

Sessaca stood without a word and left the little cabin. Dahl cursed and followed her. "Granny, look, I'm sorry. Granny!" he called as she marched across the deck toward where Xulfaril and the halfling stood deep in conversation. Mira sat to the side, a ledger spread out on the deck before her. She caught Dahl's eye as he sprinted after his grandmother.

"A word," Sessaca said as she reached the wizard and the halfling. Xulfaril didn't look up. "Yes, Swordcaptain?"

Sessaca ignored the sneering tone, addressing the halfling. "You. What's your name?"

The halfling looked at Xulfaril, but the wizard gave no signal. "Volibar," he said.

"Volibar, well met. Give me the snake."

"I don't take orders from you."

"Fine." Sessaca turned to Xulfaril. "My grandson wants to send a message to his monster lover. So get the snake out and make it happen." The wizard looked up then, her single eye considering Sessaca, then Dahl, in turn.

"Give her the snake," Xulfaril said.

"Thank you," Sessaca said. To Dahl, "There. Stop moping."

Dahl bit back a curse. "If someone's sending messages by flying snake, it ought to be Thost and Bodhar," he whispered. "They're not used to this, and neither are Meri and Dellora and Ma."

"Haslam can't go back to New Velar," Volibar piped up. "So wipe that off your slate."

"It's trained to go to particular people," Sessaca said. "Folks it knows, or folks who're playing a signal whistle to attract it. There's no one in New Velar for it to find anymore."

"Exactly," said Volibar, sounding not a little pleased that someone understood him. "Which means I can't promise you a shitting thing. Where is this . . . person?"

"Djerad Thymar," Dahl said.

Volibar cursed. "Stlarning Brume, then. Fine. We can do it." Dahl bit his tongue and filed that away for another time—the Harpers wouldn't be happy to know there were Zhentarim in Tymanther, of all places. "It's a big city, where's he going to find her?"

Dahl wracked his brain. He had no idea. "She's visiting her father's clan. She's *adopted*," he added, when Sessaca sniffed. "The clan . . . it's something with a . . . Vertha? Verthisathix?"

Farideh lying against his shoulder, tracing a finger over his knuckles. "But Nala Who-Would-Be-Verthisathurgiesh was as clever as a blue wyrm and wise as the mountains."

"And dealing with dragons who are incredibly stupid," Dahl had teased.

"Shush or you're going back upstairs."

He'd closed his hand around hers. "Keep going."

On the deck of the Zhentarim ship, Dahl shut his eyes. "Verthisathurgiesh. That's the clan. Her name's Farideh."

Volibar grumbled, and patted his pockets, drawing out a roll of parchment no wider than the end of Dahl's thumb. "That's all you get," Volibar told him. "Leave the back side blank—that's for me." He clicked his tongue, and the snake poked its dark, triangular head out of his collar. "Good boy," he murmured. To Dahl, he added, "You've got until we secure a river boat, so do it now. Choose your words carefully."

"You're welcome, lambkin," Sessaca said as she walked back to the cabin.

Dahl closed his hand around the parchment, running through Lorcan's threats. He couldn't *talk* to Farideh . . . but nothing about writing. Nothing about letters. Unless he was missing something. It felt as if he was always missing something lately. He went and sat down beside Mira.

"Can I borrow a stylus and ink?"

"Of course, lambkin." He scowled at her, and a smile danced on her thin mouth. "I cannot conceive of a pet name that suits you less."

He sighed. "I'm twelve years behind Bodhar. What they call a 'late lambkin,' in Harrowdale. She's the only one that still calls me that, because she's godsbedamned terrifying and I'm not about to tell her to stop. Stylus and ink?"

She handed them over. "So," Mira said. "Farideh. That's surprising. In several ways."

"Yes. Well." He rolled the stylus between his fingers, smiled to himself. "Things change."

"Clearly. What happened to her devil?"

He's not hers anymore, Dahl wanted to retort. But it felt so close to teasing Beshaba. "He's around."

"Ah. The urgency becomes clear." She shut the ledger. "Sounds like Sessaca's not happy about it. What about your brothers?"

"Sessaca thinks she's a dragonborn. My brothers think she's from Hillsfar."

"You haven't told them she's a tiefling?"

Dahl exhaled, as if he could stretch the tension from his chest. "I suspect it's not a whole lot better than a Hillfarian dragonborn. And . . . I'm not really in the mood to hear all the ways she's wrong for me, because they're not true and if she were here, they'd see that."

"I'll hold my tongue," Mira said. "Explains a *little* why you were so cagey. And spares my feelings."

"Don't," Dahl said. "Don't start that. You haven't had anything remotely like feelings for me since Proskur, and don't pretend otherwise."

Mira shrugged. "I could have changed my mind."

"Why?" Dahl asked dryly. "Is your father annoying you again?"

"A hit," she allowed, with a cryptic little smile. "It would have been better to let them *think* I had you wrapped around my finger. You could have been a little interested."

"Well I'm not," Dahl said. "But I am interested in what in all the broken planes is going on here. What are they after?"

"Not portal magic," Mira said. "But I guarantee they're going to pretend it's about that until they can't anymore. It's definitely about the library. They wouldn't have brought me in if there weren't a site involved. And they don't want to destroy it—whatever Grathson's doing here."

"What else is in the Master's Library?"

"Everything?" Mira shook her head. "Nothing? No one knows anymore. Sessaca's the last person to see inside. Thank the gods she's still kicking."

Dahl leaned back. The Master's Library had stood for ages, the pinnacle of knowledge, the site of Deneirrath pilgrimages. Chained to other libraries, other temples by portal spells, no one had accessed it since the Wailing Years, since the Deneirrath had given up on their god returning.

"What's Grathson do?" Dahl asked.

"Clears ruins mostly. Brings back treasure. He's the one you call when there are monsters in the way." She folded her arms. "Suggests some things."

"Xulfaril does research with you?"

Mira shook her head. "She runs a trade network of magic items, no questions asked, shipping all over. This is the first I've ever encountered her." She chewed her upper lip a moment. "It worries me that she's so . . . accommodating of your grandmother."

"Granny makes people act like that," Dahl said. "What might be in the Master's Library that needs Xulfaril and Grathson?"

"Ask your granny," Mira said.

"Do they have any idea about us?" Dahl asked. "About who I might be?"

"Not a bit," Mira said. "They think I know you from Cormanthyran artifact hunting. They think you're a backwater Oghmanyte who's maybe a little sweet on me. Or they *did*." She stood and dusted off her breeches. "I'd be ready for a recruitment attempt or two. Probably from Xulfaril, Grathson's too peeved at your granny to admit he hasn't got everything he ever needed." She nodded at the little scroll. "Don't use all my ink on bad poetry, Dahl. Stuff's expensive."

She left, and finally alone, Dahl unrolled the parchment, a strip hardly as long as his hand. A hundred words, he thought. Maybe a hundred and thirty, a hundred and fifty, if he could keep his hand tight, avoid making errors. A hundred and fifty words and they had to be the right ones . . .

He rubbed a hand over his face and cursed. No one would possibly say this was Dahl's strong suit—in fact he wondered, too often, if he'd only confessed his feelings to Farideh because of Oghma's intercession. If he would have gone on holding his tongue forever without that divine fire loosening his words, making him ramble like an overeager student.

But she loved you anyway, he thought. And you won't get another chance.

He hesitated. Setting aside Mira's black ink, Dahl fished a small bottle, green as moss, from his pocket, where it had ridden for months, a sentimental talisman. He cracked the seal and unstoppered it, the unsubtle, resiny scent of rosemary wafting off it. He dipped the pen and began to write.

• • •

MEHEN'S PLANS TO get information from Shestandeliath began to fray the moment he stepped outside Verthisathurgiesh's doors. The two young women on doorguard duty jumped when they saw him, nearly dropping their falchions. They bobbed their heads sheepishly as he passed.

"Pandjed's son," he heard one whisper. "The *outcast* one."

"The one who . . . ?" Mehen shut his eyes. Even without looking, he could sense the girl nodding.

You will be no son of mine.

Do you promise?

You say that to me, toe to toe, let's see what comes of it.

Mehen looked back over his shoulder and the guards straightened. "What have you heard?"

"Nothing," the farther one said, a tall woman with the brassy scales that suggested Vandeth's line. "Apologies."

"They say you defied Patriarch Pandjed," the other—reddish scales, broad-shouldered—said over the top of her comrade. "That you dared him to declare you clanless. That you . . ." She looked to her friend, abashed. "I mean . . . Well they say it."

"Is it true you were a god-worshiper?" the first asked.

Mehen cursed under his breath. The last thing he needed was people spitting gossip about his exile. "What in the Hells happened to this city if hatchlings have only thirty-year-old tales to tell? Get back to your posts."

He'd hoped that would be the end of it, but Anala's words haunted his every step to the Shestandeliath enclave: *You won't want to hear it, but it must be said: You look exactly like your father.* More whispers, more stares, more jumpy hatchlings dogged him. There was no hiding from his past, it seemed. If they did not know the story of Pandjed's rebellious scion, they knew enough to spot the old bastard's features in this clanless wanderer.

When he finally arrived, Shestandeliath did not take well to Mehen's intrusions. For the better part of an hour, he only sat in a small chamber—drinking cold tea and staring at the mosaic on the floor, worrying about his daughters and Djerad Thymar—until finally a woman about his own age, Shestandeliath Narhanna, arrived to tell him that the patriarch would not be seeing him today, so sorry to have wasted his time.

"Not at all," Mehen said. "You can answer questions as well as he can."

Narhanna had a pinched look about her face, and his question made it still more pinched. "I see your reputation does in fact precede you."

"I only want justice," Mehen said. He hesitated, trying to recall the proper, formal ways to go about this. "I only want to be sure no more of us are lost. Shestandeliath and Verthisathurgiesh are old friends," he reminded her. "Holders of the Breath of Petron and the Eye of Blazing Rorn, and all that."

"Are you Verthisathurgiesh now? Only I'd heard Pandjed had exiled you quite explicitly."

Mehen fought the urge to bare his teeth. "Whatever we are, the clans have this in common: Verthisathurgiesh Baruz and Shestandeliath Parvida were both killed by something in the catacombs. Why?"

"The foolishness of youth?" Narhanna's dry tone left no doubt she was referring to other, thirty-year-old tales.

"Mouthing off to your elders and calling forth a horror aren't the same things." Narhanna didn't respond. "Matriarch Anala tells me that Baruz was acting strange lately. She thought Baruz was up to something. Parvida?"

Narhanna blinked, hesitated a moment too long. Parvida was up to something too.

"Who did Parvida confide in?" Mehen asked. "Who else did she spend time with?"

"I can't say I keep track of every hatchling in the clan." Narhanna clucked her tongue. "So many lost heirs. Does the Verthisathurgiesh know you're here?"

"She's told me to get to the bottom of this," Mehen said. "However I need to."

"Well. It sounds as if she's chosen the right man for the task."

"Indeed," Mehen said. He withdrew the mangled silver chain. "Whose is this?"

Narhanna's brow ridge shifted, puzzled. "I have no idea. Where did you find it?"

"In the tomb. Among the dead. But Parvida's chain was intact and Shestandeliath had no other victims. So whose is this?"

Narhanna shrugged, but Mehen could see she was perturbed. "It might only be a piece of jewelry. A broken necklace. You have no evidence it's anything else."

"Maybe you're missing someone still."

"There are no others missing," she said firmly. "As I said, Patriarch Geshthax is very busy, particularly with Parvida's funeral to plan. He will let you know when he has the time and inclination to speak with you, Clanless."

And with that, Mehen was escorted from the enclave, feeling as if he stood in two worlds again—the one in which he could investigate a killing and the one in which he knew the futility of trying to nose around in another clan's business, *especially* when everyone knew his every sin. Shestandeliath would supervise their own and see to their own reputation. No one would be admitting anything until they were sure of what Parvida had contributed.

If Baruz and Parvida had been up to something that their elders didn't want to speak of, might they have told their friends and clutchmates? He thought back to his own youth, to his years in the Lance Defenders, to Uadjit and Arjhani and the day he realized what he was planning to do. He'd told Arjhani he meant to accept him and exile, and no one else. But that was different, a conspiracy of two.

Of one, he thought, grimly. Arjhani was never brave enough to really run.

He walked through the city, feeling alone even in the crowds of his kin. More than he hoped Farideh and Havilar had found something useful out, he hoped they were back. He wanted his family beside him, and quiet.

But even in the quiet, tensions simmered. His daughters were grown, but they weren't. Not enough. They broke their hearts on boys who weren't grown enough either, who didn't deserve them. Brin, so muddled he could hardly think straight when Havilar needed someone to keep *her* thinking straight. Dahl, blowing hot and cold and filling Farideh with doubts when she needed an anchor, a shelter. Lorcan . . .

If Farideh thought for a moment Mehen didn't have an inkling about Lorcan, she was more foolish than he'd hoped. At least the cambion stayed away, whatever had happened when they left Farideh behind in Suzail.

Trailed by more stares, more whispers, Mehen made his way back through the enclave's dragon-skull doors, back into the guest quarters. Instead of his daughters, a dragonborn woman in fine black dragonscale armor sat on the low bench before a tray of tea and sweets. She stood as Mehen froze unmoving in the doorway.

Kepeshkmolik Uadjit did not look as if she'd aged a day. Sleek, gray-green scales lay over the muscles of a skilled swordswoman. Her plumes grew nearly to her waist, all gathered together at the nape of her neck, and the row of pearly moons piercing her brow gleamed beside her dark eyes.

"A fine match," his father had said when he'd announced the contract. "A better bride than you deserve."

Once they had been comrades-in-arms, once she might have fancied him—Mehen was never sure with Uadjit. Once there had been admiration and respect between them, at the least.

But pride had a way of washing all of that away, and what remained . . . Arjhani had more than taken care of that.

"Well met," Mehen said. "Anala is—"

"It doesn't matter. I came to talk to you," she said brusquely. Far more brusquely than he'd remembered her speaking. She folded her arms. "And pardon the lack of ceremony, but what are you doing here? What are your intentions?"

Mehen folded his own arms. "Am I going to embarrass you again? Say what you mean."

Uadjit didn't flinch. "Are you?"

"No."

"You know Jhani took your place?" she said, searching Mehen's face as if his reaction would prove his promise a lie. "You know I married him? Had eggs with him?"

"How did that turn out?" Mehen said, as mildly as he could manage. Uadjit's teeth parted, the anxious edges of frost building there, and Mehen had to admit it was an unkind blow. "I didn't know. When he came to Arush Vayem. He never said a word about you or the eggs."

"I don't know what you're talking about," Uadjit said firmly. "And if you came to woo him away—"

"Please. I'm not a young man who thinks his heart is a shield and a weapon anymore," Mehen said. "I would have stayed away if only because you and he are here. But clan runs deep."

"Liar." Uadjit turned away. And for all Uadjit had been at the center of Mehen's woes, he pitied her then. Arjhani was nothing but heartbreak, even when you didn't ever really love him.

"Your son's a fine lad," Mehen said. "Dumuzi? Resourceful. I'm impressed he tracked me down so quickly."

Uadjit waved him away. "It was months."

"You forget, I've become very good at hiding," Mehen pointed out. "Plus, he was good to my daughter when she was alone. Fought by her side when he could have run. He does your clan honor."

Uadjit unfolded her arms. "Thank you. He's a good boy." She hesitated. "They say you took in tieflings. Did you . . . have them when Jhani . . ."

Mehen nodded. "Twins," he said, skimming past the sharp edges of that. "Havilar and Farideh."

"Pretty," Uadjit said, ignoring the sharp memories too. "Old names."

"I don't want him to come near them," Mehen said. "Are we clear on that?"

"Very." She tapped her tongue against the roof of her mouth. "They're investigating the murders in the catacombs with you. My father mentioned them, though Dumuzi didn't."

Mehen reconsidered Uadjit, that detail laid so carefully before him it might have been a peace offering. "I haven't been able to figure out why Narghon was there," he said slowly. "None of the dead were yours."

"No," she said. She glanced at the door, then moved around the table to stand beside Mehen, where she could watch both entrances, before adding quietly, "None of the dead in the Verthisathurgiesh tomb."

"*Karshoj*," Mehen swore. "Another one?"

"The same night, but not the same place," Uadjit said. "The southern exit from the catacombs—she was making a guard's round that night. Throat torn out . . . and one of her arms . . ." She trailed off. "You're looking for an animal. And we're looking for a second guard. One dead, one vanished."

Mehen frowned. "Narghon said nothing."

"Consider *this* Narghon saying something." Uadjit checked the door once more. "Why were the hatchlings in the catacombs?" she asked. "What were they doing?"

"I don't know."

"You don't know, or you won't tell me?"

"Both," Mehen said. "Anala's the one who called me here, Anala's the one who asked me for answers. I owe her first."

Uadjit scoffed. "I think you still owe me quite a bit."

"You, perhaps," Mehen allowed. "But not Kepeshkmolik. I'm not here to play clan politics either."

Uadjit gave him a curious look. "Did Anala tell you why she wanted you back?"

A trill of fear went through Mehen. "To recover numbers. To show she isn't Pandjed. I haven't agreed to stay," he said. "In fact, I don't plan on doing anything of the sort." He hesitated. "Why? Why do you think she sent for me?"

Uadjit's teeth bared, something between a smile and a grimace. "You tell me what I want to know, and I'll tell you what you want. Fair is fair." And *that* sounded more like the Uadjit he remembered.

Before Mehen could reply, the *smack-smack* of running feet echoed down the enclave's hallways, and Brin burst into the room. "Mehen!" he cried. "Mehen, you have to come, right away."

• • •

THE DRAGONBORN OF Djerad Thymar swarmed around Ilstan like a tide of scales and strangeness. Eyes tracked him as he passed, glassy and jewel-bright. Do they see? Ilstan wondered. Do they know? Do they mark the ghost of the god that walks among them?

. . . What are the gods if not our hearts encompassed, our hopes and fears embodied and not embodied, shadowed and silvered and undone . . . The Weave unravels, the spinner darns the breaks, and so we may find a lifeline in the darkness . . .

"Saer." Kallan took hold of Ilstan's arm, and he jumped back, lightning forcing its way into his fingers. Kallan held up both hands. "Easy. I just noticed you'd stopped. The inn is this way."

Ilstan shook the lightning out, sparks snapping from his fingers. "Oh. Yes. Do we . . . Are we to stay with your family?"

"Clan," Kallan corrected gently. "I'll have to go and present myself—make sure it doesn't filter back to my grandfather that I have no manners, you know? But we'll be staying at the Bow of Nilofer while you . . . put out some feelers?"

Ilstan nodded, eyes on the crowd. He didn't know how he'd find Farideh, but surely Azuth would help. Surely the god would not have entrusted him with this task without knowing he would complete it. Surely. Surely . . .

"Saer?" Kallan said again. Ilstan moved past him, so that he followed the gnome wizard while the dragonborn sells-word guarded his back. Through the crowds they wound, Ilstan sweeping the scaly faces for a nearly human one with mismatched eyes.

. . . There are those who are lost and those who are seeking . . .
There are those who are struggling and those who are—

The god's voice didn't trail away this time, but ended as though it had dropped off a cliff. Ilstan stopped dead in his tracks.

"Here we are," Kallan said, moving around him toward Wick. "Bow of Nilofer. How much can you afford?" he asked Wick, dropping his voice. "I think the wizard might need a rest."

Wizard! The voice echoed as if Ilstan stood in the tunnels beneath Suzail again. *Wizardwizardwizardwizard.*

Ilstan clapped his hands over his ears. "Stop it!" he hissed.

"Haven't got scaly money," Wick said.

"Silver is silver," Kallan answered. "I can get them down to six apiece, I think. Unless you want to share the room."

Something exploded beneath Ilstan's feet, and he lurched to the right, into the crowd. But the stone floor remained, smooth and intact. Not an explosion, he thought. Not an explosion, but then—

Wizard! The voice boomed again. *You are needed.*

A burst, Ilstan thought. The burst of a spell against the threads of magic. Another came, beneath the stone floor and beyond the inn. Panting, Ilstan searched the pyramid city's steeply sloping walls. An exit, a passage, something.

Quickly, he thought, or maybe the god thought, but Ilstan was already running, hoping for a passage to the deeper floors, to the spellcaster fighting for his or her life. He ran for the eastern wall, dragonborn parting for him as if they knew his errand. Ahead of him a dark passage opened in the floor. Two guards stood at its mouth, and marked him as he neared. One held up a hand and started to speak.

The spell was already leaving Ilstan's mouth in the same moment, dragging power along the Weave's remnants as he pulled his wand free. Magic wrapped the two dragonborn, heavy as a blanket, and they puddled to the floor, fast asleep but unharmed. Cries rose out of the crowd, a flock of panic, but Ilstan left them behind, diving down the granite staircase, tunneling into the city of stone.

The pulse of panic—like the crying of a rabbit in a snare—called to him along the threads of the Weave. Another wizard, another spellcaster, in danger, drawing on magic that wasn't enough. Another devoted of the Lord of Spells engaged with the forces of evil.

Below, the air was cold, and the light sparse—glowbaskets broke the dark every stone's throw or so. Ilstan stopped, listening, grasping at the bursts of magic.

Strength lies in safety, the god murmured. *Safety in strength. But strength in knowledge and there is no safety in knowledge.*

Someone collided with Ilstan, and he turned, ready to cast—a dragonborn, a dragonborn man with his sword in its scabbard and his hands held high—

"Saer?" the man said. "You have to come away from here. Come back with me."

Ilstan searched the dragonborn, his face, his hands, the sword. "Loyal Kallan," he said. His voice was breathless, panting. "Help. Someone needs help."

"No one's down here but the dead and—"

The scream came from all around them, the catacombs' construction bouncing the sound off every wall. But in Ilstan's very core, the wild cry of a spell screamed through the stale air, a signal. He sprinted away, not waiting for Kallan, not waiting for an explanation. Through corridors, through rooms and tombs and strange chapels, until he found the dragonborn wizard and the creature devouring him alive.

"*Chaubashk vur kepeshk karshoji!*" Kallan shouted, yanking his sword free.

The dragonborn stumbled. His chest was a ruin, the chains that marked his clan torn free of one nostril, which bled down his face. His right arm to the elbow was torn away, still in the grip of the creature that loomed over him.

It found Ilstan with lambent eyes sunken into a corpse's face. Gaunt and gray, with powerful limbs. Legs like a hunting cat's and claws to match. The dragonborn's blood stained its face and jagged teeth.

Too close, little morsel, a voice in Ilstan's thoughts sang, mad and ferocious and enough to make him wish he'd never left Suzail. *Hungry, hungry, hungry. One for now, one for later, and one for later still. Lucky, lucky, lucky.*

. . . the many mouths of the Abyss are never fed . . .

"Fiend," Ilstan sneered. The creature smiled, an unholy thing, just before Kallan's sword cut toward it.

The blade sliced the creature's arm, but then its terrible claws came up, and they might have been steel for all the creature seemed affected. Kallan turned the blade upward, into the thing's belly and scored a better hit.

But then its strong arm knocked the blade right out of Kallan's grip to clatter to the ground between the wizard and a sarcophagus.

"Help," the wizard croaked, trying to gain his feet again. Ilstan sprinted to the man's side. He had no healing magics ready, he had no cleric's touch. But he had the blessings of Azuth, and each step he took toward the man, they built and built and built.

. . . All work together, a chorus of action, an army of truth . . . even when we work alone, we are not alone . . .

Ilstan kneeled beside him, feeling as if his bones were turning to sugarglass, feeling as though he moved through molasses—the wrong move and all of him would shatter with power. All of the dragonborn wizard too.

"Get out of here!" Kallan shouted. His reclaimed sword scraped stone. The fiend hissed. Ilstan set his hands upon the other wizard, felt the bone and blood and muscle and *magic* in him. As the dragonborn struggled up, Ilstan glanced back at the fight.

The creature burbled something hideous and unfathomable. In their niches, the ossuaries rattled, leaped. They fell from the shelves—one, two, three, four—spilling out their contents. Their occupants.

Four dragonborn warrior skeletons stood, arraying themselves around the creature.

Endless defenders. The creature grinned. *Bones for miles.*

The skeletons advanced.

Ilstan pointed his wand over the shoulder of the dragonborn wizard. "*Ziastayix.*" A bolt of crackling force shot out of the end of his wand and shattered the skeleton nearest Kallan.

"Now you," he murmured to the dragonborn wizard. And the blessings of Azuth poured through Ilstan and into the man.

For a moment, all Ilstan knew was the surge of magic, the swirls of blue and silver light that blinded and buoyed him and the wounded wizard. Then he saw——as if he could see through the other man's eyes——how the dragonborn's hands moved as if to guide the spell into being. But the ruined arm posed beside the intact one, triggering nothing.

The creature cackled. *How weak wizards are.*

And then a voice spoke—Ilstan's, the dragonborn man's, and something greater than all of them. A word like a rockslide all condensed into sound, and suddenly the air sizzled and crackled as though the dragonborn breathed, not merely lightning but magic itself. The skeletons glowed white with the sudden pulse of power, and burst into twitching fragments of bone.

The creature shrieked in agony as the spell struck it, its skin seared away. It crashed against the farther wall, thrown by the power of the spell. Ilstan hung between worlds, between moments. In the edges of his vision, Kallan scooped up his sword and eased onto his feet.

Then the dragonborn wizard grunted and collapsed, nearly pulling Ilstan to the ground, and all at once Ilstan's mind seemed to pull together, becoming solid and real and clear. He looked from Kallan to the dead wizard to the creature, remembering.

"It's a fiend," he said, calm as ever. "You should run."

But then there were voices coming, shouting, the footfalls of a whole group. "Stay back!" Kallan called down the corridors. "For the love of every lost soul, stay back!" Ilstan turned to face the creature, wand high.

"Go," he said, drawing up a fireball. "We need assistance."

The fiend stood, still grinning, always grinning. *Another time, morsel,* it said. Ilstan released the fireball, just where it meant to turn. But slick as an eel, it twisted and fled out another door, sliding into the shadows. The fireball crashed against the wall as the footsteps reached the tomb.

"Quick!" Kallan said. "There's been—Oh!"

Ilstan turned. And there she was.

If Ilstan was surprised to see Farideh, the tiefling was nothing short of shocked. Afraid, he thought. As she should be.

. . . *We strive together even when we strive alone* . . . Azuth whispered . . . *and so every precious thing can be protected, every spell can be strengthened, every word can be saved, every tyrant brought down* . . . *and if we do not, it is the end, the end, the end in the beginning's skin* . . . The other faces didn't matter, didn't register, for here was the Knight of the Devil. The Lady of Black Magic. The Key to the prison of Azuth. The only adversary that mattered if Azuth was to live.

"Ilstan," she said. "What have you done?"

" 'Ilstan'?" Kallan said. Ilstan turned to his faithful companion, but the sellsword looked upon him with frightened eyes, his sword high. "You're that war wizard. The one who was trying to kill her. Ilstan Nyaril."

"This doesn't concern you," he said. Somewhere beside Farideh, one of her companions moved. He jerked toward it—

The glaive jutted up toward his midsection, swifter than he would have thought such a weapon could move. But Ilstan Nyaril had been a Wizard of War, and old instincts shoved him backward, away from the blade. He pointed his wand at the attacker—at Farideh, her golden eyes stern—and spat a word of magic. A globe of fire burst from the tip of the wand and streaked toward her, but she jerked out of the way, the flames only singeing the fine hairs along her crown. The fireball crashed against . . . Farideh, standing behind her, rocking her back with a sharp cry.

Ilstan blinked. Twins. Lord Crownsilver's mistress. The Lady of Black Magic and the Knight of the Devil. "You are *both* tainted," he said, realizing his mistake. "You *both* hide the key."

The shaft of the glaive hit him in the stomach, knocking the wind from his lungs. He swept the wand toward the tiefling, as someone else slammed the butt of a blade into the middle of his back.

I cannot fall, Ilstan thought, locking his legs, drawing up the magic needed to cast. I cannot yield.

Havilar pivoted, slashing the glaive toward his neck. Ilstan grabbed her fist, the point of strength, shoving her back and the blade away from him and—

For a moment, Ilstan felt as if he did not exist, as if his whole awareness merely stretched across the edge of creation, looking down into an endless void, full of the cacophony of hungry beasts, the churn of chaos.

Then just as suddenly, he was in the catacombs again, facing Havilar, who stared at him as if *he* had just crawled out of the endless Abyss. Kallan had moved toward him, and another dragonborn, a dark-scaled one with the moon sailing along his brow. And Lord Crownsilver, too, standing over the Knight of the Devil. Footsteps echoed as though all the catacombs were full of soldiers.

But none of it mattered to Ilstan Nyaril—every spark and scrap of magic in him surged forth, hungry for the blood of the only quarry that mattered now: the creature. The spell built up his arms as he turned from his previous quarry to follow the hateful fiend who had killed the dragonborn wizard.

"Guards!" the dark-scaled dragonborn bellowed. "To the tomb of Shuchir's line!"

"It's escaping!" Ilstan shouted back at him. "We don't have time."

"Stop!" Farideh reappeared beside him, her rod held in her uninjured hand. "How many more are you going to kill?"

Knight of the Devil, he thought. Lady of Black Magic. The drive to find the fiend wavered, but didn't break. "Not so many as your pet."

Ilstan twisted away from her, diving toward the exit, but as he did, he came up short against a body, a guard coming through that door. A broad-shouldered dragonborn man with greenish scales and the same moon-shaped piercings. The guard grinned at Ilstan in an unsettling way as he seized him by the right hand, crushing his wrist and forcing the wand from his grip.

"No way out, criminal."

Without a thought, Ilstan balled his left hand into a fist and slammed it into the guard's toothy jaw. All at once, the strange focus that had gripped him vanished as pain shot up his arm. The guard, surprised, loosed his grip on Ilstan, but there was little the wizard could do but fall back into the tomb, clutching his bleeding knuckles in shock.

More guards poured in, grabbing hold of him. They wrenched his hands behind his back where they could not coax magic from the Weave and pushed him down to his knees, holding his head so that all he could see were the scattered bones, the poor dead wizard, and the blood soaking his own cloak and robes.

The younger dragonborn man kneeled beside the dead body. "It's Ravar."

"Dead?" one of the guards said. The young man nodded and stood, looking away from the fallen wizard. The guard holding Ilstan's head let go, clapped the younger man on the back several times. "You did your best. And we caught the killer. Your clan will be proud."

Ilstan looked around wildly. The Knight of the Devil was bent over, messily sick on the stone floor, while Lord Crownsilver himself held her hand. Farideh's mismatched eyes held Ilstan's, her face pale as death. "Brin, can you go get Mehen?" she whispered. Her sister vomited again.

"Kallan!" Ilstan cried. "Kallan, help me! Help me!"

Kallan kneeled on the blood-slicked, bone-scattered ground, never taking his eyes off the guards. He set his sword on the ground before him, and placed both hands behind his head. "Will you contact Yrjixtilex?" he asked. "I think I have need of my clan."

163

8

19 Nightal, the Year of the Nether Mountain Scrolls (1486 DR)
Djerad Thymar, Tymanther

THERE WERE THIRTEEN HUNDRED FORTY-TWO STEPS between the Verthisathurgiesh enclave and the Vanquisher's enclave where the Adjudicators resided, and the Lance Defenders' barracks and the bat stables were—the number flitted through Mehen's thoughts as he raced toward his daughters, the memories of more recent losses, more recent heartaches fresher and realer than anything Djerad Thymar had given him. He threw wide the doors to the Adjudicators' enclave, to find Anala waiting there, hands folded with infuriating patience against her garnet robes.

"What happened?" Mehen demanded, as Brin came panting up behind him. "Where are they? Where's that *karshoji* wizard?"

Anala held up a hand. "Your daughters are being treated for their injuries. The culprits are safely imprisoned. And I'm sure the human told you more than I know about what happened. Calm yourself."

"This is as *karshoji* calm as you're going to see!" Mehen shouted . . . And then he noticed the trio of Adjudicators standing beyond Anala, watching in frozen horror. Replaying thirty-year-old tales, he thought. Or maybe watching for all of Pandjed's blood to show. His tongue rattled against the roof of his mouth.

"Take me to them, right now. Please."

Anala smiled, as if nothing untoward had happened. "Why do you think I'm waiting here?" she said. Then, in Common, "Come along."

Mehen winced. He'd slipped into Draconic again. "Sorry," he said, shaking his head at Brin. "There's too much going on."

"It's all right," Brin said, still a little short of breath as they followed the Verthisathurgiesh matriarch through the hallways. "I caught a little of it. Just don't leave me in the dark when you find out more about that serpent Ilstan."

In a small side room, Farideh sat on a heavy cot, her shoulder bandaged and packed with herbs, her expression grim and distant. Havilar lay beside her, looking faintly green, with a damp cloth across her eyes. Dumuzi sat beside her, carefully wrapping a small burn on Havilar's wrist.

"We're all right," Farideh said as soon as Mehen entered. "Minor burns. And they caught Ilstan."

"And if he's summoning demons? He hit you with a spell. He says he wants to kill you. You say he's completely mad," Mehen said, his fear racing away from him. "Am I missing anything?" He looked over at Havilar. "Is *she* in his sights now too?"

Havilar mumbled something beneath the cloth. Dumuzi looked up at Mehen, abashed. "They gave her a dose of *chmertehoschta*. For shock."

"What in all the broken planes is she shocked for?" Mehen demanded.

"Mehen," Brin said, "calm down. It's nothing worse than we've already been through."

Everything felt as if it were coming apart in his hands, and now Brin had to tell him he was overreacting. Mehen clacked his teeth together, swallowing the spark of lightning building in his throat. Worse or not, it shouldn't have happened.

"The war wizard's your murderer?" Mehen asked.

"They found him standing over the body of Shestandeliath Ravar," Anala said. "He was covered in the man's blood. We should be sure, but I suspect you've caught the culprit."

"*Nooo*," Havilar said, half a moan from beneath the cloth. She lifted a corner of it. " 'S a demon."

Mehen scowled at Dumuzi. "How much did they give her?"

"I don't know," Dumuzi said, his shoulders creeping toward his ears. "I didn't ask."

"Clearly. She's not a *karshoji* Vayemniri. You can't dose her as if she is!"

"She was vomiting a good deal," Anala said. "And you know perfectly well it will wear off."

"I just threw up," Havilar mumbled. "It's so embarrassing. But at least . . . he didn't . . . I didn't get my arm torn off, so there's that."

Mehen frowned. "*What?*"

"Ravar's arm had been torn off," Farideh said quietly. "At the elbow. No one could find it. And Ilstan . . . He probably weighs as much as Brin and he's a foot taller. Maybe with a spell—"

"He's a wizard, of course he used a spell."

"And he had an accomplice," Anala said.

Havilar shot up to a seated position and caught herself dizzily against Brin. "Kallan, Mehen. *Kallan*. He can't tear an arm off, and you would *know*."

The very name shocked all the fear and rage out of Mehen for a moment, and he grew warm at the memory of the easy-going sellsword, slim and nicely muscled, sitting at the foot of the bed, with that cheeky smile and juggling three dirty teacups. Fingers tracking over the spidery network of scars marking the scales of Mehen's chest. *Chaubask, what did you do to get those?*

How his sly expression had shattered when Mehen had told him they were done, he was heading to Djerad Thymar.

Havilar pointed an unsteady finger at her father. "He *asked* about you."

"*Thrik*, or I tell them to dose you again," Mehen said.

A knock came at the door. An Adjudicator stuck his head in and conversed quietly with Anala, his eyes darting to Mehen as he did. "I see," she said. She beckoned to Dumuzi. "Come with me, Kepeshkmolik." Dumuzi fastened the bandage around Havilar's hand and slipped out after Anala.

Mehen turned to Farideh. "Did Kallan tell you anything? Did you get any clues or . . ."

"No. Ilstan's covered in Ravar's blood, but I really don't think he killed him. *Maybe* he summoned the demon, but I don't think so. He seemed to want to hunt it down."

Mehen sat at her feet. "What else?"

Farideh winced and shifted her shoulder. "It's hard to say. He might have been in his right mind and he might not have been. But I think he might be after Havilar now too. And I think he might know more than we thought." By her look, she didn't mean the murders.

Have Anala put them someplace safe, he thought. Lock them up tight until it's all settled, until the war wizard is condemned and the murderer caught. He could already hear the girls' protests—they weren't children, they weren't helpless. They had weathered worse. You will understand when you're older, Mehen would say.

But no sooner did the words form, he shoved them aside. He couldn't think about those far-off days, not when all his heart wanted to leap backward through the hours—or even years—and protect them. Mehen's tongue hammered against the roof of his mouth again. The air tasted like fear and fury.

"How did it go with Shestandeliath?" Farideh asked.

Mehen sighed. "Poorly. They protect their own. And everyone in this *karshoji* city remembers me as a rebellious hatchling or the son of a miserable old *henish*. We'll need to reconsider how to do this."

Farideh glanced at the door. "We found out some things. The ones in the crypt were part of a group that was trying to find a way back to Abeir. Dumuzi thinks the portal was meant to go there, and that Ravar was the only one who could have likely gotten them the scroll to do it. But we didn't get to Ravar fast enough."

It was far better than Mehen had managed, though. "Well done."

"Thank you." She chewed her lip. "I have a thought, and I don't think you're going to like it: Maybe you ought to go after the clan leaders Anala's way. It seems like having her with you would help. Maybe we ought to be the ones looking at the murder scenes and talking things out of people."

"They won't talk to you."

"The clan leaders won't, but their children? Grandchildren? Especially," she added, a little delicately, "if everyone wants to know more about you and what you did."

Mehen covered his face with both hands. Broken planes, he did *not* want the youth of Djerad Thymar peppering his daughters with questions about how he'd been exiled. Even as he wondered how much of what happened in the elder's audience chamber was common knowledge . . .

"How much do you know?"

"Dumuzi told us you were supposed to marry. That you refused because . . . Well because of Arjhani. And that Arjhani married the woman you were supposed to in the end. It doesn't seem that dire," Farideh added. "Maybe it's a Vayemniri thing? Or a Thymari thing?"

"Some of it. And some of it is just missing. My father . . ." Mehen clacked his teeth. "If this life grants me nothing else, let it be that I never give you a reason to think of me as your enemy."

Farideh shifted to the end of the cot and hugged him tight. "Never."

The door opened again, Anala returning. "Mehen? Did you want to question the wizard for Verthisathurgiesh?"

"A moment." He rubbed the frill of his jaw against Farideh's head. "Do me the favor of going straight to the enclave and getting your sister to bed. Maybe you could slay a thousand demons, but my heart can't take it today. We'll shift plans tomorrow."

Outside the room, Anala walked beside him. "Do you still have your piercings?" she asked in a conversational way.

He did. No matter how many times he thought about tossing them into the sea or pawning them, he kept the plugs of deep green jade in their little box with him wherever he wandered. "I haven't decided I ought to wear them again."

"It would help you with your task," Anala said. "You are not clanless anymore, so far as Verthisathurgiesh is concerned. No need to punish yourself further. You went to Shestandeliath alone?"

"I did," Mehen said. "It felt the wisest course."

"And you see now it was not?"

"I see there's more in my way than I remembered." Mehen turned to her. "If I'm going to play this part, we have to move faster. If we wait, we lose information, opportunities."

Anala tilted her head. "I shall make arrangements then. But you will wear the piercings."

"Fine." It wouldn't decide things, Mehen told himself. It wasn't a surrender. Mehen looked off, down the hallway. "I need to question the wizard and . . . his sellsword," Mehen said. "We can talk about the details later."

Much later, he thought, following one of the Adjudicators into the prison's depths. Uadjit's cryptic question still needled at him. *Why do you think she sent for you?* He'd made the mistake of assuming since Anala wasn't Pandjed, he had no reason to fear her. But Pandjed or Anala, they were all Verthisathurgiesh, renowned for fighting too-powerful foes with cunning and trickery.

The Adjudicator he followed was a young man, pierced only by the small golden beads beneath the eyes that mimicked the Vanquisher's marks. Clans in Djerad Thymar policed their own, but when a crime reached beyond the clan's powers, the Adjudicators, gathered from every clan and dedicated to the city over all else, stepped in. They should have been brought in from the start, thought Mehen. But every clan was concerned first with protecting their own, and the current Vanquisher had no interest in fighting that.

Tarhun, he thought, shaking his head. The Vanquisher was a dragonborn only a little older than Mehen himself, a fellow he remembered from his extended service. Strong fighter, capable strategist, but disinterested in the games clans played. Probably elected easily—Tarhun had the look, the legacy of a Vanquisher, and besides, the most cunning clans would see opportunity in the gaps of his skills.

The cells lined the inner wall of the Adjudicator's space, each with a wall made of bars facing the hallway and opposite, fitted with a window too small to squeeze through—even if a prisoner could have, the fall was beyond lethal—and a low bench.

"Hold on," the Adjudicator said. "I don't have the keys." He turned back, leaving Mehen facing Ilstan Nyaril.

The wizard sat on the bench, pressed against the wall and breathing as though he'd run up every single stair from the base of the pyramid to this high-up roost. More scarecrow than man, his long fingers gripped the edge of the bench, white-knuckled.

"Have you come to kill me?" he asked.

Mehen bared his teeth, all his fear rushing back. "You hunt my daughters. I'll kill you gladly if you don't cooperate."

A wild grin cracked the wizard's face. "Oh, you poor fool. A snakelet will spill it's venom into your veins even if you're the one who warmed it at your breast. Crush them now. It's the only way. I'm sorry."

The lightning breath crackled between Mehen's teeth, built by his fury. He gripped the iron bars, reminding himself of the careful spells that prevented breath weapons from crossing their boundary. He'd only end up electrifying himself.

"You should pray to all your gods that you never get out of this cell," Mehen said. "Where is the demon?"

Ilstan stood and walked toward him, waving on his feet. His eyes wide and mad. "Ask your daughter. The Lady of Black Magic. The Knight of the Devil. The whore of the king of the Hells."

Mehen shoved an arm through a gap in the bars and grabbed hold of the wizard's robe front, yanking him hard against the bars. Ilstan's face bounced off the metal, startling him into silence. "The next words from your mouth are the location of that demon or what comes through these bars is my blade," Mehen whispered.

Ilstan smiled uneasily, blood trickling over his lip. "I don't know," he said, as if he would break into tears.

"Mehen!"

"I'm busy!" Mehen bellowed, turning on the intruder with lightning crackling in the gape of his jaws.

Dumuzi, stiff as a statue, his hands balled beside him, took several quick steps back. "You . . . you need to let him go. The Adjudicators—"

"*Karshoji arschatjamaetrishominaki!*" Mehen snarled. The Adjudicators had no hold on him.

Dumuzi swallowed hard, his eyes locked on Mehen's teeth. "And Farideh? Farideh won't—"

"What are you doing?" The Adjudicator returned, holding the lost keys. "Get your hands off him! I know Verthisathurgiesh has their ways, but you have to respect the Vanquisher's order up here."

Pandjed has his ways—the true meaning nestled in that comment, the stain of his father's anger and pride and violence tainting the whole of the clan. Tainting Mehen.

Mehen released the war wizard, who scurried back. "I lost my temper. My apologies." He looked to Dumuzi—the boy still watched him as if he were a fierce beast. "Go home," Mehen said.

Dumuzi opened his mouth to say something, then seemed to think better of it. He turned without a word and fled. Mehen cursed under his breath—the boy was blameless, even if he was irritating. "Take me to the other one," he told the Adjudicator.

The Adjudicator unlocked another set of doors, which led to a long hall of similar cells, half-filled with other dragonborn. Mehen marked their clans as they passed, out of habit—Kanjentellequor's silver skewers, Shestandeliath's silver chains, Daardendrien's bone studs. Many of them had their piercings removed, a sign of their elders' displeasure. They all watched him back, and Mehen resolutely kept his eyes on the Adjudicator's back after that.

Near the end of the hallway, Kallan sat beneath the window, on the floor. As Mehen came in behind the Adjudicator, Kallan looked up and cocked an eyebrow, and Mehen was suddenly, awkwardly aware of the fact that if he'd been a little less of a coward, things would be very, very different in that moment.

"He *likes* you, Mehen," Havilar had sung, as though she were the only one to notice such a thing. But a world of differences lay between finding time alone with a fellow you found pretty, and starting something more serious up with a pretty fellow your daughter adored. Unbidden, Arjhani rose up in his thoughts, that far-off summer and tiny Havilar holding a cobbled-together glaive of wood while Jhani caught her swings on his own weapon. His heart twisted—however pleasant he'd found Kallan and his company, however Havilar insisted that they were grown enough to weather their father's romances, leaving the sellsword behind had been the only decision he could make.

"Well," Kallan said. "I can't say this is how I hoped to see you again."

"I have to ask you some questions," Mehen blurted.

"Makes sense."

He looked back at the Adjudicator. "Can you give us a moment?"

The Adjudicator scowled at him, bunching the gold studs of his cheeks. "So you can strangle this one too?"

"I didn't strangle him. Don't be dramatic."

"You looked pretty close to it."

"Last I recall you don't arrest people for looking close to a crime. I grabbed him by the *karshoji* shirt. That man has been trying to kill my daughters. This one helped protect them."

"We have history," Kallan said, as though no one had mentioned strangling. "You don't need to worry about him, Balasar, though I appreciate your concern. It's always good to see someone taking their duties seriously."

That mollified the guard somewhat and though he eyed Mehen darkly, the Adjudicator excused himself, and moved down the hall a ways.

"You must have scared him badly," Kallan said, not moving from his spot. "I assume he's talking about the wizard?"

"I just came from seeing my battered daughters and the first thing that bastard war wizard did was tell me I had to kill them. I lost my head. And I grabbed him by the shirt, I didn't strangle him."

"Understandable." He looked up at Mehen, exhaustion written large on his face.

"I didn't know who he was, if that's what you're here about. He offered coin and polite company for a guide and guard to Djerad Thymar. He never even told me his name. I thought the one hunting your girl was dead anyhow. If I'd known . . . They're all right, yeah?"

"Minor burns," Mehen said. "Shock."

"Small favors." He sighed. "What're your questions?"

"Did you . . . see Shestandeliath Ravar die?"

Kallan looked him over again "You want to know if I ripped a fellow twice my size limb from limb?" he asked dryly. A crooked smile curved his mouth.

"I know you didn't." Broken planes, he was good-looking. Focus, Mehen thought. "I'm curious about the wizard, though."

"The wizard didn't kill him either. He was trying to save that fellow." Kallan gave Mehen a level look. "Maybe I'm no raging owlbear, but if I can't rip a man's arm from its socket, then Ilstan can't. Besides, we *saw* what did it—you need to be looking for the fiend."

"I'm trying to."

Kallan leaned back on the bench. "I can't say I'm pleased you're willing to entertain the idea that I'm in here for any good reason. Do you really think I'd get involved with a demon? Do you think I'd take a job from someone I knew was trying to hunt your daughter?"

Mehen swore to himself and crouched down beside the sellsword. "No. Honestly, no. But I don't take chances, not with them. And you know as well as I do that whatever we can do to make the Adjudicators see you don't belong here is for the best." He blew out a breath. "Could the wizard have summoned it?"

Kallan shook his head. "He didn't have time to, whether he can or he can't, or he would or he wouldn't. He got to the tomb only a few steps ahead of me, and that fellow Ravar was screaming long before that." He scratched at a loose scale behind his boot. "Did your girls think I was involved?"

Havilar's slurred admonishment. The delighted expression on her face when she'd realized Kallan was staying in the tallhouse in Suzail. The boneless shock when Arjhani had left . . .

"Not in the least," Mehen said briskly. "Though I wouldn't take that as a guarantee. They don't always make the best choices about who to trust. I trust you," he added. "If it matters."

Kallan's crooked smile spread. "So you say. You won't even tell me which clan you're with."

A beat of awkward silence, the drum of persistent heartache. *You are too old for this*, Mehen thought. "Verthisathurgiesh. I was born Verthisathurgiesh. I figured you could guess from the holes."

"Not all of us are up on the many clan piercings. But I suspect I can diagnose a sick sheep faster—don't get jealous. *And* I'm much faster at butchering."

Mehen snorted. He nearly replied that it probably caught *all* the fellows' eyes, a skill like that, but he stopped himself. He'd ended it, after all. He wet his mouth. "Ravar's not the only one dead. Verthisathurgiesh hired us to track down someone who murdered around a dozen hatchlings in their catacombs a few days ago. The girls thought it was a demon too—but we haven't laid eyes on it. So what's it look like?"

"Big," Kallan said. "Ugly. Gray skin, two legs, very strong. Talks in your head, not with its mouth." He hesitated. "It was eating Ravar alive. Pretty sure I was next on its menu."

Mehen shuddered. "A good thing it didn't. I'll do what I can to get you out of here—"

"Don't. It's really not necessary."

He scowled. "Fine, maybe I ended things more abruptly than I should have, but don't be a proud idiot—"

"I mean," Kallan said, "Yrjixtilex has been sent to speak for me. And maybe I don't know all your history, City Boy, but I do know that having a clanless bounty hunter speaking for me isn't actually going to tip the scales in my favor much in Matriarch

Vardhira's view. I appreciate the offer, but my clan's handling it." He tilted his head. "It's too much to ask what you did to end up clanless, right?"

Mehen chuckled again. "All dramatics, little substance. Maybe your clan will do the right thing, but maybe they'll do it a little faster if they think you've got some gossip about Pandjed's prodigal son." He blew out another nervous breath. "And that's *my* problem. I can't go six steps in this city without someone recognizing me and using it against me. There's something going on, the clans have a sense of it, and they're not talking for fear everyone will find out their hatchlings were plotting to escape to Abeir."

"Well," Kallan said a moment later, "that's a hatchling sort of a plan. What do you want me to do?"

"My girls are going to do the dirty work—but they're not Vayemniri. They know the language, but they're not from here. They stick out. Would you stick with them? I'd split the fee," he added quickly.

Kallan's smile flickered. "I can do that," he said after a moment. "Not what I was hoping for, I'll admit, but a fee's a fee." He shrugged. "And I think I'd like to get to know them better. They come highly regarded, after all," he added, his cheeky smile returning.

You are going to make a fool of yourself after all, Mehen thought as he left the cells and made his way out of the Adjudicators' domain. Too old or not. At least you've had plenty of practice at it.

But those were worries for another time, after the threat of killers and demons, devils and clans had faded. What would his younger self have said if someone had told him that at forty-five he would have tiefling daughters bound to a devil-god and Djerad Thymar would be somewhere he hadn't set foot in for almost thirty years? It was so far from the life he'd expected, Mehen couldn't even imagine what his younger self would have done with the knowledge.

Laughed, he thought, and vowed never to come to such a state. *Pothach* little idiot.

• • •

YOU ARE KEPESHKMOLIK, Dumuzi told himself, forcing his steps to come slow and measured as he left the cells. Forcing his thoughts away from the flicker of lightning in the ochre-scaled dragonborn's jaws, the memory of the same moment just before he fled Pandjed. Just before he was scarred. They kept circling back, indefatigable.

Dumuzi stopped in the entryway, trying to slow his breath, slow his pulse. What had he been thinking, going after Mehen? Farideh could tell her father what the Liberators were up to, what possible sources he still had. Dumuzi didn't have to involve himself at all. There was nothing to offer. He should go back to his clan and stay out of it, stay away from what remained of Pandjed.

You are Kepeshkmolik now, he told himself. You fulfill your obligations.

He squared his shoulders and went back to the room Anala and the Adjudicator had led him to shortly before. "Your counsel is your own," Anala had said before she left him. "But I would consider it a favor to your *qallim* clan if you would *politely* tell your sire that it benefits none of us for him to come around at the moment. No one needs to unearth the past."

Verthisathurgiesh Arjhani was still not waiting for Dumuzi. For a terrible moment, he wondered if Arjhani and Mehen would cross paths in the Adjudicators' enclave, one leaving, one arriving. That is probably what keeps him, Dumuzi thought, settling himself behind the table there, watching the door. Anala would have found a way to prevent it.

Dumuzi thought of the look on Farideh's face when he'd confessed to who his father was, that night in Suzail, after she'd almost died—hard and merciless and angry as he'd ever seen. He hoped Arjhani didn't cross her path either, for both their sakes.

When the door opened again, a burst of laughter followed Verthisathurgiesh Arjhani into the room. "Ah! I'll take that bet,"

Arjhani called back. "You'll see." He laughed again, shook his head. "Dokaan," he said, to Dumuzi. "Doesn't know when to quit. Well met! You made it back. You look well."

"Well enough," Dumuzi said. "I found him."

Arjhani's grin wavered. "You did? I knew you'd manage it."

Dumuzi doubted that. He couldn't imagine anything his father wanted less than the return of Clanless Mehen, and so why would he send someone he felt confident would return successful? It had stung in its own way to be asked. "Thank you."

"So he's back?" Arjhani turned around the chair opposite his son, and sat astride it. "Does anyone besides Anala know?"

"Uadjit knows. Um, the Shestandeliath and the Ophinshtalajiir have seen him. Patriarch Narghon."

"I suppose Anala didn't think it mattered much to let me know," Arjhani said, a little tartly. "Good to know everyone else has the story first. You told your mother before me?"

"I'm sorry. I saw her first."

By his expression, that didn't matter to Arjhani. Still dressed in the armor and blazons of a Lance Defender, blue wraps on his hands as he gripped the back of the chair. "How's your mother?"

"Well enough," Dumuzi said. Then, "I think she's probably been happier. They don't know if there will be a need for an ambassador come spring."

Arjhani's brow ridges rose. "But no war for us? That's a relief—High Imaskar is always too busy for our defense. Seems a shame to waste blood on their losing battle now—especially since no one *asked* for our help before."

Dumuzi nodded, but inside he winced. If High Imaskar were their allies, then why turn from them now? He remembered dimly the battles against the ash giants, the threat of war with Chessenta when he was a child. The anger that High Imaskar had not been there to aid Tymanther as promised. But also he'd remembered his mother's reaction: Diplomacy was not like lines upon a paper. It was not so simple as give and take, push and pull. It was a crisscrossing network of strings that all tugged against each other. High Imaskar's failure, preceded by their own battles, their own concerns, did not make them a bad ally. They had uses still.

But then, perhaps, their current war with the rebels claiming to refound the ancient empire they called Mulhorand saw those uses dwindling. Tymanther could not afford to make bad alliances, Uadjit had said more than once.

"Well, I'm certain they'll find something for her to do," Arjhani said. "So . . . Is he down in the enclave then?"

It took Dumuzi a moment to determine who Arjhani meant: Mehen. Mehen who he was meant to be keeping his father away from. "Yes," he said. "Matriarch Anala suggested it might be wisest for you to find things to do in the barracks."

Arjhani snorted, his teeth parting in bare annoyance. "Of course. Count *me* irredeemable. Punish *me* for Pandjed's folly."

Dumuzi said nothing. Undeniably handsome, undeniably skilled with his chosen weapon, undeniably silver-tongued when it counted, Arjhani never took well to slights. Merchants saved their best for him, because he praised their wares and their charming smiles, and perhaps—if the rumors were right—whispered just the right things in their ears, but if they were sharp with him, Arjhani would never return. The Lance Defenders kept him as glaivemaster because he was swift and observant and good with students—and if sometimes those students, sheep-eyed and smitten, stayed too late for private lessons, or spent time running errands or doing chores that had nothing to do with their lessons, it was ignored. They'd learned well enough not to stir the pot. When someone finally discovered that Arjhani's surface was not at all what lay in his core, there was Uadjit to smooth away the edges and Arjhani's insistence that none of these things were really his fault.

Arjhani watched Dumuzi, troubled, puzzled. "Did you get along all right with him?"

"We didn't talk much."

"Yeah, he's . . . Well. Strong silent type, right?" Arjhani smiled unevenly. "How does he look?"

"I don't know. He looks like Pandjed."

Arjhani folded his arms. "How much did she tell you?"

"Nothing more," Dumuzi said. It was true, what he knew of his father's past, his mother's shame and anger, he'd gathered long ago from whispers thought unheard, from unkind children, from Pandjed's cruel taunts. "I take it that you two had a falling out?"

Arjhani eyed him as if he could tell Dumuzi was lying. "You could say that." A young woman stuck her head in the room. "Master?" she said. "Commander Sepideh said to let you know your class is ready."

"Of course. I'll be there in a moment." He smiled. "Thank you for letting me know."

Dumuzi stood. "It was good to see you."

"Good to see you too," Arjhani said, embracing his son. He smiled at him, studying Dumuzi's face fondly, and then he tilted his head. "Did Mehen come alone?"

Dumuzi held his father's gaze and thought of Farideh's furious expression. "Yes," he lied. "And truth be told, I think he'll be gone within the tenday."

Arjhani chuckled once in a sad sort of way. "Well. I suppose that's for the best."

• • •

Havilar woke to Zoonie licking the palm of her outstretched hand. Her thoughts seemed too heavy to lift out of her head as she sat up, pulling her hand away. Zoonie thumped her tail against the floor and whined.

"Good girl," Havilar said, her voice hard coming. She wiped her hand on her blouse, as she looked around the room—she was back in the enclave, in the too-big bed. The stink of burnt wool hung on the air—a scattering of embers had eaten through the patterned blanket.

"Oh, Zoonie," Havilar sighed, pushing back the covers. The hellhound wagged her tail and sneezed, scattering more sparks. Havilar scratched the puppy's head, and noticed her bandaged hand.

The infirmary, she remembered. The long walk to the pyramid's peak. The tomb, the dead man, Ilstan.

Havilar stood, woozily, and dropped back onto the bed. Ilstan, in Djerad Thymar, and the sudden nausea, the sudden sickness she couldn't seem to stop. When one of the guards had offered her the tincture, she'd drunk it greedily. Whatever it took to stop vomiting. And then . . . everything was fuzzy.

Hrast, hrast, hrast, she cursed to herself. The nausea, the vomiting, that was all the same as when she'd found the dretch—but worse. There was still a demon in the catacombs. A demon that had torn the arm off a grown dragonborn. A demon that had still been near enough to make her unstoppably sick.

She had to tell Farideh and Brin. She should have told them right away—but then she'd seen Brin, and *known* that he'd flee from her if she were somehow even *more* a Chosen of Asmodeus, and then Farideh had been so upset and it had been more important to be her sister and—

A thousand excuses, Havilar told herself, standing once more, and not a reason among them. Or something like that. Moving against her still-heavy limbs, she reached the door to the sitting area before she pitched against the wall, overtaken by the drug's remains.

"Once, maybe," she heard Brin say in a low voice. "But twice? And so badly she had to be medicated?" Hrast, Havilar thought. No more keeping secrets.

"Is that *normal*, when . . . if . . ." Farideh's voice stumbled. "I mean, it might be a lot of things." Then, "Do you think that the sedative will . . . I mean, I didn't want to ask if it would hurt—"

Havilar pushed off the wall and out into the room. Brin stood as she came in, moving toward her, but Havilar caught herself against the settee and held up a hand.

"All right, look," she said. "You're right. Something's going on, and I should have said before, only . . ." She sighed. "I don't know. I didn't want it to be true and I don't want you all telling me I have to sit back 'in case,' and maybe I just really don't think it's fair, especially *right now*, you know?" She said this last part to Brin, even though he didn't and he couldn't, no matter how much she wished he did. "I didn't want to run you off."

Brin's eyes shone. "Oh gods," he said. He rushed to her, embraced her—and Havilar could only freeze. Farideh watched her, worried over Brin's shoulder. Havilar hugged him tight, imagining the worst. She'd missed something. Something *bad* had happened.

"What's wrong with you?" she demanded. "Why are you crying? What happened?"

"I'm happy!" Brin said. He pushed back from her. "I mean . . . we're not . . . Things are still unsettled, I know that. I still have so much to make up for, and I promise I won't ever stop trying to. But I love you. *I love you*, and there is nowhere I would rather be than by your side. You know that, right?"

Havilar stood stunned for a moment. It was sweet—more than sweet. And for a moment, she was so overtaken she nearly kissed him. But that wasn't what they were doing—they'd agreed. And it made no sense. "What are you talking about?" she said. She looked at her sister. "Why are you happy?"

"He knows," Farideh said, and she did *not* sound happy. "We both know."

"Know what?" Havilar took a step back from Brin. "What is wrong with you two?"

"We know that you're pregnant," Farideh said.

"*What*?" Havilar shouted. "I'm not *pregnant,* you *pothachis*! Holy gods! Why would you even think that?"

"You don't throw up," Farideh said. "And . . . the timing . . ."

Havilar colored a little deeper. "You *told* her? About the pantry?"

"I was worried!" Brin said. "You've been acting really odd and it *fit*!"

Farideh felt a flush creep up her neck. "He only told me it happened," she said quickly. "Nothing else."

"She doesn't want to know, Brin!" Havilar cried. "How could you think that was all right? Honestly, why would you two even *think* I would . . . I would have *said* something!"

"You were *just* apologizing that you hadn't!" Farideh pointed out.

Which, to be fair, was true. Havilar folded her arms tight and wished she had her glaive in hand. Brin wouldn't look at her.

"I get sick," she said, "around demons. I guess it's a sort of power from Asmodeus. I threw up the first time because that dretch was still hiding in the tomb. I threw up again when Lorcan and Zoonie flushed it out. And I threw up more than both those times together when we found Ilstan and Kallan, because I'm mostly certain there's still a demon running around down there and it was likely still in the room." She uncrossed her arms. "And next time you think I'm pregnant, *ask me.*"

"I'm sorry," Brin said. "I'm going to go, um, take some air."

Karshoj, Havilar thought. "Wait," Havilar said. "Please. I need you. I need both of you. We have to find this thing. I don't know how. But I think I know who can . . ." She looked at her sister, and if she could have willed Farideh to suggest it first, she would have.

Farideh's expression grew dark. "We can find some other way."

"Fari—"

"Look, you already know how to call him for yourself," Farideh said. "Just . . . leave me out of it, all right. Brin can help you."

The doors opened, and Dumuzi came in, carrying a tray of tea and small cakes crusted with nuts. "They're worried you might be hungry again," he said, sounding gruff. He eyed them as he set down the tray. "Am I interrupting?"

"We're just talking about whether Havilar's feeling better," Farideh said quickly.

"Don't lie to him," Havilar said. "We're going to summon Lorcan in my bedroom because there's a demon in your catacombs that's making me queasy and it's probably what killed your friends. Do you know Lorcan?"

Farideh cursed under her breath. Dumuzi blinked at her. "The devil?" he asked. "I've met him." He looked to Farideh. "Have you already rolled the rugs up? Or do you need help?"

9

LORCAN PACED THE TREASURY IN THE DEEPEST LEVELS OF the fingerbone tower, considering his mother's spoils and twisting a thin braid of purplish-black hair over and around his hands. A gift, he'd decided, was a decent place to start. It had soothed Farideh before—a spell here, a rod there. But no matter how many times he circled the treasury, there seemed nothing in it that would repair the rift between him and his warlock.

Jewels? He could picture her expression already, hard as the emerald glinting on the shelf. A new spell? No, it would have to be something more powerful than he wanted in her hands just yet. One of the many blades? *And then she stabs you through the shitting heart,* he thought. *Again.*

Lorcan considered the shelf of rods and wands, collected off the bodies of spellcasters unfortunate enough to come face-to-face with the terrible erinyes known then as Exalted Invadiah, mother of the *pradixikai.*

Bad idea, he thought. She might have appreciated the rod he'd given her, that first gift, but now it would only remind her of the second, the rod Dahl had given her, the rod Lorcan had let her think came from him.

You ought to try making amends, Sairché had said. *Admit you were wrong. That goes a lot further than it ought to.*

"Enjoying my prizes?" a voice called out, as beautiful as the nightingale's song and terrible as a vulture's rushing wings.

Lorcan froze where he stood, calculated how quickly he could grab a blade or a bludgeon from the racks before him.

"Mother," he said, as calmly as he could. "I trust you're well."

Her laughter came, too close behind him. "Well enough."

Invadiah—now called Fallen Invadiah, after her inability to secure the archduchess's schemes in Neverwinter so long ago—sauntered toward her only son, considering the jewels, the poisons, the weapons. No longer a fierce and powerful erinyes, Invadiah had been demoted to the form of a succubus, her cruel hooves only dainty feet, her red skin moonlight-pale. Her sharp horns had been traded for mottled wings and her fangs for the ethereal face of a young woman. But there was still violence in her black eyes as she approached Lorcan.

"What were you going to take?" she asked.

"Only what His Majesty requires," Lorcan said. "What are you doing here?"

"Looking for you," Invadiah said, staring at her son intently. It was enough to make him wish she were an erinyes again, and the worst he could expect was having his legs crushed. As a succubus, Invadiah had retained all her cleverness, all her cruelty, but had become more calculating still and more inclined to take the risky strike.

"Does His Majesty require a gift for a certain of his Chosen?" Her skin shivered as if it were trying to crawl away. Lorcan blinked and found himself facing his own face, his own form. "Do you need some assistance with her?" his voice asked. "Because I have quite a knack for such things nowadays."

"*No.*" Lorcan turned away, forcing himself not to shudder. "Warlocks and such things are *well* beneath you—you've made that abundantly clear." Remind her of his silly pastime, he thought, toying with a spiked chain hanging from a hook. Make her think this is about pride, about the things that had always disappointed her, when it came to Lorcan. Make her forget about Farideh. "Besides, if you manage to seduce my warlock, what does that possibly gain *you*?"

Invadiah's skin shivered, reformed into her normal face. There was still the shade of her erinyes-self there, the memory of her fierce visage. "You're right," she said. "I'm not interested in warlocks. I'm interested in the succubi."

The fine hairs on the back of Lorcan's neck stood on end. "I'll admit that's a surprise I couldn't have seen coming. Does this mean you're planning to settle into your form?"

Invadiah's dark eyes seemed as though they might sear their way through him. "Never. I'm interested in ending them."

"And what," Lorcan asked, plucking up a dagger shaped like a screaming pixie, "would *that* gain you?"

"You and I both know that there's more than what you see at first glance when it comes to the succubi and their loyalties," Invadiah said. "You and I both know that the attack on Stygia . . . let's say it obscures certain other facts. The Blood War's never just been about grinding demons into the dirt. It's as much about how our 'betters' try and trip each other up, try to advance up the hierarchy. A battle is a smokescreen to be used; a raid, a point to be won; an assassination, a sword to shove your enemy down on." She smiled, her pearly teeth edged with blood from some earlier meal. "And I wonder . . . does Asmodeus know all of that as well?"

"Does the god of sin know that his archdevils can't be trusted?" Lorcan said flatly. "Yes, I suspect he might have an inkling."

"Does he know where the Scepter of Alzrius lies?" Invadiah sang. "Does he know where it came from?"

Lorcan did not turn to consider the artifact, but he knew exactly where it was—a heavy, iron thing, more mace than ornament, lying in a case four shelves behind them, covered in cinnabar and gold leaf. "Why would he be interested in that?"

Invadiah shrugged, as if there were nothing so pleasurable as her only son's confusion. "The prize of a demon lord? There are plenty of reasons."

"Are you suggesting that Her Highness received the scepter from an unsavory source?"

"I'm suggesting, dear boy, that while she might have many reasons for you to hold onto it, few of them are in your favor." Invadiah smiled, like the crescent moon shining down on a deer in the field, showing the wolves the way to their prey. "Few of them seem to be in Her Highness's favor come to that."

He blinked. "You want me to broker your promotion."

"You are a clever child. What a fortunate mother I am after all."

Clever enough to know she might expect him to turn back to Glasya with the information her once-beloved general was trying to maneuver around her. Clever enough to know he would know to expect that much.

"I take it you mention the succubi for a reason."

"There were a lot of them in Stygia recently."

"In the attack on Prince Levistus's treasury?" Lorcan asked. Invadiah only shrugged, but the fact that the Scepter of Alzrius clearly worked the kind of fiery magics that would be very useful in melting a certain archdevil's glacier-prison lay clear in the words she didn't say. Was there any other in all the planes who would prize such a trophy as dearly as Prince Levistus?

"Those were Abyssal succubi, as I recall," Lorcan said, almost pleaded.

"Can we ever be sure of that?" Invadiah asked.

"Come to that, can we be sure of you?"

Invadiah's dark eyes seemed to deepen, until they held the heart of the void within them. "I am no succubus," she said, her sharp teeth bared. "Or do you need to be reminded, whelp?"

Invadiah's face seemed to shiver again, but the shivering extended to the rest of the treasury. Her words stretched away into a dull drone as the building dissolved around Lorcan into a deep darkness that stretched in every conceivable direction. He fell, farther than should have been possible, and an eternity later, his feet struck a stone floor. Impact shuddered up his frame, but he kept his feet, and he thanked his luck for that. He straightened—a bedroom, a stone-walled bedroom, with a balcony opening off the farther wall.

Beyond the silvery circle of runes, Havilar kneeled beside Zoonie, the great shaggy beast watching him with eyes like burning coals. On its left, Brin stood, tensed as if there were a damned thing Lorcan could do from within the circle of runes, or a damned thing Brin might do if Lorcan got out.

Farideh sat between them, behind the hellhound, her ritual book closed on her lap. Watching Lorcan with careful indifference. His gaze swept her face—the tight corners of her lovely mouth, the flare of her nostrils, the slight tension along her silvered eye. She was furious. She didn't want him here. His pulse raced once more.

"Well met, darling," he said softly. She turned away.

"We've agreed she's not talking to you," Havilar announced. "I'm the one who has a problem."

If she doesn't want to be here, why is she still here? he nearly asked. He made himself consider Havilar instead—careful, careful. You've won nothing yet. "And you couldn't send an imp again?"

"Because it's an emergency and I couldn't risk you just swatting one," Havilar said. "There's another demon in the catacombs. It may or may not be because a war wizard summoned it."

There was nowhere on any plane Lorcan was less prepared to be—but he pressed that thought down. Farideh couldn't know that. Everything would be worse if she knew that, and nothing would go back to the way it was supposed to be. Be clever, he told himself. Be everything your blood demands. "I told you to stay clear of the catacombs. That's your wisest course of action."

"It's killing people," Havilar said. "So no. I need to track it. But it also makes me throw up a lot more than the dretch. I think it's bigger."

"Not necessarily." Lorcan turned to Brin, letting his gaze slide past Farideh as he did—she was watching him once more. "So you came along? What happened? Did your Forest Kingdom get razed to the ground? Scattering war wizards?"

"She says you said it would get easier," Brin replied. "That she could be inured to it."

Lorcan's wings twitched. "I said it was possible. I said you could get used to most everything, given a chance." Farideh looked at the ground again, and he made himself smile. "So what is it you want? A parade of dretches to practice on? I don't think I'm the devil you want."

Farideh scoffed and rolled her eyes. Havilar glared back at her, and then at Lorcan. "Look," she said to Lorcan, "don't pretend that you don't know a way to do this. Maybe you can get little demons, maybe not. Maybe you can get things that have the same effect. Maybe you know some spells that do the same thing. You're in almost as much trouble as we are if we get eaten by a demon or something. So before you throw up your hands, *think*."

Lorcan didn't have to think. The answer rose up in his thoughts as swiftly as his first protestations—the Scepter of Alzrius. Forged in the depths of the Abyss by the hands of powerful demons, it would certainly give off enough of their taint to trigger whatever gift Asmodeus had laid on Havilar.

And then it wouldn't be sitting in his treasury, a beacon of guilt.

Nor would *he* need to be in Malbolge—the more time he could spend on Toril, the fewer opportunities would arise for Invadiah or Glasya or Asmodeus to make an easy sacrifice of him. Assuming, Lorcan thought as he considered Farideh, you spin this right.

"What is it you're planning on doing with such a solution?" he asked.

Havilar made a face. "What do you *think*?"

"I think if you're going to go off hunting a demon, you're asking for a lot more of my time than you might realize. I *will* be in a great deal of trouble if you get eaten by a demon after all. It might suit my needs, come to that, to simply reuse Sairché's stasis cage."

Zoonie's sudden growl thrummed through the stone-walled room. "Oh, try it," Havilar said.

"I didn't say I was going to do that," Lorcan said. "I said it fulfilled my needs better than handing you an endless sack of dretches and leaving." He paused, ordered his thoughts. "I could help," he allowed. "I have access to Abyssal artifacts. They'll likely do what you're asking. But it isn't simply a matter of handing over a soul gem and seeing what happens—you wouldn't have managed with the glaive if someone had just tossed you the weapon and left, would you?"

Both twins stiffened and Farideh's cheeks burned scarlet, even though she was still studying the floor. Lorcan tucked that away for another time.

"This is what I do, isn't it? Teach the needy how to manage strange magic?" He turned to Havilar before her sister could react. "And you will find a need for it, from the sound of things. Your wayward war wizard and his demon army."

Havilar shook her head. "Ilstan's locked up. And he might not be the one who summoned it."

"I wouldn't clear him too quickly," Brin said. "Stlarning bastard."

Lorcan frowned. "Who is this person?"

"The war wizard who wants me dead," Farideh replied. "Keep up."

The casual cruelty in her response startled him, almost as much as the revelation of another enemy, another danger. It must have shown—her expression held, but two soft spots of color burned on her cheeks.

"Well that," he said, "appeals to my concerns much more strongly. If you want my help, it's yours. For a price."

Havilar narrowed her eyes. "What price?"

"I want a moment alone. With you," Lorcan said to Farideh. Her eyes tightened. "No."

"Darling, you're angry and that's fair. But do you think you can postpone this forever? We have a pact, you're going to have to talk to me at some juncture, I say it's now. I'm still in the circle," he pointed out. "You're holding all the cards here—all you have to do is walk away when you're through." He smiled in that way that had always made her listen before.

"Except, then you'll claim it's not enough to earn your help." She bit her lip as if she were holding in a stream of curses. "Fine. Don't go far," she said to Havilar.

"We'll be right outside," Havilar promised. She glared at Lorcan. "With my hellhound."

Careful, Lorcan told himself as Havilar, Brin, and the hellhound filed from the room. Careful—you only get one more shot at this. The wrong word, the wrong gesture, and everything would fall to pieces. He'd be left grasping at what he could salvage, not claiming what he wanted.

Farideh didn't look at him, and he found himself thinking of that first time he'd been called down into a circle for her, of the chilly barn in the mountains and the innocent, wide-eyed tiefling girl who couldn't stop staring at him.

She was a long way from being that girl. And being devilish again seemed the fastest way to dig his own grave. You don't have to go about it that way, he thought.

"You look well," Lorcan said when the door closed. Farideh said nothing and his pulse started racing. "I suppose I owe you . . . an apology," he went on, trying for contrite. It didn't suit him. "I ought to have told you Asmodeus was pressuring me to keep you safe, that Glasya was watching too closely. That I was scared something would happen to you if you left Suzail. I shouldn't have taken matters into my own hands, and I shouldn't have given you shaking fever."

"Why?" Farideh said. "Because you got caught?"

He didn't speak for a long moment. Of course—but not just that. "Because you're not just my warlock, and I can't treat you like you are, whatever my reasons." She looked up at him. Good—a step. A toehold.

"I won't pretend I was entirely unhappy with the results," he said. "I got to have you to myself." She looked away again, and he wondered if she was remembering Suzail, and all those times he had her to himself.

Or if she were following the thread right to the end—if he hadn't infected her, Dahl would have remained an annoying fellow she crossed paths with occasionally.

She blushed and met his eyes as if it was difficult. "I got to see who you really were."

"As if you didn't know," he said. Then, a gamble: "How is Dahl?"

"I don't want to talk about him."

He clucked his tongue. "Has the brightbird's plumage dulled already?"

"Don't pretend that you don't know exactly where he is and how much he's talked to me."

"To be honest I have very little interest in Dahl. I only ask for your sake." The tips of his wings flicked uneasily and he fought to still them. He might prefer Invadiah's threats to this delicate battle. Careful, careful. "Did he figure out you were only using him? Is that it?"

A deep blush burned up Farideh's neck. "What is that supposed to mean?"

Lorcan shrugged, as if it made no difference to him. It didn't—it couldn't. It was only the most likely truth, its bones laid bare after much study. He told himself that over and over.

"We fight and you suddenly find yourself unable to resist whatever Dahl has that passes for charm?" Lorcan said. "*Immediately*, you throw yourself into his arms. Let's be precise: did you even wait a whole day before you're whispering sweet nothings to each other and finding whatever horizontal surface is available? That's rash. That's the action of an incautious, desperate woman. Not you.

"It seems far more likely that you were angry with me— angry enough to want to twist the knife, to make sure I hurt for wronging you. Maybe you're a little fond of him. He's not horribly malformed or anything—I'm sure it wasn't entirely unpleasant. But if you're asking me to believe you fell hopelessly in love with the man you once told me you'd rather been taken to the Nine Hells than be bound to, you'll forgive me if I'm a little skeptical."

She stared at him, horrified. "You didn't tell him that, did you?"

"He'll figure it out eventually," Lorcan said carelessly. "Probably—without you, he's a bit thickheaded."

The edges of Farideh's frame blurred with the edge of shadows, the kiss of gathering flames. Careful, he told himself. Careful.

"Do you want to see him?" he asked, in the most offhanded way he could.

The shadows fled. The flames cooled. She stared at him, lovely mouth agape as if she couldn't imagine how to respond. "Yes," she said hesitantly. "What's the catch?"

"Only that you'll have to come into the circle," Lorcan said. "And that I'm not taking you to him—I have no interest in making myself a target for a bunch of skittish shepherds and backwater bumpkins, or in making Dahl happy."

She stared at him, and there was the shadow of that wide-eyed girl who just wanted whatever answers he could give her. "What will you do?"

"Pour a little water in the basin," he said. "I'll scry him for you. Because I do care. I want you to be happy, darling. I want things to be peaceful between us again. It did hurt," he added. "If it matters."

Farideh hesitated, her eyes flicking over his face as if she could find a crack, a secret danger. But there would be none—there was no trick. Only the knowledge that this would bring her no comfort when it came to Dahl. Only questions.

He hoped.

Farideh went to the table and filled the stone basin, stepping across the line of powdery runes with care. For a moment, she was near enough to touch, and Lorcan considered drawing her to him, letting the basin fall and reminding her of all the pleasures she'd forsaken.

But she set the basin on the floor and dropped down beside it, and Lorcan reminded himself he'd have to be patient. Much as every part of him screamed for action.

"Well?" She looked up at him, her eyes shadowed.

"Have you been sleeping?" Lorcan said, kneeling beside her as he twisted one of the rings he wore around his neck onto his index finger.

"No." But she didn't elaborate.

The ring opened a dimensional pocket, from which Lorcan withdrew a few components and a book of spells. Scrying over water was a nuisance, but a few scatterings of burnt petals, a dusting of dried blood, the murmured words of Infernal, and the image of Dahl rose up clear enough to be identified, if not as crisp as a mirror would have managed.

The Harper sat on the deck of a ship from the look of things, a seafaring vessel, and Lorcan's hands curled into fists against his lap. He wouldn't be so stupid as to come here. He couldn't possibly be. He sneaked a look at Farideh's face.

She looked more surprised than joyful. Her eyes were on the shape of a woman sitting beside Dahl, leaning a bit too close for comfort. Dahl wasn't moving away from her.

"What are they saying?" Farideh asked, her voice a little tight.

"I don't know," Lorcan said. "I'd need a mirror for that." He looked at the woman too—familiar, and appealing in a reckless kind of way. "Who's that?"

"Mira. She's one of his agents."

And more, Lorcan thought. There was no denying the familiarity in the way Mira leaned in to speak to Dahl, the flirtatiousness in her smirk, the fact that Dahl didn't shift away, but smiled back. If they weren't lovers, they had been—and right now, that was all that mattered. Lorcan fought his own smile.

"Well he's clearly sailing *someplace*. Where else has he to go but to find you?" Lorcan considered the image. "Maybe Mira needed him."

"Don't," Farideh said. She stood. "I do love him. It doesn't matter what you think."

"I'd never suggest it did. But . . ." He spread his hands as if the answer lay between them. "Darling, we are what we are."

Farideh gave a sharp laugh. "A devil who speaks in half-truths and plays me like a pawn?"

"Better than the farm boy who hardly thinks you count as a person."

"That's not true."

"But you can't pretend it was never true. Are you really certain anything has changed from Waterdeep?"

She shook her head, jaw tight, as though it would keep the sharp words from forming in her mouth. "You're getting sloppy."

"Because who can say that anything's changed from that winter day?" Lorcan said. His eyes dropped to the amulet of Selûne Farideh wore around her neck. "That's ignoring quite a lot of things. I was serious when I said you and I weren't meant to break on something as trivial as this."

"There is no you and I!" The rage in her seemed incandescent, ready to explode for a moment. And then she turned on her heel. "Clap your hands three times if you want it to send you home," she called back as she stormed out. "Otherwise Havi will be here in a breath."

"Darling, wait!" he shouted. But she was already gone. "Shit and *ashes*!" He kicked the basin of water over. You can fix this, Lorcan told himself, even though he'd said it so many times he was losing count. You *have* to fix it, he thought, remembering Asmodeus's words.

He clapped his hands, triggering the spell nestled in the binding circle's magic. Another drop through eternity and he landed once more in the treasury. Invadiah was nowhere in sight as he scaled the winding staircase up to the room that held the scrying mirror. Finding the space empty, he coaxed the sinew locks across the door before stirring the surface of the mirror, bringing up the image of Dahl aboard the ship, now scribbling a note against the boards.

The terms of their agreement were simple and they should have proved more than enough. Dahl could not speak to Farideh without losing all claim to his own soul, in exchange for speedy passage to the Dalelands. The distance would surely be enough, and the realization that there were less complicated women out there for Dahl to choose might make Farideh give up whatever hope she was harboring.

Lorcan liked that less than just convincing her to come back to him. There were pieces he couldn't control, choices that weren't his to make, and the thought of being what Farideh settled for rankled him. He watched Dahl consider his words. If you weren't a devil, Lorcan thought, ignoring your promise would mean nothing. He could open the portal to wherever that ship sailed, step out, and cut Dahl's throat before the Harper realized what was happening. All the risk would be gone, and it would only be a matter of time before Farideh gave up hope. If he weren't a devil.

You have never been devil enough, Lorcan thought. Why claim that mantle now?

He took hold of the mirror's wrought-iron frame, staring into its depths and this hated foe. There's an answer, he told himself. There's always an answer, if you're clever enough and willful enough. That was what being a devil meant, after all—outwitting your rivals, overcoming the obstacles they threw you, avoiding the fallout. He thought of Invadiah's threats, the twisting narrative of the Blood War: A battle is a smokescreen. A raid, a point to be won. An assassination a sword to shove your enemy down on.

Lorcan smiled to himself. Perfect. He stepped away from the mirror, letting the image persist for anyone to see.

For—to name one—his vicious sister to see when she invariably stepped out of the portal again. Sairché would hardly be able to resist such a prize, and Lorcan would have hurt Dahl not at all.

• • •

WHEN THE BOAT nudged into the landing at the source of the Fire River two days later, Dahl was already dressed and waiting, waiting for the *clomp-clomp* of Zhentarim boots to rattle overhead. Last leg, he thought. Last chance to gather information before things get tricky.

He eased his way up the stairs, keeping his eyes on the deck above. They weren't after portal magic. They weren't secretly devout Deneirrath. What were they searching for?

Above, the sailors called back and forth from the boat to the shore, and over them, Xulfaril barked orders. Sessaca already stood on the deck, wrapped in her shawl. She spared him a dagger-eyed glance as he climbed onto the boards. Dahl tapped a finger to his lips. Everyone would be too busy disembarking to worry about Dahl—he hoped. Sessaca raised an eyebrow, but said nothing.

He stumbled, aiming for bleary, past a Zhentarim pissing over the side of the boat, as though he meant to make his own water on the farther side, but instead he darted to the left. Toward Xulfaril's cabin.

She couldn't take everything—a mountain climb and whatever they expected to bring back besides—but she wouldn't leave anything too precious either. Dahl slipped inside and shut the door behind him. The room had been picked over, nearly stripped. A chest, unlocked, sat at the foot of the bed. He flipped it open—nothing but clothes and components—and turned the bed. Nothing. He swept the bureau's drawers.

A broken ear pick. A dried-out bottle of ink. A burnt match.

A torn piece of parchment, caught by a splinter against the headspace. Just the size for a flying snake to carry, he thought as he fished it out.

I will send Grathson, the message read, before breaking off. The lines that followed gave a jagged hint at what the full message might have said.

Don't engage without
know too well what sort of threats we might be de
Apprise us of what your historian finds
we'll continue to press from the eastern

The rest was missing, thrown away or tucked into Xulfaril's belongings. Dahl slipped the scrap back under the splinter and left the room, strolling back toward Sessaca. *Threats*—A godsbedamned war of mercenaries? he wondered. A monstrous uprising in the forests of the Earthfasts? What was to the east of the Master's Library?

Doesn't matter. Up the mountains, find the library, get home, he thought. Get out before anything Grathson's here to do comes into play.

Get your hands on the portal spells, he amended. Or books about breaking deals with devils. Assuming anything of the sort existed . . .

He wondered if Farideh were making the same sort of half-managed plans, scrabbling for bits of magic that might reunite them. If she'd puzzled out the reasons that he hadn't responded to her sending. She could be awfully clever, awfully single-minded, given the right problem . . .

Or she might just assume you ran off, he thought. There was plenty to point her that way, even assuming Lorcan wasn't manipulating things.

"I just think it's safer this way," he'd said. What an idiot, he thought.

Up the mountains, he told himself. Find the library. Get back to her.

Sessaca watched the Zhentarim below, very carefully ignoring Dahl until he stood beside her. " 'Bout time," she said, her breath a cloud on the cold morning air. She pointed her chin at the Zhentarim, at Grathson in their midst. "You take any longer someone was bound to notice."

"Worth the risk," Dahl said.

"Order is we stay on the boat and out of the way until they get supplies off and sorted. But that won't take long."

Dahl surveyed the river mouth, the mountains beyond. Here, the Earthfast Mountains met the Earthspurs, two ranges narrowing around the river, like fingers pinching a thread. The dusty green of scrubby trees ran down the foothills, down onto the riverbanks.

"Where is the library?" he asked.

"Way up there." Sessaca inhaled the crisp, piney air deeply, and sighed. "Never thought I'd smell that again," she said. "Lot of memories in this place."

"Nothing like running weapons in the wilds, huh?" Dahl said a little sourly.

"It wasn't *just* weapons. That would have been a waste of everyone's time." Sessaca wrapped her shawl a little closer. "You still sulking about not knowing the secret?"

"No," Dahl said, which was mostly true. He never liked being the last to know. But knowing is better than ignorance, he reminded himself. *I shall fear no deception, but the truth remains.*

"Liar," Sessaca said.

"Thost and Bodhar didn't know," Dahl said quietly. "Does Ma? Did Da?"

"Heavens, no!" Sessaca said. "Why, by every Watching God, would I have told Barron? That's not the kind of thing you tell your children. Nor your grandchildren, come to it."

"What about Grandda?" Dahl shook his head. "Or was he smuggling poisons into Myth Drannor, pretending to be just a simple farmer too?"

"Lamhail was *never* simple," Sessaca said. The river slapped the boat's side, and for a long moment there was only that and the thud of feet on the boards. Dahl looked over at Xulfaril standing beside the gangplank, seeming to watch her agents, but if she weren't listening to every word Sessaca and Dahl spoke, he'd declare himself the bloody Chosen of Dead Deneir. Sessaca followed his gaze to the wizard. Made a dissatisfied little sound in the back of her throat.

"Harrowdale town," Sessaca said suddenly. "That's what we called New Velar in those days."

Dahl frowned at her. "What?"

"I didn't run just weapons," Sessaca said, as if he weren't listening. "Trade goods filled the gaps, covered my tracks. Little packages I didn't ask about, but paid right. Messages sometimes. I had a shipment of Tsurlagolan copper that I took to Harrowdale Town, because it seemed like a good place to lie low while I waited for orders. Sweet little town." She looked back at Dahl, smiling in a way that managed to be both fond and wily. "Sweet boy too."

"When my orders sent me west, that sweet boy insisted on accompanying me." She rolled her eyes. "As if I'd never heard that before. I kept my blades at hand, my boots buckled, my gold at my throat, but"—she shook her head, smiling to herself—"that sweet boy wasn't an act. Never laid a hand on me or my gold. Even let me stay with his family, on their little farm. And everyone was so kind and friendly. So when I came back through, I stopped again. And again. Eventually, Chauntea had her way and I turned out pregnant. When I realized, I decided to go back to that little farmhouse and try settling down. That's how it happened."

"So you got trapped on the farm," Dahl said. For all his grandmother's lies bothered him, for all her allegiances to the Black Network sat uneasy, there was no denying how swiftly the walls of a Harran life had come down on the Viper of the Earthfasts from the sound of things. He could imagine it—had imagined it. The farm wasn't where he belonged, he felt surer than ever before, and how could it have been where Sessaca Peredur belonged when she stood on the Fire River's banks and longed for the piney air? He felt a strange guilt, as if it were his fault for being born to the son who had locked her down.

"Who said trapped?" Sessaca demanded.

"What were you going to do? Leave Da behind in swaddling? You might be a blackguard, but you keep your kin close."

"The baby wasn't your da," Sessaca said. "Lost that one. So I could have escaped if I was trapped, and never mind 'kin.'

But . . . things change. People change. I loved your Grandda. I loved that farm. I wanted that life."

"But you missed this one," Dahl pointed out.

"They're not mutually exclusive," his grandmother said. "I would have thought you of all people would know that." She sighed again. "Why in the sodden Hells would anyone smuggle poisons to Myth Drannor? That's the only example you could come up with?"

"Why would a Zhentarim agent know the location of a dead god's holiest sanctum?" Dahl returned. "I clearly don't understand how you do things."

She waved him off. "I suspect you know better than you'll let on, and that's a fact. Your monster-girl send a letter back?"

Dahl watched Xulfaril gesturing at the Zhentarim below. "It's only been three days."

"Well she'd best pick up her feet, or whatever she has," Sessaca said. "I doubt very much that snake can make it down into the Master's Library."

Dahl's chest tightened. "We'll see, won't we."

Sessaca frowned at Xulfaril. "She make you want to settle down, this girl?"

"She's not the settling sort," he said. "But she's not simple either."

"And she's not a dragonborn, thank the gods. So why's she not with you?"

Dahl hesitated. "I left her behind."

"That seem like a wise decision?"

"No," he said. "It seems like the stupidest decision I've ever made."

"Well, we've established you're not too imaginative." Sessaca sniffed. "Why'd you leave her?"

"I asked her to come, because I was—I am that sure of her, but then . . . things happened. I didn't think she'd fit, and I asked her to stay behind. And by the time I realized I was being an idiot, that I'd been thoughtless . . . I found out about the Shadovar and I had to go before I could convince her to come with me."

He blew out a breath. Watched Xulfaril pretend to study Mira coming up the stairs from belowdecks, arms laden with maps. "I know," he said. "I'm an idiot."

Sessaca sniffed. "You're not an idiot, Dahl. You just think too fast. You don't slow down and ask yourself if you're considering all the pieces. It'll get you into trouble, and right here, it has. You'll figure it out."

Dahl considered his grandmother. It was the closest thing to a compliment she'd spoken in a long, long while. "Yes. Well . . . Thank you. That . . . means a lot."

Xulfaril folded her arms over her chest and crossed down the gangplank after Mira. "Gods be damned," Sessaca murmured. "I thought she'd never leave. Can put up with a lot of jabber, that one. Any idea what she was hoping to hear?"

Dahl shook his head. "Directions to the Master's Library?"

"Fat lot of good it'll do her. If it were as easy as that, nobody would be carting me out here. We're all going to have to pray I remember the way by landmarks."

The peaks of the Earthfasts blocked the rising sun, foreboding and mysterious. "How'd you find this place anyway?"

"I dreamed it," Sessaca said. "A path up the mountains, a vein of silvery metal. A voice singing over and over. Let's just say, when you see a thing you dream about like that, you have to know it wasn't *just* a dream. I was expecting treasure. Some cursed tomb or other."

Dahl frowned. "What were they singing?"

"I have no idea," Sessaca said. "I can't recall a note of it. Couldn't as soon as I walked into the place, come to think of it. Not natural," she added.

Who sent the dream? Dahl wondered. But he knew well enough to be sure it wasn't a question his grandmother cared about the answer to. The ghost of Deneir, the hand of Oghma, some wicked god hoping to entice a Zhentarim agent to ransack their dead enemy's sanctum—it wouldn't matter to Sessaca the way it mattered to Dahl. "Do you think that's what they're looking for?" Dahl asked instead. "Treasure?" Grathson's folks fought monsters, collected treasure. That could be it.

Sessaca snorted. "No. There's nothing like that up there. But if it's not old books . . ." She wrapped her shawl a little closer. "Let's hope its old books."

• • •

SHE WOULD NEVER forget the cold, the way the mud froze between her cloven hooves in the winter, the way it felt trying to pry a rock out from under the ice. Alyona wore boots after the winter of the Year of the Helm, and it looked ridiculous the way she toddled around in them, but she didn't have the same troubles with the ice between her claws. She remembered refusing to do any such thing. "We're not human," she'd say. "That doesn't mean you need to suffer," Alyona would answer, but then she was always one to look on the bright side, even when they were trapped in the dark—

"Lady, come back." The cambion's hissed voice interrupted Bryseis Kakistos's drifting thoughts. "Are you even there?"

Bryseis Kakistos shook free the thoughts of the past. Drew her attention back to the freezing room they stood in, to the wizard lying dead at the feet of a trio of erinyes. Hideous things, she thought. This was what Sairché's mother had looked like when Caisys came to her.

You cannot find it? she asked.

"Nowhere we can see," Sairché replied. Despite the thick, silver fur cape draped over her shoulders, the cambion shivered.

Look harder.

"If it's hidden beyond all the searching we've done so far, I doubt we'll find it without the man himself. And resurrection is beyond my talents and yours."

Bryseis Kakistos looked down at the tiefling man lying supine on the floor, his dark robes splayed out, his white hair soaked in the blood of a score of injuries. Her grandson.

She couldn't recall his name anymore. *If anyone had my spells, it's him.*

No, she thought. Not the spells. Focus.

"Well by your argument, no one has that spell any longer," Sairché said. "And by your claims, there's no way to proceed without it."

You already know the answer, she said. *We should seek the Abyss.*

"Absolutely not," Sairché said. "I don't dirty my hands with demons."

But you'll dirty your hands with treason? I see.

"One of these gains me the favor of the archduchess. The other only gets me killed. Although, at this juncture I question the first assumption."

Are you planning to unmask me, little cambion?

"Get me what I need with less of this chicanery."

It was always on the table. Always a risk. They'd be your faithful servants, your close companions, until something better arose. Bryseis Kakistos considered the erinyes, all ignoring their cambion sister and picking through the wizard's belongings in a disinterested way. Always a risk—and Bryseis Kakistos did not enter into plans mindless of the risks. She had contingencies. Always.

My gem, she said. *Can you find that at least?*

Sairché cut her eyes to one of the erinyes, her skin bloodless and her eyes red. "Caudine, may I have it?" The erinyes tossed her a blue-gray gem, the size of a walnut, hung on a chain. "It's not active," Sairché murmured.

It wouldn't be—another memory that fled through her thoughts as if in the dark of her mind a door hung open. The soul sapphire contained no one, nothing, but it was meant to.

"And it's not very high quality," Sairché noted, examining the asterism that marked its smooth surface.

It's distinctive. She'd changed it, shaped it to her purposes. A door that hung open . . . The thought was gone as soon as it formed.

Get the pieces back, she told herself. *Get your memories. Everything will be clear again.*

Have them take the books, the ghost said. *He might have hidden it within one.*

"He might have hidden it anywhere by that argument."

Take the books, Bryseis Kakistos said again. *If they don't have the answer, we haven't exhausted our resources.*

Sairché hesitated, a moment of pique more than anything, then ordered the erinyes to gather up the books, to carry them back to Malbolge.

The scrying mirror scintillated as they entered the fingerbone tower, its surface still stirred by magic. Sairché studied it as the erinyes piled the books on the far side of the room. The image showed a group of mostly humans, traveling through snow-dusted mountains—centered on a man with dark hair and gray eyes.

"Put them on the table," Sairché said to her sisters.

Who is that? Bryseis Kakistos asked.

"One of Lorcan's little pawns, no doubt," Sairché squinted at the mirror, then let out a short laugh. "No, wait—that's the paladin Farideh spurned him over. Which means this is a very clumsy attempt to make me interested in taking care of that for him. Idiot. He's losing his touch."

Bryseis Kakistos peered at the dark-haired man climbing the mountain slope. A paladin, she thought, with no god's mark upon him. A paladin who might challenge Caisys's spoiled son for her great-granddaughter. *Where is he?*

"I have no idea," Sairché said. "Lorcan made a deal with him and dumped him in the hinterlands."

What sort of a deal?

"Likely something to get him away from the warlock," Sairché said. "Likely something with a piss-ton of loopholes. He made that deal too fast."

Find out.

Sairché didn't move. "Is this about your replacement?"

Find out.

"In due time," Sairché said. "I would hate to leap too many steps forward and find ourselves on unsteady ground."

Bryseis Kakistos felt not the slightest bit of hesitation as she shoved Sairché aside, trapping her in the darkness of her own sleeping mind. In control of the body once more, Bryseis Kakistos rolled the cambion's shoulders and stretched her neck.

The erinyes loitered by the table, speaking to each other in low, sneering tones. The books were a waste, clearly—whatever their baby sister was up to was a waste. The flimsy steel of those who will never rise above their rank, Bryseis Kakistos thought. Jabbing at their betters and pretending they have the *real* power.

"One of you," she said, mimicking Sairché's imperious tone, "I need a copy of an agreement. Lorcan's deal with the paladin." She turned from them, sure that one would take the initiative, that waiting to see which it was would only embolden them. Unlike Sairché, she'd had plenty of experience corralling willful underlings. Indeed, a moment later, the door opened and closed once more.

Time for the search.

Bryseis went to the table, feeling Sairché's silver robes drag across the wooden floor behind her, and touched the bindings of the books. *The Road to the Abyss. The Lords of Madness. The Reign of the Demon Prince.* Know your enemy, she thought. *Summoning the Demon Lords . . .*

She'd held this book before—this same book, it was hers, from long ago, stolen from another wizard, another fool who'd thought she was something to use and discard, a puzzle to unlock. *Summoning the Demon Lords.* He'd thought to use her blood, to hook the sire who'd left his mark on her and her line. "Bisera, come on!" Alyona had hissed. Her hands were shaking . . . slick with blood, as she shoved the book beneath her shift.

"Little sister," the nearest erinyes growled. "How long—"

"Wait outside, if you please," Bryseis Kakistos said with Sairché's tongue as she turned through the familiar pages, fitting together a much more suitable plan.

• • •

EVENTUALLY, OTHERS WOULD come.

This was the only thought in Louc's head, had been the only thought for days or months or years. He'd always been here, hadn't he? In the mouth of the Underdark, at the feet of the man made of night. Other times, other places slithered through his mind, the greasy ghosts of dreams.

Eventually, others would come. More Zhentarim looking for their lost outpost, demanding to know what had closed off communications. They would find their way down into the darkness, down into the reach of the man made of night.

Who will they send? The man made of night sifted through Louc's thoughts, over and over, seeking every possible answer. At first, Louc had fought it, though now he couldn't recall why. The man made of night was a prince above them all. He would triumph, he could not help but triumph, and the world would bend itself before him. Now Louc told him everything he could, knowing that a scrap of that power could be his too, if only he pleased the man made of night.

"Xulfaril, surely," Louc told him, feeling half in a dream. "The wizard bitch. She runs what we trade up to the surface—all the dark things that darker things collect from the Underdark. If we don't answer, she'll come, thinking to punish us. She'll bring others, though. Muscle and blades. They'll expect drow or maybe duergar. They won't expect you."

Good, the man made of night said. *They'll make powerful tools.* He wasn't angry any longer—not with the Zhentarim. But with the one who had brought him here from his kingdom far away? Utter fury. The rage of a beast pushed from its rightful place atop the pecking order. The terrible, terrible moment before the pretender becomes dethroned.

A pity none of them will know how my current plans fare, the man made of night said, stroking Louc's hair. *I do not like leaving such things to their own rhythm.* Louc could no longer tell which of the bodies around them were locked in passion and which were locked in battle. Gore smeared everything. But there was only the sensation of the man made of night's fingers raking his scalp, the thin trickle of blood running down his forehead.

Whoever brought me here will lament the day they tried to play Graz'zt, the true *Prince of Demons, as a pawn.* And in his heart of heart's Louc knew it was so.

PART II

YRJIXTILEX
THE MANY ESHAM-ANA

. . .

Let us sing of one who inspired strength and kinship in our blood, of Esham-Ana Who-Would-Be-Yrjixtilex. Let us sing of the fall of the Vizier of Broken Thorns and the rise of Yrjixtilex.

While the titans slumbered and the ice lay thick on their prisons, a mine was dug at the edge of Skelkor, kingdom of the Foul Empress, and our ancestors were imprisoned there to dig ore from the mountains beneath the Dawn Titans. For long years, we toiled and died under the watch of the Foul Empress and her followers, and our suffering was great.

Esham-Ana Who-Would-Be-Yrjixtilex sought to lessen that suffering. Set as a guard, he would slip out in the night, to hunt and gather the mountains' bounty to feed the many Who-Would-Be-Yrjixtilex. The elders cautioned him, for though the wilds' plenty seemed endless, the Foul Empress was greedy and her grip like the core of the ice, cold and unbreakable. But Esham-Ana knew that the rations fed to the miners would never sustain them.

One spring, at last, the Foul Empress's regard fell upon her miners, who no longer died and needed renewing, and from there to her mountain frontiers, thinned of deer and plucked of its first fruits.

"Find me the thief," she said. "And bring me its head."

While many of her underlings flew deep into the forest with blood in their thoughts, the Vizier of Broken Thorns, Ororonymilith, a copper dragon as canny as any of his kind, was clever. He chose one of our own, a slave called Shamash, who knew his place and knew what he would lose if he defied the Foul Empress. With threats in place, the Vizier left him where he was sure the thief would find him.

Night fell and Esham-Ana, carrying a pair of does, came upon Shamash. Seeing the lost slave, Esham-Ana cut a haunch from the deer, and built a fire. "I am Esham-Ana," he said, not suspecting a trap. "I will come again tomorrow." And though Shamash's heart was heavy, Ororonymilith had the name from him by morning, and Shamash died without a clan.

Ororonymilith ordered the miners driven to the surface, too hurried to even drop their picks. "Which of you is Esham-Ana?" the copper dragon demanded. "Thief and betrayer of the Empress."

Esham-Ana Who-Would-Be-Yrjixtilex knew the steel-edge of fear, for what could he do but give in to the will of the Foul Empress and spare the rest of the slaves of the mine? He stepped forward to accept his fate, but as he did, he heard a clear voice cry out: "I am Esham-Ana!"

"No," called another. "I am Esham-Ana!"

"I am Esham-Ana!"

"I am Esham-Ana!" Ororonymilith's great head swung over the crowd, trying to single out which of the slaves before him was the thief his mistress demanded. But there were too many. Male and female, young and old. None would let he who sustained them suffer in their place—all were Esham-Ana.

And in every Esham-Ana's hands, a pickaxe.

Ororonymilith realized what all the tyrants knew eventually: Where they are one, we are many. His skull was the first to hang over Yrjixtilex's clan, cut from his loathsome body by the Many Esham-Ana, First of Yrjixtilex.

. . .

10

21 Nightal, the Year of the Nether Mountain Scrolls (1486 DR)
Djerad Thymar, Tymanther

FARIDEH DREAMS OF ARUSH VAYEM AGAIN, THE SNOW THICK AROUND her ankles. She calls for Dahl—he must be here somewhere—but she only hears the voices of her neighbors calling out, laughing, singing. She moves from house to house, fighting through the drifting snow, looking for Dahl.

"Let me help," says a voice. Arjhani walks beside her, dressed for a long-ago summer and seemingly unaware of the snow. He smiles fondly at Farideh and her sudden fury sends flames racing over her skin. The hungry damned burst from the ground, tearing Arjhani apart before she can even consider what it is she's unleashed.

"Why did you do that?" Farideh turns and finds Havilar, eleven years old, still small and scrawny, two summers before she and Farideh grew, like weeds after the first spring rain. The glaive in her hands is built of a stripped sapling, the first incarnation of her beloved blade. "Now he's gone. Why did you do that?"

"Why did you?" Lorcan echoes. He stands in Arjhani's place, amid the melting snow. A smile plays on his mouth, and she cannot speak, cannot tell Havilar what a danger Arjhani is, how he will leave, how he will never come back—

"What is the secret?" Havilar demands. "One of us knows how to defeat him — is it you?"

Farideh clutches her head. "This is a dream."

"Clever girl," Lorcan says. He tilts his chin. "Do you know who thinks you can defeat me?"

"Hey." A hand grabs Farideh's shoulder. Dahl stands beside her, his gray eyes blazing, nearly silver. He doesn't look at Havilar or Lorcan, only Farideh, and the fury melts off her like the snow under Arjhani's feet. He reaches out and fishes the amulet of Selûne out of her collar. "I'm still here," he says.

Farideh searches his face, as if she's memorizing it. "I can't find you." She looks over at the god in the cambion's skin, fearful suddenly that he'll hurt Dahl.

"Is that what you really want?" the god asks. "Another master? Another yoke?"

Yes. No. Farideh hardly knows what they're discussing anymore. She clutches the amulet of Selûne. "Don't hurt him."

Asmodeus blinks with Lorcan's eyes. The village is suddenly on fire, the cheerful voices screaming, and above them all Dahl whispers, "Remember—"

The sound of Dahl's voice extorting her to remember circled in Farideh's thoughts all morning long, chased by the scrying pool's image of him and Mira. He was fine, he was safe, she had worse things to worry about—but that only kindled a spark of anger in her. He was fine and she was worrying herself mad and still, he'd said *nothing*.

You don't know he's fine, she thought. You don't know he's not on some mission. You don't know he hasn't gone quiet to keep you safe.

But none of it felt right. None of it felt like Dahl as she knew him.

So maybe you don't really know him, a little voice in her thoughts said.

Havilar's hand suddenly closed over hers. "What did that pasty do to you?"

Farideh looked down at the mash of dough in her hands and flushed. "Sorry."

"It's not as if there's a shortage," Brin said. "Do you want another?"

Farideh took another pasty from the platter on the table, still heaped high with food. The young dragonborn who brought food to them from the kitchens seemed uncertain of how much three non–Vayemniri ate and erred on the side of too much. She set the pasty back down on her own plate, untouched. "Have you two . . ."

All three of them turned at the sound of Mehen entering, and Farideh's plans dissolved at once.

"Oh, broken planes!" Mehen spat. "Will you three stop staring?"

Farideh didn't dare make that promise. The jade plugs stretched the holes along Mehen's jaw tight. The tailored white shirt covering his arms, its cuffs and high collar embroidered in bright white Draconic runes. The new and polished breastplate, dragonscale in a dozen coppery shades. Only the falchion strapped to his back, its hilt still wrapped in white, remained a familiar touchstone—her father would never be without it.

"You look *pretty*," Havilar said, dissolving into giggles.

"It's nice," Farideh said. "You look . . . handsome." Younger, she thought, but didn't dare say. She reached up and straightened his collar, reading in the embroidered runes a lament for Verthisathurgiesh's loss. "Did she make this for you? Overnight?"

Mehen fussed with the collar anew. "It's . . . something the other lines in the clan do during mourning. Someone in Vandeth's line was apparently working on it the last few days." He grimaced. "Someone help me with this breastplate—it's too tight."

"You'll look right for Kepeshkmolik," Farideh said as Havilar went to the buckles.

"Or Kallan," Havilar teased.

"*Thrik*! There's nothing there."

Havilar giggled. "Oh, please. You could win him back."

"I cut him loose in the first place, so I doubt that. No—tighter than that." He scratched his piercings, and cursed as he knocked one of the plugs loose. "You have your plans?" he asked, popping it back into place.

Farideh hesitated. "Havi and Brin are going to track down Zaroshni and find out what she knows. I'll wait here for Kallan, and we'll go find the wizard that came with him, then look at the Shestandeliath tomb."

And then go see Ilstan about what he'd seen—and said. *You both hide the key*. He knew more than she'd realized, more than she did, perhaps, and more and more, Farideh felt certain that whatever was happening with Asmodeus, it wouldn't wait for this murder to be solved.

Mehen frowned. "You were going to leave the tombs until later."

"I know you wanted to leave that until later so you could do it. But you know perfectly well it's a bad idea to wait any longer, and you don't have much chance of sneaking down there, even if this . . . ceremony doesn't take long."

"They'll ask me to leave before it gets to that," Mehen said.

"What did you *do*?" Havilar demanded, yanking hard on the strap. "Telling your father off is not this interesting."

"It is to Vayemniri," Mehen said. "It doesn't matter—he's dead and I'm done." He stretched against the armor, swinging his arms. "Better. Many thanks. What about Lorcan?" he asked Farideh.

A little trill of nerves went through her. "Lorcan will be here later, when Havi and Brin get back."

"I'll stay close," Brin promised. He scratched Zoonie behind the ear. "We'll stay close."

"I can handle Lorcan," Havilar said scathingly.

Mehen scowled at his daughters. "You will *not* go after the demon alone."

"Of course not," Farideh said. "Don't be ridiculous. We're still gathering information—which is what you'll be doing too. Find out about the guard."

Mehen sighed and fidgeted with the cuffs of his shirt. "I'll do what I can." Then, "Are you three doing all right here? Is it tolerable at least?"

"I like it, demon aside," Havilar said. "The food's good. Nobody cares much about Zoonie. And the sparring yard is inside, which is really convenient."

"It's interesting," Brin said lightly.

Mehen looked at Farideh, his brow ridges shifting quizzically. She smiled back, pressing her anxieties down. Arjhani was still absent. Dahl wouldn't be any less silent somewhere else. Demons were likely the least of her foes. "It's fine for now."

Before Mehen could respond, someone knocked on the doorframe at the entrance to the common room. Kallan stood in the entry, armed and armored, white ribbons on his sword. His dark eyes flicked over Mehen. "Well met. Yrjixtilex sends its greetings and condolences."

"Doesn't he look nice?" Havilar sang. "Well met, Kallan. You get out all right?"

A smile curved the sellsword's mouth. "I had a little help, but yes. Whatever you said, it had the old uncles that came to fetch me impressed and quite nosy. I promise I stayed as coy as I could. So, many thanks for the sacrifice."

"The least I could do," Mehen said.

"You could improve on it," Havilar muttered.

"*Thrik*!" To Kallan, Mehen said, "Farideh's going to go with you to track down the wizard and look at the tomb." He gave Farideh a worried look. "And then you are coming back here."

Farideh exchanged a glance with Havilar. "That depends on what we find."

"You are not hunting this fiend down by yourselves."

"We already agreed to that," Farideh said. She looked at Kallan. "This is just gathering information."

"I'm sure she'll keep an eye on me," Kallan said in a friendly way. It made Farideh bristle, and she looked away, embarrassed at the reaction. Kallan was a pleasant enough fellow—but whatever had been between him and her father made Farideh's every interaction with him moorless and uncertain. Especially when Mehen kept flirting awkwardly. She made herself smile at him.

"Havi?" Mehen said sternly. "Say it."

She sighed. "I'm not hunting down a demon alone."

"Or with Brin," Mehen said. "That doesn't count. Nor does Zoonie."

Havilar gave him a withering look. "Since that thing makes me a puking mess, that would be like Brin or Zoonie hunting it alone, thanks. I'm not dumb."

"Anyway we're not taking Zoonie out this morning," Brin said. "We'll take her when we *do* hunt the demon," he added, scratching the hellhound behind the ear again, and Havilar's sour expression softened.

"She might have a chance of it," Kallan quipped. "It's a big *henish*."

Another of the younger dragonborn entered, carrying a tray of tea and cakes, followed by Anala in mourning white, her broadsword strapped to her back and her plumes in careful disarray. "Good morning to you all," she said, considering each of them in turn. She faltered on Kallan.

Kallan dipped his head. "Matriarch."

Anala smiled, but she eyed the sellsword as though he were trying to pawn a stolen jewel off on her. "Mehen, I see you're getting comfortable. Does your guest require anything?" The page set down the trays, and Mehen scowled.

"No one requires anything else from the kitchens, that much is certain. Who do you think you're feeding? A pregnant *karshoji* hill giant?"

The hatchling's shoulders hunched up to his ears, and he fled the room with a hasty bow to Anala. She sighed. "Come along. We can't be late."

Mehen tugged his breastplate down again. "Come *right* back here," he told his daughters as he followed the matriarch out.

"How many times can he say that," Havilar asked, "before he believes we heard him?"

"I think he could say it until we came back and he'd still be suspicious," Farideh said. "Good luck." Havilar and Brin headed out the door. Farideh looked back at Kallan.

"I'm, um . . . I'm not ready yet," she said. "I assumed you'd be later."

Kallan shrugged affably. "I'm in no particular rush. Got tea. It's fine. Take your time." He smiled again.

Farideh excused herself, shutting the door to her room behind her. She pulled her haversack out from under the bed, sorting out the components she needed from her stores, and the packages she'd bought earlier. Maybe a sending would go no farther than this room, maybe Dahl wouldn't be able to respond, but ever since she'd seen him in Lorcan's scrying, her every other plan seemed to hinge on facts she didn't have. Where was he going? What was he doing? What in all the planes should she do now?

Get more information, Farideh thought, kneeling on the ground and pouring metallic salts and dark powders in a careful pattern on the smooth stone floor. The magic surged, prickling along the pathways that linked her to the Nine Hells as it gathered, crossing the continent to Dahl. Farideh leaned over the faintly glowing lines, counting the words in her head before speaking.

"Looking for spells that could get me to you, but it's not easy here. Should I bother?" she whispered. "You're headed somewhere, not alone . . . I love you."

The air crackled, stirred only by Dahl's distant breath. A short sound, as if he had started to speak and caught himself. Farideh waited and waited and waited . . . until the magic collapsed. She let out the breath she hadn't realized she was holding and sat back on her heels.

He said he loves you, she reminded herself. He said he's fixing this.

The vision of him looking at Mira with dancing eyes. The memory of how obviously smitten with her he'd been so long ago. She hugged her hand to her chest.

If he left you, she thought . . .

It hurt, even testing that. You would be all right, she told herself. You'd survive.

But you wouldn't have to, a little part of her said. You have options.

Even thinking of using Asmodeus's offer that way made her stomach turn. She swept the spent components into a small pile. There were a thousand reasons he might not speak, and Mira hardly made the list. He might be somewhere he couldn't speak. He might be in danger. And here she was letting Lorcan prod her into jealousy?

She blew out a breath. Everyone doesn't need you to save them, she told herself. He saved himself fine for all those years. You will find Dahl again.

She made the bed, tidied the remnants of the spell, and folded her clothes. As she bent to pick up her haversack, her brand suddenly prickled. She clapped a hand over it as the corner of her room split with a gust of brimstone and ash, and Lorcan stepped out.

"Well met, darling," he said. "Is your sister ready?"

The sight of him made dread and lust bloom side by side in her heart, and she nearly cursed. You cannot be frustrated about Mira and look at Lorcan like that, she thought. "You're too early. Havilar's gone, she'll be back in a few hours."

Lorcan gave a rumpled sigh and flicked his wings. "You manage so many interesting things on this plane. You'd think you could work out how to make time flow properly."

"You could go back to your own plane."

Lorcan clucked his tongue. "Still upset? Shall I shower you in apologies? I had no idea that woman would be there and I shouldn't have tried to make you face it. It's not pleasant watching someone you care so much about throw themselves at someone else. What are you doing while your sister's being gone?"

"I'm busy," Farideh said.

"I could keep you company."

"I have company, thanks."

"Who?"

Farideh shook her head. "Come back later."

"Darling, whatever else is happening here, you know I can be helpful. Let me help." When she didn't answer, he said, "Why haven't you gone with Havilar?"

"Because I need to go up to the Adjudicators' enclave, and she shouldn't be up there," Farideh said.

"Hmm." Lorcan tilted his head. "Have you been sleeping all right? You look tired."

Farideh took the haversack off the floor and slid her ritual book inside. "I never sleep all right."

"Poor thing. What did you dream of?"

"I dreamt I set Arjhani on fire," Farideh said. "And then you set my village on fire."

"It deserved it," Lorcan said. Then, "Which one is Arjhani, again? The . . . midwife?"

"No," Farideh said. "Mehen's old lover. You should know that."

"Why? Have you mentioned him?"

"No," Farideh said. "But I don't think there's anyone I hate like I hate him." She yanked the haversack's drawstring shut. "That seems like something your master would have made sure you found out."

"So you loathe him, but you never mention him?" Lorcan said, not rising to the bait. "That's a powerful hate. What did he do?"

Farideh hesitated. "He showed up, made himself at home, and then when winter came, he left without telling anyone where he was going. He never came back."

"What a heartbreak," Lorcan said. "Being abandoned like that."

Like Dahl's done, he didn't say, but she heard it anyway.

You don't know a damned thing, she thought, slipping the bag over her shoulders. And the only way you have to find out is Asmodeus's offer. Take that and you'll have whatever you want. At a cost you don't dare to pay.

Farideh rubbed the pinch of tension between her horns. No matter what she did, she kept circling back to that knowledge. Maybe that was being a Chosen: impossible powers, a god who wanted your happiness and safety, and in exchange, no more choices, no more questions, no more thinking for herself.

She wondered if Ilstan had the same troubles, if he found the same chasms between what he wanted and what his god desired—but then, Ilstan had the benefit of having gone at least a little mad and having what seemed like a constant connection to Azuth.

Farideh considered Lorcan. "If I wanted to speak to . . . your lord, would I have to talk to you?"

"Why would you want to talk to him?" he replied just as carefully.

"I might want to ask him about something he said."

Lorcan went completely still. "What did he say? When did you talk to him?" A flicker, a burst of anger behind that careful expression. "A threat?" he guessed. "A promise?"

"Do I have to talk to you," Farideh said again, "if I want to talk to him?"

"What," Lorcan said, "do you want to say to him?"

She looked at him for a long moment. "Nothing," she said. "I was only curious." She looked beyond him, to the bedroom. "You can go back, or you can wait here, I suppose. But you ought to look human if you do."

"Darling," he said. "Don't listen to Asmodeus."

It sent a shiver up her spine, though there was no simpler advice on earth. Don't listen to Asmodeus—of course, you shouldn't listen to Asmodeus. Who would think you should? But from Lorcan's lips, a pale shadow of his master, it seemed sharp and cold and unavoidable as a blade. His dark eyes watched her, as if he weren't certain whether she were something to fear or fear for, and she found herself wondering how Lorcan was faring in the Hells, what had happened when he'd vanished all those days she and Dahl had been together.

"I'll be back later," she said, and turned from Lorcan and her thoughts without another word.

• • •

CLAN SHESTANDELIATH'S DOORS were just as massive as Verthisathurgiesh's, inlaid with slices of semiprecious stones and bounded by the shapes of skeletal dragons, their skulls resting on the corners.

"They're much prettier than Verthisathurgiesh's," Havilar said to the young dragonborn standing guard—in the common tongue, for Brin's sake. The girl on the right looked back at the doors, as if she'd never considered it.

"The stones are for the Breath of Petron," the boy said proudly. "The artifact Haizverad stole from the Opaline Terror, Versveshardinazar, who—"

"Broken Planes, they don't care. Sorry," the girl said to Havi and Brin. "We don't get a lot of *maunthreki*."

Havilar blinked at the word. "First off, I'm a *tiefling*."

The girl shrugged. "Well, close, right? You get bored of old stories, same as him," she said, pointing to Brin with her snout. "Ancestor stories are hard to understand if you don't learn them from the nest."

"I already *know* the story of Haizverad and the Breath of Petron," Havilar said testily. "Do I look like a *karshoji* hatchling?"

The girl looked her over as if Havilar had just declared herself the new Vanquisher. Her comrade frowned. "Honestly? I have no idea. I can never tell with *maunthreki*." He peered at her. "Can you tell with us?"

"Can we help you find something?" the girl snapped.

"We're looking for Shestandeliath Zaroshni," Brin said. "Do you know her?"

"Why are you looking for Zaroshni?" the boy asked.

"Because Kepeshkmolik Dumuzi says we should talk to her," Havilar said. Matriarch Anala's orders were on the tip of her tongue, her newly bestowed, unwieldy name. But she clamped her mouth shut around it—they were here because no one knew who she and Brin were. "Do you know where she is?"

"What do you want to talk to her about?" the girl asked.

"Ancestor stories," Havilar said icily.

"You can't talk to her now," the boy said. "She's got weapons lessons up in the barracks." The girl glared at him.

"Thank you very much," Brin said, taking hold of Havilar's arm. "You've been terribly helpful. Blessings on your clan." The boy looked at Brin with a tilted head. "I mean," Brin amended, "I hope only the best for them. Come on, Havi."

They found their way back to the walkways, to the stairs that climbed up and up toward the barracks at the pyramid's peak. Havilar eyed their steep slope, a curl of nausea in her stomach.

"Ye gods, who pissed in her porridge?" Brin muttered. "What's *maunthreki* mean?"

Havilar pushed aside her thoughts. "It's, um, it means humans. But it's kind of . . . I wouldn't say it to you. It's a little rude."

"How rude?"

Havilar hesitated. "It means something like 'those squishy ones.' "

To her surprise, Brin snorted. "I suppose that makes sense." He chuckled again. "Sorry. It's funny. I've heard people—I mean, humans—call dragonborn 'scalies' and, well, 'dragonborn,' I suppose. I never thought about the fact that we're probably horrifyingly unarmored."

"It's rude," Havilar said again. "Don't let them call you that."

He smiled at her. "I've got you watching out for me." He looked up the stairs. "Farideh told me to keep you from going up there."

That wound tension all up Havilar's back, and her tail started to lash. "Oh *karshoj*."

"She told me about Arjhani," Brin said. "A little. A very little. Do you want to go up?"

"We *have* to."

"I could go. You could wait here. If you wanted to avoid seeing him."

"I don't care about *karshoji* Arjhani," Havilar said, even though the nausea in her stomach curled tighter. She started up the stairs. She wanted to know what Farideh had told him and yet she didn't. Even after everything that had happened in Cormyr, even after Brin assuming she was pregnant of all things, knowing Brin knew about that winter would be more embarrassment than she could handle.

"Right," Brin said as he caught up to her. Havilar clung to the silence as they climbed—it was awkward, but far less awkward than talking. But then Brin said, "Are you getting any . . . indications?"

"What?"

"Have you noticed any demons, I mean? Are you feeling all right?"

"I will tell you if I'm going to throw up."

They walked on, quiet a little longer before Brin cleared his throat. "I've been meaning to tell you, I shouldn't have tried to guess. Before. I should have just asked."

Havilar's cheeks burned. "That's what I said." But she remembered the emotion in his eyes. *I love you. I love you, and there is nowhere I'd rather be than by your side.* "Were you serious?" she blurted. "Would you have been happy?"

He gave the same nervous sort of chuckle as before. "Yes. Honestly, yes. I mean, things aren't settled between us. I know that. I'm not saying we ought to rush off into things. But . . ." He shrugged. "Someday? If we get back to where we were?"

"You do know if we had babies, they'd be tieflings," Havilar said.

"Yeah, I get how it works." He smiled at her. "I'm a little fond of tieflings as it happens."

All over again, Havilar felt sick. It was too much to even think about. There were so many things she wanted before even considering the question. How soon was eventually? What happened if she opted for the herbs and the day-count? Would that decide things between them once and for all?

She wasn't sure she wanted Brin. But she wasn't sure she didn't either.

The Lance Defenders barracks were thick with the musty scent of dragonborn and the acrid, dusty odor that could only be the bats up above them. The doors opened into a wide hallway, lined with smaller rooms. Dragonborn in scarred armor, each of them wearing a medallion emblazoned with a bat, strode from place to place, none of them bothering with Havilar or Brin.

Havilar grabbed a young man by the arm as he passed. "Excuse me? I'm looking for a student taking weapons lessons."

"The training yard upstairs," he said, sounding puzzled. "Um, up there, to the left and then take the first right."

The training yard was wider than the one in the Verthisathurgiesh enclave, its ceiling much lower. And it was quite full of dragonborn carrying glaives with blunted metal practice blades.

Her blood felt as if it had turned to molten lead, scalding hot and plummeting through her veins. Arjhani's class.

But there was no Arjhani, no matter where she searched.

Every student considered Havilar with naked curiosity as she walked toward the front of the class, eyeing their piercings. Silver chains, she thought. Zaroshni would have silver chains.

"Broken Planes," a young man muttered in Draconic as she passed him. "They'll let anyone take lessons now."

"One hit and she'll snap like a twig," another voice said. "They ought to have warned her."

Havilar turned very slowly to face the teenaged dragonborn—a tall young man, pierced with jade rings along his jaw, a stocky, pale-scaled fellow with owl-shaped piercings across his cheeks, and a reddish girl with Kepeshkmolik's waxing and waning moons.

"Who's going to do that?" Havilar asked in Draconic. "You? *You*? Those glaives are so *karshoji* shiny it looks like your aunties just handed them to you this morning with your highsunfeast."

The tall boy's teeth gapped nervously, but the owl-pierced one just scowled. "This is the advanced lessons," he said. "I think you're in the wrong room."

Havilar nearly laughed. "Why? Do you think there are more-senior students who could use my help?"

The girl's golden eyes flicked over Havilar. "Like we need advice from some clanless's demonspawn hanger-on."

A murmur ran through the classroom. "*Chaubask vur kepeshk, Saitha!*" the tall boy hissed. A look of discomfort crossed the

Kepeshkmolik girl's features, but she kept her eyes locked on Havilar as she squared her shoulders.

"Havi . . ." Brin said in warning tones. "What's she saying?"

"Where's your teacher?" she said, keeping her eyes locked on the Kepeshkmolik girl.

"Master Arjhani is running late," the owl-pierced boy said. "He knows we can manage."

"Are any of you Shestandeliath Zaroshni?" Havilar shouted. The dragonborn students shook their heads.

"Zaroshni didn't come today," someone said. "She doesn't sometimes."

"Good." Havilar reached back and unhooked Devilslayer from its harness, hurt and rage and frustration itching at her bones. "I can think of a few things you could stand to learn," she said to the Kepeshkmolik girl. She backed toward the open center of the room, beckoning to her.

"Havi," Brin said. "Go easy."

Havilar grinned at him fiercely, maybe a little madly. She didn't care. "Of course," she said in Common. "It's just a lesson."

Saitha's glaive sliced toward her left shoulder, Havilar's momentary distraction, momentary cockiness, providing a wide opening. She saw just in time the blade carving toward her, the weapon not turned quite enough to glance off, and Havilar leaped back, flush with adrenaline. The Kepeshkmolik girl grinned.

Don't get cocky, Havilar told herself. Plant your feet. Watch your lines. The glaive in her hands felt as if she'd reclaimed a missing limb and she was whole and right again. She caught the girl's next strikes easily, watching Saitha's grip, her movements. She favored the slice, always tending toward the left. Good-enough technique, but *sparring* technique—each criticism came in Mehen's barked tones.

The next time Saitha went for the slice, Havilar jabbed hard at her left. It threw the dragonborn off balance as she dodged the weapon, and made it easy for Havilar to yank the shaft of the blade back against the girl's thighs, down into the hinge of her knees. Saitha went down hard on the mats, as Havilar whipped Devilslayer around to point the butt at her throat.

"Your slice is solid, but you're entirely too predictable," Havilar said. "Stop going for the left—"

She broke off, catching movement from the corner of her eye—the stocky white-scaled boy with the owl piercings. Havilar sprang back—he was quick, quicker than she would have given him credit for, more comfortable with the blade than Saitha had been. She found herself grinning—it was nearly a challenge.

The boy made a series of quick feints toward her, jabs meant to upset her balance. Havilar shifted around the attacks, the barest movements. Parry hard, push as far as you can—the boy skipped to the side, trying to stay ahead of her, keeping his strikes short.

Havilar thrust the glaive between his knees as he tried to pull back from another strike. His feet tangled around the weapon. Havilar gripped the shaft of the weapon tight, planted her feet and pulled back as he stumbled, sweeping his feet from under him.

Devilslayer caught under the edge of his boot. Havilar hardly had a chance to yank it free but the tall boy's blade chopped toward her, the side of the blade slamming into her thigh, hard enough to bruise. Havliar bashed the shaft of Devilslayer into the boy's weapon, hard enough to force him back, hard enough to let her get some space.

She'd no more than planted her feet, but there was Saitha at her back, cutting toward the left *again*. Havilar jabbed back at her with the butt of the glaive, more irritated than anything. The tall boy attacked again—chop, parry down—and she'd hardly forced him back, but Saitha was harrying her again. She stepped back, trying to force both opponents to the same side, but they'd studied that much at least and moved with her, maintaining the flanking position.

Havilar had hardly turned her attention to Saitha, but the boy was pressing toward Havi again. Havilar let Saitha hit her—the sloppily turned blade sliced a thin cut along her arm—to slam Devilslayer's shaft against the boy's weapon.

Not hard enough to throw his balance. Hard enough to make him mad. Sloppy enough to make him cocky.

Sure enough the boy pulled back, just a hair too wide, committing every bit of his bulk to the attack. In the same moment, Saitha moved toward Havilar. Havi dropped Devilslayer, reached back, and yanked the dragonborn girl forward by her weapon. The tall boy had hardly a breath to pull back his strike. Saitha plowed into him. The shaft of his glaive came down on her head. Both crumpled, panting, to the mats.

"*You're* favoring the left," Havilar shouted, pointing at Saitha, the pale boy, and the tall jade-ringed one in turn. "*Your* stance is a mess. And *you* aren't paying the least attention to your comrades. You're going to get worse than knocked on your ass if you don't start. You have very pretty bladework, but if you can't think about every part of yourself, *and* your opponent, then *karshoji* go home." She turned to the class of dragonborn. "Do any of you hatchlings still need advice from the daughter of Clanless Mehen?" she shouted, flooded with success and confidence. " 'Cause the floor is *karshoji* open!"

None of them spoke.

"I suppose that means it's my turn."

The sound of his voice stopped her heart like a glaive had been buried in it. She turned, as if in a dream, as if her blood were falling away from her ears again. Arjhani hardly looked a day different from that long-ago summer, down to the delighted expression on his face. Like she was a girl again, managing to knock a sparring dummy down.

"My very best pupil." Arjhani shook his head, smiling at her. "What a wonderful surprise! I see you've kept your practice up—I can't tell you how proud that makes me."

Havilar's ears were screaming and she felt as if she were going to boil over, as if she were going to turn into flames and smoke like Farideh did—in fact, she wished it would happen.

"How about you and I do a demonstration for them?" he went on, as if nothing had happened, as if he'd never left. He took up his glaive, twirled it in one hand. "I think you've probably progressed enough to make a decent partner."

Havilar gripped Devilslayer so hard she could picture it crumbling into splinters. She flipped it around, slid it back into its harness, and turned on her heel. A hundred words, a hundred sharp replies crowded in her throat that might have somehow evened the slate, but she didn't dare speak a one as she left the training yard, tears squeezing her throat shut.

"Havi!" Brin called, running after her. "Havi, wait!"

"I don't want to talk about it."

"Havi—"

"No," Havilar said. At the top of the stairs she spun on him. "I don't ever want to talk about what just happened. Got it? Never."

"Got it," Brin said after a moment. She turned away again, storming down the stairs. "Just tell me you're all right?"

She wouldn't, because she couldn't. She needed to go, to be anywhere else right now. *I can't tell you how proud that makes me. "Karshoj,* to him and his pride," she muttered.

Brin ran down the stairs, getting in front of her. He pulled her off the main walkway at the landing, toward an unfamiliar enclave. She swatted at him. "You don't want to talk, we don't have to talk. All right? I'll make that deal. But you have to take a moment and calm down."

"Why the burning Hells should I?" Havilar demanded.

A pair of soft *pops,* so close together they might have been one sound, punctured the air just behind her. Havilar's stomach clenched hard.

"What is it—" Mot's question turned into a muffled shriek as Havilar shoved him and Olla backward into the shadow of a column.

"Shush!" she said. "I didn't ask for you."

"Who told you that you have to ask?" Mot said. "You just have to need."

"Technically you have to need something we can help with," Olla supplied. "But you don't have to ask."

Mot looked as if he would have liked to strangle Olla with his own tail. "I said that."

"You *almost* said it," Olla pointed out. "So what do you need?"

"I *need* to be alone," Havilar snapped. "Go away."

Mot peered at her. "Someone got you angry? Is it this one?" He looked Brin up and down. "What are you doing with our Chosen?"

"Leave him alone," Havilar said.

"He doesn't seem like proper company for a Chosen of Asmodeus," Olla said. "Perhaps you need a cultist. Or several. Maybe a wizard who's morally flexible? They can be good for things."

Mot muttered something under his breath again. "She's not *that* kind of Chosen, idiot! We've been over this." He looked at Havilar again. "If someone—and I'm not saying this guy, I'm saying insulted you or something, we can help with that. We don't even have to call in favors or anything. People are really fragile when you get down to it."

Havilar's cheeks brightened. "I am never going to ask you to kill someone."

"Who said 'kill'? Killing is overrated anyway."

"Also, you shouldn't try to kill someone," Olla said to Mot. "You wouldn't manage it."

"Shut up, Olla!"

"Both of you shut up!" Havilar hissed. "Don't come again unless I ask. Don't kill anybody, and don't find me a cultist to be friends with! Got it?"

Mot peered at her again. "Lady, you are so strange." But a moment later, the air popped again, and both imps were gone.

Havilar sighed, all her anger receding like a tide, leaving her drained and feeling shaky. As if there were nothing she could do but cry, and if she didn't, she wouldn't come right again. She rubbed her eyes. Maybe Farideh had been right. Maybe she couldn't handle Arjhani.

Brin took her arm. "Come on," he said gently. "Let's go sit and have some tea before we head back."

"Lorcan will be here soon," Havilar protested.

"The priests of Torm always told me I'd have no success in my lessons with an unsteady heart. And while I know they meant for me to just stiffen up and dive in, I think it's true, too, that there's no point in diving in when you can't focus. Come on."

They walked in silence back to the Shield of Shasphur, back to the high table in the corner. The dragonborn woman brought them tea and some little cakes, complimented Brin on his improving Draconic.

"I get the feeling everyone thinks me speaking Draconic is on a level with a dog doing tricks," he said, pouring tea into the two cups. The scent of woody spices floated up on the steam as he pushed a cup toward her. "I will never talk about it, if that's what you want," Brin said. "But you have to promise me in return that you will talk to me about it if you need to."

Havilar wrapped her hands around the clay cup. "It's too embarrassing."

"Right. Because we've never told each other anything embarrassing. My opinion of you is that flimsy." He blew on the hot tea. "Don't tell me, but don't pretend I wouldn't be able to handle it."

Havilar sighed and rubbed her braid. If there was anyone who she could talk to, it was Brin, wasn't it? But should it be Brin? Maybe this was the right idea, or maybe it was making everything more knotted and complicated.

But she wanted it all out, she realized.

"All right, look, I'll tell you, but you have to promise—*promise*—that . . . that you won't . . . That you won't start treating me differently."

Brin reached over and squeezed her hand. "Never."

Havilar closed her hand around his, and curled the cup of tea nearer. "One summer, Arjhani came looking for Mehen. He was all apologies and . . . Well, Mehen's a bit of a mush-heart for him. Or maybe he was. I don't know." She let the story stop, not wanting to revisit any of it.

"I gather he's the one who taught you to use the glaive," Brin said.

"Did Farideh tell you that?"

"Yes. Although that"—he gestured toward the stairs beyond the teahouse—"pretty well confirmed it."

"What else did she say?"

"That it was hard for you when he left. That you were very attached to him."

Havilar swallowed hard, eyes on her tea. "Did she tell you I tried to kill myself?"

Brin's hand closed tight around hers like a reflex, like she was going to fall away. "No," he said, his voice as tight as his grip. "Did you?"

"No," Havilar said. "Not on purpose, anyway. But . . . I guess it doesn't matter because I did almost die and Mehen and Farideh never really believed . . . I don't think they believed . . ." Tears rose in her eyes and she stubbornly wiped them away. "It's just embarrassing."

Brin let go of her, pulled his chair around the table, closer to her. "You *do not* have to tell me this story if you don't want to," he said quickly. "You don't, all right?"

Havilar shook her head—half of it was so much worse than all of it. "I was *twelve* when he left. I was . . . maybe a little hysterical. I just . . . When Arjhani came, I started feeling like I could see my future. I had this *knack* and he could see it and I thought he loved me for it. He said I was the best pupil he'd ever had. We were going to go adventuring and I would learn everything from him and we would all be so happy. But . . . he left and it felt like I wasn't . . . Like maybe he realized he didn't love Mehen anymore, but didn't he love me?" She shook her head. "It's so *karshoji* stupid—I was just some kid. He was just *like* that, you know? Just charming and friendly and . . . I wasn't special." She drew a breath to steady herself. "So Mehen's heartbroken and not dealing with it very well, and I'm really not keeping my head on my shoulders . . ."

"You were twelve," Brin reminded her, taking her hand again. "That's a bad time for big surprises."

Havilar nodded, remembering the feeling of freefall, the terror that everything was wrong and would always be wrong and it was her fault somehow, but she couldn't figure it out. If only she could just fix it. "So . . . Farideh got really angry at me one day for being so sad. Because Mehen was the one who ought to be sad and I was just making it all about myself, when who even cared about Arjhani?"

"She said that she didn't get along with him much."

Havilar snorted. "Yeah, not at all. When he first came, she told Mehen he ought to leave, since she'd figured out Arjhani had broken his heart. I think she hurt Arjhani's pride more than anything, and I didn't realize it then, but . . . he was unkind to her after that. Not cruel. But you know, unkind." She rubbed her thumb over Brin's hand. "So she was a little glad he was gone and mad at me for missing him, but I was missing *everything*, really. And . . . Mehen had gotten some rotgut from this dwarf in the village—"

"The one who raises yaks," Brin added.

Havilar giggled, driving back the tears. "I can't believe you remembered that."

"It's a very memorable detail." He rubbed her hand as well. "Did you get drunk?"

"Really drunk," Havilar said. "*Child* drunk. I was so stupid. And . . . then I started to think that the only thing for it was to leave. To go find him and fix whatever had made him decide to leave. I put on my cloak. I took my glaive. I took a little of the rotgut and maybe a piece of bread, and I sneaked out of the village. Just as a snowstorm was starting."

She remembered still the cold, the way it ate its way into her dulled senses, as if her nerves were trying to save her. She remembered the way things started to slow and grow warmer.

How incredibly sleepy she'd become, and how comfortable the snowdrift seemed. She didn't remember anything else, until she was back in Arush Vayem again, wrapped in blankets and being fed sweetened milk, with Farideh standing over her, red-faced and weeping silently.

"Mehen found me," she said. "I knew better than to go out in a storm like that. I knew what to watch for—everyone did. And no matter how many times I told them it was just a dumb idea, that I was drunk and upset and stupid, he and Farideh treated me like I was going to shatter for months after. That's the worst part," she told Brin. "And that they think it would happen all over again."

And that somewhere deep in her heart, Havilar knew that she'd known the signs of a bad storm well enough to mark them even drunk. She knew what windchill felt like, what signs told her that her body was collapsing. She had to have known she was going to die out there, and she went anyway. To even think of it made her feel like something dark and dangerous lay within her. Something that wasn't really even herself, coiled in tight even when everything was right and happy.

She waited for Brin to point out she should have known, but he only said, "You kept the glaive?"

"I didn't at first. I put it away, but I missed it. I was *good* at it, and . . . I'm not very good at much. When the thaw came, Mehen took it out and gave me lessons. He told me it was my weapon, *not* Arjhani's. I couldn't let him get in my head and break my heart all over again."

"I think you might have broken his right back," Brin said. "A little, anyway. You didn't see his face, but he wasn't expecting you to leave, I guarantee it. And you were *spectacular*."

"But he made it about him."

"And then you *left*," Brin pointed out. "Because it's not about him. It hasn't been about him for years and years and years, so far as I can see. At this point you've learned more from Mehen than you ever learned from Arjhani. Hells, you've learned more from Zhentarim and devils and Shadovar and shades and orcs than Arjhani." He laid his hand over their clasped ones, and for a moment, neither spoke.

"You know I wasn't much younger than that when my father was killed," Brin said. "When . . . everything changed. When I stopped being a Crownsilver and I couldn't live in Suzail anymore and they sent me off to become a cleric. I do know what you mean. It feels like somebody yanked the rug out from under your feet, when you hadn't even figured out quite how to stand up."

Havilar kissed him, so suddenly she hardly realized she was doing it, and it felt, she thought, like holding the glaive, like settling into place. He pulled her close and for a moment, she didn't think about Arjhani or the demon or the Nine Hells or Suzail.

Her gorge suddenly rose, hot and metallic in her throat. She shoved Brin away so hard, she nearly knocked him off the stool.

"All right, obviously we have—" Brin started.

The demon—Havilar stood before Brin could finish, sweeping the room as she moved toward the exit, nausea building, saliva flooding her mouth. She pulled the glaive off, searching, searching.

No one screaming. No one fighting. Nothing.

She made it only a few more steps before she doubled over, emptying her stomach onto the worn granite floor. She stayed bent over, dragonborn giving her a wide berth, asking if she was all right from the edges of the street.

"*Ir bensvenk*," Brin's voice called in clumsy Draconic. *She's all right.* "*Ir bensvenk.* You are, aren't you?" He dropped his voice as he bent down beside her, handing her a handkerchief. "The demon? Is it close?"

Havilar wiped her mouth, avoiding his gaze. Her stomach had calmed. "No. I lost it." She nodded and thanked the shop-keeper who brought her another handkerchief, the woman from the teahouse rushing up with a fresh cup of something that tasted of lemon and licorice. Another shopkeeper came out and turned a stream of fiery breath on the puddle, burning it up with a cloud of noxious vapor.

"Come on, *noachi*," the teahouse owner said gently. "You should sit."

Havilar followed her slowly back, Brin's arm around her ribs not so much needed as wanted. "I didn't see anything," she whispered to him.

"It's all right," he said. "Maybe it was fast—"

"I mean no one saw anything. It was there, but no one knew it." She gritted her teeth against the fading nausea, hoping that Lorcan would be able to show her a way to make her abilities useful before someone else died. "I think I know what we're dealing with."

11

MEHEN NEVER THOUGHT HE WOULD MISS SUZAIL'S CAR-
riages—too small, too soft, too close and crowded—
but as he and Anala walked across the City-Bastion,
trailed by a pair of young guards, Mehen would have given
anything to have a carriage's walls around him, deflecting the
sidelong stares of the Vayemniri.

Which part, he wondered, made them stare? The scandalous
lover? The sharp words? The violence, the return, or maybe some
new element, woven in over thirty years of retelling? Maybe it
wasn't him at all, but the matriarch, clearly in mourning for a
son of her fourth clutch.

"The unpierced fellow," Anala said. "Who is he?"

"Kallan," Mehen said. "Yrjixtilex Kallan." A good thing
Kallan would go out into the city with Farideh—Havilar's
barely suppressed glee rattled his nerves, echoing back through
the years to the summer Arjhani had come to stay. She'd been
gleeful then, too, almost giddy. She'd loved him wholeheartedly,
and look what had happened.

Kallan's crooked smile . . . and Havilar had insisted it didn't
matter, she could handle another brightbird, another heartbreak—she'd handled things with Brin hadn't she?

Mehen scowled to himself. That was not handled at all.

"Whose son is he?" Anala asked. "Whose line?"

"I don't know," Mehen said, as they descended stairs to a
lower level. "I didn't ask."

236

Anala's mouth quirked. "You have better things to worry about in the wide world beyond? Still it seems like a question you'd ask a paramour. Does Matriarch Vardhira know he's here?"

"She knows. He comes from the homesteads, all right? One of those sheep farms. Nothing dire." His teeth parted and he closed them hard. "We're not paramours."

Anala clucked her tongue. "Oh Mehen. I never believed you then, and I don't believe you now."

Kepeshkmolik's doors were decorated with crossed single-headed axes, under a trio of carved dragon skulls jagged with spikes—the *ausiri* of the Citadel of Endings, the birthplace of the clan. The doorguards standing before them were stiffer and sterner than Verthisathurgiesh's had been, their moon-shaped piercings an unmoving line. Mehen found himself straightening too. He couldn't remember the last time he'd been within the enclave's walls, but he couldn't forget Kepeshkmolik.

Any other hatchling would be grateful for this match. Any other hatchling would know his luck.

I have my sword. I have my rank. I'm not a hatchling, and I'm not your karshoji *spy.*

The body of the Kepeshkmolik guard lay on a bier, covered to the neck in white cloth, her missing limb hidden. She was young, her plumes worn short and her scales a murky green. Kepeshkmolik Narghon stood at her head, his stern expression suddenly dark.

"You didn't tell him we were coming," Mehen said.

"I didn't need to," Anala said lightly. "The invitation is to the matriarch or patriarch. They send who they deem appropriate. I deemed myself and you. He has nothing to complain about."

"What's the dead girl's name?" Mehen asked.

"Shaysa or Sharna or something. It's not as if she doesn't deserve my attention simply because I can't recall her name," Anala added at Mehen's glare. They took their places in the line of representatives, all hatchlings without status weapons and elders without power. Beside Narghon, the girl's parents—a Kepeshkmolik man, a woman with Ophinshtalajiir piercings—stood proud and dazed-looking in their white robes. Uadjit hovered at the right of the elder's throne, her dark eyes fixed on Mehen.

Dumuzi and another young man came along the line with a caster of oil, pouring a small amount into the mourners' hands, so that they could mark the dead's mouth and eyes, a stand-in for the olden days, when it would have been blood. Dumuzi nodded awkwardly at Mehen and Anala.

"Well met, Dumuzi," Anala said. "I see they've found things for you to do." Dumuzi muttered a greeting, tipping a small amount of oil into first Anala's palm, then Mehen's, before moving down the line. "Poor lonesome child," Anala murmured.

"Does he have clutchmates?"

"A few, younger. Uadjit's first two clutches never hatched. The clutch with Dumuzi had three hatchlings—one died soon after, one died of a fever some years later. But she's had two others since then, well-spaced." She stepped forward, traced the dead guardswoman's mouth and eyes with oil, murmuring the gratitude of Verthisathurgiesh, the benediction for the fallen. Mehen mimicked her, the memory of other funerals, other long-ago dead, guiding his hands. The dead might leave this world, but their impact on the clan, on the Vayemniri, wouldn't. Her eyelids shone in the glow of the lamps.

Anala inclined her head to Narghon. "Verthisathurgiesh mourns your loss. Our condolences."

"Your very *deepest* condolences, it seems," Narghon said. "Or are your ranks truly so thin as one hears?"

"More robust every day," Anala said. Narghon's eyes narrowed further, but he did not look at Mehen.

Mehen stepped around Anala, removing himself from Narghon's presence without a word, fighting the urge to deny any involvement in Anala's scheme—that would only be worse. For him, for Kepeshkmolik, for Verthisathurgiesh. For these grieving parents. He picked his way through the crowd, carefully avoiding putting his elbow into this hatchling's back or that elder's head, until he found his way to Uadjit.

"Well met." She raised a scaled eyebrow at him, before turning wordlessly back to the crowd of guests. "This is your dead guard?"

"One and the same. Shaysa, daughter of Andjer of the line of Nilofer."

"You have my condolences."

"Why are you here?"

"I need more information to find this killer, and I can't get anyone to talk to me," he said. "This was what Anala offered—and if she had told me what she meant to do, I would have said no. I have no interest in tweaking Narghon's nose."

Uadjit's face remained a mask. "Has she laid out all her plans then?"

"Only parading me around." Mehen lowered his voice further. "I need to talk to you about that missing guard. Has he turned up?"

"Not to my knowledge."

"Who did you have guarding the catacombs the day the war wizard was caught?" Mehen asked. "Who was near to the Shestandeliath tombs?"

Uadjit frowned, but she kept her eyes on the guests. "No one. Shestandeliath's tombs are miles from ours."

"That's not what I heard. A Kepeshkmolik guard arrived around the same time as Shestandeliath's. The wizard hit him in the face. He might have returned with a broken tooth."

"I assure you," she said. "There were no Kepeshkmolik guards in that place and no one returning with tales of fisticuffs with wizards. Whatever your witness saw, it wasn't that. Did you ask the Shestandeliath guards?"

"Shestandeliath won't talk to me," Mehen reminded her. "What's the fellow's name?"

"What were they doing in the catacombs?"

"What do you care if none of them were yours?"

Now, at last, she turned to him. "They were friends of my son," she said in a voice like ice. "I would be sure he's not in the same kind of trouble."

"He's not," Mehen said. Then, "He told Farideh that they were trying to open a portal to Abeir. And he was trying to talk them out of it."

"*Chaubashk vur kepeshk karshoji*," Uadjit spat. "What were they thinking?" She cursed again. "And so that's what . . . That's where the killer came from? The old lands?"

"It doesn't look like the portal ever opened. It looks like someone interrupted it, sent something else through." He considered the crowd of guests, marked the clans there. "A demon."

"A demon?" Uadjit turned from him again. "Shall I assume your . . . daughters"— Mehen fought not to bare his teeth at that pause, the lilt of a question—"confirmed that?"

"They're clever girls."

"Dumuzi's told me a great deal about them. Especially Farideh, I believe? She's still in the city, I assume?"

"Of course," Mehen said. "Where I go they go."

"You ought to bring her next time," Uadjit said. "I think we'd like to meet her. Bring both of them, if you like."

"Why is that?"

Uadjit smiled as she turned back to him, her face a mask. "I like to know who my son's associating with. Surely you can't fault me for that?"

Among the milling guests, Dumuzi watched them with a nervous eye, as if he could hear the conversation. "What does he say about her?" Mehen asked, all too aware of the many secrets the young man might have spilled. "What is it you think you'll uncover?"

"You should bring her by," Uadjit said once more, without answer. "Before you leave Djerad Thymar."

• • •

FOR A LONG time after Farideh left, Lorcan remained in her room, trying very hard not to panic. *Do I have to talk to you if I want to talk to him?* She was smarter than that—but then there was no one better than Asmodeus at tangling the terribly wise in their wants. What did she want badly enough to be so foolish?

Dahl, he thought, his blood rising. What would it be except the paladin? Surely Farideh knew that would serve her poorly. Whatever Oghma might think of a Chosen of Asmodeus, he would have no love for her if she asked the King of the Hells to lay his blessings upon the paladin. Farideh would know that. She had to know that. It was something else. It had to be.

Lorcan considered the room. He opened the drawers and marked the spare clothing, the cluster of leather bands to tie her hair. He turned aside a blouse, a nightdress, a robe, the soft fabric hiding nothing. The same cloak she'd worn the day he met her, with snow clinging to the hem. Beneath her folded cloak he found a deck of cards, a chapbook stained with what looked like berry juice, a comb studded with rubies. Lorcan picked up the jewels, frowning as he tried to place it. A jolt of magic shocked him, twanging the fine bones of his hand like a vicious harpist.

The tower of the wizard, he thought. The one you couldn't protect her from. Adolican Rhand had decked her in such gems. She wouldn't have kept it for that monster's sake. Perhaps a reminder of Lorcan's fallibility? But no, she'd clung closer to him after that, after he'd admitted how deeply he'd wronged her.

She came to Farideh in the internment camp, only Fari didn't know who it was. Rhand wouldn't have enchanted the jewels— could the Brimstone Angel have managed it? Would Farideh have kept something so dangerous? He wondered how much Sairché knew of the ghost and her meddling.

Lorcan considered the comb—it would be a small matter to take it back to the Hells, to probe its connections and see what Sairché said or did not say—and instead put it back beneath the cloak.

Get Farideh to mention it, he thought. Get her to show him, to offer it up. If he tried to work around her too broadly, it would only remind her of the mistake with the shaking fever again. He needed something to show her he was on her side. He needed to make sure she saw how dearly she needed him.

He smoothed the cloak back over the hidden treasures.

Lorcan had no more than stepped into the humid, fetid air of Malbolge, all flowers and rotten flesh, but Neferis was waiting for him.

"Shetai sent a messenger," Neferis said. "You're free to visit."

Lorcan smiled at the fortuitous timing. "Excellent. Fetch Axona, Ctesiphon, and . . ." He sorted through his many half sisters. "Who else marches in a fury with Ctesiphon?"

Neferis didn't budge. "Shetai is dangerous," she said. "Even Invadiah feared Shetai."

"We have something Shetai wants," Lorcan said. "And only Shetai has the answers I need." He considered his half sister. "Are you afraid I'm going to get you killed?"

Neferis watched him, stone and venom. "I'm wary of it. You are no Invadiah."

"You should be glad I'm no Invadiah," Lorcan said. "A sister who doesn't want me dead is entirely too valuable to waste. For the moment, your destiny and mine are intertwined by the archduchess's order and her grace. Should I have need of a dead erinyes, there are much better candidates. Go fetch the others. Be certain they're armed."

In the end, the erinyes were a gambit, a weapon for Shetai to strip Lorcan of before he could enter the paelyrion's innermost cavern. While they stood, edgy and disused at the entrance, none of the paelyrion's minions searched Lorcan's person too closely as he entered Shetai's presence alone. They underestimate you, Lorcan thought. He could use that.

Among collectors of warlocks, none sat so high as Shetai. The Ears of Glasya, they called it. The Vulgar Inquisitor. Shetai had survived the rule of every duke to come to the throne of Malbolge, keeping its form for millennia. Even Exalted Invadiah had feared Shetai, settled in its little blind alley of the hierarchy—no one could demote Shetai, and no one who had tried remained to tell the tale.

"Well, well, well," the paelyrion rumbled as Lorcan entered its cavern. A mountain of pallid flesh encased in leather armor, Shetai shifted like a landslide, turning its great head to face the cambion. Lorcan fought back a shiver—the paelyrion's eyes were limned in garish purple, its razor-bladed mouth ringed with fuchsia paint. The mask of humanity worn like a mockery of its softness, its ineffectiveness. Humans wore paint, not devils. Not creatures that could spit you on a single fingernail and eat your heart out before you managed to die. Even if Lorcan expected the sight, it was unsettling.

"Lorcan, Invadiah's son." Shetai grinned, its mouth a slice of atrocity. "Let me guess: You want to reestablish your collection? I have a few spares I might be willing to trade for a Kakistos heir."

"When did the price of a Kakistos heir drop so dramatically?" Lorcan asked, shoving all his fear down deep. "Has someone discovered some unknown harem of tiefling mothers?" Shetai turned back to the shelf beside it, to a crystal bowl of bloody, twitching, skinless creatures, as if Lorcan bored it. "It's more about how I might help you," Lorcan went on. "How we might help each other."

Shetai laughed. "Is the cambion playing the hierarchy's game? Well, well. Where is the Lorcan we all loathe and mock?"

"It's never been all that in my interest," Lorcan pointed out. "Now it is."

"I don't purchase information of the sort a lazy cambion comes by, sweetling. Go play in the birthing pits."

"Even *this* lazy cambion?" Lorcan asked. "You know perfectly well what they're saying about me."

"And what happened to Taroth?" Shetai speared a struggling morsel with one long blood-black nail. "I'm sure you're terribly important, but I also know how to play the hierarchy. Digging up Asmodeus's buried secrets is hardly the safest way to stay ahead."

"High risk, high reward."

"High possibility that I wind up demoted back down to a spinagon," Shetai finished. "I have not risen to this state by being a fool."

"You're rather special in that regard, I think." Shetai's violet-trimmed eyes slid down to the cambion, full of suspicion. "Taroth?" Lorcan asked. "That was the bone devil? He let it slip that Fierna's eyeing the succubi as traitors."

"Who isn't?" Shetai said. "They make easy scapegoats."

"Asmodeus, to begin with," Lorcan said. "You see, a great many devils have come to me with their secrets, hoping to receive Asmodeus's by trade. Taroth was only one."

Shetai waved one saber-nailed hand. "The 'secrets' of the Fourth Layer are for lesser devils and pornographers."

"What about the Sixth?"

Shetai paused and Lorcan's guts felt as though they yawned with that eternity, before the paelyrion stabbed another morsel. "You think no one knows Her Highness has rebellion in her heart?" it scoffed.

"Even Asmodeus knows that," Lorcan said. "But I have had a very interesting discussion with my mother lately about Her Highness's desires, about the succubi. About Lady Malcanthet."

Shetai's inked eyebrows raised. "So Taroth is right."

"Not precisely. Though Invadiah would spin it that way."

Shetai sighed. "Little boy, if you want to trade for information that amounts to talking in circles, you ought to name your price, so I can decide how much of this is enough and stab you."

"I want information about the Brimstone Angel, Bryseis Kakistos."

Shetai laughed. "Go find a storybook then. Any imp knows the tale of the Brimstone Angel."

"I don't need the tale that's written down. I want to know the things we aren't told. The truth. You were here when the Ascension occurred. You have always collected warlocks."

"So long as they've been available."

"Someone held her pact before Asmodeus," Lorcan said. "If it's not you, you knew who. You knew, I'm sure, how to snatch that pact—any pact—if you'd wanted. So you know what the Brimstone Angel wanted. Why she came to him. What he didn't give her?" What does she want with Farideh? Lorcan thought.

Shetai tilted its mammoth head. "And what do you think the answer is?"

Lorcan faltered. There was no knowing, and so he'd not bothered guessing. "Power."

"Wrong. Power without purpose is a waste of time and resources. You want power, you go dance for the demons, you don't make deals with devils."

Lorcan didn't have time for this. "Wealth."

"An idiot's reason."

"Vengeance."

"Come now, you make pacts. Is that really the reason the best come to you? A moment of revenge?" Shetai considered him. "Perhaps, though, you've never had a warlock one could consider among the best."

Lorcan had had nearly a score of warlocks over the years and in that moment he couldn't remember a single one's true reason. Except Farideh. "Fear."

"Closer . . ." Shetai chuckled. "Truly, Lorcan, if you of all devils cannot guess it, then there is no hope."

Lorcan frowned at the paelyrion. What in the name of the shitting Nine was that supposed to mean?

Shetai's stubby wings flicked, and it resumed its languid pose. "Tell me about the succubi."

"There are succubi from Malbolge who used the attack on the Fifth Layer as a cover to destroy Levistus's holdings and rob him blind. There will surely be retaliation from the Fifth Layer, and if my mother remains in control, I will guarantee that the succubi will relish it, if not instigate the battle itself."

"Does Her Highness know?"

"She knows enough. But given Her Highness's wisdom, I would say she knows a very cautious portion of the truth."

"That could end Invadiah, quite neatly. Why not use it yourself?"

Lorcan smiled. "I don't play the hierarchy, remember? I doubt I could use that information as it should best be used."

"Do you have proof?"

"I have the Scepter of Alzrius that was given to a devil of the Fifth Layer called Magros, in exchange for betraying Asmodeus to Szass Tam, the Thayan lich. You use that properly, and you could make yourself ruler of the Fifth Layer, if you liked."

"Who says I want any such thing?" Shetai said with a laugh that echoed through the cavern. "Where is it?"

"Hidden," Lorcan said. "Give me the answer to my question now."

Shetai smiled. "Have you heard the name Alyona spoken?"

"No. Who's that?"

"We are all someone before we become ourselves," Shetai went on as though Lorcan had said nothing. "Find Alyona, and I guarantee you'll find everything you're looking for."

"You're giving me riddles?"

Shetai shrugged. "They're very *good* riddles. Assuming you solve them. Besides, you've given me rumors and an artifact that's still not in my hands. I'd say you're getting an excellent bargain."

Lorcan fought back a sneer. As if he'd not seen—not *made*—such "bargains" before. If Shetai still thought him worthy of pity and mockery, then there were other devils, other sources. There were other ways to find out what the ghost wanted. Other ways to make certain Farideh was safe. He turned to leave. "I won't take more of your time then. If you want to bargain further, I may still be interested."

"Come back when you can prove you're worth my time," Shetai said.

Bastard paelyrion. Godsbedamned collector devils. Calling his warlocks all second-rate.

Lorcan stopped before the cavern doors, another answer occurring to him. "Love."

"Very good," Shetai crooned. "Love is indeed what drove the Brimstone Angel to her destruction. This is the problem with mortals," it went on. "They think of love as a boon, a strength. They don't dare acknowledge it for what it is: weakness of the deepest, most unexorcisable order. Wouldn't you agree?"

Lorcan risked a look back at Shetai's blood-and-daggers smile. "You're right," it said. "I know how to snatch any pact I want. Keep that in mind."

* * *

In the Bow of Nilofer, Farideh sipped a cup of watered apple brandy while Kallan tried his hardest to coax the gnome wizard to their side. Wick didn't touch her own drink, standing on a stool so that she was level with the table.

"Abso-stlarning-lutely not."

"We got paid for a job," Kallan reminded her. "So we finish the job."

"We got paid by a lunatic who's now in dragonborn prison," Wick said. "Finish whatever you like, I'm out."

"We need a wizard," Kallan started.

"Then tell your clan to buy another one," Wick said. She nodded at Farideh. "Hells, you going to tell me you're running with a devil-child in robes, and *she's* not a caster? Anyway, don't give me this 'we' business, this stick-together nonsense when *you* ran off without so much as a backward glance. Where've you been?"

"Got locked up for a bit," Kallan said. "And the wizard—*Ilstan*—he doesn't like Farideh. He needs you."

"The crazy man I met a few tendays ago *needs* me?" Wick said. "That's rich. You are too stlarning nice for your own good."

The accusation made Farideh's tail flick, but Kallan didn't so much as blink. She'd left the enclave uncertain as she'd ever been about the sellsword, agitated by the edge of nervousness that trimmed Kallan's words. The intense politeness in the tumult of observations, of pointless questions that flowed out of him. She had no idea how much he knew about her, and the little she knew about him—specifically about him and Mehen—made her tense.

Then, at the top of a staircase, he'd stopped her.

"Look, I have to come clean with you," he'd said, with an uneasy chuckle. "Else I think I might just trip over my own tongue. I get a bit nervous around you."

"Why?" Farideh said dryly. "The tiefling part or the warlock part or something else?"

He laughed, and a little of his agitation fell away in that sound. "The Mehen's-daughter part. I told your father I was doing it for the fee, but . . . that's not altogether true. I liked his company, and I know he said you two girls were in the middle of too many things for him to start something up, but like they say, 'Hope is like a shadow and you can't outrun it.' "

Farideh frowned. "*That's* why Mehen broke it off with you?"

"You don't think it's true?"

Farideh looked away, thinking of Havilar's insistence that Mehen could have his romances, that they were grown enough to manage it. That had been before he and Kallan had started carrying on, though. She'd been sure Havilar had eased his mind. "I don't know. That's his business. And yours, I guess." The tip of her tail slashed once before she got it under control. "Did you think we told him to do that?"

Kallan laughed. "No. And if you did, it's no scales off my back—you're his daughters. I'm a month-old brightbird who never even got to hear his clan name."

"He doesn't tell anybody that," Farideh said quickly. "I didn't know it until I was twelve."

"He likes his privacy," Kallan agreed. "And he loves you two. I'm not going to deny I'd like your good opinion—even if Mehen's well and truly sick of me. I know enough to know you're someone I'd like on my side." Farideh blushed a little and looked away. "But it's not in my nature to dance around trying to keep someone from seeing something they don't like. So, blades on the table. I'll stop asking you *pothach* questions and you . . . be straight with me about whether I'm wasting my time?"

In the Bow of Nilofer, Farideh leaned toward the gnome. "You don't care if some *henish* is summoning up demons?" Farideh asked, giving the gnome a level stare.

"Some '*henish*' is always summoning up demons. Where've you been? Come to think of it, how do you owe them anything?" she said to Kallan. "You said it yourself, you're not from here. You want to put your neck on the line, there's a lot better battles to do it in."

"Every battle matters," Farideh said, "when there are innocent lives on the line."

The wizard snorted. "Where'd you get her? Out of a melodrama? I'm out." She tossed a few coppers on the table. "There, we're even enough. You want to catch up and find another job, I'll ride with you. Otherwise, enjoy your life and keep out of the way of stlarning demons." She leaped down from the stool and pulled her haversack over one tiny shoulder. A moment later she was gone, vanished into the crowds of Djerad Thymar.

"Well, *karshoj*," Kallan sighed, sliding down in his seat. "That wasn't how I was hoping that would go."

"It's all right," Farideh said. "We can think of something else. I could do it," she added. "He . . . pushed the spells into me before."

One brow ridge shifted. "Does Mehen know about that?"

"He doesn't know I'd do it again," Farideh admitted. "But . . . You can probably guess Mehen worries more than he needs to."

Kallan snorted. "I can also guess part of the reason is you take more risks than you strictly need to."

"That depends on who's deciding what's too much risk, doesn't it?" Farideh said. She set a stack of coins on the table. "Should we go?"

He laughed again, and stood. "Planes, you're the double of your father."

Farideh stopped as she followed Kallan from the inn. "No, I'm not." But he only laughed again.

So far as Farideh could tell, there wasn't a soul on Toril who would have said she took after Mehen in any fashion. Not only because she was adopted, but when there was Havilar with her quick blade and her warrior's mind, how could anyone think Farideh was Mehen's double? Havilar was the one who took after Mehen. Everyone knew that.

He's trying to get your good opinion, she thought. *He said as much.*

Shestandeliath Ravar's blood had been scrubbed from the stones of the crypt, the woken bodies of his clan's bravest warriors returned to their ossuaries, but Farideh could not help imagining each of them, long-dead and recently alive, lying upon the floor. A visible shiver went through Kallan.

"Not gonna lie," he said. "Don't want to be here."

"We'll make it quick," Farideh said. "You came in the way we did?"

"Same. Ilstan took off running for it while we were up by the inn. I caught up to him around the edge of Shestandeliath's tombs—or, I assume that's the edge. I wasn't reading all the inscriptions, obviously."

Farideh moved to stand before the door again. "And Ravar was already here? Fighting the demon?"

" 'Bout there." Kallan positioned himself in the middle of the room. He fought back another shudder. "Sorry. It wasn't pretty."

Farideh considered the room, the exits. The room wasn't large and there weren't many places to hide. "How big was it?"

"Bigger than me. Maybe a head and a half more?"

Nowhere to hide, Farideh amended. She considered the passages. "Do you know anything about demons?"

"Don't pick a fight with one unless you mean it? No. Do you?"

Farideh shook her head. The closest she'd ever come was the succubus Rohini in Neverwinter—and succubi were devils now, according to Lorcan, even if they were still mad as demons. "Not enough. Ilstan attacked it?"

"Through Ravar," Kallan said. He walked her through the rest of the fight—the thing's preternatural quickness, the clattering bones it raised. "Then you and the others came down. The thing heard you coming, though, and took off that way." He pointed at the third passage, a door that led deeper into the catacombs. "Only other person who could have seen it was that Kepeshkmolik guard Ilstan hit."

Farideh moved to stand beside Kallan where she could see the door. The corridor stretched on for some distance, unbroken by other passageways, other tombs. There was nowhere to hide, not for quite a ways. "How did he miss the demon?"

Kallan shifted his scabbard. "Come on." He took off running down the passage, Farideh hurrying after him. The hall was narrow and dimly lit, ending perpendicular to another wider passage. To the left, another long corridor, broken by other passageways to other tombs. To the right, a niche with a shrine to three Shestandeliath warriors, their ossuaries arranged around a carving of a dragonborn standing on a dragon's skull made of agate.

"Count of twenty to the end," Kallan said. "Maybe he could have missed it, but it would have been cutting things close." He readjusted his scabbard. "Up for a little exploring?"

"Of course," Farideh said. They continued down the passage. "If he'd seen something, wouldn't he have gone after the demon? I can't imagine just pretending it wasn't there." She peered into a small, unlit ossuary. "Maybe the demon can turn invisible."

Kallan shook his head. "Invisible still takes up space. Maybe it's faster than we think."

"I don't know that it would have to be much faster," Farideh said. "There's not a lot of places to hide, but there's more than none. We're going to have to find that guard."

"I guess your father will have that answer. What's with him and Kepeshkmolik, if you don't mind my asking?"

"He wouldn't marry their scion. Uadjit. She's Dumuzi's mother."

"Oh—that's *her*?" Kallan clucked his tongue. "He must have been pretty well-to-do back in the day."

"It seems like." Farideh looked around the tomb again. She'd always known that Mehen's childhood had been different than hers, that the world he came from wasn't the world they lived in. But sinking into it made her uncomfortable—it was hard to reconcile her father with the polish of Verthisathurgiesh, the half-told stories of a proud and angry young man. Especially when Mehen wouldn't tell them any of it.

Someone shouted, a frantic, scrabbling panic. A commotion of voices came around it, ahead and to the right. Neither Farideh nor Kallan said a word, but both ran toward the noise.

Ophinshtalajiir's clan name etched the posts of the entry to the tomb. Half a dozen dragonborn with jade rings stood in the crypt, clustered around one of the sarcophagi. The stone lid lay askew, and one of the dragonborn was helping a hyperventilating woman, her scales pale and her expression drawn, from the sarcophagus.

"It's all right!" the guard was saying, even as the panicking dragonborn pushed her away. "You're safe! You're safe!"

"You there!" a woman's voice bellowed. "Hold!"

Farideh turned to see a silver-scaled woman with Ophinshtalajiir's jade ring piercings in her neck and a Lance Defender's medallion pinned to her shoulder limping toward them. Her left leg was wrapped rigid in bandages from ankle to above the knee, and she hobbled on a sturdy crutch. She carried her sword bare, nevertheless. The shadow-smoke began to leak off Farideh's arms.

"Relax," Kallan murmured, stepping in front of Farideh. He smiled broadly at the approaching dragonborn, giving a polite bow. "Commander. Pardon the intrusion—we heard the shouts and meant to lend a hand."

The woman searched his face for the markers of his clan. Her sword pointed at Kallan's chest like the needle of a compass as he spoke. "Name yourself."

"Yrjixtilex Kallan, son of Ardeshisk, of the line of Esham-Ana. I'm out of the homesteads," he added, when her eyes flicked up to his bare face again. "Yrjixtilex Cayshan's place, up south of the Methwood. This is Farideh, who is newly claimed by Verthisathurgiesh, daughter of Mehen."

Surprise and recognition lit the Ophinshtalajiir's face. "Verthisathurgiesh Mehen? He was made clanless. He . . ." The sword dropped as she looked Farideh over. "She's a tiefling."

"He's had an interesting life out in the world," Kallan said. "May I know your name?"

"Ophinshtalajiir Sepideh," the woman said brusquely, remembering, perhaps, her station. "You need to clear this tomb—this is a private matter for our clan."

"Well met, Sepideh," Kallan said, not moving a muscle. "We're not at cross-purposes, I don't think. Farideh and I were searching the Shestandeliath tomb for signs of the creature that killed Shestandeliath Ravar. Wonder if you have any clues we might find useful."

Behind her, the dragonborn in the sarcophagus fainted. Sepideh sheathed her sword, not looking away from Kallan. "Maybe Shestandeliath is fine with you rummaging through their ancestors' bones, but Ophinshtalajiir declines."

"Yrjixtilex found a dead hatchling in the Verthisathurgiesh tomb killings," Kallan said. "Maybe that's a clue *you* could use?"

"Do you know why she was down here?" Farideh asked, nodding to the woman, now laid out on the floor with a folded cloak beneath her feet. "Was she with the hatchlings in the Verthisathurgiesh tomb?"

Sepideh shrugged. "Can a person not come to contemplate the struggles of their ancestors?"

"So she was just in the wrong place at the wrong time?" Kallan asked.

"Seems to be going around. Who sent *you* looking?"

"Verthisathurgiesh," Kallan said. "They're concerned about what's going on down here. And I think Ophinshtalajiir is wise enough to be concerned too."

Sepideh shook her head, the edges of her teeth clear, as if she were annoyed at the whole situation. "That well may be, but from the sound of things, we're dealing with something too dangerous for ordinary citizens . . . Rather . . . You need to go. Ophinshtalajiir has ordered the tomb closed."

"Thank you for your time then," Kallan said. "Let's go, Fari."

Up above, out of the stale air, he turned to her. "You think she knows something?"

"No," Farideh said. "I think she knows nothing and that worries her." No shortage of clues, but no sensible way they fit together. She thought of the elders in the Verthisathurgiesh tomb—and no one wanted to talk about what they knew. Except Kallan.

"That worked well. I was pretty certain we were going to get thrown out right off, but you got her talking."

Kallan shrugged. "People are generally decent. They're just scared or ignorant or frustrated. I figure you always talk to them like they're just settling onto the stool next to you and you'll get a lot further."

"What if they don't talk back to you that way?"

"Then they're hardjacks and you don't owe them," he said with a smile. "Is it time for you to go back?"

Farideh's tail slashed over the granite as she walked. "No," she said finally. "I need to take one more risk than Mehen will think I need to."

12

THE THIN, ICY AIR OF THE EARTHFASTS BURNED DAHL'S NOSE as he struggled to keep his breath. Two days into their ascent, and only Thost seemed to have little trouble. As he walked through the snowy, needle-leafed forest, Dahl listened to his grandmother's labored breath, a touchstone and a morbid timekeeper.

"Can we have a rest?" he called up the line. "She needs water."

Grathson glared back at him. "We're running behind as it is."

"Not going to be . . . any faster if she collapses," Bodhar wheezed.

They continued up to a break in the thinning trees, far enough to let Grathson feel like he'd won, no doubt. Dahl kept his tongue and started a small fire to help warm Sessaca. For the thousandth time since Volibar had released the winged snake, he scanned the sky between the branches for any sign of its return. The mountain rose up with a steep cliff face to the right, boulders and rubble from long-ago landslides littered the edges of the path ahead. Somewhere beyond the destruction, a waterfall of early snowmelt trickled.

Mira kneeled beside him, measuring out a mix of herbs for tea. "It'll help with the elevation."

"Mix it with some of that Chessentan Black," Dahl advised. "She'll toss anything else into the brush." He took out a waterskin, and Bodhar handed him a little pot out of the haversack.

"Get . . . that water . . . *boiling*," Sessaca gasped as Thost set her gently down at the base of a pine tree. "Tastes . . . like mud . . . otherwise."

"Yes, Granny."

"How much farther, do you expect?" Mira murmured.

"Gods only know," Dahl answered. He dropped his voice lower still. "What's to the east of the Master's Library?"

Mira gave him a puzzled look. "The Vast," she said slowly. "Tsurlagol. Imaskar."

"Zhentarim don't have forces in Tsurlagol," Dahl said. "Not large ones. Nor Imaskar."

"Not that I know of." She added the tea into the roiling pot. "But as established, they don't tell me everything we're doing."

He pointed his chin at Xulfaril. "Your leader there got a message saying they were sending forces along the eastern path. What's that about?"

"Add it to the list of things they don't tell me," Mira said, pouring a measure of a ruby-colored potion into the pot. "That's the first I've heard of anyone else being involved. Speaking of forces, are your folks coming soon?"

"They don't know we're here. I ran through my sendings."

"Damn."

"You keep saying 'you' instead of 'we,' " Dahl noted, dropping his voice to hardly more than the sound of his breath. "Anything you want to tell me?"

Mira turned and smiled at him in a forced way. "That we are quite surrounded by people who don't know why I wouldn't?"

She was right, and yet it didn't sit well with Dahl. Mira's father might be a High Harper. She might have sworn the oath and gotten the tattoo etched into the side of her neck, but no one could convince Dahl that at her core, Mira wasn't out for herself, first and foremost.

Beyond Mira, Sessaca watched them, a faint smile playing at her mouth even as she labored to catch her breath. Dahl scowled at her.

"Don't," he said. Mira straightened, considering Dahl and Sessaca in turn.

"Better . . . brown," Sessaca rasped, "than . . . scaly." Mira's mouth became a hard line.

"Granny," Thost said in a low voice, "you can't say things like that."

"What's she mean 'scaly'?" Bodhar asked.

"She's not a stlarning dragonborn!" Dahl said. "And even if she was, I'm not looking for my grandmother's opinion on my love life. Leave Mira out of this, please."

Sessaca snorted. "You've got," she wheezed at Mira, "a . . . brightbird . . . girl?"

"Not in the market, old mother," Mira said, stirring the tea. "Thank you for the offer."

"I still think she's Hillfarian," Bodhar said.

"A Hillfarian . . . with a dragonborn name?" Sessaca said, dripping doubt.

"A dragonborn?" Thost asked. He scratched his chin. "How does that work?"

"It doesn't," Dahl said. "She's not a dragonborn and she's not from Hillsfar, and she's not something I particularly want to discuss in front of these people, so let it lie."

"I don't know why you don't tell them," Mira piped up. She kneeled beside Sessaca and handed her a mug of the tea. "You needn't be embarrassed."

"I'm not embarrassed—"

"Why should he be embarrassed?" Thost asked.

"He shouldn't," Mira said. Then, "She's a very nice girl."

"You *know* her?" Bodhar demanded, sitting a little straighter. "She knows your mystery girl, but we can't meet her?"

"She *knew* her," Dahl said. "Before, a *long* time ago. And I didn't say you couldn't meet Farideh, I said she couldn't come."

"He didn't think you'd take to her, I assume," Mira said.

"You are not helping," Dahl hissed.

"Who said I was trying to help?" Mira replied. "These are hardly the hidden secrets of Messemprarian ruins. What's the point of hiding every detail about her?"

"Not every detail," Bodhar said. He turned to Thost and Sessaca. "She's adopted and she puts a lot of sugar in her tea."

Dahl bit back a string of curses, and turned to the Zhentarim party. A quartet of them stood, eyes on the cliff side. Grathson had his hand on his blade, tense as a wire. Xulfaril watched her unhappy subordinate, still crouched beneath the trees.

"What kind of person gets adopted by a dragonborn?" Sessaca asked, her voice stronger, but still raspy. She slurped her tea. "Seems like you'd have to go out of your way to get an arrangement like that."

"What's down there?" Thost asked. "Akanûl? She a genie?"

"That's close," Mira said. "But no."

"Not close," Dahl said, breaking his study of Grathson. "All of you, hush—"

A stone rattled down the cliff face. Another two Zhents stood suddenly, eyes toward the trees. Oghma's bloody papercuts—ambush. Dahl reached for his sword.

"What's close to a genie," Bodhar mused, "but not, but embarrassing enough that Dahl'd hold his tongue?"

"She's a tiefling, all right!" Dahl snapped, yanking his sword free. "Get your shitting blades out, now! We're under attack!"

A flight of arrows soared down from the tops of the cliffs, two of them catching the gathered Zhentarim. Goblins swarmed over the nearby boulders, stone weapons high. The Zhents rose to meet them, Bodhar grabbed his dagger, and Thost grabbed a fallen tree branch. Mira cursed and scrabbled for her pack and the long knives inside.

Dahl stepped in front of his grandmother, drawing his mind into the peace of Oghma. But it was not the prayer for wisdom that drummed through his mind.

Does the salmon demand the tide? Does the owl's wing unfurl the gale? His sword cut through the air, slamming into the first goblin and breaking one scrawny arm with a *crunch*.

My priest may name the spinning plane. The chant sounded like his own voice, sounded like Farideh's soft recitation of the words imprinted on his soul. It made him uneasy, unsettled. It made him fight harder. *The plane has never spun for him.*

Two more ran at him, holding either end of a trip line—he caught it on the sword and forced it up, over his head on the guard. One of the two lifted off its feet and landed in a heap. Bodhar cut that one's throat as if it were a lamb for slaughter while Dahl made short work of the other.

Does the owl's wing unfurl the gale? Dahl pressed forward, warding off a trio that surged toward him and Sessaca. *It is the gale that folds the wing.*

Xulfaril cast a spell that sent a crack of thunder rolling through the mountain, stones rattling down the slopes. The goblins that didn't fall redoubled their efforts, clustering around Xulfaril. Too hungry to fail, Dahl thought sweeping another with his sword.

The plane has never spun for him. And still the wise seek the axis . . .

He glanced back at Sessaca. His grandmother had gained her feet and stood with her back right against the big pine tree, three of the dirty green creatures surrounding her.

"Tough eating," she warned.

The goblin at the center, a squat creature with a blaze of white hair down the center of its skull laughed and growled something back in Orcish. They crept forward. Sessaca smiled.

Thost slammed his scavenged branch down on top of the goblins, flattening them on their backs. Sessaca nodded at him. "Next time wait," she advised as Bodhar and Dahl finished off the attackers. "You'll snap their necks. Lot cleaner."

The fight was over as quickly as it had started. The remnants of the ambush fled off into the wilds, leaving their fallen behind.

"Gods stlarning hrast it!" Xulfaril spat. "I hate goblins."

"Worse," Grathson said. He held up a dead goblin by the back of its armor. Scavenged armor, hammered down to fit a smaller body, but the embossed spider was still plain. Scavenged from drow, Dahl thought. Xulfaril hissed a curse.

Grathson dropped the goblin. "If they're on the surface—"

"We need to keep moving." Xulfaril turned and found Dahl watching. He didn't look away. "Get your grandmother up and ready or we'll leave her behind, understand."

"There's no point in heading on without me," Sessaca called, as loudly as her struggling breath would allow. "It's not a stlarning inn. If you could just push in and wander around, there'd be nothing there to find."

Xulfaril watched her stonily. "Don't be so sure."

Dahl surveyed the damage. Bodhar had a hand pressed to his forearm, blood seeping through the sleeve. Sessaca and Thost remained unharmed, but the tea had been kicked over, the mug shattered, and the waterskin's cork knocked free. The crust of snow melted at the loss.

"So . . . what's that mean?" Bodhar said, as though the fight hadn't happened. "Does she have goat feet?"

Dahl sighed. "She doesn't have stlarning goat feet."

"Didn't think you could do worse than dragonborn." Sessaca's dark eyes held him like razors to his throat.

"You know you're not . . ." Thost began. He looked awkwardly to Bodhar. "I mean, we all joke, but it's not as if you don't have *options*."

"Randar's youngest daughter's still at home," Bodhar offered. "She's . . . a good seamstress?"

"I'm perfectly aware of the options I have." Dahl rubbed his face. "I'm going to refill the waterskin."

"Are you?" Bodhar asked. "I mean . . . No, I don't think there's many a woman out there thinking, 'My, but I'd like to be married to a Harper agent up in Waterdeep!' but I can't believe the number's . . . so . . ."

At the word Harper, Dahl's hand grabbed hold of his sword. He kept his eyes on Bodhar, carefully watching Mira from the edges of his vision—she had the wisdom to look surprised, to grab her own weapon.

Bodhar turned almost purple. "Oh, naed."

Dahl turned slowly. The Zhentarim were all watching him. Grathson's sword was still out. "Hands on your head, Harper."

"I don't think that's necessary," Xulfaril said. She eyed Dahl with a speculative smile.

Grathson narrowed his eyes. "Have you lost your mind? You've been letting him send messages—"

"All of which have been read."

"And we know they use codes. Who knows what they know by now? This is why you're here—I shouldn't be the one telling you to stlarning think about these kinds of outcomes!"

"Precisely," Xulfaril said. "Go fetch your water, Harper."

Waterskin in hand, Dahl stormed through the crowd of staring Zhentarim. The snowmelt splattered down the cliff, past the boulders, where it curved in toward the mountain peak. Out of sight from the Zhentarim and from his family, Dahl propped the waterskin's mouth under the fall and crouched against a boulder, out of the icy spray, waiting—surely—for Xulfaril.

In Suzail, before he'd let his fear and doubt run him off the path, he'd been sure that his family would take to Farideh. How could they not? He loved her, after all. He still wasn't sure what to credit to the chaos of war and the shock of their near deaths, what to the changes wrought by the blessings of Oghma, and what was the pure unaltered truth—but it seemed that the moment he realized he loved her extended, forward and backward, through time. He'd always loved her. He'd always be surprised he loved her.

Except for a moment where she'd channeled the powers of the god of sin, and Dahl found a kernel of doubt.

Or was he simply being sensible for once? Without Farideh beside him, Sessaca and his brothers could assume all manner of things about her. And what if they convinced you? he thought. You doubted yourself once. You might again.

"Oghma's bloody papercuts," he muttered up at the sky. Focus on the Master's Library. Focus on finding a way out of this deal. Focus on keeping everyone alive. You can be a weeping mouse later.

He pulled the flask out, held it in both hands.

The magic of a sending crackled in his ears like a shower of ice. Farideh's voice floated on the brittle air. He sat up straight.

Looking for spells that could get me to you, but it's not easy here. Should I bother? she whispered. *You're headed somewhere, not alone . . . I love you.*

I love you too, he nearly said. He bit down hard on his tongue. Don't come here. Stay where you are. Stay away from the Zhentarim. I can't stop thinking about you. I'll find you. The spell dissolved in the same icy crackle and Dahl cursed and cursed and cursed.

A shadow fell across the rocks and Dahl turned, expecting to find Xulfaril creeping up on him. But a woman he'd never seen before stood at the cliff's edge.

No, not just a woman. A devil. A cambion like Lorcan. A silver gown trailed off her narrow shoulders into the muddy rocks, and her shaven scalp was tattooed with matching silver figures. Her wings curved around her, a niche for a dark idol.

Dahl drew his sword as he stood.

"Well met," the devil said. "My apologies for eavesdropping."

"Lorcan could have come himself," Dahl asked. If the letter had broken their deal, well at least that was settled, he told himself, even though his pulse was racing. "Where is he?"

"I am an agent of nothing but my own desires." She smiled at him in an unbroken way that made Dahl grip his sword all the more firmly. "And what I desire requires assistance. You have a deal with Lorcan. A deal you might prefer to be free of?"

Dahl took a step toward the clearing. "I've had my fill of Hellish deals, thanks."

"Better to go the rest of your days without once speaking to your beloved?" She clucked her tongue. "No. That's not it. You think you can break the deal, don't you? You think you're clever enough to find a path around it."

Dahl said nothing, and her smile grew. "Let me guess: you have a plan. You've probably worked out a way to return to her—that's not too difficult if you're determined—and you think given that you'll surely be able to untangle the deal." She shook her head. "You're out of your depth, Dahl Peredur."

"Who are you?"

"An interested party," she said. "What if I said I could fix this for you? I could take control of the deal, revise the terms, and make certain you're reunited with Farideh."

Dahl didn't lower his sword. "I'd say the price is probably too high."

"But you would want to hear it, wouldn't you?"

Oghma, Mystra, and Lost Deneir, he did. Some part of him shouted that it might be enough, it might be fair. Who knew what this woman wanted, what she had against Lorcan? Maybe it was about harming him, not about Dahl or Farideh at all?

"What do you want?"

She smiled. "Your firstborn child."

Dahl's blood turned cold. "I don't have any children."

"Not yet," the woman said. "Let us say you'd be required to perform certain tasks once I have the deal in hand."

"That's monstrous."

She laughed. "You're a very innocent little boy, aren't you? All I'm asking you to do is bed your brightbird—are you going to pretend you weren't going to do that already? The child wouldn't be harmed. The child wouldn't even have to leave your sight. But she'd be mine."

For a moment, Dahl turned the offer in his head, boggling at the woman's insistence that it was nothing, a trifle, a reasonable act. Just as Lorcan had spoken of giving up the right to speak to Farideh—he'd live without it, the alternative was worth the price, no one could possibly turn this down. That was how they caught you, Dahl thought.

But what this woman was suggesting moved beyond that, and a rage at all the Nine Hells boiled up in him.

"Stlarn off," Dahl said. "I'm not making any shitting deal with a shitting devil, regardless of how 'reasonable' it is, when you're talking about creating a child for the sole purpose of damning it—behind Farideh's back no less. And yes, I said that the way I did for a reason—because I *am* clever. I am not out of my depth yet. Take your deal back to the Hells."

"It's not going to get cheaper," she said. "Think about it."

"I've thought," Dahl said. "I don't want it."

"Very well," she said. She never stopped smiling at him as she held up one ringed hand. "It's not as if I don't have options."

Dahl started to shout—what was *that* supposed to mean? Had he put Farideh in danger? But the woman twisted the ring on her thumb and she vanished out of existence.

Oghma's bloody papercuts, Dahl thought, letting his sword drop. That small part of him screamed that he'd lost a chance, however monstrous it had been, and the very thought of any of it made him sick. He grabbed the waterskin, hardly feeling the splash of the chilly water. His hands shook. There had to be an answer. A better answer than this.

"Well, well, Harper." Xulfaril stood at the edge of the boulders, a smile threatening her thin mouth. "Looks like you might have more to offer than rituals after all."

"I don't know what you think you saw—" Dahl began.

"Please," Xulfaril said. "Don't insult my intelligence and I won't insult yours. Do the Harpers know you're dealing with the Nine Hells?"

"Are you asking if you need to tell them?"

Xulfaril chuckled once. "I don't intend to tell the Shepherd and his flock anything. Does your family know? I assume the creature was speaking of your other little secret. The tiefling." She smiled. "You've been awfully skilled at hiding such a lot of things."

Dahl swallowed against his suddenly dry throat. "What do you want?"

"Is that what you think we're doing? Goodman, let me assure you—while I wouldn't hesitate to extort you given the right circumstances, we are not the Harpers. Your indiscretions are your own business, so long as they do not impede our business. No, I came to offer you an opportunity."

There it was. "How is that different?"

The wizard smiled. "I need historians. You've worked with Mira before, she says. She's coy about details—not exactly what you'd call easy to work with. I can't imagine she'll be much easier now she knows where your allegiances are."

Relief flooded him. They weren't questioning Mira's cover—yet. "You'll hear the same from my side about me."

"Not the same," Xulfaril said. "You dislike unnecessary conflict. You'll volunteer yourself to make certain your grandmother survives. You'll try and stop my snake handler from wasting resources. I don't doubt that if, say, Grathson were to try and even the slate with your brother for that punch he got in, you'd have your sword out and ready. And while you'll keep your allegiances secret, you're not going to hold things back just because it suits you—obviously you told your brothers the truth, because you thought they needed to hear it. I think you have a better sense, perhaps, of what's important. What the rest of us need to know."

"Like why you might be traveling to the Underdark?"

Xulfaril's single eye searched his face a moment. "See? Clever. And since you aren't fond of unnecessary conflict, I think you'll keep in mind what might lie in the Underdark is no worse than what slinks out of the Nine Hells. And that I still have Grathson's leash in hand—as much as anyone can. Be wise about the rumors you spread." She turned, unperturbed. "My superiors have a very long list of artifacts they want, and quickly. What do you know about giants?"

"Enough," Dahl said slowly. What did the Zhentarim want with giant artifacts? "Depends on what exactly we're looking for."

"And we can get to that once we've found the Master's Library." She smiled back at him, and it made Dahl want to look away. "Welcome to my team."

• • •

DON'T PANIC, ILSTAN Nyaril told himself, staring at the crisscross of iron bars, the single guard in the room beyond. Don't panic, don't panic, don't panic . . .

. . . the demons of the Abyss cannot be said to be bold, Azuth, the Lord of Spells, murmured in Ilstan's thoughts. He'd been too long from another caster, Ilstan dimly realized, too long from sharing the gifts of the Chosen of Azuth. The voice of the god grew stronger and stronger, and Ilstan's headache built and built.

Don't panic. Don't panic. *What should I do, Lord?*

. . . To be bold, the voice went on, *implies comprehension of what meekness is. They are force. They are chaos. They are will and hunger embodied . . .*

And the devils of the Hells, Ilstan responded in his own thoughts, are their match in every way, only worse. The creature that attacked might have been either—and with the Chosen of Asmodeus appearing right after, how could it be anything but a devil?

. . . They are the wolves baying at the edges of the village. They are the wolves who cull the sheep . . . And the devils are the shepherds . . . but what difference does that make to the lamb, in the end?

What was her plan? Ilstan thought frantically. He began to pace. What was she going to do, and who was going to help her, thinking she was nothing to be frightened of, no one to mistrust? Even when Farideh had appeared on the stairs, Ilstan's first thought had been gladness. Reinforcements. She had a way of making you think she was on your side, after all.

But was it her? Ilstan wondered. She wasn't there when the fiend was feeding—or was that a trick to make her seem innocent?

She blocked you, he thought. But she didn't try to harm you. She could have, and who would have thought her wrong? Him, covered in the dragonborn's blood. Her, wounded by his missiles. A perfect opportunity, if one were bold enough . . .

The door opened a moment later or an eternity later. Time was rushing past him at points, crawling over him like ants on a corpse at others. He risked a look up and saw Farideh and Kallan the Traitor enter.

. . . There is treachery and there is treachery . . . the tale of the unfaithful servant tells us . . .

"I am faithful," Ilstan murmured, holding Farideh's mismatched gaze. "I am faithful. I am faithful."

"*Kallan, akison?*" the guard said, each word needling its way into Ilstan's mind. He clasped the Traitor's forearm. "*Wushzarath sathi?*"

"*Sjath vethkeshka,*" Kallan replied. He pointed at Farideh. "*Irth Verthisathurgiesh Farideh.*"

The guard's pierced brow rose higher. "*Thyr irth?*"

"*Ariverthisathurgiesh.*" Kallan shrugged. "*Irth ir-okhuir tuorth. Irth renthizhath Munthrarechi. Akison?*" The Draconic itched through Ilstan's brain like worms crawling around his skull. He covered his ears.

Farideh stood right up against the bars, peering at him, while the lines of magic shivered over her, threatening to expose what she was at her core. "Ilstan? Can you understand me?"

"Do you know where you are?" Kallan asked.

Ilstan glared at the sellsword, and Kallan took a step back. "I know where I am, O Traitorous One. I know where I am and I know who put me here."

"*Karshoj,*" Kallan spat. The guard rattled off some more Draconic, and Kallan replied. "Fari, I don't know what you're going to do. He's not well."

"But I think I know why," she said. The magic across her buckled and puckered, pulling up her skin to reveal the terrible creature beneath, a fiend of unparalleled cruelty and avarice . . . which twisted and melted to show a kind and peaceful young woman, the face of an angel.

. . . *Illusion is deception . . . illusion can be the only way to speak the truth . . . We cannot trust our eyes, so trust the mind, the heart, the soul . . .*

"Ilstan," she said again. Her features flickered from girl to fiend, from angel to devil. Ilstan covered his eyes, unable to bear the distortion. "Lord of Spells, forgive me, I am too weak, I am too weak."

"He gets like this," Kallan said. "He needs a wizard."

Farideh blew out a breath. "Well, then I'll have to do it. *Zhvori ir. Ir tuorth arcanish.* Um, *lefanthish. Ya lefanthish. Deshkrouth?*"

The guard waved a hand. "*Thrik. Thrik. Ghorosh ir Verthisathurgiesh ir svent-sinti!*"

"*What?*" Farideh cried. "Who?"

"Thrikominaki Mehen." The guard shifted. "I did not see it," he added in Common that rolled like stones from his mouth. "It's why Adjudicator Sirrush moved him here."

You should always engage a fiend directly, the voice said. Ilstan stopped. The Lord of Spells had seldom been so clear, so certain. So mellifluous . . .

Who else can stop it, the voice crooned, *if not you, o Chosen One? You have the strength, the wherewithal . . . You just have to free yourself . . .*

Something pulled on Ilstan's thoughts, toward the iron bars. Toward the spaces between. Toward Farideh.

Even iron melts, the voice said, *if it's hot enough . . .*

The fireball built in Ilstan's hands, kindled by magic he hardly sensed he was drawing. Bigger, hotter, enough to melt the bars and end the guard. He had to escape—one death was a sacrifice.

The dragonborn guard shouted at him in Draconic, one hand on his weapon. Farideh turned, eyes widening.

Straight on, my lad, the voice said. *It's what must be done.*

Bigger . . .hotter . . .

"Ilstan! Don't!" Farideh shouted. Her voice seemed to snap the tugging line upon his thoughts, his headache vanishing and leaving Ilstan cold and dizzy. Something shoved him in the side, knocked him off balance. The fireball peeled itself off his hands as he stumbled, streaking toward the door of the prison.

The space between the prison's bars crackled as the fire hit, and the orb ricocheted off at an angle, crashing against the stone wall. The heat of it scorched Ilstan's skin, sizzled the ends of his hair as he threw himself to the floor.

He heard Farideh shouting in Draconic as well, heard the door open. "Hey," she said. "Are you burned? Are you all right?"

"Don't touch me!" Ilstan said. But suddenly his skin was a sheet of pain as his nerves woke again to the burns. "My lord! My lord!" he screamed, as if his cries could pierce the prison of the Nine Hells. He could not be alone. He could not be—

"Here," a man's voice said. And then he was choking on a syrup that tasted of bitterness and anise, wintergreen and old wine. The screaming edges of his body quieted. Kallan stood over him, the guard's spear in one hand, the instrument of Ilstan's failure.

A feeling like a sigh rolled through his thoughts.

. . . One must never assume, the voice went on, as if nothing had happened, *that a demon may be kept in hand. One binds them as one binds the gale . . .*

Ilstan wept. Azuth remained.

"The bars are protected against the dragonborn's breath," Farideh told him. "That fireball would have turned right back on you."

"No," Ilstan said. He struggled to sit, but the potion made his movements sluggish, his muscles weak. "Azuth wouldn't have let it. He would have destroyed my prison." You must cast, he told himself. You must end her. "You distracted me."

"Did Azuth tell you to do that?" she demanded. "Does he talk to you?"

Ilstan sneered. "You cannot trick me."

"Did he tell you to melt the bars?"

Ilstan shook his head weakly. His vision was swimming—they'd drugged them, the beasts! He pulled at the Weave, magic crackling into his form "You cannot trick me, devil-child."

"Listen to me!" she shouted. "I think . . . I think we can help one another. I think you're already being tricked."

"You cannot trick me," Ilstan said again, before he passed out of consciousness

• • •

FARIDEH STEPPED ASIDE as two Adjudicators moved Ilstan's slack body to a bench, the pieces of the mystery not set together, not ready to knit into something whole and true. She sat perfectly still, as if moving might scatter her thoughts . . . or give her the answers she was afraid to have. Ilstan's arm drooped, dangling off the bench, displaying ugly rows of runes in thick thread along his sleeve.

Find a wizard, the embroidered words read. *Give the magic to another caster.*

Find Farideh.

Rescue the Lord of Spells.

End the Lady of Black Magic.

Farideh swallowed hard. He wants you dead, she thought. He thinks you're the hand of Asmodeus.

Asmodeus, who burned with the sigil of Azuth.

Asmodeus, who wasn't a god until the same year when Azuth stopped speaking to his followers.

Azuth, who drove Ilstan mad.

Who told him to cast a fireball at a shield of magic that would turn it right back at him and burn him alive.

Who had told Ilstan to kill her.

She read the embroidery again. Were those the words of Azuth, or were they Ilstan's? Or were they Asmodeus's? Azuth, after all, was dead—dead since the Spellplague almost a century ago. Was it more likely he was alive and mad and trying to murder his purported Chosen or that it was never Azuth at all?

Dahl would know, she thought. Or at least, Dahl would have something to add, something that might shift all these pieces around in her head into an answer.

A memory flooded her—Dahl, his arms around her, late, late in the night, mumbling sleepily, "You should be a Harper. Do you want to be a Harper? I wonder if I can convince Tam."

Farideh had stirred from the edge of sleep. "Why?"

"For one, I figure things out faster when I have you to talk to." He nuzzled the back of her neck. "Besides, for another, you figure out plenty on your own—"

"I think you have those backward."

"See look, you spot what I don't," he teased, and he kissed her. "Besides, if you join, we could run missions together. Thwarting blackguards by day. By night . . ."

"You'll run around on more missions?"

"The exact schedule is not the important part here."

"Are you all right?" Kallan asked.

"Fine," Farideh said. Dahl was safe, because Dahl wasn't here. Put him aside. She considered Ilstan's sleeve again, blew out a breath. "I have to come back here. How long before that wears off?" she asked the guard in Draconic.

He shrugged. "A few hours. I don't know. It's made for Vayemniri and sometimes it hits . . . the others kind of hard. Except dwarves." He looked at Kallan, shaking his head. "*Karshoji* dwarves, *sathi*. *Karshoji* dwarves."

They thanked the guard and left, winding through the Adjudicators' enclave, back toward the center of the city. *Rescue the Lord of Spells. End the Lady of Black Magic.*

All I want is your happiness, Farideh, Asmodeus's nightmare promise echoed through her like a thunderclap, and she shuddered. If you don't touch this puzzle, she thought, he'll leave you be. He'll give you whatever you want. He'll rescue Dahl. Everything will be safe.

And you might be responsible for something unspeakably evil, she thought. Leaving aside Dahl is much safer away from you. She thought of the image Lorcan had conjured in the basin—much safer. And happy.

She kept her eyes on the mottled granite beneath her feet.

"Look, I'm sorry about back there," Kallan said as they left the Adjudicators' enclave. The light of Djerad Thymar glowed low, the pale of early evening. So close to the city's peak, the stairs were uncrowded, only a handful of Lance Defenders climbing toward home. "Jumping after you. I'm not your keeper. You're not a hatchling."

"It's all right," Farideh said. "You were worried about Mehen."

"I was worried about *you*. That wizard's completely mad—do you realize that?"

"I've dealt with madder," Farideh said. Truthfully, it had been a risk—a risk she didn't relish telling Mehen about, but worth it if she'd managed, even a little, to break down Ilstan's fear of her. Which she wasn't quite certain she had. "Thank you for coming with me. Getting me in."

"Don't mention it." Kallan nodded at a dragonborn man staring at them as they passed. "What's your father going to say if I tell him?"

It shot a bolt of panic through her, but it dissipated quickly. "If you do," she had said, "he'll be upset, but he'll get over it. You're not my keeper, and I'm not a hatchling."

Kallan chuckled. "Too true."

They crossed the walkways before Farideh spoke again. "I don't think you're wasting your time."

"How's that?" Kallan asked.

"With Mehen. I don't think you're wasting your time." Farideh blew out a breath, the shadow-smoke unfurling off her sleeves in little curls like sprouting seeds. "But you should know he's . . . kept mostly to himself for . . . well, for a long time. I think. He hasn't carried on with anyone seriously for . . ." She fumbled at the count of years—there were seven and a half missing from her thoughts, after all. And you don't know what he did while you were lost, Farideh thought. "We were twelve. He's not used to it. And sometimes . . . Sometimes he forgets . . ."

"He forgets you're not twelve still?" Kallan said. "My granny has the same trouble. And none of her kin chase down mad war wizards or run with hellhounds."

Farideh blushed. "I just mean his reasons might not be firm enough to completely count him out. Unless you want to, I mean."

Kallan gave her a gentle smile and patted her shoulder. "I'm no hatchling either, but I appreciate the advice. What's your plan with the wizard?"

"Try again," she said. The shadows dissipated—the man who thought a god wanted her dead was less nerve-wracking than her father's romances. "He might be mad, but I think he knows more than I do at this point. He just doesn't realize it."

Kallan started to answer but stopped dead, thirty feet from the entrance to the Verthisathurgiesh enclave. The same two dragonborn girls were standing guard beside the massive doors, but they held their weapons more like they could do some harm and less like they were merely supports. A tall tiefling man with pale skin, blackened horns like a ram's, and brown hair stood a little too close to them, speaking a little too loudly. He wore a dark coat with a high collar that he kept pressing a hand to.

"The message goes in her hands or it doesn't leave mine," the tiefling man was saying. "So you can tell me where to look or you can go and fetch her."

The dragonborn guard started to reply, but she looked over his shoulder and spotted Farideh. "There," she said. "That's who you're looking for."

The man turned. His pale eyes, blue as a summer sky, fell on Kallan first, puzzled. But then he found Farideh and he laughed once. "Well," he said as she approached, the shadow-smoke leaking off her skin. "You're no dragonborn. Farideh, is it?"

She'd seen him before—the first day they'd come to Djerad Thymar. "Who are you?"

"The name is Brume," he said, with a florid little bow. He straightened, eyeing Kallan. "Might we talk in private?"

"Depends on what you want to talk about," Farideh said.

His smile twitched. "Cagey, aren't we? I have a message for you. It seems you know someone who knows my friends."

Farideh studied him. Devils. Harpers. Dragonborn clans. Cormyrean nobles. There was hardly any telling who he meant or what sort of a message he'd mean. "You're going to have to be more specific."

Brume pressed a hand to his collar once more, and plucked a tiny roll of parchment from his sleeve. With one hand he unrolled it an inch or two. "Someone called Dahl."

For a moment, Farideh's legs felt as though they'd vanished, as if she'd plunged through the granite floors of Djerad Thymar, nothing but a ghost. "Give it to me!" Brume closed his hand around the scroll and smiled again. "Might," he said, "we talk in private?"

Farideh felt the powers of Asmodeus creeping up her bones. "Kallan, you know the way back to the rooms, right?"

"Fari, I don't know—"

"I'll meet you in a moment." She beckoned to Brume, passing through the doors and winding her way to a little sitting room whose latticework screen overlooked the city below. Brume shut the door behind him, and handed over the note.

"Compliments of the Black Network."

Farideh said nothing. There was only the tiny sharp green lettering, a hand she knew better than most, and the faint scent of rosemary hanging over the letter. Dizzy, dreamlike, she skimmed the words twice, afraid to sink into it, afraid it would crumble to dust or figment.

I don't have space to tell you everything I want to: I wish you were here—not a day's gone by that I haven't wished you were here. How could I have possibly been so stupid as to think we would've been fine apart? It's been 12 days & it feels like a lifetime & I am so sorry I ever suggested it. I realized that in Suzail—I swear—& I was coming back to tell you so when I was interrupted. Now my brothers & I are hostages of the Zhentarim & we're heading to the Vast. I'm hoping I can find a way to you soon, through them & end this. I love you. I miss you. I am sure of that. Please tell me you're all right & that you haven't given up? Yours always, Dahl

He was fine. He wasn't running. He was safe.

For now, a little part added, because he's looking for you and now you know where he is, so will Asmodeus. She read the note again and was glad for it anyway. Farideh looked up at Brume. "How did you get this? Is he near here?"

Brume reached up and unhooked the fastener at the collar of his coat. As the fabric parted, something slithered out, separating and flapping into the air above them. Farideh startled and the Zhent chuckled as she watched the dark shadows course over the ceiling like eels through water.

"Winged snakes," Brume said. "Haslam and Keetley won't bite, never you mind. Sweet as kittens. They'll even bring back a reply if you ask nice."

Farideh narrowed her eyes. "What's the price?"

Brume settled in one of the chairs. "My superiors are very interested in how the elections for Vanquisher are going to fall together. It happens that you're the foundling daughter of the Verthisathurgiesh clan's most infamous exile. You seem like someone who might know a thing or two about who the Crippled Mountain is going to have stand for them."

"I don't know why you'd think that," Farideh said. "I don't know the first thing about electing the Vanquisher."

"But you have ears, don't you? You have eyes?" The snakes spiraled down to his outstretched arm, slithered one after the other into the sleeve of his coat. "You promise to find out who the matriarch is pushing for Vanquisher, I'll let Haslam ferry back your love notes. Deal?"

"What if I can't find anything out?"

"Then we'll have to renegotiate," Brume said, handing her another tiny scroll, then ink and a stylus. "But to begin with, there's a lot of murmuring about this returned scion. That doesn't happen much."

Farideh's hand shook as she dipped the stylus, her thoughts a rambling mess. What did she say? What could she say? *Why did you leave? Why aren't you here? Why didn't you mention Mira? You have to stay away for your own safety.* She shut her eyes.

You only get a handful of sentences, she thought, setting pen to page. *Don't waste them on what might not matter.*

She scribbled her message as quickly as she could and handed it back to Brume. "How long?"

He shrugged. "Wind's good. A day or two to get there."

She nodded and took a silver coin from her pocket. "Here. My thanks."

"You've already agreed to pay in talk."

"But not for bringing me the note," she said, thinking of Kallan's way with the Shestandeliath commander. "So here. My thanks."

Brume grinned as he pocketed the coin. "Any time. I'll tell you if you get an answer back." His eyes flicked over her. "Ask around if you get bored with the scalies. I'd be happy to show you the city."

She walked him back to the entrance, clutching Dahl's note. He'd written the letter before she'd made the sending, before he'd been unable to respond. What if something had changed? What if he was in danger? What if she'd unmasked him with that sending or called attention to him in the wrong moment? What if—

Stop, she told herself. Imagining every horrible possibility wasn't going to keep Dahl safe. What would keep him safe were his wits and his skills. She blew out a breath. *You have to trust him*, she told herself. *You have to remember he can take care of himself.*

Besides, there was plenty to worry about right in front of her—demons and murderers and Ilstan and all the Vayemniri politics. She read the note over several times as she walked back to their rooms, dwelling instead on the warm, fluttery feeling in the base of her chest. *I love you. I miss you. I am sure of that.*

Zoonie scratched feverishly at the door to Havilar's room. Farideh rolled her eyes and went to let her out. It wasn't until the hellhound had pushed past her into the common area that Farideh noticed Lorcan, stretched out on one of the low sofas and staring at the ceiling. He wore his human guise and an irritated expression that he turned on her as she stopped.

"Have you been sitting here since this morning?" she asked.

"No, I found another problem to bang my head against," he drawled. "And you still haven't figured out how to make time run properly on this plane."

Farideh chuckled and tucked the note into her sleeve. "Sorry, I didn't have time. Did Kallan come in here?"

"No one's come in here." Lorcan propped himself up, eyeing her. "How was your terribly private outing with the sellsword?"

Farideh blew out a breath. "Useful in some ways and confusing in others." She sat down on the couch beside his. "Do you know of demons that . . . stick people in coffins or something similar?"

Lorcan tilted his head. "Not personally."

"I mean, specific types. Before we go running around after it, it seems like it would be a good idea to figure out what else it might do. So is that something a kind of demon does?"

"Possibly," Lorcan said. "What I know about demons comes from my sisters—what does an erinyes need to know on the battlefields of the Blood War? No one stuffs living bodies in coffins in the Blood War. Or at least they didn't. No one ever said the Abyss was known for its consistency."

Farideh bit her lip. "If you were going to trap someone in a stone sarcophagus, why would you do it?"

"I'm not a demon," Lorcan returned.

"I know, I'm just looking for answers. Why would I do it? To stop them from doing damage and keep them where they are so I could bring the guard—the Adjudicators," she corrected. "So why would you?"

Lorcan tilted his head again and was silent for a long moment. "I would do that if I couldn't kill someone, but I needed them to die."

"That's gruesome."

"I didn't say I'd done it," Lorcan pointed out. "But assuming you're talking about the same stone box that Zoonie found the dretch in, you're taking quite a risk stashing a person inside. Bad air, no water. People panic in a situation like that. Unless you somehow put them to sleep."

"Then I suppose we wait for Havi." Farideh sighed. "What's your problem? The head-banging one."

Lorcan sat up, repositioned himself to lounge against the sofa with a kind of preternatural ease that made Farideh's stomach tighten in a very different way. His dark eyes swept over her. "You're in a good mood. Did the sellsword help you shake your bad dreams?"

She thought of the note in her sleeve and felt a peculiar, giddy mix of gladness and guilt. "I guess it's good to have some direction. Even if it's making you frustrated."

He laughed once. "As if you've ever let a problem stymie you, darling."

It was almost easy. It was almost normal—as if he'd never betrayed her, never tricked her, never broken her heart. As if he meant his apology were true and everything might be all right. She couldn't deny a part of her still felt fond of him, still mourned what they'd had in Suzail. That a part of her still looked at his lean body, stretched artfully across the couch and felt hungry and possessive.

A slow smile curved Lorcan's mouth as though he sensed the tide of her blood, the shift of her thoughts, and she ran her thumb over the edge of the note, protruding just beyond her shirt cuff.

Then someone entered the common room and a voice she never wanted to hear again sliced through Farideh's thoughts.

"Havilar, I know you don't want to talk to me . . ."

Farideh stood and turned, slowly, slowly—wanting to see for herself, not wanting to see at all. Not wanting to be noticed and wanting to demand to be noticed. The powers of Asmodeus twined up her nerves, building with rage. Arjhani fell silent as she looked on him—and it *was* Arjhani, looking every bit as he had sixteen years ago, sleek and bronze and self-assured. A thousand words rose up in her mouth, but she could speak none of them. Her feet felt glued to the mats. All of a sudden, she was eleven again and powerless, completely powerless.

"Farideh." He fell back on his rear foot. "So you're here too."

Too—he'd seen Havilar, spoken to her maybe, and she wasn't back yet. Old fears, old furies scrabbled up through her thoughts, trying to gain hold, trying to steer her. "Where is she?" Farideh demanded.

Arjhani looked to Lorcan, back to Farideh. "I have no idea. I came looking for her."

"Don't you *karshoji* look for her," Farideh said. "Don't talk to her. You need to leave before Mehen gets back."

Arjhani snorted, as if there were nothing more absurd than Farideh ordering him around. As if the very possibility of Mehen wanting him gone was a joke. The powers of Asmodeus surged up inside Farideh, and she was not eleven, not powerless. But neither was she calm.

"What?" she said. "Did you think he'd just wait for you to change your mind again? If he comes back and finds you . . ."

Arjhani looked at her as if she were small and telling tales, his smile returning. "Don't be dramatic," he chided. "He'd never hurt me."

From behind the couch, Zoonie's growl sent a trembling through the air and made the powers filling Farideh shiver. If she stayed, if she spoke another word, she wouldn't be able to hold onto the powers. Her dreams would come true. *There is nothing you want to say to him. There is nothing he can say to you,* she told herself. And still she felt as if she were burning from the inside out. If she ran, where would she run? Where could she hide in this city where everyone was on top of each other?

Lorcan stood swiftly and slipped past her. "Darling, I'll handle it. Arjhani, was it?" Lorcan put an arm around the dragonborn. "Your reputation precedes you."

Arjhani's nostrils flared. "Who in every broken plane are you?"

"Doesn't matter," Lorcan said, guiding the other man toward the exit. "You're going to leave. Because you don't want to find out the answer to that question. I don't like when people upset Farideh. I don't like when people get in my way. You're managing both. So you're going to leave, and we're going to go on being polite strangers, Arjhani. It's really for the best."

Farideh squeezed her eyes shut as they left the room, focused on her shuddery breath. He was no one. He was nothing. If he hated her, it didn't matter—she had nothing left for him.

Lies, the blessings of the Raging Fiend trilled. *You owe him vengeance.* Zoonie's growl deepened.

"Darling? Are you all right?"

Farideh shook her head—there was no way she was going to tell him, no way she was going to put that ammunition in his hands. Lorcan's hands on her shoulders. Lorcan's hands guiding her away from the furnishings.

"It's fine," she said. "It's fine."

"It will be," he said. "You're on stone. I won't burn. Let it go."

She shook her head. "It's not worth—"

Lorcan folded his arms around her, holding her close. And for all a part of her knew it was dangerous, Farideh put her arms around the cambion, laid her head against his chest, and the flames rolled out of her, burning over her skin. She felt Lorcan tense as if he wanted to run, and she clung to him more tightly.

Farideh burned until her nerves began to soften, to quiet. The fire guttered out, and she felt nothing but foolish. What an idiot. What a child.

Lorcan's hand glided down to the small of her back, and in the absence of Asmodeus's blessings, lust rushed through her like a sudden wind. Her face tilted toward his, her hips easing toward him, before her thoughts could grab hold of the rest of her.

Farideh pushed away from Lorcan. "This is a bad idea."

"Who's having ideas?" he said, all innocence.

She locked her eyes on the floor. "Thank you. I appreciate your help. Don't do that again."

"Fari!" Havilar's shout from the doorway sent Farideh back another step from Lorcan. Her sister stopped just inside the room, and Farideh found herself searching Havilar for some sign of what Arjhani had said, why he'd come back, what had happened. Havilar looked stoic—maybe surprised . . . and Farideh realized her sister was staring right back, as if she'd seen that moment in Lorcan's arms. As if she were saying, *What is wrong with you?*

Farideh gave a little shake of her head. There was nothing there, and there was no point bringing Arjhani up.

"There you are," Lorcan said. "Was there a purpose to your dallying?"

Havilar glared at him. "That demon is possessing people. And it's walking around the city."

13

HOW LONG DO YOU INTEND TO STAY?" MEHEN SAID TO Anala. She turned from the elderly Clethtinthtiallor man she had been speaking with, her smile stiff.

"As long as it takes to make certain I've spoken to everyone," she said. "You could help, instead of skulking at the edges."

Mehen resumed his post against the wall. He had attempted to speak to enough people to realize that he wasn't going to get anything useful here. Faces with a dozen different piercings stared at Mehen, whispering, wondering. Uadjit avoided him and he couldn't blame her. The past and Verthisathurgiesh trailed his every move, echoed his every word.

Narghon strode toward him, powerful still despite his advancing years, and Mehen found himself calculating how fast he could draw his falchion, how much space he'd have to get himself before Narghon had his own blade out. How fast he'd have to leave Djerad Thymar if it came to that.

"You have quite a lot of nerve showing up here," the Kepeshkmolik said.

"I'd be happy to leave," Mehen said. "But I've promised to find Baruz's killer."

Narghon's eyes flicked over Mehen's face. "I'm sure those piercings are relevant to your search."

"According to Matriarch Anala they are," Mehen said. "Your scion has her match. Pandjed is dead and has no hold on you. My presence ought to only increase Kepeshkmolik's standing,

since obviously"—he gestured at a staring cluster of hatchlings—
"everyone knows Verthisathurgiesh harbors the disrespectful and
the dispossessed."

Narghon's expression twisted. "Don't play the fool. You know
exactly the damage you do."

The patriarch walked away before Mehen could reply.
Enough, he thought. There was nothing for him here, and so
he left. Anala caught up to him at the walkways.

"If you wished to leave," she said, "then you should have said.
There are appearances to consider."

"That's about what Narghon said."

"Of course he did. Look, you can hardly expect to make
any headway if you leave people thinking you're still the sullen
rebel of your youth."

Mehen didn't respond—it wasn't worth the response. It didn't
matter if Anala thought him a sullen rebel, a spoiled boy, or a
hero. "Does Narghon know everything that happened?" he asked.

"I assume he knows everything Pandjed told him, perhaps
more if he asked Arjhani."

"So let's assume I'll never find myself on Narghon's good side."

Anala waved this away. "It's not that valuable a place."

"You say that as if you've ever been on Kepeshkmolik
Narghon's good side."

"I don't like Narghon," Anala said, adjusting her scarves.
"And I don't mind flicking his snout, given the option. Uadjit is
hardly the perfect heir he pretends her to be."

Mehen left that alone too—he didn't care. Kepeshkmolik
could do what it liked and it didn't affect him, not anymore—

Uadjit's interest in Faridech came back to him. A mother's
worry, he thought. An elder's concern. It almost sounded likely.

"To the tyrants with Narghon," Anala said. "Did you find
out what you were looking for?"

"Some," Mehen said. He scratched his piercings, fumbling
over the smooth stone plugs. He'd gone longer not wearing them,
he realized, than he'd worn them in the first place. "No one

wants to talk about the murders because it would reflect badly on them," he said. "Which of them would balk at finding out their children were planning to run away to Abeir?"

"Enough to unleash a monster?" Anala asked. "I would level such a charge at no one. Besides, you can't be sure that's what was happening."

Mehen swallowed a sigh. "Fair. But you cannot pretend it's a wild assumption. Others might come to it." They climbed stairs toward Verthisathurgiesh's enclave. "Did you know Baruz was interested in Abeir?"

"No," she said tersely. "And neither do you." Her teeth gapped, a glimpse of nerves. "There are plenty of elders who might react badly. I can't believe any of them would go to these lengths. You know the families who deal in magic. Why not look at them first?"

Kanjentellequor, Yrjixtilex, Shestandeliath—and there were others. But there was magic, and there was this. "It *is*," Mehen admitted, "a monstrous step."

"Some people take *omin' iejirkkessh* quite seriously," she said, coming to a stop beside an archway that overlooked the market below, thick with plants. "Which returns us to the ceremony— don't embarrass me like that again. You may feel you are not Verthisathurgiesh any longer, but when you wear that jade, you are my responsibility and you will act like it."

Mehen popped the jade plugs from his jaw. "Fair enough. Take them back."

"Is your pride that precious?" Anala asked. "Worth the lives of a dozen hatchlings?" She walked away before he could respond, leaving Mehen holding the piercings in the cup of his hand.

It's no different than following the fool rules of some cara-vansary, Mehen told himself. No different than dancing for the sake of Cormyr's long-past mistakes. He didn't put the piercings back in, though.

In the enclave's entryway, he was struck by the sudden sense of *home,* sneaking up out of his memories, like a bandit sliding through the shadows only to spring out in ambush. He moved into the wider atrium, lit through grates to the center of the city and smaller magical lights. He stood, looking up at the carvings of Reshvemi, of Clever Nala, of Khorsaya and the thighbone sword, and the warrior-twins.

You come from here, he told himself, whether you like it or not.

"Any luck?" a voice came from behind him. Mehen turned to see Kallan standing before the double doors.

"Some," Mehen said. "Where's Farideh?"

"Meeting with some fellow who brought her a message."

"What fellow?"

Kallan arched a brow ridge. "Am I your spy now? Just some tiefling fellow. There are guards right *there* with them."

A pair of gangly hatchlings with swords they're still learning to use, Mehen thought. At least he trusted Farideh more than those.

Probably, he amended. "Did you take her to see the wizard?" Mehen asked as he started walking again, through the atrium, heading after Anala.

Beside him, Kallan's smile flickered. "I would say she took me. For all the good it did."

"Is she all right?"

"He tried to throw a fireball at her, but the bars bounced it. Fellow's madder than a mouther. My opinion is moot here, but she's going to have to get someone else to go with her if she's going to do that again." He hesitated. "You angry?"

Mehen rolled the jade plugs in his hand, grinding them against one another. "I know my daughter. And like you said, you're not my spy."

"Well you *look* angry." Kallan moved in front of him. "Anywhere in this place that makes you *less* angry?"

Mehen stopped, ready to snap back that the whole day left him rattled and irritated and the whole *karshoji* enclave did too. He rolled his shoulders, as if he could shake off the ghosts. "Yes," he said after a moment. "Come on."

They wound through several passages until they came to a little alcove near the elders' audience chamber. It was nothing much—a pair of couches beneath a carving of a man called Ana-Patrin, some long-dead patriarch without much to say for himself. "No one notices this," Mehen said sitting down. "Almost like it doesn't exist."

"Cozy," Kallan said, sitting opposite him. He nodded at the archway that led to Anala's audience chamber. "And convenient if you're watching for someone."

"Did you find out anything about our fiend?" Mehen asked.

Kallan's expression sobered. "Figured out the guard couldn't have made it into the tomb without passing the demon. We ask the guard, maybe he saw something that didn't seem dangerous, or some other clue."

Mehen cursed quietly. "One problem: he doesn't exist. Kepeshkmolik says there were no guards of theirs in that part of the catacombs, and they're right—the Kepeshkmolik tombs are miles away, on the other side of the pyramid. That guard had no reason to be there, and he hasn't turned up since he went missing."

"Well there's a clue in its own right," Kallan said. He shook his head. "Weirdest job I've ever taken, this."

Mehen laughed once. "You get a little used to it."

"Don't worry, I got no reason to settle." Kallan's laugh faltered as if he'd heard the rebuke in that. "This is . . . awkward. Isn't it?"

Mehen rolled the jade plugs against each other. "It really wasn't you. I mean that. I'm just a poor option, historically. My daughters . . ."

"Your adult daughters?" Kallan said skeptically. "*Noachi*, you don't have to dip it in honey. You want to have done with me, I can take it. But don't tell me you wish it didn't have to be this way, that your girls can't cope with it—like they're too innocent to understand."

Mehen looked away, off down the corridor. "It's more complicated than it sounds."

As if the point needed proving, as if the very ghost of Verthisathurgiesh Ana-Patrin had reached down the corridor himself just to make his mark, the doors banged open and Arjhani stormed down the corridor.

It would be a lie to say that in sixteen years Mehen hadn't thought of Arjhani, of what he might look like now, of what he might say if he saw again the man who'd broken his heart twice, who'd broken his daughters' hearts without a word. Age hadn't softened him. He seemed smoother, harder, the edges of his scales silvered but not dulled. He did not wear his glaive, but there was no doubt he'd kept at it—the power in his stride, the muscles of his narrow chest.

He would be quick, Mehen thought without meaning to think. Get him off his feet, fast as possible. Arm around the neck, up against the wall—

"Who's that?" Kallan asked.

At the sound of his voice, Arjhani turned and finally saw Mehen.

What did he see? Mehen wondered. Doom or passion or some old man? Their doubles ran rampant in his own thoughts, bandits at ambush once more. *Kiss him. Break him like you swore to. Pass him by.*

Arjhani said nothing for a moment so long and terrible Mehen forgot everything else. He took a step toward the alcove. "Mehen?" he breathed. "Is that really you?"

But Mehen could say nothing.

The doors to the elder's audience chamber beyond him parted for Matriarch Anala. She did not have the same hesitance as the younger men. She spied Arjhani and her eyes widened with alarm. She sprang forward and grabbed him by the arm. "*You* are meant to be in the barracks," she hissed. "Into my chambers this *instant*."

Arjhani shot a look back at Mehen—alarm, apology, longing. Mehen wondered what his own expression betrayed. Anala shoved Arjhani toward the elders' chamber and pointed a clawed finger back at Mehen.

"I will deal with this," she said. "And find you later."

And they were gone, leaving Mehen feeling as though he'd shot back through time and then forward again. He exhaled hard, as if he could drive all the unwelcome emotion out of him. He had not been prepared to see Arjhani again, but in that moment he had to accept that there was never any being prepared to see Arjhani again.

Havilar, he thought. Farideh. He needed to find them, right now.

"So," Kallan said.

Mehen turned, embarrassed. "It's, um . . . He's . . ."

The sellsword stood and clapped a hand on Mehen's shoulder. "Let me save you a few steps: *noachi,* don't tell me it's about what your daughters can handle and then look at that fellow like you just did right where I can see."

It's complicated, Mehen started to protest, but how complicated? How gnarled? He couldn't pretend he was done with Arjhani. His tongue rattled against the roof of his mouth and he cursed softly to himself.

"I need to find the girls," he said.

"All right," Kallan said. "You need me, you know where to find me."

Mehen watched him leave, all too aware of the stern glare of Ana-Patrin looking down on him. Verthisathurgiesh is never soft, he thought. Verthisathurgiesh knows its own mind. So what the *karshoji* Hells do we call you?

• • •

YOU ARE HERE for a reason, Lorcan told himself as Havilar faced him down, as if she were planning to pin him to the wall with her glaive. Zoonie settled herself along the wall and watched him with softly glowing eyes. He rubbed his thumb against the flat gold ring he wore around the second finger of his left hand. "I'd assumed your sister would be joining us."

Havilar's glare deepened. "I'm *not* cheering you on," she said. "Don't think I am."

"Odd—weren't you the one giving me advice on how to warm her feelings to me again?"

"*Don't.* You made her cry again. You want her back, you have to stop being awful first, otherwise there's no point."

While crying wasn't *good*—though one didn't cry about something they were truly finished with and without care for—the fact that in only a span of days she'd gone from refusing to look him in the eye to nearly falling into his arms again was promising enough that he felt sure things weren't as hopeless as Havilar painted them. You can fix this, he told himself. The shape of what they had was *there.* Only to nudge her back into it. Brin came in and shut the door behind him.

"While that's all very interesting," Lorcan said, "I meant it would be useful to her. If one of you needs to wait for Mehen to return, why not the one who has no business fighting demons?"

Brin looked to Havilar, who didn't break her glare, and chuckled. "She asked to be the one to wait for Mehen. She doesn't want to be in here with you."

Lorcan smiled to cover the sudden fury that wrapped around his heart. That's how you get into trouble, he told himself. You have to act human. "Fine. This should be quick enough."

He turned away, twisted a magic ring onto his left hand. A shimmering appeared beside him and he plunged both arms into it. He withdrew a case as long as a bone devil's thighbone, made of joined wood and decorated all over with cinnabar and gold-filled runes of Nar. "Here," he said, offering the Scepter of Alzrius to Havilar. "Just remember, if you're going to vomit, don't do it on my mother's treasures, if you please."

She eyed the box with plain distrust. "What is it?"

"It's an Abyssal artifact," Lorcan said. He unlatched the case and opened it. Havilar winced at the golden scepter, heat shivering the air over it. "It should give off the same sort of power or energy you're reacting to. Just sit with it a few times a day, until you get used to it."

Havilar frowned, the skin above her lip speckled with sweat and her face a little drawn. "It's not that bad," she said, although her voice was a little choked. "I think I could handle that a lot longer than the demon. Don't you have anything stronger?"

Lorcan snapped the case shut. Shit and ashes, he thought. He had prepared for this, but really, there was no preparing. He steeled himself. "I do have a few more items," he said, "in case this one wasn't suitable. They're all mostly weaker . . . Just one stronger."

"Well give it to me."

Lorcan set the scepter aside. This was the only way to make certain the scepter found a new, temporary holder. He reminded himself of that piece, of Invadiah's threats, of the sword Glasya had set upon his throat, of his gamble with Shetai, as he pulled the third artifact free of the dimensional pocket and opened the case.

He had hardly revealed the treasure inside—a star sapphire the size of a chicken's egg, the asterism shivering as though alive—but Havilar turned pale. She took a step back. Beside the wall, Zoonie leaped to her feet and gave a growl that seemed to shake the room.

"Close it," Brin said.

Lorcan wished he could. He took a cloth from his pocket and picked up the gem. A muffled, primordial scream suffused his thoughts. He focused on Havilar, holding the gem out to her. Seal it. Make sure that everything's safe. Zoonie's growl became a snarl, and sparks crackled from her bared teeth.

Havilar's eyes focused on the stone, her lips white with the force of clamping them shut. She drew a long breath through her nose. "Put it away," she said in a small voice. "That's all I can manage."

Lorcan put the star sapphire back into its case, latched it, and slid it back into the dimensional pocket. The screaming stopped, and a faint buzzing sensation bloomed in its place. Lorcan winced. Still growling, Zoonie put herself between Havilar and Lorcan, settling down only when Havilar put her hand on the hellhound's shoulders.

"Which one?" he managed.

"The scepter," she said. "I can handle the scepter."

"Very well," Lorcan said. His stomach curdled and the buzzing grew clamorous. Shit and ashes. "I'll leave it with you. Sit with it as long as you possibly can, first thing in the morning. Better if you try to do something else at the same time."

Havilar nodded, still faintly green. When Lorcan kneeled to slide the case under the bed, she spoke. "Why did it make me sick around the ghost? If Abyssal things make me sick . . ."

"Because she's a demonborn tiefling of course. Apparently, you're a little sensitive."

Havilar frowned. "But . . . wouldn't that mean *I'm* a demonborn tiefling? Why doesn't Farideh make me throw up?"

"Don't be ridiculous," he said. "You were born after the Ascension. You're devil-blooded. Anyway you would have gotten used to Farideh by now."

Havilar frowned. "How long does it take?"

"I haven't the faintest idea," Lorcan said. "Something under nine months." He rubbed his forehead, his neck—the soul sapphire had been a gamble and it had worked. But the price was worse than he'd anticipated. He needed to sit down. "A good sign."

"It has to be faster," Havilar said, dropping onto the floor herself. "The demon's still out there."

"That's what the next lesson's for." Lorcan started to stand. He caught the footboard of the bed and dropped onto the mattress, before vertigo caught him.

"Are you all right?" Brin said.

"No." His eyes felt as if someone were trying to burst them like grapes, via a pair of iron spikes driven inch by inch through the top of his skull. "Abyssal magic doesn't agree with me either."

"If you throw up, *I'll* throw up," Havilar said.

"All right, I'm fetching both of you some water and a draught," Brin said. "Don't get up while I'm gone."

"Lordling, divine magic is not going to be better."

"Lucky for you the dragonborn just know their herbs better than most. Well done, Havi," Brin said. Lorcan heard the door shut behind him, Brin speaking to Farideh beyond.

Havilar was quiet a moment, scratching the hellhound's coat. "What is that thing anyway?"

"A kind of prison."

"There's someone *in* there?"

"There's someone in there with a demon," Lorcan said into his hands. "I don't know who. It wasn't labeled."

"That's awful."

"The Blood War was awful. Is awful. Just . . . you don't want to dabble with demons, all right? You should thank us for keeping them at bay."

"Are you still going to help me?" Havilar said after a moment.

"I said I would. It doesn't benefit me in the slightest if you get torn up by a demon or captured by a cultist."

"True," Havilar said. "Farideh would *never* forgive you."

"That's not what I meant."

"Please. You're in love with her, whatever you say."

"How long are you planning to lead Brin down the primrose path? Just until you find someone more your . . . class?"

Havilar snorted. "I don't know if I'm getting used to you or if you're slipping. Brin and I are perfectly fine with the way things are."

Lorcan lifted his head, the glowing lights on the walls as sharp as lightning bolts through his eyes. "Are you? I'd ask him about that."

Havilar considered him with an unmistakably savage glint in her eye. "She likes Dahl better, you know. In bed."

Rage poured through him, swift and hot enough to still his breath. Lorcan laid his head in his hands again. "You are very lucky," he said, "that I can hardly stand breathing right now."

"Fine," Havilar said. "Truce."

"Truce," he agreed, though he resolved to discover what exactly Farideh had told her sister when he wasn't listening. He glanced at the door, waiting for her to stick her head in, to ask where Brin had run off to—she might as well have not been there.

"Who's Alyona?" he asked offhandedly.

Havilar lifted her head and frowned. "Never heard of her. Should I have?"

"It would be simpler," Lorcan said. "Do you have any idea what kind of name that is?"

"What name?" Brin asked, returning with a glass flask and a pouch of herbs. "She said put it under your tongue," he told Havilar. She opened her mouth, and he stuffed a pinch of the medicine there and handed her the water flask. Brin turned to Lorcan again, expectantly.

"Wha kine uff name is Alyona?" Havilar said.

"Alyona?" Brin tilted his head. "Sounds Damaran. Maybe Vaasan. Who is that?"

"A puzzle," Lorcan said, taking the herbs from Brin. Their flavor resembled the underside of a shambling mound, and even with the water, it left his mouth puckered and muddy-tasting.

"What's the next lesson?" Havilar asked.

Lorcan gritted his teeth. The herbs did almost nothing for his headache, though they seemed to calm the spinning nausea that came with it. He ought to set a magic circle first, but the pain of getting down on the floor to draw it wouldn't be worth the danger of the dretch. He pulled out a scroll. "Get your glaive ready. You're going to practice."

Havilar stood, still pale, and took the weapon from where it rested against the wall.

"Wait," Brin said. "Truly? You nearly threw up all over—"

"Better throwing up than getting possessed. Stay back," she said grimly. Then, "If I do vomit, please don't watch."

"Get ready." Lorcan cast the spell, a simple scroll, of only the most limited practical use. The air within the room seemed to contract violently, then shiver. The scent of corpses and roses and the edge of ancient ice filled the room. A wave of heat burst out of the center of the circle, and when it passed, there was another dretch, squat and stinking at the end of the room.

"Kill it," Lorcan said.

The dretch might not have understood Lorcan's words, but it clearly understood the language of a blade advancing toward it. A screeching voice scrambled over Lorcan's thoughts, protesting in Abyssal that they would regret it. It threw itself against the wall, shrieking. A noxious cloud rose around it.

The hair on Zoonie's back stood up straight and she slunk beside her mistress. Havilar had eyes only for the dretch, her knuckles white around the glaive.

"Zoonie," Lorcan said. "*Tarto.*"

"*Tarto,*" Havilar repeated.

The hellhound dropped back on her haunches and whimpered, eyeing Havilar and then Brin as if one of them would rescind the order. Havilar pressed on. The dretch bared its gummy stumps, its claws curling against the granite.

A few feet short of her glaive's reach, she stumbled as if she were fighting against an invisible tide. Her lips pressed together white, her eyes watering, she stood, drawing breath through her nose as if the air were thick as mud.

Despite her demands, Brin darted to her, and despite her insistence, Havilar reached almost blindly for his shoulder.

All the fine hairs along Lorcan's wings stood on end. In that moment, the room itself seemed electric, alive. He blinked and it passed, but there was no denying it happened. The dretch bunched its legs under it, as if it meant to spring.

But before Havilar could stop it, Brin lunged toward the dretch, sword suddenly in hand. He plunged the weapon into the creature and its squeaks broke off abruptly. Before he'd pulled the sword entirely free, it burst into flames and vanished.

"Gods damn it!" Lorcan shouted. Havilar suddenly straightened, her cheeks flushing, her breath rattled. Brin stared, dumbfounded at the blackish blood oozing down his weapon.

"I don't know. I just . . . It happened." He turned to Lorcan. "Was that your doing?"

"No," Lorcan said. "You can thank Havi for that." He muttered a curse under his breath. "*Why* didn't you tell me you could do that?"

"I don't know!" Havilar panted. "I didn't *do* anything."

"Really? What just happened then? Hmm? Brin?" Lorcan gestured to the lordling. "Care to enlighten her?"

"I don't know," he said. "It was . . . I was here, and then I wasn't. There was a breath where I could have sworn . . ."

"That you didn't exist?" she asked softly.

Brin nodded. "Something like that. And then all I could think of was the dretch. Killing the dretch. I don't think it's exaggerating to say I couldn't have done anything else."

"It's possible you couldn't have," Lorcan said. "Let's say the blessings of the Raging Fiend have their own schedules. Use it now or it's not for you."

Havilar cursed softly, over and over, before straightening. "I did that before, I think. With Ilstan. Whatever it is, this time it made me feel better." Brin wiped the blood from his sword and sat down beside her.

An interesting development. Another element to consider. He handed Havilar the glass of water. "Here. Take it out into the sitting room. You're going to want to let the air clear out for a bit."

And Lorcan was going to need to find more answers.

• • •

DAYS PASSED—FEIYEN ONLY realized that they'd left the outpost far behind when the man made of night turned the Zhentarim against some mind flayers and their thralls. There was no asking what the creatures were after, where they were coming from when they had strayed so near the Zhentarim's routes.

Feiyen fought, tooth and claw. A vague part of her mind wondered where her arrows were, where her poisons had gone. She watched her hands, calloused from the bow, crush the throat of an emaciated man. She watched a mind flayer fall to its knees, shattered by the magic of the man made of night.

After, there was no asking how many had died—the thralls, the Zhents, or even the mind flayers. *The fallen are weak,* the man made of night said, as though she were a child for having such thoughts. *They are but rungs for the strong to climb.*

"Yes, my lord," Feiyen heard herself say. His fingertips trailed down her spine, burning like frost against her skin. Pain in her shoulder evaporated in that strange sensation, and it was only then she realized she'd been wounded.

And if do you fall, the man made of night said, one strong hand kneading her breast, *you have no choice but to strike upward. One . . . last . . . chance.*

The sound of his voice made Feiyen's thoughts dip and soar, plunging down into nothing more than an awareness of pulse and nerves one moment, then scattering everything so wide that she forgot she existed, forgot she needed to breathe. The more he talked, the more she felt as if she were changing into something else. A more bestial, more calculating version of herself.

Of course, he went on, *my foes think I've fallen, trapping me here like this. But they're fools, whoever they are. Already I've grown an army. I've found an exit. I will make this place my fourth kingdom, and whichever of them has struck against me—it is Demogorgon, though, mark it—will find that I cannot be unseated so easily.*

He gestured then to the cavern before them, a tumult of rock and rubble. Feiyen's attention focused as he pushed her forward, her eyes catching the edge of a scroll, dusty and torn, that protruded from the earthfall. Neat runes of High Shou lay faded against the ancient parchment, and a whispering part of her mind read them in her grandfather's voice: *All the world is a valley from the mountain's peak.*

The man made of night's breath curled against her neck, the smell of blood and sulfur and dense perfume assaulting her as he whispered, *Start digging.*

14

23 Nightal, the Year of the Nether Mountain Scrolls (1486 DR)
Djerad Thymar, Tymanther

D UMUZI IS CAUGHT IN THE BELLY OF A THUNDERHEAD LIKE A *fish in a whale. He swims through dark clouds as the lightning hems him in. He twists, flips, but the lightning spears him through the back, out the belly and he's falling, falling . . .*

Out of the cloudbank, Tymanther spreads out beneath him, rushing nearer by the heartbeat—the bulk of Djerad Thymar against the Ash Lake, shining Djerad Kethendi standing over the harbor, the homesteads scattered over the northern plains, the lush farmlands to the south all centered on Arush Ashuak, the village that's quickly outstripping its name.

Suddenly, the coastline shifts as though it's a pulled string. Djerad Kethendi falls first, it's shining white walls crumbling into sand along the rising water. Djerad Thymar flattens into the hills, the homesteads' lights wink out as the storm clouds whirl faster. The green fields shift and reshape. All over the plains, the ziggurats rise.

And Dumuzi keeps falling.

Cities sprout out of the ground, clusters of mudbrick and stone. Where bustling Djerad Kethendi once stood, an enormous golden city rises. At its center, a ziggurat.

Dumuzi tries to scream as he crashes into the city, tries to get his feet beneath him, as if that would stop his fall. But before he can do any such thing, he is thrust into a body standing on the steps of the ziggurat, looking down at an unfamiliar street.

Humans stroll past dressed in loose clothing and heavy gold, eyes traced in dark kohl. Proud-shouldered guards pass, nodding at the citizens walking by. There is something of Djerad Kethendi in its flower boxes and whitewashed walls, but Dumuzi's never been here. No dragonborn has ever been here.

Still, the people who pass him don't stare. They pause and bow, and he bows back—a little gesture that makes him feel as if he has been here after all. As if he belongs in this place, this . . . this . . .

Unthalass—*its name is suddenly in his thoughts, as though he has always known it. Unthalass. City of Gems.*

No, he thinks, remembering his waking life. You mean Djerad Kethendi, the Fortress of Gems.

That moment of confusion makes everything change.

The windows are shut tight, the flower boxes long gone. People move, quick and closed off, eyes on the ground while ornate palanquins ferry other men, heavy with gold and marked by blue circles on their foreheads. The guards are thickest around these, and not much else. It's a poor, frightened place. Fear presses in on Dumuzi like a physical thing, and deep in his heart that fear curdles into anger. They will obey him, or they will die. That is the order of things, that is—

Then the dragon screams.

Dumuzi flees down the side of the ziggurat, leaving behind the tyrant's spirit that gripped him there. The streets flood with soldiers, and he runs and runs and runs. In the chaos, he can hear the voice of dead Pandjed shouting—

He runs full into the man with the curly beard. The man considers him, as though he's a puzzle. Dumuzi tries to shout—they have to run, there's a dragon! But he cannot speak. The man turns him around and Dumuzi sees they're on a rooftop now, overlooking the city, the battlefield swelling out of the ground. At the head of the humans is a golden king, his shoulders as broad as a dragonborn's, his skin shining as new scales. He is beautiful and terrible and foolish as he strides toward the five-headed dragon and her endless invaders.

Tiamat, Toril's own Tyrant Queen, fire and ice and lightning and acid streaking from her many jaws, burning through her own armies and Unthalass's. People flee. The tyrants and their armies crash and crush the city, striving for supremacy. Bolts of magic fly alongside arrows, alongside the Tyrant Queen's murderous breath. One will win. And so Unthalass will lose.

The golden king is the one to fall, and Tiamat claims his body in her ungainly claws, leaving the armies to battle beneath the burning sun. Unthalass collapses, ruined, and Dumuzi suspects that it isn't alone. All the lands of Unther, broken, because of one man.

Not a man, *ushumgal-lú, a voice rolls through his thoughts. Dumuzi turns, surprised, to face the bearded man. He looks up at the sky over Unthalass, where the clouds are scarlet and bristle with gilded lightning.*

"Then what?" Dumuzi asks.

A storm is coming, *the man says.* And so this will happen again, unless you listen. Ushumgal-lú-en ur-sag enlil-la-ke? . . .

Dumuzi woke to a cold room, feeling as though his body had turned to lead in the night and now his soul was trapped within it. The lightning breath crackled in his lungs, and he swallowed it.

The brazier went out, he told himself as he dressed. You had a bad dream. That's all.

The lights were still dim, too early to be up without reason, but Dumuzi washed himself and dressed anyway. He stopped, shirt in hand, and moved before the looking glass, turning back over his shoulder.

The scars the lightning breath had left over his back, feathery patterns of silver where all the color bleached from his scales, remained as bright as ever. "They'll be gone in a month or so," the healer had said. But whatever scales he shed, the mark of Pandjed's displeasure always returned.

A storm is coming . . .

"Ush-um-ga-loo," Dumuzi murmured. The rest jumbled in his thoughts. It wasn't Draconic and it wasn't *Munthrarechi* and he didn't have an ear for anything else. He thought of the languages he'd heard in the months that he'd searched for Clanless

Mehen—it must have been one of them, but he couldn't place it. "Ush-um-ga-loo en . . . sag . . . enlil . . ."

Dumuzi sighed and pulled his shirt on, dressing and tidying his room, the phrase seeming to dart past his thoughts too quick to catch hold of. What did it mean?

It's a dream, he told himself. It's just nonsense your mind tells itself while you sleep. Not the sort of thing, after all, that Kepeshkmolik gave credence to.

He made his way through the enclave toward his mother's chambers, wondering if there would be anything for him to do today or if he'd be free to seek out Zaroshni and the handful of Liberators they'd not tracked down.

Or head to the training yards again, he thought glumly. Zaroshni was avoiding him, there was no denying it, any more than there was any way of knowing why. Perhaps she'd devoted herself more wholly to the Liberators, and the fact he thought them fools meant he wasn't welcome. Perhaps she was angry he'd listened to his father's request and left. Perhaps she'd met someone else.

That doesn't matter, he told himself briskly. She was always going to find someone else. He was always meant for someone else. That was how things were.

As he came near to the hallway that led to Uadjit's rooms, raised voices broke into his woolgathering.

"What about Chessenta?" his father's voice came. "Or . . . I don't know, Aglarond? Akanûl?"

"There are ambassadors in those places already," Uadjit answered.

Dumuzi froze. He ought to keep walking. He ought to make his presence known. In a space as crowded as the enclave, the only proper thing was to pretend you couldn't hear what you heard, to remove yourself when it could be done or interrupt to make it clear the speakers had forgotten they shared space with so many. Dumuzi leaned against the wall instead, listening to his parents argue.

"Besides," Uadjit said, "you've never come with me before. People will talk."

"It's not about me, it's about you," Arjhani said. "You have skills that are a benefit to all of us—why waste them on entertaining overtures from Verthisathurgiesh?"

"Why waste them on Mehen, you mean."

"Oh *karshoj* to Mehen!" Arjhani shouted. "I don't need to hear about Mehen from you of all people."

"Lower your voice," Uadjit snapped. Dumuzi leaned his head back against the stone. "And face what trails you, Jhani. None of this is about you."

"It's about you, so it's about me."

"Why would I leave? Why would *I* leave *now*?"

"Because you know as well as I do that Anala did not call Mehen back out of the goodness of her heart or for the sake of the rolls. She means to ruin you."

"If you believe that so strongly, Jhani, then why did you send our son out into the wilds to find him? Unless, that is, you meant to ruin me too?"

A dense, chilly silence. "I'm trying to help."

"From where I stand I see few options," Uadjit went on. "Either Anala wants to break me and you sided with her, you want this to happen. Or you don't side with her, and you sent Dumuzi—our son, the only choice for my scion someday—out into the world, believing he would fail and possibly never come home to us. Or you are a *karshoji* liar and you have no idea what Anala intends or what Mehen wants. So which is it?"

Dumuzi waited, dreading the answer.

"How can you think I'm not on your side? *Noachi*, I might not be the one you wished for, but I'm your ally—you can't doubt that. *Irthiski*," Arjhani crooned the endearments like a charm. "*Vorellim.* I just want you to be happy."

Uadjit sighed. "The happiest you can make me involves not having this conversation and getting me gravid like you came here to do."

That's what you get for eavesdropping, Dumuzi thought, once he'd left the enclave doors behind him. An earful of his parents' troubles, a glimpse into their private lives, and now he had nothing at all to do. He couldn't go back and interrupt—and truth be told, he didn't want to either.

He meandered over the walkways, as if looking for a path to catch his feet. *Ush-em-gal-lù-en-ur-sag.* With every step the alien syllables popped in his thoughts. *Ush-em-gal-lù-en-ur-sag.* He found himself heading toward the Verthisathurgiesh enclave without meaning to.

To his surprise, Farideh was already awake—or mostly so. She sat curled on one of the divans in the sitting area, her eyes hollowed by fatigue, reading a little scroll to herself. She startled visibly when Dumuzi came in, and closed the note between her hands.

"You slept badly too?" he said.

"Worse and worse," she said with a half smile. She spoke in a mishmash of Draconic and *Munthrarechi*, leaping from one word to the next. Dumuzi found it strangely easy to follow. "No one's brought morningfeast yet. I think Mehen scared them the other day. Do you know where the kitchens are?"

"Yes," Dumuzi said. But his stomach knotted at the thought of wandering the halls of Verthisathurgiesh enclave, every step feeling as though it would plunge him back into his frightened youth or into imaginary Unthalass. "I owe you a visit to the Horn of Shasphur. We could just go there. Let the others sleep."

Farideh looked past him, at her sister's door. "All right. But let me leave a note."

"What did you dream about?" she asked as they reached the market floor.

Dumuzi pretended not to hear her, turning before a shop selling bolts of colorful linen and wool to head toward the teahouse. Farideh sprinted up beside him.

"What did you dream about?" she asked again.

"That's . . . personal," Dumuzi said. Then, "Vayemniri don't talk about that. They're just dreams."

He didn't say anything else until they were seated, alone, in the Horn of Shasphur, after many exchanges of greetings with his cousin, Yehenna, to be passed on to his parents and siblings and to hers.

"I'm sorry," Farideh said finally. "I didn't know." She tilted her head, as if she were considering him with her silver eye alone. "Do you get a lot of nightmares?"

"Sometimes," Dumuzi said. "It depends."

She was quiet a moment, as Yehenna returned with an iron pot of tea and a basket of *farothai,* hot off the griddle. "Is it because of what happened to your friends?"

Dumuzi took one of the stuffed flatbreads. "They weren't exactly my friends."

"Were you in their . . . group?" Farideh asked. "The Liberators—"

"Don't." He glanced back at Yehenna greeting another customer. "Don't talk about that. Please. I wasn't. I was . . . I was friends with some of them. One of them. I was trying to convince them they were being fools. If I'd been here . . ." He pulled the *farothai* into pieces, until his fingers were slick with oil.

"Maybe you would be dead too," Farideh pointed out as she took one of the breads. "What's in these?"

"Um, sheep's cheese and chilies." He took a belated bite as she poured the tea.

"What about your friend? Zaroshni?"

"We're not—" Dumuzi's tongue hammered nervously at the roof of his mouth. "Shestandeliath Zaroshni. Although I don't know if she would say we were friends."

"Did you fight?"

"We argue. She wanted to convince me, I think, of their . . . hopes. That we . . ." He set the flatbread on the plate and clasped his hands together. He could almost hear Zaroshni's teasing tones, laying out why he was obviously deluded by Kepeshkmolik's iron hand. "They wanted to go back to Abeir. She thought . . . we fought so hard to make a safe haven, to make our own destiny, and now? Now Uadjit comes back from Imaskar and all she has in hand are half-made trade promises and requests for more military aid. We don't matter in this world. It's not ours." He dropped his eyes to the table. "That's what she says, anyway. Said. I haven't talked to her about it since . . . it happened."

"Do you agree?"

"No. A little. I don't know anymore."

Farideh was quiet for long moment. "Do you love her?"

Dumuzi shut his eyes. "I don't know that either," he said. "I'm already promised anyway. And I've seen how badly it goes if you fall in love before you're married off. It's for the best."

Farideh's eyebrows rose. "You're engaged? To who?"

"No one specific. I have to marry back into Verthisathurgiesh. Matriarch Anala has to make the offers to the . . ." He squinted. "*Shuk-qalli?*"

"'Maybe' . . ." Farideh shook her head. "I don't know the other part. What's it mean?"

"The girls I might marry."

"Brides."

"Brides," Dumuzi said, testing the word. "So I don't have a *bride.* I have just a vow."

"Is that usual?"

"It's . . . a little old-fashioned." Dumuzi said, wrapping his hands around the clay cup. "I was what's called a *koshqal.* A . . . 'bride cost,' I suppose. In a marriage contract some eggs are set aside for the *anurithominak.*"

"The . . . under name?" Farideh said.

"It's . . . One clan is by tradition the initiator of the agreement. The higher-ranked, more powerful clan usually. The eggs are mostly theirs then. But some are *koshqalli.* Some are considered the cost of the bride."

"Or the groom," Farideh said.

Dumuzi frowned. "What's the difference?"

Farideh chuckled and explained it. "You know I would have thought I spoke Draconic completely before I came here. But there are so many words I don't know, and so many things I feel like I'm missing." She sipped her tea. "So you were supposed to be Verthisathurgiesh?"

Dumuzi turned his head and pulled the frill of his jaw taut, so that she could see the small holes left behind by the jade plugs. They'd never close, not completely.

"What happened?" she asked.

"It didn't work out," he said brusquely, "and so my mother negotiated the marriage contract." The crackle of lightning echoed in his memory. His tongue rattled against the roof of his mouth to match. "What did *you* dream about?"

"I thought that was personal."

"It's personal for me," Dumuzi said. "*You* asked, so I assume it's not personal for you."

She looked down into her teacup, as though the leaves were full of answers. "Lately when I dream, it's the same, or nearly the same. I dream I'm in Arush Vayem and it's snowing. Dahl is somewhere, but I can't find him. I can hear people laughing and shouting, but every building I find is empty and cold. Like no one's been there for ages. Sometimes Lorcan's there. Sometimes Havi. Sometimes Arjhani turns up. Sometimes the village catches on fire." She rubbed the back of her neck. "I don't know if they're really dreams."

"What else would they be?"

"Messages." Farideh looked up at him, her mismatched eyes solemn. "Warnings."

"They're just dreams."

She shrugged. "These are odd times. The gods are . . . very present."

Dumuzi pressed his tongue against the roof of his mouth hard, as the image of the human with the curly beard flashed in his thoughts. *Ushumgal-lú.* The feeling of the tyrant's heart beating inside him. "How can you tell the difference?" he asked.

"I think you just know. Are you worried about something?"

"No," Dumuzi said. Then, "Sometimes my dreams . . . echo lately. The same things again and again. And I don't always know what they are."

Farideh bit her lip, and Dumuzi pressed his tongue more firmly against the roof of his mouth. It's nothing, he thought. You shouldn't have mentioned it.

"I know a spell," she said, all caution, "that can tell if a god has . . . an interest in you."

"Not here!"

"It won't hurt."

"I'm not afraid of it hurting."

"No one will know what I'm doing. Promise."

He tapped his tongue a few times. Yehenna was in the back. The other customers were engrossed in their own conversations. *A storm is coming . . . Ushumgal-lú.* "Fine. But quick?"

"Quick," she agreed.

For a moment, Farideh only stared at Dumuzi, her flat eyes shifting colors as if they were slicked with strange oil. He fluttered his tongue within his closed mouth, hiding his discomfort. A moment later, Farideh blinked and smiled awkwardly.

"All clear," she said. "I suppose they're only nightmares."

"Of course," Dumuzi said, oddly relieved. "I'm Vayemniri."

Farideh shrugged, and Dumuzi had the distinct impression that he'd said something wrong. But he held his tongue—he was already acting too familiar. It would only be worse to try and drag things out of her.

"These are a lot better than Mehen's," she said, plucking another of the *farothai* from the basket. "I'm going to ask you something, and if it's improper, I apologize. Someone was asking me about the election for Vanquisher. They wanted to know if Verthisathurgiesh had a candidate yet. Is that something I'm likely to find out?"

Dumuzi eyed her a moment before he remembered there was no way she knew any of this. "If you mean is Anala going to tell you before the official announcements in a few months, no.

The elders can change their minds right up to the announcement anyway."

"But people can usually guess?"

"Right. For example, my mother came back because Imaskar is at war, but she was coming home anyway. Kepeshkmolik means to put her forward as Vanquisher."

"How often does that happen?"

"Every ten years," Dumuzi explained. "Tarhun is Vanquisher until next year, so all the clans put forth their candidates and a new one's elected. So this year everything's getting . . . tense. Everyone's getting ready. Trying to make sure their candidates look best."

"Do you think she has a chance?"

"A fair chance," Dumuzi said. "It's not a very powerful field. Ophinshtalajiir will put forward Sepideh—she's a Lance Defender commander, and she'll never, never defeat Uadjit. Fenkenkabradon will bring up Dokaan who is in charge of the Lance Defenders, but a lot of the older clans don't like how he's run things. They say he forgets our roots and leads us into battle looking like hatchlings. Daardendrien is a gamble. They have a scion, Medrash, who made a name for himself, in battle and in foreign courts. But he's young and he's a god-worshiper—that will hurt him badly, so I don't know if they won't put up someone less risky. Shestandeliath is anyone's guess, but there's no one obvious enough to point to. Uadjit would likely win over any of those."

"That's why they're all being so cagey about what happened in the catacombs?" Farideh said. "Because it would reflect badly on their clans and then candidates?" Dumuzi shrugged—but it was almost certainly true. "Who's Verthisathurgiesh's choice?"

"Mehen, I assume."

"*What*?" Yehenna and the other customers turned at the sudden burst of Common. Farideh looked as if he'd told her they were planning to throw her and Havilar off the pyramid later. Dumuzi frowned.

"Why else would Anala ask him back?" he said quietly, hoping she'd take the hint. "Verthisathurgiesh doesn't have many candidates who could win out over Uadjit—Arjhani wouldn't dare stand, and he's probably their best option. I can't say it's wise . . . Is that why you didn't think it important to stay away from the wizard? Because you didn't know?"

Farideh only shook her head. "I can't imagine why she'd . . . Why she'd think . . ."

"There's no forcing him to do it if he's elected," Dumuzi said. "Maybe she'll tell him what she intends and you'll leave straight after." The thought gave him a pang of sadness—he covered it by pouring them both more tea. Farideh dropped several lumps of sugar into hers. "I doubt he will defeat Uadjit either, come to that."

Farideh smiled. "Your mother sounds formidable."

"That is an excellent word for her."

"Is she happy to have you home again?"

Dumuzi shrugged. "I don't think she was too happy I was sent out. She's been asking me questions every time I see her, about everything I did or saw or thought. Looking for things that might reflect poorly on Kepeshkmolik, I think. She asked me a lot of questions about you," he added.

Farideh set her tea down, eyes on the cup. "Oh? Did she know who I was already?"

"No," Dumuzi said. "I mean I don't think Arjhani told her. She seemed surprised about that. She's . . ." He hunted for the right words. "She can be a little overconcerned with who my friends are. When she's in the City-Bastion, anyway. She's probably worried you're going to try and turn me into a god-worshiper."

Farideh giggled at that. "I think there's more chance you'll convince me to swear allegiance to the line of Khorsaya and go out hunting dragons."

"That is *not* how it works." She only giggled more, and despite himself, Dumuzi laughed too. "Not everybody kills a dragon, anyway. They're hard to come by these days."

"What about Zaroshni?" Farideh said. "What's your mother think of her?"

"She doesn't know about Zaroshni. Not really." Dumuzi sighed. "Not that it matters. She's been . . . distant lately. Two conversations about who was still alive and who wasn't, and . . . well, let's say before I was sent after Mehen, she would sometimes make . . . compelling arguments about defying the *qallim* agreement. Obviously things must have changed since I left. Not that it matters," he said again, hastily. "Like I said, I'm promised."

But Farideh's expression had shifted into something blank, something Dumuzi couldn't read beyond the look of fear that transcended the lack of scales and ridges.

"She's acting odd," Farideh said. "We can't find her. And she was supposed to be there, with the others that night."

"Yes," Dumuzi said, dread building in him. "Why?"

Farideh shook her head. "Oh, Dumuzi. I think she *was* there. I think she might be possessed."

• • •

"YOU CAN'T BE mad at Bodhar forever," Sessaca said as Dahl built her another fire. They had stopped atop a ridge overlooking a snow-filled valley and the higher peaks beyond, and settled Sessaca against a heavy column of rock. The sunset blazed behind them, painting the Earthfasts in shades of red and gold. Thost and Bodhar had been set to work with the Zhentarim pitching tents against the growing cold. "Are you letting her hold that over you? Or is it something else?"

"That depends on who you're talking about," Dahl said, trying to coax a spark from the steel. "But the answer's probably that it's not your business."

Sessaca snorted. "I mean our one-eyed friend," she said quietly. "Which is all of our business, and might I add, you avoiding your brothers like a sulky boy because they wrecked your cover and hurt your feelings over some tiefling is not helping matters. There's no girl on Toril who's worth playing mum with your own kin over."

The sparks from the firesteel finally caught the edge of the charcloth he'd laid in the kindling, erupting into greedy flame. "You giving Bodhar and Thost this same talk?" he asked. "Or does that only go the one way?"

Sessaca drew the blanket around her closer. "You haven't answered my question."

"You don't want to know what she has over me."

"Listen, lambkin, whatever you get up to, I'm going to come out and guarantee I got up to worse. So unless you want to get into a pissing match with me and find out, answer the question."

Dahl said nothing, only feeding twigs and bits of bark to the fire. Since Xulfaril's threats to tell his family about the devil woman, he'd bounced between calling her bluff, telling them everything—he *hadn't* made anything like a deal with the strange woman after all—and resigning himself to becoming a Zhentarim agent completely—because how could he explain anything without revealing his agreement with Lorcan?

Don't worry about any of this, he told himself over and over, until you get to the Master's Library.

"Fine," Sessaca snapped. "You want to keep your secrets, I'll leave them be. But I expect you're going to say *something* before this ends with our blood on your hands."

"Don't be absurd," Dahl said. "There's nothing she could hold over me that would make that acceptable."

Sessaca's stony expression softened. "Then go make up with your brothers because I've got no interest marching with a divided force, understand? Finish the fire first," she added.

Dahl added the fuel he'd collected as they'd scaled the peak, out of the thick forests, enough to get the fire hot enough to get a pot of water boiling, at least. They'd have to go down through the valleys tomorrow. And then? Sessaca was still being coy.

"What lies to the east of the Master's Library?" Dahl asked her quietly.

Sessaca's dark eyes pierced him. "Lot of things. You can read a map, can't you?"

"What lies to the east *beneath* the Master's Library?"

Just as it had back in New Velar, a certain cunning overtook his grandmother's expression, even though not a muscle of her face moved. "A lot of dirt, I suspect. You have a different idea?"

"I think these folks have that idea," Dahl said. "I don't think they want the library, I think they want what's down below it. Those goblins came up from the Underdark, and that spooked Grathson. So what is it we're heading for?"

Sessaca was quiet a moment. Then she shrugged. "Nothing."

"They can't hear us right now."

"Truly, lambkin, nothing of note. It's the Underdark. It's all strange. It's all beyond your wildest nightmares. You think it matters if there's a lake here, a city there, but it's all made for someone, some*thing* that's not you." She considered the backs of the Zhentarim grimly. "You sure that's what they're after?"

"I'd stake every drop of whiskey I have on it," Dahl said. He frowned at his grandmother. "You've been to the Underdark?"

"I told you," she said. "I've done a lot more and a lot worse than you. Put a little of that whiskey in the tea. There's no way I'm sleeping on these rocks otherwise." She was quiet a moment as he set up the pot, added the tea, debated keeping his dwindling whiskey to himself.

"I don't remember where everything within the library is," Sessaca suddenly said, "but . . . there's a statue of an archon on the floor above the entry. You can see it when you go in. The shelves beside that have scrolls, samples of a godsbedamned great lot of spells. Schools of magic marked on the rollers. Best ones are gone, but you could probably find a portal spell among them."

"How do you know the best . . . No, you know what? Never mind. Add it to the list." He stirred the tea. "You think we'll need a swift escape."

"It never hurts to be ready."

Dahl sat back on the cold ground, listening to the water bubble in the pot. "How long were you in there?"

"Long enough," Sessaca said.

"Gods, Granny, are you going to be cryptic the whole trip? You dreamed a path up the mountains and then you heard a strange voice and you found the Master's Library and wandered around a bit? Why's no one gone back there?"

"Because it's sealed shut." He turned to see Mira behind him, her dark eyes full of warning, and Xulfaril beside her. "People have found it since—or said they found it," Mira went on. "They just can't get in."

Sessaca folded her blanket closer, her eyes hard. "Not my sort of gossip."

"I assume *you* can," Xulfaril said, "else I don't think you'd be foolish enough to lead us up here, where no one will find your body or your grandsons'."

"You making *more* threats?"

"I'm making reminders," the wizard said.

Sessaca's dark eyes glittered. "I can open the door. I helped seal it, I can unseal it." She turned to Dahl. "I don't know who did the singing, but when I found the place, there was still a priestess there. An old woman, the last of the Deneirrath who held the Master's Library. She told me she'd been praying and praying for someone to come assist her—there was no one left and she had to seal the library. She thought I was the one the gods sent. I laughed at her."

"Well, that sounds about right," Dahl said.

"Don't insult the gods like that, and I won't laugh. Her prayers were answered by a blade-ferrying sellsword with a rotten heart and a bad demeanor?" She made a face. "Turns out she was asking for trouble, that one."

Dahl knew better than to argue, even if there was nothing about Sessaca's opinion that made sense. She'd come on the suggestion of a vague and prophetic dream, after all, to a place on no one's maps, and whatever had happened, she'd clearly helped the Deneirrath priestess—

"Gods' books—did you *kill* her?"

Sessaca gave him a withering look. "She wanted help and I gave it to her. She had a magical way of closing it off, but it needed two people to work. One inside, one outside." She fished the heavy locket she always wore out from her shirt. "Gave me the key and a few instructions. And the Master's Library was sealed."

Dahl narrowed his eyes. "She gave that to you?"

"More or less," Sessaca said, tucking the necklace back in place. "So," she said to the Zhentarim, "that's all the assurances you're getting. For your records, I'm fair sure that it's got to be me that wields the charm. Though if you're feeling lucky, your swords could always pluck it off my corpse and see if they're good enough."

Xulfaril narrowed her eyes. "I'd suggest you not give Grathson any excuses."

"I'm surprised you haven't found his leash yet," Sessaca said. Xulfaril only smiled at her, and left their little fire to return to the rest of the camp.

Mira smiled. "Fair winds, old mother." She fished the pouch of herbs out of her bag and crouched beside the fire. "I won't let them do any such thing, and neither will your grandsons."

Sessaca looked at Dahl over Mira's dark head. "Sometimes you can't help it."

"If anyone can, I'm sure it's your boys." Mira stood and gave Dahl a significant look. "Xulfaril's making noises like you've volunteered your expertise."

"Volunteered is an odd word."

Mira raised an eyebrow. "Is it bad?"

"It's enough."

"Well," she said. "Could be worse. At least you and I know we . . . work together well."

Beyond Mira, Sessaca smirked in a triumphant kind of way.

Dahl cursed to himself, but kept his tongue. "Your tea's ready," he told Sessaca, and strode off toward the rest of the camp, without so much as meeting Mira's eye.

It stung when it shouldn't to have her humoring Sessaca like that. He didn't mourn the loss of her—there was never any road that didn't lead to Mira growing bored of him or him becoming frustrated with her constant indifference—but *she'd* been the one to end it, and in the intervening years, she'd not shown one spark of affection.

It still wasn't affection, he thought. But there was no pretending Mira wasn't acting a little less than indifferent. Or that Sessaca hadn't noticed.

"Lord of All Knowledge," he muttered under his breath as he watched the sun slip behind the horizon. "Binder of What Is Known. Make my mind open, my eye clear, my heart true."

There were a hundred reasons he ought to be fond of someone like Mira—someone human, someone who was intimately involved in the secretive parts of his life, someone his family was already charmed by. Someone who didn't bring devils to his door.

Devils aren't worse than Zhentarim, he thought. But the devilish woman's words rang in his head: *It's not as if I don't have options.* Because you aren't what she wants, he thought. Farideh's the key. And options meant Lorcan—it had to mean Lorcan.

She can take care of herself, Dahl thought—made himself think. If only to stem the surge of memories, proofs that—once, at least—she had been more than a little taken by the cambion, and Lorcan had been more than a little willing to put her best interests to the side. He turned back to the Zhentarim and his brothers, and cursed again.

Beside a second fire, Volibar suddenly jerked up, scrambled to his feet. He pulled a little metal flute out of his pocket and played a fluttery trio of notes. Dahl's heart skipped as the dark shape of the winged snake slipped down the air currents and settled itself around Volibar's neck. He ran at the halfling.

"Good boy," the halfling crooned. "Who's a good, strong boy?" The snake licked his chin. In the little harness it wore, there was a tiny scroll case.

"Give it to me," Dahl said, trying to keep the urgency out of his voice and failing. "Please."

Volibar glowered at him as he removed Haslam's harness, checked the snake's wing joints, and finally opened the scroll case. "Looks like you got an answer."

Dahl snatched the note from the halfling's hands, unrolled so quickly he tore the edge and cursed. Both sides of the paper were covered in Farideh's jagged handwriting.

I haven't given up, though I have no idea what's going on. Why didn't you answer my sending? Why did you go? I trust you. I know there are reasons, but I wish I knew what they were. I wish you were here. My nightmares are worse & now Ilstan has turned up in the city. There's a demon loose, murdering people. (I suspect you would say I should stay inside given that, but the joke is on you—the whole city is inside.) More than once I've thought, "Dahl would be such a help here." And besides, I'm lonely for you. I don't know if you can write again, but now I know where the Zhent in the city is, I will use him to track you down if I must. I love and miss you more than I can say. Be careful. Farideh.

Ilstan, Dahl thought, feeling his stomach knot, demons, murderers. And still Asmodeus. And here he sat, on the edge of the Vast, too far to do anything at all. She didn't mention Lorcan, and that was something—the memory of Lorcan kissing her rose up again and he shoved it away. What in the name of Oghma, Mystra, and Lost Deneir would he say to her now?

He couldn't answer any of her questions, after all, not without breaking his agreement with Lorcan. But how many letters could he send without saying a word?

And where was Lorcan?

"How long before I can send another message?" he asked.

"Haslam's not a magic faerie," Volibar snapped. "He's got to recover."

"Before you go in," Dahl said. "I want that before you go into the ruins."

Volibar chuckled to himself, as if Dahl were a little mad. "Run that by Xulfaril. Pretty sure we'll be able to package up what's left of you and ship it snake-back to your ladylove."

It would have to do. And if not, he told himself, you can find the means to make a sending. You can pass a message through Havilar or Mehen. Maybe Brin, if he was still with them. Farideh was already picking up the pattern, already being resourceful with scryings and sendings. All is not lost, he told himself.

I will use him to track you down if I must. I love and miss you more than I can say.

A hundred thousand reasons to love someone else, Dahl thought, folding the note into neat quarters. And none of them were true.

His brothers stood, considering the lines of a tent, the dusting of snow blowing up its side. Thost kicked a stake. "Sturdy enough."

"I suppose," said Bodhar. "Assuming that wind doesn't pick up. Gonna have to bunk in together to keep her warm, though. You still snore?"

"Like you don't."

They both looked up as Dahl came to stand beside them, Thost greeting him with a wordless nod. Bodhar looked awkwardly down at the tent stake.

Dahl rubbed his thumb over the note in his hand and tucked it into his pocket.

"One," Dahl said, feeling like an idiot, "she makes me happy. Happier than I think I have any right being, sometimes. And when I'm not, when I feel like I could just fall into the stlarning gutter and quit and no one in the world would care, she does care. And that's enough, right, but I said three. So two, I love the way she laughs. It's ridiculous, because it's just a laugh, but gods' books, it feels like I could do any godsbedamned thing in the world when I hear her laugh. When I hear how happy she is. And three, I love how much she loves her family, because I know that when I tell her that I had to come here, that I had to make certain you were all safe, she understands because she would do the exact same thing.

"And I do think it's adorable how much sugar she dumps into her tea, even if that's ridiculous too," he added. He spread his arms, making a target of himself. "So let's hear it."

Bodhar shook his head. "Look, you're a man grown. You make your choices, good and bad."

"Have you thought about Ma?" Thost asked. "She's not going to like it."

"Bodhar didn't think she'd take to Dellora either," Dahl said. Thost turned, surprised, to Bodhar who threw up his hands.

"I was wrong, obviously! But don't tell me you weren't nervous about telling Ma you were marrying a lady sellsword out of Cormyr? Mind," he added, shaking a finger at Dahl, "that's not 'tall the same as a devil-child, and you can't pretend otherwise. You can't deny blood."

Dahl felt as if his heart had grown still as a mountain pool. "She is the truest person I've ever met. She once saved my life by hauling me out of a ballroom full of shadar-kai and Zhentarim assassins, *after* I'd dragged her there and left her with a lunatic. There was nothing stopping her from saving her own skin—I would have deserved it at that point—and she still got me out. She's better than she has any reason to be. Whatever bad her blood brings, I will stand and fight it with her because she doesn't *deserve* it—not for being born to the wrong parents." He paused. "Do you want some help?" he said, nodding at the tents.

"No," Bodhar insisted. "You . . . You take a load off. We'll finish up." He scratched his beard, quiet a moment, before he pulled a short stick of wood from his belt. "Um, here. It's a good, straight piece. Lellthorn. Won't split. Found it on the way up. You could . . . whittle maybe a knife from it? Couldn't hurt, right?"

Dahl took the bit of hardwood from him. "Yeah, sure. Thanks."

"Course. Shoulda kept my wits about me. Before. I wasn't thinking. I hope it's not put you under treefall or anything."

"Nothing worse than what I've put myself under."

"We good?"

Dahl turned the wood in his hand—solid, straight. "If you call her a devil-child again, I will punch in your stlarning face."

A moment of silence, Thost and Bodhar watching him, and Dahl felt surer than ever that if there was anything at all that might drive him from his family, this was it—and it wrung his heart out to know that.

Then Bodhar snorted, a half-swallowed laugh. Thost's shoulders shook, and as one they burst out. Thost slapped Dahl on the back and Bodhar put his fists up as though they would brawl right then and collapsed into further laughs.

"Ah, Hells," Thost managed. "Sodden Hells."

"Clearly you mean it," Bodhar said. "Punch me in the stlarning face." And burst into laughter again.

Dahl gritted his teeth, but at least they were brothers again. At least they were united as they headed into the last day of travel before they reached the Master's Library.

• • •

THE CATACOMBS AT evening were no darker than in day, no more twisting or solemn, but to Farideh, they felt inarguably different. The shadows seemed more solid, more secretive, as they threaded their way in twos through the first of the tombs. As they descended a set of stairs, she found her way to Mehen's side.

"This is too many people," he said gruffly. Ahead of them, Havilar and Brin, Kallan and Dumuzi, Lorcan and Zoonie moved through the shadows. He tugged on the hood of the cloak he'd worn to help him pass unnoticed through the city. "We might as well be bellowing, 'Here, demon, demon,' while we walk."

"You could have stayed," Farideh pointed out as mildly as she could. She might have too—Havilar was necessary, Lorcan required, and there was no chance of telling Dumuzi to stay behind.

And no chance of leaving Mehen or Brin or Farideh back, once Havilar agreed to help him rescue Zaroshni.

"Lorcan's exercises are kind of rubbish anyway," Havilar had said. "That scepter is creepy. It's not *that* hard—even if it's not that pleasant either. *And* it's boring." She drummed her fingers against the shaft of her glaive. "Besides, it seems like the whole thing's *less* about finding demons and *more* about making people want to fight them for me. And I can't practice that on a *karshoji* stick."

Lorcan had been less pleased about the sudden insistence that they needed to track the demon down—though clearly a *little* pleased that Farideh had called him down herself to do it.

"What's the situation with Lorcan?" Mehen asked as they walked along, as if they were talking about something as simple as a bounty.

Farideh kept her eyes on the cambion's back. "He's helping Havilar."

"Is that *all*?"

A blush crept up her neck. "I don't know what you mean."

"Do you think I'm an idiot? That I have no idea you are— or *were*—infatuated? You don't need to tell me everything that happened in Suzail, but don't think I haven't got eyes and a mind."

If Mehen ever knew even a fraction of the details of what happened between her and Lorcan in Suzail, Farideh would curl up and die on the spot. "What happened then has nothing at all to do with what's happening now. If it weren't for these murders, I'd be done with him."

Liar, she thought. If it weren't the murders, it would be something else. It would be collector devils or Shadovar or Asmodeus himself. It would be the unshakable worry that something bad would happen to Lorcan because of her. Could she ever truly be done with Lorcan?

Maybe not, she thought. But that's got nothing to do with who you go to bed with.

Mehen sighed. "Fari, trust me when I say this: keep your wits about you. The heart's a foolish thing . . . other . . . parts more so."

"Gods, just . . . no. We're done." Farideh resolutely did not look at her father as they wound through the catacombs, watching instead the slim dragonborn sellsword ahead of them. As they'd armed and armored themselves, Havilar had sent the doorguard to fetch Kallan, it felt rude and disruptive to suggest *he* alone should stay. "Are you avoiding Kallan?"

"I'm not avoiding anybody," Mehen muttered. "Where is she taking us?"

"Did you tell him you had to break it off because of us?" Mehen said nothing for a long moment. Farideh cursed to herself. "That's not fair. What happened to 'my, you girls have grown'?"

"You *have* grown," Mehen said. "And that's got nothing to do with whether it's a good idea for me to take up with a fellow."

Farideh hooked her arm through her father's. "You deserve to be happy."

Mehen pulled her close, but said nothing, and Farideh wondered if he believed a bit of that. "Arjhani was in the enclave," he said in a low, apologetic voice.

"I know," Farideh said. "He . . . we argued."

"*What?*"

"I'm fine. It was nothing. Lorcan got rid of him." She wet her mouth. "I think Havi saw him too. He was looking for her. Like he was trying to finish a conversation."

Mehen stopped dead in the corridor and turned his daughter to face him.

"I haven't talked to her about it," Farideh protested, before he could say a word. "She seemed fine and . . . well, it would be worse to bring it up again if she'd shaken him, right?" She searched Mehen's scowling features. "Did you talk to him?"

"No," Mehen said. His teeth parted, tongue tapping against the roof of his mouth. "You are grown," he said after a moment. "But . . . I have not been the best judge of character. It's my decisions that have left you girls in range of heartache you didn't deserve. I don't think Kallan is Arjhani, but I don't know." He snapped his jaw again. "Havilar liked him too much. I panicked."

Farideh put her arm through his once more. "Havi likes more people than not. And it's not your fault. No one blames you."

"Maybe you should."

Farideh shook her head. "Sometimes you want to kiss someone, and they're awful. That doesn't make *you* awful. At least I hope it doesn't."

"*That* is where this conversation stops," Mehen said. "Kallan tells me you went to see the wizard."

"The guard tells me you almost killed the wizard," Farideh returned.

"And I'd do it again. Do not go up there again."

Farideh shook her head. "Mehen, all this Chosen business . . . He knows something, and I think he doesn't realize it. If I don't find out, we could all be in a lot more trouble."

"And if you're in his sight, you'll be in one of these ossuaries before long."

Farideh sighed. "What if you come with me? If we go together, then you can keep an eye on Ilstan, and you'll know what's happening." Mehen hesitated. "You know I'm going back, one way or another."

Zoonie jerked suddenly toward the right-hand passage, ears pricked. Havilar handed the chain over to Brin and went a few steps down the dark hallway.

"It's—" A high-pitched scream echoed through the catacombs and suddenly cut off. Havilar cursed and sprinted toward the sound.

"*Karshoj*!" Mehen shouted. In Draconic, he ordered Dumuzi, "Run for the guards!" But the younger dragonborn ignored him, racing after Havilar.

"Got it," Kallan shouted, sprinting toward a side passage.

Zoonie yanked hard on the chain, and Brin had no choice but to run after, the rest of them chasing.

The passage ended in a small, disused tomb, the clan's name—*Churirajachi*—etched over the lintel, unfamiliar to Farideh. At the far end, something hunched over a body, the sound of cracking bones echoing loudly as cannon shot.

Zoonie growled and the shadow went rigid, whirling to face them: a dragonborn girl with dark green scales, the silvery chains of Shestandeliath hanging along her cheek. Blood, nearly black against her scales, smeared her snout.

"Zaroshni!" Dumuzi shouted.

"That's not Zaroshni," Havilar said, her voice starting to shake.

The dragonborn girl smiled, and suddenly her body stretched, as if the bones were outgrowing her joints, reshaping her bit by bit. Her scales became hairless skin leached of color, like a dead fish drawn off the bottom of a lake. Powerful muscles bunched across its chest, over its thick thighs, its dangling arms. The sight of it stopped Farideh dead.

Baatezu . . . a purring voice rumbled through Farideh's thoughts. *You want this prize too?*

Beside Farideh, Lorcan tensed. "Not particularly. But I have agreements to uphold."

Mehen gestured at Farideh, at Brin—get to the sides, surround it. He moved toward Havilar, slowly, slowly.

The creature laughed, and Farideh's scalp crawled at the sound. *This one tastes like the old days. He has your master's stink upon his flesh.*

Farideh moved up beside Zoonie, where she could see the man lying on the floor, in a pool of blood. Brume's pale blue eyes, wild with pain, found hers. His throat had been torn out in such a way that he could not scream, but he had not died.

No, Farideh thought. No, no, no.

"Lords of the Nine," Lorcan swore, drawing his sword.

"Zoonie," Havilar managed in a shaky voice. "P-*parosh renoutaa*." Her hands gripped the glaive tight, but a fine sheen of sweat showed on her face. "One . . . of you . . . get . . ."

The creature grinned, its teeth long and yellowed as finger bones. It spread its bloody, clawed hands, and all around, the ancient ossuaries rattled on their shelves and smashed open on the stone floor.

"Zoonie! *Renoutaa*!"

Dry bones bound with magic recombined into eight Vayemniri warriors, their claws lengthening into weapons themselves, fed by the demon's magic. Farideh's powers stirred in response.

Havilar had hardly spoken the order but Zoonie leaped at the demon. Two of the bone warriors, just combined, threw themselves into her path. Their claws drew blood, even through her thick coat.

The skeletons formed a wall before the demon, protecting it and its terrible meal from attack. Farideh pulled hard on the powers of the Nine Hells, drawing missiles of burning brimstone out of the air, raining down on the skeletons and the demon beyond. One hit Zoonie, thrashing against a clinging creature. Behind the iron cage she wore, her teeth were bared.

"Muzzle!" Farideh shouted.

"Shit!" Lorcan cried. He slashed at the skeleton that lunged toward Havilar, still gray-faced and leaning hard on her glaive. Farideh cursed and shifted her aim, drawing another cluster of missiles over the skeletons that menaced her sister.

Lorcan shouted something in Infernal at the hellhound, grabbing for the muzzle's latch. Zoonie ignored him, slamming down on one of the dragonborn skeletons with the full force of her front paws. Bones clattered, twitching, to the stone floor.

Farideh released another blast of energy, threading the streak of bruised-looking power through the gap Brin and Dumuzi formed as they pressed their attack. A skeleton slammed against the wall. Mehen shoved forward, toward Havilar, toward the wall of skeletons.

"Somebody!" Havilar bellowed. The gift of Asmodeus, Farideh thought. She could leap through the planes, come out behind the skeletons. She darted forward.

Mehen's roar, the crack and flash of the lightning breath, made the air in the tomb fizzle and cling to Farideh's skin. Lightning leaped from skeleton to skeleton to skeleton. Dumuzi scrabbled backward, wide-eyed and fearful as if he'd been hit too, nearly dropping his sword.

Havilar, unharried now, still took a step back, reaching back for an ally to take the blessing. The fiend, seeing its army shattering, noticed this. Noticed Havilar, and perhaps the building magic, that seemed to shiver on her frame. It moved forward, a terrible smile spreading over its bloody mouth.

Farideh pulled hard on the powers of the Hells, even as she sprinted forward.

Several things happened altogether: Lorcan yanked the pin holding the muzzle loose, stumbling as it came free. Zoonie shook the cage off, grabbed one of the skeletons by the leg and swung it over and into the ground, straight toward Lorcan. Farideh shoved him hard, out of the way of the skeleton that crashed between them.

And into Havilar's outstretched hand.

He flinched. When his eyes opened, Farideh thought she could see a flicker of horror at what Havilar had done, but it was swallowed up by a sudden ferocity, as though Lorcan's erinyes blood were bubbling up to the surface. His dark eyes locked on the demon.

Farideh threw a spell at the skeleton before him. The burst of dark energy boiled out of the rod she held, slamming into the creature's sternum and shattering what was left of its torso, opening a gap for Lorcan to leap forward and stab the demon through the back.

It screamed, the sound of a score of voices in startled anguish, arching against the sword, the splatter of blood. It twisted, its clawed hand striking Lorcan across the face, hard enough to knock him off his balance.

Havilar, freed for the moment of the burden of her gift, lunged with the glaive, driving the blade into the creature's belly. It twisted, hissing, retreating. It flung one muscular arm at Havilar, and she ducked under it, but she'd no more stooped but she clapped a hand to her mouth.

Blessed of the blessingless, its mocking voice slid through Farideh's thoughts. *Are you too soft for the Raging Fiend's—*

"*Adaestuo!*" Farideh cast another burst of energy through the crowded room, but the demon yanked one of its skeletons into the blast's path, and it destroyed the soldier's arm instead.

Farideh threw another blast of energy at the demon, pushing it back from her sister. All around the clatter of bone shards marked the nearing end of the demon's defenders, and it seemed to realize this. It turned and fled deeper into the catacombs, still bleeding, but quick on its powerful legs.

"It's getting away!" Dumuzi shouted, racing after it. Mehen swore and followed. Havilar stood, furious and woozy. "Zoonie!" The hellhound looked up from shaking one of the skeletons' still kicking legs. Havilar hauled herself onto Zoonie's back. "Go! Chase it!"

"*Ahdiseqa!*" Lorcan shouted. At the Infernal order, Zoonie took off like an arrow after, followed by Lorcan, cursing a steady stream.

Farideh ran instead to the tiefling still dying on the floor.

Brume's throat was a ruin of meat. Farideh pressed both hands to the wound. "Brin! Get over here! *Karshoj*! It'll be all right," she told Brume. "He'll fix it, it'll be all right!"

Brume's mouth gaped, fishlike. "Please, look at me!" Farideh said. "Look at me! I can't let you die, *karshoj*—I haven't got any other way, you can't die. Brin!" she screamed. "Get over here!"

He couldn't die. Not like this. And not now.

Someone yanked on her shoulder.

"Fari!" Brin was shouting. "Fari, *stop*! He's dead. He's dead."

Farideh blinked. Brume's lifeless face looked up at her, blood running into his pale blue eyes. She stood. Throat torn out. Belly half-gone. One of his legs had been eaten to the knee. There was no saving him. There had never been any saving him.

"*Karshoj*," she said, feeling her eyes well with tears. "*Karshoj*." She went to wipe them and realized her hands were covered in his blood.

"Did you know him?" Lorcan asked from behind her. Brin met her eyes over the body.

"I met him," Farideh said. A man was dead, and what went through her head but, *I haven't got any other way.* Brin handed her a handkerchief. Her hands shook when she took it. Brume was dead, and so the snake had no one to find. Her only link to Dahl was gone. She wiped her hands on the cloth, as if she could wipe away her guilt too. "I don't know . . . He might have family . . ." She looked up at Brin. "He was Zhentarim."

Brin's eyebrows rose. "We have to search the body," he said, with evident care. She nodded and kneeled down beside Brume. Their heads together, Brin whispered, "He's the one with the note, isn't he?" She could only nod again. "Don't give up, all right? You're tougher than that."

She felt about as tough as the bone ash scattered on the floor. She reached up and closed Brume's eyes. "I'm sorry," she said, before she began digging through the pockets for trinkets, messages, anything that might lead her to the Zhentarim and back to Dahl. A whistle, a handful of coins, a note of promise in Draconic for one trade bar. Half a slab of sweet almond cake wrapped in a handkerchief. A lump formed in Farideh's throat.

"Here." Brin kneeled beside her, grim and solemn. He cut the lining of Brume's coat, turned it out. A small black disk clattered to the floor. Brin picked it up with a look of faint disgust. "Token." He pulled a sheaf of papers out. "Take it all. There's no telling what's useful." He picked up the whistle. "He's got a snake of his own?"

Farideh nodded. "He called it Keetley."

Brin blew a short note on the whistle. Something rustled, high up in the ossuaries. He tried again, a trio of flickering pitches. The winged snake poked its blunt head out, its black tongue tasting the air for trouble.

Farideh reached out to it. "Here! Come here, Keetley." The snake eased out and seemed to consider Brume's body, torn apart on the floor. Farideh pulled her collar open. "Come here!"

Brin played a little tune with the notes of the whistle. Keetley flew out of its hiding place, circling the tomb twice, before slithering down through the air, and into Farideh's collar. It was smooth and heavy, looping twice around her shoulders. Its wings draped on either side of her branded arm.

Brin ventured out a hand to stroke the creature's nose. "Do you know anything about caring for snakes?" Farideh asked.

"Not a damned thing," he said. He looked back to the tunnel. "Hrast."

Mehen returned, one arm around Lorcan, bloody-faced and favoring his right leg. Dumuzi was close behind, steadying Havilar, while Zoonie whined and pulled against her chain.

"We lost it," Mehen said.

"He's dead," Farideh said.

Mehen looked down at Brume and cursed. "The guards will be here soon."

"It won't matter," Lorcan said, wiping the blood from his cheek. "Your demon is a *shitting* maurezhi."

"What does that mean?" Farideh said.

"It means that someone is trying to bring this whole city down."

15

DUMUZI RETURNED TO THE VERTHISATHURGIESH ENCLAVE in a fog, feeling as if language were falling away from him like shed scales. Bits of *Munthrarechi* slid off his ears without meaning. The devil's explanations like dream-speak with their unfamiliar words.

"The maurezhi," Lorcan said, from the couch where his injured leg was propped, "were created to be the corpse collectors of the Abyss. What Orcus can't use, what the Abyss doesn't consume, they devour. And because nothing in the Abyss can be simple, what they devour, they become. They consume thoughts, memories, experiences, and they replicate them."

Devour, Dumuzi thought. He thought of Zaroshni, bright and buoyant, sharp and magnetic. A light even in the crowd of their friends. She knew what she wanted, she said what she meant, and what the elders wanted was a suggestion, not a lead around her neck. Do I love her, Dumuzi wondered in an inane way, or do I wish I could be like her?

Did, he told himself. You mean "did." The creature growing out of her skin. Zaroshni was gone, all that promise just meat.

"Replicate them how closely?" Kallan asked from beside the door.

"Exactly," Lorcan said. "The maurezhi can appear to be anyone it's consumed. It can mimic them all but perfectly. It knows where they would go, what they would say. Who they would know."

Exactly, Dumuzi thought. But not exactly. Dead-eyed Zaroshni who didn't laugh, didn't care about the missing, didn't argue with him when he called her out for being so foolish. That was not Zaroshni, and shame on him for not seeing that his friend was gone, that she needed vengeance, that he owed her better.

Brin sat down next to him with a roll of bandages. "Here," he said, taking Dumuzi's arm. It was raked and bloodied, the scales torn away in great rents. Dumuzi blinked as the human dripped some tincture on the wound. It hurt, but it didn't matter, didn't make its way into his thoughts.

"Every time it consumes someone," Lorcan went on, "it becomes more powerful. Stronger, faster, tougher. At this point it could be anyone, and you cannot defeat it alone."

"How do we stop it?" Farideh said, slicking her sister's shoulder with the same tincture.

Lorcan smiled as if she were trying to be funny, shook his head. "You have to find it first."

Find it. The gray-skinned beast fleeing into the darkness, the last edges of the glowlight from the disused Churirajachi tomb. Running as hard as he could, even as he felt the creeping sense that he'd miscalculated, that he wouldn't keep the pace without suffering. And if he'd caught up? Mehen shouting at him to drop back, *karshoj,* you fool—and the sound of Pandjed haunting his words made every other sense fall away. He'd run until he died, for one reason or another.

"But we have me," Havilar said. "I mean, I can track it, can't I?"

"That's the assumption," Lorcan said. "But how many people live in this city? *Any* of them could be the maurezhi. Any of *you* could be the maurezhi."

Any. It could look like Uadjit. It could look like his little siblings. It could look like Patriarch Narghon, all stern and thoughtful. He thought of his teachers, up in the barracks. Fenkenkabradon Dokaan, the Lance Defenders' commander. Ophinshtalajiir Sepideh, who taught tactics and thrown weapons. Arjhani with his glaive. Could they fall? He looked around the room considering these, his new friends, his new companions. Would he even be able to tell if one of them were dangerous? Mehen caught his eyes, frowning, and Dumuzi considered the floor.

"*You* could be the maurezhi," Farideh said. Lorcan smiled at her.

"Precisely," he said. "And beyond that, if you want a hope of surviving, you have to capture it, not kill it."

"Because it's serving someone worse," Mehen said. "An invasion."

"And I cannot tell you who," Lorcan said. "But you don't send a maurezhi into this world for minor matters. And the sort of demons who send them are . . . very bad things to have after you."

"So it's trying to replace people?" Farideh asked. "That could be to unsettle the city leadership? To . . . find some secret out?" She turned to Lorcan. "Where would you send one?"

"I have absolutely no shitting idea," Lorcan said. "You can hardly predict a demon's decisions. They're little more than hunger and fear given limbs. And whatever orders it was given, it's been carrying them out in its own way."

"But it's been sent for a reason. You said it was a harbinger of an attack—so what's it here to do?"

Lorcan sighed and was silent a moment. "Gather intelligence. Or what it thinks is intelligence anyway. At this point—assuming it's the source of your massacre—it's most definitely had the opportunity to devour as many as a score of people. Which means it's getting cleverer. Less demonic. More focused. And stronger."

"So whoever sent it probably isn't in the city," Kallan said. Everyone turned to him, and he shrugged. "Can't control it once it's loose," he said counting off on his fingers. "Have to take out a lot of not-so-powerful folks to get at the ones you want. It showed up and left a trail a league thick. And again, let's all be honest—Vayemniri don't truck with this *aithyas* in general. This isn't something you do to steal the Vanquisher's piercings or upset someone's trade agreements, it's too blunt a tool. Maybe you got a lunatic running wild in here, but they're not working for themselves. The real threat is going to come from outside."

"Who would want to take down Djerad Thymar?" Brin asked. "I mean, people out there don't much bother with you."

"Dragons," Mehen said grimly.

Brin shook his head. "Maybe. But I'd assume a dragon sent a demon only just before I'd assume a drago— a *Vayemniri* did."

"We have to find out who else it took," Farideh said. "Zaroshni? The Kepeshkmolik guard? There have to be others. That could point us toward what it's trying to do."

"The maurezhi can certainly fight a group, as seen," Lorcan said. "But it needs time to consume its victims—it has to devour every part and quickly—so people it can lure away in ones and twos are certainly preferable."

Dumuzi cleared his throat. "If it wants information, it would head for the Lance Defenders. Maybe clan elders."

A heartbeat of silence followed, and Dumuzi filled it with such grief and shame.

"That's a good point," Mehen said. He stood. "We need to alert Shestandeliath and Kepeshkmolik that they have weak points, the Lance Defenders as well, and . . . *karshoj* every clan in Djerad Thymar."

"I'll take Yrjixtilex," Kallan said. "Should be able to spread that out to . . . Ophinshtalajiir, Kanjentellequor, Daardendrien, and . . . maybe Fenkenkabradon."

"Anala will want Fenkenkabradon," Mehen said. "But . . . Let me know. Who you talk to."

Dumuzi sat motionless as plans were made, destinations assigned, a buzz of activity that didn't reach him. Farideh sat down beside him. "Are you all right?"

"No," he admitted.

"Come on," she said. "Mehen and I will walk you home."

"I'm fine," Dumuzi said. "I can go myself."

Mehen suddenly stood before him, and the memory of the lightning breath crackled along Dumuzi's nerves. He held his breath. "You're not going anywhere alone," Mehen said. "After all that? *Karshoj,* none of us are the monster."

"We have to go to Kepeshkmolik anyway," Farideh said. "You're not putting anyone out."

"They don't want you there," Dumuzi said. "Forgive me for saying so, but Patriarch Narghon—"

"I am well aware what the Kepeshkmolik thinks about me," Mehen said. "And if he asks, I will tell him you've said all the right things and made all the right gestures, and I do not give a dead dragon's *aithyas*. If you were my son and Narghon made you walk alone after what just happened, I'd rip his *karshoji* piercings out. Now get up," Mehen said. "We have a lot to do."

Farideh folded her arm around Dumuzi's as they walked, following Mehen. "He's scared," she murmured. "He shouts a lot when he worries."

"I know," Dumuzi said, even though he didn't. He held her arm close as if she would keep him upright. This is not how Shasphur would react, he thought. This is not the way Nerifar would have faced her trials.

When they reached the Kepeshkmolik enclave, Mehen did not hesitate at the decorated doors. The guards looked wide-eyed at Dumuzi, and Mehen yanked them open without so much as acknowledging the young dragonborn. Dumuzi nodded, out of instinct more than anything, as he followed Mehen into the enclave, wondering what more could happen.

As if in answer, Uadjit came out into the entry hall. She stopped dead as she saw them. "Dumuzi?" She sprinted toward them, a fine edge of frost growing around her jaw. "What happened?" she shouted at Mehen. "What did you do?"

"We found the creature," Mehen said. "Your son fought very well, but it's a *karshoji* monster . . ." He faltered. "The guard, the one I asked you about. He's dead. And so is Shestandeliath Zaroshni."

Uadjit's eyes flicked to Dumuzi, to Farideh . . . where they caught and lingered. "That's not possible. I saw Zaroshni the other day. Dumuzi said she wasn't there."

"It was the maurezhi," Dumuzi said. "The fiend. I was wrong."

"The demon takes the form of those it eats. You need to tell *everyone* to be on the lookout for that guard," Mehen said. "To be watchful for people acting out of the ordinary. People shouldn't be wandering around alone. And stay the Hells out of the catacombs."

Uadjit frowned at him. "Have you informed the Vanquisher?"

"It's on the list," Mehen said. "You want to go tell Tarhun for me, I'd be obliged. We still have to tell Shestandeliath, and I expect that to take the better part of the day. Come on, Fari." Farideh hugged Dumuzi's arm once, and slipped free.

"Wait!" Uadjit said. Mehen turned. "I told you. I need . . . We need to talk to your daughter." She nodded at Farideh. "That one."

"No, you don't."

"Mehen, this isn't what you think," Uadjit said. "Believe it or not, it has nothing to do with you." Uadjit's penetrating gaze found Farideh, and if she was surprised or upset or even amused, there was no telling. "I'm Kepeshkmolik Uadjit, daughter of Narghon of the line of Shasphur. Dumuzi's mother."

"Farideh," she said, nodding to Uadjit.

Uadjit smiled. "I believe you mean Verthisathurgiesh Farideh, daughter of Mehen, claimed by the line of Khorsaya. A pleasure." Her eyes lingered on Farideh's face. "You'll get the hang of it, I don't doubt. In the meantime, the patriarch wants to speak with you. And my great-great-grandaunt." Uadjit gave Mehen a significant look and nerves started curling up Dumuzi's stomach.

"Ashoka?" Mehen said. "She's still alive?"

"For the moment," Uadjit said a little lightly. "So you see the matter's a bit pressing." She snapped her teeth, nervous. "Please," she said. "Please. It won't take long."

Dumuzi reached over and squeezed Farideh's hand, already sure he wouldn't be allowed into this meeting, already sure whatever was coming for his friend, it wouldn't be simple. Not with the last daughter of Thymara involved.

• • •

THE VEIN OF mithral seemed to glow in the gloom of the valley, reflecting and refracting scraps of light, standing bright against the ice-coated rocks around it. There was no path—only a long scrabble up a rocky slope—but as near as they must have been to their goal, no one complained as they set out, aside from Volibar, who did not like sending the snake off once more to Djerad Thymar.

Seven Zhentarim, Dahl counted. Including Xulfaril and Grathson. Against himself and his brothers. And Mira—who more than usual had him on edge.

"Why are you cozying up to my granny?" Dahl asked as they climbed.

Mira shrugged. "So? I like her. She's interesting."

"So I wish you wouldn't," Dahl said. "I mean, hrast, it's bad enough I have to convince my *very* Dallish family to accept my tiefling lover when she's not even here to convince them—"

"Why *isn't* she here?" Mira asked. "I don't think you've ever explained that very well. Why are you sending her snakes?"

Dahl scowled at her. "Are you doing this because you think it's funny?"

"It's not funny," Mira said calmly. "*I'm* not a child, so no, I'm not asking to torment you. I'm asking because none of this seems like you. You don't go for tieflings. You don't pine for anyone. Every word I've ever heard about your family makes me wonder why you'd possibly run at them, horns out, pardon the pun. This isn't you. At all. And what are we for but made to watch where things don't fit?"

"Maybe I am," Dahl said. "But you're also meant to destabilize, aren't you? Isn't that what the Zhentarim specialize in?"

Mira raised an eyebrow. "You think this about choosing sides?"

"Your superior is extorting me into working for the Zhentarim. You're playing some odd mix of jealous or heartsick or coy and getting my grandmother on your side. Your murky conscience is a lot more likely than Farideh compromising me, or whatever you're trying to imply. I'm not joining the Zhentarim."

"No one said you should," Mira replied with infuriating mildness. "You're very testy about this, aren't you?"

"Given my choices here are my agent has flipped entirely to

the enemy *or* my former lover who broke things off in a stlarning field report suddenly cares so much about my happiness, yes. I'm testy." He shook his head. "Decide what you're doing, Mira. I've got enough on my plate to worry about without picking at why your actions don't fit."

Mira's accusations dogged his thoughts like a predator in the shadows. She was right, even if she wasn't, and wasn't that worth considering? Was there harm in second-guessing? Of course not.

That just made you more certain.

Made sure you were right.

My champion, my wayward son. Oghma's words cut through those runaway thoughts. There was no harm in being sure, but he was sure already, and letting others push him away from what was true so that he could feel right was a path he'd already stumbled down, losing the god of knowledge in the process.

Mira does not know you better than you know yourself, he thought as he climbed. Whatever she thought about him, about Farideh, it was old and obscured and knew nothing about what had happened in Suzail, about who they'd become to each other.

"What do you call people from Harrowdale?" Farideh had asked, her eyes on the chaos of the overcrowded taproom, his thoughts on his knee pressed against her thigh.

"Harrans. Why?"

"Because you need to talk about something and you keep getting quiet," she said. "Tell me about Harrans. Tell me about two hundred years of Peredurs. What do you farm?"

"Rye. Sheep. Peas. Flax." He hesitated, turning the flagon against the table. "Do you want to know a secret?"

She smiled, even as her eyes were on the crowd. "Do you want to tell me a secret?"

"Peredur . . . It isn't my family name. I don't *have* a family name. I didn't," he amended. "Until I went to the Domes of Reason and it was pretty clear going around without one made me look like some haynose Dalesman off a farm who didn't belong."

She'd turned, puzzled, her knees brushing his. "Aren't you some Dalesman off a farm?"

He sipped the ale. "Thanks."

"Don't be like that," she said. "I mean you can call yourself whatever you want—but if people are going to think coming from a farm means you don't belong, does it make a difference? You're still you, aren't you? It doesn't erase that. It shouldn't." He bristled but before he could respond, she waved it away. "Says the woman who goes about disguised as a human—sorry. We all do things to smooth the way, I suppose." She gave him a tight smile before turning back to the crowd. "*Karshoj* to those snotty apprentices. If a second name made you quicker-witted, they're lucky you had only one. I don't see the draw personally."

Dahl's irritation evaporated. "You don't have a Draconic surname you trot out for special occasions?"

She'd laughed. "*Thrikominari,*" she'd said. "Clanless Farideh." Which even then he'd thought was a cruelty. It made her sound like she was all alone.

At the peak of the slope, a crevasse opened in the mountain, and they wound through it, single file. Above, only a ribbon of the sky, the color of the ice coating the walls, showed.

"It's close," Sessaca said, just loud enough for Dahl to hear.

"Good," Thost replied. "I could use a sit."

"Keep walking," Xulfaril said.

The crevasse closed over, and beneath the overhang a doorway had been carved into the stone, etched only with the scroll of Deneir. No lock upon it, no handle to grasp—it looked more like the false idea of a door than the entrance to the greatest library in Toril.

A shiver ran down Dahl's back, and the faintest presence of Oghma prickled at the edges of his mind.

"Well," Xulfaril said, turning back to Sessaca. "That's promising."

Thost crouched to let Sessaca climb down, and Dahl and Bodhar gave her their hands. She kept a grip on Dahl's and he led her around the Zhentarim, over the crusty ice. Her eyes never left the doorway.

"Is that how you saw it?" Dahl whispered.

"No," she said. "It was open then. This is where I met her. Where she told me she needed help." She pulled the heavy locket out from under her furs. "Help me with this?"

Dahl unfastened the necklace, while Sessaca turned back to the Zhentarim. "Swords in their scabbards, mind," she said.

"Of course," Xulfaril answered, before Grathson could protest. "We need to know if this works, after all."

Sessaca shot Dahl a look that said clearly he oughtn't trust the Zhentarim. Dahl returned it—what had he been doing the whole trip but gauging their captors? He glanced back at the Zhentarim, flanked by himself and his brothers. Mira in the middle. Not odds he liked, but odds he could deal with.

"There's a possibility," Sessaca admitted, "that this won't work without someone on the inside." She turned the locket in her wrinkled palm and considered the door. "But I suspect she wouldn't have done that."

The locket, made of bronze and the size of a flattened walnut, etched with runes that spelled out a long-lost prayer on every side, fit into the carving of the scroll's roller end. She pressed upon it, trying to wriggle it into the seating just right.

"Ah, hrast," she spat. "Help me here." Dahl put his hand over hers and pushed hard. The locket sank into the door with an audible *click*.

A wave of power rolled over Dahl, over the door, over the mountainside. A rumbling, so great and deep, shook the stones beneath his feet. The door began to vibrate, to blur, and then it was gone. The rumbling passed.

Sessaca looked back over her shoulder. "Well, there'll be a draft. But it's open. Come along." She took hold of Dahl's arm once more.

This was not the main entrance to the library, Dahl thought as they entered. The shelves crowded close around the dusty, cracked circle of mosaic tiles, blocking any view of the library beyond those impossibly high shelves. The only acknowledgment that anyone might enter here was a pair of benches and the remains of a carving in Draconic along the opposite shelves. The shelves themselves were half empty, fallen books and scrolls littering the ground around them.

Even from this unflattering quarter, the Master's Library sent shivers all through Dahl.

"Watching Gods," Mira breathed. "This is . . . How is it still intact?"

"People gave a care for things back then," Sessaca said.

Dahl kneeled and picked up a tome. *From Heavens to Hells: A reflection on the names and natures of the planes,* by Brother Itherius, priest of Oghma. Dahl's shivers turned to a faint and persistant *hum.*

My priest may name the spinning plane, Farideh's voice came to him, reading the lines of Oghma's mark. *The plane has never spun for him. From Heav'ns to Hells the planes will ring.*

He looked at the Master's Library as though it might come to life around him. Was he supposed to come here? Was the answer to Oghma's riddle hidden in these long-abandoned tomes?

"Spread out, in pairs," Xulfaril ordered. "Mira and I will stay here with the swordcaptain and her fellows."

Sessaca shrugged. "Take them too. Just tell them what you're looking for."

Giants, Dahl thought. Underdark. Who stlarning knows? He searched the tops of shelves, considering how many answers were hiding in the Master's Library, how many paths. He should be studying Xulfaril, he should be calculating the truth in her words, but his every thought dwelled on the thrumming presence of the god of knowledge, just out of reach.

Xulfaril hesitated before answering. "Somewhere in this library is a room that's collapsed. A sinkhole. We suspect that if anything remains within the library, it's going to be a room that holds mostly texts from Shou Lung, regarding philosophical notions and the gods. It might be this floor, it might be one of the upper floors, it might be below. Our understanding is that the library was shaped around the mountain itself. It might be that we must go up to go down. Find it, come back here, and mark the path you took." She looked at Sessaca. "Anything you want to add?"

"Walk carefully?" she said. "It was unstable sixty years ago. Watching Gods know what's happened since."

"Monsters?" Grathson asked.

"Yes," Sessaca drawled. "Every beastie that can break through a seal that kept every godsbedamned treasure hunter in Toril out. Think it through, donkey shit."

"Granny," Dahl warned. Grathson was not one to be riled— especially not as Sessaca was coming near to the end of her usefulness. She gave him a sharp look.

"And don't you go getting distracted now that I've vouched for you," she said. "Knowing you, we'll find you elbows deep in spells to draw your monster doxie back or leap off across the planes to her."

That broke Dahl's distraction, a retort on his lips, but then he caught the clever glint in his grandmother's eye: the portal spells. The angel statue on the floor above the entry. A quick escape.

Focus, he told himself, though it was Farideh's sharp tones.

"Gods' books, Granny," Dahl said, hoping his delay wouldn't show. "Lay off." He scowled at Xulfaril. "We find this, we all go our separate ways?"

Xulfaril smiled at him. "If that's what you really wish."

Which meant he needed that portal spell, Dahl thought, as one of the Zhentarim handed out sunrods. Xulfaril waved Volibar and Mira over to follow him.

"Ye gods," the halfling spat as they worked their way around the library's outer edge. "Be all day with you two. Mira Turn-Me-Every-Stone and a stlarning Oghmanyte walk into an ancient library. It's like a bad tavern joke."

"You can go search for yourself," Mira said, her eyes wandering the stonework. "It's not as if we can't manage." From the corner of his eye, Dahl saw her glare at the halfling and tap her dagger. Dahl's pulse skipped—a threat for the halfling? a sign for a fellow Zhent?

Volibar hesitated. "Xulfaril sent me after you."

"Then come along," Mira said, as if she couldn't imagine anything mattering less to her. "You heading somewhere particular Harper?"

"Up," he said tersely, as they came to a staircase.

"What happened?" Volibar called. "You two have a falling out? You need to send *her* a love note too?"

"Look at these carvings," Mira said, crouching on the stairs to examine the spindles. "Late twelve-hundreds. Dwarven. You wouldn't expect to see that. Must have been a later addition."

Dahl walked quickly, searching for the Zhentarim's hole or the statue of the angel, dreading the possibility of finding them in the wrong order. The shelves on this level were more disheveled than below, cracked and leaning. Dahl clambered over more piles of lost wisdom than he dared think about. The gods only knew what remained in the Master's Library.

"Slow up there, longshanks!" Volibar shouted, as Dahl made his way over a fallen shelf and around a column. And found himself facing the angel statue.

A planetar, to be specific—though if his granny had known that, Dahl would have given up ever being sure of anything else ever again—a muscular winged woman bearing a sword, her skull as smooth as an eggshell, her features merciless as her blade.

Behind the statue, a shelf of scrolls reached nearly to the cracked ceiling, untoppled by time, the Spellplague, or Sessaca Peredur. Dahl glanced back, listening for Volibar's grumbling, gauging the distance. Not much time. He scanned the ends of the rollers, hunting for the marks of conjuration. Top four shelves, all the way against the wall. He climbed as high as he dared and pulled scrolls from the shelves one after another, hoping one would be castable, one would be the right spell. You can come back and look for the perfect one once you're free. You can come back and search for the answer to the riddle.

And if you believe that, Dahl thought, his bag reaching its limits, then Mira's right. You've gone right off your mind.

He jumped down, pulled the bag shut, and turned as the sounds of the halfling and Mira came closer. Strolled back as if he'd only realized he'd gotten ahead of them and needed to turn back. "Will you hurry up?" he called as they climbed over the broken shelf beside the column. "I think there's more up ahead."

A sharp whistle resounded through the library, amplified by magic. Mira grimaced. "I suppose it will have to wait for another time," she said. "Sounds as if we've found our sinkhole."

● ● ●

HAVILAR FELT A sort of relief once Mehen and Farideh had left. That might not have gone the way she'd hoped, but it was a lot better than the last two times, and it wasn't as if she'd collapsed. She'd handled herself.

"Are you sure you're all right?" Mehen had asked once again, just before they'd left. "You should be lying down."

"I'm *fine*," Havilar said. "It's hardly more than a scratch."

A scratch that definitely still burned. She rotated her shoulder, feeling the skin stretch around the wound, itchy and aching. A scratch, and maybe she felt a little antsy, a little unsettled. But at least she'd *done* something. Stabbed that *henish* right in the gut. And then it had outrun even Zoonie.

"*Ah-di-say-ka*," she murmured under her breath. The word tasted off in her mouth. "You have to teach me the commands," she said to Lorcan. "It's stupid my dog knows all these things and I don't."

"What's stupid is that we're making due with mud and herb water while Brin has not once gotten his little amulet out," Lorcan drawled. "What happened, Tormite?"

"You *hate* being healed," Brin said mildly as he worked a salve into Zoonie's cuts. The hellhound lay on the floor, once again muzzled. She didn't seem to notice Brin, burning eyes locked on the dark space between the cushions of the unused couch where the winged snake had retreated.

"I hate this itching more," Lorcan said. Havilar agreed, but said nothing. The last time Brin had tried to heal someone, it had not gone well. Maybe he was avoiding it, and maybe he knew it wouldn't do any good.

"I suspect Torm would say you are capable of withstanding it," Brin said. "Builds character and focus. Or something." He smiled at Havilar. She thought about kissing him again.

You are doing a very bad job, she told herself, of figuring things out.

"Don't be bad-tempered just because Farideh left," she said to Lorcan.

Lorcan narrowed his eyes at her. "Who was that fellow? With the snake?"

Havilar schooled her features into carelessness. Farideh had slipped into her room again the other night, asking if Havilar was all right in a way that made Havilar suspect she knew about Arjhani. But when Havilar had made her change the subject, Farideh had told her about the Zhentarim with the winged snake, and the note from Dahl.

"Let me see it," Havilar had demanded.

"No!" Farideh blushed. "It's private."

That had surprised Havilar. She didn't have any notes like *that*. "Is it that racy?"

"It's not racy, it's just private," Farideh had said stubbornly. She'd smiled. "But he's safe—safe enough, rather. He's all right and he's sorry and he loves me."

Very easy things to say, Havilar thought, from the other end of the world. *Karshoji* Dahl.

"A Zhentarim," Brin answered, when Havilar had sat silent too long. "His name seems to have been Brume." He stood, scratching Zoonie behind the ear. Zoonie stopped her vigil over the snake long enough to happily rub against Brin's hand.

"So she's crying over some Black Network tiefling."

"If she was crying," Havilar said, "it's probably because she's worn out of *karshoji* devil gods and murder demons and a certain someone who is still not sorry."

"I apologized, not that it's your business." He sat up, flexing the foot of his injured leg. "When you were traveling in Cormyr, out of curiosity, did you tell Sairché about the ghost?"

"No," Havilar said. She thought a moment. "She was there when Brin was . . ." *Possessed*—she couldn't quite bring herself to say the word. Brin sat down beside her, fist full of unused bandages, and said nothing. "The, um, I think the ghost talked to her then, and before then. She kept calling her . . . That thing the maurezhi called you. Batty-zoo."

Lorcan glowered at her. "*Baatezu.*"

"It's another word for devils," Brin told her.

"It's not important." Lorcan drummed his fingers against his leg. "Did she recognize the ghost?"

"No," Havilar said. "Should she have?"

"That would be odd," Lorcan said. He glanced back at the door. "I assume this isn't finished. I assume you're going back out after it."

"Sooner or later," Havilar said. Then, "I appreciate your help."

"I think you don't need it so badly as you insisted."

Havilar made a face at him. "Well then take that creepy scepter back."

"You aren't done with it," Lorcan said, standing. "Tell your sister I want to talk to her when she gets back. And try to survive in the meantime since the Tormite's spells are too good for you." Before Havilar could reply, Lorcan had opened the portal back to the Hells and vanished in a gust of sulfurous wind.

"*Gods,* he's insufferable." Havilar turned to Brin. "How did you know that?" she asked. "*Baatezu.*"

Brin focused on rolling bandages. "I read a *lot* of books. When I was looking for you. It came up."

A wave of guilt rolled through Havilar, perversely settling the edge the demon had left her with. It was a familiar guilt, a familiar sadness. One she might be making worse . . . or maybe saving herself from drowning in. "Sorry," she said, and it was such a stupid thing to say. "I forgot."

"Demons," Brin said, as if he were changing the subject, "call themselves *tanar'ri*. Three sounds," he added, with a smile. "Tah-nahr-ree."

Havilar giggled. "That does sound better than 'demons.' "

Brin's attention returned to the bandage roll. "How come you keep trying to get Lorcan to make up with your sister?"

"Because," Havilar said, "he was awful to her."

"Right. But he's Lorcan—he *is* awful. Apologizing doesn't change that. Your sister's probably better off without him."

Havilar wasn't sure she could agree, but at the same time she wasn't going to argue. Lorcan could be awful—worse than awful—but he could be kind too, in his own strange way. More, she couldn't quite imagine him *not* being around. How he'd gone from an intrusion to a fixture in their lives, Havilar couldn't have said. Wouldn't have said, she amended. She knew Brin was right, even if she didn't believe it completely.

"He's not a lot worse than Dahl," Havilar said.

Brin looked at her as if she were a little mad. "You can't really think your sister ought to prefer Lorcan to Dahl."

"She ought to prefer neither of them," Havilar said. "I don't care what he said, he left without telling her and he's said nasty, snipey things to her and he's a drunk."

"I think you might be a little biased," Brin said. "Didn't Farideh say things like that about me? And it made you furious."

"I shouldn't have told you that."

Brin shrugged. "That's what I mean, though. For both of you, no one's good enough for the other. You just have to trust that she's got her own life in order, and if she needs you, she'll say so." He looked down at the bandages again. "I mean, it's not that either of you are necessarily wrong . . . if you think . . ." He cleared his throat, and Havilar took his hand.

"This is all pretty stupid, isn't it?"

"No, it made sense. It's hard to make decisions without knowing what's out there." He cleared his throat again. "Though if you were planning to find another fellow or two, you certainly picked a terrible city to come to."

Havilar squeezed his hand, but there was nothing she could say to that that didn't sound worse. She didn't want to find another fellow—she wanted to have already had other lovers, to have enough life under her feet to feel like she stood equal with Brin. To know she was making the right choices.

Zoonie trotted up behind them and laid her muzzled head between theirs, whining. Havilar wrinkled her nose. "She needs a run," she told Brin. "I think she might have eaten a little of the skeleton."

"I doubt your knee's better yet," Brin said. He scratched Zoonie's enormous head. "Could you heal it?" Havilar asked. "Or do you think . . ."

Brin considered her leg, before blowing out a breath. "I don't know. And I don't know if I want to. I pretty well spat in Torm's eye back there. It doesn't feel right to ask for blessings from him." He set his hand upon her injured knee, gentle and familiar. "If you really need it . . ."

"It's all right," Havilar said. "It's just a twist."

Brin left his hand against her leg. "I could take her. If you think she'd listen."

Havilar smiled. "That could work."

It took some persuading—Zoonie didn't like to leave Havilar behind—but when the hellhound puppy seemed to grasp that the only way she was getting out of the pyramid was with Brin, she relented, glancing back at Havi mournfully, but leaving slack in the chain as she followed Brin from the room.

Havilar's heart twisted. Brin had relaxed a great deal about Zoonie after the hellhound had defended both Havilar and the now-Queen of Cormyr during the siege of Suzail, never turning on the Cormyrean army. And now Zoonie had clearly settled on

Brin as someone she ought to listen to, in the absence of Havilar, more so even than Farideh or Mehen.

But you have to send her back eventually, Havilar thought, even though she hated it, even though she'd rather hide from it. Zoonie couldn't be happy penned up and kept from her natural urges. Would she be happier, though, Havilar wondered, in a pack of vicious, evil hellhounds—and nearly snorted at the image.

Maybe you just don't know what she really is, Havilar thought. She's not going to be a puppy forever.

What Havilar *needed* was a spell to keep Zoonie a puppy forever . . .

On second thought, no—such a spell might be too tempting for Mehen. And then they'd never find the *pothach* maurezhi.

Havilar stood, testing her twisted knee. She could work around it. She took up the glaive and limped away from the sitting area. Her weight on the uninjured leg, sweep the glaive down, through an imaginary attacker. Shift back onto the injured leg, just enough to skip the good leg backward, tail pressed to the ground for balance.

Havilar wrinkled her nose. Not perfect. Good enough for skeletons, maybe, definitely dretches. But she wouldn't be cutting down the maurezhi one-legged. She imagined another fight with the creature, staying back and letting Mehen and Farideh and Brin and Dumuzi handle the front—and she couldn't even picture herself, loitering around the edges, passing blessings off.

Havilar went through another pass, trying to pivot on the uninjured leg. Whatever it was *supposed* to be like, being the Chosen of Asmodeus was just *pothach* through and through. What a stupid set of powers to give her! Better Farideh have the demon sense, the blessing against them, and Havilar be the one to burst into terrible flames. She paused—she'd look *amazing* with fiery wings—and then shook her head. She didn't want Farideh's powers. She didn't much want any of these powers.

Except Zoonie, she amended, which meant except the imps. Except Mot, she added. She rather liked Mot at times.

Someone behind her cleared their throat, and Havilar whirled on her unhurt leg, glaive ready. Anala raised an eyebrow.

"Has no one shown you the training yard?" she asked. Beside her stood a dragonborn man who seemed vaguely familiar. Broad-shouldered as Mehen and with similarly bronze scales, though with a wider face and dark green eyes. Instead of piercings along his jaw, the ridge above each temple had been fitted with small branching shapes, like steel antlers. His eyes settled on Havilar's glaive and a faint smile broke his gruff expression. The man from the barracks, she thought.

"This isn't *really* training," Havilar started.

"Never mind," Anala said. "Where's your father?"

"He and Farideh are walking Dumuzi home," she said. "He said he'd find you soon."

The man stepped forward before Anala could speak. "Well met," he said, in easy Common. "I am Fenkenkabradon Dokaan. I take it you're Verthisathurgiesh Havilar."

Havilar frowned. "*Who*," Havilar said, "is calling me *that*?"

Dokaan blinked at her, startled. He cleared his throat. "Well. Regardless . . . Arjhani has spoken well of you. Seems you brought his students down a few notches? Showed them what they hadn't mastered?" He turned to Anala, shaking his head. "They get younger every year and seem like they already know everything a month earlier than the last. Hatchlings."

Havilar twisted her glaive against the floor. "If they got hurt at all, it was only a few bruises. I didn't use the blade."

"He's offering you a position," Anala said to Havilar. "Not chiding you."

"A position? Doing what?"

"Teaching," Dokaan said. "The glaive is not the most popular weapon, but we like to make certain the cadets have a range. Arjhani has . . . enough on his hands. And from the sound of things, he may be leaving our company for a time. He suggested I consult Anala and see if you'd be interested in the position."

Havilar frowned, sure she was missing something. "You want *me,* to teach Vayemniri hatchlings how to use a glaive?"

Dokaan nodded once. "It would be a few classes a week. And you'd have to enlist, so you'd have other responsibilities as well. We would waive the two-year service. You'd be career. And clearly we'd have to work out what that means. We've had mercenaries serve alongside us, teach cadets a time or two, but . . ." He shrugged. "This is tidier."

Havilar wasn't sure what that meant. "Would I live here?"

Dokaan looked at Anala. "Most live in the barracks at the peak. That's included."

In all her days, Havilar had never imagined anything like this conversation coming to her—the very idea that a person could make coin just telling people how to be better with their weapon seemed so peculiar that she might have dreamed it up.

"Would," Havilar asked carefully, "I get to ride a bat?"

Dokaan frowned at her. "You'd . . . you'd have to take some lessons. But it could be arranged. Your father probably recalls how it's done. A pity he's not here. The Lance Defenders could easily find a place for Verthisathurgiesh Mehen."

Anala's smile never warmed. "Where did you say he'd gotten to?"

Havilar realized everything they hadn't told Anala yet. "Um, he's gone to tell the other clans about the maurezhi." She wet her mouth. "We found what killed your son."

* * *

"We don't have to stay," Mehen told Farideh. She tapped her fingers against the arms of the chair, looking up at the frieze of dragonborn, riding, attacking, dismembering three white dragons. Blue chalcedony, red jasper, and pale citrine marked the dragons' eyes, setting them apart from one another as they struggled and died under the onslaught.

"Anala won't be happy if we leave, will she?" Farideh asked. "It would be rude?" And I want to know what this is, she thought. I need to. She already had more than enough mysteries hanging over her.

"She won't be happy we got ourselves caught here either."

Farideh studied a dark blue dragonborn, posed with one end of a chain knotted around the the yellow-eyed dragon's neck. "You're curious, aren't you? I mean, if they wanted to talk to you, that would be one thing, but me? Why should they want to talk to me?" She wet her mouth, and tried not to think about the dark powers twining up her nerves. "Do you think they *know*?"

Before Mehen could answer, the doors opened once more. Kepeshkmolik Narghon entered first, bearing a case about the size of Havilar's scepter's and a ferocious sneer. Mehen stood swiftly, and for a moment Farideh feared he would pull his falchion out. Narghon's eyes never left Mehen as he set the case down on the table.

Behind him came Uadjit, leading a very elderly dragonborn woman, her moon piercings loose along her pale, coppery brow, the ends of her plumes white. She moved slowly, Uadjit pacing her with mincing steps all the way to the chair opposite Farideh, but her eyes held Farideh's—one dark as night, one silvered by a cataract.

"This is Kepeshkmolik Ashoka," Uadjit said. "Daughter of Thymara. Honored among elders." Ashoka smiled and squeezed Uadjit's hand.

"My great-great-grandniece," she said, patting their shared fist. She settled her hands in her lap, considering Farideh in a puzzled sort of way, before turning to Mehen. "So you're Pandjed's boy? The pugilist?"

"There's no reason for you to be here," Narghon started.

Mehen's nostrils flared. "You want to talk to my daughter, Kepeshkmolik, then that's reason enough." Narghon started to retort, but Ashoka waved a hand at him.

"Narghon, hush." Ashoka leaned forward, smiling at Mehen. "Our patriarch is ever ready for battle. A good trait, but one that costs him at times." She turned to Farideh and the row of moons across her wrinkled brow shifted. "Do you know what an ancestor story is, hatchling?"

Farideh glanced at Mehen, but her father only folded his arms grimly. "Yes," she said, cautiously. "My father told them to us as children."

"Good boy," Ashoka said, nodding at Mehen. "Did he ever tell you of Kepeshkmolik Thymara and the Gift of the Moon?"

"It's Kepeshkmolik's story," Uadjit reminded her great-great-grandaunt gently. Ashoka waved her off.

"It belongs to all of us," she said, her dark eyes on Farideh.

Farideh felt a shiver run up her back. "Thymara was your mother."

Ashoka gave a solemn nod. "Mine was the last of her clutches. The ancestor stories are the lessons of our past, the path that leads to the Vayemniri's present, the path to our future. I would tell you this one, so you understand why you're here."

Farideh glanced at Mehen, Uadjit, and Narghon again. None seemed eager for Ashoka's story. None seemed ready to stop her. "I would like that," said Farideh, unsure of whether she should be afraid of where this was going. The powers of Asmodeus were a constant hum in her veins. Mehen sat again, and took her hand in his.

Ashoka rubbed her hands together and began, crooning the tale as though it were half song, the way Mehen had told his ancestor stories when they were small. Farideh shivered down to the tip of her tail.

"Let me sing of one who gave home and hearth to the Vayemniri, cast into a strange land, the praise and promise given the fallen warrior, the steps we took into Toril. Let me sing of the voyage that nearly broke us, and the rise of the Fortress of Thymara, the bastion of the Vayemniri, and the debt of Kepeshkmolik.

"It was not long ago by the count of stones that the Blue Fire came and tore our fledgling kingdom from the breast of Abeir." Ashoka's hands spread, the worlds splitting apart. "The sky burnt the color of an *ulhar* tyrant's scales, the titans' artifacts ignited like beacon fires with this strange power, as though all the strength and magic would burn out of them. The earth shook, the air vanished, and Tymanchebar was no more.

"In those days, each clan kept its own *djeradi*—clanholds ready to fight for their fellows, united against the tyrants, but caring foremost for their own. When the Blue Fire came, there was no warning, no foe to fight, and so the *djeradi* were thrown across the planes and shattered against the face of Toril. They were ruined to a one and many died, such was the violence of the Blue Fire.

"We were scattered. Elders could not find their hatchlings, warriors could not find their holds. The Blue Fire burned on the strange new plane, giving rise to monsters and other terrible things." Her hands made claws as her wrists twisted, like strange beasts rising from the ground. "We fought and we survived.

"Kepeshkmolik Thymara, daughter of Kharadin, of the line of Shasphur, arrived from a smaller holding, heavy with eggs and near to her time. The Blue Fire had spared her, but not her kin—all had died or been deformed by the wild magic. She fought her own blood, and survived to sing over their bones. Alone, she surveyed this new world, wondering what would come next.

"*You walk*, said a voice in Thymara's heart."

Ashoka smiled in a strange, knowing fashion, and Farideh shivered again. There were no strange voices in ancestor stories. There was so little magic as to make people assume that dragonborn could not touch that sort of power. This was something different.

"Now, Thymara had heeded the stories of her ancestors. She knew that the dragon tyrants could whisper into a person's mind. But the burning sky dimmed for a moment and the sphere of the moon appeared.

"*Walk,* the voice said again. *I will give you shelter.*

"Thymara walked until she was certain her legs would sink into the ground below her, but wherever she went, the moonlight left a path that led her past the worst dangers of Toril. Soon she came to another ruin, an enormous granite structure partly collapsed. Thymara knew that nothing of this kind lay so near to her holding—this place came from the new world. Sword in hand, she entered the ruin.

"The stone made a safe place, and more, magic worked upon it drove away the terrible monsters. At its heart lay a tomb, revealed by the broken stone. A bearded man, twice Thymara's height, a human by his look and freshly dead by any indication. Across his chest lay an axe as black as the inside of a *vutha's* skull. Thymara knew a warrior's rest when she saw it, and sang the dirge for the lost in gratitude for the shelter. Her eggs she laid that very night, the firstborn of the Thymari, warmed in the dust of newborn Tymanther.

"She woke again the next night and stood at the entrance to ruins, considering again the moon. 'You have my thanks as well,' she said to her strange rescuer. 'But I do not wish to be in debt, especially to one I do not understand. What may I do to earn the balance?'

"*Thrive,* said the gentle voice. And it told Thymara to claim the warrior's black axe. 'Who was he?' Thymara asked. *Myself,* the voice said. *My son. My comrade. It is hard to understand.* The axe, the voice said, would lead Thymara to the other Vayemniri, who could make this place into a new *djerad,* a fortress to protect the Vayemniri in this new world.

"'Again, my thanks,' said Thymara, 'but this does not even the scales, only creates more debt on my heart. What must I do?'

"*Hold the axe,* said the moon. *Pass it down, until its true bearer arrives to guide you.*

"'Many might claim that title,' Thymara said. 'How will I know?'"

Ashoka fell silent, the last words of Thymara's question trembling as she spoke them. Farideh found herself holding her breath and exhaled too noisily.

"What did she say?" she asked finally.

Ashoka's tongue fluttered behind her teeth a moment. "My dear," she asked, "how is it you came by your silvered eye?"

16

WITH EVERY WORD OF THE ANCESTOR STORY, MEHEN'S pulse seemed to quicken, the phantom taste of peril filling his mouth. As Ashoka, Last Daughter of Thymara, waited for Farideh to answer, he felt dizzy, breathless. Desperate for enemies he could cut down.

"I think there's been a mistake," Farideh said. "Selûne isn't . . . I'm . . . I'm not a god-worshiper."

"Neither is Kepeshkmolik," Narghon said severely. "We are merely fulfilling a promise."

Kepeshkmolik is like a nest of vipers, Pandjed's voice echoed in Mehen's thoughts, *masquerading as a warrior. That's why you will marry Kepeshkmolik Uadjit.*

"You were born with it, weren't you?" Ashoka said. She tapped her own silvery eye. "I was too."

"That means nothing," Mehen said, nearly shouted. "Do you think she's the only child born with a silver eye since you hatched?"

"She nearly is," Ashoka said mildly. "The only living one."

"And not Vayemniri!" Mehen said. "It's a mistake."

Polish on the outside, Pandjed had said, *venom on the inside. They play at honor but they're slippery, gutless. Dangerous.*

"Believe me," Uadjit said, "the possibility's been discussed."

That is why you will marry Kepeshkmolik Uadjit.

"It's just…" Farideh drew a deep breath. "I'm not the sort of person Selûne would… appreciate, I think," she said. "And I don't particularly need more gods in my affairs."

"Be grateful," Ashoka advised. "Insofar as deities go, she is a generous one."

"And better suited to your kind than ours," Narghon said.

Farideh laughed, a little wildly. "You've got that *all* wrong."

Narghon stood and retrieved the long casket from behind the elder's chair. He set it on the table between them and opened it.

Inside lay a jet-black axe, its long, tapered blade as glassy as a mirror. A trio of jackal heads were carved in the stone along the back of the axe head. Strange glyphs marked the haft, strange figures of animals, wide-eyed human men and women embedded in gold along its length. Mehen had never seen its like.

"What . . ." Farideh faltered. "That's it?"

Narghon held the weapon out to her, and Mehen fought the urge to knock the axe out of his hands. "The Black Axe of the Moon's Champion. Take it."

"It's not mine," Farideh protested, holding her hands up. "You have the wrong person."

"No we don't," Ashoka said firmly. "Tell her we have fulfilled Thymara's covenant, and we will honor her aid in our symbols."

"I don't talk to the moon goddess . . ." Farideh's protest fell away in a helpless sort of way. "What am I supposed to do with an axe? You can't think I'm supposed to guide you?"

"No one thinks that," Uadjit said gently.

"Hatchling," Ashoka said, "one doesn't have to worship the gods to acknowledge their existence and the things they claim to be gifts. Sometimes a power cannot be denied—titan, god, or tyrant. Sometimes a gift is only a gift. My time is far past when it should have ended. If you're not the true bearer, then you have only to guard it until another one comes who is meant to be."

"Kepeshkmolik sees to its debts," Narghon said, thrusting the artifact at Farideh. "Take it and fare well."

Mehen yanked the axe out of Narghon's hands. "There," he snarled. "You're through."

Narghon eyed Mehen coldly, but the transfer seemed enough. "Give Anala my regards, and kindly tell her I won't be available for her to vent her inevitable ire at for the next few days." He swept from the room. A younger dragonborn slipped in and took Ashoka by the arm, to lead her from the room.

"Very nice meeting you, dear," she said, as though they'd done no more than talk about the weather. She smiled at Mehen. "And you I wish well, even if you make some terrible choices." Leaning on the staring young dragonborn's arm, she hobbled from the room.

Mehen considered the axe. Blacker than the dead of night and polished to an edge so keen it looked as if it could split a mountain without the slightest hesitation. More like the weapon of the Chosen of Asmodeus than the Moon's Champion, he thought with distaste.

And yet . . .

He wrapped both hands around the axe. At a glimpse, it was darkness and death. The humans gilded into its haft looked ordinary, the animals unfamiliar but quiescent. The jackals along the butt of the axe head looked fierce and stern, not wild. He turned the blade, shifting the reflection from his own face . . . to Farideh's stricken one. To her silver eye.

"Should sink fast enough," Mehen said.

Uadjit folded her arms. "That's your answer? Take a priceless artifact, a well-loved weapon, and chuck it in the *Kuhri Ternhesh*?"

"It's not your grandmother's greatsword, it's the gods' *karshoji* yoke!"

"It's payment for a favor done. 'Never lay in debt to one who might crush your clan.' "

"Don't you quote *omin' iejirkkessh* at me like we're at *karshoji* lessons."

"Stop cursing at me and lower your voice, if you please."

Farideh stood swiftly, crossing to where they stood. "Give me the axe."

Mehen broke off and turned to his daughter. Farideh held out her hand with a grim expression. "There's no reason—"

"Yes, Mehen, there's a reason." Her voice had the faintest tremor to it, but she meant what she said. "You can say it's a mad one, you can say you don't agree with it, but you cannot say that the gods are acting at random."

Mehen's nostrils flared. "So you're arguing this one's like the other one? Nothing to worry about, just a little favor. Is that it?"

"I don't know," Farideh said. "You won't give me the only clue about *this* one that we have." She dropped her voice, switched to Common, for all the good it did. "And as for the other, that should tell you clearly enough that I'm not taking this lightly."

A retort was on his teeth—she was taking it all too lightly— but Mehen crushed it. He thought of his daughter, burning by the riverbank, solemn as a statue. He thought of how hesitant she was to seize those powers, how *fearful* she was when Havilar began to use hers. How determined she was to coax the truth from the mad wizard, who called her a viper, who wanted to crush his daughter for something she was trying so hard to control.

Mehen tapped his tongue to the roof of his mouth. "Better—"

"Better I should ignore them all, I know," Farideh said. "But I don't get that luxury, and I need every weapon afforded me. Give me the axe. Please."

Uadjit snorted. "Verthisathurgiesh Mehen has a daughter indeed." Mehen glowered at her, but Uadjit only smiled and nodded at Farideh. "She may not be you, scale and breath, but she has the breath close enough. Only she says 'please.' "

Farideh flushed, which made Mehen bristle. "None of this is your business anymore. Your debt is paid, as I recall." He handed over the axe.

Like most weapons, the great black blade looked lost in Farideh's hands. His daughter had a way of taking hold of a blade in the same way she took hold of curious branches or mislaid ladles. With the axe laid across the flats of her hands, she frowned, studying the runes.

"Well?" Mehen asked.

She shrugged. "Just an axe."

Half a weight came off him—maybe the thing was nothing more than an old family heirloom, Ashoka's failing memory twisting it into something supernatural and cursed. But there was still an obligation attached to the weapon, another hook in his baby girl. She turned it, scrutinizing the shining head.

"Have you used an axe?" Uadjit asked. Farideh looked over the blade at her.

"I-I've chopped wood," she said. "But not as a weapon, no."

"She uses the short sword," Mehen said. "And as we have a lot to do—"

"You don't want to carry it loose." Uadjit pulled a belt from the case. She helped Farideh into it, and slipped the axe into the loops. "Watch your thumbs," she advised, before turning to Mehen.

"I would help you," Uadjit said, her chin high. "This concerns Kepeshkmolik as well. It concerns me," she added, "and my son."

Mehen tapped his tongue against his teeth. Once upon a time, he would have counted Uadjit among his closest allies. Once upon a time, he thought grimly, you were an idiot. But here, at least, was a matter he felt sure that she and he could be steadfast on—they would not let their children fall, not for clan, not for elders, and that was where Uadjit's slipperiness would come in handy.

"Shestandeliath," he said finally. "The last time I called on the patriarch, it didn't go as planned. But someone needs to get in there quickly, to warn them about Zaroshni and lock down their enclave."

Uadjit nodded once. "Have you told Anala?"

"Not yet," Mehen said. "And she can go complain to Khorsaya if she doesn't like Tarhun finding out before her. This is beyond hatchlings spitting on their ancestors. The city is in danger."

Uadjit chuckled. "I doubt she bargained on you being so forward. I'll send runners to the other enclaves," she added.

"In twos," Mehen said. "Leave no one alone."

"Where are you two going?"

Mehen regarded Farideh with a grim expression. "To the Vanquisher himself.

• • •

IT MUST HAVE been a reading room once, Dahl thought, considering the collapsed room. The way the shelves framed the space, the capitals of columns still clinging by their mortar to the ceiling. Beside him, Mira aimed her glowstick toward the ceiling and peered at them.

"That looks Shou," Mira said. "But not—they don't . . . Their pillars aren't built like that. Has to be another repro—"

"No one gives a shit about the stonework," Grathson snapped. "Aside from which bits can hold ropes."

Mira lowered the glowstick. "Well, certainly not the collapsed sectioned column."

Grathson looked down the shaft, hand still on his sword. Dahl pictured shoving the Zhentarim over the edge—and everything that would fall apart once he did. "Any idea how far down it goes?"

"Obviously that's where we need to begin," Xulfaril said, magic cloaking her arms to the elbows. "Any words of wisdom, Swordcaptain?"

"I think you can get yourselves down a hole," Sessaca said. "Shall we wait up here, or may we start our journey home?"

"Why oh why, Swordcaptain," Xulfaril said, "do I find myself suspecting you're not being entirely forthcoming?"

"I'd lay my guess on the company you keep."

Xulfaril studied the sinkhole, ignoring the barb. "Mira, dear, where can we anchor?"

Mira edged around toward the farther side of the hole, gravel spilling down into the void with each careful step. "Nothing's safe to tie on to in here," she said, searching the stonework. "I'd go back out—lash the main ropes to one of the monolithic pillars near the entry, set some anchors and smaller ropes into the walls here. Might take a while."

"This is all going to take a while," Xulfaril said. She turned to Sessaca, "So get comfortable." Dahl didn't like the smile that split Grathson's scarred face at that.

He took hold of Sessaca's arm, as if to guide her back to a seat, and whispered in her ear, "Got them. I need to read them, though."

"Any idea how long they'll take?"

"None. But portal spells aren't simple. Half an hour, maybe more."

Sessaca cursed and stopped walking. "You're taking the long way," she called back to Xulfaril. "No idea what you're up to, but you seem in a hurry."

Grathson and Xulfaril's quiet conference cut short. "What do you mean the long way?" Grathson asked.

"It means," Sessaca said, "that you're going to be digging for a very long time if you head down that shaft. Half a mile down it's packed with rubble—or at least, it was sixty years ago. Can't imagine it's loosened up much since."

"We know about the slide," Grathson started.

"Shut up." Xulfaril narrowed her eyes. "You spent a lot of time mapping paths out of the library?"

"I had to," Sessaca said. "That Deneirrath bitch sealed me in here. 'One inside, one outside.' Last to see it, and last to flee it."

Turns out she was asking for trouble, that one. Dahl felt sick at the thought of a priest of a god so near to Oghma's grace sacrificing someone like that. Even "a blade-ferrying sellsword with a rotten heart and a bad demeanor." *How long has she been in here? Long enough to remember where the portal spells were, sixty years later,* he thought.

"You didn't mention that part," Xulfaril said.

Sessaca smiled. "You didn't ask."

The wizard and Grathson exchanged glances. Grathson let go of his sword. "What are we looking at?" Xulfaril asked.

"That's cute," Sessaca said. "Here's what's going to happen: my grandsons and I are leaving. You can send one of yours along—"

"Old woman," Xulfaril interrupted, the end of her wand lighting with foul-looking magic, "you're trying my patience. I've got the magic to get it out of you, come to that. How did you escape?"

Sessaca's eyes flicked to Dahl, calculating. "The shaft you've found is bigger, but as I said, the rubble fills it well before you get to the Upperdark. It's as if the whole core of the mountain fell in. You dig down very far and it's practically solid rock, even though the bottom's coming loose—clear there's something big blocking the way. There's a second shaft. That's what you need if you want to get down there."

"Where is it?"

"It starts in a room with a plaster painting of Candlekeep on the back wall, six rows to the east. Just a crack, you'll have to go in one at a time. Follow it down and then take the right-hand passage, then the leftmost. Squeezes tight about a mile down, but it jogs enough there's no reason to fear falling. It's not very difficult—least if you're young, spry, and determined—but it'll take you some days. It comes out almost on top of the slide, so you'll know where you are.

"Now," she said, rubbing the fingers of her right hand, "you don't need to haul me down there. I'm just going to slow you down all the worse."

Xulfaril laughed once, short and sharp. "At this point, Swordcaptain, you've shown me at every step of the way that you have one more secret in your pocket. So no—you won't be leaving until we're absolutely sure there's nothing left to discover. I hope the climb down is as easy as you've promised, for your sake."

"And when we reach the bottom?" Dahl said. "You need her for what's down there, or are you going to make us climb back up?"

"She hasn't said," Mira remarked.

"Something to do with the outpost," Volibar added. "That much we can all guess."

Grathson drew his sword. "Take your orders and shut your—"

"No," Xulfaril said. She stepped in front of the mercenary. "The outpost in the Upperdark has gone silent. A snake carrying a distress call got out to the aboveground checkpoint, and the decision was made—too hastily, I might add—to collapse the passage. Now we can't contact the outpost, the paths to it through the Underdark are either blocked or too dangerous at the moment. The collapsed shaft was marked on maps, as well as its probable connection to the Master's Library. We get in, we find out what we're dealing with, we get out."

"Slowly up a crack one-person wide," Dahl said.

"Do you care so little for your people, Harper?" Xulfaril said. "We'll get out. But first, we have to get in."

• • •

"WHAT IS THIS going to be like?" Farideh asked Mehen as they climbed the wide stairs toward the rooms at the peak of the pyramid called the Vanquisher's enclave. "Is it more like court in Suzail or like heading into a tavern or Tam's offices?"

Mehen glanced back at her. Even as she walked, Farideh fidgeted with the black axe at her hip. The edges of the shadow-smoke had begun to tatter the edges of her arms.

"I don't know," Mehen said, honestly. "It changes, Vanquisher to Vanquisher. But if it's Tarhun that's in the throne . . ." He sniffed. "Court mixed with tavern."

"So he's not exactly a king?"

"The trouble with the Vanquisher's seat," Verthisathurgiesh Pandjed had been heard to opine, "is that by the third year, they think themselves kings and queens. They forget they are but trumped-up arbiters, commanders who've been given airs. Watch the fools remember the day after they're told to hand the piercings back."

There was truth in it, Mehen had to admit. But like anything Pandjed said, the truth was poisoned—he had been passed over when his chance arose, in favor of an Ophinshtalajiir, an aunt of Sepideh's called Shaushka who'd led a bloody raid against the ash giants that everyone had said was doomed before it started. Only three Vayemniri were lost. Every clan head voted for her, save Ophinshtalajiir, which by tradition could not. By the time Shaushka's term had ended, Pandjed's father had died and he'd been elevated to patriarch, no longer eligible for the Vanquisher's throne.

"Not exactly," Mehen said. He scratched at the jade plugs—there was no going to the Vanquisher unmarked. "The Vanquisher is elected every ten years. Each clan puts forth a candidate and then each clan votes for someone else's candidate. In that time, the Vanquisher is the final authority in Djerad Thymar. So like a king, but you're not stuck with any of them."

"But the clan heads don't like going to him?" He looked back at her curiously. "The ones in the catacombs didn't want to bring it to the Adjudicators," she reminded him, "which sounds like it means bringing it to the Vanquisher."

"More or less."

"Do you know the Vanquisher?" Farideh asked. "Tarhun?"

Mehen snorted. "Yes and no. He's clan-kin to Uadjit. Kepeshkmolik, but a line called Akkadi. He's not much older than I am. I was certainly aware of him, and I'm sure we patrolled together in the Lance Defenders. We weren't friends, but I can't say anything bad about him." He knocked one of the jade plugs loose as he scratched, and he cursed. "That's not true. He was always a bit of a prig. Wants everything to be straightforward and honorable, and because he's a skilled warrior, things shake out that way *for him*. Never mind a thousand years of ancestor stories make it clear that's not how things usually go. And people wonder how their hatchlings start falling for the Platinum Dragon's line." He shook his head.

"But he'll listen," Farideh said. "He'll help to stop the maurezhi?"

"He's not a monster," Mehen agreed.

They crossed the threshhold of the enclave that housed the Adjudicators' and the Vanquisher as well, high up the pyramid and intertwined with the Lance Defenders' barracks up above. The double doors were wide-open beneath a carved row of dragon skulls and the words: Never forget what clans may do as one.

"Did you ever want to be Vanquisher?" Farideh suddenly asked. "Growing up, I mean?"

Mehen sighed. "Children want a lot of things. Come on."

The Vanquisher's Hall of Mehen's memory did not resemble the room he stood in now. In Shaushka's reign it had been everything Kepeshkmolik prized—ordered, mannerly, as if the dragonborn had gotten their hands on one of Havi's chapbooks about Cormyrean kings and queens. Her successor, a grizzled Churirajachi veteran called Versengethor, scattered his chamber with warriors ready for battle.

Tarhun's court, by contrast, was crowded—too crowded— with petitioners and elders and warriors, all mingling in their finest as though it were a gathering or a wedding or a hatching.

Pandjed would have loathed the court of Tarhun, Mehen thought. He grabbed the nearest Adjudicator, her square gold piercings mimicking the Vanquisher's own. "I need to speak with someone. It's an emergency."

The woman cocked her head. "The Vanquisher is hearing grievances. You can tell him yourself."

"It's an emergency."

"Then go and tell him," she said slowly, as if Mehen were simply not hearing her. "Give your name to Shikari over there, and wait to be called." She squinted at him, and then at Farideh. "Are you visiting from somewhere?"

Mehen muttered a curse to himself. "Thank you." He turned to Farideh, still standing in the doorway, studying the dragonborn with a faraway expression. The soul sight.

"Anything?" he whispered.

She shook her head and blinked twice. "Nothing extraordinary," she said in a quiet way that made him worry she'd seen something upsetting. "I'll wait here."

"Don't be silly."

"Mehen," she said, as if he were being obtuse, "I'm the only tiefling—the only non–Vayemniri—in the whole place. They'll listen to you."

Mehen looked out over the Vanquisher's Hall—scaly bodies in a hundred shades all like enough to himself that he hadn't even hesitated.

All like himself, and not a one like his daughter—he couldn't remember a time when they hadn't both been outsiders.

"If they don't, I'm coming to fetch you," Mehen said. "Anyone gives you trouble, say you're Verthisathurgiesh and we'll see if we can call Anala's bluff." He left her and strode into the audience chamber, feeling a number of eyes follow him.

Tarhun, at least, looked like the sort of Vanquisher Pandjed would have appreciated. A broad-shouldered, bronze-scaled pinnacle of Vayemniri masculinity and physical prowess.

Don't karshoji *say it like that,* he could hear the ghost of his father's voice say. *This is why everyone thinks you're a blasted clutch-dodger.*

Your type, old man, not mine, Mehen thought as he gave his name to the adjudicator. "It's a matter of critical importance," he said. "Lives are at stake."

Tarhun glanced over, frowning at Mehen. He did not have to wait long.

The moment the conversation Tarhun was having with a Kanjentellequor man ended, the Vanquisher descended the dais, studying Mehen as he did. By the time Tarhun stood opposite Mehen, his eyes had lit with recognition. He clasped Mehen's forearm.

"Broken planes," he said. "Mehen, yes? We were in Shaushka's honor guard together. *Chaubask vur kepeshk,* it's been, what? Twenty years?"

"Thirty," Mehen said.

"Thought you were old Pandjed for a moment," Tarhun said. He turned grim. "Terrible what happened." Whether he meant Pandjed's death, Mehen's exile, or some fanciful vision of what happened in either case, Mehen didn't know and didn't care.

"There is a demon running lose in Djerad Thymar, a creature called the maurezhi. You need to send out as much of your force as can be spared to search for it before it kills again. Majesty," he added a little reluctantly.

Tarhun looked surprised. "Right to it then." He glanced at the Adjudicator, the reddish-scaled man called Shikari. "Did you say a demon? As in one?"

"So far as we know."

Tarhun waved this away. "I'll get my sword and armor. We can take care of this—you, me, a few others. Dokaan will be up for it, when he returns. Do you remember him?"

"It's not merely a demon," Mehen said. "It's a shapechanger. It's capable of moving among your people, disguised as one. And we think it might have been sent as the vanguard of an attack."

Tarhun shook his head. "A single demon is the harbinger of an attack? By whom?"

"We haven't figured that out," Mehen said. "There are more than a dozen dead at this point and probably more. Seven of us couldn't pin it down. You need to sweep the catacombs, tell the clan elders to take this seriously."

People around them were starting to whisper. Tarhun's expression shifted. "Very well," he said. "I'll discuss it with Dokaan. Speaking of elders," he went on, "where is the Verthisathurgiesh? I would have assumed Matriarch Anala would have come herself."

Mehen cursed to himself, and from deep down the horror he should have felt at this error, this appalling misstep ghosted through him. *Some people take* omin' iejirkkessh *quite seriously,* Anala had said. The whispers thickened.

People are dying, he told himself. *Karshoj* to etiquette.

"I came here first," Mehen said. "This is a matter for all of us, not just Verthisathurgiesh. Had I waited for the matriarch, precious time would have been lost."

That seemed to satisfy the Vanquisher well enough. "A wise choice. But I would strongly suggest you head straight back to your enclave. Anala is not one to trifle with."

"Of course, Majesty," Mehen answered, gritting his teeth as the whispers continued all the same.

• • •

. . . THE GREATEST MEASURE of strength lies in patience . . . the voice of the god murmured. *. . . Though urgency would suggest otherwise . . . And there is no enemy like urgency . . .*

Any moment now, Ilstan thought, you will burst into nothing but magic and power and the scattered scraps of a once-whole mind. Your bones will be the Weave and your blood will be an offering to Mystra herself. Any moment. Any moment.

. . . Then perhaps it is madly wise to lay an offering to Urgency . . . or wisely mad to ignore her . . .

Here was the edge, here was the precipice, the moment before he tipped into madness and Ilstan remembered, still, every moment of the last time, deep in the tunnels of Suzail, trying to hold his thoughts together. And then the moment when he escaped the powerful pull of the god's promise, of the lines of magic and destiny that bound Ilstan to Azuth, Azuth to Ilstan, in a flood of spells.

"What am I meant to do?" he whispered, frustrated tears welling in his eyes, as the cell began to vibrate with the once-invisible magic of the Weave. "Why can't you free me?"

. . . Freedom isn't necessary. Only patience . . .

Ilstan froze. "My lord?" he murmured. But there was nothing. Only the growing crackle and hum of magic bleeding through the stone walls, the whine of the barrier spells anchored between the bars. His guard—a pale gold one this time, with silver skewers protruding from his jaw—watched him with a quizzical, mocking expression.

"Lord of Spells forgive me, I am too weak, I am too weak."

. . . Strength in weakness, weakness in strength. Power in all things—it is easy to forget when you wield the gift of Mystra herself . . .

Ilstan straightened. The wizard. He pushed his sleeve back, saw the shivering runes embroidered there—*Find a wizard.* That was how he staved off the madness. That was the only way to remain sane as more power than he could contain roiled through him.

But here, trapped in the clutches of terrible dragon-men and at the mercy of his greatest enemy, and Wick . . . where had Wick gone? Betrayed him like Kallan?

. . . Our dearest allies may be our nearest friends . . . but a wizard is often alone, and so it must be that a wizard seeks allies in the strongest of his peers . . . for a time at least . . .

He lost time, he was sure of it. The guard's scales became pale then coppery then red, the piercings leaping around as if they were flies alighting on that changing face. But when the door opened, when Farideh came in, time gelled around him.

"Not again," he murmured. "Not again."

An axe as black as the hidden face of the moon hung at her hip. The guard snapped orders at him, the words rockfall and crackling ice. Farideh retorted, storm clouds and broken glass. She came close to the bars, staring at Ilstan, eyes unreadable. Demon axe at hand.

"You should not have come," he panted, the god threatening to crumble out of his words. A warning, a threat—both, if he were honest. "You should not have come."

"I have to ask you something," she said. "When Azuth told you to cast the fireball, did he sound like himself?"

"You will not turn me against the Lord of Spells."

The voice in his thoughts echoed back, eerily mellifluous: *Even iron melts if it's hot enough . . .* Ilstan found himself mouthing the words, for hours and hours and hours. He blinked. She was still staring at him.

"Is Asmodeus the one talking to you?" she whispered.

Ilstan blinked again. Asmodeus. " 'And perhaps, then,' " he recited, the words of Azuth, " 'it was a fitting punishment, for the wizard who forgot what it was to want, that he landed broken at the feet of one who was nothing but want incarnate.' "

Her eyes widened and for a terrible moment, Ilstan feared he might fall into them and felt the world shift. He grabbed hold of the bars, and she jumped back, startled.

"You have the key," he said. "You or the Knight of the Devil—he said so. You have the key to free him, and you do *nothing,* minion of evil. You know he would split your would-be god in twain! You would rather there were sin in the world than to have the Lord of Spells walk anew."

"I don't want any of those things," Farideh said. "When was the last time you . . . when did a wizard last come?"

His head spun—the feeling of the Weave bursting out his fingers, the dead dragonborn, the fiend in the catacombs . . . *Our dearest allies may be our nearest friends . . . but a wizard is often alone, and so it must be that a wizard seeks allies in the strongest of his peers . . . for a time at least . . .*

Another dragonborn burst into the room, an ochre-colored male who filled the door, shouting thunder and thrown stones. Lord Crownsilver's bodyguard. Farideh's guardian. Ilstan released the bars and scrambled back, out of reach.

"What are you doing here?" he shouted at Farideh.

"Running an errand," Farideh said. "Mehen—"

"We need to go." He shouted something at the guard. The guard snapped back. A storm of Draconic, vicious and violent. Farideh interrupted, over and over. Her father ignored her, and so she turned to Ilstan.

"Ilstan!" Farideh shouted over the arguing dragonborn. "Don't listen when the voice changes! Understand? Don't listen!"

"We're leaving," the dragonborn said. "Come on."

Ilstan blinked. He was alone once more, but for the guard, who had turned into a female with greenish-bronze scales and brass owls pinned to her face. She regarded him with distaste as he studied her.

"Don't listen to the voice when it changes," he mouthed, and wondered if he'd know when he heard it.

• • •

From the grave of the pyramid up to its peak—the city hums, it buzzes, it rasps, but I am silent as a ghost, sliding up out of the graves in the skin of the girl. The guard has his uses, foremost of which is the names and the faces of the ones who know how the city protects itself, how this jewel is guarded, how the king of dust might pluck it. Up to the peak, to where the soldiers stand guard, to find another body, another batch of memories, another burst of strength. The taste of the devil-touched is still sweet-sour on my tongue, and my belly is aching for the stolen meal. Worse, my body is battered, bloodied. Unrepaired.

I cannot return to the catacombs.

Do not fail me, *my dark lord instructed.* The gains are too important. *And what has the maurezhi done but grow distracted with sweet flesh and too-wily prey? If I am called back soon, there will be nothing to show for it, and my torments will never end. I want to run and run from this city that is nothing like I was told, to where I might not be found.*

There is no such place, for all my fear says there is.

And running free through the buzzing, rasping, boiling city will unmask me, and my mask is my greatest strength, the reason the Dark Prince has a use for me. I pull myself deeper into the girl's skin—I cannot wear this much longer—I have to be clever now while the hunt and hunger screams in me. I have to feed, or I will die.

So I hurry up and up and up where my crowded memories say the defenders of this strange city live.

She had lessons here—the screaming one—and these feet on the padded floor kick up memories of blades and bruises and bodies. Young ones, clumsy ones, to-be-honed ones, and their teachers too— the ones who fill their heads and muscles with the ways of soldiers, the ways of protecting the city. Fenkenkabradon Dokaan—the old general with a booming voice. Verthisathurgiesh Arjhani—the slim man with the glaive. Ophinshtalajiir Sepideh—the silver woman with a brusque manner. Vanquisher Tarhun—the sweetest prize. Devour them and I'll fill my mind, my muscles, with those answers, learn their secrets with my teeth and my gullet. Bring them to that king of dust and my Dark Prince will be pleased and I will not suffer.

The slim man with the blade-stick, I find, foolishly tucked away in a training room no one uses. He sees me and smiles—she missed her lessons the other day. He has time for her to make it up—stern- ness in that offer, annoyance. He holds out another blade-stick.

I smile, weapon enough myself. I reach not for the offered blade but for his arm and yank with all my strength, the joint separates with a delicious crack. The man shouts in surprise, pain, but he doesn't pull away like he's supposed to. He twists, slippery as fresh intestines, and my hand is forced to open.

He is fast, the glaive sharp. I dart around it. He's frightened—he is prey, after all, and this sweet, sweet girl isn't supposed to be a predator—but the glaive isn't afraid. This was what it was forged for, and in some part of his shivering mind the man knows it—the knowledge floods his eyes, squeezing out anything sensible. He cuts the girl across the chest and it burns, but I grab his other arm and twist—

Pain—the room spins—

The glaive's blade, slammed across my borrowed face, I realize.

"Arjhani!" a woman shouts. And there by the door, a better prize, a silver one, a ring-pierced one, her leg bandaged up and hurting her as she walks. Ophinshtalajiir Sepideh, my new memories say. A teacher of tactics. Wounded by an overeager student who is still polishing tack for the sloppiness. Her blade is elsewhere, but she charges in. "Drop your karshoji weapon! Are you all right, Zaroshni?"

"Just learning," I say, and in a moment it will be true.

"Sepah!" Arjhani shouts. "Don't!"

I turn and I change—the panic that overtakes this broken soldier thickens the air. I reach for the Abyss, and my own army comes running, obedient and fearful. Eight loathesome dretches burst out of the air, and, just after, a cadre of ghouls. I will not lose again.

"Block the doors," I order. "Don't kill them yet." A thud, a crunch, pain—Sepideh's crutch hits me like a bludgeon in the base of my breath. A lesser demon would fall to that. But the maurezhi lashes out, tooth and claw, and I rake her deep, deep, through the armor that is no armor. She limps back, but I am furious, unstoppable. And the poison in her veins is taking hold.

She manages half a shout before her tongue stills, her leg buckling. Half a heartbeat more and I am on her, the tear of flesh, the crack of bones, the spray of blood—yes, yes, yes—

Pain. Again. The blade in my back. I dip into the space between spaces, leaping to a safe distance.

Half the dretches are gone, half the ghouls. Another vanishes in a burst of flames as it tries to intercept the glaivemaster—he is quick, *too quick, even with one arm hanging useless. Strike and strike and strike, never slowing. The glaive carves up my ghoul as though it's made of tissue, and now he's coming for me. My prey behind him, trying to gain her knees, to crawl away, to reach the glaive I dropped.*

I can only have one, only one can make a meal before both souls flee.

Unless the maurezhi is clever.

The glaivemaster defends his fallen comrade, winnowing my army—putting them to their true purpose, but if I'm to claim both these prizes, I need some preserved.

Fear is my weapon, as much as the mask. Not even the glaive-master can defeat the dread gift of the Abyss. It slows him, and when the glaive hits me again, it comes just after I've yanked his useless arm wide and bitten deep into the muscle.

Cloth and scales peel away and my poisons sink into his blood. I let go. One step back, two, and Verthisathurgiesh Arjhani collapses, boneless but alive. For the moment.

"Don't let him get up," I tell the remaining ghoul as I return to the silvery prey reaching for the fallen weapon. "I'm going to need him later."

∙ ∙ ∙

THE FOURTH WARLOCK had proved the trickiest to pin down. Pacted to a paelyrion called Shetai and bound to the seventh layer of the Nine Hells, the tiefling had hidden himself in plain sight. A wise scheme.

He has Elyria's eyes, Bryseis Kakistos noted as Sairché watched the man argue with a fishmonger. *The shape of them, I mean.*

"The most powerful descendant of Caldura Elyria and he's bargaining for salmon," Sairché replied. "What a waste."

Visibility is a poor indicator of power, Bryseis Kakistos said. *The scorpion outlasts the butterfly.*

Her thoughts buckled again. Watching herself gasping, delighted, at a cloud of pale green moths in the moonlight. Staring at a brilliant orange butterfly, dying on the side of a building, its wings twitching as it fought the grip of Kelemvor. Standing over a grave mound, watching the swirl of lemon-yellow wings, mocking the hollowness in her heart and knowing she wouldn't stand for it. She would tear the world apart instead.

"You have such interesting sayings in this world," Sairché said. "When do you expect to snatch him?"

All in good time, Bryseis Kakistos said. *There's still much we need to do.*

"Of course," Sairché said. She triggered the portal back to Malbolge. Bryseis Kakistos still couldn't have said whether Sairché could be taken at her word—whether she wanted her mistress's favor returned by giving Glasya the means to topple her father, or whether she intended to hand Bryseis Kakistos over to gain the princess of the Hells' good graces.

"Where's the fourth?" Sairché asked.

He was the fourth, Bryseis Kakistos said.

"Was he?" Sairché was quiet a moment. "Yes . . . I suppose I just lost count."

Half the capsules remained, and still Bryseis Kakistos had not secured a new body. She had not found the spell to separate out her soul's parts. And already Sairché seemed to be noticing the gaps left in her memory.

When Sairché went to the scrying mirror and drew up not the image of another warlock but Farideh's human lover, Bryseis nearly overtook her out of panic.

Why are you interested in him? Bryseis Kakistos asked. *I thought you found your brother's baiting insulting.*

"I do," Sairché agreed. "But if Lorcan wants him dead, then it stands to reason—assuming all else is neutral—I want him alive. The sands are running down on this pact between us. I'd like to have my arsenal ready. You understand, of course."

Of course. The mirror shivered, and the dull reflection reshaped to show the human man, amid his fellows, standing in an ancient and tumbled-down library near an enormous hole, its edges hemmed by leaning columns and dangerously tilted shelves.

Sairché's puzzlement swarmed around the ghost. She swirled her fingers over the hole and the mirror shuddered, the blackness of the hole folding around the image as though the whole mirror were being swallowed. Down, down, down. Through rock and earth and mountain, faster and faster, and then—

The mirror stopped amid a group of humans who seemed to be digging through the rubble at the bottom of the great hole. Bloodied, dazed, not noticing either the dead that lay around them nor the couples locked in ferocious passion.

"What by the shitting Nine . . . ," Sairché murmured. She swirled the ring again.

The image held, focused on the center of the humans, the deep shadows there . . .

Eyes opened in the shadows, an impossibly handsome man, his skin as black as charred bones. He looked directly at Sairché as though he could see her, through the spell, through the planes, through the mirror. He met her eye and he laughed.

Sairché waved the trigger ring over the mirror as though she were slapping it, falling back several steps as though the man were going to leap out of the mirror before the scrying could be dispelled. As soon as the mirror returned to its resting state, she tore the ring from her finger, hurling it across the room.

Was that who I think it was? Bryseis Kakistos asked.

"No one," Sairché said. "It was no one. Put it out of mind."

You are not that lucky, little devil, Bryseis Kakistos thought. And I may not have to go down to the Abyss after all.

PART III

VERTHISATHURGIESH THE TALE OF THE CRIPPLED MOUNTAIN

...

Let us sing of the battle that spilt the blood of the Tyrant of Tyrants and burnt his bones to ashes. Let us sing of Iskdara and Shurideh Who-Would-Be-Verthisathurgiesh, the descendants of Khorsaya, of Reshvemi Who-Would-Be-Verthisathurgiesh, whose descendants we claim. Let us sing of the battle that birthed Verthisathurgiesh, the Crippled Mountain.

Rhodrolytharnestrix, the Tyrant of Tyrants, laired high on the peak of a volcano called the Celestial Mountain, ancient and canny and cruel. Uncountable lives were lost to his ambition and greed, as he waged war against other dragons and unearthed the titans' treasures from their graves, our ancestors' merely tools and toys to the Tyrant of Tyrants.

We craved his death and our freedom from the very shell.

Iskdara and Shurideh brought their band, still heady from the victory at Arambar Gulch, strengthened by the band of Thuchir Who-Would-Be-Shestandeliath, of Haizverad's line, and bearer of the Breath of Petron; by the band of Mirichesh Who-Would-Be-Ophinshtalajiir, of Caysh's line and killer of the Frostborn Duke; by the band of Nerifar Who-Would-Be-Kepeshkmolik, of Shasphur's line, whose descendants would found Djerad Thymar, and many more.

But the Tyrant of Tyrants upon the mountain peak could rain fire down on our ancestors, long before they ever reached him, and from so high, Rhodrolytharnestrix thought himself unassailable. He watched the massing armies—thousands upon thousands armed and armored—with the cruel amusement of a hatchling considering ants upon the stones.

But at the battle of Arambar Gulch, where Iskdara and Shurideh, sister-warriors, had felled proud Asativarainuth, the Silver Death, they had gained from his treasury a weapon beyond all of Rhodrolytharnestrix's imaginings: the Eye of Blazing Rorn, a ruby imbued with all the rage, all the heat of that terrible Dawn Titan.

"What good is even a titan's fire-jewel against an old, wily charir?" asked Nerifar Who-Would-Be-Kepeshkmolik. "He could swallow it whole and never feel a thing."

"It is not for the Tyrant of Tyrants," said Shurideh.

"It is for the Celestial Mountain," said Iskdara.

As the battle stirred, the sister-warriors, brave Reshvemi and Thuchir Who-Would-Be-Shestandeliath found their way into the belly of the volcano, through old lava tubes and caverns that opened for the Breath of Petron, that precious artifact of the titans' power. The armies massed, the Tyrant of Tyrants gloated and circled his lesser dragons. The Eye of Blazing Rorn plummeted into the belly of the volcano, tipped from Reshvemi's hand, stirring the fires that kept the Tyrant of Tyrants warm, into an inferno.

The Celestial Mountain conspired with them, they say. The eruption did not flood the old lava tubes and burn and boil away Iskdara, Shurideh, Reshvemi, and Thuchir. Lava and ash and stone exploded into the air, breaking the peak of the Celestial Mountain so that—ever after—it bent, away from where the ancestors hid, as if it were crippled by the explosion. Ever after, we honor the intent of the sacrifice and the luck of the Crippled Mountain by our name, Verthisathurgiesh, so that we draw strength from deep within and surprise our foes when they least expect it.

The ashes rained down for forty days, the death of the Tyrant of Tyrants coating the scales of all who had faced him that day, all *who fought the armies that survived the eruption. Ever after, we named ourselves—no longer the slaves of the tyrants, their unlucky progeny—the Vayemniri, the Ash-Marked Ones, so that we shall never forget what clans can do as one.*

. . .

17

25 Nightal, the Year of the Nether Mountain Scrolls (1486 DR)
Verthisathurgiesh enclave Djerad Thymar, Tymanther

ARIDEH SAT UP IN BED, WATCHING THE WINGED SNAKE zigzag across the ceiling. If she stayed pressed against the headboard, the urge to duck and cover her head as Keetley passed over was manageable. Zoonie had not adapted yet, pressed to the floor beside Havilar's edge of the bed and whining.

"How many of the enclaves are locked down?" Farideh asked Havilar.

Havilar, still curled up on her side, groaned. "Six? Five? I don't know."

"Maybe the maurezhi is already in one of them," Farideh went on. "Maybe it's biding its time and that's why no one's found it?"

Havilar rolled over. "They're looking. The Adjudicators, the Lance Defenders. Why are you awake?"

"Nightmare," Farideh said. This time she could see Dahl, standing amid the empty houses of Arush Vayem. Between her and him, though, was the Lorcan who wasn't Lorcan, and the ghost of Bryseis Kakistos.

We could be very helpful to each other, he'd said, while the ghost faded in and out of reality, baring bones and viscera and sinews. *The enemy of my enemy is my friend.*

"Do you ever get them?" Farideh asked her sister. "Nightmares about . . . you know?"

Havilar regarded her blearily. "No. But you always have more dreams than me anyway."

Except Farideh could not shake the suspicion they weren't dreams at all. So why did they trouble her and not her sister?

"Which of the clans are locked down?" she asked. Keetley looped around the bed twice and landed at the foot. It slithered up the blankets and coiled itself in Farideh's lap.

"I don't know," Havilar said. "I can hardly keep them straight."

"Shestandeliath. And Ophinshtalajiir. You said six?"

"I don't know!" Havilar said more forcefully. A faint, rising tune floated in from the sitting room beyond. Keetley lifted its head, swaying. "Brin's up," Havilar noted.

Farideh scooped up the winged snake, letting it coil around her shoulders, considering the last few days. "Are you avoiding him?"

"No," Havilar said. Then, "Sort of." She threw back the covers and climbed out of bed, dressing quickly.

"Do you want to talk about it?" Farideh asked.

"No. Not now." Havilar strode from the room, Zoonie trotting after. The hellhound's shoulders nearly brushed the edges of the doorframe as she passed, and Farideh frowned. Around her shoulders, Keetley tightened at the sound of Brin's flute.

The message from Dahl had included instructions for the winged snake's care—in case, the note explained, the creature was stopped in its progress. They were sparse but seemed to satisfy Keetley well enough: a large shallow basin of water, access to rats, a warm stone close to the brazier, and time outside each day. The snake moved through the room on its own schedule, sliding out of the shadows to curl up against her around the same time each day. But Farideh's shoulders didn't seem to replace Brume's voluminous cloak.

The snake's tongue flicked alongside her jaw. There were no instructions for how to send a message somewhere using Keetley.

"Do you know how to get to the Vast?" she murmured. The snake flicked her jaw again. Farideh rubbed her eyes and sighed. She climbed out of bed, dressing around the settled snake.

The black axe sat on the floor beside the bed where she'd tucked it the night before. She kneeled to retrieve it, still hesitant about the whole business. If this was Selûne's gift, the moon goddess's overture to her, Farideh thought, then where was she when Asmodeus made his claim? Where was she when Farideh was left with only monstrous powers to save Dahl? Where was she when Havilar's safety was so in danger Farideh sacrificed everything to protect her?

Still, she kept it at her side, as if the axe would give up its secrets just by being near. She pressed her palms into the unfamiliar runes, and thought, not for the first time, of how they reminded her of the runes in the failed portal circle that the dead hatchlings had made. She stood and slipped the axe into the loops of the belt Uadjit had given her.

Out in the sitting room, platters of food for morningfeast already waited, beside a pot of tea. Havilar nibbled at a *farothai,* while Zoonie watched her faithfully.

"Mehen's already left," Brin explained.

"Has he gone to see what's happening in the maurezhi search?" Farideh asked.

Brin shook his head. "He had the piercings in. I think he was going to see Anala. Again."

"Maybe this time she'll talk to him," Havilar said.

Matriarch Anala had not taken it well that Verthisathurgiesh had been told of the maurezhi's identity and possible motives so late after its rivals and the Vanquisher himself. She would not speak to the twins at all since then, and Mehen had not returned from her summons with anything more than a foul mood.

"Has anyone come back from the Lance Defenders?" Farideh asked. "The Adjudicators?"

"No one," Brin said. "The only person who's been here is the boy who brought the food up from the kitchens. Hencin," he added.

"I wish Mehen hadn't yelled at him about the food," Havilar said, taking another *farothai* from the stack. "It *was* too much, but now we never get *yochit*, and it's not like you can get that just anywhere."

Brin made a face. He spotted Farideh watching him, and dropped it. "You look exhausted," he said. "Sleep badly?"

"She had nightmares," Havilar said. "Eat something." She shoved a pasty at Farideh.

Keetley flicked its tongue at the pasty. "It's ridiculous we're shut up in here like we're just visiting," Farideh said. "We took a job. Havi and I can help in ways no one else really can. This is just stupid."

"The Lance Defenders are searching," Brin said.

"They're not finding it, though," Farideh said. "And we have to stay until they find it, right? So we need to find it."

"Can you *hear* yourself?" Havilar asked, curious. "You sound like a lunatic."

Before Farideh could retort, Havilar went on. "You ought to ask Lorcan where it is. He probably knows if it would hide in an enclave."

Farideh said nothing. Chalked on the stone floor of her room was a circle of runes she'd made the night before, stopping just short of the ritual's completion. There were a score of questions she wanted to ask Lorcan: about the maurezhi, about the things Ilstan had said, about her dream, about whether he could scry Dahl for her again. She'd stopped, considering the runes, considering the way her pulse had picked up, the way old urges nearly had her in his arms again. The way just talking to him made her temper run rampant. The way she couldn't be sure the urges were all that old.

She sat for so long, perhaps it shouldn't have surprised her when the sensation of someone tracing a fingertip over the lines of her brand came, slow and certain. She closed her eyes.

You will never be free of him, she thought. Not like this. She'd gotten up then and slipped into Havilar's room. But she hadn't swept the runes away.

"Well," Brin said, suddenly, and Farideh realized how silent they'd all become. "I suspect the menagerie needs to take its air. Shall we go out?"

Behind the sofa, the great bulk of Zoonie suddenly rose, eager to leave. Havilar giggled, and even Farideh had to smile.

In addition to the hatchlings standing ceremonial guard, there were now two seasoned warriors standing at Verthisathurgiesh's gates. Havilar told them where they were going, when they were likely to be back, and that Mehen would surely come looking for them before any of that.

"What sign will you give when you get back?" one asked, a young man with glossy black scales. "How will we be sure it's you?"

Havilar squinted at him. "That's not how it works."

"If you agree on a sign," Brin said, "then if the maurezhi gets one of us it will automatically know the sign. It won't make a difference." The young guard frowned.

"Look," one of the veterans, an older woman with a Lance Defender badge said. "There are three of them plus the snake-thing and the dog-thing. They come back together, you know they weren't ambushed. Got it?" To the rest of them, she added, "You shouldn't be going out."

"We have to let the dog-thing out," Brin said. "We won't be long."

When they were farther down the stairs, Havilar muttered, "You'll know we're us because I'm not falling to that *karshoji* thing."

However much it felt as if the Thymari dragonborn weren't taking the threat of the maurezhi seriously, there was no arguing that the City-Bastion didn't feel abandoned. The market was subdued, half-shuttered. The gates had twice as many armored guardians as they had when the caravan had first arrived, and the village beyond the pyramid crawled with armored dragonborn bearing the badges of Lance Defenders, the gold piercings of Adjudicators, the marks of clans upon their shields.

Outside the City-Bastion, the rising sun painted the road to the east and the field it cut across in a cool, crisp light. The moon, still high overhead, moved slowly through the sky. Keetley unlooped itself from Farideh's shoulders, slithering up the side of the pyramid, until it reached a height it could launch from. Farideh took the axe from her belt and sat leaning against the side of the pyramid, as Zoonie raced to the Road of Dust and back again.

Farideh rolled the axe's shaft against her thighs. Overhead, Keetley slithered, wings wide. You're just collecting other people's things, she thought. Brume's snake, Thymara's axe, Asmodeus's blessings.

Havilar sat beside Farideh, stretching her long legs out on the sandy ground as she settled back against the pyramid. "How about you give me the axe, and I'll give you the creepy scepter?"

"No."

"Come *on*! I could *do* something with an axe. Maybe I'm *supposed* to have the axe, you don't know."

"It's not for chopping things," Farideh said. "Or, I guess it could be, but it sounds like it's the symbol of the thing."

"I don't understand that," Havilar said. "The dragonborn clearly don't know or care about the axe. You walk around with it on your *belt*. Raedra had that glittery short sword, and as soon as she drew it the whole *karshoji* army knew what it meant. The axe's not a symbol. It's a secret." Havilar drummed her hands on her knees. "Do you like living here?"

"In Djerad Thymar?" Farideh watched Zoonie race along the river for a few moments. "No. I don't. Not on the whole. Some things are better, but I'd trade them all to live somewhere I can see the sky, I don't have to think about falling, and I don't worry about running into Ar—"

She broke off, pursed her mouth around the name.

Havilar dragged a finger through the dust between the grass. "You saw him too?"

"I didn't want to bring it up." *Are you all right?* the question begged to be asked. *Are you all right?* and *What did he say to you?* and *What did you say?* and over and over, *Are you all right?* Her sister tensed beside her, as if Farideh had spoken all of these questions aloud, so she didn't. She took Havilar's hand and squeezed it.

"I like it all right," Havilar said abruptly. "I could live here. Maybe."

Farideh looked askance at her. "Do you know something I don't?"

Havilar took her hand back and folded her palms together. "Not exactly."

"Did Mehen tell you he wants to stay?"

"No."

Dumuzi's offhand remark stirred an eddy of dread in Farideh. "*Karshoj.* Gods. So he knows? About Anala making him Vanquisher? And he told you? Does he mean to—"

"*What?*" Havilar cried. "She wants to make him Vanquisher?"

"That's what Dumuzi said." Farideh frowned. "Wait, if that's not why you're asking—"

Havilar waved that away. "Because I got offered a position with the Lance Defenders. Why does Dumuzi think Mehen's going to be Vanquisher?"

"You took a *position?*"

Havilar grabbed hold of her hand. "I said I was *offered* a position," she hissed. "Don't change the subject. Why in the *karshoji* Hells does Dumuzi think Mehen's going to be Vanquisher?"

"Dumuzi thought that was the clearest reason for Anala to call him back. There's an election soon and Verthisathurgiesh doesn't have a very good candidate."

"Why would she think Mehen's a good candidate? Everyone is still all gape-faced about how he got exiled, which I *still* don't understand. Which part is so stareworthy? The fact he didn't get married? The fact he smarted off? The fact he doesn't like women that way?" She shook her head. "I like it all right, but this is a weird *karshoji* place."

Farideh shrugged. "I don't know. And I don't know if Mehen knows. I assume he'll just laugh at her. Or I did before he put the piercings back in and went and let her yell at him two days running." She yanked a blade of grass from the dusty ground. "You got offered a position? Are you taking it?"

Havilar sighed. "I don't know. I mean, what am I going to do the rest of my life? Sellsword? I would be getting coin to tell people how to fight with a glaive. That actually sounds fun."

"But you'd have to live here," Farideh said.

Havilar's hand curled around hers. "Yeah."

Farideh swallowed against the sudden lump in her throat. There's nothing decided, she told herself. Don't worry now. You're too tired to worry.

"What does Brin think?" she asked.

Havilar winced. "I haven't told him yet. It feels like I should make up my mind about one thing or the other first." She bit her lip. "He was with me when I ran into Arjhani. He was really sweet. And I kissed him. *Really* kissed him. I'm not doing a good job of keeping my space."

Farideh kept her thoughts to herself, but she found herself wishing for the days when Havilar and Brin had been a couple. She watched Brin throw a bit of wood broken off a cart for Zoonie to chase. She wondered if Havilar had warned him about Asmodeus, if Havilar even thought to worry about that. If it would make things worse to make Brin aware of the god of sin's potential interest.

It would be wiser, she thought, to leave him out of it. To leave Dahl out of it too. That was safest, wasn't it? Tell him it's over, tell him you're through—he was so close to doing it himself, wasn't he? Who's to say it wouldn't be for the best? Who's to say you haven't already doomed him?

She blew out a breath. Dahl is fine, she told herself. Dahl is safe. He is clever enough to get back to you, Zhentarim or no Zhentarim. She pressed her hands into the axe, hard enough to impress the runes into her skin. Dahl is fine. Dahl is—

Farideh started, eyes on the axe head. For a moment, the reflection on the axe head had seemed to be not the flicker of the pyramid's stone, the dried-out dirt—instead it was Dahl's reflection, dirty-faced and grim, somewhere dark, somewhere lit by sunrods and nothing else. She turned the axe, back and forth, but there was nothing.

You're tired, she reminded herself. You're dreaming on your feet.

"You should probably tell Brin," she murmured to her sister.

"I'm angry at you, you know," Havilar said suddenly. "You shouldn't have told Brin about Arjhani."

For a moment, Farideh didn't know what to say. "I didn't tell him much. He was worried and . . . and so was I."

"I know," Havilar said. "I understand why you did, but it wasn't yours to tell, not to him."

"I'm sorry," Farideh said. The calm way her sister spoke, the *direct* way she spoke—there was nothing about it that should have unnerved her, but it did. "I was worried," she added lamely.

"You're always worried," Havilar said. She took Farideh's hand again. "I'm all right. You really don't have to worry about me."

Farideh's eyes welled with tears she was too tired to stop. "I can't help it."

"I know that too." Havilar sighed. "Maybe I worry about you too much too. How bad is this dreaming business?"

Farideh shook her head and laughed nervously. "I don't know. Maybe nothing, maybe inescapably terrible. I don't know if it's better or worse if you know."

"You weren't going to keep secrets anymore," Havilar reminded her. "Tell me anyway." Farideh told her, in careful bits and pieces, about the possibility the god was really two gods. About the ghost. About the cryptic way Lorcan spoke in her nightmares.

Havilar made a face. "*Karshoji* gods. Does Mehen know?"

"He knows a little."

"A very little," Havilar said. "*He* worries worse than you do. If he knew all that, we would *not* be here, we'd be locked up in those rooms *forever*. Maybe he can get over what might happen with boys, but godsbedamned gods . . ."

Brin's flute drowned out her cry, a shrill flickering tone. Zoonie's barks echoed off the pyramid, sending Havilar to her feet, her glaive to her hand.

Not Brin's flute, Farideh realized. Brume's.

She was on her feet before she identified the source of the sound, running before she was aware she'd stood. Silhouetted against the purplish sky, two winged snakes spiraled down toward the sound of the flute.

Her hands closed around the new snake as it dropped low, pulling it close. Its scales were cool, its wings pulsing with over-exertion. In a little leather harness buckled between its wings and the blunt triangle of its head, a tube of paper peeked out.

She tucked the exhausted serpent into the crook of her arm, yanking the note free.

Was it idiotic to think you might get a moment of quiet? Be safe. I don't know much about demons. Although by the time this reaches you, I'm sure you'll have figured everything out. As for your questions, it's more complicated than it seems & part of getting back to you is finding how to answer them. Don't trust Lorcan!

He'd underlined it over and over, until the ink bled down into the next line.

Another worry: a devilish woman tracked me down. She knew about us & other things. I would guess she is a cambion, but her head is shaved & silver tattoos cover her scalp. She offered to reunite us. I said no, suspect she'll return. She heard your sending—wait on those until field clear. A happier note: My brother has been insisting I tell him 3 things I love about you, which was none of his business, but your letter overwhelmed me, & I told him 4, & have thought of at least a score for myself. Love always, Dahl.

Farideh curled the note back into a cylinder. Sairché had found Dahl—and there was no warning him, no sending back a message without someone who knew how to give the snake orders.

"Brin, what's 'field clear' mean?" she asked, trying to keep the panic from her voice. "If he says not to do a sending until field clear?"

"It means wait until he says no one can hear him," Brin said apologetically. "Silence until then, for safety."

"He's in trouble?"

Brin shrugged. "Not necessarily. I never got sendings unless I initiated them, because Suzail's a city of eavesdroppers. It's not good, but it's not a sign of anything terribly dire."

Farideh unrolled the note again. *Don't trust Lorcan.* Because Lorcan had done something? Because Sairché had named him? Because he didn't trust Farideh to keep her head straight?

Maybe he shouldn't, she thought.

Brin and Havilar were staring at her. "I have to . . . ," she started. "I have to get the snake inside."

And I have to talk to Lorcan, she thought. For better or worse.

• • •

THE ELDERS' AUDIENCE chamber, filled with Verthisathurgiesh's veterans, the commanders of the clan's emergency army, was nowhere near as crowded as it had been in Mehen's youth, the commanders all ancient or else shockingly youthful, Anala's court of advisors a paltry handful of uncles and aunties. The swath Pandjed had cut through Mehen's generation apparent as the track of a marauding army.

Anala listened to their reports, their elaborate ways of saying, "We've found nothing. We're running in circles. But no one else has found it either, so there is that." Here, she seemed the matriarch without question, stern and cool and stony. No sign of her earlier ease and humor. Clad in new-made mourning white, she did not so much as look at Mehen, even though she'd demanded his presence.

In some deep, ungrown part of Mehen, the chastisement burned the way she meant it to, and that annoyed him. Though not quite enough to leave.

"As much as I would like to advise that you increase your search," Anala said after all the commanders had spoken, "we cannot justify Verthisathurgiesh overreaching thus. Remain within a few tombs of the clan crypts. Do not divide your force any further than groups of three. Offer unqualified assistance to the Lance Defenders if you encounter them."

"What about the Adjudicators?" a young man who couldn't have been any older than the twins called out.

A dark look crossed Anala's expression. "If you're asked, do not slight them either. Those of you not instructed to remain, return when the light dims. To your posts."

As the army of Verthisathurgiesh filed out, the old ones avoided looking at Mehen, while the young ones watched from the corners of their eyes, as if Mehen would not spot it. When they had been gone long enough that the silence felt thick and smothering as a burial shroud, Mehen spoke.

"Pandjed would have torn down that boy, asking about giving aid to the Adjudicators."

"It is more of a question than it would have been in your father's day." Anala regarded him with the solemn distaste of one of the ancestor statues. "Verthisathurgiesh is no longer strong enough to sneer at the strong arm of the Vanquisher's law-bringers. Besides," she added, "you've already signaled us as the Adjudicators' trained ponies."

"This is not Verthisathurgiesh's crisis," Mehen said. "It affects every person in the city, clanless or scion, Vayemniri or not."

Anala said nothing, only folded her long sleeves back, descending the dais for a side table, as though Mehen were not even there.

"This is a waste of time," Mehen said, crossing his arms reflexively, feeling like a sullen hatchling. "My girls are the only ones who can absolutely identify the maurezhi. We should be down there, hunting it."

Anala poured tea—spiked with apple brandy, Mehen knew—into two clay cups before speaking. "Do you know how large the catacombs are?" she asked. "How many rooms and tombs and dead ends and tunnels are currently being searched? Are your girls somehow capable of being in all of them at once?" She blew across the surface of the tea. "Swallow your breath, hatchling. The Lance Defenders will gather up anyone who might be the creature, and your tieflings can sort through them."

Mehen bared his teeth. "It makes no sense—"

"It does, actually," Anala interrupted. "You've been gone too long. You forget how things are done in Djerad Thymar. Vayemniri don't deal with gods and fiends and other outsiders. We do things with our own two hands. And we don't stomp around ignoring clan to declare a demon is running rampant and every enclave should bar its doors."

"You're exaggerating the matter."

"I assure you, I am not." Anala set her cup down on the table once more. "If you've truly forgotten what it signals to have my newly returned nephew, the last patriarch's exiled scion, running off to Kepeshkmolik and Shestandeliath and Yrjixtilex and karshoji Tarhun to tell of this grave threat before he ever breathes a word to me, the leader of his clan, well, then you will just have to trust me: you have made yourself noticeable in all the wrong ways."

I have been noticeable in all the wrong ways since I set foot in this city, Mehen thought. Guilt still gnawed at him for not telling Anala first, for not confirming the identity of Baruz's murderer the moment he'd discovered it.

He could tell her of Dumuzi's sick-shocked expression, of the way the creature had taken the form of the Shestandeliath girl, even as it had fed. How the boy had fought bravely, but after . . . after he had seemed so close to collapse, that Mehen could do nothing but think like a father: get him home, get him safe, get him dosed with *chmertehoschta,* and put him to bed. He's too young for this, for any of this—and it had rattled his heart that his own daughter faced the maurezhi and the Black Axe besides with a grim solemnity beyond her years.

"You have my apologies," Mehen said. "Again."

"Ah, I don't want your apologies," Anala said. "I want your amends."

The doors parted, and a young man stuck his head in. "Matriarch Anala? You have a visitor."

"Hencin, dear," Anala said, oozing false patience. "I'm with someone."

The doors opened wider and a stout woman, broad-shouldered and round-bellied slipped around Hencin. Her scales were coppery-tinged with a silvery-gray patina, and the bright axes of Yrjixtilex traced her brow ridge. She wore plate over a white mourning shirt, a cape of lavender capping her shoulders.

"Oh, Anala, don't be silly," she said in a surprisingly breathy voice. "If it were a private matter, I would have said so." She turned to Mehen, her smile and her stare so persistent, so expecting, that he fought the urge to bow unasked. A pair of pierced Yrjixtilex, armed and armored and too old to be hatchlings on guard duty, came in behind her, followed by Kallan, looking vaguely annoyed. Mehen raised an eyebrow at him. He smiled and shook his head—don't ask.

Anala's stony expression had returned. "Mehen, may I present Yrjixtilex Vardhira, daughter of Chamnatis, of the line of Esham-Ana, matriarch of Yrjixtilex; her scion, Laivesdeh; and her son, Sirrush." Anala gestured to the woman and the man flanking the elder in turn. "Vardhira, my nephew, Mehen."

"Pandjed's son," Vardhira added, cheerful and guileless. "Yes, I know. A pleasure. Kallan speaks well of you." Mehen made a little bow. She smiled at Anala and gestured to Kallan. "My youngest brother's—Cayshan? Do you remember? He's his grandson. From the homesteads, obviously."

"We've met," Anala said. "I trust you haven't come to trade sheep."

Vardhira's eyes took on a dangerous glint, and Mehen reconsidered the Yrjixtilex matriarch. "If you want to strengthen your herds, there are better times to talk about that," Vardhira said. "But this is far more important—Kallan brought it straight to me, and I said, 'If this isn't a matter for elders, well, I don't know what is!' "

"I'd heard you'd locked down your enclave," Anala said.

Vardhira nodded. "Considering the circumstances, it seemed wisest. But Kallan has convinced me that matters have progressed beyond what we were previously told."

Unasked for, Kallan skirted the guards and came to stand beside Vardhira.

Anala's brow ridge arched. "Did he?"

"Ophinshtalajiir has a survivor," Kallan said, his impatience with the slow politics of these two clans colliding evident to Mehen. "I talked to her."

"How?" Anala demanded. "Kaijia locked the enclave down immediately."

"He's very clever," Vardhira said in a way that meant she might be annoyed and she might be delighted, but either way she was pleased to have one up on Anala.

"Ophinshtalajiir's got a clan-kin called Perra, who travels regularly up to Chessenta for diplomatic business. She's good friends with my mother *and* one of her daughters has eggs with my first cousin on my father's side." Kallan spread his arms. "And so I explained things and asked very nicely. She talked to Kaijia."

"What things?" Anala asked.

And here at least, Kallan knew his place and looked to his elder.

"All blades on the table, Anala," Vardhira said. "We're not talking about some monster those hatchlings unleashed from the old world. Something's running wild and someone sent it. Whatever your nephew told the Lance Defenders, it's not clear to me that it took—not that anyone asked me, but it wouldn't be the first time Dokaan and Tarhun got a little prideful about what could and could not be managed by their warriors alone."

"The maurezhi's particular about how it feeds, right?" Kallan said, to Mehen and to Anala. "This much we know: the body's got to be fresh, and it can't be interrupted before it polishes off every bit. Otherwise the whole scheme falls apart and all it's got is a full belly. But think about that—it's only so big. It can't bolt down a few at once, unless it wants to split its guts."

"So it stashes others for later," Mehen finished. "The Yrjixtilex boy in the sarcophagus—"

"Died lucky," Kallan said grimly. "The Ophinshtalajiir girl—Rimi—she said she was on patrol, the same day Ravar was meant to meet the maurezhi. She saw Zaroshni, told her off for wandering through Ophinshtalajiir's tombs. The next thing she new, some invisible thing had grabbed her and she couldn't move. Then it stuck her in the sarcophagus, and she was trapped there."

"It knew it was heading to meet Ravar," Mehen said. "And it couldn't go back once you'd chased it off—that area was swarmed with guards." He cursed. "It can turn itself *invisible*? What is this *karshoji* thing?"

"Every clan needs to ascertain their every member's location," Vardhira said. "It's not just who could be the fiend in a mask, but who might be missing and need recovery. We do not leave our own behind."

"None of us do, *noachi*," Anala said, folding her wrap around herself. "Not if we can help it. Who have you warned?"

Vardhira shook her head. "You. I set my sisters to checking our rolls. Next we go to Ophinshtalajiir, make sure they understand the matter. Kanjentellequor and Linxakasendalor will hear me. We have ongoing *qallim* agreements, on good terms."

Anala tapped her claws against her folded arms. "Fenkenkabradon. And Prexijandilin, Churirajachi. We don't have as many allies as we used to—obviously—but those I can be certain of. Can you warn Geshthax?"

"Do I look like I came carrying a battering ram?" Vardhira asked.

"Kepeshkmolik," Mehen said. Anala gave him a sidelong look, and Vardhira raised her brow ridges. "I'll go," he said. "No one else is going to break through Shestandeliath's damned blockade but Narghon and Uadjit. Besides, whatever you think about Narghon, they should know people are missing."

"We know." Mehen turned toward the opened doors. Uadjit stood there, Dumuzi beside her. The boy looked so agitated and exhausted that Mehen felt sure he hadn't slept. "Arjhani's missing," she said, with such forced crispness that her own anxiety could not be clearer. "Should I take it that you haven't pushed him to leave the city once and for all?"

The fear that surged in Mehen seemed a separate thing, divorced from the core of him, but no less real. Who was Arjhani to him now, after all? A heartache, a betrayer twice over. If he'd gone all the rest of his life without seeing Arjhani again, a colder, older part of him reasoned, then Arjhani would have died and he'd never know it, never shed another tear.

But that distant surging fear made the ghost of his youth scream.

"When's the last time you saw him?" Mehen asked.

"Two days ago," Dumuzi supplied.

"He went up to the barracks," Uadjit said. "People saw him there, but he was supposed to return to Kepeshkmolik that night and he didn't, nor the next. No one's seen him."

"That's one for Verthisathurgiesh," Vardhira said grimly.

Anala turned to Mehen. "A full accounting, if you please, of our assets, before we go tearing through the pyramid. Havilar can spot the creature."

"She can tell when it's close," Mehen said. "Her hound can track, though—anything she can get the scent of. If we can get something of Arjhani's to Zoonie, she'll track him down." And Havilar will have to come, he thought, fighting not to tap his tongue to the roof of his mouth. And you will have to explain everything.

"Farideh," he said instead. "She might be helpful too. She can see . . ." He weighed the best way to put it, and there really wasn't one. "She can see the state of people's souls, which means she can tell if something's missing one, the way a demon would be."

Anala cursed softly. "Well, as I've said before, Verthisathurgiesh is nothing if not adaptable. Vardhira, if you will go with yours to those clans, I will go with mine. Uadjit, if you would be so kind, we need every clan to make an accounting of their members so we know how many we might be missing, and you have already slipped past Geshthax with that gilded manner of yours."

Uadjit did not so much as smile at the compliment. "I should look for Arjhani."

"Mehen and the hound are going to have to do that, dear. You'd be extraneous."

"I'm going," Dumuzi piped up.

"You are going back to the enclave," Uadjit said.

"Mehen and the hound will handle it," Anala repeated. "He's in good hands."

"Your pardon," Dumuzi said, very properly, "but it's partly my fault the maurezhi has run so free. You can't ask me to go home and wait when I've got that to make amends for. And he is my father—whatever you should do, Uadjit, I should do tenfold."

Mehen frowned. The lad had a stoic quality that looked fairly ridiculous on a lad of fifteen, but there was nothing affected in it. He had a duty to Arjhani, but no affection—an oddity, when Arjhani could make almost anyone love him so easily.

"He can come," Mehen said. "I'll keep an eye on him."

"Kallan, go with them," Vardhira said. "That will make two pairs. Much safer if something goes awry. Uadjit, you come with us—Kepeshkmolik is not so far from Ophinshtalajiir. And it will give us a chance to talk."

"Hencin!" Anala called. The young man lurking just outside the door poked his snout in. "Rouse me a guard of three, and go fetch your mother and tell her you are both tasked with accounting for every member of this clan." She sighed and looked to Mehen. "I think we will come to curse Pandjed and his tendency for making enemies by day's end."

• • •

Lorcan handed over a small stack of coins. "A pleasure doing business with you," he said, taking the pouch of herbs. The woman smiled at him in a way that made Lorcan suspect he could have gotten a better deal still, and for the briefest of moments, he considered other ways to exploit that smile.

Not worth it, he told himself, pushing out of the shop and into the snow-crusted market of Waterdeep. You have more important things to see to. He pulled the collar of his cloak up and wound back through the alleys to where he wouldn't be disturbed.

He had watched Farideh for the better part of half an hour, late into the night, waiting for her to take action. Waiting, waiting—he felt as if that was all that she'd left for him to do. Wait until she realized she'd made a mistake. Wait until she realized he wasn't the enemy here. Wait until she realized everything could work out fine.

Lorcan was not good at waiting.

The tea would be a good overture—a reminder he cared about her well-being. It might also stop the dreams that seemed to plague her and give her ideas she ought to avoid. The less she slept, he thought, as he withdrew the portal ring, the more reckless she got. Nobody needed that.

First, he told himself as he stepped into the Nine Hells, help her sleep. Let her see reason again. Second, find Sairché, find out how serious this Brimstone Angel threat was—

His third thought dissolved into the hum that filled the fingerbone tower. He was surrounded on every side by hellwasps, the dog-sized insects rubbing their sword-arms against one another. At the center of the room, Glasya, Lord of the Sixth, Princess of the Nine Hells sat perched upon a throne of brass.

"Well met, little Lorcan," she said, her voice like the roar of the endless ocean forced into a song. "Where have you been?"

Lorcan dropped to his knees. "Your Highness. Just a minor errand in Toril, procuring components."

"For your Chosen?" she asked lightly.

"She will make use of some of them, Your Highness. What can I do for you?"

"You can start," Glasya sang, "by not pretending you are nothing but my erinyes' spoiled son. The scepter I gave you is missing. And I think you've been asking too many questions."

Lorcan's hand closed tight around the pouch of herbs as if it had the power to do anything at all for him. "Which questions are those?"

Glasya stepped down from the throne, her coppery feet stopping just before Lorcan. "My father may have an interest in you," she said, "or, at least, that to which you provide the conduit. But you are desperately mistaken if you think that will save your pitiful life, cambion. You know what the scepter is."

She hadn't mentioned the Vulgar Inquisitor, Lorcan noted. Shetai was still holding tightly to its cards. His thoughts spun, clicking bits of knowledge together like ivory tiles, searching for a play that would let him survive.

"I beg your pardon, Highness," Lorcan said. "I did not dare trust Invadiah."

Glasya paused, the span of a butterfly's heartbeat. "Invadiah has redeemed herself of late," the archduchess said. "Unless there's something I don't know?" One razor-sharp nail lifted Lorcan's chin. Lorcan met the Lord of the Sixth's terrible golden gaze—he could not risk looking away.

"Her overreach led to her downfall," he said. "Her current form encourages that same recklessness to a new degree. I saw the signs of it in her decision to inform me of the scepter's provenance. The artifact is safe. Away from prying eyes. Away," he added, "from Fallen Invadiah."

Glasya's placid expression did not shift, and the longer Lorcan stared at her, the more certain he became that he was about to die, devoured like a vole in a falcon's talons. "Why did you visit Shetai?" she asked a moment later.

Lorcan's thoughts spun—there was no part of what had happened within Shetai's lair that he wanted Glasya to know, and nothing would twist easily away from the information he'd tried to deal, the knowledge that the Brimstone Angel still roamed Toril.

You don't have to tell her the truth, Lorcan thought, a little giddy.

"There is no devil in Malbolge who Invadiah hated like Shetai," Lorcan said. "I felt if the situation was what it seemed, if I needed to prepare for my mother's gaze to fall upon me, then Shetai was an ally I needed to cultivate."

Glasya's eyes narrowed. "And?"

"And the Vulgar Inquisitor seemed to feel I was no more than Invadiah's spoiled son after all," Lorcan said. "I was sent away with nothing but Shetai's derision."

Glasya released his chin and tapped his cheek, just shy of slaps. "Let us call this a warning then," she said. "Remember, little Lorcan, you were not made for the hierarchy."

"Yes, Your Highness." He dropped his gaze, and did not dare look up until the buzzing of hellwasps had ended, the throne and its queen vanished from sight.

Beshaba shit in my bloody eyes, Lorcan cursed to himself. His breath wouldn't slow and his heart seemed likely to burst out of his ears, the way it seemed to climb his chest. *He had lied to Glasya*. And he still lived.

A miracle, he thought. A shitting miracle.

Or the missed blessings of his ignoble birth. Was it that he was not made for the hierarchy or that the hierarchy was not made for one such as him?

How long until some greater devil noticed?

He did not have much time to ponder that question before the *pop* of an imp arriving disturbed the air. Lorcan leaped to his feet, but not fast enough to prevent the imp from seeing his cowering position. It giggled at him, baring a serrated grin.

"Oh, don't get up for me."

"It's much easier to cut you from the air from up here," Lorcan said. "Who sent you? I thought I had a forbiddance on this room."

The imp giggled again and handed Lorcan a tasseled envelope, sealed with ink-black wax that seemed to shiver and reshape, as though it were alive. Lorcan broke the wax, ignoring the tiny howl that gusted out of it, and unfolded the parchment note.

You have exceeded my expectations, it read. *You may return at your earliest convenience.*

18

Malbolge, the Nine Hells

Y OU'RE QUIET," SAIRCHÉ SAID. "SHOULD I BE CONCERNED?"
Bryseis Kakistos pulled herself away from her careful
plans. The hour was at hand, and she could think of little
else beyond making certain she was properly armed and armored.
No more than I would expect you to be usually.

Sairché was quiet a moment, as they walked through the
palace of Osseia, trailed by a pair of erinyes. "How many
are left? Four?"

Three now. That was the tenth.

Her thoughts smeared over the cambion's and for a moment
she could only see her assembled coven, and among them Pradir
Ril, the progenitor of the last tiefling warlock they'd sought out.
Where his great-grandsire had been the unremarkable descendant
of a rakshasa, a thoroughly human boy with only his reversed
hands to mark his blood, the warlock looked much as they all
did now—horned and tailed and every inch Asmodeus's. The
eyes were the same color, though—black and soft. She wondered
if he'd cry when the time came—Pradir Ril had.

"What is it you're going to do with them all?" Sairché asked
in a casual way.

I will tell you as soon as you need to know.

If you survive that long, she added to herself.

They came at last to the door at the base of the fingerbone
tower. As Sairché reached to unlock the door, Bryseis Kakistos—
giddy with anticipation—shoved her aside. Where Sairché had
intended to climb once more to the room that held the scrying

mirror, Bryseis Kakistos steered her instead down into the cellars of the tower.

"What are you doing?" one of the erinyes asked.

Bryseis Kakistos looked back over her shoulder. "Gathering tools." She set her hand upon the sinewy lock that held the door closed.

She would need shielding—plenty of it. She found a box of rings and selected three that hummed with protective magic and an amulet of retribution besides. A chain shirt clearly made for an elf, slim enough to fit the fine-boned cambion, and bracers besides, charmed to absorb spells. A blade—she selected a short sword that glittered with a soul sapphire. Turning the blade in the torchlight, she smiled to herself, imagining how quickly the next steps would come.

"Well, well, well," a silky voice said. "You are a brazen one, aren't you?"

Bryseis Kakistos turned and found herself facing a succubus with black hair and mottled brown wings. The creature paced toward her, the easy gait of a predator approaching wounded prey. Bryseis Kakistos looked her over with a dismissive flick of the eyes.

"I'm a little busy," she said. "Whatever nonsense you're peddling, take it out on the plains."

The succubus smiled in a mad, ragged way. "A little busy stealing my bounty? You always were a deceitful child. Creeping and scheming. How long did you think you'd last, after you betrayed me?"

Ah, Bryseis Kakistos thought. Exalted Invadiah. She returned the succubus's smile. "What line did he feed you, when he'd called you down? I've always wondered what he said."

Invadiah's eyes narrowed, reassessing her treacherous youngest daughter for a moment. "Whelp," she finally spat. "What are you talking about?"

"Caisys, of course. Was it all business—all about the monstrous children he could get you—or did he seduce you the way he did mortal women?"

A slow, terrible smile spread across the succubus's face, and in it Bryseis Kakistos could almost see the fierce erinyes she had once been.

"You aren't Sairché at all, are you?" she said, starting to pace around Bryseis Kakistos. "What did she let in to the mistress's house?"

"I'm sure you can guess," Bryseis Kakistos said, buckling the sword in its scabbard around her hips. "From what your daughter's told me, you are quite clever for your kind. Do you have anything suitable for—ah! There." She crossed to a rack of rods, ignoring the succubus entirely. She selected two—one charged with fireballs, one humming with the kinds of enchantments that would give her spells an additional edge—and tucked them into the cambion's belt.

Skritch.

The softest of sounds—a blade against a hard surface. A sound that every flicker of the ghost, every borrowed nerve knew. Bryseis Kakistos twisted out of reach as the sword cut through the air where she'd been standing. She hardly had a moment to wake the rings on her fingers before Invadiah pressed her attack again, forcing Bryseis Kakistos back, forcing her to stumble. She pulled the sword with the soul sapphire free and caught the long sword on it. A succubus was nothing to the Brimstone Angel.

But Invadiah was no mere succubus. She might have lost her form, her monstrous strength, by failing the archduchess in some manner or another, but her cunning remained, her speed, and her skill. The stalwart leader of Glasya's elite erinyes army. Mother of the *pradixikai.* These things didn't vanish just because you changed your form.

Fortunately, the ghost thought.

"I've heard you were an admirable swordswoman," Invadiah said, attacking again. "I always assumed that was just flash to the legend."

—A sword in her hand, a cheap battered thing. An old man with horns—Titus Greybeard, watching, unmoving. *No one's going to guard your back like you will.* Sighting him down the pitted blade, thinking of someone who would have had her back, no question. The pull on her soul. *Not even you?* He smiled wickedly. *Now you're catching on—*

Invadiah's blade sliced toward her, straight down to cut her hand from the wrist. Bryseis Kakistos shook free of the memory as the blade hit the shield she'd crafted around herself, sending magic crackling into the air.

"Do you really think I'm stupid?' she said. "Do you really think I reached where I did by leaving my guard down and trusting in devils?"

Invadiah laughed, a sound both musical and somehow virulent, as if it were growing in Bryseis's ears. "You ended up dead. Just like the rest of them."

Quick as an adder, her hand shot out, grabbed hold of Sairché's wrist with her free hand. Bryseis Kakistos felt the pulse of magic from the succubus, the will of Invadiah washing over her. A charm to subvert her will. A charm to make her compliant.

Bryseis smiled as the ring on her middle finger burned hot. "Maybe," she allowed, "you don't know who I intend to go after next."

Invadiah pulled her hand back and cut her sword across before Bryseis Kakistos could grab hold. Pain shot up Sairché's nerves from where the blade had sliced along her forearm. Bryseis Kakistos pushed magic down those same nerves, squelching the pain before it could stir Sairché's consciousness, as Invadiah stepped back repositioned, and then pressed forward in a motion so quick Bryseis Kakistos could not split it into steps.

There was no denying Invadiah had earned her title and her status.

There was no pretending it would save her either, Bryseis Kakistos thought. She retreated, letting the succubus attack and chase her back across the arsenal, toward the suppurating wall. She kept the long sword away mostly by escaping, counted her steps until her heel struck the bone wall and Invadiah pulled her weapon back to cleave her daughter's head from her body.

Bryseis Kakistos released a burst of magic Sairché had kept stored in the ring of her smallest finger. A gust of wind caught the blade, and Invadiah overbalanced. In that moment, Bryseis Kakistos plunged the sword into the succubus's midsection, driving the blade with all Sairché's strength. The long sword slipped from Invadiah's hands.

Bryseis Kakistos drew upon the remnants of her pact—that it remained showed how little Asmodeus really thought of her—pulling power from the Nine Hells and waking the soul sapphire.

But Fallen Invadiah was no weakling. Rage burned in her dark eyes, even as inky blood poured from her mouth. As the magic imbued in that relic of the Blood War sapped away the very essence of her being, Invadiah pulled a dagger from her belt and plunged it up under the chain shirt, deep into her daughter's abdomen.

That woke Sairché. Bryseis Kakistos gritted the cambion's teeth as her soul screamed and thrashed, shoving her back down as hard as she could, as a spell, freezing and burning together all along her veins, slipped past her damaged defenses.

"You cannot win the hierarchy, oathbreaker," Invadiah sneered. "My vengeance will . . . chase you . . . to the . . . grave . . . again." She withered on the blade until, a useless corpse, she slid off it, crumpling to the bone-tiled floor.

Bryseis Kakistos gasped and wrenched the dagger from her belly. A trickle of blood spilled out. Not a spray, she thought. She had a few hours at least. She tore a strip of cloth from Sairché's robes and bound her belly tightly enough to staunch the bleeding. She held the pommel with the soul sapphire close to her face. "As I said," she whispered, "I'm a little busy."

Not bothering to wipe the sword, she sheathed it and stepped over the succubus's body, armed and armored and ready for battle with a far more worthy opponent.

She had no more than crossed the threshold of the treasury but the two massive erinyes were waiting for her. Blades out. Dark eyes burning over predatory grins.

"Oathbreaker," the one on the left said. "You've been marked."

Bryseis Kakistos raised an eyebrow, even as she took stock of her magic, stolen and otherwise. "Is this the best use of your lives?"

"This is the role and purpose of the *pradixikai*," the one on the right told her. "The glory of the erinyes. We kill you, we secure ourselves among them."

Bryseis Kakistos gritted her borrowed teeth. That damned dagger. "You want your mother's fate?" It made no impact upon either erinyes—it wouldn't. Fallen Invadiah wouldn't bother with anything weaker, not in curses and not in daughters.

Swiftly Bryseis Kakistos drew both rods, leaping back out of the erinyes' reach. She cast a burst of blinding light, a little nothing of a spell that still made the erinyes pause, reposition themselves. These were not, after all, *pradixikai*.

She'd no sooner cast the spell but she'd pointed the other wand straight up, shooting a fireball toward the fleshy ceiling. The ghost of the layer's previous ruler screamed in the walls of the fingerbone tower as the magical flames ripped a hole through the tissue and bone. The erinyes had no more than gained their feet but Bryseis Kakistos launched herself in Sairché's wings through the still-burning passage, up to the next floor. The wound in her belly screamed with pain, and a gush of new warmth soaked the bandage.

The Brimstone Angel paid it no mind and ran her borrowed body up the stairs, the thunderous hoofbeats of the bloodthirsty erinyes chasing her up to the peak of the fingerbone tower. She paused only long enough to lock the door, and then to wake the scrying mirror, to pull the image of the dark-haired paladin wandering the Underdark up to the surface.

• • •

DON'T LISTEN TO the voice when it changes, Ilstan told himself, over and over and over. Farideh's warning, made into a sort of prayer, a kind of mantra. Don't listen to the voice when it changes.

. . . The goal and gift of the gods above and below is the care and dedication of mortals below . . .

Don't listen to the voice when it changes. Only that felt like it tied him to reality—all around, the world blurred and bled. Time slowed to a crawl, then blew past him in an instant.

. . . To care of the care, dedicate to the dedicated . . . but the greatest gods know, these are your children and not your children . . . They must grow and thrive alone, despite terrible odds and the gods must let them . . .

Don't listen to the voice when it changes, Ilstan thought, magic prickling all up and down his sleeves. It was coming, his whole body braced for the shift that would signal the presence of the god of wizards receding and what might be his captor rising up. His captor. Farideh's master.

Is the warning for you? Or for the god of sin?

For all his preparation, for all the times it had happened even since Farideh's warning, Ilstan did not hear the change in Azuth's voice at first, only as it continued did the mellifluousness, the coaxing tone come clear. Only as it continued did he coil away from it.

If you know, then he can surely find you . . . She has handed you over, bound and paid for to the king of the Hells—can you be sure she hasn't?

The strange voice trailed off into silence, almost more terrible than its presence. Ilstan held his breath.

. . . What pain it is to see your children suffer . . . the god's true voice returned, and Ilstan breathed a sigh of relief. . . . *What wisdom it is to grant them their freedom . . .*

Ilstan was dimly aware of the door to the cells opening, lost in the words of the god and the humming of the Weave, but when the guard stopped before his own prison, the key clanking in his own door's lock, Ilstan shot to his feet, flattening himself against the far wall as if he might melt into the stone as the door swung wide.

"You can go," the guard said, loud enough to crack the foundations of the city.

"Go where?" Ilstan asked.

The guard, a reddish-scaled man with jade rings in his jaw, only shrugged. "Go where you want. You've been cleared of all charges, so 'not here' is as far as my orders cover. We need these cells for whatever the Adjudicators bring back. Now move along, before I come in and drag you out."

Ilstan crept through the long, stone hallways of the strange city, the eyes of dragonborn following his every step, wondering who this shabby, ragged, hunched, and haggard thing was. He felt as if he were curling into himself with every step.

. . . *And from the vantage of a god one may see . . . the present doesn't erase the past . . . the present builds upon what came before . . .*

Ilstan stopped in the middle of the hallway, a moment of clarity smoothing the shuddering passage of time, the shapeless edges of reality.

"I am a war wizard of Cormyr," he said, softly to himself.

"Good-man?" the dragonborn guard said, the word weighted all wrong. "Good-man, keep moving, you're not out yet."

Ilstan stood straight, his spine crackling as it unkinked. He turned to face the guard, now looking down at the dragonborn's scaly pate. "I am a war wizard of Cormyr," he said, as calmly as he could. "And I've been falsely imprisoned. You will return my things—my wand, my spellbook, and my robes. And I expect an apology."

The dragonborn guard gaped at him a moment. "Yes . . . all right. Um . . ." He looked around the hallway, as if he might find the spellbook on the floor there. "This way, please."

. . . *the past lifts the present into the light . . . and the present prepares for the future . . . but the past is never gone from us . . .*

Settled on a bench, Ilstan watched the dragonborn passing back and forth, their steps in time with the rhythm of the god's words, his breath slowing to match. He looked down at the sleeves of his robes, eyes ticking from rune to rune, reading the words stitched there. *Find a wizard. Give the magic to another caster. Find Farideh. Rescue the Lord of Spells. End the Lady of Black Magic.*

. . . the past lifts the present into the light . . . and the present prepares for the future . . . but the past is never gone from us . . .

The sensation of the spell that made the stitches ghosted through his thoughts. He frowned—he couldn't remember stitching them, but clearly he had. He imagined the thread creating itself, finding its way through the cloth to shape these runes by force of the Weave and the god of wizards.

. . . the past lifts the present into the light . . . and the present prepares for the future . . . but the past is never gone from us . . .

. . . can you trust what you see? Ilstan stiffened. *Can you trust any of this?*

Ilstan wrapped his arms around himself, searching the dragonborn for the guard returning with his things. They blurred together, like a school of fish too thick, too similar for Ilstan to pick apart the individuals. A rainbow sea of scales.

Then a woman cut through them—a dragonborn with silver scales, bright as moonlight, sharp as a knife. Ilstan stared at her, hard enough that the taunting words stopped making sense.

Then the silver-scaled woman paused. Stared. Smiled.

. . . can you trust what you see? Can you trust any of this? . . .

A cold tendril of horror unfurled in Ilstan. The Weave unfurled along with it, wrapping Ilstan like a cloak. The pull of Azuth, suddenly stronger, enough to smother him in madness and magic. The Knight of the Devil? The Lady of Black Magic.

Let her try and stop me, Ilstan thought. Let the powers of evil try and crush the spark of the divine. I am a war wizard of the vessel of the Magister, and though the words are missing, I have the powers—

"Here." The dragonborn guard had returned with Ilstan's spellbook and wand, his cloak neatly folded around them. Ilstan blinked, focusing with some difficulty on these precious things. He took them, crushed them to his chest. "Thank you."

The dragonborn nodded. "And . . . we're sorry. I suppose. Best of luck."

"Blessings of the Magister upon you." The dragonborn muttered something under his breath that skittered away through the Weave, like spiders across an endless web.

Ilstan turned back to the strange woman, weapons in hand. The silver-scaled woman was gone.

Had she ever been there? Had he dreamed the whole thing?

The Knight of the Devil, his thoughts murmured without meaning to. The Lady of Black Magic. He looked down at his sleeve. *Find Farideh.*

Don't listen when the voice changes, he could hear her saying. But was that her or was that the god of sin mimicking his Chosen? Was it only a taunt, since there was no not-listening? What terrible plans were hidden in the possibility of not listening?

. . . all work together, a chorus of action, an army of truth . . . Azuth's words? Or Asmodeus's? Or one god speaking with the other's voice? *Even when we work alone, we are not alone . . .*

She holds the key—Ilstan clung to the thought like a lifeline as he plunged into dizzying Djerad Thymar. She holds the key and that doesn't mean what you think.

. . . power for the mighty . . . More power than you can imagine . . . I can offer that . . . No one will ever deny you again . . .

Ilstan shuddered as the voice changed, and found himself seized by vertigo as he crossed a bridge, suddenly flush with more magic than he could remember. He clutched the balustrade, imagined tipping into the void.

. . . power makes the weak mighty but can make the mighty weak . . . a wizard never rests . . . a wizard never forgets the reach of that might . . . without suffering ramifications greater than can be imagined . . .

His hand was off the balustrade. He stood before a pair of enormous doors, a carved dragon skull leering down at him. Where the time between had gone, he couldn't guess. A smear of dragonborn guards stood between him and the door. Him and the Lady of Black Magic. Him and the key.

What do you want? the streak of dragonborn and blades demanded.

"I need to speak to Farideh," he managed.

Other battles, other battlefields stuttered through his thoughts—marshes and ruins and forests of Cormyr. Facing wizards and goblins and bands of sellswords. They crystalized around this passageway, this entry, under the auspices of the wooden dragon.

Lord of Spells, Ilstan prayed. *Give me the strength to bend the Weave to this most glorious purpose, your freedom.*

Farideh parted the doors, looking as dark and terrible as an angel of battle swooping down upon this meager plane. At her hip hung a weapon of nightmares, a black axe of uncanny glassiness and evident sharpness that twisted with magics not of this world. The shadows of the Nine Hells twined around her. Ilstan was ready.

Her hands came up. "Ilstan? Wait, are you all right?" Her voice shimmered like moonlight on the water. "Ilstan, you have to stay calm."

Don't listen to the voice when it changes, Ilstan told himself. He drew his wand and began to cast.

The words made time slow again, the magic growing thick around him. Farideh's eyes widened, and in answer he saw magic build throughout her frame.

He did not see the dragonborn guards separate from their scaly blur of flesh to tackle him to the ground. A ball of fire streaked from his wand, arcing toward the stone ceiling as he fell, the wand knocked from his hand. He cast again, a spell sure to strike, and the motes of magic curved as they arced off his hands, striking two of his attackers in the back with a chorus of *smacks.*

"*Henish!*" a voice snarled. "Stop struggling!"

"I am blessed by the Lord of Spells!" he snarled, hauling hard against scaly hands even as he drew up the power to recast the spell. "You cannot stop me, beasts!" He started to speak the words to trigger the spell. One of the guards wrapped an arm over his mouth, smothering the words and filling his nose with a musky scent.

"Ilstan!" Farideh's voice cut the hum of magic, the grumbling Draconic. Her face—one silver eye, one gold—swam into view. Angel. Demon. Angel. Demon.

Lady of Black Magic, Ilstan thought. Don't listen when the voice changes.

"Ilstan!" she shouted over his struggles. "Ilstan, you need a caster! You need to—stop it! You need to pass the gift on! Give it to me! You did it before!"

Find a wizard, his sleeves said. *Give the magic to another caster.* You go mad when you don't, he remembered.

The powers of Azuth yanked him toward her. This was supposed to be—whether it saved him or ended him, this was what the god wanted. The dim memory of his hand on her shoulder, then his hand on her shoulder again. He flexed his hand toward her, the little movement he could manage as the guards held him. She grabbed hold of it, squeezed tight.

The pulse of magic that went through them both made his vision black. He heard Farideh shout, "*Karshoj! Oshvith! Oshvith!*" Hands released him, and for a moment it felt as if he were floating, falling slower than ever possible.

Then the heat and roar of lava seared his ears and drove his eyes open. Farideh caught him around the waist, hauled him to his feet, even as she pulled a great rift of burning magma up through the planes. Even as fireballs peeled off her other hand, streaking toward the lava, one after another. Screams echoed all around them, but Ilstan smiled as magic surged through them both—he could almost imagine he felt the bare threads of the Weave against his skin. Every piece, every particle of magic in reach, seemed to surge through him and into her.

It tapered away, the final notes of the last musician on a stage, as the glowing coals of the lava vent went out, the last of the fireballs swallowed up in that gap of the planes. Ilstan searched, by reflex, for casualties. A line of dragonborn stood twenty feet from the scorched boundary of Farideh's spell, weapons out, eyes wary.

No one had been hurt.

Farideh released him, her own legs buckling under her. "*Karshoj*!" She shuddered violently, as if every nerve in her body had suddenly woken again. "*Karshoj*. Is everyone all right?" she shouted back to the guards, then shook her head. "I mean . . . *wuyethi bensvenk*?"

"*Akison*." One of the guards—a female, he saw now, with waist-length plumes of red, and jade plugs in her jaw—helped her to her feet, while the other three stood close to Ilstan. "Nobody was near it, whatever the broken planes it was. Good aim . . . one of you."

Farideh nodded, too quickly, still agitated by the flood of magic. "Good."

Good, Ilstan thought. She warned you. And she warned you. And when you tried to kill her, she reached out a hand.

. . . a wizard is often alone, and so it must be that a wizard seeks allies in the strongest of his peers . . .

"Thank you," Ilstan said, clinging to the all-too-brief clarity he'd gained. "I'm sorry." He clutched his hands together. "I heard the god all wrong. I thought you were my enemy. I thought I had to kill you before you killed me. I don't, do I? You've never tried to kill me, unless I was trying to kill you. You keep helping me and I keep forgetting. I'm so sorry."

Farideh shook her head. "You were mad with magic. It's not your fault."

"But it is," he said, and he felt his eyes well with tears. "I mistook you from the start. Before I could ever blame the madness. Oh gods, I'm so sorry."

Farideh looked away. "It's all right."

"I have nowhere to go," Ilstan told her. "And you're right, the voice keeps changing. What is happening? Do you know?"

Farideh glanced at the guard who'd helped her up. The woman gave a small shake of her head. "Matriarch Anala won't like it."

"Well she won't like it if he stays out here gaining an audience," Farideh said. She rattled off more Draconic, her tone sounding as if she were bargaining. "*Deshkrouth*?"

The guard looked to her fellows and shook her head again, handing over Ilstan's dropped implements. "*Deshkrouth*. Your burial."

Farideh considered him gravely a moment. "You can come in. But I need to keep your wand and your spellbook. For the moment."

"That's very fair," Ilstan said, handing over both, even though a tiny part of himself panicked at being so disarmed.

"Come on," Farideh said. She guided him through the warren of hallways beyond the wooden dragon doors. For a moment, Ilstan thought of the Royal Palace of the Purple Dragon in Cormyr, its corridors as mazelike, as natural to Ilstan as this place's seemed to be to Farideh.

"Is there somewhere safe you can keep me?" he asked. "Somewhere where I won't . . . well, I'd prefer someplace I won't go mad, but that's asking for the moon, I suspect."

"How long do you think you'll be all right?" Farideh asked.

Ilstan shook his head. "I have trouble with time since . . . since all of this started. That was risky," he added, "a spell that big. But it might persist longer."

"Did it, the first time?"

Ilstan looked down at his feet. The first time he had been days past the kind of madness he'd reached at the dragon-skull door. Maybe tendays. But he'd been sane enough to escape, to know he needed healing, to know he would steadily lose his grasp on reality—and after Azuth had guided him to channel the magic through Farideh, Ilstan had time to address all of those things before he'd started slipping again.

"Was the spell you cast in the sewers stronger?" he asked.

Farideh hesitated. "It's the most dangerous spell I know."

Bits of that night flashed in his thoughts, jagged as a broken mirror. The nobleman who'd found him and his oily grin. The sight of the explosion racing past the shielded door. The moment of panic when it became clear the compulsion hadn't taken on the Harper. The moment of triumph when it had worked on his colleague. His stomach churned sick as Farideh reached a door.

"How many of them did I kill?" he asked in a small voice. "The war wizards. How many died because of me?"

Farideh paused at the door. "I don't know," she said quietly.

"But Devora? Drannon?"

"Yes. And others." She sighed. "Ilstan, I know it won't help, but you weren't the evil down there. Someone was just using you—if Pheonard Crownsilver hadn't been there, they wouldn't have died."

He wasn't so sure. "I thought she'd betrayed me. Devora. She was doing her duty, but I'd spun it into something cruel and spiteful. And I made her walk to her death."

Farideh sighed, a sound so full of grief Ilstan wondered at it. "I'm not going to tell you not to think about it—you'll always think about it. But Pheonard is dead. Shade was crushed at Suzail's gates. You can never erase what you did, but you can make certain it doesn't happen again." She considered the door. "And make amends with the people you've hurt. Come on."

• • •

HAVILAR PEERED AT the winged snake, lying coiled and unmoving a few feet from the iron brazier, its wings folded tight. Zoonie whined and pranced a little, not sure what to make of it. "Do you think it's dead?"

Brin came to stand beside her, peering past her shoulder. "No. I think they just do that." She considered it a moment longer, watching its scaly sides for some sign of movement, before she realized Brin was watching her.

"Are you worrying about Farideh?" he asked.

"No," Havilar said. "I sort of figured it was Dumuzi at the door. Or maybe the Kepeshkmolik people changed their minds about that axe and came back for it." She cursed to herself.

"I forgot to sit with the scepter today. I would rather do a hundred drills than Lorcan's stupid practice."

Brin chuckled. "That's not saying much. You drill every day."

"But not a *hundred* times. That would be stupid." She looked at the still-closed door as she walked toward the bedroom. "Do you think we *should* be worried about Farideh?"

"Always," Brin said, following her. "But what are you actually worrying about?"

Hands on the closed case, Havilar blew out a breath. "Anala brought someone here. Dokaan. He's . . . I guess he's in charge of the Lance Defenders." She pressed her hands to her thighs. "He offered me a position."

Brin frowned. "With the Lance Defenders?"

"Teaching glaivework," she said. "I haven't . . . I haven't said yes. I haven't figured out the details."

Brin could no more hide the surprise on his face from her than she'd been able to hide her worry from him. "Ye gods. That's fantastic."

"Is it?"

Brin nodded, too quickly. "Of course. I mean, you'd be wonderful at it. Of course it's fantastic. They'd be lucky to have you."

"But I'd have to live here," she said. "In Djerad Thymar."

That hadn't been lost on him. Brin looked as if she'd hit him in the kidneys. "Well, yes. But . . . You always wonder what you're going to do, where life is going to send you, right? This is perfect."

"It's not perfect."

"Well, it's so godsdamned suited to you that I can't really make an argument that it's no good," Brin said with a nervous laugh. "Look, we're not . . . You don't know what you want from me. Let's just be honest. I shouldn't be the thing that keeps you from an opportunity like this. You should take it."

She wanted to ask if he'd stay, but even if he'd said yes, it wouldn't settle her nerves. She'd watched Brin's humor wearing thin as their days in Djerad Thymar stretched. A tiny part of her wanted to seize it, to say *See? This is why I hated Suzail so much!* But only a very tiny part—he understood, and so did she. And she didn't want him to be unhappy any more than she wanted to be unhappy.

Before she could say anything more, though, Farideh returned, her hair looking as though she'd run into a gale on the way back.

"What happened to you?" Havilar said.

Farideh hesitated in a way that made Havilar very sure it had not been Dumuzi at the door. "We have a guest," she said after a minute. Havilar frowned and looked around her. Ilstan, looking like a lost scarecrow, stood in the middle of the sitting room, staring at the furnishings as though they were insulting his robes. His eyes fell on Zoonie and he leaped backward.

"Is the dog yours?" he called. "The . . . one dripping fire?"

"Just sit down," Farideh said. "She's not going to attack you."

"She *will* attack you," Havilar said, pushing past Farideh, "if you try anything funny. What is he *karshoji* doing here?" she whispered to Farideh in Draconic. "Was he or was he not trying to kill you?"

Farideh pursed her mouth. "Was," she answered back in the same language. "I don't know. Things are getting worse—for both of us. We have to figure this out, and for the moment, he's sane, he knows what he did was wrong, and I have his wand and his spellbook."

"I owe you an apology as well . . . Havilar," Ilstan called from his perch at the very corner of the sofa. "I did not think well of you when Lord Crownsilver brought you to Suzail, and I did assume I should also kill you in order to fulfill my destiny. I was wrong. I beg your forgiveness."

Havilar glared at Farideh. "What did Mehen always say? 'Don't bring home *karshoji* wounded animals'?"

"He's a person, not a skunk with a broken foot," Farideh said. "We can keep him sane. *I* can keep him sane. We just need somewhere safe for him in case he slips."

"*How?*" Havilar demanded. Brin edged around her, eyes hard, mouth tight. Lord Crownsilver again, every inch. He'd never liked Ilstan, even before the Chosen business had caught them all.

"I haven't read my spellbook in days," Ilstan said. "Right now what I can cast is very minor. If you give me the spellbook back, I can cast an antimagic spell upon myself. It would take repeated castings, but in between it would render me safe, and I wouldn't read any other spells—"

"Clap him in irons," Brin said. "Bind his hands and he can't cast."

Ilstan recoiled. "That seems unnecessary."

"You tried to murder Farideh repeatedly," Brin said, without an ounce of pity. "You tried to kill me, and now you've tried to kill Havilar. You can't prove you won't do it again." He turned to Farideh. "If they have finger-cages, they should use those. Otherwise manacles behind his back will do in a pinch."

"I'll still be able to cast," Ilstan said. "There are spells that have no somatic requirement." He pursed his mouth, his eyes darting from side to side as if searching some invisible book. "Light," he said. "I can cast light without gesture."

"We'll take the risk," Brin said witheringly.

"It's just until we find a way to stop it," Farideh said.

"I'll go fetch some," Havilar offered. She didn't want to be in the room with Ilstan anyhow. But before she could get far, Mehen stormed through the doorway, and Havilar's heart jumped into her throat. When Mehen saw Ilstan—

But he didn't make it far. When he saw Havilar, he stopped dead. For a moment, Havilar was sure he had some terrible news, but then he gave her a level look.

"Arjhani's missing," Mehen said. "Dumuzi's gone to fetch something of his in the hope Zoonie can track him down."

"All right," Havilar said. "I just need to do something and I'll be ready."

Mehen's teeth parted. "I think it's best if you stay here."

The words failed to sink in for a moment. "That's stupid," Havilar said, a knot growing in her stomach. "She doesn't listen to you. She certainly doesn't listen to Dumuzi. I have to come."

"Brin could come," Mehen said. "She listens to him."

Havilar felt her cheeks flush, hot and angry. "I am not," she said, "sitting here and *waiting* while you use my dog."

"Havi, I'm just trying—"

"I can handle it."

"I'm sure you think you can," Mehen shouted. "It's that I don't think you should have to spend another moment worrying about Arjhani."

Her blood felt as if it were boiling. "*Karshoj* to Arjhani," she said coldly. "I already saw him. I already spit in his eye. And *karshoj* to you, too, if you're going to keep acting like I can't be trusted not to lose my mind again. I am *not* a little girl anymore and you are not taking Zoonie without me."

Mehen seemed so startled by the outburst that he took a step back from her. Brin's hand settled on the middle of her back. "I'm fine," she whispered, fighting the urge to shrug him off. Fighting the urge to keep yelling at Mehen.

She didn't get a chance—it was then Mehen spotted Ilstan, crouched at the end of the sofa.

He spat a slur of Draconic, crackling with lightning, even as he reached for his weapon. Ilstan put his hands atop his head, trying not to flinch. Farideh stepped between them.

"What the *karshoji* Hells is he doing here?"

"He wasn't the killer," Farideh said. "So they let him out."

"He might not have killed Shestandeliath Ravar, but he's a *karshoji* monster all the same!"

"Gods!" Havilar cried. "Do you think we're just letting him settle in? Do you think we're that stupid? We have a plan!"

"So does he." Mehen switched back to Common, shouting at Ilstan, "Do you remember that, madman? 'Crush them now. It's the only way.' " Ilstan flinched, as if he could become smaller by sheer force of will. Mehen reached back as if to grab his sword. "Maybe I should take that advice, and remove the viper in our midst."

"Mehen!" Farideh shouted. "Calm down!"

"No," Ilstan said, easing shakily to his feet. "I cannot undo what was done in madness. I cannot unsay what I said without understanding. But you have my apologies, and so do your daughters. You are my only allies in this world."

The anger didn't leave Mehen's expression—he did not forgive Ilstan, although Havilar would be shocked if any of them *really* forgave the war wizard. But his hand came off the falchion.

"We need him," Farideh said. "We need every ally we can gain."

"Tell me that when he does something useful."

Ilstan fidgeted with the hem of his sleeve. "I don't know if this is useful, but if you're missing someone, you should use your scrying surface," he said, pointing to the axe at Farideh's hip. "If you wish to leave . . . Havilar"—he stumbled at her name again, as if he didn't know how to call her—"out of it, that could be a solution."

Farideh's hand went to the axe. "The axe is a scrying surface?" Havilar rolled her eyes skyward—of *course* it was a scrying surface too. Farideh had all the luck.

"Fari, he's not well," Mehen said. "Don't listen."

"I am not well," Ilstan agreed. "But I am a war wizard of Cormyr, and I know a scrying surface when I see it." He peered at the axe, as if looking at some invisible surface just inches from the shining black metal. "That one has a condition. It doesn't work all the time."

"What's the condition?" Farideh demanded. Ilstan only shook his head.

"If you give it to me, I might be able to figure it out," he said. Then he added, ahead of her father, "But I don't think it's wise to give me a weapon just now."

Farideh blew out a breath. "No, that's true." She pursed her mouth. "The axe can be the backup. I'll try and figure it out, but if we can't find Arjhani, maybe that's a use for it. Maybe we can use it to find the maurezhi." To Ilstan she said, "How long will you be all right?"

Ilstan shook his head. "Maybe a day? I can tell you when it's starting."

"Can you make scrolls in the meantime?"

"It depends upon the spell you want."

"A magic circle. One that can bind the demon. If more of us have it, ready to cast, then we have a better chance of stopping the maurezhi when we find it."

Ilstan's nervous gaze darted from Farideh to Mehen to Brin, and Havilar found herself thinking of the smug war wizard he had been, the one who'd greeted her with just enough effusiveness to make her distrust him. Gone? Or only hiding?

"It will be expensive. The components won't come cheaply—I suspect they will be dearer still in this place."

"How dear?" Mehen asked Farideh in Draconic.

Farideh turned to him, a heartbeat delayed. "Double," she said. "Maybe not so bad if a Vayemniri bargains for it?"

The door opened for Uadjit and Dumuzi carrying a dark red wad of cloth. He nodded stiffly at Havilar, as if they were now comrades-in-arms, and she fought the urge to sigh. If she had the slightest idea how to shake Dumuzi loose of his properness, she would.

Considering his mother, though, it might do no good. Uadjit's gaze fell on her and there was no shaking the sensation the dragonborn woman was judging Havilar, and no telling what for.

"A shirt," Dumuzi said, holding out the cloth.

"He wore it a few days ago." Uadjit considered Havilar grimly. "I trust that's enough for your . . . animal."

"She can track him," Mehen said, before Havilar could protest. "Thank you," he added, "for setting aside all this rivalry. You didn't tell Narghon you came, did you?"

"I'll tell him," Uadjit said. "Now that I'm agreed and it's clear this isn't some gambit of Anala's to claim the Vanquisher's piercings."

Mehen folded his arms. "Even Pandjed wouldn't have unleashed a fiend just to get Verthisathurgiesh in the Vanquisher's throne."

Uadjit gave Mehen a skeptical look that made Havilar wish she knew the stories behind it . . . and made her wonder about Anala. "One thing is certain at least," Uadjit said. "Neither of us will be Vanquisher if we can't stop this creature."

A stab of panic hit Havilar in the heart—Farideh was right— but when she looked to Mehen, to gauge his response, there was nothing but shock there.

"What did you say?"

"Be sensible," Uadjit went on. "You're tied to this now. If we can't—"

"Who *karshoji* told you I was standing for Vanquisher?" Mehen bellowed. Beside Uadjit, Dumuzi tensed. Havilar traded a glance with her sister—someone was in trouble.

But Uadjit didn't so much as blink. "I suspect," she said, "you'll need to talk to Anala about that. Later, though." She clapped him on the shoulder. "You have too much to do to waste time with clan politics, I suspect."

19

DAHL TURNED SIDEWAYS TO SQUEEZE AROUND A SHARP outcrop, focused on his feet against the crumbling rock beneath. Higher up the shaft, where the crack intersected with an existing pocket in the stone, the rest of the group still slept. Sessaca hadn't been exaggerating—the crack went down miles, and they were all crammed close enough the whole way that Dahl had no space to read the scrolls he'd stolen, to see if he'd secured their escape.

"Get yourself out of here," Sessaca had murmured to him while they were still waiting for the Zhentarim to shift supplies, secure ropes, whisper over messages to be sent. "Find the one we need." But Grathson's toughs kept a constant vigil, and Dahl could not so much as escape to take a piss before they were crawling down the shaft.

Where the crack bent to the left, it widened enough for Dahl to sit down, back against the sharp-edged stone. Out of sight of anyone who might come looking, he thought, wedging a sunrod between his head and shoulder. He pulled his haversack open, and withdrew the first of the scrolls—a teleportation.

Peering at the runes in the dim light, tracing the spell, the way the magic would unfold, his thoughts raced ahead to the result—where would a portal be able to take them? Where would he ask it to take them?

Harrowdale, he told himself, even though it wasn't the answer he wanted. If he went back, he was as stuck as before.

No components, no coin, and no messenger snake. There was an argument to be made for staying with Xulfaril after all.

Not much of one, Dahl thought. Whatever Mira found in her albeit false service to the Zhentarim, he doubted he'd find it too. The spell spiraled into a final function—it wouldn't take them far enough, not even out of the tunnels. He rolled it back up and pulled another. He made it only a few lines before it became clear it was for summoning.

The third . . . the third was more promising. A portal—a true portal—to anywhere on the plane Toril occupied. He studied the spell's threads of magic, the way it would fall together, the way it played out in his own thoughts . . .

The spell didn't include the caster. Once they moved from the point they cast at, the portal would collapse. "Godsbedamned simbarchs," he muttered, recognizing the handiwork of Aglarond's ruling wizards.

"Good morning, Dahl Peredur."

Dahl reached for his dagger as he looked up, the only weapon he could reasonably draw in this space. Farther down the passage, the bald devil woman stood, her wings curled close around her in the tight space.

"Do you trust me, Dahl Peredur?" she asked.

"Are you mad?" he returned. "Why in the world would I trust you?"

She gave him a strangely beatific smile. "Fair. Though I assumed by now that you'd realized by comparison I am quite the ally. I brought you a gift."

"I don't want it."

"Are you certain?" She held out another scroll, this one dense and capped with copper end pieces. "It's your contract with Lorcan. I thought it might sweeten the pot." She tapped the copper cap. "There are such a lot of ways to make certain he suffers. I have to imagine, right now, you want him to suffer."

Yes, Dahl thought, but also he thought of Farideh, of her asking him not to hurt Lorcan, because of what worse things might come after her and Havilar in his absence. Would she still say that, if she knew the bind Lorcan had put him in?

Dahl wet his mouth, considered his words carefully. "How do I know you're holding what you say you're holding?"

"You won't," she said, "until I have a little show of good faith."

"What's that?"

She held out a hand. "Come with me. Leave this place."

"I can't. My family—"

"They can manage without you, I'm sure. You come with me, we'll get you out of the way of things. I'll deal with it, and they can make their way home, I'm sure."

"Oh I'm sure," Dahl said. "My ninety-year-old grandmother and my brothers who've never left the dale can manage fine. I'm not going anywhere without them."

"My powers have limits."

"As does my patience," Dahl said. "You don't get my imaginary child and you don't get to haul me off to gods-know-where. But I'm guessing the other thing with limits is your luck in dealing with Lorcan, since you're back here."

The woman snickered. "I haven't even begun to make Lorcan dance. To be frank," she said, "I do prefer you to him. His father was a nightmare to deal with and I'd rather avoid any connection I possibly could." She smiled thinly. "Perhaps you'll reconsider when you see what you're up against."

Dahl hesitated. "What's that?"

She gave him a sly smile. "Do you trust me?"

"Not in the slightest."

"Then you'll have to see for yourself."

With that, she vanished in a gust of wind.

A very similar gust of wind, Dahl thought, to the one that marked the portal Lorcan had used to ferry him to Harrowdale. He sipped a little whiskey from his flask. Lorcan had a sister, he knew, but then she'd said "his father" and sounded more a contemporary of that man than Lorcan's.

Likely it's a trick, he thought bitterly, a little torment to make it all worse.

Something higher up the tunnel clattered against the stone. Dahl cursed, shoved the scrolls and the flask back into his haversack, and climbed back up the narrow passage. Grathson was waiting for him, sharpening his dagger.

"Where'd you go?"

"Do I need to wake you up and tell you I'm going to have a piss?" Dahl asked dryly.

"You might," Grathson said. "We're close enough to the Underdark that strange beasties might have a mind to crawl up if they hear you moving around." He considered the edge of the dagger, and over it, Dahl. "You need your haversack to take a piss?"

"Easier to carry down a waterskin to wash the rock down. Like you said: don't want to attract strange beasties."

"Watch your tongue, Harper," Grathson said. "Godsbedamned Underdark doesn't care how clever you think you are. Only gives it new and better ways to break you down."

Dahl frowned. "How so?"

Grathson chuckled to himself, but did not explain.

"Don't stlarning listen to Grathson," Sessaca said later, as they eased their way down the steep path. "Less sense than a ram in early spring, trying to measure horns with the godsbedamned back end of a bull."

"Right, I know his type," Dahl said. Much as it pained him, he was the same way more often than he cared to admit. "I'm asking what he means about the Underdark."

Sessaca shook her head. "I told you. It's all made for something that's not you. You don't belong in the Underdark."

The change was subtle at first: a fuzziness to the air; a sensation as if someone were humming tunelessly, irritating Dahl beyond measure but without any actual sound. As they descended, he found more than once as his hand reached for the rock wall, it wouldn't be where he expected, but a finger's breadth farther or nearer. The gloom seemed to grow thicker, smothering their sunrods.

"You have a plan, right?" Bodhar asked, as Dahl slowed to creep around a turn in the path.

Dahl hesitated. "Stay back," he said. "Let them get ahead and see to their outpost. We'll head back up the shaft when we have the chance." And pray, he added silently, that you managed to grab the right scroll.

They had certainly been climbing for hours, but it still surprised Dahl when the crack ended and one by one they eased free of the narrow passage into a wide cavern.

The Underdark.

At a glance, the cavern beyond the light of their sunrods seemed like nothing more than a cave, but the longer Dahl searched the space, the more *wrong* it felt. The stone seemed to have somehow oozed into place. The fluorescent fungi that smeared the rocks came in more virulent shades of purple and orange and yellow than he had ever seen. The sense that had struck him in the shaft, the sense that something was wrong, something was just two steps from how it ought to be and he couldn't see it, had built into a powerful urge to get out right now.

"You're going to want to cover those sunrods," Sessaca said. "Things down here will come toward the light. Figure you for a treat."

"Keep them out," Xulfaril said, drawing her wand. "Better we fight off some monsters than fall down a hole."

Volibar came to stand beside her, turning a map, looking for a way to match it. "We're a little turned around," he whispered, though the cavern made every sound ring as clear as if he had spoken much louder. "If I've got this right, the passage we were going to use should be . . . to the left, maybe three bow's shots?" He rolled up the map. "Once we find that, we'll have a much easier time orienting for the outpost."

"Excellent," Xufaril said. "At which point, I think our business will have ended, Swordcaptain." Her eyes flicked to Dahl. "At least, some of our businesses. This way. Weapons out."

"Don't you go with her," Sessaca muttered, as they moved through the Underdark, Grathson's heavies on every side of them. There would be no slinking back to the passage. But, too, there would be no taking Xulfaril up on her offer—maybe Mira was right, maybe he was compromised, maybe Farideh's allegiances weren't so innocent as he thought. He found he didn't care. If the Harpers rejected him, he wouldn't turn against them. And he wouldn't forget Farideh.

None of which mattered in that moment, with the Underdark playing upon his nerves like a clumsy harpist.

"Why not?" Dahl said. "You did."

"I worked for myself, thank you very much. It was a different time, and you're a different person."

"Stop talking," Grathson hissed between them. " 'Less you want to be what I throw to the hook horrors."

"Is that what you think it is?" Sessaca asked mildly.

Not hook horrors, thought Dahl. He'd never consider himself an expert at the bestiary of the Underdark, but he knew enough to eliminate most of what he did know. Something that could block off the access routes. Something that would scare goblins to the surface. Something strong enough to silence the Zhentarim of the outpost.

Not hook horrors, he thought. Not kuo-toa. Not goblins.

The Zhentarim stopped as they came around the corner to where the library had collapsed. Stopped, frozen and staring, all in a line.

Dahl spotted the leader before he registered the masses of bloodied and torn Zhentarim, the bodies of the dead: the shadow of a man, so rich and vibrant that he seemed in his darkness to invert the space, to will the shadows into solidity and the Underdark around them into fluttering, negative phantasm.

He saw the man, and the man saw him, saw within him the furious dread, the desperate need, the dark things that had overtaken his mind in his pursuit of Oghma's favor. Arrogance, ambition, ego. He saw the hunger in him, and the pure rage that coiled around his every thought of Lorcan. The man saw all of this, Dahl felt sure, and he smiled, as if someone had left a great gift in his hands.

A smell like strong, cheap perfume sliced through Dahl's nostrils, a smell like salt and brimstone. His mouth suddenly tasted of ashes and his mind seemed to break apart.

Oh my boy, a voice like velvet said in Dahl's thoughts. *What a rich and fertile field you make.*

• • •

HAVILAR WALKED ALONGSIDE Zoonie, keeping the hellhound to an easy pace and keeping herself out of Mehen's reach. He tapped his tongue nervously, memories of that long-ago autumn night on the edge of the hardest winter Arush Vayem had ever seen circling through his head. They would find Arjhani and he would be alive, and then what?

"I have to ask," Kallan said quietly, falling in beside him. "Did you really think you could get the dog and not the daughter?"

"I hoped."

Kallan shook his head, eyeing the darkness of a crypt off to the left. "The way you all tiptoe around this fellow, I'm half expecting some kind of charm-casting, mind-controlling vampire."

Mehen kept his eyes on his daughter's back, the memory of a long-ago late autumn night playing over and over in his memory. Maybe, he thought, Arjhani will be dead.

The thought stung, and he wished he hadn't had it. Just behind Zoonie, Dumuzi marched, straight-backed and solemn. You are too old to think the world is all about you, Mehen thought.

"Are you that hung up on him?" Kallan asked in a curious way. "Afraid you can't keep your head on straight?"

"I'm not hung up on him!" Mehen snapped.

Kallan held a hand up in a gesture of surrender. "Obviously I read that wrong. Sorry."

Mehen's chest squeezed tight. "No, I'm sorry. It's . . . Did the girls tell you anything? About him?"

"I think I overheard once from Havilar that Arjhani had nothing on me," Kallan said with a playful smile. "Beyond that, nothing."

Mehen kept silent, not wanting to air out the past, not wanting to go any longer holding tight to it. *How many years have you let all of this rule your life?* "I don't like talking about . . ." He bit off the end of the thought.

"Anything?" Kallan said. "I get that. You're a private fellow."

Because it's nobody's *karshoji* business—but that, too, was a lie. Maybe at the start, but Pandjed, Arjhani, Uadjit, the snowstorm—these moments and decisions and memories pushed and pulled him, and in turn pushed and pulled his daughters and Brin and even Kallan.

"I'm not hung up on Arjhani," he said again. "No more than . . ." He shook his head, feeling foolish. "I loved him. That never goes away completely."

"Fair." Then, "You don't look at him like that's it."

Mehen snapped his teeth in annoyance. "Are you jealous of someone who might be dead?"

"A little," Kallan said matter-of-factly. "Although dead or not's got nothing to do with it. I certainly don't wish him ill."

Mehen said nothing for a long time, while the memories of that autumn night ran through their steps like players at a fair, over and over the same lines. *You have to come back. No one else can stand against him.* The little bottle of mud-brown syrup falling out of the haversack. *How could you think I would use it?*

You have to come back . . . wouldn't you leave them here?

"You can wish him a little ill," Mehen blurted.

Ahead Zoonie jerked against the lead, heading down a right-hand corridor. They followed—this passage was wider, winding toward the center of the city. "Is he the reason you were exiled?" Kallan asked.

"I'm the reason I was exiled." The words were no more out of his mouth, but he regretted their cheapness. "My father agreed to a marriage contract with Kepeshkmolik Uadjit. I refused, and so he exiled me." Still cheap, he thought. Still little better than a lie.

"He didn't care you weren't keen on women?"

Mehen snorted. "Maybe in the homesteads you can use that as an excuse not to get eggs for your clan, but in the city, you knuckle down and do what's needful." Then, "Our clans have never seen eye to eye. Kepeshkmolik is a bunch of self-important upstarts, Verthisathurgiesh breeds tyrants. This would have been a bridge. Anything that would have given either side room for scrutiny would be dangerous."

Kallan made a face. "So why make the contract?"

Why indeed? Kepeshkmolik had made the offer, because Narghon doted on his scion and Uadjit had examined all her options and asked for Mehen. At the time it had infuriated him—they were friends, she knew about Arjhani, she knew he wouldn't want this, Uadjit was forcing his hand, making him do what she thought was *right*. Now, looking back, he wondered if she'd been trying to protect him. He wondered if she'd been fond of him in a foolish, teenaged way, or if she'd seen, as he could see now, how she and he could have leaned on each other, each making the other stronger at the cost of some happiness.

The agreement is made. You live at my pleasure. You will wed her, or you will be no son of mine.

"I don't know," Mehen said. "I only found out after it had been made without my say."

You say that to me, toe to toe, let's see what comes of it.

"I refused," he said, avoiding all the rest. "I was exiled. And Arjhani didn't come with me. That's it."

Kallan looked at him sidelong. "*Aithyas.* You don't need to tell me a damned thing, but that's not *it*. None of that has to do with Havilar. You went back to him?"

How could you think I would use it? The little bottle of mud-brown syrup falling out of the haversack. Arjhani, playing with Havilar and a pair of makeshift toy glaives. *Wouldn't you leave them here? With their own kind? It's probably for the best.*

"No," Mehen said, feeling that unwelcome anger rise up through his blood. "He came and found me."

"And the girls?"

"And the girls." Mehen tapped his tongue to the roof of his mouth. "The thing about Arjhani is that everyone adores him. Even you—if you met him, you'd wonder what I'm so angry about. And Havi . . ."

"Havi doesn't like someone halfway," Kallan finished as Mehen let the thought hang, half-made. "He didn't stick around?"

The lie Mehen had told so many times sat ready in his mouth. But this time, to Kallan—this man who didn't have a disingenuous bone in his body, who wouldn't take the easy lie, who still thought there was something worthwhile in him—Mehen couldn't tell it.

"No. I threw him out." He kept his eyes on Havilar's back. "I let the girls think he left on his own. It was simpler. The whole business . . . My father was more than fearsome. He was a tyrant in his own right, the kind of person that slips up unnoticed, until you look around and realize you're living in a *karshoji* ancestor story, only the dragon's one of you.

"I don't know where Pandjed heard I'd made a new life in Arush Vayem, but he was still so angry at me. He sent Arjhani. He sent him to kill me. 'To wipe the stain from Verthisathurgiesh's rolls.' "

How could you think I would use it? But there was the little bottle of mud-brown syrup in Mehen's hand, not bumping down the river, not at the bottom of a ravine, not broken on the rocks of the Smoking Mountains. *I was afraid—is that what you want to hear? He said kill you or he'd kill me. I wasn't going to do it, but . . .*

"Your father sounds like a *karshoji* lunatic," Kallan said. "And I can't say much for Arjhani at this point."

Mehen shook his head. It was all more complicated than that. "Arjhani . . . he was terrified of Pandjed in a way he couldn't even name. Sometimes I think he didn't love me, he only stuck with me, because I could defend him. And then I was gone. He

430

begged me to come back, to depose Pandjed. Said I was the only one who could. I pointed out that I could never be patriarch with my daughters so young and so far from being Vayemniri."

Had it been Pandjed's plan all along that Arjhani wouldn't be able to kill Mehen? That he would lure Mehen back by confessing the whole awful situation, and Pandjed would get another chance to make his son bow? What had Arjhani suffered when he'd returned without Mehen and without proof he'd been dealt with?

"Someone told me once a fellow had best know going in that he'd always come second to your daughters," Kallan said. "I'm going to guess no one warned Arjhani."

You have to come back. No one else can stand against him.

Jhani, you're not thinking. Nobody's making me patriarch this young—nobody's making me patriarch after what happened! And all that aside, nobody's going to accept the girls.

Wouldn't you leave them here? With their own kind? A blade in his heart. The words stirred up an animal rage in him even all these years later, a moment where he saw with perfect clarity how people could say he was his father's son, breath and scale.

What did you karshoji *say?*

Don't take it like that. I didn't say they weren't fine. Just that they're not really *yours—they're not like us.*

Ahead, Zoonie stopped at a crossway, sniffing the air in an agitated way. Havilar glanced back at Mehen, then turned to scratch Zoonie's shoulder.

"Shouldn't need a *karshoji* warning." Mehen said. "They're my daughters. Not my pets." He started toward Havilar.

"Hey." Kallan tugged him to a stop out of earshot, pulling him closer. "You know that's not going to go well. She's still angry. Now you're angry." He rubbed Mehen's arm in a comforting way. "I don't think anyone with half a brain would say you didn't do exactly the right thing. The hard thing, but the right one. Also, I think Havilar's clearly right," he added. "Arjhani has nothing on me."

That jolted a laugh from Mehen, and much of his tension with it. He glanced ahead at Havilar, who was still carefully not watching him. "I've never told anybody that," he said. "Not even the girls."

"Well I'm flattered. I don't know what you're keeping exactly."

Mehen looked away. "The girls think he left on his own. And two tendays later, my heartbroken little girl chased after him, into the heart of a snowstorm, because she thought it was her fault. She almost died."

"*Chaubask vur kepeshk*," Kallan swore. He looked after Havilar, the full horror of the situation evident in his features, and Mehen found it harder to forget the handsome sellsword. "All right so *that's* why you're trying to keep her back."

"I have to tell her, don't I?"

Kallan shook his head. "No. Bite your tongue. She thinks he left because he didn't love her enough? Why confirm it? All you'd give her is the knowledge you love her beyond measure, and she knows it. Besides, she seems all right."

Mehen shook his head. "She says so."

"You don't believe her."

"I will never believe her," Mehen said. "I've seen what happens when I'm wrong."

"You're leaving things out, aren't you?"

"Some. Let me have it." He hesitated. "I meant it, when I said it wasn't you."

"But you were lying when you said it was your girls," Kallan said in a mild way. "How long you planning to punish yourself for someone else's crimes?"

"I don't know," Mehen said honestly. Then, "How long can you wait?"

Kallan chuckled. "I've got nothing else in my sights. But as fine as you are, I'm not the kind to pine forever. So, you do know most fellows aren't interested in breaking up your family?" Kallan said. "Even if they want more than a tumble."

"Course not," Mehen said grimly. "Nobody plans for that."

432

Suddenly, Zoonie pressed her nose to the wall, going stiff all over. She threw back her shaggy head and howled, a sound that shook Mehen's bones. Havilar grabbed hold of the hellhound's thick fur, and—as the beast bunched her legs to run—pulled herself up onto the creature with one smooth motion.

All three of the dragonborn took off running after the hellhound. She slowed at another crossway, letting Mehen get within arm's reach before taking off down a shallow set of stairs. They were into the oldest parts of the catacombs now, the resting place of those who'd died in the Blue Fire, down far enough that each ancestor had their own tomb to protect their bones from dark magics, instead of the ossuaries above.

Zoonie skidded to a stop, whining and prancing.

Havilar rubbed the side of her neck. "It's all right, good girl. It's all right. She held out Arjhani's shirt again. "Just that. Find that."

Zoonie sniffed it again, eyeing the long hallway mistrustfully. She shook her head once, sneezed, and backed down the narrow hallway, turning with a little trouble. She snuffled along the stone hallway, stopping beside an ancient Linxakasendalor tomb. Havilar slipped from the hellhound's shoulders, and the beast padded into the dark space. Here a trio of Vayemniri, ended by the violence of the planar shift, had been interred together.

Zoonie lay flat in front of the center sarcophagus, growling deeply enough to shake the whole city. All four of them went to the corners of the stone lid, heaving hard to move the heavy granite slab. Mehen's heart climbed up his throat.

Arjhani bolted up as the slab moved away, a broken bone in one hand, his other arm pressed up against his chest. He lunged, blindly, toward the open end of the tomb. Toward Havilar.

For a brief terrible moment, everything seemed to slow, as if Mehen were trapped in a dream. His hands wouldn't let go of the granite slab, even as the sharpened weapon arced toward his daughter.

Havilar dodged to the side, her hand shooting out to grab Arjhani by the wrist and yank the bone down, away from her.

On the opposite side, Dumuzi reached out and grabbed his father around the shoulders, pulling him close.

"It's me!" he shouted as Arjhani started to struggle. "We came to rescue you. You're safe! You're safe!"

Gasping for air, Arjhani searched their faces as though any one of them might wear a mask. His whole body stayed tense, as if he were preparing to throw off Dumuzi as soon as he'd decided which of them was the worst threat.

"Easy, *sathi*," Kallan said gently. "We can't all be the maurezhi."

"None of us can be the maurezhi," Havilar said irritably. "I would be throwing up so hard."

Arjhani blinked at Mehen. "I . . . ," he managed. "I . . ."

"You're safe," Mehen said. "You're safe now. Come on." He held out a hand, and Arjhani took it, stepping out of the sarcophagus as Dumuzi released him. His whole body shook and the scales of his hand were burning with fever. Mehen cursed and his arms pulled Arjhani closer. "He needs a healer."

Kallan pulled a little bottle from his haversack. "*Chmertehoschta?*" He tossed the sedative to Mehen who helped the fevered Arjhani take some.

"Sepideh," he wheezed. "Help."

"*Karshoj*," Kallan said. "That's a Lance Defender commander. We have to move." Mehen helped Arjhani over to Zoonie, no small feat as the other man shook violently with shock and fever and as the *chmertehoschta* started to take hold, his knees weakened. Havilar watched, stern and worried, as Mehen helped Arjhani onto the hellhound's back. He couldn't shake the feeling that he'd failed them both.

"Let me help," Havilar said, getting her arm around Arjhani's chest and helping balance him facedown on the dog's back. Kallan produced long strips of cloth, which they bound Arjhani down with. Mehen stepped back, watching Havilar. Nothing he'd feared showed in her, and despite the situation he smiled.

"Where's Dumuzi?" Kallan asked.

Mehen looked around the tomb and cursed. The edge of panic was just beginning to take shape around his heart as he stormed out into the corridor. There, at the far end where Zoonie had balked, Dumuzi stood staring up at a larged sealed tomb door.

"Hey!" Mehen shouted. "What part of don't go off alone did you mistake?"

Dumuzi startled. "Sorry. I just . . . I needed a moment."

Mehen came to stand beside Dumuzi. The tomb door had been painted in now flaking blue and red, the shape of a crescent moon spanning the width of the doorway. Beneath it an epitaph of sorts could still be read: Here lies a great warrior of this world. Claimed as clan-kin by Kepeshkmolik and all the Vayemniri of Djerad Thymar, now and forever more under our protection.

"Have you ever seen this?" Dumuzi whispered.

Mehen shook his head. "I've never been this deep into the catacombs. Did Ashoka ever tell you the story of the black axe?"

"Narghon doesn't like that story," Dumuzi said. "Says it muddies the waters when it comes to gods. Who do you think he was?"

Ashoka's story flowed through Mehen's thoughts. "Your clan-kin," Mehen said. "And mine too, I suppose."

Dumuzi shook his head. "Narghon won't like that."

"*Karshoj* to Narghon," Mehen said. "We weren't blood-kin when we formed the clans—any and all who would stand against the tyrants. We survived because of that. Because anyone who would be an ally, could. Come on."

Dumuzi kept glancing back at the tomb as they hurried back through the catacombs, and Mehen couldn't shake the feeling that the Gift of the Moon was not through being given.

• • •

FARIDEH MADE HERSELF consider the golden glyphs along the shaft of the Black Axe of Thymara, even as her thoughts drifted elsewhere—to Havilar, to Dahl, to Lorcan, to Ilstan. Focus, she told herself. People are going to die if you don't. "Maybe it says what we need to do on the axe itself."

"Likely," Brin said. "Have you got the components to cast a language ritual?"

Farideh shook her head. "I doubt it. I haven't cast that spell since . . ." Since before they'd been locked in the Nine Hells. Since back in the arcanist's library-tomb.

"Pity Dahl's not here," Brin said. "He's always got a damned apothecary in his bag."

If Dahl were here, Farideh thought, how many things would be better? Another pair of eyes, another mind, another way of looking. Someone who could remind her to stop panicking—he was good at that.

Or if Dahl were here, would he even be *here*? she wondered. Would he be able to think of twenty things about her, or would he have only thought of one: Asmodeus?

"We can send Hencin out for them when he comes back," Farideh said, pushing it all aside and dipping her stylus in ink. "What else could we try?"

"Anything," Brin said. "It could literally be anything."

"Well, what's common? What have you seen before?"

"Holy water," Brin said. "Or maybe a blood sacrifice. Maybe . . ." He bit his lip, eyes on the axe. "Did she tell you? About the thing with the Lance Defenders?"

Farideh set the stylus down. "This morning. I suppose that means . . . She made a decision about everything then?"

"No." Brin blew out a breath. "I don't think so."

"Maybe she won't."

"I told her she should. And she should. She really seems to like it here." Brin smiled. "You should have seen her. She knocked those little plinth-heads on their backsides, never broke a sweat, and told them exactly how she'd done it. She could be amazing at this. She would be so happy. I can't keep her from that." He dropped his eyes. "But I can't stay here, any more than she could have stayed in Suzail."

And if Havilar stayed in Djerad Thymar—or worse, if Havilar *and* Mehen stayed—did that mean Farideh would stay? The thought made her feel as if she couldn't breathe. She squeezed her eyes shut. Calm. Calm.

"Perhaps it needs a different wielder?" Ilstan piped up from the sofa.

Brin scowled. "Wonderful, we'll run down our list of, oh, everyone in the stlarning world. That should be simple enough."

Farideh thought of Ashoka's admonition. If there was a true bearer of the axe, maybe it would only work for them, and all of this was nothing but wasted time. She wrapped a strand of hair around and around her finger, tight enough to hurt. There was no way to know—except to keep guessing or let Ilstan study the axe.

Make Ilstan study the axe, she corrected herself. He had so far refused to so much as touch the weapon. "I cannot be trusted at the moment." He considered the axe grimly. "Perhaps ever."

Proper wielder. Farideh added it to the list.

"What about the story?" Brin said. "Are there any clues in it?"

Farideh rubbed her eyes—it was all muddled now, mixed in her dreams and everything else. "Thymara found the tomb of a warrior and the axe and she used it to gather the other Vayemniri." She bit her lip. "Maybe you have to be from Thymara's line."

"If that's the case," Ilstan said, "then why did they let it pass out of their hands. Why give it to you if it must be borne by one of their line?"

"What else?"

"The moon told her to . . ." Farideh went completely still, recognition flooding her. "Oh gods. Oh. *Dahl.*"

"Hrast," Brin said. "What now?"

"I . . . I think I used it. When we were outside, I was holding the axe and I was thinking about Dahl, and there was a moment—just a moment—where I would have sworn I saw him reflected in the axe head. I thought I was just seeing things, too tired, you know? But what if that's it? It would make sense. The moon protected Thymara, told her to take the axe and keep it safe. *Karshoj,* how could I not think of that?"

Farideh snatched the axe off the table. Even in the morning light, the moonlight had been enough to wake the axe, her thoughts of Dahl enough to direct the scrying. If it were that powerful, it should take nothing at all to find Arjhani, and thereafter the maurezhi. "If we get up to the top of the pyramid, we should be able to—"

"What is the date?" Ilstan interrupted.

"The, er, twenty-fifth of Nightal," Farideh said. "Why?"

"The time?"

"Tharsun." Brin said, folding his arms. "Late afternoon."

"Then the moon has set already," Ilstan explained. "Assuming nothing else has gone awry in the world, it will not rise until some hours after deepnight."

Farideh cursed and sat back down. So close, so close. And now what was there to do, but worry about Havilar, about Dahl, about Asmodeus and everything else?

"We could just try what's on the list?" Brin said, as if he'd had the same thought. "Can't hurt, right?"

Farideh shrugged. "I guess not." She considered the list. "Should we start with fire?"

"I beg your pardon?" Ilstan called. "If it is tharsun, then it occurs to me I haven't eaten since morningfeast, and that's likely why this pain in my belly—"

"You're hungry. Got it." Brin stood. "Are you all right alone with him for a moment?"

Farideh nodded. Shackled as he was, sane as he seemed, Ilstan appeared to be nothing of a threat compared to everything else. Brin left, and for a long moment, the room was so quiet Farideh felt as if the silence were about to break through her ears.

"How are you doing?" Farideh asked Ilstan.

Ilstan bobbed his head. "He speaks," he said, "though not as much. And . . . the other one is quieter. But I would not say he's gone. Sometimes I can feel . . . I don't know how you contend with his presence."

Farideh frowned. "He doesn't talk to me. Except when I dream, maybe. I don't really know what's real and what I'm imagining. Azuth just . . . talks to you?"

Ilstan looked surprised. "Constantly. I mean, I cannot say it always is coherent. Or that I can be sure of who is speaking. But I believe."

"And he tells you to free him?"

"He tells me many things." Ilstan sighed. "I worry I'm not hearing any of them right."

Farideh returned her attention to the axe, leaving Ilstan to his thoughts. What more could she say? What more *should* she say—most everyone would say she was mad for trying to comfort Ilstan. He'd tried to kill her multiple times. He'd hunted her all the way to Djerad Thymar. What had he done to deserve this sudden alliance?

But for all that made sense, Farideh knew she didn't believe Ilstan was wicked. There was good in him as much as anyone, and it wouldn't be right to throw him away. Especially when he might be the only one who knew what was happening to her and to Havilar.

The shivery sensation of a finger gently tracing the edges of her brand interrupted those thoughts. Lorcan. Farideh steeled herself. Now or never.

"I'll be right back," she said, standing and making for the bedroom.

"The Knight of the Devil," Ilstan intoned. Farideh turned, the shadow-smoke of her pact and the racing flames of Asmodeus's gift chasing each other up her frame, ready for another battle.

But the war wizard only sat, staring into the middle distance, an expression best described as vague annoyance on his face. "The Lady of Black Magic. She has the key. With it the prison unlocks."

"Ilstan?" Farideh asked. "Are you all right?"

The wizard whipped his head toward her. Something unnatural seethed behind his eyes and her brand started to prickle. "You know," he said in that rushy voice. "And you do not. But what you do not know, she knows. Which is the greater danger, to he and I and all of you."

Snow began falling all around them, a blizzard that blurred away the ceiling and walls. She stood as if she could run and found herself sinking to the ankles in a snowdrift. Djerad Thymar was gone. There was only Arush Vayem and the lonely winter wind. Farideh turned in a slow circle.

"Ilstan, what have you done?"

Suddenly he was standing so close, nearly on top of her. "What you do not know, she knows. Which is the greater danger, to he and I and all of you."

"Who?" Farideh managed.

Ilstan smiled at her, in a fond, grandfatherly sort of way that didn't fit his features at all. "The Lord of Spells," she murmured. "What's the key?"

"You're a funny little thing, you know that?"

She turned, the wind whipping the snow up around her. Lorcan stood in the path—but gods, it wasn't Lorcan. "I wish you wouldn't do that," she said, numbly.

"I gave you the chance to stay out of this," he said. "To be happy. Until it was clear that you don't want to be happy. You want to be virtuous, right, *good.* I let you uncover enough to see your enemy clearly and yet you become so focused on something that isn't your concern."

Farideh watched him through the swirling snow, unsure if she was awake or asleep. "But I think it is. I think . . . I think . . ." She turned again, considering the empty village, the thickening snow.

Suddenly Lorcan stood beside her, nearly on top of her. "You think. You think. Do not think. Do not act. You are given a great gift, my dear, but only if you obey. I am not an enemy you want to make. The one who gets hurt doesn't have to be you."

She looked into his fathomless eyes. "What happens if you die?"

He chuckled softly and tilted his head. "What did he tell you?"

" 'The Knight of the Devil. The Lady of Black Magic. She has the key. With it the prison unlocks.' " She swallowed, the snow almost too thick to see through, cocooning them in a blanket of white. "I don't know anything about a key."

A burst of light illuminated the snow, so bright, so sudden, that Farideh flinched, and when she opened her eyes, her vision was seared in spots.

For the briefest of moments, she saw an elderly human man, leaning so close to her there was nothing else. And then she blinked and he was gone—the *world* was gone. She could see nothing but white, the snow becoming shards of ice that abraded her skin. She turned and turned, but the wind moved with her, trapping her in place, herding her like a lost lamb. She forced herself against the gale, and—

Found herself lying on the floor of the common room, staring up at the ceiling, one hand clutching her burning upper arm.

"Darling!" Lorcan shouted. He was kneeling beside her. "Darling! Can you hear me?"

Farideh, all impulse, shot to her feet, shoving the cambion away. The snow was gone, Arush Vayem was gone. Ilstan still sat on the couch, staring into the middle distance, and there was nothing of either god in his eyes or in Lorcan's.

"Darling," he said, holding his hands high, "what happened?"

You know. And you do not. But what you do not know, she knows. Which is the greater danger, to he and I and all of you.

"He and I and all of you," she murmured.

"Farideh?" Lorcan said again. "What happened? Tell me you're all right."

No, she thought. None of us is all right. And I can't stop it.

20

NONE OF THIS IS RIGHT.

The thought rose in Dahl's mind, like a swimmer breaching the surface of a rough and rising tide, and for a moment, he saw everything: the Zhentarim mindlessly digging through the rubble, the bodies trailing back into the Underdark, Mira staring blankly into the darkness. The man made of night staring back into Dahl's soul.

The darkness pulled Dahl down again.

What an interesting specimen you make. The man did not so much speak as his voice echoed in the space between Dahl's heartbeats, stretching them out to make his point. *You don't belong with these fools, this rabble, now do you?*

The demon's efforts struck the thought like a plow against a fieldstone, sparking fears Dahl didn't know were still in him.

He didn't belong here—his ears seemed to fill with years' worth of his brothers poking fun at his borrowed books, the freedom offered in Jedik's suggestion Dahl be sent to train in the Domes of Reason. His father's puzzled expression. He had risen above his upbringing. He would make something of himself. He had bested Oghma's puzzles. He would show them.

His thoughts jolted as if his mind were a rough and rocky road. There was Farideh—considering him with a faint frown. "I mean, you can call yourself whatever you want—but if people are going to think coming from a farm means you don't belong,

442

does it make a difference? You're still you, aren't you? It doesn't erase that. It shouldn't."

It shouldn't. It didn't need to. Finding Oghma wasn't a weapon to cut down his doubters. His family weren't his enemies.

Oh, how naive. The man of night eased through the new crowd of would-be followers, Grathson's sellswords, Xulfaril's minions. *Look around you. You are a lackey to your lessers. Have you fallen so far as that, or did you ever stand anyplace higher?*

Anger surged in Dahl. That's how it always went, wasn't it? He would go where he ought to fit, where things were sure to be right and he would be valued, and what would they do but grind him down? His family—they didn't understand him or what he was. The Oghmanytes—there was no help there, no support in his time of need. The Harpers—how many still held his mistakes against him? How many thought he was without merit, without redemption?

A secretary, the man finished. *That's the best they want you to be, because they fear what you could become.*

Yes.

"Dahl," his grandmother's voice said. His thoughts shuddered once more.

No—*I wish you were here,* the note had read, *You would know what to do.*

Vescaras, who antagonized him like no one could, fumbling in the doorway. "Goodwoman, I don't mean to speak out of place, but I think you ought to know that . . . Dahl's a good man, a good agent." Stepping up for him.

They don't fear you, he thought. *They value you, even if it's not always the way you want.*

He blinked and saw the cavern for what it was, saw that people had moved—or maybe he had moved without realizing it. Bodhar with a blackened eye, a bleeding lip. Suddenly his knuckles were throbbing—he looked down at the ragged bloody scratches. The marks of hitting someone in the mouth.

Of course you hit him in the godsbedamned mouth, Dahl thought, balling his fists again. He doesn't respect you. Laughed when you made clear he couldn't talk about her like that. He thinks you're still some kid, some stupid kid.

Farideh—squeezing Dahl's shoulder down to the bone, down through muscles tensed for another such fight. *"Martifyr,"* she hissed in Draconic. *Peace.* "He's baiting you."

Dahl looked up and saw the man made of night, his attention on Xulfaril, on Grathson strangling under some magical spell. He's baiting you, he thought.

You're in a lot of danger, he managed. He couldn't move his feet. He turned to see Sessaca glaring at him, as if she were the only one who wasn't in thrall. "Think," she said.

He tried to reach beyond himself, out to the presence of Oghma, hoping the god of knowledge might arm him, might give him some strength against this creature.

You know that won't work, the man said.

Why would he arm you? Dahl thought. He left you before. He led you on a merry chase. And for what? To make you grovel? To make you humble? What do you need to be humble for?

My champion, my wayward son . . . the path's well-trod, the hunting's poor.

Farideh—streaked and dusty and puffy-eyed and the moment he'd realized he had it all wrong. He loved her and he'd wasted so much time pretending that he didn't, because someone like him didn't fall for someone like her. Because he already knew the answer, even though he hadn't thought about the question.

So turn your face into the wind . . . My champion, my wayward son. The echo of the god's presence, a memory held by every corner of Dahl's being shivered through him.

Dahl blinked. Saw his brothers fighting one another. Gods' books, he swore at himself. Keep it together. He managed four steps toward them—grab Thost around the neck, get him off-balance, get him to listen—

Do you know why your god isn't here? the man asked. His fingers slid through Dahl's hair, grabbing a fistful and tugging his head back so that he stared up at the cavern's ceiling, traced in eerie fungal lights that made his eyes swim. *He is not here, because you are mine, Dahl. You have always been mine. Who else prizes you? Who else sees you were meant for greatness? To scrabble up this rotting heap they call civilization. Deep down, you know your worth. You know your strength. You could crush them all.*

"Dahl." Sessaca's sharp voice cut the rhythm of the demon's threats. "Think."

Who else prizes you?—He shut his eyes, remembered Farideh, remembered the fear that gripped him when he'd come back to her after that first night, unable to quiet the voice that whispered in his thoughts: *She's changed her mind. You've said all the wrong things too many times. It's too late to undo them. She knows you're a fraud.* And then he'd seen her, voiced that fear that she might not want him still, and she'd laughed like she knew the worry too, and she'd kissed him.

She values you, he thought, holding to it like a talisman. Even if everything else was false, that was true.

Is it?

"Well met," Mira murmured, and his thoughts filled with cold nights in Proskur made warmer by their embrace, the taste of whiskey, faint in both their mouths, and the flinty taste of cave water this time as she kissed him. Everything dissolved again—everything but the moment, and memory, and this woman in his arms.

See? the man crooned. *You can have whatever you are willful enough to take. Why are you playing by other's rules?*

"Dahl," he heard his grandmother say.

None of this is right.

Dahl pushed Mira away—or tried to. The demon seemed to fracture his mind and his will and his body, and making them work in concert would have been simpler if they had been three completely separate people. "Mira," he managed, though he murmured it against her lips. "We shouldn't."

"I won't tell if you don't tell," she teased.

He'd never not wanted her—from the first moment he'd met her, he'd been struck by how sharp, how clever, how striking she was. She knew what it was to be a Harper. Or close enough. And she was here, in his arms, and human—what could anyone say about Mira?

Here and now, Dahl thought, are all that matter after all. Someone had said that.

Mira shoved him up against the wall, his collar in her fists. Dahl hooked his fingers in her waistband—

The crash of glass beside his head startled Dahl—he pushed away from Mira. The scent of rosemary hit him next and he gasped.

Farideh—"It smells like rosemary," she'd said, not knowing how intimate a gift she'd given him, just wanting to make him happy, to make things right. He pushed Mira farther back— maybe it would be easier, it wasn't what he wanted.

He blinked. The cavern, Mira at the end of his arms, eyeing him in a glazed and sultry way. A shaking, bony hand, green with spilled ink and red with blood, inches from his face.

"*Think*!" his grandmother shouted.

He blinked. Think. It would be easier to give in, it would be easier to let the demon drive him like a horse to whatever fate the demon craved. Or he could get one of the scrolls out and make an escape. Even if it only sent them farther into the tunnels, it would give them a chance.

Think, he told himself, reaching back for the pack. Think of Thost and Bodhar. Think of Granny. Think of Mira. Think of the Harpers. Think of Farideh.

Farideh—arms around him, legs around him. "I don't want you to leave."

Who is this?

Farideh surged up in Dahl's thoughts again, and even when he opened his eyes, he could see her, as if the demon had summoned her to stand beside him. Dahl didn't answer, and the demon laughed.

I'll have it out of you sooner or later.

Farideh—sitting on the opposite side of the table, deliberately adding lumps of sugar to her tea, watching him over the cup like she was daring him to tease her again.

Farideh—lying against him, her head on his shoulder, her horn falling into the gap. "Gods you fit there perfectly," he'd said.

Farideh—burning like a bonfire, surrounded by the wings of a Hellish angel, pulling souls from the very stones beneath her feet.

Farideh—"I'm one of the Chosen of Asmodeus!" she'd shouted. "You cannot possibly love me.

Well, the man made of night said. *Well, well, well.*

Farideh—kissing Lorcan in the snow, like Dahl wasn't even there.

Farideh—saying, "I want you to promise that if he doesn't try to hurt you, you're not going to try and hurt him."

Why do you think that is? the demon asked. *A devil*—that *devil? He has to be protected?*

"He protects her," Dahl said. "He has to."

From what? A cold bed?

Why are you answering? Dahl's thoughts screamed. But he couldn't stop himself: "From the rest of the Nine Hells."

I see. A cambion against the full might of Asmodeus. For a clever boy, you're easily duped. Even I can see she loves that thing. *Even I can see he's going to win her in the end, unless . . .* He turned Dahl's face toward his with one long finger, lingering on his cheek. *Unless you are something special after all. Unless you can do what must be done.*

Anything, Dahl thought. Anything.

The man made of night grinned the grin of a crashing moon. He moved his hands in careful concert, shaping a ball of magic and power. Dahl watched it, transfixed, as it built to the size of an apple. The demon held it in one hand for a moment.

Here is everything you need, everything I need.

Then slammed it into Dahl's chest.

He felt the magic suffuse him, reaching every inch of his skin. For a moment he could not breathe. For a moment, he was sure he would die.

Never say, the man chuckled, *that I am not generous with mortals. That should give you a fighting chance when your rival comes to call.*

"What have you done?" Dahl managed.

Made of you a most fearsome weapon, the man said. *Now tell me what you know about Asmodeus, and his Chosen.*

No, Dahl thought.

The demon clucked its tongue. *That wasn't a question.*

"My lord, Graz'zt!" a woman called. The man made of night turned, and Dahl followed his gaze to the far edge of the cavern, where the cambion woman who'd tried to lure Dahl into another deal stood, wings outstretched, expression imperious. "I'm here to make a deal with you."

• • •

DUMUZI KNEW HE should be worried about Arjhani as four cousins helped his sedated father off the hellhound's back, but he found himself curiously numb, as if he were looking at an injury that his nerves hadn't yet caught up to.

The bits of conversation he'd overheard in the catacombs bounced around his thoughts, taking advantage of that empty-feeling space.

"Where's Anala?" Mehen demanded.

"She's not back yet," Lanitha said, straightening as she laid Arjhani on the stretcher. She glanced at the group of them. "Which of you are coming up? We need two for the stretcher." She gave Dumuzi a look that said she clearly expected him to volunteer.

No one said a word. Arjhani's head lolled to one side, his eyes half-lidded with the *chmertehoschta.*

"Well, I suppose that's me," Kallan said. To Mehen he added, "I'll be back in a song. Can I come find you?"

Mehen's expression didn't soften. "You might be waiting. I have words for the matriarch."

"Sounds like I'll track you down later." He smiled at Lanitha. "Which end do you want?"

As they carried Arjhani off, Mehen watched the sellsword go, and Dumuzi made himself avert his eyes. It wasn't his business. It was too close to his father's business.

Havilar, on the other hand, stared shamelessly. "Are you and Kallan brightbirds again?" she hissed.

"That is not your business," Mehen said. "You and I and all of us have better things to worry about. Go see if your sister and Brin have cracked the secret of that *karshoji* axe. I assume you," he said to Dumuzi, "will want to carry word to Uadjit." He looked back at the doorguard, a skinny fellow a few seasons older than Dumuzi. "When the matriarch arrives, tell her I'm waiting in the elders' audience chamber to speak with her." With that he stormed off, down the hallway.

"Gods, he's impossible." Havilar considered Dumuzi a moment. "Is . . . your father like that?" she asked, more subdued than Dumuzi could ever remember seeing her.

"We don't talk very much," Dumuzi said. "I don't interest him. And . . ." He shut his mouth around the words. "Sorry, I'm not feeling well."

"You and me both," Havilar said. She scratched the hellhound's neck. "I wish the Lance Defenders would hurry up and get rid of that thing. You'd think they weren't even trying."

Dumuzi shook his head. "This city is a warren. They built it out of rubble with the magic of a relic—not everything lines up right and not everything was constructed together. There are tens of thousands of places to hide. The catacombs alone are far bigger than you'd imagine."

Havilar squinted at him. "How many people can have died in a hundred years?"

"Not just them," Dumuzi said. "Everyone who died in the Blue Fire. Everyone who died in the other world, whose bones made it through. And room for every descendent who will one day pass."

Havilar made a face. "That's kind of morbid. You know exactly where you'll be buried?"

Dumuzi blinked at her. "You *don't?*"

"I try not to think about it," she said. "Are you coming back to the rooms or what?"

Dumuzi looked down the hallway, toward the elders' audience chamber. "I have to get a message to Uadjit. I assume I'll see you later."

Once Havilar and Zoonie had passed out of sight, Dumuzi blew out a long slow breath.

My father was more than fearsome. He was a tyrant in his own right, the kind of person that slips up unnoticed, until you look around and realize you're living in a karshoji *ancestor story, only the dragon's one of you.*

In those stories, the elders praised the values of *omin' iejirkkessh*—what the clan writes in your blood. What you should know to do, to say, without being taught. You didn't speak poorly of your sire, your patriarch, like that, not if you knew *omin' iejirkkessh*.

But if you were exiled? If you were cut loose?

Not even certain of what he was hoping to discover, Dumuzi strode down the halls of the Verthisathurgiesh enclave, not daring to stop. He slipped in through the audience chamber's double doors. Mehen sat with his head in his hands on the edge of the platform, before the center throne and the great red dragon's skull. He looked up as Dumuzi came in.

"I hope you haven't come to tell me Arjhani wants to talk. I have no interest in making my way through the *chmertehoschta*-addled babbling of anyone else."

"I," Dumuzi began, not sure *how* to begin. "I wanted to ask you . . . If it's not impertinent? If . . . if it's not overstepping?"

"Lad, *what* is making you so *karshoji* nervous?" Mehen demanded. "Every sentence out of your mouth takes three tries these days. What in the Hells do you think is going to happen?"

Dumuzi shook his head. "I'm sorry."

"It's that *karshoji* story, isn't it?" Mehen folded his arms over his chest. "You didn't tell the girls everything you know about how I got exiled, did you?"

Dumuzi held himself as straight as he could. "Not all of it. It's not mine to tell."

"Oh, so just some of it is? Well, out with it. What nonsense have you heard that's left you quaking like I'm some sort of *karshoji* warlord in an ancestor story?"

Dumuzi's tongue rattled nervously against his teeth. "I think you've got the wrong impression about me. I don't—I haven't spread gossip about my father and you, if that's what you mean."

"I asked what you've heard," Mehen said. "Not if you passed gossip. What do they say?"

"They say . . . They say that when Pandjed ordered you to marry my mother, you refused, because Kepeshkmolik wouldn't let you . . . That is, you had other entanglements, and . . . Agreements—"

"I was in love with Arjhani," Mehen said flatly. "Is that all they say?"

"They say you told Pandjed you'd rather be exiled and when he threatened to do it, you urged him on. They say before you left that you struck him. That you hit him so hard it knocked the tooth from his upper jaw. He did have a gap there," Dumuzi added. "A missing tooth."

Mehen said nothing for a long moment. "I'm surprised he never had that fixed."

"Is it true? Did you hit him?"

He laughed once, unfolding his arms and leaning against his knees. "No, I didn't hit him. I beat him nearly dead."

A thrill of horror, of *righteousness* went through Dumuzi. "While he was patriarch?" he blurted, as if that made a difference. The idea of attacking one's elder, one's own sire—to say it wasn't done was like saying people didn't leap from the pyramid's peak to get to the market.

But Mehen just nodded, grimly. "He was patriarch and I, his scion. He brokered a marriage with Kepeshkmolik and had it in his mind that I would settle down, quit 'dallying with boys,' and be his little spy, bring back the sort of information that would make Narghon fall.

"I told him I wouldn't marry Uadjit for that, that I wouldn't cut ties with Arjhani, and he tried to shame me. I told him I didn't care how that reflected on him, and he threatened me with exile. I told him I would gladly take exile, and he stepped down from his throne and challenged me. Like a *karshoji* rival. Like he knew he was going to crush me.

"He struck me for the last time, and then I beat him to a bloody pulp in return. Right in front of the other elders. I left without knowing or caring if he survived. That's why the very old ones won't tell the story, not even to make a lesson of it. It might give you young ones the wrong ideas." He shook his head. "He was a cruel man."

"I know," Dumuzi said, too quickly. "I knew him too."

Mehen straightened and let out a soft curse. "He was always hard on hatchlings. Probably harder on you for descending out of my mess. You have my apologies for that."

Dumuzi hesitated, and then it seemed as if his mind were elsewhere, floating, while his body turned itself, unbuckled his brigandine, bared the lightning scars to Mehen.

"I was *koshqal*. It shamed Kepeshkmolik that I begged to be returned," he said, his voice shaking in a way that shamed them all over again. "But after . . . after this, I couldn't remain."

"Ah, *karshoj*," Mehen swore softly. "That's not just from once."

Dumuzi pulled his brigandine down with a sharp, embarrassed tug. "No."

"How long did you last?"

"A few months."

"Does your mother know?"

"Some of it."

"What about your father?"

Dumuzi was silent a long moment. He had gone to Arjhani first, nearly blind with the pain of the burns on his back. Arjhani had pulled him into the farthest room of the enclave, salved the burns, told him he shouldn't worry, Pandjed would give up soon, everything would be all right. *Don't tell Uadjit.* He wasn't angry, he was afraid.

"He did nothing," Dumuzi said. "He was a coward."

Mehen gestured to him to come and sit on the dais beside him. When he had, it took several breaths before the other man spoke again.

"You have to give your father a little bit of slack," he said. "Not a lot. You don't have to like him, you don't even have to love him. But for your own peace of mind if nothing else, you have to forgive him for this. He grew up here too. He lived under Pandjed's thumb, less than you or I did, but all the same. It shapes you whether you like it or not, and maybe it forges some of us into stronger stuff, but you cannot make tin into steel no matter how it's tempered."

Dumuzi gave the smallest of nods, keeping his eyes on the tiles. None of this was proper. But none of this was fair. Maybe Arjhani was as afraid as he was—but why couldn't he have been better? None of that was proper either, and the words filled his mouth like river rocks jostling against one another, unable to settle.

"I still think he's a coward."

"You're right," Mehen said. He sighed. "But it's who he is. Your father is a coward and mine was a tyrant. There's nothing either of us can do about that."

"Why did you love him?" Dumuzi demanded. "Why give up everything for *him*? He's so . . . false, so selfish."

Mehen sighed again, his nostrils flaring. "You'll understand when you're older, when you've had some heartbreaks and some distance. You fall in love with someone and it doesn't always make sense. You fall in love because maybe you need something they can give you, or you think they can give you. And you don't see, until you've let it go, the flaws and the failings in that."

He didn't mean to think of Zaroshni then, but he did, his throat closing tight. All the confidence, all the joy, all the sharpness he didn't have. He loved her after all, or maybe just the parts of her he couldn't be.

"And you'll understand one day that your parents are just people. They make mistakes. They fail." He cursed again. "A great deal of them seem to leave me to have these conversations with you all, so that's one enormous failing so far as I'm concerned. But—and, mind, I have no reason to say a single kind word about your father just now—they have goodness in them too."

Dumuzi nodded, eyes on the carpet. "Your pardon, but I don't much care anymore."

"The problem I have always had with Verthisathurgiesh," Mehen went on, "with Djerad Thymar, truth be known, is that you have so little choice in where you belong. You are born, and that is that. But if your clan is wrong, if your patriarch is a monster, what do you do? It's cut yourself off or swallow it all, but out there? You have other choices. You can make your own family. You can tell your clan to piss into the wind."

Dumuzi folded his hands in his lap. "What about 'we are strongest together.' "

"We are. And that means you tell a fool when she's a fool, and a tyrant when he's a tyrant and you remember that all these things about saying and doing the right and honorable thing are guidelines we gave ourselves, nothing else. You don't owe your mother your silence because she's your elder." He shook his head again. "Pandjed's lucky you didn't tell her. The Uadjit I knew would have found a way to break him right down and never torn a scale. She'll make a formidable Vanquisher."

"You won't stand?" Dumuzi asked. Mehen only snorted.

"If it matters," he said a moment later, "I know those scars too." He patted his chest. "Quite a lot up here. I hate to tell you they'll probably never fade."

Dumuzi began to protest that he knew that, that he didn't hope they would, even as the pit of his stomach dropped at the confirmation he would always bear the scars of Pandjed's wrath.

Before he could, the doors opened once more and Matriarch

Anala swept in. Dumuzi sprang to his feet, bowing to her. Mehen stood more slowly, not seeming to notice Anala's perturbed expression.

"Run along," Mehen said. "Go see if your father's woken."

Upstairs, Arjhani still lay sleeping. Kallan sat on a chair beside the door, arms folded as he considered the farther wall. He shifted slightly as Dumuzi entered, hand brushing his sword hilt. He recognized Dumuzi and nodded.

Dumuzi frowned. "Are you really guarding him?"

Kallan shrugged. "I don't know what you think of me, but I don't want him eaten any more than you do. Plus—I'm not going to lie—that Lanitha said she'd bring me some tea and sweet *farothai* while I waited." He dropped his voice, "Between you and me, I think she has ulterior motives. I don't like breaking a girl's heart, but it's a little easier when I've got a full stomach."

Dumuzi made a face, and Kallan's smile fell. "What's that?"

"Nothing," Dumuzi said. Then, "Lanitha's one of the girls they're considering marrying me to. I have to marry back into Verthisathurigiesh."

"Ah. *Qallim* clause?" He clicked his tongue. "Nice thing about coming from a far-flung clan is you get far out enough, your parents' contracts come down to which homestead you have to wrangle livestock on which season."

Dumuzi nodded, considering Arjhani lying so still and slack he might have been dead. As they'd slipped deeper and deeper into the catacombs, Dumuzi kept imagining what it would be like to find him: long dead, freshly dead, desperate and injured, or even perfectly well with a bragging, roundabout tale of how he'd bested the maurezhi himself. He'd shied from every one of these, not wanting any of them to be true. The truth was not much better: seeing Arjhani, wasted and wild-eyed, spring from the tomb ready to kill. Feeling his father struggle against his grip, too weak to break free. Wishing—for a horrible moment—that he could have just been dead.

It took the breath out of him, that thought.

You don't have to like him, you don't even have to love him. But for your own peace of mind, if nothing else, you have to forgive him for this.

"That was brave, what you did," Kallan said. "Going down after him."

"I did what was required."

"Yeah, I think you believe that, but all those rules? They don't make you do a *karshoji* thing. They certainly don't make those catacombs any less creepy."

Dumuzi laughed once. "They're just a part of the city. It's scarier going out in the world, having no idea of what's done or not done."

"Which you also did," Kallan pointed out. "And which was also brave." He nodded at Arjhani. "He's lucky to have a hatchling like you. Hope he knows it."

The way he said it—as if he knew already that Arjhani didn't appreciate Dumuzi and Kallan thought less of him for it—made Dumuzi want to protest. But Mehen's words echoed back to him. It would be a lie to pretend it wasn't true.

"You want this spot?" Kallan asked.

"Yes," Dumuzi said, even though it wasn't exactly so. "Thank you."

• • •

FOR ALL MEHEN would have said he hated his first life, he found Djerad Thymar wrapped around him, like a mold closing on its casting. He remembered why he loved this city, why he'd sworn to defend it, why he'd dreamed—yes—of being Vanquisher when he was young and foolish, like every hatchling born under the pyramid. He'd said he had to come because he owed Anala, because he had to see Pandjed was well and truly dead, but those were only reasons to justify the pull in his heart.

But whatever his heart murmured, his eyes were clear. Thirty years he'd walked the world beyond the City-Bastion, with only his daughters for clan, with only the respect he'd earned himself following his name. And so all the days he'd been in Djerad Thymar, Mehen felt as if he were walking in and out of two separate worlds. One moment, perfectly at ease, the next finding everything foreign and false.

Anala walked into the elder's audience chamber, her gold-chased breastplate polished to a shine, her greatsword strapped to her back—every inch the matriarch of old—and Mehen felt for once as though he stood in both those lives at the same time.

"I take it you found Arjhani?" she said. "Is he well?"

Mehen nodded. "Shocked and in need of rest and care, but alive. He's upstairs, waiting for healers. When he wakes, he might be able to tell us who else the maurezhi is masquerading as."

"Well, that's something," Anala said. "You're not waiting here just to tell me that, though, are you?"

Mehen folded his hands together. "I've heard rumors you brought me here to stand for Vanquisher."

Anala's brow ridges rose. "And?"

"And tell me it's not true."

"Well, I won't *lie*."

"Have you forgotten everything that happened?" Mehen demanded. "You're supposed to lead this clan to victory and strength. You can't possibly think I'd be elected Vanquisher."

"To be honest, no," Anala said, removing her gauntlets. "I don't believe you'll be Vanquisher. But thanks to Pandjed, my options are thin on the ground and there isn't time to build up a truly viable candidate. You're the best option Verthisathurgiesh has."

"I can't imagine Arjhani wouldn't suit."

"With Uadjit standing for Kepeshkmolik? That would be poor form." She set the gloves on the side table and poured herself a cup of tea. "Besides, do you honestly think you're the only one whose trust he's broken? Narghon might make a lot of noise about you, but Arjhani's the one he'd like to toss off the pyramid. He's a vain little peacock and selfish as they come. He'll never be elected Vanquisher."

"He has a damned better chance than I do."

Anala chuckled to herself. "You're not seeing the entire picture. I think you'll build your reputation back," she said. "I think you'll end the elections better off than you started. But most important, while you won't be Vanquisher—you're right: too many scandals, too many old memories, too much gossip—when people start to talk, neither will Uadjit. You will bring her down even as she lifts you up. And who knows? You'll be a bit old when the next elections come, but we've had grizzled Vanquishers before. Is that settled?"

"You brought me all the way back here to spit in Kepeshkmolik's eye?"

"Not exclusively," Anala said. "Besides, that's a glib way to frame things. I would say instead it's preserving our clan, our city, and our way of life from their proud and near-sighted declarations."

"Kepeshkmolik has the city's best interests in mind, just as—"

"Please. Do you think for a moment we're better off trying to make ourselves more like the *maunthreki*?" Anala shook her head. "Ten years of a Kepeshkmolik and where are we but begging the Imaskari for their aid, the Chessentans for their attention. Put another on the throne, we'll be heading to *karshoji* Aglarond with shoes on our feet and our shields held out like beggar's bowls. Is that clear to you?"

"I think it's *karshoji* clear you're not so different from Pandjed after all."

Anala waved the condemnation away. "I'm different from him in all the right ways. Pandjed might as well have been the Starshine *karshoji* Duke for all he looked on this clan with anything approaching sanity. A patriarch who kills off his generations—a tyrant who devours his own limbs, and then wonders why he can't bloody walk. We would be *dying* if he hadn't passed first."

Mehen grew very still. "You killed him."

"No," Anala said. "He died of a heartstop."

458

"There are a lot of things that cause heartstop."

Anala's dark eyes glittered dangerously. "Quite. Many terrible, terribly handy things. We are at war, Mehen. My brother left us in the midst of our enemies with only our fists for weapons. You'll forgive me, I hope, if I make use of every tool I can get my hands on for the sake of the clan."

"I'm not standing for Vanquisher."

Anala chuckled again. "Hatchling, all I have to do is declare you. You can deny it, if you wish, but you won't save Uadjit—why ever you think *that's* worth doing. You forget your place. You forget where your strengths are."

Those two lives scrambled over each other—Djerad Thymar pressing him back into place, the world beyond urging him to roar and spit and storm out. "You can't declare me if I'm not here."

"True," Anala said. "You can always leave. But there are things to keep you. The handsome Yrjixtilex lad. The demon you can't find—"

"*Karshoj,*" Mehen swore. "You called it down?"

Anala looked startled, hurt. "I would not. You forget my child died in that thing's first attack."

"The child who risked humiliating you."

Anala set her teacup down, so hard that the sound of it clunking against the wooden table might have been a weapon itself. "I am not Pandjed," she said again. "And I am not Kepeshkmolik. What do I have to fear from hatchlings playing ancestor stories in the catacombs? I would not call Baruz my favorite, I would not name him my scion, but I would not have killed him. I loved him. I'm not a monster."

"But you'll use it to keep me here."

"If it works—even long enough for you to reconsider—I will take it. Maybe Arjhani didn't tempt you. Maybe the reminder of what being Verthisathurgiesh means didn't. Perhaps my offers of a kinder *qal* agreement, of taking in your foundlings won't affect you. And maybe you will find the demon and be ready to leave." She unbuckled the harness for her sword. "But before you start packing your things, I would suggest you ask your daughters what their plans are."

Mehen stood, all panic. "What have you done?"

"Given Havilar a destiny she might prefer," Anala said. "You should discuss it with her, though. If you'll excuse me, the first bands of hunters will be returning soon. I'll need the room to hear reports. And you have quite a lot to think about."

Mehen left the elders' audience chamber, feeling almost as disoriented as the last time he'd left Pandjed there. He should have seen this coming—every bit of it was there, plain as day. He found the little alcove and sat beneath the bust of Verthisathurgiesh Ana-Patrin, trying to get his bearings. Too many dangers, too many dice not thrown—sorting them all out would not be a simple matter, especially when it wasn't only about him.

You are not overwhelmed yet, he thought. After all, he knew what Anala wanted, what she had planned. And if Pandjed had taught him nothing else, it was that knowing an enemy's deepest desires was nearly as useful as knowing their greatest weakness.

• • •

Bryseis Kakistos traced a deep bow, though the demon lord only cocked his head as if she were a particularly odd sort of cave rat. The madness he exuded seemed to press upon the shield she'd made around herself before she'd descended into the Underdark. She marked the paladin among the milling mortals. A pity, that.

I'm busy, he said.

"You haven't heard my offer, my lord," Bryseis Kakistos said with careful deference that belied her impatience. The erinyes would not be able to trigger the portal by its usual methods, but they were clever enough to know there were unusual ways to make it suit their needs. "I think you will be quite interested."

The demon lord's lambent eyes swept over Sairché's borrowed body in a way that would have made a lesser soul shrink away or perhaps succumb to the Dark Prince's arguable charms. Bryseis Kakistos only gave him a mild smile.

"What I'm offering, my lord," she continued, "is the chance to destroy the Raging Fiend."

Violence danced in the demon lord's eyes, and the mortals behind him, the ones well under his thrall, reflected it—what had just been moans of pleasure became shouts of anger and pain and mastery. Graz'zt remembered the treachery of Asmodeus and the Nine Hells—not even the Abyss could scrape that from him.

Is it Asmodeus then who's played this little prank? Who thinks to bring Graz'zt to his knees? The Dark Prince smiled, a pleasant atrocity. *Does he forget I have long since mastered this plane? Once I reach the surface, he will find all his attempted torments are turned to my utmost advantage.*

Bryseis Kakistos guarded her tongue. How had the demon lord come to Toril, if not by his own wiles and accord? Interesting. She tucked that bit of information away. "It sounds like him, doesn't it?" she said. "Lording his so-called might over others in ways that hardly matter. Reigning like a madman from the heights. I wouldn't be surprised, and I think you wouldn't either."

Do you? Graz'zt tilted his head, considering the cambion from toes to horns to the tips of her wings. His smile spread, wider than his handsome face ought to have allowed. *And what do you ask in return?*

"There is a spell," Bryseis Kakistos said, "which can divide a soul from itself. Powerful magic that all upon this plane seem to have forgotten. One trusts, my lord, you have forgotten nothing."

How clever of you, warlock. Bryseis Kakistos hid her surprise. Graz'zt would know more than she said, she reasoned. He would make a point of trying to unsettle her, of course. *So I give you this spell, this gift, and Asmodeus will suffer?*

"He will *fall*," Bryseis Kakistos said.

The demon lord leaned forward. *And the others? The archlords? His conniving daughter? How complete is this vengeance?*

"When the king comes down," Bryseis Kakistos said, "all his vassals collapse. The very Hells will quake. What you do after is your own design."

Truly a revenge for all the Abyss.

"Every layer, but yours most especially."

All for a spell. How cheap a deal.

"It will take more than the spell, but I have all else I need."

You're very bold. He tilted his head. *Or is it just very angry?*

"Asmodeus deserves nothing less," she said. "Destruction comes to us all, one way or another, isn't that the song of the Abyss? His time has come. Asmodeus has plotted and dealed and made himself more enemies than even a god can handle."

And how do you plan to handle a god then?

"Believe me," Bryseis Kakistos said savagely, "I know how to divest His Majesty of that little boon. I will break him, I will *punish* him, I will see you have your revenge—for your betrayal, for the loss of your brood, for every slight the Blood War brought. And I will have mine. You can trust in that. Do we have a deal?"

Graz'zt began to laugh, a sound that echoed throughout the cavern, down through the Underdark, and into the very lacunae of Sairché's bones.

I don't trust anyone, he said. *Least of all you, Bryseis Kakistos, child of my loins.*

He snapped his fingers, and the shield surrounding Sairché disappeared in a burst of flames. Every mortal in the cavern straightened, turned to her.

Destroy her, Graz'zt said, and settled back down on his throne.

21

25 Nightal, the Year of the Nether Mountain Scrolls (1486 DR)
Djerad Thymar, Tymanther

THIS BODY IS A WEAPON, A TOOL LIKE NONE OF THE OTHERS. I keep the *crutch and the limp—it's a mask, a joke. It takes effort to keep from laughing. What they see is a liability, a weakling, a broken sword. They trust, but they pity. They don't know the maurezhi has been nibbling at their edges, indulging in a half-dozen souls as Ophinshtalajiir Sepideh, Commander of the Lance Defenders. I could pick them off, one by one, for days and days, and they'd never, never suspect Sepah.*

But time is short. I cannot return to the catacombs, not while they swarm and seethe with armored dragon-folk. I think of the meals I have, dropping like flies in the catacombs. I think of the Dark Prince. I have to press on.

I know enough—the defenses, the defenders, what will happen when the attack comes, what will need to be done to prepare the way—but, too, I know how to make certain there is no way that king of dust won't claim this city of primordial-twisted stone, this tomb-turned-city-turned-tomb.

So Sepideh limps through the hallways, nodding to her colleagues and students, heading for the Vanquisher's audience chamber.

The day is growing long at last, and the crowd around the broad-shouldered dragonborn on his throne is thin. Every muscle urges action—I could tear through them, bathe in their blood and their memories. They are few enough—

I remember the fight in the catacombs, over the unfinished meal of the tiefling, and choose caution. For now.

Tarhun smiles at the sight of the woman waiting. He stands, gives his regrets to the man still talking at his side, and descends the dais.

"How's our fiend hunt going?" he asks.

I smile. They know each other from years and years ago. They were comrades, peers. They've dallied with each other, in their youth and more recently, though nowadays they only speak of that passion with faint fondness, perhaps an eye to the future, but nothing more urgent.

"I need to talk to you in private," Sepideh says.

Tarhun grunts. "Nothing private for me. I've agreed to go nowhere without guards close by, until the creature's caught." He shakes his head. "I can't say I understand why. I can't imagine it would risk the Vanquisher's enclave. But I've agreed."

"Let them come," Sepideh says. "It will make them feel better."

"Just two," he says.

I giggle as we leave the audience chamber, walking down a wide hallway lined with trophies, dragon skulls, and claws, weapons of old. It's more than I can help. I pause as if my leg pains me, let the guards pass by. The doors close behind us and it's the easiest motion in the world to slide the heavy crutch through the ornate handles.

The leftmost guard turns at the sound, but he doesn't know quick the maurezhi is. Before he realizes Sepideh no longer limps, I am even with him. Before he can cry out, I've run him through with her sword. The other guard shouts to the Vanquisher, and Tarhun turns. I stride toward him, even as he draws his broadsword, even as the guard tries to flank me.

This one will be fun.

"Sepah," Tarhun says, not understanding what's happening, "what are you doing?" He's going to be difficult, I know, he's fought his way to this place, stronger, cleverer than many others. "Who put you up to this?"

The guard charges me, and I move too fast for Sepideh, tripping him, slamming him into the granite floor. I plant my foot on his head, plant the sword in his back.

"The True Prince of Demons," I say sweetly. Someone deserves to know, after all of this. "Graz'zt the Dark Lord."

Half a dozen souls are fresh in me, and with the power of them all, I wake the dragons on every side. The ancient bones rattle off the walls as I strip away poor Sepideh's form, as I re-call the ghouls and the dretches to my side. Tarhun could kill the maurezhi, but not even he can fight an army like this one.

There is something glorious in the way he fights, though—the surety that he will prevail. My master would prize this one, who has clawed and climbed his way to greatness, to the precipice of tyranny. He would tip so easily, I suspect. He would be a prize more precious than many who have sought out the Dark Prince.

But as the Vanquisher said, agreements are made, and I will suffer if that king of dust doesn't get his prize.

Tarhun ends the dretches as they force themselves forward, spears two of the ghouls. The dragon claws he strikes from the sky like troublesome bats. His expression is fearless, his sword sure.

But the skull of a horned dragon that snaps over his shoulder is swifter than it was in life and far less afraid. Tarhun bellows, tears the head off him, hurtling it to the ground, but the champion is wounded. The end is begun.

The urge to attack is more than I can master. The dragon trophies batter and break him. The ghouls rend his scaly flesh. The dretches snap and whine. Each sword stroke brings him nearer to me, and in my stolen memories I am sure I am witnessing an ancestor story unfolding. It's unbearable.

So I leap. I tear. I am torn in turn. The pain is bliss and fuel and fear—how can something so minor stop me, when the Dark Prince still reigns? For the Vanquisher this should be a fight that tests him, that pushes him to his limits, that sees him spring back a hero.

It isn't. It never would have been.

At last, he lies still.

"That one must be gone," I say, pointing at the nearer guard. "Someone will come searching soon." I set myself to my task.

Every bit—every bone, every sinew, every slippery organ—all must be mine to gain the power, the soul, the memories. They build as I eat, and he and I blur together with each step. The kidneys—and

I hear the names of every elder in the city. The muscles of the calf—and I smell the ordure in the bat stables. The eyeballs—and I taste the tea he drank with breakfast. Words build in my brain, stacking upon my earlier faces'. Strategy. Defenses. Sepideh's knowledge of what the city would do if attacked increased to what the city will do, and who will do it, and how to spur them into action.

When I finish, someone is trying to break down the door. The ghouls look to me, waiting for orders. I take his skin from the moment of the first injury—blood down the arm. With the Vanquisher's sword, I cut both ghouls down—my need for them is ended. I open the farther door, and lie down in the blood near there, as the doors burst.

More guards rush in—see the carnage, see their dead fellow, see me. They race forward. "Majesty? Majesty?"

"It was here," I pant. "It was one of the guards. It overpowered Shestandeliath Sepideh—I barely fought it off. Quickly! You must go after her!"

Poor Sepideh—poor injured Sepideh—she taught all of them and they respect her. This one they'll fight for, they'll run after. The other guard would not have spurred them so. They shout orders back down the hall. One helps me up, offers me a healer.

"No time," I say, clutching my falsely injured arm. "I must speak to Fenkenkabradon Dokaan immediately."

• • •

GET HER OUT, Lorcan thought as Farideh stumbled a second time. Shit and ashes, get her out of here. He caught her and steered her toward the bedroom, ignoring the silent wizard—a problem for another moment.

"Stop it," she said, her voice distressingly hoarse. "I'm not an invalid. I only fainted." She dropped down on the bed all the same, as if her legs had given out.

"You were absolutely under some sort of trance, and then you fainted, and you're bleeding from your nose." He gave a silent sort of thanks that she was clearly still dazed and unlikely to notice the tremor in his voice. "What in the shitting Hells happened?"

She didn't answer, only daubed at her bleeding nose with careful fingers. Lorcan's worst fears raced to the fore. He shut the door, closing out the wizard and anything else.

"Did the Brimstone Angel come to you?" he demanded. "Did she possess you? You need to tell me if she—"

"It wasn't the ghost." Farideh looked up at him, blood smeared across her upper lip. "It was the god."

Lorcan's whole being went cold. *There is nowhere to get her to,* he thought. *Nowhere that is safe.* "What are you talking about?"

"Would you be worried if . . . if your master were in danger?" she asked, still sounding hoarse and bleary.

"My master is never truly in danger, assuming you mean Asmodeus," Lorcan said. "He has a plan for every situation, a plan for every outcome within those situations, and another for every counter and reaction his enemies might have. Asmodeus always wins." He made himself pause and in the delay, asked, "What sort of danger?"

"I don't know," she said. "What if someone were trying to kill him?"

"What did he tell you?" Lorcan did not want the answer, but without knowing, without understanding Asmodeus's demands, how could he know how to stop her, if he should stop her, how he could protect her.

Farideh did not speak for a long moment, lost in thoughts Lorcan wished he could tear out of her head. "What did he say?" he demanded.

Farideh looked up at him once more. "He's not always himself," she said in a low voice.

She cannot die, the king of the Hells' terrible voice echoed through his memories. *She cannot be allowed to ask too many questions.*

It will be you that determines if she succeeds or she succeeds, the same voice saying—but not the same, not the same at all.

"What in the world does that mean?" Lorcan asked, slow and careful.

"You know what it means," Farideh said. "That vision didn't start out coming from Asmodeus. It was Azuth speaking to me." Her voice was surer now, though uneven, as if she understood at least that what they were talking about shouldn't be given words.

"Ilstan," she went on, heedless, "says Azuth told him to cast a fireball at a shield that was meant to deflect breath weapons. He nearly died."

"A pity it didn't work," Lorcan said. "I would suspect this isn't the god so much as the wizard." The wizard who heard the voice of Azuth. Azuth who *could not* be the strange and dreamy voice that Asmodeus sometimes spoke with.

Azuth who could only be the strange and dreamy voice that Asmodeus sometimes spoke with.

"I think they're connected," Farideh said. "I think sometimes Asmodeus is Azuth and sometimes Azuth is Asmodeus. And—"

"And when you started putting that together," Lorcan said, "the god of sin forced you into a waking vision. Does that not suggest anything to you?"

Farideh pursed her mouth. "It suggests," she said, "that he wants me to stop. But I don't think he knows—"

"He knows. Trust me, he knows."

"I don't think he knows," she said more firmly, "what Azuth overwhelmed him to say." She wet her mouth. "He told me, 'You know. And you do not. But what you do not know, she knows. Which is the greater danger, to he and I and all of you.' It sounds like maybe, just maybe, Asmodeus isn't ready for everything."

"Or maybe," Lorcan said, "just maybe, you are losing your mind. What's to say that any of that was Asmodeus's doing? What's to say it wasn't *all* his doing and *this,* darling, is his punishment for nosing around in his affairs? Darling, believe me, please believe me, the only way you survive Asmodeus is by avoiding his attention."

Farideh shook her head. "What happens, if he dies? What happens if *she* is actually a danger to him?"

"He isn't going to die. He's a god."

"Gods die all the time," Farideh said. "What happens if Asmodeus dies?"

"Asmodeus always wins, darling. If he dies, then I daresay that was his plan all along. Leave the gods to their own ends, whatever that means."

She didn't flinch, and that as much as anything unnerved Lorcan. "Who is *she*, do you think?"

"A figment," Lorcan said, even as his thoughts sped away: *Glasya. The Succubus Queens. Bryseis Kakistos.* The voice saying, *It will be you that determines if she succeeds or she succeeds.* "You should lie down. Perhaps sleep. Here"—he pulled the musty little pouch of herbs out of the pocket of his belt—"I brought you something. That tea you drank before, when you were having so much trouble with your nightmares. I thought it might help."

She took the pouch and made an awful little sound, half laugh, half sob. "Do you know he looks like you? In my dreams, he looks like you."

That startled him, and it made a new swirl of fear churn up through his chest. "Why would he do that?"

"I don't know. To make me trust him?"

Lorcan tilted his head. "Do you trust me?"

She laughed again, covering her mouth as the laughs broke apart into sobs. Lorcan did not move as she mastered herself, wiped her eyes. "Why are you like this?"

"Like what?"

"Like a devil," she said bitterly. "I want to trust you, but I know better . . . You don't have to be like this. You have a choice." She looked up at him, as though *this* were the greatest tragedy in either of their lives. "He offered to change you once. To make you a decent person for me. Give us a normal little life."

Lorcan carefully schooled his expression. "What did you say?"

"I said absolutely not. That's monstrous. You can't just make someone be someone they aren't."

You can if you know what you're doing, Lorcan thought, but he knew well enough not to say so. He let the silence stretch, too long. She wiped her lip again, brushed the blood from her fingers. "Why are you so concerned about the Brimstone Angel?" she asked.

Before Lorcan could think of an answer, before he could shake off her odd confession, Brin's shouted voice came through the closed door. "Stlarning hrast! Farideh!"

"In here!" she called back.

Latch the door, Lorcan thought. Grab her, get out of here. Away from the wizard, away from the maurezhi.

When was the last time that shitting worked? he thought, as Brin pushed the door wide, bringing with him the fragrant scent of food.

"What happened to Ilstan?" he demanded.

Farideh's eyes met Lorcan's. "Complicated. Is he still sitting there?"

"No, he's asleep," Brin said. "Knocked over on his side, snoring."

Before Farideh could answer, wisely or otherwise, the door beyond opened again, and the jingling of the hellhound's harness rang through the room. Havilar stuck her head in the door. "What's going on in here?"

"Did you find him?" Farideh asked.

"Yeah," Havilar said. "He's upstairs. Mehen's waiting to yell at Anala. Or something. Did you figure out the axe?"

"What axe?" Lorcan asked.

"It's a dragonborn artifact," Farideh said. "The head is possibly a scrying surface."

"We're pretty certain the axe has to be in the moonlight to work," Brin said. "It's what makes sense. But the moon's not coming up until after deepnight."

"*Karshoj*," Havilar sighed. "I was hoping this would end quickly." She frowned at Lorcan. "You can scry things. Can't you find the maurezhi?"

"And say what? 'Show me the maurezhi'? Do you have any idea how many maurezhi there are?" Lorcan peered at her. "Do you have any notion of how scrying works?"

Havilar scowled at him. "No. You find people all the time. You did it before—Mehen, Farideh. Hells, you found Dahl in a bowl on the floor."

"Because I *knew* them," Lorcan said. "The spell understood who I meant. Better if you have something of the subject—an object, some blood or hair, a signature. Better still if you have a more powerful scrying surface than a bowl on the floor."

"I think we do," Farideh said. A shiver ran down Lorcan's spine. *Beshaba shit in my eyes*, he thought.

"Let me see the axe," Lorcan said. Farideh stood and led him back out into the sitting room, where the lanky wizard was indeed sleeping deeply on the settee. She took up the weapon: a single-bitted axe, black as a spinagon's underbelly, glinting with gold leaf. The head gleamed like obsidian, unnaturally reflective.

His hands had no more than curved around the shaft but a cold so deep it shocked his nerves went through Lorcan. "Shit and ashes," he spat, jumping back.

Farideh clutched the axe nearer. "Are you all right?"

Lorcan rubbed his hands together, trying to sooth the lingering ache. "That's a holy relic," he said. "If you don't want gods in your hair, then I suggest you not take the bait."

"But does it work?" Mehen's rumbling voice startled Lorcan. How in the name of the Nine that man moved so quietly, Lorcan would never know. "That's all that matters, gods or not. Does the damned tool work?"

"You will have to ask someone else," Lorcan said. "It doesn't agree with me."

Farideh told him about the moonlight, about moonrise. "We can only wait."

Mehen's nostrils flared as he sighed. "And rest up. If it works, we're going to be off and running and *karshoj* to the time of night. I'll tell Kallan to keep watch—if Arjhani wakes first with a name for the last victim, that will be faster than the axe." He glared at Lorcan. "What are you doing here?"

"Checking on my warlock," Lorcan said.

"Then it sounds like you're done." He looked over at the sofa. "What in all the broken planes happened to Ilstan?"

The wizard was fine, so far as anyone could assess. Havilar and Brin laid him out flat and covered him with a wool blanket. Mehen left, presumably to update the sellsword, after giving Lorcan such a prolonged glare that the cambion had to turn away. Havilar followed, trailing the hellhound. Farideh went back into the bedroom and nestled a kettle in the coals of a brazier.

Lorcan followed her, standing close behind. "I could stay," he said. "Keep an eye on you. We could share that protection spell, just like old days." He thought of Shetai's summons, of the lie he'd told Glasya. *You don't have to be like this*—Farideh had no idea how terrifying, how terrible that truth was. "Things are not . . . easy in the Hells," he added, "it would be a welcome holiday."

Farideh turned, studying his face. Behind that frank appraisal were too many things, too many ideas. He could beg her for all his days not to think of Asmodeus, not to worry about Azuth, not to trouble herself with the struggles of gods. It wouldn't do any good. If she were happy to let the troubles of others pass her by, Farideh would never have become a warlock in the first place.

One would assume that you understand your position, Lorcan. That you understand what is required of you. You tempt, he thought. You corrupt. You find the thing they'll do anything for, and make it possible.

All our wants align, he thought bitterly, even as he leaned in and kissed her. One hand on the small of her back, just above her tail, one hand between the shoulder blades. Persistant, not rough. Her mouth parted and his plans frayed as she pressed close. For all the rest of the world mattered, to Lorcan, they might have stood in Suzail once more, everything neat and right.

Then she pushed him away. "Lorcan—"

"I'd stay," he said quickly. "Didn't you always want that? You share the protection and I would always stay."

But she only shook her head. "That's not what I want now. That's not . . . Right now, I need to go to sleep."

He leaned close, kissed her temple. "I know what helps you sleep."

His breath on her neck sent a shiver through her. But then she pushed him away. "You can stay. If you really need to. But I'm sleeping with Havilar, so not in here." She gestured to the door. "Go. Please."

Fury built in Lorcan. "How many times do you think you can tell me to go before I stop coming back? I'm not your shitting dog." He left before she could respond, burning with an erinyes' pride and rage.

Beyond, the sitting room was empty but for Brin, playing a flickery tune on a wooden flute, and the sleeping wizard. Brin stopped as Lorcan paused, considering the sitting room and trying to decide his next steps. Trying to get his feet under him again.

"Troubles?" Brin said coldly.

It's a step, Lorcan told himself. It's a process. You are not defeated—not yet.

"Nothing you need to worry about," he said, waking the portal that pulled him back into the Hells.

. . . right into a squadron of erinyes.

Lorcan froze—as much as he might have outranked his half sisters in that moment, he'd lived too long not to know when this many of them stood together, he was going to hurt. Four of the *pradixikai*—Sabis, Tanagra, Ctesiphon, and Zela, who wore their mother's mantle as the leader of the elite erinyes—plus six more of the lessers—Caudine, Axona, Pandosia, Numantia, Plataea, and Illipa. Neferis stood against the far wall, watching. She pursed her mouth as Lorcan regarded her.

Three makes a fury, he thought, counting them all. Nine makes a curse. And Zela to lead them—something catastrophic was happening.

Zela separated from the others, looming over him like a living thunderhead. "There you are. Unlock the portal."

Pale Caudine and red-eyed Illipa both crouched beside the gash in the wall, Caudine with an orb in one hand, a knife that crackled with magic in the other; Illipa with a staff pressed to the portal's edge. The walls gave off a low-pitched whine.

"What is it you're trying to do?" Lorcan asked.

Zela regarded him in a way that made Lorcan remember Asmodeus's good graces were but a paper-thin barrier to the *pradixikai*. "Hunting an oathbreaker. Invadiah marked Sairché. She fled through the portal."

Beshaba shit in my eyes, Lorcan thought. That was the purpose, the true calling of the *pradixikai*—to hunt down those who broke their oaths to the archdevils, and Glasya most particularly. If Invadiah marked Sairché as an oathbreaker—he thought of her cursed dagger, always tucked into the small of her back, always ready to mark the target of the *pradixikai*—then she was moving. Lorcan owed her his aid, but in the same moment he had made a deal with Sairché, to protect her from danger until her claim on Farideh had passed.

Danger like this, he thought, feeling the edges of that agreement tugging on his thoughts. If he broke it, would it break him? Would he be human enough to avoid the fate that waited for devils who did not keep their words?

"Where is Mother now?" Lorcan asked.

Zela bared her tusks. "Dead. Open the portal."

"*Dead?* How?"

"Open the shitting portal."

Lorcan fidgeted with his rings, trying to buy time. Invadiah, dead—Invadiah *dead*. He could say it until the planes all flipped like cards in a deck, and it wouldn't feel real. "You"—he had to wet his mouth—"you know where she went?"

"Through the portal!" Zela bellowed.

Focus, Lorcan thought. Keep your place. You faced the Vulgar Inquisitor, you lied to the archduchess, you can stall Zela. "Well if you don't know where she is, it isn't going to help matters for me to unlock the portal. It's not like it's a damned door to the next room." Eleven pairs of eyes glared at him. "Give me a moment," he protested. "I didn't say I couldn't find her."

He moved toward the scrying mirror, trying for unconcerned, trying for ease. He waved the ring over it and thought of Sairché, hoping the mirror would show his sister at the head of a particularly vast army.

The mirror shivered, right to the edges of the frame. An image rose halfway out of it, like a soul struggling its way out from the Birthing Pits. Zela leaned close, her face appearing in the mirror over his shoulder.

"Sairché's mucked with it," Lorcan said, waving the ring over the surface again. "Too many adjustments."

"Fix it," the erinyes hissed.

Lorcan hit the frame of the mirror with an open hand, then waved the ring across the surface once more. His reflection split to reveal a cavern—an Underdark cavern—crowded with bodies. There was Sairché standing at one end—

"Make it go there," Zela ordered.

But Lorcan's attention could not be torn from the scene in the mirror, from the man standing beside the object of Sairché's focus—Dahl Peredur, shabby and battered. There was a moment, slim as an eyelash, where all Lorcan could think of were the ten thousand ways Sairché must be trying to unmake his deal with the godsbedamned paladin.

And then he saw who Sairché was speaking to, and he understood why the mirror had fought him. He waved a hand frantically over the mirror, as if he could wipe the sight of the demon lord from the mirror. Beshaba shit in my bloody, stlarning eyes! he nearly screamed.

"Little sister trucks with Azzagrat?" Sabis said. "That's unexpected."

"Hardly," Tanagra said, baring her tusks. "Cambions always have an eye out for a way up. No discipline."

"Open the portal," Zela said. "I'm not asking again."

Lorcan's agreements pulled on him—nearly a year more of protecting Sairché, and there was no chance she would survive a demon lord. Moreover, he might lose Dahl's soul to the paladin being conscientious about his agreements and find the archduchess annoyed—if he lost it to Graz'zt the Traitor, he wouldn't live to make another deal, leaving aside whether breaking such a contract spelled his doom.

You have only one choice, he thought.

"Give me some room." The erinyes moved away from the portal, each fury of three lining up behind the four *pradixikai* erinyes. Neferis moved to stand behind them, as if she intended to follow Lorcan too.

He found himself thinking of Farideh as he took hold of the trigger ring. *You wouldn't be here if not for her,* he thought—even though he doubted any part of this path would have changed. He opened the portal, hesitating long enough for the spell to stretch, for his half sisters' hooves to clack impatiently upon the bone-tiled floor.

Cursing his luck one more time, Lorcan rushed through the portal, sealing it shut behind him as he did.

• • •

FARIDEH STUDIED THE glowing coals in the brazier beneath the kettle, picking out the shifting shapes in their embers, the fanciful forms in the steam and smoke that curled up toward the vent in the wall above. She studied them with a dedication they didn't deserve, because every corner of the rest of her thoughts was a riot of competing panic. If it had been hard to concentrate on the immediate problems of the maurezhi, of Thymari politics, and her family's happiness, then the current situation was flat-out untenable.

I gave you the chance to stay out of this. Farideh flinched as if to shake it from her thoughts. Just listen to him, a part of her urged. Just do as he says, hide your head, protect yourself. Protect the ones you love. You don't even know what's happening.

You know. And you do not.

Farideh flinched again. A nightmare, she thought. That's all. She could almost believe it. Except the way Lorcan had pled with her to take it to heart.

And then there had been that kiss.

"*Karshoji* gods," she whispered, burying her face in her hands. How had she let that happen?

Easy, she thought. You were there. You wanted it too. *Why are you like this? You don't have to be like this.*

She pulled Dahl's last note from her sleeve. What would happen to Dahl and her if Lorcan weren't a devil? How could she even suggest he ought to change for her, when she had Dahl.

Maybe that's what you want, a little part of her thought. Maybe you're just that cruel, just that shortsighted. She didn't want Lorcan. But she did. She felt trapped, like some dreamkisser, knowing it was poisoning her to keep taking the drug from him.

What if there was nothing for it? What if she would always feel that way? That wasn't fair to Dahl. Did it even matter, a little part of her asked, when he's on the other side of the continent? When he's running around with Mira—who he hasn't once mentioned—and you don't even know if you'll see him again? If he even wants to find you again?

Something lay between the fear in his voice when he'd left her in Suzail and the sweet words in the snake notes, and Farideh couldn't begin to guess what it was. She smoothed the last note flat, unrolling it between the pinch of her hands. *Your letter overwhelmed me, & I told him 4, & have thought of at least a score for myself.*

Don't trust Lorcan.

She eyed the shifting embers of the brazier. It would be safest for both of them if she burned the notes. It would be safest for both of them if she stayed far away from Ilstan, if she listened to Asmodeus.

From under the mattress, she took out the first note, read them both together.

Mehen returned before the water had grown hot enough. He sat down next to Farideh, his bulk tilting the thin mattress and pulling her toward him.

"Lorcan wasn't here to check on you," he said.

Farideh felt a blush burning up her neck, even though Mehen couldn't know about the kiss. She shifted higher up on the tilting mattress. "No. I mean, I think he was at first, but . . . something happened."

"With the god business."

"It might not be such a conjurer's trick after all," she said.

"What happened?"

"I don't want to tell you. If you don't know, it might be safer."

Mehen cursed softly. "Where does this stop?"

"When it stops," Farideh said.

"No," Mehen said. "Don't give *me* that. I've known you all your life. You've obviously made the decision that you're not going to sit still and let this pass you by. You've obviously decided to do something, never mind the rest of us. Now, have you done that with a plan in mind or not?"

Farideh stopped. "I'm still figuring that out."

Mehen shook his head. "Since you were tiny, you've been the sort to rush in and rescue, and worry about the consequences after."

"No one's rushing in!"

"No one is considering consequences!" Mehen roared. "You say it stops when it stops, but you don't have a plan to tell you when that's happened. You don't know who your enemy is or even what your victory conditions are. You have the mutterings of a madman, the messages of a *karshoji* archdevil, and a fear that you won't be able to save everyone—am I close?"

Farideh looked away. "I don't want to be the kind of person who sits on her hands when she could have done something."

"Take it from me," Mehen said, "you also don't want to be the kind of person who rides into battle without a plan, without a thought for what you can achieve. With only righteousness for a shield. At best, you're going to get hurt, and I can't sit on my hands and bear that."

Farideh considered the coals in the brazier. "I just want it to make sense. Doesn't it bother you that none of this makes sense?"

"Some things don't make sense," Mehen said. "Some things you need to walk away from because you will make yourself mad trying to fit them into a box." He pulled her into an embrace, rubbing the frill of his jaw against her head. "Asmodeus doesn't deserve your help."

Farideh hugged her father back, but kept her tongue. It wasn't Asmodeus—it was her and Havilar and Ilstan and Lorcan and more. Azuth. All the world, maybe—who knew what happened if a god died? Not Farideh.

"Which is worse," she said, releasing Mehen, "this, or panicking about one of us being pregnant?"

"Not funny." Mehen sighed. "Don't go back to him. There's not a man alive I'm going to think is worthy of my daughters, but . . .You light up when you're with Dahl, whatever it is you see in him. When you look at Lorcan, you look afraid."

I am afraid, Farideh thought. Loving Lorcan was like looking down over the edge of a chasm. Dizzying, intoxicating, but there was no way to see where it ended. Unless you leaped.

"Dahl isn't here," she said.

"Then there are a hundred thousand other fellows for you to bother with another day," Mehen said. "And all of them will be less dangerous than Lorcan." He rubbed his jaw against her head again. "Get some rest."

After he'd left, Farideh opened the pouch of tea. The smell took her right back to eight years earlier, when Tam had given her a similar pouch to help her through a bout of battle-shock and anxious dreams of Lorcan being tortured. It smelled like summer and fear and meeting Dahl, a time when the sparks between them only bit and stung, when if someone had suggested she'd be pining for Dahl Peredur, Farideh would have laughed hard enough to injure herself. Farideh flipped the lid off the kettle and added three fat pinches of leaves to the steaming water. The memory of being so irritated by him felt foreign now—he could certainly rile her and be riled right back, but there was a care behind it, an awareness of where they needed gentleness.

She tried to imagine Lorcan being gentle like that.

Havilar slipped in the door. "Gods, I thought Mehen would be in here forever." She sniffed the air. "Oh, gross! Where'd you get more of Tam's tea?"

"Lorcan." Farideh plucked the pot out of the coals and poured the tea into a clay cup. "Do you want some?"

"It's from Lorcan and you're just going to drink it?"

"If it was poisoned or something he would have made sure I drank it," Farideh said. "He's just trying to be nice. Do you want some?"

Havilar sat down beside her. "Maybe half a cup. I told Brin. About the Lance Defenders."

"He, um, mentioned." Farideh passed her the half-filled cup.

"What did he say?"

"That he really does think you should. He thinks you'd be happy."

Havilar wrapped her hands around the mug. "Do you think he means it?"

"Yes. But I think he's . . . sad that . . ." Farideh bit her tongue. "I think you should just talk to Brin. Or decide on your own. Do you want to be a Lance Defender?"

Havilar sighed. "I don't know. I don't know what I want. Would you stay if I did?"

Farideh drank the tea down to the bitter dregs before replying. "I don't know. I don't want to leave you here, but—"

"Right? I don't want to make all my life about where you and Mehen and maybe Brin are, but I don't want to leave you. I might like it," she said. "But I'd be so lonely."

Farideh squeezed her arm, feeling the tea start to seep into her veins. "If that happened, you'd make friends. You'd be all right. And it's not as if we'd never see each other again."

I am not an enemy you want to make, Asmodeus's words rattled through her slowing thoughts. *The one who gets hurt doesn't have to be you.* Farideh flinched.

"But you wouldn't stay."

"Mehen might still."

Havilar sighed. She knocked back her tea. "I'm angry at Mehen right now, so that's not a good argument."

Farideh blinked, her eyelids growing heavier. "Go to sleep. You won't have a choice in a minute."

I let you uncover enough to see your enemy clearly.

Which enemy? Farideh thought. There's too many to count.

What you do not know, she knows. Which is the greater danger, to he and I and all of you.

How many dangerous women did she know? Glasya, she thought, her thoughts shattering into broken sounds. Invadiah. Sairché. Mira. The Nameless One. Rohini. Helindra. Havilar . . .

. . . One moment all is blacknesss, the next Farideh dreams, but this time is different: she's not in Arush Vayem, there is no snow, and she's certain from the moment she looks across the landscape that this is a dream.

Under a full moon, she crosses a field, a desert, the ruins of a stone-paved road. Something slips beneath her feet and she realizes the ground is littered with Wroth cards, like fallen leaves. She picks one up—the Adversary. On one side, the true version, the archon chasing the devil chasing the archon, a never-ending circle. On the other, the dream-form, the tiefling woman who looks like her—one gold eye, one silver—framed by burning wings and pulling the grasping souls of the damned from the earth. And when she turns it once more, it's not an archon but the maurezhi, sprinting after an erinyes who pursues it, forever and ever.

Farideh turns it over and over, and the face changes. Not Farideh, Chosen of Asmodeus, but a woman with short, sharp black horns and hooved feet. Bryseis Kakistos, holding a baby by one ankle in one hand, holding a knife in the other.

Do you know who you are? *Farideh looks up at the ghost of the Brimstone Angel, hovering over the stone-paved road.* What you can master? You have let a weakling—a robber, cloaked in magician's robes—outwit you by playing on soft feelings. He cannot afford to lose these people—you know that and so does he. Steel yourself— a few more dead, a score of dead, it is nothing compared to what he'll do. He cannot afford to lose you.

Farideh turns the card in her fingers. "What's the secret?"

The ghost drifts, in and out of the dreamscape, her skin peeling back, her bones baring to the moonlight. I don't know. I know the past. I know the path that brought us here. Alyona and the broken vessel. Chiridion and Adrestreia. I don't know the secret. Ask Caisys. He lies and he does not. Ask the other.

"Do you hold the key?"

Her skin layers back over her face, revealing a hideous rictus before smoothing into Bryseis Kakistos's implacably lovely face. Farideh blinks and the ghost is doubled, as if the world is folded over itself like a sheaf of parchment.

The key is the secret, *the left-hand Brimstone Angel says.*

You were supposed to be safe, *the right-hand one says.* He gave you that, at least. Be careful.

Farideh lets the card fall, fluttering to the ground.

When it lands, He is there.

This time is different: he comes as if she's called him, he comes as if he's called to battle, and the god doesn't walk in Lorcan's skin. It's the shining archdevil she saw in the internment camp, in the tunnels beneath Suzail. Asmodeus, the Raging Fiend. The ghosts fade, the layers of their selves peeling away and away and away.

"Are we to battle now?" *he says, and his voice is a terrible song that threatens to crush her heart into a pulp, shrivel her soul.*

Farideh seizes the powers twining up her spine, the powers of the Nine Hells flooding her, leaping from her skin to form an armor of flames, the wings of the burning angel. The terrible fear abates as the flames build, and the avatar of the archdevil laughs as though he's never seen such a thing. The wind picks up, swirling the Wroth cards in little dust devils.

"I'm not your enemy," Farideh begins.

Asmodeus laughs. "You are not my ally. I am the champion of happiness, the patron of desire—and what do you do? You run from what you want, you hide from your desires. You sublimate them, burning them out of you like a farmer ridding a field of pestilence. How could you think we were anything but opposed?"

Farideh knows she should be afraid, but the fire, the gift of Asmodeus pushes it all out of her. "Then why did you Choose me?"

"Because I honor my agreements," he says slyly, "in the way that best benefits me."

"I know Azuth is still alive."

"Alive is a funny word to use, when we are speaking of gods." He twirls a hand over the cards, and they rise in a column of wind. His hand snaps shut on three and he tosses them at her feet: the Firetail; Draevus, the Trickster; the Godborn.

"Do you know what happens when the spark is stolen out of a god? The god is killed. Destroyed. You cannot pluck something so fundamental from a being and not expect it to collapse. Did she tell you that?"

"Who?"

Asmodeus only smiles. He tosses a fourth card at her feet: Tethyla, the Dark Lady. *It slides, top-first beneath her burning boot, and catches ablaze.* "It's not an easy thing to achieve either," he says. "Imagine using only your smallest fingers to tear the heart from your father's rib cage, whilst blind. You might imagine it—you are imagining it, my dear—but you cannot manage it."

"You managed it."

"And are we equals suddenly?" He closes a fist around empty air and the fire ebbs from her. She clings to it, but it's his to take, not hers to hold. As the wings fold in and gutter out, he says, "Do you know what happens when the king is stolen out of the Nine Hells?"

"It collapses?" she guesses.

"Very good. I am the linchpin, the core. My vassals may scheme—that is their very nature, so they must. They may try to pull themselves up into my throne, but I have been ready for that since the beginning of time. They pull, and their plans, their greed, their ambition break with their weight and fall upon them, so that the one beneath may climb up their failure to their seat of triumph. Everything is carefully balanced, carefully ordered. If you were to steal the divine spark from me, I would die and all that order would be lost. All that greed and ambition and carefully leashed wickedness would burst out—the Hells could not contain it, oh no—and so you would damn your whole world by doing what you thought was good. You would gain nine kings and queens of nine warring Hells to show for all your heroism, and two dead gods beside. And that's presuming you succeed—you cannot imagine there aren't contingencies in place."

The fire is nearly gone now. "What happens when he finally wakes up?" she asks. "Will it hurt you?"

The avatar shimmers like a heat mirage. Asmodeus tilts his head in a way that reminds her so much of Lorcan that for a moment she's afraid he'll change once more.

"This much we can both agree on," he says. "I cannot afford to lose you, or your sister. Stay alive."

22

THIS BODY, THIS SELF, IS THE SIMPLEST OF ALL—EVERY YEAR that he has *been Vanquisher seems to have stripped a little more of his true self away. The man is the role. The role is all they see. Every choice, every action he takes is because* that *is what the Vanquisher would do. If I had only been strong enough out of the gate, I could have taken this one and not a soul would have noticed, he is so easy to mimick.*

Not even the guards who trail me notice, as I march them up to the highest part of this city of stone. By now I know that king of dust is bound to be surprised—this city isn't what he's bargained for, but it should do.

Tarhun knows Fenkenkabradon Dokaan better, perhaps, than anyone else. They are comrades. They are friends. They have the city in a stranglehold and never once reflect upon it—they simply have more power between them and too many of the same thoughts. In their minds all is perfect, but what that means is the city's weaknesses are so easy to find.

The leader of the Lance Defenders is still awake—too long awake. How easy he would be to overtake, to add to my collection of souls . . .

No—I am full still. And I have orders.

"Majesty?" Dokaan says. "What's happened?"

"I was attacked by the creature," Tarhun says in a low voice. "But that will be its undoing."

"Chaubask vur kepeshk!" *Dokaan spits.* "Are you all right?"

"Of course," Tarhun says dismissively. "The creature hinted at a threat coming from the north, near the Smoking Mountains. Deploy the bat riders immediately. All of them."

"All of them, Majesty?"

"Of course," Tarhun explains, and paints a picture of a demon-augmented army riding from the north. "The creature is an advance scout," I add. "Sent to break our defenses."

It would never occur to Dokaan that everything Tarhun says is not true. It would never occur to him that it might all be true, every word, and yet it might also be what destroys him.

He nods gravely. "I'll send the order to the war drummers. We'll launch within the hour."

"No, you ready the Lance Defenders," I say. "Let me give the orders."

● ● ●

DJERAD THYMAR IS the ziggurat. The ziggurat is Djerad Thymar. It's Unthalass's streets and houses, stacked into the pyramid's shape, linked by its pathways and bridges that dark-eyed humans and Vayemniri alike march across, never looking down, never looking at Dumuzi. Through the crowds, he glimpses the dark gray shape of the maurezhi, slinking between bodies. Dumuzi's sword is in his hands, but as he turns, he cannot track the fiend.

The planes are thinning. Dumuzi turns to find the bearded man standing beside him. His Draconic is accentless, but stiff, as if he must place deliberately each word beside the last, like bricks in a wall. The old world and the new collide. The tyrants are reborn. You have to listen.

The drum of feet makes it hard to do that. "We've fought before," Dumuzi says. "We're ready to fight again. Always. We never forget." The stories of his clans, of all the ancestors, rumble through his thoughts. The stories persist because any hatchling might be the next. One day they might need such heroes. Shasphur. Nerifar. Thymara. Esham-Ana. Iskdara and Shurideh. He knows them all.

The man's dark eyes are full of anguish and lightning. Dumuzi stops. He knows the stories because he listened.

"Tell me," he says.

The man takes a step back, his eyes never leaving Dumuzi's. The pyramid spins and melts and turns into the plain, the ziggurats, the cities of dark-eyed humans.

I brought them here, *the man's voice rumbled.* I made this their home, their sanctuary. I breathed the law and civilization into them. They were my children.

In that moment, Dumuzi feels as if the man has bled into him. As if the dark-eyed humans are his *children, his charges, and what's left of his self will drown in that endless pride and love.*

I gave my crown to another, *the man says.* My scion. My heir. He betrayed me. He betrayed my children. I didn't know this and I should have.

The maurezhi slinks through the crowds, unnoticed and unstopped.

A storm is coming, *the man says.* Powerful enough to wake me, to draw me back from that farther place. I saw what had become of Unther. I saw what the Blue Fire brought. I see that the world is unstable again and you, who are the heirs of my children, are in grave danger.

The air crackles, the storm building all around them. "What does that mean?" *Dumuzi asks.* "What sort of storm?"

The man looks out over the city, consternated and silent, as if he lacks the words, or maybe Dumuzi is the one who can't understand.

I am close, he says. I am so close. But I have no children anymore. Do you understand?

Dumuzi shakes his head, and thunder rattles the city. The people scream and stumble, and the maurezhi slips out from the shadows again, leaving a trail of blood. "What do you need?" *he demands.* "I can help you if you ask, but there's so much going wrong. I can't even stop that."

The man frowns at the maurezhi, as if he's just noticed it. If a fire consumes the house before the flood comes, the house is still destroyed. I see. I know what you need.

He gestures to the sky. Dumuzi blinks and the city is gone. The storm is all around them, and nothing is making sense. The seething

*clouds split as the prow of a ship cuts through them, sailing through
the night, the full moon its passenger.*

*The ship dips low and a man leaps from it. He is dark-eyed as the
humans, but his skin is paler than a Cormyrean's, almost silver. He
strides toward them and Dumuzi realizes he is carrying Thymara's
black axe as he bows to the bearded man.*

*The dark-eyed warrior turns into a woman with an angled
face and softly pointed ears, her silver hair sweeping to her waist,
her eyes the luminescent gray of the moon. Dumuzi blinks and she
becomes a dragonborn woman, silver-scaled and lithe, a full head
taller than Dumuzi. She holds the axe out. "Not all with power are
tyrants," she says, and her voice sounds so like Ashoka's. "Not only
blood makes a tribe."*

*Dumuzi takes the axe. He looks back at the bearded man, but
he's gone. In his place, a dragonborn, as tall as Pandjed or Mehen,
his scales black as night, his eyes gold as the sunset. The blood of the
storm is in his veins and lightning sparks between his teeth.*

"Listen," he says, "Trust me. Ushumgal-lú-en ur-sag enlil-la-ke?"

Dumuzi jolted awake, grasping for a weapon that wasn't
there, gasping air that felt too thick, too humid. A storm is
coming, he thought. Someone was hissing his name, shaking
him awake. He blinked and Arjhani's narrow face resolved
from the darkness.

"Wake up, lad!" his father said. "We have to hurry."

Everything felt slow and disjointed. Everything felt as if he
were moving at the wrong speed, as if his thoughts would never
fit together in the right order again.

And all the while a little part of him screamed, *Go get the axe.*

"Hurry where?" Dumuzi said.

"The thing, the creature." Arjhani winced and rolled his
shoulder as if testing the joint's limits. "It looked like Zaroshni.
It killed Sepideh. It . . . it made itself look like her. After."

The maurezhi. Dumuzi forced himself to his feet. "Right."

"We have to wake Mehen?" Arjhani said it as if he wanted
Dumuzi to contradict him, as if he wanted another option.

"We have to wake Mehen," Dumuzi agreed. Without the twins, without the hellhound, they would only be cutting their own legs out.

And they have the axe, he thought without meaning to. *Ushumgal-lú-en ur-sag enlil-la-ke?* He shuddered even in the unseasonably clammy air, and buckled his sword belt.

"Are you all right?" he asked his father belatedly.

Arjhani nodded and shrugged in the same gesture. "Still have a shadow. I don't think I'll dream well for some time yet." He took up his glaive from where it rested against the wall, avoiding Dumuzi's gaze. "It's a fast *henish,* but it's rotten at keeping its guard up. I might have beaten it back, if Sepideh hadn't interrupted, but . . . I don't know. I might as easily have died."

That acknowledgment, so far from his father's usual boasting, unnerved Dumuzi. "Well," he said, "we'll find it. I'm sure we'll find it. We should go."

Arjhani led the way, winding through the dark corridors of the Verthisathurgiesh enclave, as the bearded man's voice went around and around in Dumuzi's thoughts. *Ushumgal-lú-en enlil-la-ke?* The woman who'd given him the axe made him think of Ophinshtalajiir Sepideh, with her gleaming silver scales. She'd given him lessons up in the barracks, praising his skill with the bow and the dagger. Said he was a credit to Kepeshkmolik and to Arjhani too. His chest squeezed tight. *Another dead because you couldn't see what was happening,* he thought.

Dumuzi slipped around Arjhani to knock on the door to the guest rooms. In the middle of his head, a growing pressure nagged at him, the beginnings of a headache. Havilar yanked it open and frowned. "You're not Kallan." She saw Arjhani beyond his son, and her expression grew stony.

"He saw the maurezhi," Dumuzi told her. "He knows the last victim."

"May I come in?" Arjhani asked.

Havilar turned on her heel without answering, leaving the door open and retreating to the sitting room where Brin, the wizard, and the hellhound waited. Dumuzi took a few steps into the room, searching for Farideh, searching for the axe. Trying to ignore the bare distaste in Brin's eyes, the tension in the helhound's crouch.

Havilar pounded her fist on the door nearest the exit. A few breaths later, Mehen yanked it open, scowling and half-dressed. "What?"

"He woke up," Havilar said.

"He knows the maurezhi's last victim," Dumuzi said more severely.

Mehen's gaze fell on Arjhani, as if he were looking at a ghost. Dumuzi thought of snippets of confessions he'd heard in the catacombs, of his own father's haunted expression when he returned—it was like looking at a ghost. Dumuzi turned away—he ought to have brought the message alone. He had let the dream distract him, let him forget what was sensible.

Arjhani cleared his throat. "Well met, Mehen," he said, all fragile formality. "You're, um, you're looking for Ophinshtalajiir Sepideh. That was . . . that was the, uh . . . *tiamash,* sorry. There's not really a good way . . ."

"It's all right," Mehen said, not moving from the doorway. He folded his arms over his scarred chest. "Ophinshtalajiir Sepideh. Same Sepah from our service?"

"Same. Can you track her the way you did me?"

"She won't smell like herself," Havilar pointed out. "Zoonie only found you because we had a shirt. We don't have anything that smells like the maurezhi."

"Right," Arjhani said. "Clever. Do you have anything—"

"The axe," Brin said.

"Might work. We still need to test it." Mehen scratched his jaw. "All right, we were going up to the pyramid's top regardless." He turned to Havilar and Brin. "Keep an eye out for her. Silver scales. Jade rings."

"She has a limp at the moment," Dumuzi added. Mehen frowned.

"One of her students let an arrow go wild," Arjhani said.

Ilstan stood, staring at the table. "A silver-scaled dragonborn woman," he repeated. "With a limp. I have seen her. Passing through the crowds of her fellows. A shark among the—"

"Where?" Mehen demanded.

Ilstan blinked and looked up at Mehen. "In the place where I was kept, of course. This morning, after I was released. I thought her a vision. There was something very unnatural about her. I was right."

"Someone has to have seen her then," Havilar said. Then, "*It*, I mean. If we're going up through the barracks to test the axe, we should be able to ask on the way. Or at *least* warn people."

Mehen rubbed a hand over his jaw. "Fine. I need to wake Anala, tell her we're going." He started to go back into his room, but Arjhani caught his arm.

"We should talk," Arjhani said quietly. "I think I owe you an apology."

In that moment, Mehen looked so like Patriarch Pandjed, that Dumuzi was sure he was about to strike Arjhani. "We don't have time," Mehen said instead. "Go send a message to your *qal*. Tell Uadjit you're awake and we're heading to the Adjudicators'." He pulled away and shut the door.

Arjhani turned back, his startlement swiftly hidden. "Well, I shouldn't go alone." From the corner of his eye, Dumuzi could see his father looking to him, waiting for him to volunteer or to offer his company. Mehen's words came back to him: *You have to give your father a little bit of slack.* He heard the truth in them, felt the quiet suffering of his father echoed in the bearded man's guilt at failing his children.

But there were other things he had to attend to that night.

"I have to take care of something," he said. He crossed quickly to Havilar before Arjhani could say anything more. "Where's Farideh?"

Havilar peered at him. "*Asleep*. It's the middle of the night."

Brin was eyeing them. The wizard had gone back to the magic he was working by the lamplight, his hands unbound while he crafted scrolls. Dumuzi dropped his voice. "I need to talk to her. Right now. Please. Can you wake her?"

Havilar cocked her head. "All right."

The door opened again—Kallan, ready for their trek up the pyramid. Arjhani, not yet left, frowned at the sellsword.

Dumuzi's attention snapped back to Havilar, heading into the farthest room. "How about I just come with you?"

He followed her into the bedroom without waiting for an answer. Farideh seemed to have stirred at the door's opening, propped on one elbow and looking blearily at her sister. The black axe lay on the floor beside the bed. "Is it time already?" she asked.

"Almost," Havilar said. "Dumuzi says he needs to talk to you first."

Dumuzi shut the door behind him as Farideh sat up, arranging the blankets around her "What is it?"

For a sharp, terrible breath, Dumuzi couldn't speak, couldn't tell her. This was all a mistake, he thought. He was having nightmares and giving them the credence of a hatchling.

The air clung to him. The lightning in his throat seemed to spark, and he swallowed it down, putting it out as he always did.

"I had a dream. I think . . . I think you might have been wrong about the kind of dream. Will you look? Again?" Dumuzi said, unable to keep the fear out his voice.

You already know the answer, he thought. She checked once. You cannot be afraid of what you know.

Farideh's strange eyes searched him. She frowned. "There's . . . something."

Dumuzi balled his hands into fists, his ears ringing. "No."

"It's a mark . . . but not exactly. It's as if it's not entirely there. But it's as if . . . It's like someone wrote it on a glass. Like it's over you, but not on you."

"Not yet," Dumuzi said. His breath was coming too quick, sparking in his throat. He swallowed hard. "What happens? What happens when I get marked? *Karshoj*!" He snapped his teeth as if he could bite off the rising panic. "The patriarch will exile me for certain. Uadjit will—"

"Dumuzi," Farideh said firmly. "You haven't done any-thing—wrong or right. You're not Chosen. And if you become Chosen, that's nothing you've done. The gods choose people for their own reasons."

Not this time, Dumuzi thought. "He says he comes to me because I listen. Because no one will." All his dreams were churning through his thoughts together. "Maybe it doesn't need to happen. I think I have to take it or he won't give it, because . . . because . . ."

I don't know, he thought. I don't know about any of this.

"Who?" Havilar said.

Dumuzi shook his head. "He's never said his name. I think . . . I'm afraid he was a god here, before the Blue Fire, before the Vayemniri came. He showed me . . . cities that were here, that don't exist. He said he left the world behind, left another god in charge. His scion. The scion turned out to be a tyrant."

A shudder went through him at the memory of the earlier dream, of standing on the ziggurat's steps with the cold oppressive mind of that lost son. "And then everything went wrong. He lost his children. The ones that survived the tyrant were taken away in the Blue Fire. He's all alone. I think he . . ." He tapped his tongue against the roof of his mouth. "I think he wants me to have the axe."

"Not fair," Havilar said.

"He's a human god?" Farideh said.

Dumuzi nodded. "I think. He looks . . . he looks . . ." He unclenched his hands to touch the axe, the carvings along the shaft. "Like these. Dark eyes. Dark hair. Heavy beard. But then, just now, he turned into a Vayemniri—dark scales, gold eyes. Lightning in his teeth. I think . . . he has something to do with the lightning. The dreams always have lightning. And he asks the same thing." Dumuzi closed his eyes. "*Ushumgal-lú-en ur-sag enlil-la-ke?*"

Farideh frowned. She climbed out of bed, crossing to the dressing table, and pulled out her ritual book, a fistful of compo-nents: a bottle of ink, a bone-white feather, a fistful of pouches.

Murmuring a spell, she poured a silver powder into a square around the bottle, then a second grayish dust into a line across the square. Dumuzi shivered as Farideh dipped the feather into the bottle of ink and then brushed it against her eyes and her ears.

"Say it again," she told him. "The words he asks you."

Dumuzi hesitated. He didn't want to know. "*Ushumgal-lú-en ur-sag enlil-la-ke*?"

Farideh shut her eyes, the air suddenly denser, thick as if it were full of lightning. Dumuzi's pulse sped at the sensation. He felt as if his throat were closing shut, as if he might cry or choke or burst with the lightning breath.

"Dragon-man," she said, carefully, "Are you the warrior of Enlil?" She opened her eyes, surprised. "Enlil?"

"Where's Enlil?" Havilar asked. "Is that a homestead?"

Farideh shook her head. "No, it's a person. A god. I've heard it before—it was a name in the Supernal book Dahl and I were using to find out what Ilstan's Chosen mark said. Dahl told me a list of names it wasn't, and Enlil was one. He's definitely a god." She gave Dumuzi a solemn look. "He might be your god."

"I don't *have* a god!" Dumuzi snapped.

"Does he say why he's pestering you *now*?" Havilar asked. "Handing you amazing axes because you dream too much?"

Dumuzi let his teeth gap, full of nerves and worry. He could feel the lightning building again, fuzzy in the back of his throat. "He says there's a storm coming. He says he can't let it happen again. He doesn't say when it happened before, so I don't know if that's something else, something worse, or if he means the tyrant or if he means Tiamat, who destroyed the old city." He clacked his teeth. "He didn't give me the axe in the dream. There was another god this time— another man, a warrior with a boat who sailed the moon across the sky. Then he turned into a woman, an elf maybe? Then *she* turned into a Vayemniri, a woman with silver scales. She said 'Not all with power are tyrants; not only blood makes a tribe.' And she handed me the axe."

The twins stared at him for a long, uncomfortable moment, before Havilar shivered visibly. "You can have the axe," she conceded. "*Karshoj.*"

"Are there two gods claiming me?" Dumuzi asked.

"No," Farideh said. "I promise."

That was something. "I think . . . I think the axe is supposed to help us stop the maurezhi." He told them about the maurezhi in his dream, Enlil's curious metaphor about the house. "It might be a sort of overture," he said. "A gift so I trust him. So I listen."

So I yoke myself, he thought.

"Maybe." Farideh held out the axe to him. "Ilstan says it's a scrying surface. But it only works under particular conditions. We think it has to be used in the moonlight." She held it out to him. "Maybe it has to be you too."

Dumuzi eyed the axe, every lesson he'd ever learned insisting he not take it. Vayemniri didn't yoke themselves to tyrants like dragons or gods. Vayemniri didn't grasp at easy answers.

But Vayemniri, he thought, don't leave their own to die.

"I'll come with you," he said, a compromise, "but you try it first, please. If I don't need to encourage matters, that will be for the best, I think."

Farideh pulled the axe back to her. "Fair enough." She looked over at Havilar. "Everyone else ready?"

The sudden pulse of drums echoing through Djerad Thymar, vibrating the very stones, startled Dumuzi, stopping his answer. He jumped to his feet without meaning to.

"What is that?" Havilar demanded.

"War drums," Dumuzi said. "They're calling the Lance Defenders to attack."

• • •

Every breath felt as if Dahl's lungs were going to explode. He clutched a hand to his chest where the demon lord had struck him, trying to get his heart to stop beating out of his throat. The cavern spread around them, real and solid, and filled with bodies all angled toward the winged devil woman who'd addressed Graz'zt.

Graz'zt, Dahl thought, and his lungs seemed as if they were trying to invert themselves again. The tide of violence rose in the cavern, threatened to wash him away with it.

"Dahl." Sessaca stood beside him, seemingly unaffected by the demon lord. "That's enough."

He shook his head, hand pressed so hard to his sternum he felt he might crush his own heart back into his spine.

"You need to think," she went on. "You need to stop this. What's he telling you? That you're special? That there's the right kind of strength in you?"

"Yes," Dahl gasped.

"Well then prove it, lambkin," Sessaca said. "Look at all these sheep around you. Look at these godsbedamned dummies waiting for someone to hold their stlarning hands and walk them through this. Piss and hrast, it doesn't even seem to occur to your brothers that they can fight back. Who in the Hells is going to save them if it's not you?"

The scrolls, Dahl thought. Whatever remained unstudied, there was the portal—he could get most of them out of here. There was the teleportation—he could get his brothers free, Sessaca and Mira, perhaps more. *Martifyr,* he told himself. Think.

Dahl reached for the scroll again, his fingers fighting him as he slipped it from his belt loop. He'd have to read it, to cast it without the demon lord's notice. He'd have to keep his head on straight.

I don't believe anyone, he heard Graz'zt say. *Least of all you, Bryseis Kakistos, child of my loins.*

Oghma's bloody papercuts, Dahl thought, his blood cold. The Brimstone Angel. She wants a new heir. She wants you on her side. He'd nearly gone with her.

The man made of night snapped his fingers.

The pull toward the devil woman nearly brought Dahl to his knees, as his mostly cleared mind fought. Even Sessaca seemed to bow under it, grabbing hold of Dahl's shoulder with her bony hand.

The Zhentarim who'd been under Graz'zt's thrall for the better part of a tenday adjusted their stones, their makeshift shovels—weapons when held another way. Some carried swords still. A Shou woman brandished fistfuls of arrows. They plunged toward the cambion in a ragged mass. Magic coalesced around Xulfaril, and Grathson gave a battle cry. Mira pulled her knives. Bodhar drew his dagger. Thost heaved up a stone.

"Stop them," Sessaca whispered. "Hurry."

Keep them close together, Dahl thought, riding the compulsion that drew him closer to Bryseis Kakistos. Keep them all in arm's reach. He grabbed at the scroll with one hand, hooked Mira with the other, yanking her back behind Thost whose stone made him slowest. He unrolled the scroll with one thumb, getting into Bodhar's way and turning him back toward Mira. Teleportation. Fine—get them away, plan better later.

Lord of All Knowledge, Dahl chanted to himself. *Binder of What Is Known: Make my eye clear, my mind open, my heart true.* A warm glow grew in the base of his brain, the presence of Oghma breaking through the demon lord's aura like the dawn slipping through the thick forest. *Give me the wisdom to separate the lie from the truth,* Dahl prayed. *My word is my steel, my reason my shield.*

Then the air near the devil woman shimmered and split, and there was Lorcan.

Dahl nearly crushed the scroll in his hand. Whatever plan he'd had was gone—there was only the cambion, only the searing rage in Dahl's chest, the sureness in his step as he followed the pull of Graz'zt's power toward his hated enemy.

And Graz'zt has made of you a most fearsome weapon, he chanted, his prayer perverted. *So I may do what must be done.*

• • •

MEHEN CLIMBED THE stairs, following behind most of the party where he could watch his daughters, his charges, and give Arjhani a wide berth. Only Zoonie trotted up the stairs behind him, too big to walk abreast. An army to face down a single demon—a demon who'd bested not only Arjhani but Sepah as well.

Ophinshtalajiir Sepideh had been older than Mehen by a year, had been the one to show him and Uadjit and Arjhani where the cadets kept their hidden stash of apple brandy and the one to sit back smugly when they'd overdone it the next night. That she'd become career, that she'd become a teacher, surprised Mehen at first, but then, she had the kind of temperament that would have meant letting her cadets have enough rope to hang by, but cutting them down when it happened. Would he have done the same, if he'd stayed?

If you'd stayed, you might well have taken Anala's route and made yourself patriarch by now.

With everything bare before him, the frayed parts of Mehen that regretted leaving all of this had begun to mend, to knit back into the whole of himself. Verthisathurgiesh meant strength and cunning, yes—also ruthlessness and severity. Djerad Thymar meant blending in and belonging to something greater than one's self, fitting in damned chairs and having food that was properly spiced. It also meant being locked into his clan and his past in a way Mehen found untenable. Especially when it came to his daughters.

He sped up enough to fall into step beside Havilar. "Anything?"

She shook her head. "Just nerves. Nothing else."

Mehen glanced over his shoulder at Zoonie, who nearly took up the width of the stairway. "You remember those commands?"

Havilar rubbed her arms. "Some of them."

"I don't know if I'm the last to know about your Lance Defender position—"

"I haven't decided anything yet," Havilar said. Her tail slashed the steps behind them. "I mean, I should. It's a good position. Better than I'm likely to get somewhere else, right?"

"Anybody talk coin to you yet?"

"No," she said. "I figured when it came to that, maybe I could use some help. I don't know what's reasonable here." She kept her eyes on Brin, walking ahead of them. "Fari says Anala wants to make you Vanquisher. Do you want that?"

Mehen sighed through his nostrils. "Do *you* still want to be a brigand princess? That's a dream for hatchlings and the very determined. And Anala."

"So . . . once we've caught the demon, you're not staying?"

"We're not going to abandon you," Mehen said.

"That's not really better," she said, with a sigh of her own. "I'm still thinking."

Someday they'll be grown enough to leave, he thought. And that would be right and true—a sign more that anything that he'd done well by them. Still, it was hard—he could see all the ways the world had left to hurt them, but he couldn't stop a one.

He glanced back at the hellhound again. "Zoonie seems to know you don't like Arjhani."

"She's smart."

"Make sure she doesn't get him confused with the demon. He's fast with the glaive."

Havilar made a face. "I'll bet I'm faster."

"You're not," Mehen said. "But you're smarter. It's more than a glaive in your hands at this point—Arjhani's got a better technique, but he's always going to fight like a scroll of methods. You'd beat him, not that it matters." He hesitated. "Don't challenge him to a fight."

Havilar gave him a sidelong look. "Waste of my time." Then, "You and Kallan seemed . . . cozy down in the catacombs."

"Still not your business."

"Then don't make it my business," she said. "You don't want to carry on with him, don't, but don't blame me, thank you very much."

Mehen tapped the roof of his mouth in irritation, thinking of all the things his daughter didn't understand. Thinking . . . perhaps she had a point. "Fine. We're done talking about it now."

This late at night and with the hunt for the demon still on, the Adjudicators' enclave was less crowded than it had been in earlier days, but the dragonborn who remained behind sprinted back and forth as if to make up for their missing comrades. They looked awkwardly young to Mehen's eyes.

"Anything?" he asked Havilar. She shook her head again.

The sheer mass of their party stopped one of the gold-pierced dragonborn in her tracks—a broad-shouldered gold woman with a sharp scar across one scaly cheek.

"What's happened?" she demanded.

"Well met," Kallan said. "We're looking for anyone who's seen Ophinshtalajiir Sepideh. It's a matter of extreme urgency."

The woman's teeth gapped briefly. "We're all looking for her. Any trace. But I'm sorry to say we haven't found anything."

"Who did she attack?" Mehen demanded.

The woman gave him a curious look. "She was attacked. We fear she fell to the creature when it attacked the Vanquisher earlier today. It killed two of our own as well."

"That's not possible." Arjhani stepped around Mehen. The Adjudicator's brow ridges rose in recognition, and Mehen recalled Arjhani had a ranking now. "The demon attacked me, three nights ago. Commander Sepideh intervened, but she was killed then. I was . . . carried off," he added reluctantly.

The Adjudicator shook her head. "The Vanquisher was very clear. Adjudicator Khrish transformed in the Hall of Trophies. It took control of the dragon bones—tore them right off the walls. Tarhun was barely able to fight it off before it overcame Sepideh and fled with her body."

"I watched her *die*," Arjhani said, and Mehen felt a pang of guilt. "It couldn't have been Sepideh."

"*Karshoj*!" Farideh swore. She clapped both hands to her mouth, eyes wide. "It's not Sepideh."

"This is not the sort of place for that language," the Adjudicator admonished.

"Don't mind her," Arjhani said. "She's excitable."

"It's *not* Sepideh!" Farideh said more loudly, and Mehen realized what she meant.

"Tarhun."

"It must have gone in as Sepideh," Farideh said. "Killed one of the guards—or both—and then killed Tarhun."

Mehen cursed. "And covered the fact that its attack would absolutely be heard and noticed by setting everyone on a false trail. After all, who can best the Vanquisher?"

"It's getting cleverer," Farideh said. "This isn't the same maurezhi that left all those hatchlings to be found, that killed the Zhentarim in an obvious place. It planned ahead. It waited until it had its strength back. It gathered the resources it needed to overpower someone like Tarhun and then it set things up to make everyone run a different way."

"Where's the Vanquisher now?" Kallan asked.

The Adjudicator shook her head. "He said he had to speak with Dokaan. I'll go and get him." She sprinted off and returned swiftly with a harried-looking Fenkenkabradon Dokaan. Age had treated Mehen's old swordwork teacher well—but for the gray edging his scales, the sag around his eyes, he looked just the same, thirty years on. Down to the fierce expression.

"What nonsense are you spreading?" he demanded of Arjhani. "The Vanquisher is no imposter—I would know him!"

"Uncle," Kallan said with all his homestead manners, "to be frank, that is just how the creature works. It mimics like none other."

"I *watched* Sepah die," Arjhani repeated. "The thing paralyzed me, and I watched it devour her—*she* was the maurezhi when the Vanquisher went walking. If Tarhun is saying otherwise . . ."

"We have ways to be certain," Mehen added. "If you show us to the Vanquisher."

Dokaan shook his head. "He's not here. He went down to the market, to give orders to the war drummers." His teeth gapped in agitation. "*Chaubask vur kepeshk*—what have I done?"

"What orders did he give?" Mehen asked.

"They're sending the bat riders north," a new voice said. "That's the rhythm."

501

Havilar looked back over her shoulder—Kepeshkmolik Uadjit stood in the entryway, armored to the edges and wearing enough blades to make Mehen want to turn and tell Havilar not to get ideas. She was flanked by a handful of armed Kepeshkmolik guards.

"You have a plan?" she said.

"Girls?" Mehen asked.

"I'm fine," Havilar said.

Farideh considered Uadjit and the guards, then nodded once. "They're fine."

Uadjit gave Mehen a sour look. "We cannot be too careful," Mehen said. He looked back at Dokaan. "Have all the riders left?"

"Most of them. I'll ground the remainder. Tell the drummers to give the order to land. Do we have any idea where this *henish* is?"

"Not yet," Mehen said. "But that won't last long."

23

LORCAN KEPT HIS EYES CAREFULLY OFF THE DEMON LORD. Don't pay him mind. Don't pay him mind. He scanned the swarm of enchanted mortals, dodging a shower of thrown stones. Thirty, maybe, forty? All aimed at Sairché.

This is adorable, Graz'zt chuckled. *Two little cambions, playing at archdevils. Each of you thought—all on your little owns—that you'd come to me and leave alive? How droll.*

The power of the demon lord ate at the edges of Lorcan's thoughts, Graz'zt's very nature dissolving everything devilish in Lorcan bit by imperceptible bit. The diabolic and the demonic could not coexist. The Blood War had raged too long not to etch itself into their every fiber.

Speed would be everything if Lorcan was going to snatch a few lambs back from the jaws of this wolf.

"Sairché!" he shouted, never letting go of the trigger ring for the portal. His sister looked at him, annoyed beyond measure. "You shitting idiot—give me your hand."

"You need to get out of here," she said, calm and measured. "In fact, take the paladin. She'll be so grateful you might stand a chance. And I'll have a little less to do." The first of the charmed humans scrambled up the rocky slope. She pointed a wand at him. A fireball streaked from the tip, and he tumbled into his fellows, a smoking hole in his chest.

Lorcan grabbed hold of her wrist. "I don't shitting care what you think you're doing—you've gotten yourself *marked* and I'm not about to let you damn me—"

"Ah, the agreement. I'd forgotten," Sairché said. "You can have her back in just a moment. I can't say the curse won't come with her, though—better you should think of a way around that."

Lorcan let her go, leaping back. "Shit and ashes."

Oh, have you caught up to us, cambion? Graz'zt said. *It's far more amusing still—don't you agree? She comes to beg a boon and this is the sad little armor she claimed.*

Four Zhentarim, their uniforms still intact, rushed Sairché and Lorcan. Lorcan flung a bolt of bruised-looking energy their way, slowing one enough to give him time to draw his sword. But Sairché calmly pointed her wand at the attackers. A line of spirits, doomed souls, boiled out of the air, meeting the line of sellswords head-on.

"You can be squeamish or you can be helpful," the ghost he hadn't been able to find said to Lorcan. "And if I were you, I'd keep in mind that, unlike Sairché, I have a vested interest in reuniting you and dear Farid—"

She broke off with a yelp as a bolt of lightning hit her in the back. A woman with short-cropped hair and a missing eye advanced grimly toward her. Before Bryseis Kakistos could retaliate, the wizard spat another word of power and a handful of bluish missiles streaked through the air, striking Sairché with a series of meaty *smacks.* Lorcan leaped back again as she turned—a stone sailed through the air, cracking against the side of his sister's head.

The air near them shimmered again, the air jagged as if strands of reality were being pulled this way and that. Zela stepped free, followed by the curse of erinyes. Zela marked Sairché—or what was in her skin—pointing a sword at the cambion that immediately burst into flames.

"Oathbreaker," she said, even as the rest of them took notice of their full battlefield. Without Zela's orders, they reorganized, spreading out into a V.

Only a curse of erinyes? Graz'zt said in a pouty way. *Don't I warrant the full* pradixikai?

Bryseis Kakistos scowled at the intrusion. Blood running down the side of her borrowed head, she shouted to Graz'zt, "You've made a worse enemy than you realize!"

He clucked his tongue, the sound of an executioner's axe resounding through Lorcan's skull. *Prove it.*

She plucked up Sairché's portal ring and blew through it once, vanishing into the whirlwind that pulled her into the Nine Hells before Lorcan could grab hold of her again.

Graz'zt sighed. *At least she brought me more interesting playthings. Look alive, cambion.*

Lorcan turned to gauge his half sisters' progress—

And found himself instead facing Dahl, storming toward him with a look of single-minded fury on his face. Driven by Graz'zt or driven by his own anger?—Lorcan had only a moment to curse before the Harper's fist crashed into the center of his face.

Fifty-eight erinyes half sisters and there was nothing novel about getting punched in the face for Lorcan. His vision briefly crowded with sparks, his face went numb then hot, and the first thought in his head was to run like mad.

The second punch, Lorcan had his hands up, deflecting the strike. "He's gotten to you, hasn't he?"

Dahl's answer was an uppercut that broke through Lorcan's guard enough to knock his teeth together. Lorcan lashed out with one arm, striking the Harper openhanded. The edges of his promise to Farideh traced his thoughts like a knife. Careful, careful—he scrambled back. The Zhentarim had fallen into violent disarray— some attacking the erinyes, some still surging up the rocks toward Dahl and Lorcan, some tearing into each other, given the chance.

"Harper, you have all of a"—he ducked another punch— "shitting song to break out of this"—another hit slammed into his arm—"before I opt to test the limits of my promise to Farideh."

Something in the paladin's expression shifted, and for a moment, Lorcan thought he'd found an opening.

Then Dahl's fist slammed into the unguarded center of his chest. Suddenly, Lorcan was dying.

• • •

THE PRESSURE BEHIND Dumuzi's eyes had grown steadily worse, until it was all he could do to concentrate on his breath, to avoid the sensation. You're not Chosen, he thought. Not yet. Farideh watched him from the corner of her eye. Because you keep watching her, he told himself. That's all.

"Are you all right?" Uadjit asked him as they descended to the market floor.

I see that the world is unstable again and you, who are the heirs of my children, are in grave danger . . . a storm is coming. "I'm only worried," he said.

Uadjit considered him for a long moment, even as they hurried toward the war drummers, the monster that had walked among them all this time. "You can tell me if there's something wrong."

What would Uadjit say if he told her? *If you are going to be Kepeshkmolik, then you must never refuse your duty like this again. The clan is only as strong as the weaknesses each of us shows.* And how weakened would Kepeshkmolik be if Dumuzi became the Chosen of a god? "Just nerves," he said. "I want to be useful." Uadjit frowned again, but let him fall away from her.

You're not Chosen, Dumuzi thought as they wound toward the drummers. This time of night, most everything was locked up tight, and what would have been opened had been shut by the cadence of the war drums. She never said you were.

"What were you talking to Farideh about?"

Dumuzi startled. When had Mehen come to walk beside him? "Just . . . I had a dream. Silly things."

He could feel Mehen's eyes boring into him. "So you told Fari?" he asked, in a skeptical way. He knows, Dumuzi thought. He has to.

"It seemed wise," he said.

"Are you having the same sorts of dreams she does, then?" Mehen asked.

Dumuzi swallowed. "I don't know what that means."

Mehen snapped his teeth. "*Karshoji* gods. Not everyone wants your yoke."

The pressure behind his eyes seemed to bloom into a deep sadness that poured through Dumuzi. *Not a yoke,* he thought, or maybe Enlil thought. *It should not be a yoke. It should never have been a yoke. You are our children. We are not your masters.*

Dumuzi thought of the tyrant-scion. "What if it's not a yoke so much as a . . . an agreement?" he asked. "What if it's more like a clanship? A *qal* agreement? An adoption?"

"Don't listen to them," Mehen said. "Whatever they're selling."

"Not all with power are tyrants," Dumuzi murmured. "Not only blood makes a tribe. You can make your own family. You can tell your clan to piss into the wind."

Mehen scowled. "What are you talking about?"

Dumuzi shook his head. "How am I supposed to know who to listen to when you all make sense?"

The war drums stood at the open end of the market, facing out onto the plain beyond. Standing at an angle, their stretched-sheepskin heads as wide as a firepit, the drums echoed with the furious beats of a score of drummers, a tattoo that sang orders out to the cavalry beyond and the citizenry within. An attack, far to the north, be ready. At every quarter of Djerad Thymar, Vayemniri would be waking, checking their arms and armor, assessing the forces they could muster if the attack reached the City-Bastion. We are strongest together. Vayemniri stand alone.

But the curl of anxiety building in the space behind Dumuzi's eyes didn't abate. We are strongest together, but what good is that if we march into battle unarmed?

The lead drummer's rhythm faltered as he noticed the small army hurrying toward him.

"Where is Tarhun?" Arjhani demanded.

The lead drummer frowned. "He was just here."

"Stop the drums," Arjhani said. "Call them down, call them *back*. There's been a mistake."

"Where did he go?" Mehen said.

The drummer looked from one to the other. "Outside, and what about the Vanquisher's order?"

"That wasn't the Vanquisher," Uadjit said.

Dumuzi looked over at Havilar. "Anything?"

Instead of answering, she walked out the open side of the pyramid, into the streets beyond. Farideh chased after her, and Dumuzi found himself following, looking for the shape of the demon, or another Vayemnri. The air tasted like lightning, and whether it came from his own throat or the clouds that seemed to gather on the horizon, he couldn't have said.

Havilar stopped at the edge of the next street. "It was here," she said. "It's somewhere . . . I can't . . ."

Farideh yanked the black axe free of its place at her belt, searching the sky. The moon, nearly full, had only just breached the horizon, sailing slowly over the scattered buildings surrounding Djerad Thymar, painting a silver path across the grasslands beyond. She held the axe at an angle, trying to catch the beams of moonlight just so. Dumuzi watched, his breath caught in his teeth—maybe it would work, maybe it would show nothing. Maybe Farideh would be the bearer. Maybe it would be just an axe.

A flash.

A flicker—a bronze-scaled man, broad-faced, broad-shouldered. Stooped? Reaching? The image was gone before Dumuzi could tell, before he could see any hint of where the Vanquisher was. Farideh spat a curse, trying to catch the moon just so again.

Again, the Vanquisher; again, he was gone before anyone could make sense of him, his strange posture. Farideh looked up at him.

"Try again," he said.

"Take the axe, *pothachi*," Havilar yanked the axe from her sister and shoved it into Dumuzi's hands. "This is what your dream was about."

Dumuzi's hands closed around the axe—it was a weapon, after all, you didn't let a weapon drop. A strange jolt went through him, as if all the muscles of his arms and back had twitched together. It felt warm in his hands.

Tapping the roof of his mouth, he tilted the glassy blade toward the moon.

A flash.

A flicker.

A clutch of panic in his chest, and the pressure behind his eyes seemed to spread.

You want to be an ally, he thought. *Show me. Help me. Something terrible is about to happen. Help me, and I'll know we are comrades.*

The full moon's light poured down on him, painting a path across the plain, the way it had for Thymara so long ago. There was no voice in his thoughts, however, no indication that a god would take him by the hand—

A flash. A flicker. An image.

The Vanquisher's form scaling a hill of stone, the edge of him traced in the moonlight.

Dumuzi turned. The dark shape of a body, crawling up Djerad Thymar stood out from the fainter shadows, two-thirds of the way to the platform at the peak.

Hurry! This time, Dumuzi felt sure it was the god. *Listen. Listen, and I can help you.*

"Up!" he cried. "It's climbing the pyramid." The shortest route to the peak—and without thinking, he began to climb after it. *I am listening,* he told the god seeping into his head. *I am listening if you can help me. But no one else takes the yoke. No one else makes this agreement.*

Anguish again, frustration—*not a yoke, not a yoke.* The tyrant-scion—a name, Gilgeam—the five-headed dragon queen—anger and anguish. How badly the world hurts because of ones like them.

Dumuzi gritted his teeth and sprinted for the pyramid's stones. He thought of his dead friends, and his new ones, his clans and the people at the pyramid's top who didn't know what was coming for them. His father shouted at him, but he ignored it. *Give me the yoke, I will take it if this stops.*

The god grew calm behind his eyes.

Climb, Ushamgal-lú, *and I will climb with you,* Enlil whispered in Dumuzi's thoughts. *Your heart is strong enough for both of us.*

509

• • •

As Dahl's fist struck Lorcan, the same surge of power went through him as when Graz'zt had slammed the ball of magic into his own chest. It sucked the air from his lungs, the pulse from his blood, the strength from his marrow.

The cambion fared worse. His black eyes widened, the breath going out of him. For a moment, every vein in his face stood out, a tracery of black lines like tributaries on a hideous map. A web of grayish, clinging magic seemed to coat him, to drag *through* him. Lorcan gave an ugly grunt and convulsed once as the spell seemed to pull something vital out of him. His legs buckled, sending him to his knees.

Oghma's bloody papercuts. Dahl took a stumbling step back.

"I want you to promise," Farideh had said, "that if he doesn't try to hurt you, you're not going to try and hurt him."

You haven't hurt him, the demon lord's voice echoed through Dahl's head. *You've evened the field.*

No, Dahl thought. The cambion regained his feet, but looked like little more than a corpse. If he dies, Dahl thought, you might have doomed her.

"You have to get out of here," Lorcan rasped. "You fall to him, and I lose my head."

"I'm not making any more deals with you."

"You already made this one," Lorcan said, as though every word were an effort, but stopping would be impossible. "You stupid bastard—you keep your soul by holding to the deal, it's not my shitting fault. You lose it to a demon lord, and you might guess we're both damned!"

The demon lord. The pull down to some base, animal version of himself. Fighting his way out only to be swamped under again by the sight of Lorcan.

Lorcan reached out a hand. "I'll pull you out."

His brothers. His grandmother. Mira. The Zhentarim— he looked back over his shoulder at the seething mass of them. Thirty-five? Forty? He looked down at the scroll, still crushed in his fist. Too many to teleport, he thought. Too many to save. He found Thost and Bodhar and Sessaca in the mass of bodies between the rock shelf and the line of erinyes pressing toward Graz'zt.

The demon lord laughed, and every hair along Dahl's spine stood on end. *Zela, Zela, deadly dealer. More like mantle-stealer, now, eh? When'd your mother fall from grace? Same time Asmodeus turned your lot into boar-faced land-things?*

More interesting playthings, Dahl thought. He shoved the crumpled scroll into Lorcan's hands. "Cast it. Cast it as soon as you see me coming back, or I will throw myself in front of that godsbe-damned monster, drag his attention over here, and damn us both."

As many people as you can grab, he thought, drawing his sword. But it wasn't as simple as just hauling bodies nearer to Lorcan. He couldn't pull himself up out of Graz'zt's thrall unless his thoughts ran to Farideh. Unless he thought about the one he loved? The one he would sacrifice for? If he couldn't get them out of that dark place, then they couldn't stop following the whims of this tyrannical demon lord.

Sessaca must have followed him when Lorcan appeared—she was much closer to the shelf than they'd been. She gave him the dagger eyes as he approached.

"Granny," Dahl shouted over the chaos, "think about Grandda. Think about Lamhail. You have to—"

"Oh Watching Gods, Dahl, don't waste your time," Sessaca said. "He's got no hold on me—I've got nothing to prove. Help me up the rocks and then talk your brothers down."

He lifted Sessaca up onto the relative safety of the shelf. Nothing to prove, nothing to prove—of course it's not as simple as it seemed, he thought. Letting his thoughts fall to his brothers—the family he'd sacrifice everything for—had done nothing but rile him and bloody Bodhar's nose.

Not Farideh, he thought, dodging an emaciated Zhentarim's wild strike. You don't need to prove anything to her. When Lorcan had mentioned her, his thoughts had even cleared briefly—he'd wanted to crush Lorcan, but not for anyone's sake but his own.

That's the key. Someone you care about, someone you have nothing to prove to.

Thost stood over one of Grathson's sellswords—a sallow man with a torn ear and a newly broken leg—a rock in his hands. Dahl leaped over the sellsword, shoving his brother backward as he raised the rock. Thost almost toppled.

Dahl grabbed the outer edge of his sleeve, racking his brain. "What would Dellora say if she saw you like this?"

Thost's eyes narrowed, his lip curled. "Don't you stlarning start—I know you've got eyes for her." He pulled the rock back and swung it toward Dahl.

Dahl darted out of the way, backing into another of the Zhentarim. The erinyes were far too close for comfort. "When I was six, plinth-head!" he shouted.

Gods' books, that was it: "Like Wilmot is! Six like Wilmot is! What would Wil think if he saw you, throwing rocks at an injured man? Screaming about your baby brother's tenday-long crush on his new sister-in-law?"

Thost startled, as if he'd woken from a nightmare; stared, as if he were suddenly seeing the cavern around them. "Wilmot," he said. "Hrast . . . Dahl—"

"Help me get to Bodhar," Dahl said. "Keep thinking about your kids."

Bodhar had gotten into a three-way battle with one of Xulfaril's favorites and a bedraggled man with shaggy hair—as if all three had intended to make a run at the pale-skinned erinyes nearby, now engaged with a pair of casters, and none would share the glory.

"Bodhar!" Dahl shouted. His brother made no move to acknowledge his presence, only took another swing at the bedraggled Zhentarim, dagger in hand.

"Bodhar, is this what Sabrelle would want to see?" Dahl tried.

That time Bodhar heard, but unlike Thost, Bodhar only turned, eyes wild. His free hand flew out, striking Dahl across the chest with his forearm, faster than Dahl would have credited his brother. "Stlarn off," Bodhar said. "You think she wouldn't believe her father has a chance in a fight? Of course you would, 'little' brother. Think you're the big man, too good for the rest of us?" He lashed out with the knife this time, fierce but clumsy. Dahl grabbed the wrist, knocking his strike aside and twisting his arm away—Bodhar moved with him, slippery as an eel, forcing Dahl to release him.

"Meri's going to cry her damned eyes out if we have to tell her you're dead down here," Thost said. " 'Specially if you die of acting like an ass."

Bodhar seemed to forget his previous opponents, eyeing his brothers as if they were his attackers now. "Don't *you* tell my wife I'm the foolish one."

Shit, Dahl thought. If Bodhar's kids didn't pull him out, if Meribelle didn't pull him out, what was left? It struck him that he might not know his brother well enough to save him.

Or maybe there was nothing he or Thost could say—*'little' brother*—Dahl had grown taller than Bodhar while he'd lived in Procampur, coming back one Greengrass a handspan over his older brother, much to Barron's delight. Bodhar was always the cheerful one, but a hundred teasing barbs came back at Dahl. Maybe he wasn't the only one who struggled in his family.

"Your friends in Harrowdale," Dahl blurted. Someone outside the farm, someone Bodhar didn't have too much history with. Bodhar didn't answer, only launched himself at Dahl again, stumbling past when Dahl ducked out of the way.

He glanced back at Lorcan—the cambion had the scroll out already. Oghma's bloody papercuts.

"Stlarn it, Bodhar!" Thost shouted. "You're going to break Ma's heart!"

Bodhar froze. Where nothing else had cracked the demon lord's madness, that seemed to strike their brother in the very core. Maybe he'd been as anxious as Dahl to gain Barron's approval—but he'd never doubted for a moment that his mother loved and treasured him with all her heart, and always would.

Xulfaril's lackey swung wildly at him, but he ducked instead of striking back at her. Thost shoved her off her feet with one good push, while Dahl grabbed Bodhar by the elbow, pulling him back toward Lorcan and the shelf. Nearly there, nearly done.

"Come on," Dahl said. "We're getting out."

He caught hold of Mira, just as she was about to run at the erinyes. She tensed—ready to slam her elbow into his gut, he was sure. But Mira, at least, would be easy to distract.

"If you don't run with me now," Dahl said in her ear, "the Master's Library will be lost again. Forever." She looked at him, alarmed, as the tension in her shifted.

Thost boosted first Bodhar, then Dahl up onto the rock shelf. Mira scrambled up unaided, while Thost came last, hauled up by his brothers. Behind them, Dahl could feel the spell binding itself together, the magic sparking and snapping as it gathered its strength. Dahl grabbed hold of Sessaca and Thost as they chained themselves together.

"Volibar!" Mira shouted. The halfling dashed at them, blade high. Grim-faced, Mira broke the chain of hands, rushing out toward the halfling. He swung the blade at her as she tried to catch his hand, and she dodged, twisting her ankle too far and tripping over a rock. The halfling raised his sword.

"Haslam!" Mira shouted, as Dahl ran to intervene. "Come on, we'll save your damned snake!"

Volibar stumbled. Looking puzzled at the blade in his hand. Dahl hauled Mira up under her arms, then grabbed Volibar by the arm, yanking the halfling close.

Oh little mice, are you trying to skitter away? The demon lord's attention fell upon them, dark as a bank of rain clouds, smothering Dahl's good sense—

Dahl shut his eyes. Farideh, walking under the rain clouds in Suzail from one terrible tavern to another, her arm around his, telling him an ancestor story called the Crippled Mountain. "But the Tyrant of Tyrants thought himself undefeatable," she said.

"He watched the massing armies—thousands upon thousands armed and armored—with the cruel amusement of a hatchling considering ants upon the stones."

"Honestly," he'd said, "this is a bedtime story?"

The taste of wintergreen and old wine filled his mouth, overlaying the bitterness of ashes and thick perfume. He squeezed Thost's hand hard.

You think you're escaping, Graz'zt sang in Dahl's head. *But you can't flee your own true nature . . .*

The magic clutched tight around them, so tight Dahl found he couldn't breathe. A moment later, the flavor of ashes and perfume, the electric taste of the portal was gone, as were the sounds of fighting. Thost's hand was still in his, Mira still leaning on him. He opened his eyes and found himself facing Lorcan.

"Tluin and buggering Shar," Volibar swore. "What happened?"

The cave around them was quiet but for the gentle sounds of water brushing against rock. Dahl's eyes adjusted to the soft, sickly light of the fungi on the wall—a lake of dark water nearly filled the space. He helped Mira to the ground. On the cave wall behind them, the rock had been roughly chiseled into a crude altar, sinuous pillars around a wide, curved niche.

There were bones in the niche. There was also no exit to be seen.

"Where in the Hells are we?" Dahl demanded.

Lorcan had limped backward away from the others to lean against the wall. In his hand was a ring. "I don't know," he said panting. "I don't care."

Dahl's stomach clenched. "What happened to 'we're both damned'?"

"Do you see a demon lord? You die, it doesn't matter. All that counts is that I don't lose your soul to the one shitting entity my mistress hates more than the Lord of the Fifth. All that counts is I didn't break my word to Farideh." He inched up the wall. "Actually this all works fine for me—not hurting you, not losing your soul, not breaking the deal."

"I don't think Farideh would agree."

Lorcan laughed. "I don't think Farideh's going to know. You shitting bastard. You had to get in the middle of everything. You had to think you knew best." He raised the ring to his lips. The portal ring. "I don't have enough to spare what you want to take from me."

Dahl ran at him, but he wasn't quick enough. Lorcan blew unevenly through the ring. A terrible wind, reeking of brimstone, pulled the cambion out of the plane, out of Dahl's grasp, leaving them behind, lost in the Underdark.

• • •

BRYSEIS KAKISTOS HELD the struggling consciousness of Sairché off with the very last shreds of her power as she stepped into the Nine Hells once more. The room was clear, the erinyes too driven by the lure of the curse to think about covering their retreat. She released her control on Sairché's limbs, her voice, her self.

Play your shitting part and you don't die, Bryseis Kakistos said to Sairché, a coil of magic around the delicate vessels at the base of the cambion's skull. *I can always find another body.*

"You've made me an oathbreaker," Sairché said in a small frantic voice. "Dying now would be quicker."

But more certain. Your brother's agreement means he can't let the erinyes have you. Go to the mirror. As Sairché limped over to the scrying surface, Bryseis Kakistos took stock of what reserves she still had, of how much Sairché could still manage.

The demon lord had been quick to blame Asmodeus for his state—but in a way that said Graz'zt had no more notion of how he had come to the material world than the mortals in his thrall. To bring a demon lord out of the Abyss against his will took massive power. To do so without that demon lord knowing you were the one who had done it? That suggested massive power and an even more massive error.

"What do you want?" Sairché asked.

Ask it to show Demogorgon. The one they called the Prince

of Demons—if someone had thrown Graz'zt from the Abyss, it would be that most hated enemy of the lord of Azzagrat.

Shaking, Sairché did as she was told. The scrying mirror's surface wavered and buckled, as if it didn't want to find the Prince of Demons. The vision came in bursts: the two-headed demon lord roaring over a drow settlement too minor and murky to place anywhere but the Underdark. Curious.

And promising.

Sairché let the image drop and Bryseis Kakistos considered the myriad enemies of the Dark Prince. The one enemy she knew might not kill her on sight. If Demogorgon walked the Material Plane, so might he.

"I know where there's a healing potion," Sairché said in a small, rasping voice. "It would only take—"

Ask it to show Orcus.

Sairché hesitated, as if Bryseis Kakistos would reconsider. The ghost of the Brimstone Angel nudged the vein, enough to give Sairché a flutter of lightheadedness. The cambion complied with shaking hands.

Again, the mirror managed. Again, the demon lord was not in the Abyss. Orcus, Prince of the Undead, perched upon a throne of gathered bones, a whole cemetery of bodies to support his massive bulk. At his cloven feet, a crowd of shadowy figures— stolen denizens of the Underdark made temporary vassals—gave the appearance of an ever-shifting floor around a pool of water that glowed with an unsettling amber light.

Bryseis Kakistos chuckled. *Someone has made a very grave mistake.*

"That's fairly rich," Sairché said. "Coming from you."

Bryseis Kakistos did not grant Sairché a response but gathered all her remaining strength and seized the body once more, one tendril of magic still looped around that vital vein. As she came into it, all the pain that wracked Sairché came into the ghost—she could no longer keep that from herself—and the legs beneath her nearly buckled.

You don't have time, she told herself. From the table beside the portal, she stole parchment and quill, scratching out the key to her success. Then, grabbing the portal ring and focusing on the image of the dank, crowded cave, she activated the portal. The gash in the wall split with a scream, and the ghost and her borrowed body were yanked through, into the Underdark once more.

Deeper than Graz'zt had been—Bryseis Kakistos marked the twisted stalagmites, the faint hum in the air. The fact that there were far more illithids among the milling minions than one would otherwise have expected. That the glowing pool seemed to pulse with a life—or *un*life, perhaps—of its very own.

Orcus's eyes glowed like moons above a burning plain. His wings spread, blacker than the shadows beyond him. *Who dares trespass?* a horrible voice echoed through her skull.

"Bryseis Kakistos," she said. "We had a deal once. Or the beginnings of one."

That deal was finished. The phylactery made for another. Still counts.

"Yet Asmodeus stands. I have another deal for you," she said, panting through the pain. "Simpler, maybe, but sweeter." The demon lord shifted in his new-made throne, and every sunken eye in the cavern fell upon her.

"You're not the only one down here, my lord. The bastard Graz'zt is within your reach and making for the surface. Just as weakened, just as cut off from his realm. Maybe more so. I'll trade you his location." She held up the scroll. "The only way you'll get it. Make me a deal"

That gave undead Orcus pause.

What do you want? the horrible voice whispered in Bryseis Kakistos's thoughts, but she had come too far and seen too much to shiver at it. Graz'zt would regret the day he underestimated the Brimstone Angel.

24

26 Nightal, the Year of the Nether Mountain Scrolls (1486 DR)
Djerad Thymar, Tymanther

MEHEN REALIZED WHAT DUMUZI WAS PLANNING TO do a moment too late. One moment Uadjit was shouting her son's name, the next Mehen was trying to catch Dumuzi as he raced by, bounding up the pyramid's blocks as though they were only steps. Beside him, Kallan eyed the slope.

"Give me a boost," Kallan said.

"You'll never make it," Mehen said. The pyramid's slope was steep and nearly a half-mile to the peak. He'd been made to climb it more than once—punishment for insubordination doled out by instructors—and even at his fittest, the climb was punishing. Two-thirds of the way up the pyramid, someone was climbing, and in spite of all sense, Dumuzi was gaining on them.

Let him—the thought went through his head, before he could catch it and crush it. Let him—because there were bound to be others at the peak who would stop the maurezhi, eventually. Let him—because what problem was this of his? Of Verthisathurgiesh?

The thought went through him before he could recognize the echoes of his father's voice.

Farideh and Havilar came up beside him. "How do we get up there?" Farideh demanded. "The stairs? The side?"

"Zoonie," Havilar said. She whistled through her fingers and the hellhound came loping up. "You want to ride, or do your jumping-in-the-planes thing?"

These are the voices you listen to, he told himself. These are the voices you helped shape. His girls would never *think* to leave Dumuzi to his own mad decisions, to leave a city that wasn't even theirs to a monster's predations. Pandjed may have shaped you, he thought. But you shaped them. *This* is Verthisathurgiesh's true advantage: determination, defiance, adaptability.

The drumbeats started up again and Mehen glanced back. Uadjit had snatched the nearer drummer's sticks, pounding out a beat he was surprised she still remembered—*bum ba babum bumbum*—the emergency order to land, to return to the city. Above, the last few bats to lift off wheeled around. Arjhani ran out, waving his arms at them.

"It's not as big a space up there as you imagine," Mehen said. "Don't let her run off the side of the pyramid, and *don't* let her eat anyone."

Havilar pulled herself up onto the hellhound's back with a wicked grin. "Except demons."

"You're cleaning it up," Mehen warned.

A moment later, one of the giant bats landed, wings spread against the ground.

"What's at your back, *sathi*?" the rider demanded. He seemed to recognize Arjhani and straightened. "I mean, Commander."

"Get us up to the platform," Arjhani ordered. "Your comrades and the city itself are in danger. I need three bats down, now."

Brin had pulled himself up onto Zoonie's back behind Havilar. Farideh looked from the hellhound to the giant bat, going faintly pale. "Havi? Can we switch?"

For a moment, Mehen was certain Havilar was about to leap off the hellhound and onto the bat, she stared at the creature with such bare excitement. But instead she reached down and unlocked Zoonie's muzzle. "She doesn't listen as well to you," she added apologetically. She nudged the dog's ribs and the hellhound howled, a sound that threatened to snuff the spark in Mehen's chest, before bounding up the stepped side of the pyramid.

Another bat had landed, taking on Uadjit and Arjhani. A third was swooping toward Kallan. Mehen climbed on beside Farideh.

"How do we make sure we don't fall off?" she asked in a rush.

"You hold on very tightly," Mehen said. He hooked an arm around her waist. The bat's wings pressed against the ground, lifting its body high enough for the wide wings to flap and catch in a jerking, bouncing flight. Farideh was as rigid as a steel rod, her tail trying to tangle itself around Mehen's right ankle.

"Go low," he shouted at the rider, "but don't stop. We need your squadron back." The drums still pounded out the order to return, but whatever lay to the north, they needed to pull back as fast as possible.

"Fari," he shouted over the bat wings and the wind, "we're going to have to drop. Keep your knees soft and roll—toward the center. I'll tell you when." She nodded tightly, hands knotted in the beast's coarse fur as they rose in a spiral.

Below, what seemed to be Tarhun gained the platform—the wide, flat peak of the pyramid, the size of a village square. For a moment, the thought left Mehen disoriented, his references inverted. Lance Defenders standing guard at the platform's corners turned from their stations. A half-dozen more—first-years tasked with preparing the giant bats and assisting with launches, no doubt—scattered over the platform, looked confused. He spotted Dokaan near the stairs, heard his distant shouts.

It wasn't enough to save the eastern sentinel, or the hatchling unlucky enough to approach. The maurezhi killed them swiftly, striking while they still thought it the Vanquisher.

The bat swooped low. "Now!" Mehen shouted. He gave Farideh a little shove and dropped to the granite platform. His knees crunched angrily as he landed, forcing him into a roll. Farideh landed with a little less grace, but perhaps better intent—she rose to her feet in line of sight of the creature, drawing her rod and spitting a word of power. "*Adaestuo!*"

The ugly burst of power hit the demon in the shoulder. It hissed, baring Tarhun's teeth, and vanished from where it stood, reappearing deeper into the crowd of Vayemniri. It yanked one first-year's sword away, stabbing it deep into a second's gut and twisting, before teleporting again to reappear along the southern edge of the platform. It grinned at Mehen, making Tarhun look as if he had no idea how to shape a smile. The southern sentinel loosed two arrows in close quarters, one sinking deep in the maurezhi's flank—it hardly flinched. The smell of brimstone and ash and cheap perfume suddenly thickened the air. A chorus of pops and six repulsive little creatures, like hairless dog-goblins, dropped out of the air, encircling the maurezhi. Two leaped at the archer—she swung her bow and knocked one aside, scrabbling at the platform's edge—and in that moment of distraction the maurezhi reached out and ran her through with the stolen sword.

Where is my challenge? The creature's voice echoed in Mehen's thoughts. *Where is my trophy? Bring me the baatezu and you might all survive to be slaves of your new conquerors.*

Mehen brought his falchion down on one of the little monsters hard enough to break its leathery skin and possibly its back. It screamed and let off a cloud of noxious gas. Another strike and it burst into flames. Beyond more gouts of flames as the Lance Defenders made short work of the little demons, one by one. The maurezhi surveyed the damage as if recalculating. Six steps, Mehen thought, starting forward, and then—

"Back!" Farideh shouted at him. He pivoted on his heel, keeping the maurezhi and his daughter in sight. She had the scroll out, unfamiliar words tumbling from her like a rockslide, piling magic in their wake. Mehen's scales prickled. The final words burst free of Farideh, the circle etching itself upon the granite—

—In the same moment, the maurezhi vanished. The circle snapped to the rock, around a single dog-demon. The little creature tried to flee, screaming as it hit the invisible wall.

Dokaan cried out. The maurezhi stood behind him, holding a bloodied sword. It grinned again, this time at Farideh.

Blessed of the Blessingless. If I cannot bring a baatezu down with me, then you at least will do. What secrets can I suck from your marrow?

Dokaan turned and hit the false Vanquisher in the throat with the full force of his elbow. The maurezhi staggered back, startled but not ended. When the northern sentinel rushed it, the maurezhi twisted out of reach, forcing the man to the side, stumbling over one of the first-year's corpses.

Another bat swooped low—Uadjit and Arjhani dropped from it, weapons ready. The maurezhi hardly had a chance to notice Arjhani before the glaive whipped toward it in a high slice. Whatever grace and speed age had stolen from him, Arjhani was still a master of the glaive. The maurezhi fell back, dodging the blade but catching it every other strike. Uadjit, her own long sword free, sprinted past to flank the beast.

Another bat swooped low, dropping Kallan who landed spryly behind Mehen. "Dog's nearly to the top," he shouted, drawing his swords. "Dumuzi's close behind, little madman. Did I miss much?"

Sheer numbers will end this, Mehen thought. Not a pretty strategy, but a hard one to defeat.

As if it had heard him, the maurezhi teleported again, away from Arjhani and Uadjit—right up to the southern edge of the platform. It spoke a dark and tangled word and all four dead Lance Defenders suddenly rose swaying to their feet.

I seem to recall you find this unsettling, the maurezhi said. *Reminders of another time, another tyrant.* The Lance Defenders turned on their former comrades, only the baleful glow of the Abyss behind their eyes.

• • •

ZOONIE SCRAMBLED UP the edge of the pyramid's platform, and suddenly, it was all Havilar could do not to throw up. The pyramid's platform was crowded with bodies—dragonborn, demons, dead things. She spotted Mehen and Farideh on the farther edge of the crowd. She climbed down to one side, Brin to the other.

"Zoonie," she said. "*Parosh—*"

Zoonie snarled and grabbed the shoulder of the nearest Lance Defender, a lithe gold-scaled woman, stumbling toward them. Havilar had no time to shout—and hardly enough time to register the woman's already broken neck, the blank look in her eyes, the fact she'd been heading straight for Brin—before Zoonie tossed her like a toy off the side of the pyramid.

And before the undead creature landed, before all the pieces could come together, a burst of panic hit Havilar, and the two imps appeared as if from nowhere.

"Blistering archlords!" Mot yelled. "What the ever-burning—"

"This is a mistake!" Olla shouted over him. "A mistake. You didn't mean to call us."

More undead dragonborn crowded the platform. The living Lance Defenders harried the maurezhi still wearing the Vanquisher's skin. It made them slower, more careful, like they didn't quite believe he wasn't Tarhun. One jabbed a spear at the maurezhi and it grabbed hold, pulling the man closer, grabbing his arm and twisting it swiftly from the socket.

Beyond it Farideh had pulled the second scroll out, watching the maurezhi with a pinched brow, as if she were waiting for something.

Come on! Havilar thought.

Kallan broke past one of the zombie Lance Defenders, slashing his sword down against the maurezhi's arm. Before the blade could connect, the creature had vanished, reappearing several feet away.

It raised both arms, hissing something that made Havilar's spine feel as if it were about to slide down her tail. A crackle of magic filled the air and five ghouls rose out of the stone, crawling up through portals to some other world that leaked the same stink of brimstone and salt and cheap perfume.

"*Karshoj* to this. Mot!" she shouted. The red imp swooped low. "Zombie things, ghouls, dretches—go annoy them and see what you can trick into falling off the pyramid. Don't get too close," she added. "And *don't* push Olla into one."

Mot gave her a sidelong look that said he knew she'd said it because she was considering it too. Both imps flapped off. Havilar started toward the maurezhi.

Or tried to—every step felt as if she had to fight against some invisible force, pulling her back or maybe pushing her away. The nausea rose and rose and rose. Don't throw up, she told herself. Don't throw up. Every step made it worse.

"Havi!"

Mehen's shout pulled her attention back. The broken mantra had Havilar so distracted that she didn't see the ghoul that broke away from its fellows to attack her. She only just caught its reaching claws on Devilslayer's haft, keeping their poisons from her. She whipped the point of the glaive up, smacking the ghoul in the crotch.

A blast of flames struck the creature in the back—it turned its baleful glare back at Farideh, giving Havilar another chance to hit it. Slice, step back, force the point in. A wave of nausea hit her again and she held her breath. The stink of dretches was not helping. The ghoul turned back to her—

Zoonie leaped on it, ripping away one arm and shaking it like a rag. The ghoul tried to scratch at the hellhound with its poisoned nails, but her thick fur deflected the attack. Havilar brought the blade down on the thing's neck, severing its head enough to stop it from attacking again. Zoonie threw the arm aside, sniffed the ghoul twice, wagging her tail.

"Don't . . . eat . . . ," Havilar started to say. Her vision suddenly contracted, black stars around a hazy point of light. She didn't realize she was falling until she noticed Brin had caught her. She nearly grabbed his arm to pull herself up, but remembered what would happen if she did.

"Don't touch me," she warned Brin. "You don't want to get blessed on."

"You have to pass it," Brin told her. "If it's not me, choose someone else, and hurry!"

Don't throw up, she told herself. Don't throw up. Mehen rushed up to her—give it to Mehen. And then watch him bull in and get killed while everyone else wonders what he's *karshoji* thinking.

Dumuzi climbed over the edge of the pyramid, behind everyone else but still looking fresh and ready to fight. Dumuzi could take it—but how would that work with whatever god-blasted nonsense he was dealing with?

This should have been Farideh's gift, she thought. Don't throw up.

Uadjit slashed a ghoul, hardly flinching as it screamed its horrible, bowel-shaking death cry. She spotted Dumuzi, and Havilar almost cursed. Head in the right place, heart in the wrong one. She forced herself to stand, to spring to Uadjit.

"You get to kill it," she said, and pressed her hand to Uadjit's bare cheek. "Be smart."

For an awful moment, Havilar felt as if she'd disappeared, as if she were nothing but the power surging through her and the world was only a ledge overlooking a terrible abyss. She focused on Uadjit's scaly cheek under her hand, as if it would drag her back. The moment seemed to stretch out hours, but when it passed, no more than a heartbeat could have passed with it. Uadjit narrowed her eyes at Havilar, then turned to the maurezhi.

The absence of the building blessing made Havilar feel so light she nearly toppled again. Glaive in hand she forced another ghoul back before gesturing to Mehen. Uadjit was already in the hold of the blessing, fighting her way through the wall of ghouls. If Mehen came around the other side, he could give her cover, help pinch the maurezhi in place.

Already, Havilar could feel the blessings building up, already she knew it would have to be passed along again. Several feet away, Arjhani skewered another of the ghouls.

Which meant they were at least even, and Havilar could not let that stand. She gripped Devilslayer, and grinned at the nearest ghoul—to the Abyss with the Chosen of Asmodeus, *this* was how Havilar fought ghouls.

• • •

THE PYRAMID'S PLATFORM felt as uncontrollable as a tavern brawl, there were so many bodies crowding the space. Farideh tried to keep her eyes on the maurezhi, the scroll ready for the next time it faltered. Its minions kept claiming her attention, and she sent spell after spell streaking through momentary gaps in the crowd. Nothing more powerful than a blast or a burst of fire—spells like the lava vent would do more harm in the chaos than good.

You could burn, a little voice inside her murmured. Cow the creature. Remind it of who you are, what strength you possess.

The powers of Asmodeus climbed up her spine, pressing upon her chest, almost closing her throat. Tatters of shadow-smoke kept leaking off her arms, as she fought to keep the flames from bursting forth and turning an already chaotic scene into a massacre.

Uadjit lunged at the maurezhi. Before her long sword could reach its target, the maurezhi teleported again to land behind Mehen—not as far, Farideh thought, it's slowing down. But it wouldn't hold still, and she only had two more scrolls to use. She pulled on the powers of the pact, opening a rift in the plane and leaping through it to land lightly on the other side of the fray, gaining a clearer line to the maurezhi.

Concentrate, she told herself.

A wounded ghoul rushed her—she had only a moment to raise her rod, to scramble for a spell before its sharp black claws were on her. Before she could cast, Kallan slammed into it, knocking the ghoul off its course. The undead turned on him, lunging once more, but Farideh cast a burst of flames, wreathing the walking corpse in enough fire to send it screaming back to the grave.

"All right?" Kallan asked. She nodded tightly, her knees locked from the ghoul's death shriek. "You planning to use that circle soon?"

She turned back to the knot of the battle—the maurezhi had shifted again, deeper into the knot of fighters. "It's moving too quick," she said. "I can't waste the scrolls when it keeps jumping out of the way."

Kallan cursed, considering her view of the demon. Between them, Mehen broke away and punched one of the risen Lance Defenders across the jaw with his off hand. "If I'm in there when you cast it," Kallan asked, "am I stuck?"

"No," Farideh said. "Why? What are you planning?"

"Can't be too much worse than wearing down a bull, right?" He gave her a quick grin, and sheathed his sword. "You ready?"

Farideh nodded, unrolling the scroll. Kallan darted through the crowd. Just as Uadjit surged forward, catching the maurezhi's eye, Kallan leaped onto its back, wrapping both arms tight around Tarhun's neck.

Farideh started reading, the words of the scroll streaking out of her like hornets gathering into a great cloud. The maurezhi screamed, the sound echoing in her skull loud enough to threaten her concentration. Farideh glanced up as Uadjit's sword cut an arc toward the demon's belly, slicing deep into it and splattering the stones with a thick, yellowish blood.

Tarhun no more. The dragonborn man's bones seemed to stretch, to break, and suddenly he rose in height, his arms and legs hideously stretched. One clawed hand lashed out at Uadjit, who had the presence of mind to throw herself backward, out of reach and onto the stones. Mehen charged at its back, and the other clawed hand raked him, tearing through the scale plate as though it were cloth, and knocked him back.

Farideh kept chanting, kept filling the angry cloud of magic with more words, more power. It flowed from her around the maurezhi, shaping a wall to lock the demon in. Meanwhile the maurezhi reached back, trying to scrape Kallan from its back as though he were a tick. Suddenly it paused, eyeing the edge of the spell Farideh was casting as though the growing circle were visible. It looked up at Farideh, its eyes endless and cold. A smile grew on its hideous face. It raised its hands—

A *crack* of thunder broke the maurezhi's concentration and threatened Farideh's. She kept at the spell—she knew very well the sound of Mehen's lightning breath. The last of the ghouls would be smoking.

But it wasn't Mehen who streaked past her vision—it was Dumuzi, lightning still snapping between his teeth. Never slowing, he leaped over the edge of the growing circle, to bury the Black Axe of Thymara in the maurezhi's chest.

The maurezhi looked down at the blade, perched above its earlier wound. In the same moment, a low *whoomp,* went through the air, a pulse of power that sent lightning crackling over Dumuzi's armor, and seemed to sap the strength from the maurezhi. Its endless eyes widened as it sank into the stones, staring at its injury. Dumuzi yanked the axe free.

Farideh spat the last words of the spell. A circle of glowing runes erupted around the maurezhi, trapping it in place. Kallan limped away toward Mehen. Dumuzi remained, at the edge of the circle, still crackling with lightning. It surprised Farideh to see he had the lightning breath, same as Mehen, though she wasn't sure why.

"Zoonie!" Havilar shouted. "Zoonie, down! *Tarto!*" The hellhound, bounding toward the trapped maurezhi, the last of the demons, dropped to her belly just behind Dumuzi, teeth bared, sparks raining from her glowing maw.

Perhaps you are a challenge after all, the maurezhi's voice echoed in Farideh's skull. It's gray, corpselike face shifted, its bones pulling into a mockery of Zaroshni's face for a moment, before its strength failed it. *Too bad it took you so long.*

"Who sent you?" Dumuzi asked, brandishing the axe.

One greater than yourself, the maurezhi said. Farideh could hear the pain compressing its terrible voice. *On behalf of one lesser than him.*

"Who?"

The maurezhi chuckled. A syrupy yellow liquid streamed from its mouth. *I call him the king of dust. He is no one, and you are less than no one.*

"We are Vayemniri," Uadjit said. "Forged in hardship, tempered in war. We have survived millennia of tyrants—your king of dust can be added to the list with room for more still."

You are fractious and flawed as every other creature on this plane. One demon in your midst, and how many die? Your greatest warrior crushed in his own hall of trophies? You are weak and you are lucky, this time. He doesn't even want you. But taste the air—you're the ones he'll get. Tell him how the maurezhi brought you low. Tell that king of dust how it did his work.

"Who's the king of dust?" Farideh said.

The maurezhi turned to her, its eyes half-lidded, its movements slow. *You'll discover. Soon enough. Taste the air. He comes soon . . . His army . . . swells . . . Not even allying . . . with the hateful Hells . . . will save you.*

The maurezhi succumbed, bursting into a bonfire that hit the limits of the circle. The scrabble of bodies darting away from its heat came from every corner, but Farideh didn't move. Neither, she noticed, did Dumuzi.

After, there was silence. The maurezhi was finally dead, and whatever it had taunted them with, it had been powerful enough. Farideh knew she ought to feel a measure of relief now that it was dead—but instead she felt even more anxious.

Taste the air—the sudden emptiness that came before a storm and yet the skies were clear. A strange electricity, a curious clamminess. What did it mean?

Calm, she told herself, and she could imagine Dahl saying, "We'll know when we know." Meanwhile there were wounded to be healed, dead to be buried. In the light of the moon, the dark shapes of the bat riders returning—what had been in the north? Anything? Only a distraction? She looked down at the platform.

At Dumuzi, ineffably changed, still standing at the edge of the protective circle. He looked back at her. "Will you look again?" he whispered.

She didn't need to. "It will be all right," she said. "I promise."

But then there was Uadjit staring at Dumuzi as if she hadn't the first notion of what to do with him. Then there was Arjhani not even considering his son. There was Mehen, still down and pressing a hand to his wounds, watching Dumuzi in a most unsettled way. It would be all right—it was true in the long run, but for now, Dumuzi's world would be upended.

Maybe we're all being upended, she thought. She searched the horizon, looking for an army, a monster, a portal—some sign of this threatened attacker. The air made the magic of the pact prickle along her skin. It felt as if something was about to happen.

And then Lorcan dropped out of nothing, landing in a heap beside her, and looking for all the world as if he were dead.

25

26 Nightal, the Year of the Nether Mountain Scrolls (1486 DR)
The Underdark

T HERE'S NO EXIT," THOST REPORTED BACK, AFTER WALKING the perimeter of the cave twice. "Best chance is something's feeding the lake under the surface and maybe someone could swim for it." Dahl cast a worried glance at Mira, binding her ankle with torn pieces of her cloak and the scrolls Dahl had ruled out, rolled tightly enough to make splints. She kept her attention on her injury in a way that made him suspect she knew he was watching.

"Granny's not swimming either," Thost said. Their grandmother stood off to the side, considering the wall of the cave, her injured hand wrapped in bandages made of Volibar's cloak and held up. Pretending she's not listening, Dahl thought.

"We've got a little food, little water," Bodhar said. His jaw was swelling badly, his words thick around it. "Enough for a few days. But once we're through that, it gets dire. The water's sweet, but I can't say for sure it's safe past that."

"I can fix the water," Dahl said.

"And food? 'Cause all there is are the lights." He gestured at the glowing fungus on the walls. "I can't say I'm too eager to give 'em a try."

"Not edible," Volibar piped up from the lake's edge. "You'll shit yourself to death if you try. Fish in the water?"

Bodhar shook his head. "Too dark to tell. How're the spells coming?"

Dahl rubbed his hands over his face and cursed. "We've got one bad option. I haven't found anything better yet."

532

"Still a few to consider," Bodhar said. "Why don't you work your magic, and Thost and I will see if we can't find a trace of a current. See if there's any hints about where our secret exit might be." He fished a bit of wood out of his pocket and pulled out his knife. He and Thost retreated to the far edge of the shore to flick wood shavings into the lake.

It won't matter, Dahl thought. You know what you have to do.

He unrolled the next scroll—a summoning to bring a monster to your side—and rolled it back up again.

"How's your ankle?" he asked Mira.

"Fine," Mira said, avoiding his eyes. Then, "Not fine. Broken." She tied the makeshift bandage off and sighed. "We're not fine either, are we?"

Dahl hesitated. "One of these is a portal spell," he said quietly. "But it's not written to encompass the caster. I'd have to stay behind."

Mira cursed. "You don't need to. Someone else—"

"Who here stands the best chance of getting out of here—alone—alive?"

"I've handled worse."

"Your ankle's broken and you don't know how to cast a scroll," Dahl pointed out. "It has to be me." He unrolled another of the scrolls: another summoning. His heart sank. Only two more.

"If I'm going to die," Dahl said, "I want to be clear about something. I didn't kiss you because I'm . . . It wasn't you. There's a lot of things that, apparently, I'm scared of when it comes to Farideh. A lot of things that would be easier if she were human, and I think he seized on that. But when it comes to her—"

"Stop," Mira said. "You weren't the only one he was tormenting. That wasn't about you. It was me." She blew out a breath. "Look, we weren't a good match. I know that."

"*You* ended it."

"I ended it, because I don't want a brightbird. But maybe I assumed that if I changed my mind in the future, you might be interested. I'm not jealous," she added quickly. "Or at least, I wouldn't have said I was jealous. But clearly I was wrong."

Dahl was quiet a moment. "We were really awful, you and I. I think you're forgetting how awful. You wouldn't want me for a brightbird." She kept her eyes on the water. "I once started a fight because you didn't leave a personal note in your field missives," he reminded her.

"I seem to recall implying you were only sleeping with me to get into my father's good graces."

"I think I told you the same."

"I suspect he does like you better," Mira said. "I once came to Waterdeep, and didn't tell you."

"I knew," Dahl said. "I got very drunk over it. You're not missing anything. Neither am I."

Mira sighed. "I didn't hate it, you know. I wouldn't have held on to the possibility if I really hated being with you." She chewed her upper lip a moment, the way she did when she was thinking. "We were less awful in bed."

Dahl snorted. "It did keep us going a lot longer than we should have."

He unrolled the second to last scroll: a teleportation good only for inanimate objects. He took the last one from the bag. If it couldn't be a portal, could it at least be some kind of scrying? If he couldn't return to Farideh, if he couldn't speak to her again, then, gods, if he could see her, hear her—

"If I give you a note for her . . ." Dahl broke off, coughing to clear the lump in his throat. "Do you think you could get it through? Please? Just in case?"

"Of course."

He unrolled the last scroll. Another summoning. He read it twice, as if the runes would somehow change for him. "Hrast."

At the far edge of the lake, his brothers discussed the wood shavings spinning in the non-existent current. Volibar crouched beside the water, looking for fish. Sessaca kept studying the carvings.

"Dahl," Mira started.

"I have to go get ready," he said, standing. He scooped his haversack from the cave floor, walking to the farthest lit spot he could reach. Don't think of it ending, he told himself. You could still escape. You have the best chance of escape.

He pulled open the haversack, and drew the scroll out, but found he couldn't read it. He shut his eyes.

Lord of All Knowledge, he prayed. *Binder of What Is Known. Make my mind open, my eye clear, my heart true.*

Footsteps, light and shuffling, stopped beside him. "Give me a moment, Granny," he said, hating the thickness in his voice.

"I know what you're planning."

"It's what makes sense," Dahl said. "Of all of us, I'm the most likely to find a way out. I can cast the ritual. There's no reason to discuss—"

"You're not getting out of here." Sessaca sat down on the rock beside him. "You don't even know where that beastie dropped us. Even if you try and swim down through that lake—which I *know* you're planning—you'll be alone in the godsbedamned Underdark."

Dahl kept his eyes on the scroll. "There's options. This isn't the worst thing I've figured a way out of."

"Which of us has escaped from the Underdark?" Sessaca said. "And that was the Upperdark, *and* I was younger, *and* better equipped, *and* I had a sense of where I was. Trust me, Dahl. You do this, and you're not getting out. Not by yourself."

"Granny, there's no food. Mira's injured. You're not doing well—"

"Exactly. Give it to me. I can read a damn scroll—been ages, but I can't imagine they've changed all that much."

Dahl startled. "What? But . . . you'll die."

"Yes, lambkin. I'll die," Sessaca said patiently. "It's not my favorite option, but I like it a good deal better than you dying or your brothers. Besides, it's not as if you haven't all been waiting for it."

"Granny that's . . . . None of us . . . You can't say that like we've been impatient for it."

"But you're *ready* for it. You're all ready, and you should be—you've got a lot of life before you, Dahl, and the end of my path is very near." She sighed and turned to consider the still, black lake. "Not the view I would have chosen. Better than some. Better than a back alley."

"I can't let you do this."

"Oh, don't give me that. You think I think you're out there stitching pillows and trimming quills? You know this life. You know what the risks are. It's nothing more than Tymora forgetting to check her sister's dice. You of all people know I'm right."

Words failed Dahl. Never in his life had he considered his grandmother would have two words to say to him on her dying day. Never in his life had he considered he might have anything at all in common with her, save his stolen surname.

"It's good to know," he said, swallowing against a sudden lump in his throat, "who you were. Who you are. I'm glad . . . It would have been a shame if . . . if you left without any of us knowing. Understanding, I mean. Thank you."

Sessaca said nothing, the both of them staring across the glassy lake, watching the distant dancing motes of light. Each moment that slipped by felt as if it were slicing a part of him away.

"Folks like to call Thost 'Barron's son,' " Sessaca said abruptly. "You've heard them say that?"

"Yes. And Bodhar's Ma's."

"Well, they've got that same damned constant cheer." Sessaca sighed and shook her head. "Wanted to smack them both the whole way to New Velar. Creeping through the forest, stopping to pick ruddy herbs in the dark and cracking jokes. But," she added, "it's their way. Comes in handy, too, given the right opportunity. Same with Thost and Barron's manner. Pays to have someone who can work the day without yammering about everything, or stare a blackguard down." She cleared her throat.

"Folks say that, and I see it too. I see you hearing it. You don't like it. Makes you feel like you don't fit, I suspect. But what I've come to say is . . . well, you might not be so like your da or your ma as for folks to comment, but if Thost is Barron's and Bodhar is Eurdila's, I think it's fair to say that you're mine, Dahl. You're my grandson like neither of them are."

Dahl covered his face with one hand, as if he could press the tears that welled up in his eyes back in. He couldn't thank her. He couldn't say a word.

She covered his other hand with her gnarled one. "Sometimes," she said, her voice uncharacteristically gentle, " 'specially when you're like us, it takes a certain someone to make you look up. Keeps you from getting lost in your own head. Never think there's shame in that. Never think that's a weakness. That's your anchor. Your axis. Other folks are just too slow already to need slowing down, I'd say. That's why I stayed with your grandda and took to a farm life."

Dahl cleared his throat. "Mostly."

"Mostly," Sessaca agreed. "If she does that for you, I couldn't care less if she's horned or scaly or Hillfarian."

Dahl swallowed hard. "Thank you."

"Now give me the scroll," she said, all business. He handed it over, wishing it didn't have to be this way, wishing he did have more time with her, even though she made him madder than a mouther. Sessaca yanked the scroll from his hands. "Quit bawling and figure out what in the Hells you're going to tell your brothers, because I'm not having this argument again."

• • •

The rhythm of scroll-making lulled Ilstan into a calm he hadn't found in longer than he could remember. Even after Farideh collected the four he'd crafted, he'd continued, locked within the little room for safety: one to craft a sentry, one to call forth a modest swarm of missiles, another protective circle. The piles of components vanished, bit by bit, and he tried not to notice how close he was coming to stillness again.

. . . a wizard's wits are the difference between a magister and an ever-apprentice . . . a wizard's eyes must be clear, their ears open, their senses attuned to every possible scrap of information . . . elsewise a wizard risks spell madness or worse . . .

The air in the little room felt closer than it should have—Ilstan looked up from his work, searching for a window—only ventilation grates high up on the walls. Perhaps, upon the others' return, they could find another place for him, a room with a window. Maybe a view. Maybe if he just kept crafting scrolls, he would never go insane, he would stay focused and calm and the powers of Azuth wouldn't surge up beyond his control.

. . . power has a rhythm, has a pattern, has a flow . . . a true wizard knows before something becomes uncontrollable . . . when the pattern changes, when the flow reverses, when the rhythm shatters . . . a true wizard knows . . . but most people do not . . .

Ilstan focused on the magic knitting together under his hands, on the way it seemed to cling to his knuckles, like silk in dry weather clings to one's legs. He fed it back into the components, into the ink and the parchment. One more scroll to make food in the wilds. A good use of magic, he thought.

Then the voice changed: *You are in danger,* it said, bluntly. *The planes grow unstable, and we can hear him shouting it on every plane.*

Ilstan froze. Was *that* Asmodeus? It had the other god's directness, the melodious lilt. If he left this room, what would happen?—knowing the god of sin's other attempts at controlling him, nothing good. Don't listen to the voice when it changes, Ilstan thought. Even though the prickle in the air was clearly not sweat upon his skin. Even though the buzz of building frantic magic was growing steadily more apparent by the moment.

. . . a wizard is often alone, the voice drifted on, *and so it must be that a wizard seeks allies in the strongest of his peers . . . a true wizard knows . . . when the pattern changes, when the flow reverses, when the rhythm shatters . . . . a wizard's eyes must be clear, their ears open, their senses attuned to every possible scrap of information . . .*

Ilsan stood.

The Blue Fire comes again, the other voice said. *Stop dithering. Find the other Chosen and tell him. Now.*

Which one? Ilstan nearly screamed. Which one? He didn't mean Farideh and he didn't mean Ilstan. Lord Crownsilver? A dragonborn? He had no weapon, he had no wand, no spellbook. He dug his hands into his hair—

He looked down at his hands. They hadn't bound them again. He'd been so engrossed with the scrolls, Farideh hadn't used the manacles. He was free. He had cantrips. He turned to the locked door, saying a little apology to his hosts. Fire bolts seldom made tidy door-openers, but time was of the essence.

• • •

WHATEVER HAD HAPPENED to Lorcan, it wasn't good—even Havilar could tell that much. If she didn't know better, she would have said he'd gone a month without sleeping or eating—but the cambion didn't need sleep or food. A month, a year, a decade without wouldn't make a difference.

He'd been awake when Farideh screamed and dropped down beside him—barely, but still, barely counted. She'd tried to haul him up under the arms, which was when Havilar intervened, insisting that they put him on a remuzzled Zoonie's back. Mehen and the others would go down to the Vanquisher's Hall to have their wounds seen to, to bring the elders up to speed. Havilar and Farideh and Brin would take Lorcan somewhere quiet and find out what the *karshoji* Hells was happening.

Even as they hurried down through the pyramid, Farideh kept a hand on Lorcan. Havilar frowned.

Mot and Olla flittered uneasily around her, a pair of pesty nursemaids. "I don't know if you should be near him," Olla said. "I don't know if *we* should be near him."

Havilar didn't think any of them should be near Lorcan, on the one hand. On the other, well, she owed him a *little*. "We don't leave allies lying in a heap," she told Olla.

"Technically," Olla said, "that is very much a done thing."

Mot scowled at her. "Are you planning on getting into any more lunatic battles on top of buildings in the future?"

"I don't think you *plan* that," Havilar said, which made her think of all the things she did have to plan. She thought about catching Brin's hand as they walked, and decided against it.

When they'd reached the Verthisathurgiesh enclave, Anala had just left by another staircase, hurrying toward the others.

"Just as well," Brin said as they reached the guest quarters. "I can't imagine she wouldn't have had a thousand questions about this."

Farideh helped Lorcan slide off Zoonie, one arm around him. "That's the problem," he slurred, "too many questions and you get too many answers and you get too many consequences."

"What happened?" Farideh asked again, her voice shaking. Lorcan met Havilar's gaze, but there was something oddly diminished about his dark stare. Farideh pursed her mouth.

"I'll put him to bed," she said. "Wait here."

Havilar wanted to protest, but Lorcan could barely string a sentence, let alone talk Farideh into something stupid. Besides, she thought, feeling a curl of anxiety rise in her already tender stomach, it suited her own needs. When the door had shut, she went to the imps, hovering over Zoonie who was trying to pull her muzzle off once more.

"You can go," Havilar said to Mot.

The imp shook his head. "Doesn't feel right. I don't think you're safe yet."

"That's an order," Olla pointed out. "You're supposed to follow orders."

"Follow away!" Mot fixed his dark eyes on Havilar. "Do you feel it? The air . . . feels off. Like you're standing in a portal."

Havilar shook her head. "Feels like a storm's coming. If you feel better staying, I don't mind. So long as you don't make trouble and you give me some space." She looked over at Brin. "I have to do something."

She left the imps perched on the back of the couch, and went to sit beside Brin. "Are you doing all right?"

"Well enough. You?"

"Queasy," she admitted. "But better than before."

"I was surprised you didn't jump on that bat with Farideh," Brin said. Then, "I guess you have plenty of opportunities for that. Should be fun."

"That's not why I didn't." Havilar wet her mouth. "Um . . ." She drew a deep breath. "I don't want to live in Cormyr, all right? Visit, fine, but I can't live there."

Brin blinked. "I know. I'm surprised you'd still visit."

"I mean, we can visit," Havilar went on. "We can't live there, and I know we can't live here. You'd be miserable here, wouldn't you?"

"I wouldn't love it," Brin said carefully. "Havi—"

"Where would be good?"

"Havi, what . . . I don't know. Waterdeep? Neverwinter? Why?"

Right. *Karshoj.* She was doing this all wrong. "I'm going to tell Dokaan I don't want to stay and work for the Lance Defenders. I just, I want some assurances that . . . that I'm being practical. Or really, not *impractical.* I don't want to live in Neverwinter, I don't think."

Brin shook his head. "Don't do that. Not for me."

"I'm not doing it for you, *pothachi.*" She took hold of his hands. "I'm doing it for me. And a little for you. For us, I guess then. I love you. I didn't stop loving you, I just . . . Things were so . . . "

"You just had to put up with me being a git," Brin said. "And you lost so much."

Havilar shook her head. "Right, but . . . Whatever I lost, whatever I couldn't get the hang of, I fought for you *really* hard because I didn't want to lose you too. Maybe we don't make any sense. Maybe we're really poorly suited, but I don't care. I want you. I like the idea of being a Lance Defender, but I *hate* the idea of doing it without you. And I wish I had a little more experience at everything, but . . . not if getting it means I can't have you. So if you were being a git before, maybe I was being a git this time."

"Maybe both of us deserve a bit of slack," Brin said, his voice a little thick. He took her face in both hands and kissed her, and Havilar felt certain this was the right decision.

"Maybe I can come sleep with you tonight?" she said, holding him close.

"I would like that. I would stay here. If that's what you wanted," he said. "I would try it."

"No," Havilar said. "There's plenty of other things we could do."

Brin smiled at her. "Maybe you can be an exhibition fighter. And I'll be your piper?"

"Maybe . . . you could start a caravan, and I'll run the guard?"

He intertwined his fingers with hers. "Maybe we'll just get a writ and adventure? *Maybe* we write chapbooks."

Havilar broke into laughter. "I'd like that . . ."

"If we have babies, they have to learn Draconic," she blurted. "I mean, I'm not saying we will or even that I definitely want to, but I'm not going to be the only one speaking it, and so I think you ought to learn."

He smiled. "*Akison*," he said, with only a little accent. "Just promise me you won't make me eat *yochit*?"

"*You* made me eat frogs in cream," Havilar reminded him.

"I introduced you to a beloved Marsembian delicacy at a high-quality hearthhouse," Brin said with mock haughtiness. "Also, there are eels and other things in fishdice too." Havilar made a face and he laughed.

"What made your mind up?" he asked.

She took his hand in hers and rubbed her thumb over his knuckles. "It's not very romantic. You didn't tell me to stay back. It was a good reminder that you know me. You love me. And I love you."

He kissed her again and reminded her of many more things, giving Havilar plenty to think about until Farideh came back.

• • •

FARIDEH STRAINED TO keep Lorcan upright as she hauled him into her bedroom, his wings drooping listlessly behind them. He seemed exhausted—but Lorcan didn't get exhausted, Lorcan did not sleep—and maybe drunk—but Lorcan didn't drink, couldn't even *get* drunk the way mortals did.

"What happened?" she asked again.

"What *happened*," he said, trying to stand on his own and falling back against her, "is that I made stupid deals. So many stupid deals. I managed it. I managed to save them. For the moment anyway."

She helped him sit down on the edge of the bed. His face was a mess—blackish blood streaked him from nose to chin, an ugly bruise growing on one cheekbone. She touched it gently, testing the swelling. "Have you got any other injuries?"

He tilted his head toward her, not flinching at her fingers. "Bruises. Sairché got it worse."

"Did someone give you something?"

"Your shitting brightbird," he said. "I saved him—you're welcome. I didn't want to, obviously, but you wanted it, so I did it. And other reasons. And then he did this."

Dahl—her blood ran cold. "What did he give you?"

Lorcan shook his head. "That wasn't his magic. I know that. I think . . . I think . . . Do you feel sorry for him or something? Because this plane is filled with women. He could *trip* over another woman—that Zhentish . . . Zhentil . . . Zhentarim . . ." He made a disgusted noise. "That Mira. She's right there. And if that's who I think it was, I will lay a balance of twenty souls that he absolutely bedded her while they were down there."

Farideh felt the powers of Asmodeus simmering through her. "I don't care what you think—"

"I know you care," he said. "I know you do because if you didn't, you wouldn't be angry at me. You only get angry when you think you can change something, and if you can't, you don't care."

"I don't care what you think," she said again. "He wouldn't do that. Why were you and Sairché with Dahl?"

Lorcan shook his head. "You don't even know what he'd do. You hardly know him, and . . . is that it? He's got such a shine, 'cause you haven't seen the ugly parts. At least I'm up front about mine. I think you were up front about yours. That's why he left after all."

Farideh held her tongue, burning with embarrassment at the memory of their awkward conversation in the garden. But then:

It's been 12 days & it feels like a lifetime & I am so sorry I ever suggested it. "He left because his family was in trouble," she said.

"Oh right. He left," Lorcan slurred, "because some people he *happens* to share blood with *might* be in trouble—he abandoned you for them. I would never do that. I would cut the throats of all forty-eight of my remaining half sisters, and Invadiah *and* Sairché, once the deal's done . . . Shit and ashes, that's a lie—I'd kill her right now if you needed me to, damn the consequences. Do you realize that? How can you think I don't love you?"

Farideh's throat grew tight. "You don't love me."

"I do. I love you," he said. "I just don't love you the way you want, because I am who I am, but I'm not myself now, am I? So what do you do with that?"

"Lie down," she said. "Whatever happened to you, you need to rest."

"I don't sleep."

"Well, you're not yourself." Farideh sat down beside him, unbuckling his studded armor with as much distance as she could muster. Trying to think like a healer and not about the myriad times she'd helped him out of this same armor in very different circumstances. Lorcan caught her hands in his, brought them to his mouth.

"Stay," he said, kissing her knuckles. "You could stay and I could stay, and isn't that everything we both want?"

Two months ago, in Suzail, she would have been elated at the offer. In Djerad Thymar, in the dark little room, she touched Lorcan's cheek. "Lie down."

He pulled her close, a glimmer of that old, wicked smile on his features. Echoes of other nights stirred her thoughts, as Lorcan kissed her, once, twice. She wondered if he was right, if Dahl had slept with Mira, and a little part of her thought she would understand if he had—even if you didn't mean for it to happen, there were ways to fall into old wants, old patterns, never knowing how dangerous it was.

But there was no danger this time, even if she stumbled. Lorcan was falling asleep as soon as he lay down.

"Tell me where Dahl is," she whispered.

"Somewhere safe," he murmured. "Somewhere no one can get at his soul."

Farideh waited a few moments, until Lorcan's breath had slowed and steadied into the rhythms of sleep. She closed her eyes, listening to him. This had been all she wanted once, this closeness, this safety. A part of her wanted it still, but that part felt weak and small and shriveled, trying to strengthen itself on the feeling of his arm around her.

I love him, she thought, and it will kill me.

When Lorcan's breath had gained the rhythm of sleep, Farideh slipped from the bed. She took the last of Ilstan's scrolls from her pack. The protective circle swept around the bed, not set to bind Lorcan in place but to keep out whatever had done this to him.

Dahl—he'd said Dahl had done this. But with a spell that wasn't his. And Lorcan hadn't given her any explanation of what he and Sairché had been doing where Dahl was. For a moment she wished there were a way to cast the circle pointing both ways—keeping Lorcan in and keeping demons and other dangers out.

At least you can solve this next problem from somewhere else, she thought, going back out into the sitting room. As she did, Brin and Havilar sprang apart, and Farideh blushed. "Sorry," she said—so they were back to that.

"It's fine," Havilar said. "How's Lorcan?"

Farideh's heart squeezed. "I have no idea. Something's definitely wrong with him, but I can't figure out what. He's sleeping for now."

"Sleeping?" Mot said. "Why?"

"You must have seen wrong," Olla said. "Devils don't sleep."

Farideh sighed. "Let's just go back up and get Mehen. Maybe one of the healers can figure out what's wrong with Lorcan."

As she turned to go, the air ripped with a gust of brimstone-tainted wind. A flash and Sairché stood between them and the door, bloodied, battered, and looking more than a little wild. In one hand was a scroll, dangling tassels of fresh skin.

"Good evening, my dear granddaughters," she said, and a chill skittered up Farideh's spine. "We have a lot of catching up to do."

26

S IT DOWN," BRYSEIS KAKISTOS SAID WITH SAIRCHÉ'S VOICE.
"There's a lot to say, and as you can see, I'm a bit short of
time." Farideh felt for her rod, tucked into her sleeve. Her
nerves were shot, stretched thin by the battle, but the strongest
spells remained in reach.

The blue-skinned imp launched off its perch. "That is not how
you're supposed to talk to us, cambion. This is the Chosen of
Asmodeus you're ordering around, you know, and we are her—"

Bryseis Kakistos pulled a wand from her belt. "*Loxiferi.*"
Bluish flames streamed from her wand, engulfing Olla completely. When the spell faded, nothing remained of the imp but
a fine sifting of ashes drifting toward the floor. Mot let out a
little squeak, ducking behind Havilar.

"Sit down. We haven't been introduced," the woman said,
lowering the wand. "At least, not properly."

Farideh kept the tips of her fingers on the rod. "You're Bryseis
Kakistos. The Brimstone Angel."

"Possessing someone's friends seems like introduction
enough," Havilar said. Zoonie slunk up beside her, growling
low and dripping flames.

Sairché's bloody face twisted in a fond smile as she pointed
the wand idly at the helhound. "Clever girls."

"What do you want?" Havilar asked, stepping in front of Zoonie.

"The same thing you want, ultimately: the end of Asmodeus."
She tilted her head. "Unless you enjoy being a slave to his whims?"

"We know about the Toril Thirteen," Farideh said. "You made all of this happen."

"Then you know he played me for a fool? I'll admit to it—you don't know what it was like in those days. At least the devils offer structure, rules."

"And power?" Farideh said.

Bryseis Kakistos smiled at her as if she were a stubborn child. "You don't know anything about power. Sit down."

"What did he promise you?" Farideh asked, not moving.

Sairché's dark eyes suddenly grew unfocused, her expression softening as if she were suddenly daydreaming. Farideh and Havilar exchanged a glance—if ever there was a time to attack, it would be now, while she was distracted, while she wasn't ready with a spell. Farideh shook her head—she might be ready, she might not.

Sairché's eyes blinked, suddenly clear again. "That's where you come in," the ghost went on, as if nothing had happened. "You see, you aren't supposed to be here. You were meant to be my vessel, the body for my soul so that I could walk Toril again and bring the god of sin low. But something went wrong—I have my guesses—and there were two of you. In that moment, my soul was destroyed, scattered to the winds. It's taken nearly twenty-seven years to pull myself back together, to come to something approaching my former strength, and without you I can go no further.

"There are two pieces still trapped inside you from that moment of error, buried in the layers of your own souls. That's what makes you interesting to the devils. That's what makes you interesting to Asmodeus."

Farideh's pulse pounded in her ears, full of the flames of Asmodeus. She wasn't supposed to be here. She wasn't supposed to exist. She was only the tool of a long-dead maniac. She let the rod slide out of her sleeve another inch.

"I thought we were Chosen because we were your heirs," Havilar said. "Why would he do that if—"

"You aren't the Chosen of Asmodeus," Bryseis Kakistos said. "I am.

"That was the deal—I gather the coven, I perform the rites and the sacrifices, I deliver unto him an entire race to carry on his bloodline, to amplify his power, and in return, I would be seated at his right hand, given powers unlike any mortal . . ."

She trailed off again, staring into space. Havilar cut her eyes to Farideh once more—*now?* Farideh shook her head again, even though she knew they should. She wanted to hear the rest. They weren't supposed to be here. They weren't supposed to be Chosen. What else?

This time, Bryseis Kakistos returned to herself with a wince, as if she'd noticed. "I'm sure you've discovered by now that devils always keep their word," she said, "they just make a point of keeping it in the way that suits them best. I wasn't endowed with power until after he killed me, after I'd escaped the Hells, after my soul was shattered, after . . ." Another moment of blankness crossed Sairché's features, briefer but no less complete. "Those powers flow to all parts of the soul," Bryseis Kakistos said. "And a great deal of them flowed straight to you two—to the fragments of me that are buried in you. That's how I found you, despite whatever meddler laid that protection."

Who? Farideh wanted to ask. Who laid it?

"I don't know if you noticed," Havilar said, "but these powers aren't that impressive."

"No," Bryseis Kakistos agreed. "They're not. Not separately and not in you. I don't care about your powers as Chosen. I care what they cling to. I knew how to defeat him and now one of you knows how to defeat him."

"We don't," Farideh said. "Don't you think we would have done something if we had?"

"You know. You just don't know that you know. You need me. Sit still, let me cast my little spell, I'll take back what's mine and deal with this problem. The first step is nothing."

It sounded reasonable, benevolent even. A way to right the wrong. "What's the second?" Farideh said, knowing nothing was so simple. The ghost hesitated.

"I need a body. Just temporarily. I'll give it back, perhaps in better shape than I found it." Here, she smiled at Brin in a way Farideh found unsettling.

"You have other heirs," Farideh said. "You found someone to make you a vessel the first time. They must be willing."

Bryseis Kakistos shook her head. "It needs to be one of you. You were made for me. It won't be so difficult to maintain control. It won't damage you so badly. But you have that barrier on you. You have to be willing. You have to ask me in."

"If we say no?"

"Then, my dears, I'm going to remind you of exactly how determined I am." She smiled at Brin. "How's your finger, your lordship?"

Brin pulled the symbol of Torm out of his collar. "It's working fine," he said. "Back off."

Bryseis Kakistos clucked her tongue. "That didn't help you last time. Willing to risk it?"

"You're injured," Havilar said. "We're no hatchlings. We won't go down easily."

"*I'm* not injured," Bryseis Kakistos pointed out. "Sairché is. And while I don't wish to roam the world incorporeal again, I can and I will. It won't take much time for me to, say, return to your dear Dahl. We've had several enlightening conversations. I think I'm getting through to him." Farideh's chest squeezed tight, the flames of Asmodeus yanking on her every nerve. Cast, she thought. Tear her apart.

And let Asmodeus go free. Do you know what happens when the spark is stolen out of a god? The god is killed. Destroyed.

"Though," the ghost went on, "it needn't come to that. We're on the same side. And the longer we argue about these details, the greater Asmodeus's predations become."

Burn her down, a little part of Farideh thought. But then, she'd only be freed—she had no magic to completely destroy the ghost. Then Dahl would be in terrible danger, everything she feared. She might possess Brin again, or Mehen, or Lorcan—and Asmodeus would keep haunting Farideh, and Azuth would still be in peril and—

Karshoji gods, what was she supposed to do?

"So," Bryseis Kakistos said, "which of you is it to be?"

The shadow-smoke poured off Farideh. She'd have time to think at least, she told herself. Although would she? Would she remember anything? Would it just be a wall of blankness, another empty gap in her life like when Sairché had yanked her and Havilar out of the world for seven years? You have to do this, she told herself. You have to remember and find a way to stop her.

Do you know what happens when the king is stolen out of the Nine Hells?

Havilar took hold of her arm. "Make sure someone takes Zoonie for runs, all right?"

Farideh looked up at her, baffled. "What?"

"I have to go," Havilar said, with a firmness that didn't match her trembling voice. "It should be me."

Farideh shook her head. "No. I can't let you."

Havilar gave her a withering look. "Pothachi, you don't let me do anything. It's the only thing that makes sense. You know what's going on better than I do. You're the smart one—you'll find a way to stop all of this. To fix it. And I'm the strong one. I can . . . I've done this before." She squeezed her sister's hand. "Just figure it out, all right?"

"Havi," Brin started. She turned and laid a hand against his chest, stopping him.

"I love you," she said. "I *love* you, Brin Crownsilver, and I will come back. But I think this time it has to be me."

He clung to her hands as if he could keep her right there. "You can't trust her. Even if she says you'll come back, what is there to be sure?"

"Nothing," Havilar agreed. "So you'll figure it out, or you have to beg a miracle from Torm." She kissed him. "Be careful, all right?"

"You want to stand back, your lordship," Bryseis Kakistos unrolled the scroll. "I can't make guarantees for the radius of this spell." She drew another scroll from her pocket, with a necklace wrapped around it—a chain with a fat blue-gray stone—and held it out to Mot, still flapping agitatedly beside Havilar. "Would you bring this to Havi?"

"Piss off," Mot said. "I don't work for you."

"Not yet," Bryseis Kakistos reminded the imp. He hesitated, glancing back at Havilar, then did as he was bade.

"This is a bad idea," he hissed at Havilar. "You should know that this is a very bad idea."

"Shut up," Havilar said, taking the scroll and the pendant. "And thank you. For your help." She looked over at Farideh and took her hand.

"You don't have to do this," Farideh whispered.

Havilar squeezed her hand. "My turn for a bad idea."

Bryseis Kakistos began to read the scroll, and the room's air began to vibrate, as if it were suddenly filled with a thousand errant souls, all of them angry. Farideh's skin crawled, as if it were trying to peel off of her, to escape the magic's intrusion. She squeezed Havilar's hand, and Havilar squeezed hers, their bones crushed against each other as the magic built and built.

The spell snapped together with a high-pitched whine that rose into a scream, and Farideh realized the screaming was her. As the spell ripped the soul fragment out of her, the pain was so deep, so far beyond her own body that she couldn't recognize it.

She watched helpless as images flickered past her, the memories of the fragment—a younger version of Bryseis Kakistos, a crowd throwing stones, a man who looked terribly like Lorcan, a woman she'd glimpsed in the fountains of memory with a cloud of red hair. Asmodeus, incarnate and terrible. Yellow butterflies on a cairn.

And then: the wordless, imageless knowledge that Asmodeus had not been able to tear the spark out of the Lord of Spells.

That's the secret, a little part of Farideh whispered. That's what Asmodeus fears.

The spell completed and Farideh's legs collapsed under her. She hit the floor only a heartbeat before Sairché did, the ghost remaining over her, traced in the dim light. She looked exactly as she had in the prison camp, cool and terrible and not entirely of this world, as she drifted nearer.

She gestured to Havilar, hands opening like a book: *Read.*

For a brief, absurd moment, Farideh felt sure her sister would refuse, would find some way to thwart the ghost.

But Havilar took the chain off the scroll, unrolling it with one hand. The words shivered as she spoke them, and Farideh found herself remembering another time, Havilar practicing Garago's lessons, the old wizard of Arush Vayem perpetually annoyed by Havi's cadence. This had been how it all started, Havilar reading a scroll to summon an imp but calling Lorcan instead.

Farideh pushed herself up onto her knees, limbs shaking. It felt as if the whole world were shaking. She looked up and saw Havilar's mouth open, the ghost stretching into something almost unrecognizable as she flowed into Farideh's twin. Zoonie howled and Farideh's marrow shook.

The magic ceased, though the shaking continued a few moments more. Havilar blinked and put the chain around her neck. She looked over at Farideh, and for the briefest moment, Farideh thought perhaps this was still Havilar. The sneering expression that had twisted Sairché's face was nowhere in evidence. Only a vague confusion. But as the moment stretched, Farideh felt surer and surer, this wasn't Havilar.

Bryseis Kakistos looked down at Havilar's hands with Havilar's eyes, but her expression shifted from puzzled to horrified. "Oh Watching Gods," she whispered. "I'd forgotten." Again, the expression on her face grew distant, dim. Farideh pushed to her feet, weaving.

Bryseis Kakistos shook her head. "No. I have to finish what I've started. I have to . . . Yes, whatever the specifics, I have to destroy him." She considered Farideh. "Believe me when I say, I intend to give her back. But I will need a body. Bodies." She searched the room, anxious and nervy. "That is your task, my dear—difficult and simple together. If something goes awry, I will do the same for this one. That's fair." She nodded as if to convince herself.

"I don't understand," Farideh said. "You have to explain."

Bryseis Kakistos blinked at her. "If you want Havilar back, you have to make us new bodies."

"How?"

"The usual way."

Farideh recoiled. "You want me to stay here and get pregnant?"

Bryseis Kakistos frowned at her. "It's what you are for. Do you think I bore heirs because I wanted children? You are a precaution. This way we can start over." Her eyes flicked over Farideh's shoulder. "You have the cambion. He would do. If I can free the Harper, all the better. Not as handsome, but steadier." She turned, flexing her hands.

Zoonie whined and pranced, as if she knew this was not Havilar, as if she couldn't decide what she ought to do. She grabbed hold of Brin's jerkin, tugging him toward Bryseis Kakistos. His eyes were red, Farideh noticed. He grabbed Zoonie's muzzle, clearing his throat.

"Let me come with you," Brin said. Bryseis Kakistos looked back over her shoulder. "She and I have an agreement, right? You need to know something about her, I might. And . . . you want heirs? Worse comes to worse, you'll have me."

Bryseis Kakistos narrowed her eyes a moment, and again it seemed as if she were somewhere else, as if Havilar's body were vacant entirely. Then she frowned. "Where is it now?"

Brin paused before answering. "I haven't had the chance to determine that," he said, every bit Lord Crownsilver. "But I'm probably the best one to find it, don't you think?"

"Stands to reason."

"I need resources, though. I assume . . . I assume you can help with that."

"Better than anyone alive."

Farideh felt as if she were in a dream—none of this made sense. Brin shot a glance at her, and she knew, he had no idea either. He was bluffing like mad in the hopes he could stay close to Havilar.

"We were going to try the hellhound," he said. "Zoonie. She can track like nothing. I need to bring her too."

Bryseis Kakistos smiled with Havilar's mouth. "Of course." She held out a hand. After a long, distrusting look, Brin took hold of it, his other hand on Zoonie's muzzle.

"Where are you going?" Farideh cried.

Havilar's eyes regarded her, cool and distant. "Somewhere safer than this." And with that, Bryseis Kakistos and her hostages vanished.

• • •

DESPITE THE NUMBER of wounded Vayemnri, no one asked Dumuzi to help as they made their way down to the Vanquisher's enclave. He followed regardless, still feeling the echo of the pulse of power that shook his very bones, the crackle of lightning that danced on his skin. Wherever he looked, it seemed as if he were seeing things but also seeing their ghosts—as if stones and statues and banners and even empty air could have ghosts. He walked as if he were dreaming or maybe watching himself dream. He came into the Vanquisher's enclave not sure of who he was.

The enclave was half-filled with elders—Dumuzi spotted Narghon and Anala, Geshthax and Vardhira and more. Healers, still hollow-eyed from interrupted sleep, swarmed Dokaan and Mehen and Kallan with herbs and bandages, helped Arjhani to sit.

"What in all the broken planes is going on?" Anala demanded.

A storm is coming, the voice in his thoughts repeated. *A storm is coming.*

The sky above the pyramid had been clear. What few clouds remained were too far away, moving too swiftly toward the sea to be any kind of danger for Djerad Thymar.

A storm is coming.

The air, though, felt like a storm. Humid, but thin—somehow. Electric as the taste of nerves in his mouth. *A storm is coming.*

"What do you mean?" It took a heartbeat for Dumuzi to realize he'd spoken aloud. His mother watched him with concern etched across her features.

"Dumuzi," she said gently, "are you all right?"

He wet his mouth. "I've done something," he said. "He says it's not a yoke." Uadjit's frown deepened.

The lanky wizard—Ilstan—appeared in their midst. One moment there was a gap between Anala and Dokaan, the next the wizard was there, frantic and wild-eyed. Both Anala and Dokaan leaped away from him. The Adjudicators' swords came out quickly.

"I have to warn you!" the wizard shouted. "I have to tell you! There's a significant disturbance in the stability of the planes. We must find a way to shelter or we'll be doomed!"

"Shelter from what?" Dokaan demanded. He looked at Uadjit. "Your *Munthrarechi* is better, Kepeshkmolik. What's he mean?"

Uadjit frowned. "The planes? What do you mean the stability of the planes? Are you talking about the old world? Are you talking about Abeir?"

"How do you shelter from another plane?" Mehen demanded. "What are you warning us of?"

A storm is coming, Dumuzi thought. *The Blue Fire is coming.*

"That can't happen!" one of the patriarchs shouted.

But the pressure in Dumuzi's head became exultant and fearful all at once, as if now, *finally*, Dumuzi understood him. As if now, finally, the warning was clear: The world is about to end. Tymanther is in grave danger. He cannot let it happen again.

I have no children. He needed believers. He needed someone to anchor him to this world. You have to take the yoke, Dumuzi thought.

"Help us," Dumuzi implored. "What one cannot do, many can manage. Be one of ours, please, one of our many." He reached beyond himself, for the growing presence of the god.

And the god reached back as Abeir returned once more.

• • •

THE LAND REMEMBERS what the people forget: where the mountains were, where the shoreline lay, where the grasslands stretched flat and where caverns crawled beneath the surface. Where magic pulsed within it. It remembers what was, what is, what shall be again. When the planes unite, it knows what will come and what will go.

From the vantage of overgods, the planes kiss as they pass, but the land remembers this violence: earthquake, flood, unnatural fire. For the people, some will survive while some will take the brunt of Abeir's return—it doesn't matter to the land. It was, it is, it shall be.

But from the vantage of overgods, one thing is changed: an island in the storm, a city born of both worlds. The force of the planes passing through one another is enough to level it, the way it leveled the tower that once stood in its place. Magic, birthed by union and disunion, rolls toward the stone city like a tidal wave . . . only to break upon a wall of lightning that curves around the city like the wings of a mother vulture.

• • •

THE FARTHER EDGE of the shore held the only place wide enough to wake a portal. At loose ends, Dahl kicked bits of stone into the lake, out of the way, making the surface smooth when it didn't need to be. His brothers were deep in conversation with Sessaca, who sat like a queen hearing grievances, upon her throne of a rock. Dahl had taken the brunt of Thost and Bodhar's protests—she was too old to leave behind, she was too frail to cast the spell, she wasn't in her right mind always.

"You can't possibly believe that anymore," Dahl had said. "She was playing us all those times." Sessaca listened, but there was no swaying her.

Volibar came to stand beside him. "The others are up the wrong end of the tluinstick, aren't they? The Zhentarim?"

"It's in Tymora's hands," Dahl said. "We'll weight the dice all we can, once we're out."

"Yeah, they're up the wrong end." The halfling sighed. "Appreciate you bringing me along."

"Again, thank Tymora not me," Dahl said.

"I'll thank her when I get Haslam back."

Dahl shook his head. Where the snake was now would be anyone's guess. By now Farideh would have gotten his letter, would have written her own reply. Haslam would have been sent on its way to its master's last location, winging along the path Volibar had given it. Maybe it would curl up in the Master's Library and somehow survive the cold winter of the Earthfasts. Maybe Tymora would roll high again.

Thost and Bodhar approached, helping Mira limp her way to where the portal would be. Dahl nodded at his brothers. "Ready to go home?"

"No," Thost said.

"We've been talking," Bodhar added. "Granny's going to aim the portal for . . . ah, hrast, how do you say it?"

"Djerad Thymar," Mira supplied.

Dahl's pulse sped. "That's a bad idea. You'll be at least a tenday from home—"

"They've got boats," Thost said. "Right?"

"And a better market for your spell components, I'd wager," Bodhar said. "We can tell the womenfolk where we've gotten to with another little casting."

"And Zhentarim contacts," Mira said. "Which means we can warn them faster of Graz'zt and the fallen outpost."

"You've been doing a lot more for us than I think any of us appreciated," Bodhar said. "Now we're doing this for you."

Dahl shook his head. "I can't let you—"

"Lambkin," Sessaca called. "You've been outvoted. Let it go and stand in your spot."

Feeling dazed, Dahl found his way to the middle of the group, hemmed in by his brothers. He could not have felt more uneasy if they'd stood on the edge of battle. In a moment, they'd be free of the Underdark. In a moment, he'd be near Farideh again. But he'd still be caught in Lorcan's deal.

One thing at a time, he told himself. Get yourself rescued first.

Sessaca unrolled the scroll, holding it high over the assemblage of components meant to help it focus along the still-mending Weave. The words left her, a singsong chant half demand, half prayer, that pulled together all the magic within reach as if it were swiftly training vines of power to wind around the cluster of people. His mouth took on the taste of wintergreen and old wine again. Sessaca looked up.

Good-bye, he mouthed. She nodded once, spoke the last word. The cave dissolved in a flash of light.

Dahl felt as if he dissolved with it, and suddenly he was falling without the pull of the ground, flying without wind in his hair. He was everywhere and nowhere but *moving*, without motion. The clammy air was gone, replaced with a sense like none other—not hot, not cold, not even there.

Suddenly, that nothingness became *somethingness*, as if the air had become gelatinous all around him, squeezing him down into nothing. An impossible vortex pulled at his very self, knotting him, twisting him, threatening to break him apart.

Lord of All Knowledge, Dahl prayed, reflexively. *Binder of What Is Known.* He reached for his sword, but he had no sword, no hands to reach. His mind filled with flashing colors—silver, red, violet, blue. So much blue.

His body hit a solid wall—

Then he slammed against a parched, grassy ground as if he'd fallen from a height, knocking all the breath from his lungs. He rolled over, all his senses coming back and reminding him of exactly how many bones he possessed and exactly how hard they were. He heard others around him, and forced himself up. Thost, Bodhar, Mira, Volibar. Every one breathing, moving. Alive, at least.

"Gods be damned!" Bodhar gasped. "You do that often?"

Dahl climbed unsteadily to his feet. They'd landed on a ridge of sorts, where a long berm of land had crumbled away into the wide grasslands beyond. The moon hung high to the east, over the sea. Still winter, Dahl thought. But south, far south. He scanned the horizon—a rolling plain, a river . . .

There. Far, far to the southwest, a dark mountain alone and sharp, gleaming silver in the moonlight. Djerad Thymar. It had to be Djerad Thymar. Two day's ride, he guessed. Four or more walking. He looked down at Mira—maybe more, given her injury.

Mira watched the plain with a grim expression. "Army," she said. Dahl followed her gaze out to the west. A dark patch of bodies, clumped into groups, between them and the river to the south. Flags, almost unreadable in the darkness, flapping in the occasional breeze. Dahl pressed himself down against the ridge again, trying to make out the emblem.

"A fist?" he said. "That's a fist. Banites?"

"Wrong color." Mira peered into the darkness. "Red fist on a golden sun," she said. She frowned. "Nobody's used that symbol on the Alamber Sea since before the Spellplague. Before the Time of Troubles, even. Who's stlarning resurrecting an Untheran battle flag?"

• • •

In the first heartbeat after Dumuzi's outburst, Mehen heard the roar, a windstorm in rapids in the mouth of a fathomless beast.

In the second, only whiteness, a light that burned away Mehen's vision, bursting from where Dumuzi had stood. Lightning-white, he thought, but lightning would never linger so long, nor would he be standing if it came this close. He was blind, defenseless. Dumuzi was surely dead.

In the third, a singing through the roar. Strange words, strange cadence: *Enlil aga-ush kur-kur-a ab-ba numun-numunre-ne-ke . . . Enlil-e kur-Thymar-ah ba-gi-shey.* And chasing it, Draconic—*Enlil, soldier of all the lands, father of all children, to Djerad Thymar, Enlil comes.*

In the fourth, the lightning ended, Mehen's vision slowly returning in patches. While all else was still a blur, for a moment, he saw Dumuzi his head still thrown back, clear as day. And a man, behind Dumuzi—black scales, golden eyes, no piercings. He looked over at Mehen, and nodded once, the curt respect of warrior to warrior, or father to father. Comrade to comrade. Mehen's tongue tapped frantically against the roof of his mouth. *Soldier of all the lands, father of all children.* Suggestion, that was all. The same thing that made his legs think they should bend.

He nodded back instead of bowing. The man set a hand on Dumuzi's shoulder, and the boy seemed to relax, all the force of what he'd channeled seeping out of him. The black-scaled Vayemnri patted Dumuzi's shoulder in an oddly fond way—

Five heartbeats after Dumuzi had shouted a prayer in the middle of the Vanquisher's Hall, Mehen stood at the edge of a circle of elders and Lance Defenders, all staring at Dumuzi, as if the boy could offer some explanation of what had just happened.

Dumuzi for his part, only stood, staring down at the floor and shaking. But not dead.

Not all with power are tyrants. Not only blood makes a tribe. Ah, Dumuzi, he thought. What have you woken?

"I don't want to be the kind of person who sits on her hands when she could have done something," Farideh had said. The gods were present. They were becoming more present by the day, it seemed. How long could the Vayemnri hide?

We can't, Mehen thought. So we can't sit on our hands.

It was Uadjit who broke out of the circle first, rushing up and grabbing her son, as if he were new-hatched and she could protect him—as if she knew she could not protect him, not from this.

In front of everyone, Mehen thought, numbly considering the staring elders. Not Uadjit's sort of careful move. Rash. Instinctive. But as complicated as things were guaranteed to become in Djerad Thymar, not even Kepeshkmolik Uadjit's silver tongue and smooth manners could save things.

Beside him, Anala watched with the same bewilderment that had struck Mehen. There would be no denying a god had briefly manifested in the Vanquisher's Hall. There would be no stopping the chaos that would chase the revelation that Tarhun was dead, that the Blue Fire had returned, that an enemy with no name was heading for Djerad Thymar. That Kepeshkmolik Dumuzi was in the middle of it.

"I will stand for Vanquisher," Mehen told her. "On one condition."

Anala's attention snapped to him. "Go on."

"I will stand for Vanquisher," he said again, "and you will set Verthisathurgiesh behind Dumuzi. You will protect him, even if that means standing alongside Kepeshkmolik."

Her eyes narrowed. "I don't care for your conditions."

"You don't do it, I'll be his first *karshoji* convert, as soon as your declaration that Mehen stands for Verthisathurgiesh finishes," Mehen said. "You protect that boy like you couldn't before, and I'll be your candidate, piercings and all."

Anala considered him a moment. "I'll think about it," she said. "But I have a counteroffer. I still don't think you'd win, in the end, but I wonder"—she nodded at Kallan, who still watched Dumuzi and Uadjit with wonder and apprehension—"if the man who hunted the maurezhi, who leaped upon it like a runaway horse and brought it down, might make a better candidate overall?"

27

26 Nightal, the Year of the Nether Mountain Scrolls (1486 DR)
The Underdark

THE VIPER OF THE EARTHFASTS WAS NOT SENTIMENTAL, Sessaca Peredur reminded herself as she sipped her grandson's whiskey and contemplated the eerie black lake. It was practical to pray for her grandsons' happiness, to pray for her daughter-in-law's grief to be easy, for the farm she had made her home to be safe without her skills. It was a matter of preparedness to think back on her life, to consider the good deeds and the bad, to consider what god might open their gates to her soul once she'd passed. What the chances were of seeing her man, Lamhail, again; her lost baby; her boy Barron again.

She remembered Tsurlagol and Lyrabar and how many times she'd had to scrub someone's blood out from under her fingernails. The wars that thrived on the blades she ran. The deaths on her head.

She took another swig of whiskey. I'm sorry, Lamhail. I'm sorry.

But would she have done a damned thing different? Here or there maybe. If she thought too hard about that, what would she find but the ten thousand ways she would have lost a life she dearly loved. Perhaps the good would outweigh the wicked. Perhaps her soul would be light enough to escape Bane's grasp. Perhaps, she thought. Perhaps.

Ten thousand choices. Ten thousand escapes. But not this time.

Another sip of whiskey—good boy, Dahl. She thought of the demon lord, how close she'd come to losing him. How hard he'd fought his way back. A pity she couldn't meet this devil-child.

She hoped this Farideh had a measure of her Lamhail's patience, his loyalty, his kindness. Gods above, she missed that man.

A song floated through her thoughts, like a tune she couldn't shake—although it had not been in her head for more than sixty years. The lure of the Deneirrath priestess, come back to tempt her again? She hummed along with it. She had whiskey to finish.

The surface of the water shivered. A dark gray head broke the surface, bulging eyes first. Sessaca drew the little knife. Death was coming. The Viper of the Earthfasts would not go easy.

A rough triangle of heads, a dozen in all. The creatures lurched out of the black water, making croaking sounds of Undercommon to one another, their slick gray skin pale in the light of the glowing fungus. Nearly all of them carried spears—one though, one carried an offering, a bloody drow head.

"Who are this one?" the one carrying the drow head croaked in broken Common. "How you make to the Lady's shrine?"

"I am the Viper of the Earthfasts," Sessaca said, and readied herself for death. "I came because I was brought."

The kuo-toa looked at one another, mad eyes wide and puzzled. The attack didn't come and didn't come. Sessaca said a little prayer to herself, the song in her head given words.

The one with the offering suddenly dropped to its knees, laying the drow's head at her feet. Sessaca raised an eyebrow at its grotesque, upturned face, as the other eleven kuo-toa dropped to their knees behind the priest.

"The Viper of the Earthfasts," the priest croaked.

"The Viper of the Earthfasts," its guards chorused.

"Well piss and hrast," Sessaca said. Perhaps she was not finished with adventures quite yet.

• • •

HAVILAR BLINKED, BUT it did nothing to clear the haze from her eyes. Wherever she was, there seemed to be nothing but a pale fog—no ceiling, no floor, no walls, no end. She looked down at her hands—at least she still existed, in some way. She had her armor on, but no weapons, no supplies. Every pouch and pocket was empty.

Gods, I hope this isn't being dead, Havilar thought. An eternity of nobody and nothing. She was already bored.

She searched the fog again, but this time found a woman floating in the haze to her right. She grabbed for her glaive before she remembered it didn't exist here. The woman was the ghost who'd peeled away from Sairché, the same one Havilar had glimpsed before awaking here, in this place of nothingness. Unlike the ghost, though, this woman seemed more solid—as solid as Havilar anyway—from her sharp little horns, to her cloven feet. She smiled at Havilar in a bashful sort of way.

This could not, Havilar thought, be the Brimstone Angel.

Who are you? Havilar asked, but the words formed without breath, without effort. The woman's smile faltered.

Alyona, she said. *And you're Havilar. It's nice to meet you, properly.*

How do you know my name?

Alyona laughed, bright and happy. *Because I know you. I have known you all your life, and your sister too. I'm part of what she took out of you, before . . . Before.* Her expression turned grim. *This wasn't the plan. She had seen the error of her ways, I thought. I thought . . . Maybe my faith was misplaced . . . Maybe what she promised was never meant to . . . This madness with the heirs . . . People will be hurt . . .*

Havilar had no idea what the woman was talking about. She seemed to lose track of her thoughts as she spoke, not quite present. *How likely,* Havilar asked, *is it that everything is going to turn out all right?*

Alyona's silver eyes regarded her, all solemnity now. *That depends upon your sister and mine.*

A twin, Havilar thought. The Brimstone Angel had a sister. Did Lorcan know that? Did *anyone* know that? Alyona watched her in a worried way. Havilar tried to smile back. *Is your sister as stubborn as mine? She might be in trouble.*

• • •

FOR A MOMENT, Farideh's world was the silence enfolding her own panicked breath. Havilar was gone. Brin was gone. Even Zoonie was gone. The fear that gripped her was an animal's, intense and mindless. She couldn't even scream.

"You will be weakened," Bryseis Kakistos had said, and Farideh wondered if that were it.

Near the door, Sairché stirred, lifting her head from the stones with a terrible moan. All Farideh's shock turned to rage—Sairché had colluded with the Brimstone Angel, Sairché had brought the ghost here, Sairché had failed some way so that Havilar had been taken. She expected the powers of Asmodeus to engulf her, to burst out of her skin as flaming wings and send a wave of terror racing out over the cambion.

But nothing of the sort happened. Her powers had vanished. All that remained was the pulsing line of her pact. For all she'd wished for this, it left her feeling unmoored and incomplete.

Think, she told herself. Think. To the Hells with vengeance— the wrong decision could cost lives. It could cost her Havilar.

Bryseis Kakistos means to kill Asmodeus, she thought. Asmodeus will do all he can to stop her. And if he stops her, Havilar dies.

Sairché managed to roll over onto her back. "Help me," she said, her voice a ghost of its own. "I've been cursed. The erinyes will be searching."

Even without the blessings of Asmodeus, Farideh's temper would not cool so quickly. "How can you ask me that?"

"You don't want this place full of erinyes anymore than I do." Sairché swallowed with effort. "I know how she's going to do it—a ritual. I know she wants to unseat Asmodeus, maybe kill him. But I don't know how. Find me a potion, get me somewhere safe, we can compare notes."

That stopped Farideh. "You don't know what she's doing?"

Sairché gave the smallest shake of her head. "I know who she needs. I know where they are. I know where she intends to take them."

But not about Azuth and Asmodeus. Not about the spark of the god. "Do you know where she's gone now?"

Sairché hesitated. "I could guess."

"Guess."

"Fortress in the Snowflake Mountains. She doesn't have allies, but that . . . that one was close. She might hide there."

Might, Farideh thought. Close. It wasn't the answer she needed. Sairché reached out a hand as if she sensed Farideh's annoyance. "You could scry her. You could check."

She couldn't—she couldn't work a scrying and she couldn't use that kind of magic on Havilar, if Lorcan was telling the truth. And Sairché didn't know that.

But Lorcan can work a scrying, she thought. And Brin has no protections on him. She crouched down, scooping Sairché from the floor with an arm under her shoulders. "I have a magic circle," she said. "You can suffer in safety at least."

At least, Farideh thought, for a moment. Every one of their enemies was about to collide.

• • •

WHEN THE WORLD stopped shaking, when the sky stopped falling, the first thing Namshita became aware of was the blood-red eyes of one of the bull-headed monsters that surrounded the golden god. The goristro held her gaze as it lifted one of the slack bodies that lay beside it—a young man, thrust into ill-fitting armor and given an unfamiliar blade in advance of the attack. Dead, without a doubt. The demon sniffed him once.

Namshita looked away, willing herself not to flinch at the crunch of bone. The price of the god-king's madness. She searched the horizon over the heads of her soldiers for the break in the cliffs that would mark the meeting place, the point of their escape. She looked and looked and looked, as if somehow by searching, the land would change back to the sunset-painted cliffs she'd been considering only a moment ago.

But it didn't. We've left, she thought, feeling numb.

She stood stiffly, as if her limbs weren't her own, as if her armor were suddenly made of stone, it took so much effort to move. The cliffs were gone, and so the canyon was gone, and then there was nowhere to lead the deserters, the rebels who had heard the lunacy in the Son of Victory's revelations. Her heart felt as if it had crawled up into her throat.

"My lord," she heard one of the god-king's warpriests cry, "where is Shyr? Where are the armies? Where have you brought us?"

Namshita watched from the edge of her eyes as the golden god-king rose to his feet, unscathed by earthquake—nay, by the unseating of their world. He, too, searched the rolling hills, hunting for the walled city of the genasi slavers, his army's prize-to-be.

Instead, on the edge of the horizon rose a pyramid of granite that throbbed with the beat of a thousand war drums.

"Home," Gilgeam said, with a cruel smile. "I've brought you home."